NOT MY TIME

RIVERPEAK HEROES
BOOK 1

JESSICA SALINA

To my husband, Anthony, who has acted as both my biggest cheerleader and fight scene coordinator.

And to my best friend, Michele, for all of your support and helping me find Kane Kelly lookalikes on TikTok.

CONTENT WARNINGS

Not My Time is an adult superhero romance featuring physical violence, gun violence, stalking, drug use (mentioned), blood, and consensual sexual content.

CHAPTER 1

Rory Miller all but jumped when she heard a whistle from the shadows. Her breath quickened as she glanced around campus, looking for the source of the sound. In the dark, it was hard to tell. Some of the streetlights that normally illuminated the sidewalk were out, making it harder than usual to see on their way back to her friend Naomi's dorm from the library. Naomi, who was with Rory, reached for the keys in her purse, in case she'd need the pink tube of pepper spray attached to them.

A male voice called, "Haven't seen you in a while."

Rory's anxiety hadn't been for nothing, despite the university police's claim that she was just being overdramatic about her stalker. Her stomach sank further and further into her body, along with any courage she might have had left. She wanted to find those officers and scream, "I told you so!" in their faces, but it was too late now.

"Why haven't you been showing up to class? I've been looking forward to seeing you, you know," the familiar voice said.

The answer to that question was that their professor let Rory finish the course online, but Daniel didn't need to know that. In fact, their professor was the only person, other than Naomi and her friends, who took Rory seriously. The light Daniel now stood beneath cast a long shadow, making his already towering stature that much more intimidating. His baggy T-shirt made his lean frame billow out, appearing as though he were wider. His casual attire helped him blend in as he followed her around campus, and if anything was in the large pockets of his cargo shorts, no one would ever tell from a quick glance of his appearance.

Rory could hear her heart beating faster in her own head and tried to focus on the way her feet felt beneath her, since her vision was so dizzying. She glanced at Naomi, and they both took steps back away from him, inch by inch, in hopes of not alerting him. Naomi nodded at her, her silent way of saying they needed to be ready to run and stick together. Being alone was dangerous for both of them right now, but especially for Rory.

With her hand still in her purse, Naomi opened her phone's voice recording app she kept handy for her journalism classes. She made sure it was on and then held onto Rory's hand to comfort her friend.

Before they could think of a response, another voice—gruff and muffled—rang through the night. It almost sounded electronic, as if a modifier was changing the man's voice. "Do you know him, miss?"

Rory looked at the sound of the new person. A man wearing black and dark blue came from what seemed like nowhere. A mask covered his entire face, except for his eyes, and a scarf and cowl that wrapped around him a few times covered his mouth, neck, and the top of his head. His shoulders were narrower than Daniel's, and the stranger was significantly less stocky, so Rory wasn't sure what to think just yet of any potential odds.

"Unfortunately," Rory answered. She wasn't sure if she should be afraid of the presence of this new man, but something in her gut told her he was there to help them. She hoped she was right about the newcomer. Her gut was right about Daniel following her around campus, trying to find her alone late at night after their classes wrapped, and sending cryptic text messages hinting at her location.

"Aw, Rory, don't be like that," Daniel said. He took a few slow steps toward her, and his pasty skin seemed to shine beneath the streetlight he was now under, almost making him glow. "I don't know why you don't talk to me."

"Don't even fucking think about it, pal," the mystery man said, as he held a hand up. Without looking away from him, the man asked, "Rory, was it? Is he bothering you?"

Rory nodded. She felt a lump in her throat where she once felt her heartbeat, but she wasn't entirely convinced she was even breathing at that point. She wanted to speak, but her voice was frozen in fear.

"He's been stalking her since the start of the semester," Naomi said. She held her head up high, making the two braids in her black hair look even longer. "Campus police haven't exactly been helpful. His name is Daniel Sanders."

"Oh, shut up," Daniel retorted, wasting no time defending himself. "I am not stalking her. That's just being extreme."

The guy in the mask scoffed. "Then what the hell do you call this?"

"Can't a guy get out there and pursue a woman? I thought chicks liked that," Daniel said.

"Oh my God, ew," Naomi reflexively said under her breath. Rory had been too stunned to say anything at all, feeling quite like a deer in the headlights. She glanced around, hoping someone else might show up to intervene and scare Daniel away—a teacher, an administrator, anyone who might show some authority. The man in the mask wasn't scaring him; she wondered if anything would.

"Choose your next words wisely," the masked man replied. "Or else we'll have a problem."

Daniel rolled his eyes and reached for the large side pocket of his cargo shorts. Before he could grab whatever was in there, the man in the mask was on him in a second. Rory jumped at the sudden movement. Naomi stayed grounded and gripped her hand tighter. Suddenly, the man in black and blue had Daniel pinned down and unable to move. Daniel reached for his pocket again once he was on the ground, but the other man beat him to it, as he pulled out a handgun.

"What are you doing with a gun, buddy?"

The masked figure made quick work of disarming Daniel and whacked him across the face with the handgun, hard enough to knock him out. Naomi held her friend close to her side after the sound of the man hitting Daniel made her jump again, but the fight was over before it even began.

The masked man kneeled over Daniel and examined him for a moment to make sure that he was, in fact, unconscious. Once he determined Daniel was out and would be for a while, he stood, taking the gun with him. He kicked Daniel again for good measure, this time in the shoulder, in a surprisingly casual way.

The stranger held his hands up as he slowly approached the women so they could see where the gun was with his finger away from the trigger. Naomi noticed that Rory's trembling had slowed down as she held her, but Rory's breathing was still labored and her eyes were wider than Naomi had ever seen.

When the masked man was closer to them, he nodded his head toward the hand holding the gun. "I'm going to take this apart now, okay? I promise I won't hurt you. No funny business."

Rory nodded. He gradually lowered his hands and then detached the slide from the top of the gun and tossed it. The slide clattered across the ground until it landed right at Rory's feet. She stared at it for a moment and then looked up at the masked man, trying to say something but bursting into sobs instead. Naomi took a hold of the slide as Rory's body caved in on itself.

"Hey, hey," the man whispered at Rory's crying. His voice was still gruff and hard to make out, but his tone was gentler. He reached for his cowl and tore off a small piece of fabric. "I, uh, don't have any tissues or a handkerchief or anything. So, I hope this will work."

Rory smiled at him as she cried, attempting to say her thanks and hoped that it would be a sufficient means of communication to him. She accepted the second offering from him and wiped her face with the tattered fabric.

"That pathetic asshole won't bother you anymore," the man said. "I'll personally see to it. Okay?"

Through her tears, Rory asked, "Who are you?"

"I don't have a name. But some people call me Hematite."

The name was familiar; she had heard of him on the news, but she wasn't sure if he really existed. Hematite was as good as a local cryptid, the local vigilante superhero that no one ever got a good look at but everyone seemed to have a story about. Rory's breathing had been heavy and labored; however, she finally found her voice again. But before she could even say thank you, he was gone without a trace.

While Naomi called the police on her cell phone, Rory just stared at the spot where Hematite had been standing. She glanced around, trying to see where he hid in the shadows or how he disappeared like lightning, but there was no trace of her savior.

———

Rory pulled her car into park and gasped as she realized where she was. She looked around and saw that she reached her destination, a parking lot of the small plaza in Denver where the rooftops only partially blocked her view of the Rocky Mountains. She wondered how long she had been lost in her thoughts. The flashback from eight years ago felt as real as the car she was sitting in; she guessed driving out here for her first therapy appointment triggered it. She cursed to herself as she unbuckled her seatbelt and hoped she didn't run a red light without realizing it.

The snowfall was delicate, like it wasn't in any rush to leave the skies. It left thick flakes on her windshield that were piling up now that the wiper was turned off. She took a deep breath, hesitant to abandon the warmth of her car to venture into the therapist's office. She reached for her scarf in the passenger seat and put it back on to brace herself, both emotionally and physically, for heading out into the cold for a moment and into her first therapy appointment. Despite the light snow, the sky was still clear enough to get a decent view of the white-tipped mountains and rolling pines. Even though Rory preferred the summer, she always loved the way they looked like larger-than-life paintings in the winter, especially as the afternoon sun sparkled across the snow.

At her appointment, Rory wasn't sure where to begin once she sat on the sofa in the therapist's office. As she looked around, she felt uncomfortable trying to gauge the environment and ground herself. She reminded herself that she drove here all the way from Riverpeak, about a ninety-minute drive, and only had an hour with Dr. Marissa

Thornton. As nervous as she was, she hated the thought of wasting precious time.

Dr. Thornton was a straight-haired brunette with a warm smile. Tattoos covered both of her arms, and her white dress shirt failed to hide them; the designs were still visible through the sheer sleeves. The lack of frills or stiffness helped Rory feel more at ease. Her office was pleasantly warm, with plenty of plants and books on a mahogany shelf, but Rory's overall discomfort came from within.

―――――

"So, let's dive right into it. What brings you in today?" Dr. Thornton asked. The steam from her fresh mug of coffee billowed over her face in wisps as she drank, but Rory found the aroma soothing.

"I've been putting off therapy for a while now," Rory confessed. "At first, I thought I was managing just fine. But after a few years, my friends and I have noticed I've been getting progressively more paranoid and nervous."

Rory knew that her feelings never went away but had just been buried. However, she wasn't sure how to articulate that in a way that made sense. Her eyes darted over to glance out the window for a second until she snapped her gaze back to the office and tried to put what she was feeling into words.

"Sorry, I'm new to this," Rory said. "This is surprisingly difficult for me."

"It's okay," Dr. Thornton said. "It can be nerve-wracking at first."

Rory swallowed a lump in her throat. She cracked her knuckles a few times as she nodded.

"Why don't you tell me how you've been feeling to start?"

Rory liked that; having to verbalize what happened to her felt like too much right off the bat.

"Have you been sleeping?"

"I couldn't tell you the last time I got a full night's sleep," Rory said with a nervous laugh. "I'm pretty much fine during the day; it helps that I keep busy. But once I'm alone at night and lay down to sleep, the anxiety or flashbacks come rolling in. I take melatonin to force myself along, or I'll play a game on my phone to keep myself distracted until I pass out, but it still sucks. I told myself that this year would be my year for healing."

"What does that mean?" Dr. Thornton asked. There was no judgment in her voice.

Rory took a second to think about it. "I … I guess I've been hiding from what happened in the past instead of allowing myself to feel it." She rolled her shoulders back. "I guess I'm finally ready to feel normal again."

"Are you experiencing any other symptoms?" So far, Dr. Thornton's style seemed straightforward, as she probed Rory for more information. Rory appreciated that.

"I'm very jumpy. Can't even stand to be jump-scared on Halloween," Rory said. "If I watch a horror movie with friends, I have to be cuddled up to one of them and have a blanket handy for comfort. But we avoid those."

Dr. Thornton wrote something down on the notepad resting on her lap. "Sounds like your fight-or-flight is always turned on."

"Oh yeah. A few months ago, I started boxing classes to feel powerful again. I was, uh, stalked in college," Rory said. "Probably should have started with that so this made more sense. I don't think I ever got over it."

"I'm sorry to hear that happened to you," Dr. Thornton said. Rory could tell from the softness in her voice that she meant it.

"Thanks, I guess." Rory shrugged. "You know, I didn't even know the guy," she recalled. "Some random dude from one of my Gen Ed classes. He was obsessed with me, and I couldn't even say why."

The therapist frowned. "That sounds like cause for post-traumatic stress disorder."

"That's sort of what I suspected."

"Does he still live in Denver?"

"No, no. He's long gone," Rory said. She brushed some of her tight, highlighted curls back with her fingers to push them out of her face. "He, uh, got arrested. He followed me and my friend Naomi home one night. Had a gun on him and everything." Rory paused and took a deep breath. Even just recalling the memory had her feeling tense and her heart rate increasing.

"You're okay," Dr. Thornton reminded her.

"Have you heard of Hematite?" Rory asked, as she felt some warmth return to her face.

"The vigilante?"

"Yeah."

"I have. He's been working in the Denver area for a long time now, hasn't he?"

Rory nodded. "He saved me. Hard to believe, I know. I tried getting help before it escalated to that point, but the cops on campus didn't take me seriously." Rory exhaled after recalling what happened to Dr. Thornton. Her knee was bouncing subconsciously. "I wish I could thank him, but I don't think that's going to happen, given there's no way of knowing who he is. So now we're here."

"Maybe try writing a letter to him, even if he never sees it. It can even be a simple message in your phone's notes app or a Google doc. That may help you find some closure."

"I don't even know what I'd say. That's the funny part," Rory admitted. "Like, I feel like there's so much I'd want to tell him. But if I ever came face to face, I'd fall flat."

"Writing your feelings down may help you start," Dr. Thornton said. "Start small. Maybe a feelings journal or one of those daily mood log apps you can get for your phone."

Rory nodded again. "Not a bad idea."

Dr. Thornton then asked, "Where was your family during all this?"

"They, uh … they physically were here but weren't emotionally. Some of my friends were there for me. My friend Naomi, the one who was with me? She and her now-fiancé, Brad, were super helpful. So was my friend Kane. He and Naomi pretty much took turns that whole year making sure I was never alone."

Rory smiled at the memory of waking up the following morning to Kane in her dorm room. Naomi had let him in after Rory had gone to sleep, so Kane was sitting in a chair by her bedside. Before Naomi woke up, he must have fallen asleep, as she found him slumped over with his head resting on Naomi's knee.

However, as Rory continued answering Dr. Thornton's questions, her smile turned back into a frown. "But my family sort of suggested to me it was my fault for attracting the attention," she said. "Which is weird because, like I said, I don't even know why this guy picked me of all people. They helped me through the motions, but part of why they moved to Riverpeak when I was born was because it's safe. Maybe they were just too shocked to process it. I dunno."

Rory was certain that Riverpeak wasn't even on the maps, but after her college experience in the city, she didn't mind returning to her roots. Everyone from Riverpeak somehow stayed in Riverpeak. Even if they left for university, the residents always found their way back to the tiny mountain town. The familiarity of a small town that no one had ever heard of was comforting to Rory and helped her feel secure in times of distress. Rather than feeling stuck, she felt at home there.

"There are crappy people everywhere; it's not your fault," Dr. Thornton said. "Do you believe me when I say that?"

Rory didn't have an answer.

———

Dr. Thornton's words rang through Rory's head with each hit of the punching bag that afternoon. She couldn't hear her boxing gloves making an impact, but the meeting with her new therapist replayed with every punch or jab.

Rory made a mental note to never go to boxing class after therapy again. Now that she had a name for her feelings, and some first steps to proper healing, she thought she might burst because coming to grips with her emotions was too much for her to handle.

Rory kept asking herself if she believed it when Dr. Thornton told her she was safe and what happened to her wasn't her fault. However, at that moment, she didn't have an answer, and as much as she wished it would come with each hit of the bag, it never did.

She hoped her workout would have cleared her mind, as it often did, but her head still felt like it was spinning. She did nothing all those years ago to warrant what happened to her with Daniel, but Rory still had those doubts that plagued her from time to time. Every time she hit the punching bag that day, she imagined it was her stalker. Rory remembered the tension in her body that night, as she inevitably waited for something to happen and remembered the way her jaw felt stuck when he whistled at her from the darkness. Had it not been for Hematite, she didn't know what might have happened—and she was too frightened to think about what that alternate reality might have looked like. She didn't snap out of it until the class switched to some ab workouts to end the class, where she was forced to focus on nothing but keeping herself steady during long planks.

Rory put some music on once she returned to her single-family home. She lived in a modest one-bedroom in the suburbs of their small town, not much larger than a studio. Rory didn't want to be alone with her thoughts anymore, so whipping up dinner would serve as a pleasant distraction. Her mind usually wandered, often in directions she didn't like for it to go, so at least she could focus on her meal and the lyrics of the song playing. Background noise meant she wasn't alone with her thoughts; it didn't matter what it was to her, so long as it kept her mind occupied.

When she stared at herself in the mirror as she brushed her teeth later that night, she saw more than just her reflection of olive skin and curls, but a culmination of life experiences. Looking into her own eyes snapped her out of her nightly disassociation from herself, so she tried not to stare in the mirror for too long.

After she finished in the bathroom, Rory frowned at the stack of papers still facing her. On a normal day, she was on top of grading her high school students' work, but she had been putting off grading their history assignments for the last few weeks. It wasn't her intention, but she'd been zoning out more and more frequently. She wasn't sure why now, of all times, to be thinking about her stalker, as it had been years since he tried anything; having to get bailed out of jail was enough to spook him out of Colorado entirely. The New Year meant she was even closer to approaching a decade since the attack, but it seemed as if everything was coming out of the shadows of her mind where she had tucked it all away for safekeeping.

The days were starting to all blend into one in Rory's head. Her rhythm of waking up, picking up Kane, teaching at school, and then going home to drown herself in busy work was making her lose all track of time. The only things keeping Rory aware of the day of the week were her lesson plans and school holidays. As much as she hated being alone with her own thoughts, the idea of letting the time pass around her and doing nothing about it didn't sit quite right with her either.

This isn't fair to my students, Rory thought. *They deserve a teacher who is always present.*

Thankfully, her disassociation presented itself as part of her routine that night. She'd check the answer key, grade a quiz, and then take a swig of hot tea. The routine was easy to fall into, and before she could even realize what she was doing, she was in a rhythm that kept her out of her own head and grading her papers. She wished every night could come with such ease.

When Kane texted her around 10:30 that night, she'd been so in the zone that she was caught off guard. Kane Kelly was one of her closest friends whom she met through Brad and Naomi. Kane had a full ride at the university, thanks to scholarships and grants for low-income, first-generation students. He played the part of a carefree party boy well, but Rory knew the moment she met him, he was a lot smarter than he'd ever give himself credit for. Since then, Kane hadn't changed much. His weekend routine comprised of spending time with his friend Shawn Jameson at the bars downtown and drinking away like they were still 21, not 27. He rarely texted her while he was out, so she wasn't sure if she should be excited or worried.

KANE: You home?

Its shortness was unlike Kane's, and the cryptic words had Rory concerned.

RORY: I am, what's up?

She tried to continue grading the last of the quizzes while she waited for Kane to answer, but she could feel her anxiety spiking in the way her knee bounced up and down again.

KANE: Ok good. I'm out with Jameson. We heard some gunshots nearby. Just making sure you're safe.

Rory sighed as she texted him back.

RORY: Are you guys okay?!

KANE: Yeah, we're fine. I'll see you tomorrow!

Rory groaned. She knew Kane well enough to tell that something was off, but she wasn't sure what. On any given day, Kane was an open book with Rory, so the uncertainty of his text had her a bit on edge. She chalked it up to Kane likely being under the influence of alcohol, but she turned the news on to see what may be happening.

"Breaking news," the anchor kicked off. "At least one person is dead after shots were fired in downtown Riverpeak. We have not confirmed his identity, but the victim appears to be the local masked vigilante Hematite."

Rory dropped her remote in shock and suddenly snapped out of her dissociative state. She felt a lump in her throat when she tried to swallow a sip of chamomile tea, her hand shaking as she set the mug down.

"Police tell us that the victim's description is in line with Hematite, a street fighter who has remained a mystery to Riverpeak for more than a decade," the other anchor said. "The suspected shooter is now in custody. Police say he claims another anonymous figure hired him."

"They tell us the suspect blamed a man named Stone Breaker. We have a crew on their way to the scene now for more updates."

"What?" Rory asked herself. She wasn't sure why a stranger would want to kill Hematite, never mind hurt him. And with a name like Stone Breaker, she thought this had to be a targeted attack.

Rory rushed to grab her phone, desperate for more information. It was hard for her to accept that Hematite was dead, and she had never heard of anyone going by the name Stone Breaker, so she felt too shocked to process what was happening right away. She went to Twitter, hoping for live reports from bystanders and found the video of the suspected shooter being arrested with little hassle.

"This was for Stone Breaker! There's more of us!" the suspect shouted. Despite the suspect's anger, he didn't seem as if he was inebriated or tweaking out. In fact, it was a sort of calm rage—the type that scared Rory the most.

"What the hell kind of name is Stone Breaker?" she muttered to herself with disgust as she Googled the name on her phone. She found a new YouTube channel belonging to someone of the same name and tapped into it, afraid of what she might find.

There was only one video, a trailer for his channel. Stone Breaker's video opened up with a tacky lightning bolt transition and sound effect. He too was masked, wearing what looked like a 3D-printed face shield that hid his identity. However, Rory could see the pale color of his neck, showing that he wasn't wearing anything beneath his face covering. A bright yellow lightning bolt was painted across the stone-gray mask, but the outline of the lightning bolt looked messy as though they tried to patch it up with a marker.

"Masked vigilantes are ruining our city," he began. The monotone, deep sound of his voice hinted that Stone Breaker was using a voice modifier to disguise himself. "If you agree, then you're in the right place. It's about high time we let the thin blue line do their work rather than take matters into our own hands. It's time we stop people like Hematite once and for all."

Rory couldn't believe what she was hearing. While she understood that vigilantism wasn't everyone's cup of tea, she thought all of Riverpeak considered Hematite a hometown hero, especially considering it was the community who named him.

"Hematite claims to protect this city," Stone Breaker continued. "But I think that he's just getting in the way and inciting crime."

Rory couldn't bear to watch it anymore, even though there were still three minutes left in the video. She closed out of the YouTube app and tossed her phone onto her couch. She decided instead to focus on the news, hoping for word that Hematite wasn't dead and that there was some huge misunderstanding. When the local news channels were on a commercial break, she grabbed her phone again and opted for panic-scrolling through social media.

The night felt like a blur to Rory. The hours felt like they were moving in slow motion, but when she looked at the time on the corner of her phone screen, she saw it was already three in the morning. She realized the news she was hoping for would never come and accepted that his death was true. Filled with grief, Rory opened her jewelry box in her bedroom and removed a small, torn piece of dark fabric from it. She held it with care in her fingers, letting the softness soothe her.

Rory clutched the fabric to her chest and, for the first time in years, let herself weep. Her sobs racked her body to the point of sharpness in her lungs.

So much for a year of healing, she thought.

CHAPTER 2

Kane Kelly woke up with the worst headache of his life on Monday morning, already feeling the effects of Sunday night's events. He could tell that he was getting closer to thirty; he was still young, but not as quick to recoup as he used to be ten years ago. He rubbed his temples, sighed, and grimaced as he got out of bed. His entire body ached, but he'd have to just pop some painkillers and carry on with his day to conceal his current state.

He made the short trek from his bed to his bathroom in his studio apartment, finding the cold of the fake hardwood floor beneath his feet soothing. There wasn't much on the walls of the small apartment, but he didn't mind. The few things that were there were old house-warming gifts or recycled from his college dorm, which he thought made the space a little more special. Because he had little to decorate with, the studio felt anything but cramped. Rory liked to call his studio apartment minimalist, but he just called it being poor.

Kane tried to remember the events of the night before, but it was hazy. He remembered getting in a fight, and then it all came flooding back when he looked at himself in his bathroom mirror after washing his face. A fresh, round scar rested on his ribcage. He pushed back his long blonde hair, turned around, and craned his neck so he could check his back. It didn't take long to find the scar's twin, as the pink popped against his ivory skin.

Of all the ways Kane had been attacked, getting shot was one of his least favorite. *At least the bullet went clean through this time,* he thought. He'd had to fish out some bullets before and hated having to get some help from his doctor.

Immortality had its perks, but he considered moments like this to be a real drag. He had worked with a specialist at a lab on the more rural side of town who was helping him determine the likely cause of his immortality. But so far, they'd only been able to guess that it had to do with his mother's drug addiction; the dealers were putting something in the methamphetamines, but he still hadn't found out what. Kane used HIPAA laws to his advantage to make sure they swore to secrecy over what they found.

The knocking on his door startled him. He looked at his watch; Rory was there thirty minutes before her usual time. In only his boxers, he didn't even bother to put the rest of his clothes on and answered the door while he continued brushing his teeth. She was holding a bag from the local cafe and two cups of coffee.

Rory looked ever the academic, as per usual. Her curls were down today, with only a few pieces tied back to stay out of her face, and she kept her makeup simple. Some liner rested on her lids to distract from bloodshot eyes, and she had some foundation on, but Kane could tell the flush on her cheeks was natural, not from whatever blush she used. She was the social studies teacher at Riverpeak High and someone could tell that just by looking at her, with her wide-leg black trousers and brown button-up blouse tucked into it. Kane always teased her, saying that she looked like she belonged in a gender-swapped remake of an *Indiana Jones* movie. He never told her this part, but he thought it suited her well.

Kane noticed Rory was wearing her glasses today; on a normal day, she would opt for contacts.

"Don't hate me for being super early," Rory said as Kane let her through the door. She looked Kane up and down before she concluded, "And you're as good as naked. Shit, Kane, did I..." Rory dropped her voice to a whisper. "Did I fuck up? Is someone—?"

Kane's laugh was stifled by his toothbrush. "No, no one's here. I never score, you know that. Come on in; I don't give a shit," he said with a shrug.

"I come bearing breakfast," she said. "So, I hope that makes up for my being early."

Rory and Kane both worked at Riverpeak High School; his apartment complex was on her way there, so she was always his ride. Kane had made his old Honda Prelude functional and he took pride in it, but Rory insisted they just carpool to prevent his work of art from falling to pieces in the street.

Kane just patted her shoulder in response before he walked back to the bathroom. Despite having known each other for years, Rory had never seen Kane shirtless before. She took the opportunity to check him out as she sat down on a barstool in his kitchenette. Rory only got a quick glance before he moved into the other room, but seeing his strong back, he was more muscular than she thought he'd be. Beneath his clothes, he looked fairly scrawny, but she realized she was mistaken.

"Don't hate me for not having any pants on. In my defense, you're super early," Kane replied once he spat out his toothpaste.

He sounded extra exhausted, Rory thought. "You're lucky you're cute," she retorted. "Everything alright, Kay?"

"Yeah, yeah." He walked over to his bureau to get dressed. "Rough night last night. The usual."

He couldn't see it as he reached for some pants and an undershirt, but Rory frowned at his confession. "Well, I got your favorite coffee and sandwich. That should help you out, I hope."

"Always does. You're the best. I might ask you to marry me if some other guy doesn't snatch you up before we're thirty." He winked as he joined her at the counter. Kane brushed his blonde hair, which reached halfway down his neck, out of his face. "I'd be a terrible husband, so you better be careful."

Rory laughed; Kane had been telling her that for years but she often wondered if he would ever actually propose.

Had it been anyone else, the behavior would have annoyed Rory. She rarely associated with flirts who cracked sex jokes often and were unafraid of dirty talk being part of casual conversation. But Kane was Kane, and his delivery always toed the line between charming and over the top. Rory couldn't remember a day where Kane didn't make her laugh at least once.

"I can never tell when you're flirting with me for real anymore."

"Eh, I can't either." Kane shrugged and took a sip of coffee. "Why breakfast today? You always cook at home."

"I wanted a pleasant start to the day and figured I'd treat myself."

Kane noticed her brief pause as he chewed his breakfast.

Rory then asked, "Did you watch the news last night?"

Kane shook his head. "No, you know I don't have cable."

"I mean, me neither, Kay, but it's all over the local channels. Facebook, TikTok, everywhere. They found Hematite dead last night. I think I cried myself to sleep. I took a *lot* of melatonin gummies to help the process along, though."

That would explain why she's wearing glasses instead of her usual contact lenses, Kane thought. *Rory never wears her contacts after a good cry.*

"Oh, shit," Kane said. "I'm sorry, Rory. I know he meant a lot to you." Kane took a bite of the breakfast sandwich that Rory brought him and took his time chewing it. He felt his heartbeat speed up and struggled to look into her dark eyes, which only appeared darker with her mood.

Now he remembered every detail of last night. He also remembered texting Rory in his dying stupor last night and mentally scrambled to recall what he may have sent her. She wasn't saying anything out of the ordinary, so he allowed himself to relax. *Clearly*, he thought, *I didn't out myself.*

"Yeah. The cops found him after someone reported some gunshots downtown. It was breaking at eleven. They think it was someone working with that Stone Breaker prick, whoever that is. What a stupid, fucking name."

"Yeah, that guy sounds like a real piece of shit." Kane took another bite. He did everything in his power to pretend that he did not know what Rory was talking about. He found that eating and drinking his coffee was helping him mask his expressions.

"God only knows the cops in this town are totally useless, so."

Rory sighed, then sipped her coffee. "It's weird, though. When I was driving here, the radio station was talking about it, and they said his body actually went missing. They think someone broke in overnight to steal it. I'll have to see if Naomi has any info that they aren't sharing yet."

"Maybe he's not really dead." Kane hoped the suggestion would cheer her up.

"I dunno. The news said he got shot in the lungs. I'm not sure how anyone could come back from that."

Kane had so much he wanted to say to comfort her, but he knew he couldn't. He wanted to explain to Rory that Hematite was fine, and his outfit was in the dryer, waiting to be hung up. He wanted to say that he simply woke up in the coroner's office and was the one to bust a window, no body snatchers involved. Hematite was, in fact, very much alive, and he wanted nothing more than to tell her that with the utmost confidence.

But Kane couldn't explain last night to Rory. He would much rather she think his behavior this morning was from a hangover instead of getting the shit kicked out of him, because Rory did not know that Kane was actually Hematite; and Kane would prefer it stay that way.

Kane didn't even know what else to say at that moment. He was always so afraid he would slip up or say something that gave away too much. If he wasn't careful, one misplaced word would be all it took to clue Rory into his secret identity, but he prioritized her safety over anything else—even if it meant lying to her for the last eight years. Rory was one of the wittiest people he knew, though, so it hadn't been an easy task.

He was relieved when Rory continued the conversation. "When I heard the news, I thought I was gonna puke. I've spent almost a decade on and off trying to find him again, hoping I'd see him. I never got to thank him for the night he saved me, and that's all I've wanted to do. Now I can't. I should have taken this more seriously while I could have."

Kane moved his hand to her back to rub small circles to comfort her. Every time he touched her, he felt his heart swell, but he tried to just push his feelings down like he had since day one. Their friendship and her safety both meant too much to him to risk stating his feelings for her.

"I'm sure he doesn't need your thanks. That's not why heroes do it, you know."

Rory's smile was a sad one. "Yeah, I guess you're right."

———

When they arrived at Riverpeak High School, they hadn't even started the homeroom period before an assembly was called. All students and faculty were to report to the gymnasium right away.

Rory took attendance as her class made their way back out their doors and led her students through the halls. It was a small school, only one two-story building for classrooms, since it was such a small town wedged between the mountains. The gymnasium was detached and was separated by the football field on campus.

One of Rory's students walked alongside her, not having checked in for the day. "Hey, Miss Miller! Long time, no see. Do you know what the assembly is about?" Jordan asked. "It seems kind of random. They've never done one right after winter break before."

Jordan was a normal teenager, not quite nerdy enough to hang out with the bookworms and not quite trendy enough to be invited into the popular cliques, since her parents kept her busy at their local cafe. Jordan always wore her dark hair in twin braids in a way that reminded Rory of her friend Naomi, except Jordan's hair was naturally curly whereas Naomi's was silky and straight.

"Your guess is as good as mine, if I'm being honest. If they told us anything, I missed the memo." As they walked, Rory made a note of Jordan's attendance, not wanting to forget later.

"Hey." Rory turned to her left and saw that Kane caught up to her. "So, uh, what's this assembly? Did they tell us, and I just missed the email or something?" he asked.

"I dunno either." She shook her head. "Glad it's not just me."

Kane turned as he walked to look at his English students behind him. "Sorry, guys. The smart one doesn't know either." He looked back at Rory, patted her shoulder, and shot her a wink before returning to his class to make sure no one snuck off. "I'll see you inside."

A few of her students whispered, but Rory ignored it. A lot of the kids theorized that she and Kane were dating over the years, but it was amusing at this point. She separated from her class once they reached the gymnasium to join Kane and the rest of the faculty. They sat together as they always did, not helping their case against any dating rumors that their students were spreading.

The gymnasium hardly looked any different from when Rory and Kane were students there; despite both growing up in Riverpeak, they never had classes together until college, where they met through Naomi and bonded over their undergraduate teacher program. The bleachers showed their age and even though the floor was freshly waxed over winter break, Rory could still see years of scuff marks and scratches from basketball games. A few banners hung up on the wall behind them, highlighting basketball championships they won over the years. Their success had been the only thing to put them on the local maps.

A man with balding brown hair and blue eyes was standing at the podium, accompanied by the school principal, who looked like his polar opposite, with her tight, voluminous blonde curls.

Rory recognized him from a few stories Naomi had covered for Channel 10: Councilman Tom Stevens, best known for a few scandals that were mostly forgotten about by the public. His green shirt was about half a size too small for him, with his white tie hiding the buttons threatening to pop open.

"Good morning, Riverpeak High School." The principal's tone lacked any of the enthusiasm one would expect from her words. "We have a special guest today. Please give a warm welcome to Tom Stevens from our town council."

The students partook in a polite golf clap. Rory and Kane did not.

"Thank you for sharing your time with me this morning." His voice boomed with overconfidence already. "I come here on behalf of the city council to talk to you about some concerning trends in our town."

He paused as he straightened out his papers on the podium and then continued. "As many of you may have heard, the masked vigilante Hematite is dead." He sounded like a perfect, polished politician who kept his emotions in check, but Rory could see the slight upturn of his lips.

This news caused a few students to whisper, which resulted in a gentle shushing from the principal. Her mouth was stuck in a thin line, as if she wasn't happy about the situation at hand but that she had no choice and had to go along with it.

"We do not want to see this trend of vigilante violence rise. Our police force does a wonderful job keeping Riverpeak safe. Vigilantes do not help our city; rather, they inspire and incite violence."

Rory's mind flashed to what Stone Breaker said on YouTube; the word choice couldn't have been a coincidence. Before she could get too angry, she felt Kane's hand on her leg. Kane gave her knee a gentle squeeze.

"Should any of you be interested in pursuing a path of law enforcement, I have partnered with the University of Colorado's criminal justice program and our local police department to spread awareness of how you can help keep Riverpeak safe. We'll be by the cafeteria all day today to answer any questions you may have. Thank you."

They played a short video advertising the university's criminal justice program to finish up the assembly. Rory couldn't bring herself to watch it. From what she heard, though, it wasn't even pretending to be anything but the propaganda that it was.

"You okay?" Kane whispered. Even if he hadn't known her, it was obvious she was in anguish just from looking at her. Her jaw was tight, and her shoulders hunched inwards.

Rory almost nodded but remembered she was trying to heal after everything that happened to her. She couldn't move on if she didn't face her feelings, so she shook her head and hoped she didn't draw any attention to her and Kane.

"We know the truth." Kane felt like such a liar for saying it to Rory, so he tried to remind himself of the context to feel less like a hypocrite. *Juggling my costume changes is about to become a lot more difficult,* he thought. "Don't worry. I'm here."

"Thanks, Kay." Her voice almost cracked.

Kane pondered his next move as the video played and paid no

attention to it; he knew from experience how much of a joke the Riverpeak Police Department was. If they were half-competent, he wouldn't be searching for answers about how he got his powers and why he was getting shot at in the process.

There was a reason Kane couldn't die from the shooting last night beyond just pure luck at birth, and he was determined to figure out why. He couldn't put his finger on it, but he felt like Stevens was part of that answer.

After the assembly ended, Rory returned to her classroom with a smile on her face, but nothing about it was genuine. She adjusted her glasses on her nose before she said, "Alright, time for current events, though I could probably guess what most of you have picked." She placed her hands on her hips as she asked, "Show of hands, who picked Hematite's death as their topic for the day?"

Two-thirds of the class raised their hands. Rory allowed her smile to drop at that and exhaled as she looked out at the sea of hands before her.

"Alright, let's handle this a little differently today. You guys can lower your hands," she said. "How many people here have been personally affected by Hematite or know someone who has been? Close your eyes and then raise your hands."

Rory already felt like she had taken a knife to the heart with the news, but it cut even deeper when she saw every single hand raise up.

"Okay, open your eyes before you lower your hands. Look around."

Her class was silent as everyone glanced around them, seeing every single hand in the air. Rory sat on the top of her desk as she thought of what to say next. She had never seen them all so quiet, as they all brought their hands back to their sides.

"I don't want to spend the entire class talking about Hematite. But it's clear that he's had quite the impact on all of us, myself included. If anyone needs to talk, my door is always open, okay?"

A few voices chimed together, "Thanks, Miss Miller."

Jordan raised her hand.

"Yes, Jordan?"

"Why would anyone want to kill Hematite? He stopped some guys from mugging my dad when he closed up the cafe one night last year, and people are *still* coming in to offer to pay for

Hematite's drinks. Not that he ever comes in."

Rory bit the inside of her lip. "Well, I'd bet that Hematite gained a few enemies by doing what he does. But I don't know what might have sparked it now."

"My mom says that crime's gonna get worse here."

"It might," Rory said with a shrug. "I won't lie to you guys. We can't be sure. But you all are safe here, okay?"

Rory swallowed after she said it, hoping that it was true. She wasn't even sure of it herself, but as she looked at the crowd of concerned teenage faces before her, she knew she had to be strong for them

CHAPTER 3

Kane, dressed as Hematite, dropped a stack of blankets by the front door and then wandered through the halls of the long-abandoned two-story office building on the east side of the city. Some company once considered moving their headquarters here, but their office was overrun by a handful of the unhoused people that used to pop their tents up over the lot. The city never stopped them, and they weren't why Kane was there—he was just glad they had a roof over their heads in the winter, even if it wasn't ideal.

Kane sauntered the halls, trying to not alert anyone to his presence until he reached a cubicle in the back corner. He ghosted his knuckles over the cubicle wall and knocked to see if the person he was looking for was inside.

"Hematite?" Their head popped up from beneath the desk. "Holy shit, you're alive?"

"Shh." Kane put his finger to his mouth, though no one could see his mouth beneath his many layers. He crouched down to be at eye level with them. The teenager had blonde hair like Kane's, but longer and more unruly. They reminded Kane of himself, and he realized just now that he didn't know their name.

Kane reached into one of his pants pockets and handed them a water bottle and a peanut-butter-and-jelly sandwich that was covered in plastic wrap. The teenager grasped it with a quiet thanks before they snagged their first bite of food. They closed their eyes in contentment.

"Anything?" Kane asked once they finished chewing.

The kid nodded. "Yeah, it's been weird. A bunch of guys have been coming in here trying to sell drugs. If people say no, they ask if they want to make them so they can get some extra cash."

Kane held back his groan. "What do they look like?"

"The one that's here the most is really tall. Clearly works out and has short brown hair. What day is it?"

"Wednesday."

"You might see him; it's his day today. Be careful, okay?"

"You too, kid. Your parents doing alright?"

He nodded. "Their withdrawals have been something wicked, but they're managing. They're sleeping two floors up. My mom said she feels way less productive, but I think she knows it's for the best."

Kane smiled beneath his mask. "Good. Thanks again, bud."

Kane made his way back to the front of the office, careful to stay away from the windows to stay in the dark. He heard a few whispers as he walked through but paid them no mind. After all these years, he was bound to get caught dead somewhere; he just hated the aftermath of it.

When Kane reached the entrance and the front door swung closed behind him, he came face to face with the man his teenage friend warned him about.

"Well, I'll be damned," the man said with a smirk. "I thought Stone Breaker had Shatterstone and his buddies take care of you."

"Yeah, I think they thought that too." He held his arms out. "But here I am."

As the man approached, Kane put his hands up to cover his face. The man was taller and bulkier than Kane was, so Kane knew what was coming next; these types usually assumed they'd have the upper hand. Just as Kane predicted, the man swung first, trying to get a punch in, but Kane bobbed and weaved away just in time. He shifted his footing to switch positions with the man, wanting to lead him away from the office building. Kane mentally thanked God that it worked, as his attacker took some steps toward him, throwing punches but missing because of poor, sloppy technique. Kane's long pants and hoodie helped him blend in with the night, which only helped his case as they moved away from the building and close to the shadows.

Just as Kane let his guard down, he flew back into a building after being kicked in the shoulder with a steel-toed boot. Kane felt his shoulder pop when he hit the wall with a force he hadn't expected. Kane groaned as he reached for his shoulder. He rushed to crack it, grateful that it wasn't dislocated, and then grabbed for one of the billy clubs clipped to his belt. Even with his boxing wraps and the black wool gloves that he wore over them, the metal was cold to the touch in the frigid January air. His adrenaline was pumping now, but he knew his back would hurt like hell in the morning.

As he swung at his attacker with the club, Kane thought about everything that culminated up to this moment. He thought of how he was getting pretty sick and tired of everything he put up with. After years of working to clean up his city, he had only scratched the surface; the long road ahead was far from encouraging.

The man's instinct was to protect his face after being whacked with the club, leaving his body wide open for Kane to hit. Kane sighed, thought of Rory and his sister Kayla for some much-needed motivation, and punched his attacker in the ribs with a left hook. Kane knew he could take the hits and make it out okay, a luxury most others didn't have, so he carried on with the fight. The man spat out blood, which stained the snow beneath their feet, and he popped a tooth out along with it. Kane whacked him again with the billy club, which finally knocked his attacker down.

His opponent was twice his weight and a few inches taller than him, so having the man on his knees would make his job easier. Kane grabbed him by the collar of his shirt.

"What do you want, man?" the attacker asked in pain.

"Who sent you?" Kane was already out of patience for this guy before the fight even began. "Who and why?"

"He'll fucking kill me, man." He seemed to have accepted his fate. If he was afraid, he didn't show it.

"Answer the question." Kane pulled the man's head back a bit to get a better look at him. "Who and why?"

"He's no different from you. He's just looking out for him and his own, you know?"

"Who, Stone Breaker?" Kane scoffed. Stone Breaker was new on the scene, having been around the east side of town for maybe a few months, but he'd been a major pain in Kane's ass since he arrived. "He's delusional if he thinks we are anything alike."

"Just knock me out. You won't kill me, right?" His voice shook now, and his lip started quivering. Kane would never tire of seeing how quickly they mentally broke. "That's not your style, I know that. But he *will* kill me, man. I'm serious."

Kane didn't see a point in asking any more questions; he got as much as he could. This wasn't the first junkie that Stone Breaker sent after him, and he was sure it wouldn't be the last. He hit the man one last time in the jaw, and it was enough to knock him out. He dropped him and called it a night.

"Stupid fucking name, anyway," Kane muttered to himself.

As he made his way to the closest fire escape to travel by rooftop through the east side, he paused on the street corner. Someone had spray-painted a memorial for Hematite, including a portrait of him in his disguise of black masks, scarves, and hoods that took up much of the brick wall. A few people laid flowers by it, and someone had lit a candle that had already burned out and melted down. Kane frowned at the sight as he moved on.

Kane scaled the fence of the storage facility to not be detected and made his way to his unit. It had been under a pseudonym, using his old fake ID from college so he could avoid raising any suspicions when renting the storage unit out. His unit was plain, only decorated by a few news articles on the wall that he had pieced together in hopes of finding answers to why he could not die. That question plagued him the most, and the closer he got to figuring it out, the more criminals seemed to pop up to stop him from uncovering the truth.

When he was inside his storage unit, Kane sighed as he sat down in the metal folding chair. The chair had been as cold as the brick wall earlier, but the chill felt nice on his back after his fight. He glanced up at the camera he had set up in front of him and took a moment to compose himself.

Once he felt ready, Kane straightened his posture and confirmed that his voice modifier was on. He double-checked that he'd tucked his blonde locks into his balaclava before recording. He then lowered his hood further over his face, making sure it cast a shadow over his eyes, and then he spoke. Being a public figure wasn't his thing, especially when he donned the Hematite getup. But he knew the people were mourning and if he didn't say something, things would only get worse at the hands of Stone Breaker.

———

Rory had the local news station on as she did her dishes to support Naomi; it was her friend's first time as an in-studio reporter, finally getting a cushier gig instead of being out in the field. Rory wouldn't miss it for the world. She dried her hands to grab a quick photo of Naomi, sharing it on her Instagram Stories with the text, "THAT'S MY GIIIIIRL!!!" and the heart eyes emoji over it.

"And breaking news," Naomi read from her spot, standing by the monitor with the station's logo flashing on it. Naomi looked sharp, her black hair curled and her makeup the perfect combination of glamorous and natural. Rory could detect focus and fierceness in Naomi's dark eyes, which was how she could tell this story was serious. "We have confirmed that Hematite is alive. This just came into our station within the last few minutes."

Rory dropped the sponge into the sink.

"We received this video from Hematite. Take a look."

Rory was frozen in place at her kitchen sink as she watched the video roll. Hematite was in a dark room, wearing the same clothing as always. He'd changed his voice in the video's post-production even more than it was in real life, but he included captioning. Rory didn't need the captions; she could make out every word.

"My name is Hematite," he said. His eyes weren't visible, but you could tell he was addressing the camera in his posture. "And I'm here to let you know that you can't kill me so easily. Corruption has allowed our town to house a dark underbelly for far too long." His tone was serious, even with the voice modifier, and Rory sensed this was acting as both a threat to whoever was after him and as reassurance to those who stood behind him. "The ones who hired my attempted killer are none other than Stone Breaker and his crew, who I believe are directly connected to our city government. Mark my words: I'm not going anywhere, so you can end your little propaganda tour."

The video cut to black, so the news switched back to Naomi in the studio. She said, "For those of you just joining us, Hematite is alive. There is no confirmation that this is the real Hematite, whose body went missing after he was found dead last week, or if it is a copycat vigilante. The video sent to us had a lot of security locks on it, so we couldn't confirm the validity of the sender's information. Either way, you can rely on us to keep you updated the second we can confirm."

Rory heard nothing the news anchors said after that. She was in a complete daze, shocked at the news report and video. She could tell from his voice and build that this was the same Hematite who saved her when she was in college; Rory felt it in her gut. Seeing him on the screen was enough to bring her back to that day on campus. The memories made her body tense up, starting at her jaw and shoulders and moving downward. She tried to just focus on the surrounding room instead, rattling off a few mental notes about her safety and her surroundings to try and ground herself at the moment. The last thing she wanted was to relive the scariest day of her life in vivid detail twice in one week.

She was in her apartment.

She was safe.

Hematite was alive.

After all those years of wishing she could have thanked him, Rory realized that now she was given her chance. She grabbed her phone with shaky hands she could not control and sent a simple text to Naomi, asking her to call her once she got off work. When Naomi did, Rory was quick to answer.

"Hey! Glad you called."

"Hey. Sorry, I didn't mean to hit FaceTime. My thumb must have slipped," Naomi said with a laugh.

"Eh, no biggie." From the video call, Rory could see that Naomi was still in her car and hadn't left the news station yet.

"I take it you saw the video?"

"Yeah. Good job, by the way. Listen … do you want to help me find out who Hematite is?"

Naomi grinned. "I would love to. I was wondering when you'd ask me that."

"It's about time I get some closure. I don't even know what I'll say when I find him, but I have to."

"Have you practiced at all?" Naomi asked.

"My therapist suggested writing him a letter, even if I never get to deliver it to him. The note in my phone that I set aside for it has been sitting blank," Rory revealed.

"I'm sure it'll come to you when you meet him again. He saved our lives, after all! Yours especially." Rory could hear the excitement in Naomi's voice when she said, "Can you imagine if we actually found him?" Naomi had that sparkle in her eyes that she got whenever she had something new to research; she was an investigative journalist through and through.

Rory closed her eyes and tried to envision meeting him again. She pictured herself standing before him, unsure of his face or unfiltered voice, but able to say thank you once and for all—but the words still felt trapped in her throat.

"What if we reveal him to the world by accident?" Rory asked.

Naomi sighed. "Don't tell me you're having second thoughts. Rory, you've wanted this forever!"

"And I don't want it at the expense of ruining his career. What if we mess this up for him?"

"I doubt we will. And if you're really unsure, why don't we start with Stone Breaker? It'll be a good test run of our sleuthing skills, and then there won't be any harm done if we reveal a secret identity. If anything, it'll help the cops get a guy wanted for an attempted murderer … and help Hematite find the guy after him." Her smile hinted at her confidence, something Rory desperately wanted to borrow.

Rory nodded. She liked Naomi's idea, and though she could not care less about helping the police, who never helped her when she needed it, she wanted more than anything to help Hematite. Naomi knew that this compromise would appeal to Rory's need for closure after everything that happened to her in college.

"I'm in." Rory felt a sort of conviction she hadn't felt in a long time. "Hematite helped us. It's time we help him."

CHAPTER 4

Kane was sitting atop the local pharmacy with a peanut-butter-and-jelly sandwich in his full Hematite regalia when Rory called. He shoved part of the sandwich in his mouth and, as he chewed faster than he ever had in his life, reached for the off switch for his voice-changer. He somehow picked up the call just before the last ring.

"Hey!" He still kept an eye below to continue his patrol. He normally went from town to town but had been focusing more on Riverpeak lately to hone in on Stone Breaker, since he suspected he was close; all the attacks had been happening in Riverpeak. "What are you doing up this late?"

"I could ask you the same thing," Rory said. "Hey, listen, do you wanna help me and Naomi out with something? We could use all the help we could get."

"What's going on?"

"Well, there's a sort of vigilante video war going on. Have you seen it?"

"I mean, who hasn't?"

"Naomi and I want to figure out who Hematite and Stone Breaker are. You down?"

Kane had a feeling this would happen eventually, but he was still unprepared for it. He buried his nerves and kept his composure when he said, "Like, right now?"

"I mean, she and I are, at least. But you don't need to head over here or anything if you're busy."

"Yeah, I'm on my way to meet up with Jameson at the bar." Kane winced at himself; he hated lying to her, but it was a necessary evil. "He and his girlfriend are having some issues again, so I promised him I'd come out. You know how they get, can't stop fighting. But maybe some other night, okay?"

"Oh, okay." Rory sounded disappointed, and it killed him to hear her voice drop like that. "Have fun with Jameson. Call me if you need a ride home, alright?"

"Thanks, Mom," Kane teased. "Have a good night. Tell Naomi I said hi." He sighed as he hung the phone up. "Shit," he muttered to himself. He paused as he tried to think through his panic. He questioned how far Rory could actually go down the rabbit hole before reaching a dead end.

Kane knew Rory well enough to know that if anyone could figure his identity out, it was her. She was stubborn and resourceful enough, plus she never knew when to quit. With Naomi helping her too, their likelihood of discovering who Hematite was just skyrocketed. Kane thought that if Rory was going to uncover who Hematite was, he'd rather she heard it from him—and he wasn't ready to tell her just yet.

He opened the YouTube app on his phone and quickly found Stone Breaker's channel. There was a new upload from only a few minutes ago, so Kane clicked on it. The video opened with a lightning bolt sound effect; Kane thought it looked cheesy, especially since it matched the mask's haphazard paint job.

"This video is for Hematite," Stone Breaker said. He was sitting in what looked like an office. Kane could only see him from the chest up; Stone Breaker had darkened the room, but it looked like he wore a black hoodie and a light blue beanie to hide his hair from view. "I've about had it with you wreaking havoc on my town. You can talk about Riverpeak's underbelly all you want, but the people need the stability that we're providing them. Let's see how you like me when I don't hold back, Hematite—and let's see how many times it'll take for me to take you down. If I can't kill you, maybe I can unmask you."

"What a fucking asshole," Kane said with a roll of his eyes. He pocketed his phone and knew he only had one place to turn to right now. The last bite of his PB&J sat forgotten in his lap after answering his phone and watching the video, so he took one last bite of his sandwich, tossed the crumbs for the pigeons sitting on the other end of the roof, and left.

———

Elijah Baron did not expect to hear a knocking at his back door, of all places, at nearly midnight. He walked to his kitchen to peer out the back window, only to see Hematite standing there in his full regalia. If it weren't for the large hood, Elijah might have been able to see his eyes, but the shadow from the fabric covered them.

Elijah answered the door right away. His full lips curled up into a smile. "It's been a while since you've been here."

"Yeah, well, I need your help again," Hematite said. "Is now a good time?"

Kane assumed the answer was yes, based on how Elijah was dressed. His loose auburn curls, usually tucked beneath a hat, were on full display, something that Kane had tried to tell Elijah would be beneficial to show in his search for a girlfriend after years of being single. Elijah was still wearing jeans and an anime T-shirt, officially off the clock from his IT gig but not going to bed soon. His five o'clock shadow made his typically light, golden skin take on a much paler hue, but his dark green eyes looked lively despite the late-night hour. Kane always ran the risk of running into their mutual friend and Elijah's roommate, Brad, when he showed up unannounced in need of tech support like this, but it was a risk he was willing to take.

"Sure, come on in. Brad is already asleep since he has an early shift at the clinic tomorrow, so it's just us." He closed the door behind him and was sure to lock it. "One second." He jogged to the front of the house to close the blinds that were still open. "Okay, you're good."

"Thanks. I have a few people who are trying to figure out who I am."

"Isn't that half of the Denver area?" Elijah ran a hand through his hair. "Especially after your video that you sent me to encrypt for the news stations?"

"I mean seriously trying to find out who I am and who can actually figure it out," Hematite stressed. "Can you let me know if that's possible? These people are equal parts determined and capable."

Elijah furrowed his thick brows. "And what if it is possible and I find out who you are in the process? Doesn't that go against our agreement?"

"Fuck the agreement," Hematite said without a second thought. "You've been helping me since we were kids, Elijah. I can trust you, and I don't think anyone knows that you've been helping me. You should be safe, even if you know. And I'll still hold up my end of the deal."

"Alright then. Suit yourself."

The agreement was something they established when Hematite first came on the scene. Elijah had been the most intelligent kid in their class since kindergarten and Kane recognized this. He considered Elijah one of his best friends, so he went to him whenever he needed help with anything tech-related—something that especially came in handy when he was first starting out as Hematite and didn't have his own computer, only an old flip phone. Despite being friends since they were kids, Kane never revealed his identity and he had no idea how Elijah would react once he knew.

In return, Elijah and his family had 24/7 access to Hematite in the event they needed help, so long as they asked no questions or tried to find out who he was. Elijah found value in the deal since his family was the only Jewish one in their backwoods mountain town. Their neighbors were accepting people, and the town was diverse enough, but he'd rather be safe than sorry against any antisemitism.

However, it had been twelve years since they made the deal, and a lot had changed since they were in high school.

Hematite cleared his throat and dropped the hood of his cowl. He yanked off his balaclava, messing up his blonde hair beneath it, and sighed. Elijah watched him turn off the voice changer beneath it, which rested by his neck. He then said, "It's me, dude."

Elijah's eyes widened. "Kane?"

"Yeah." Kane shrugged. "If you're gonna make sure no one knows … you've gotta know."

"Holy shit, man." Elijah took a moment to process the revelation. "Of all the people I would have guessed, it was not you."

Kane laughed. "That's kind of the idea."

"Come on, we can head to my office. Let me just check the blinds upstairs." Elijah felt shellshocked but knew they had work to do if people were trying to crack Kane's code. He ran upstairs, double-checking the blinds and making sure Brad was still asleep. After a moment, he came back down to let Kane know it was all clear.

Elijah's home office had more monitors in it than Kane knew what to do with. His desk was one of the large corner ones that took up considerable space in the room. Elijah's office always sent Kane down memory lane, what with the photos of them throughout the years and the different basketball and baseball trophies Elijah earned in high school.

"Alright, let me log in to my personal laptop here." Elijah grabbed a laptop on the edge of the desk that was connected to one of the many monitors, so it had a second screen effect. The laptop had two stickers on the back: one that he bought from one of the high school fundraisers featuring the school mascot, a mountain goat, and the other being from an anime that Kane didn't recognize. "I have an extra chair in my bedroom if you want to bring it over so you can sit down. Let me get to work here."

"Yeah, thanks."

When Kane returned, Elijah asked, "So, who is trying to figure you out? That'll help me know where to start in our search. If I can try to trace their likely footsteps, I can see if it'll work."

"Stone Breaker is actively threatening me, for starters. He filmed a video and uploaded it on YouTube earlier tonight."

Elijah rolled his eyes. "He used YouTube? What an amateur. There's a way to dig out an IP out of just about anything online." He pulled up the website. "Who else?"

"Rory is getting serious. She's always been curious, but I think my temporary death the other night lit a flame under her ass."

He stopped in his tracks and turned to look at Kane. "Rory?"

Kane nodded as his lips formed a thin line. "Rory."

Elijah raised a brow. "Rory Miller? The Rory that you have been madly in love with since our freshman year of college?" Elijah sounded a bit annoyed, but he didn't bother to correct his tone. "*The* Rory that you work with at the high school?"

"Yeah. That Rory."

Elijah rubbed his temples as his expression dropped. "Why is it so awful if she finds you out, dude? I take it this," he said, as he vaguely gestured at Kane in the Hematite getup, "is why you haven't told her, right?"

"Can you imagine what would happen if word got out Hematite had a girlfriend?" Kane countered. "Especially now that I have someone actively trying to kill me at every turn?"

"Dude, you said it yourself. I've been helping you since we were in high school. No one has found us out and probably never will," Elijah said. His voice went monotone, the telltale sign he was getting aggravated. "Even with all this Stone Breaker stuff, I've been fine."

But Kane was standing firm. "I can't risk it, Elijah."

Elijah shook his head and said, "I think you should tell her either way. Regardless of if you date her, you know? You spend more time with her than you do with any of us anymore. Don't get me wrong; I'm not mad about it, especially since we're about to spend a lot of time together again with Brad's wedding coming up. I'm just sayin'."

"Us" referred to Elijah, Brad, Shawn, and Kane. The four of them had been tight-knit since grade school, and despite life taking them in different directions, the four of them were still in Riverpeak—as was everyone else in their high school—and thus they still had strong friendships. Their time together was briefer than it had been as children, but they all took comfort in knowing the others were there.

"But how do I just tell her that?" Kane asked. "I can't just say, 'Hi Rory, I genuinely care for you and want to be completely honest with you, so I thought I should tell you I'm a masked vigilante that goes by the nickname Hematite. You might have heard of him. Sorry that I've been lying to you for nearly a decade.'" He rolled his eyes. "Yeah, that would go over well."

Elijah sighed. "I mean, maybe you could try that, but just a little less blunt? Like, 'Hey, I have something I've been meaning to tell you for a while, just never really had the right moment. May come as a shock to you. Viewer discretion is advised,' sort of thing."

Kane groaned. Elijah had always been the type to be honest, so much so that it was often what got them in trouble as kids. Before Kane could object, Elijah changed the subject.

"Luckily for us, Stone Breaker is right beneath our noses. The IP address in the video is actually from here in Riverpeak. I was expecting him to be closer to Denver, but I guess he's here."

Elijah pulled the video up again and hit play. Stone Breaker's voice was, similarly to Kane's when he wore his Hematite disguise, modified from some form of electronics when he was in his uniform. It was hard to tell who it was by voice alone, but Elijah grabbed the URL and plugged it into a video downloader.

"He's filming these on Main Street," Elijah said. He took a screenshot of the video as he waited for it to download, opened Photoshop, and then brightened up the shadows. "This looks like the offices in City Hall."

"How can you tell?"

"If you zoom in, you can see a plaque of their logo behind him a bit." Elijah did exactly that and pointed it out to Kane. "See?"

"Can you tell whose office it is?"

"It's barely decorated. Let me see what else I can find. We're on the right track. Oh, good, this download is ready."

"What are you doing with it?"

"I'm going to try messing with the playback settings and see if we can get this voice to sound more natural. I have a feeling he's using an audio filter over this, though, besides whatever he's using to mess with his voice."

Kane watched closely as Elijah threw the video into editing software and adjusted the pitch. After a few different tries, Elijah sat back in triumph at the final result—a much more natural-sounding audio. It was significantly higher in pitch than the modification, but that didn't surprise Kane.

"Sound familiar to you?" Elijah asked. "I'd be willing to bet this is his actual voice."

"Unfortunately, no. I feel like this is a guy I've never met in my life." He sighed as he put his head in his hands. "I'm sure they're wrapped up in this drug ring. It's been driving me fucking crazy lately."

"You've gotten pretty deep, huh?"

Kane nodded. "That's an understatement. Some little twerp called Shatterstone killed me the other night, alongside some random junkies he brought to tag team it. He's working with Stone Breaker. The only reason I didn't kick his ass was that he brought a damn gun to a fist-fight and then ran." Kane was grateful that Elijah already knew about his immortality; it was one less thing he had to explain tonight.

"What a coward," Elijah said. "It didn't sound like him?"

"No, and I don't think he was changing his voice. It looked like his outfit was kinda half-assed. Pretty sure he grabbed whatever he could at Goodwill and ran with it."

"Hmm. Weird." Elijah's brows furrowed and his nose scrunched up subconsciously as he worked. "Okay, this could be helpful. Here's a full list of everyone who works out of City Hall. I'll keep this open so we can see who is old enough to have a son around our age. Maybe younger?"

Kane shook his head. "They're runts, but they're close in age to us."

"Good to know," Elijah said. "Every bit helps. But first, time to do some research on you, my friend."

Kane thought his eyes would go crossed if he tried to follow what Elijah was doing closely, so he just let him get to work.

"Nope, nothing on the internet connecting you to Hematite," Elijah said. "Now let's see what happens when I look up your identity..." Kane waited with bated breath before Elijah announced, "Nope, you're good. I think if anyone will find out, it's Rory, since she knows you. But if I'm some guy's dickhead son, who doesn't know you from a hole in the wall, I won't know what to look for."

"Wait, what's that supposed to mean?"

"It means that I wouldn't put anything past Rory. You two are best friends, dude. Have been for years. There's nothing here, so you don't have to worry about that. I've been doing my job well for you," he said with a chuckle. "But Rory's ... well, she's Rory."

"Yeah. That's for sure."

———

Rory felt less unnerved heading back into Dr. Thornton's office. She wasn't still feeling completely vulnerable since her last visit two weeks ago, but Dr. Thornton was slowly yet surely earning her trust.

"How's everything been the last few weeks?" Dr. Thornton asked.

"I just feel really weak, mentally and physically," Rory confessed. "Everything's been catching up to me. My boxing classes are helping with the physical aspect, but not as much of the mental as I was hoping."

"You're a lot stronger than you think, Rory," Dr. Thornton said. "After all, you're here. This takes a lot of courage."

"I guess so," Rory said. "I tried writing a letter to Hematite; it didn't exactly work. But I have been logging a feelings journal every night! I got an app on my phone like you suggested."

"That's great," she said. "Why don't you think the letter to Hematite worked?"

"I dunno," Rory said. "I think it's hard for me to envision him like he's real, you know? It's so hard when I don't know who he is, and I have no idea how he'd take it. It's not like Kane or Naomi, where I know them and can guess how they'd respond. I don't really like not knowing what to expect."

"Are you afraid of being alone again after your family wasn't emotionally there when you needed them?" Dr. Thornton asked.

Rory released a deep breath that she didn't realize she was holding in. "Probably. I just didn't know how to put the words to it. But the thing is, I don't even care what Hematite is like behind the mask. I just know I'm grateful, you know?"

"That makes sense, yes." Dr. Thornton jotted down some notes.

"This is the second time you've mentioned Kane. What's your relationship again, exactly?"

"He's one of my best friends. He was there for me through it all. We're still super close." Rory wrestled with her feelings, and then she said, "If he'd just settle down for five minutes, I might ask him on a date."

Dr. Thornton smiled. "Why don't you try writing a letter to him, then, instead of Hematite? You mentioned Naomi, too, yeah? Write one for each of them. You don't have to send it to them if you're too embarrassed."

"Sure, yeah," Rory said. "I'll try. That might be easier."

"And you said the feelings journal has been working out for you?"

"So far. It's become easier to identify what's making me jumpy or paranoid." That was true. She realized it was little things that set her off, even if it had nothing to do with the stalking incident. "I think once my fight-or-flight mindset gets set off, it doesn't wanna turn off."

"I want you to try some grounding techniques next time you feel that way," Dr. Thornton said. "I think it'll help you. Try to find all the items in a room that share the same shape or color, for starters. This will remind you that you're not reliving the trauma, which will help you calm down and relax."

"Thanks," she said. "I think I'll need it."

What she didn't tell Dr. Thornton was how she was hoping to get directly involved with Hematite. She sensed that the news may be met with words of warning or caution, but Rory didn't want to hear it. No matter what anyone told her, she was going to find him—no matter what it took.

CHAPTER 5

R ory hadn't even finished making her coffee when Naomi called her on Saturday morning. She was half-awake, having brushed her teeth and showered but still waiting on her coffee to brew. The smell was helping her perk up, but she was looking forward to that first sip of sweetened caffeine.

"Hey girl," Naomi said. She was so fast to answer that Rory didn't even have a chance to greet her. There was a strong sense of urgency in her voice that was hard to miss. "FaceTime on purpose this time. Do you have a moment?"

Rory's interest was instantly piqued; Naomi normally cut right to the chase, and she appreciated that about her friend. "Yeah, I just got up, like, twenty minutes ago. Why, what's up?"

"You'll want to come over here and see this. I think I'm onto something big."

"How big? Like Hematite big?"

"Almost." Naomi grinned at the collection of newspaper clippings before her as she switched the camera's view to show Rory. "I think I know who Stone Breaker is."

Rory nearly dropped her phone. "I'll be there in five minutes, tops."

Rory had never gotten her belongings together more quickly than she had at that moment. She nearly forgot her coffee but was quick to pour some into a to-go tumbler. Rory all but sped down the road to reach Naomi's home, opting to drive instead of walk to not waste a single second. It was only a ten-minute walk through the suburbs, but Rory wanted this information right away.

Naomi lived in a house that was simultaneously modest and nicer than average. Her father, who owned his own stand-alone restaurant-turned-chain, gifted her one of the rental properties he owned when she graduated college. Brad, her fiancé, would move in with her eventually but still had about a year on his lease with Elijah, so for now, it was just Naomi and Rory in the house.

"I'm so excited for you to see this," Naomi said when Rory arrived. She'd thrown her hair up in a messy bun and wasn't wearing any of her usual makeup. "There's a little self-doubt in the back of my mind, so maybe you can let me know if you think I'm onto something here, but it all adds up."

A myriad of paperwork littered Naomi's dining room table. There were so many that Rory couldn't even see the wood beneath it, but all the important ones with lines highlighted in pink were on the top.

"How long have you been at this?" Rory asked before she took a sip of her coffee. "Don't you work the night shift? Are you not exhausted?"

"I will sleep like a baby come lunchtime, don't worry," Naomi said with a wave of her hand. "Anyway, at first, I didn't believe it. I thought there was no way. But the more I found, the more I realized all signs pointed to him." Naomi pointed at a printed-out photo of a reporter for the local newspaper. His thin, blonde hair was gelled back, and he seemed awkwardly stiff in his headshot.

"Do we know him? He doesn't exactly look familiar."

"I think I do more than you. He was in a few of my journalism classes at school. I think he went to school in Riverpeak too. It's Mark Stevens."

"Okay, that name sounds familiar, at least. Wasn't he that geeky kid in your classes? His dad was the politician?"

"The one who got caught sleeping with Chief Daniels, yes! Listen, I can't confirm it, but I'm sure there's a way we could if we keep going in this direction. And if you look in this video that Stone Breaker posted," Naomi grabbed a printed-out screenshot, "in the background is the city council logo. It's the same one right outside of City Hall. People have also reported seeing him drive a Harley, and the only person in town I know with a Harley is Mark."

"His dad shacking up with the police chief is enough to convince me, to be honest." Rory began shuffling through some of the documentation. Articles Mark had written for his newspaper were included in the mix. Rory began scanning them and then furrowed her brows when she saw how a few of the words stacked.

Stone Breaker
   rising
   19
   January

"Hey Naomi," Rory said, "do you have a highlighter?"

"Yeah, let me grab it." Naomi jogged over to her bedroom and shortly returned with one. "Did you see something?"

"Maybe it's just my history teacher brain over-analyzing something, but I think there's a message in this," she said. "It could be a coincidence, but I wanna see if this checks out. My juniors are learning about World War II, and we talked a lot about spies and how they sent codes, so I had them write a report with a hidden message inside. They had to get creative with how they hid everything. If I wasn't in the middle of grading those, I don't know that I would have necessarily picked up on this."

Rory went over the words that stood out to her. She hoped it would, in fact, result in a secret message. She blindly highlighted the stacked words in Mark's article until she reached the last line and then read over it to see what it resulted in.

. . .

Stone Breaker
  rising
  19
  January
  Riverpeak
  attack
  plans

"What day did Hematite get killed?" Rory ask^{ed}. "Was it January 19th, by chance?"

Naomi shuffled through a few more papers and grabbe^d one dated January 20th. "Yup. This one from the next day is covering it since it happened the night before."

Rory set the article aside and grabbed another newspaper, doing the same thing. She followed the same pattern as the last piece, using the second word in each row to see if it lined up to form a sentence.

Stone Breaker
  fight
  Valentine's Day
  downtown
  night

"He's hiding messages in his work," Rory said. "If he's not Stone Breaker, they're certainly working together."

"Holy crap," Naomi said. "Good catch."

"We gotta get this to Hematite. We still have about a week before Valentine's Day. He could seriously use this, and we could stop something big."

"If I get caught getting involved, my journalistic integrity will come into question, unfortunately," Naomi said. "Our news director has insisted that we stay as non-biased as possible. I think this situation falls into that category."

"That's fine; I can bring it to him. You know, speaking of journalistic integrity, this Stevens guy is pretty anti-Hematite," Rory said. "For hard-hitting vigilante stories, these all seem really soft on Stone Breaker and the city government. They've gotta be linked, which would make sense if that's his dad."

"How are you going to get this to Hematite?" Naomi asked. "It's not like anybody knows where he is."

"No, but we can find out his beat. How often does he come up on the scanners?"

"All the time. Every night the cops say the caller mentions him, but by the time they get there, he's gone."

"When you tune in next time you're at work, keep me posted. I'll be up late so just text me whenever. You know I barely sleep anymore." Rory checked her watch. "Shit, Kane will be at my house soon. I gotta go. We grade homework together every Saturday."

"Aw, cute! Here, if you're going after him, take this." Naomi slid all the papers together. "I have copies of everything. Don't sweat it."

"You sure?"

"Positive. Just stay safe, okay?"

Rory grinned and felt a renowned sense of determination she hadn't ever felt. "I promise."

———

Kane smiled every time he entered Rory's house. It was a clear upgrade from his and felt more like home to him than his own place, considering how often he was there. Her single-story home was small but still made his studio apartment look like a shoebox. White curtains draped across the window in the living room and were held together at the ends with a gold rope. There was a large sill for someone to sit and look out the window at the town, which was often Rory's go-to spot. Even Kane had to admit that the view of the mountaintops from her window was beautiful and enough to almost make him forget about the problems that lie beneath them.

The open floor plan allowed for the kitchen counter bar stools to face the living room, making for an ideal space to share with company.

The coffee table in the living room had a vase filled with fresh-cut flowers from the grocery store that made the whole apartment smell like summer, even in the dead of winter. Assorted photos and artifacts littered the walls, some from travels and others of her with Naomi, Brad, and Kane in college.

Kane took his usual spot on the floor of her living room, with his students' homework on the coffee table and his back against the couch as Rory made her way to the windowsill. But unbeknownst to Rory, he couldn't take his eyes off her. The sunbeams coming through the window fell on her skin and her hair, making her highlights pop in their trajectory. Her expression showed she loved how it warmed her skin, and Kane could see it in the way her lips rested in a soft smile while she worked. Every now and then, she would toss some hair over her shoulder or tuck some behind her ear. The sight of her in her element, focused on her work and basking in the sun, made Kane feel a pang of longing in his chest.

Rory, breaking the silence, interrupted him from his admiration. "What would you do if you were a superhero?"

"Me?" Kane took a sip of water to hide his nerves. "I'd probably be like Robin Hood or something. Steal from the rich but give it to the poor."

"Ooh, very noble. I like that. Anything else?"

"Eh, maybe I'd get laid for once."

Rory poorly stifled a laugh. "You'd go through all that just to get laid?"

"Hell yeah! Come on, Rory, think about it. The school pays us peanuts, and you know my family is broke as shit. That's not exactly great for a love life. I'm chronically single."

"Not all of us care about a guy's wallet, you know."

"Alright then. Can I ask you a serious question and have it not fuck up our friendship? No judgment allowed."

"Sure. I'll even pinky-promise if you want," Rory said, matching his mischief in her tone.

Kane held his finger out, and Rory interlocked hers with his. His finger was calloused, but his skin was otherwise fairly smooth. She noticed that Kane's hands were quite larger than hers, something so obvious yet somehow new to her. *Maybe,* she thought, *therapy has me seeing things in a new light.*

"Let's pretend we weren't friends and haven't known each other for years. I try to pick you up. Let's say we're out at a bar or whatever. Would you sleep with me?" Kane subconsciously licked his lips and then said, "You can say no; I won't be offended."

"Kay, you know I don't do hookups."

"Pretend you did. Don't try to skirt around the question."

"You want my honest answer?" Kane nodded and then, to his surprise, she said, "Yeah, I'd let you take me home."

"No fuckin' way, dude," Kane said, as the corner of his mouth curved up into a smile. He leaned his head back against the couch. "You would?"

"Yes, Kane, I would! You're a fucking pervert sometimes, but you're funny and ridiculously good-looking, so you can get away with it."

"You think I'm ridiculously good-looking?"

Rory huffed. "You've got this, like, mid-90s-Ethan Hawke-thing going on. It works."

Kane laughed. He wanted to kiss Rory right then and there, but he settled for holding on to her pinky with his own. "I don't think I'd hook up with you."

"Ooh, ouch." Part of her felt disappointed, but she wasn't totally sure why. "Why not?"

"You're *way* too good for me. Especially morally, but in every way possible. You're the type of girl I'd intend to hit once and then end up falling in love with, only to never hear from her again."

"That is oddly specific. Thank you, I think."

"I'm glad we got that out of our systems," Kane said. He pulled Rory's pinky to his lips and gave it a playful kiss before letting go. While he hadn't been serious, it still felt good for him to let some of his feelings out, even if it was in a roundabout way.

The softness of Kane's lips on her finger surprised her. In truth, it always surprised her when Kane shared a rare moment of tenderness with her, even if it was something he tried to hide in a sea of jokes.

"What would you do if *you* were a superhero?" Kane asked. "Your turn."

"Hmm. I'd probably help other women. Beat up their shitty boyfriends and dunk the ones who catcall in the sewer."

"That is rather on brand for you. Maybe I could be your cool sidekick."

Rory smiled at him, and Kane thought he was going to melt. "Say, are you ever gonna help me and Naomi with this Hematite thing? I think we're onto something here."

Kane raised an eyebrow. "Oh yeah? What have you found?" He was genuinely curious about what Rory had to say, his own personal biases set aside.

"We're starting with Stone Breaker. I think I know who he is, but I want to get everything over to Hematite either way. I think he's this reporter that Naomi went to school with; his dad's a politician."

Kane felt a sense of relief when he heard that their focus was on Stone Breaker rather than himself.

"What would a journalist and a politician have to do with Hematite?" Rory asked. "I mean, I get they're super pro-police, but it seems excessive. What the hell are they hiding?"

Kane soaked her in as she spoke. He loved seeing the gears turn in Rory's head like this. "All I know is that he's got a really dumb name," Kane said. "Stone Breaker. What is he, twelve?"

Rory laughed. "I don't like it either. Naomi is going to be narrowing down when Hematite patrols downtown Riverpeak so I can get all these goodies to him. Maybe I can finally meet him."

Kane did his best to not tense up. "And what will you do when you meet him?" In truth, Kane was wondering what *he'd* do when he saw Rory. "What if he isn't everything he's cracked up to be?"

Rory furrowed her brows. "What do you mean? He saved my life, Kane; you know that. Your sister's too!"

"I know, I know! But what if he turns out to be just some ordinary dude? Or what if he doesn't want any help?"

"Then too bad for him," Rory said. Kane could see how strong her conviction was now. While she always wanted to meet Hematite, she had never actively done much of anything about it. Now, though, she held confidence she lacked before.

"Just be careful, okay?" His teasing nature from a few moments ago faded. He kissed her pinky again but with more pressure this time. "You're my best friend, Miller. I worry about you."

"Then help us. Come on, Kane. I know you like to play dumb, but you're so much smarter than you like to lead on."

Kane couldn't help but smile. No one ever told him that before.

"I'll help in my own way," Kane said, with the hint of a promise in his voice. "I'm not about to be running into gunfire with Stone Breaker. And you shouldn't either." He was painfully self-aware of the irony in his words, but he bit it back.

Something is off with Kane, Rory thought. That left her something else to get to the bottom of, but it was clear from his half-baked responses it wouldn't be today.

————

That night, as he changed, Kane couldn't stop hearing Rory's voice on repeat in his mind. He pulled his hood over his head as he walked out the door, ran down the stairs of his apartment complex, and then lurked off into the shadows. He was surprised no one spotted him coming in or out of his apartment over the years, but he supposed that came with the territory. Riverpeak was a small, quiet town and much didn't happen after nine o'clock, unless you looked closely enough.

Kane entered the east side of the city with trepidation. He stopped fearing death a long time ago, but still hated the unpredictability that came with the streets. City Hall was at the far end of the road, marking the division between the east side and downtown. Most of the times he had been attacked or even killed were right between the two. He even saw some spots where his old blood still stained the sidewalks.

It was eerily quiet tonight and with no real reason why, Kane was more on edge than usual. He glanced twice at each alley before turning down any intersections, trying to find any sign of life beyond the occasional prairie dog that scurried by when spooked. Based on his own chill he felt shooting down his spine, he figured most people would be bundled up indoors somewhere. But even on the coldest Colorado nights, there were still a handful of people looking for a way to get their next hit on the streets.

Kane decided after walking a few blocks that he needed a higher vantage point. There was no luck on the ground, something that usually wasn't the case. So, he found a fire escape for an apartment complex and used it to climb up a few stories before hopping over to the Chinese takeout restaurant next door, where he'd have more room to patrol. He could smell the residual sesame oil from earlier in the night, even through the multiple layers of fabric that covered his nose.

The last few times he came to the east side, there had been at least a handful of Stone Breaker's hired help waiting for him. He walked the perimeter of the restaurant's flat roof, avoiding the vents and trying to not be blinded by the neon lights of their sign, and saw no one. After doing a full lap around the roof, he sat on the spot where he started, letting his legs swing over the side of the roof as he waited for something to happen. He grabbed his burner phone and called Shawn, one of the few people in on his secret.

"Hey, dude. Where are you stationed up tonight?"

"Just a few miles outside of downtown Denver. Why?"

"It's fucking weird, man. I'm on the east side of Riverpeak, and there is literally no one here. Barely even a light on. I've never seen it this quiet."

"I think they're all here," Shawn said. "I'm keeping an eye on some pick-up trucks and beaters moving in and out of the South Main Burgers up here. Something tells me it's not just college kids with the munchies."

Kane checked the time. "They should have closed an hour ago. I'll let you go, then. Don't lose them, Jameson."

"Yeah, yeah. Whatever, dude. Don't die or whatever."

Kane hung up and sighed. Knowing Shawn, that would, unfortunately, be the last he heard of it. Shawn wasn't shy about his super strength, which was the only reason Kane had approached him in the first place. When he first told Shawn that he was Hematite, Shawn laughed in his face, but believed it once Kane showed the scars to prove it. Their partnership began in college, but Shawn seemed to always seek more. As much as Shawn denied it, Kane knew it was jealousy over local fame that Kane never wanted for Hematite in the first place.

Kane squinted as he spotted someone in the distance coming from what seemed like out of nowhere. Once they were closer, he cursed to himself.

Kane knew who it was right away when he saw voluminous, tight curls he could spot in any crowd. *At least,* he thought, *she had the sense to dress plainly.* He turned his voice modifier on as he made the leap back over to the fire escape, slid down the interior of the tube, and then ran as silently as he could toward her.

Walking along the sidewalk in plain sight with a backpack over her shoulders was Rory Miller. He wasn't sure what she thought she was doing, but he had to get her the hell out of there

CHAPTER 6

Rory sighed as she walked through the relatively abandoned part of town on the east side. She always got the creeps heading through this dusty corner of Riverpeak. A few people still lived here, but the city government, who viewed it as just a money pit, had largely ignored the area. Their blind eye made itself clear with the various potholes in the street, the cracked sidewalks, and patches of dead grass trying to peek out through the snow, desperate for some sunlight. There was a cop car sitting at a corner she passed, but no one was inside. Someone had tagged it with a symbol Rory didn't recognize in red spray paint.

The spookiest part of the town, in her opinion, was the abandoned burger takeout restaurant with its windows boarded up and covered in graffiti. She wasn't sure why, but she felt like she was being watched when she walked past it. It was Naomi's dad's old place, but she never was totally sure why he abandoned it.

She adjusted her backpack straps as they fell down her shoulders a bit, eager to share the evidence she and Naomi collected with Hematite. Rory monitored her surroundings to stay alert, not because she was afraid of the community but because she knew Stone Breaker could be anywhere. As she wandered, she hoped she would find

Hematite camping out. She had no luck with a police scanner, but Naomi dug up some police reports that mentioned him being here this day of the week and at the late hour. Rory was going off of nothing but hope and a prayer, as she tried to ignore the chill that wouldn't seem to leave her spine.

The last time she had been to this part of town, it was much busier, with people just trying to make ends meet no matter what it took. But it seemed like the victims of the corrupt government had gone into hiding. It was actually more fear-inducing, Rory believed as she glanced around, with no one walking the streets. She hated the unpredictability of the quiet roads and run-down buildings. *What a shame,* she thought, *because it could be a charming district.* The local government just didn't care, no matter how much the people spoke up or voted for change.

Suddenly, in an instant, someone wrapped an arm around her torso. Before she could scream, a hand covered in boxing wraps and a wool glove was over her mouth and nose. The unseen figure jerked Rory into an alleyway and just as she thought she was making the biggest mistake of her life in coming down there, the person gently placed her against the wall of a building.

Her lower back felt the cool brick through her clothes; it was cold and late enough to be felt through her multiple layers, but her backpack provided some relief. Rory's eyes widened in panic, but she immediately felt relaxed when she saw it was just Hematite standing before her. He removed his arm from her body to hold his finger up to where his lips were beneath his scarves and balaclava, showing she should be quiet. Rory nodded, trusting him, and he dropped his hand.

As Rory caught her breath and let her heart rate slow down, she took in the sight of him. Hematite looked exactly as Rory remembered him, but was broader now, especially in his shoulders. His frame was still lean, though, and his outfit was more or less the same as it had always been. The only difference was the hoodie he was wearing over his usual black or navy shirt; the hoodie had a fish-mouth-shaped high neck that helped him cover his face beneath his usual balaclava and cowl. She couldn't fully make out his eyes, which were the only part of him she could see. Between the dark of the night, the shadows of the alley, and the hood over his face, it was hard to tell what color his eyes were.

"Sorry about that," Hematite said in a whisper. "We can't be seen. Follow me."

Hematite took a hold of her hand and led her down the alley. He took care to check around every corner and periodically looked up too to make sure no one was hiding on any rooftops. Before Rory knew it, they were at the storage unit facility at the edge of Main Street. Hematite led her into a unit in the back, and he was quick to close the door behind them.

The unit was mostly empty. An old laptop rested on a desk and a few newspapers hung up on the wall, all featuring stories of Stone Breaker or the town's drug ring.

"What the hell were you doing out there?" Hematite asked. "That's Stone Breaker's territory. You know that, right? You could have gotten seriously hurt."

"I was looking for you!"

"Don't look for me," Hematite retorted. "It's dangerous."

"Like I give a shit! Listen, I can help you. I have info. Like, a good deal of it."

"And what do you want in return?" Hematite asked. He already knew the answer, but he had to keep the front up.

"Nothing," Rory said. "I want nothing in return."

"Nothing comes free. Why are you really here?"

"You saved my life a few years ago and wanted nothing in return. Is it so hard to believe that maybe someone wants to help you for once?"

He didn't respond. This was not how Rory expected this to go. She could feel the adrenaline moving through her body and in their silence, she became hyper-aware of her increased heart rate as Hematite looked her up and down.

After a long moment, he finally broke the pause. "I remember you."

The tension she was subconsciously holding in her face released. She didn't realize how tight her jaw had become. "You do?"

Hematite nodded. "Rory, right?"

She smiled. "You remember my name?" Rory didn't think he'd

remember her at all. It had been years, and he had helped more people than she imagined he could count. Rory never considered herself special enough to be worth him remembering.

"What can I say? You left an impression." He sat in the cheap, metal folding chair that was in front of the computer and leaned forward, his elbows resting on his thighs. "Alright, fuck it. You're already here. What do you got for me, Rory?"

As much as she wanted to ask him what he meant by her leaving an impression, she knew she needed to stay on target. Rory swallowed the lump in her throat and looked at the newspaper clippings of Stone Breaker. One of them caught her eye—the one written by Mark Stevens. She took it off the wall and handed it to him, pointing at the byline.

"That's Stone Breaker." As she rattled off the information, Hematite blinked at her as he comprehended what she said. She was so confident and said it so quickly that it took him a moment to digest the information. "I have proof," Rory said, as she reached for the paperwork resting in a folder in her bag. "My friend Naomi is fantastic at digging up dirt on people. She may have fallen down a rabbit hole here. Any and every kind of supporting documentation that you could possibly have is all right here. I am 100 percent positive when I say that Stone Breaker is Mark Stevens."

"I … wow," Hematite said. "Thank you. This will help me track him and try to figure out what he's up to." He shuffled through the papers in the manilla folder. He was looking forward to telling Elijah about this information. "How did you two do all this?"

"Naomi is a reporter for Channel 10. She has access to a lot and knows who to call," Rory said. "I'm just a nosy bitch."

Hematite chuckled. "I think the word you're looking for is inquisitive."

Rory's smile grew. "Well, that certainly sounds a lot nicer. By the way, the highlighted stuff in yellow, the reports spell out a message. I found out that he stacks the second word on every line. It's been consistent, but worth noting for future articles in case he does this again. He might attack on Valentine's Day in Downtown Riverpeak. Hope you don't have a date."

He scoffed. "Guess I do now." Kane thought about how this must have been what Rory referenced when they graded papers together the afternoon prior. He was impressed—he knew Rory was sharp and that Naomi was resourceful, but he hadn't expected them to crack the Stone Breaker case so quickly. He hoped they couldn't crack his own.

"Is there any way I can help?" Rory asked.

"No, no," he said. "You've already put yourself in harm's way enough. Stone Breaker is dangerous, and I don't want you getting hurt. This is a tremendous help. If I can get ahead of Stone Breaker and Shatterstone, I might stop them for good."

Rory furrowed her brows. "Wait, who the hell is Shatterstone? There's two of them?"

Hematite nodded. "Shatterstone has been keeping a lower profile. He's the one filming all of Stone Breaker's videos."

"And I thought Stone Breaker was a stupid name. Shatterstone is even dumber."

Hematite chuckled. "Shatterstone was the one that tried to kill me. He ran before I could even talk to him and strikes me as a complete coward."

"I'd say both of them are for wearing a mask, but you know," Rory said with a nervous chuckle, "it's different when you do it."

He shook his head and grinned beneath his facial coverings. "I get what you mean. No offense taken, don't worry."

"Why is he going after you? You can't be the only one trying to clean up Riverpeak."

"Actually, I think I might be. But to be honest, I'm not entirely sure," Hematite said. "I have a theory that he's somehow profiting off the drug problem in this city. If he isn't, his father definitely is. That and the fact that he failed to kill me is probably driving him fucking crazy." He looked at Rory and set the papers down. "Let me take you home."

"Oh, no, I couldn't ask—."

"I'm not asking."

"Oh." Rory released another nervous laugh; he didn't make her uncomfortable, but she still couldn't believe this was happening. "Are you sure? I'm sure you have better things to do."

Hematite smiled at her, even though she couldn't see it. "I'll feel better if I know you got home safely. But we're going my way. Do you trust me?"

Rory nodded. "With my life."

"Follow me and do as I say. Got it?"

Rory nodded again.

Hematite led Rory outside. As he closed the storage unit behind them and locked it, she made a mental note of the number to look it up later. Hematite led Rory out of the facility through the back, and once they reached the fence, he crouched down a bit.

"Hop on my back," he said. "I'll carry you over."

Rory didn't question him and just did as he said. She felt incredibly close to him as he carried her over the fence, with her arms around his shoulders and her legs around his waist. His effortlessness was a testament to the strength and stamina he'd built from years of street fighting. The muscles that Rory could feel beneath her were solid and defined, even through the layers of clothing.

Once they were back on the ground, Hematite set Rory gently on her feet. They ran behind buildings, with Hematite keeping a close eye for bystanders or anyone who might be watching. She held his gloved and wrapped hand as she trailed close behind him, so as to not get lost. The entire time they ran through the alleyways of Riverpeak, she could hear her heart pounding in her ears. Despite the risk of danger and the way the cold air stung her face, Rory couldn't stop smiling.

———

Once they reached her neighborhood, Kane stopped and realized he had to be careful: if he took Rory to her home, then he'd practically be giving his identity away to Rory.

"Where do you live?" he asked with feigned uncertainty.

"Come on, it's not far. Everyone's probably in bed by now."

He nodded, letting Rory walk him the rest of the way there. Now that they were out of the east side of the city, and away from Stone Breaker's reach, he felt a bit more relaxed. Rory's corner of the suburbs was quaint and sleepy. The homes lined the street in perfect rows, more or less the same style but all in different colors and sizes. Kane glanced at Rory and saw that her shoulders were rolled back, and the corners of her lips were curled upward, likely subconsciously. She let him walk on the outside of the sidewalk, further from the streetlights that illuminated the path.

"Thanks for walking me home," Rory said. "And for everything else."

Kane nodded. "Yeah, of course." He cleared his throat as quietly as he could. "Safety first."

She fiddled with her thumbs. "Sure, sure. But for real. I've been wondering what I was going to say to you if I ever came face to face with you again. You saved my life, you know?"

"Don't mention it," Kane said with a small shake of his head. "Like you said, I'm just trying to clean this place up. Cops don't seem to want to do it, so someone has to get their hands dirty."

"Well, I'm glad it's you." Rory rubbed the back of her neck. "You're a good man."

Kane smiled beneath his mask and scarves. "Thanks." He wasn't used to this; normally he was gone before anyone could even acknowledge him, but he couldn't find the desire to walk away from Rory.

She stopped in front of her house and pointed at it with her thumb. "If, uh, you ever need anything, this is me," she said. "You're welcome here anytime. You don't even need to ask; just show up."

"I'll keep that in mind," he said. "Be careful out there. Good night, Rory."

Rory's closed-lipped smile was so wide that she felt it in her cheeks. "Good night, Hematite."

He didn't leave until Rory went inside. When she peeked through the blinds, she saw him linger by the front door before making his way back down the street from the way they came. She walked over to her couch, picked up a pillow, and screamed into it to release the adrenaline still pent up inside her. She thought maybe when she removed the pillow from her face, she'd find out it was all a dream, but nothing changed when she did.

She thanked him as she had always wanted, but now, Rory realized she wanted more.

———

"Good morning!" Rory greeted cheerily as Kane got in the passenger seat of her car.

"Morning, sunshine. You're certainly chipper today," Kane said. He noticed the pep in her tone right away.

"Aren't I always?" Rory asked with a bit of a pout. She waited for him to buckle his seatbelt and then took off for the school.

"I mean, you're definitely more of a morning person than I am, but you seem extra awake, I guess." Kane already knew why but wanted to hear what she had to say.

"You wouldn't believe what happened last night," Rory said with a goofy smile. "I found Hematite."

Time to play dumb again, Kane thought. "No shit? That's great. How'd that go?"

"I can't believe it, Kay. He actually entertained the idea of me helping him. I was hoping for a slightly less ... broody response, so to speak, but he took all the info that Naomi and I have been gathering."

"I'm glad to hear you found him. Just be careful out there, alright?"

"You're sounding like him," Rory teased. Kane didn't miss the irony. "He says Stone Breaker is dangerous, and I'm sure he is. But we found him, Kay! We can fight back if we know what to expect, you know?"

"I suppose that's one way of looking at it," Kane said. He had been up all night debating on how much he should tell Rory today, if anything at all. He took a swig of his coffee as he pondered it again and then decided ultimately against it.

Very few people actually knew who Hematite was behind the mask. He had told Elijah, plus his doctors were aware since they were the ones to discover his power with him after a near-death experience in his parent's drug shed as a teenager. The only other person who knew was Shawn Jameson, who had some powers of his own. Shawn's physical prowess was out of the ordinary and likely from the same source as Kane's inability to die. Neither of them told Brad, their childhood friend, and Elijah only knew about Kane's identity at this point.

Kane wagered that if Rory knew it was him, she'd only want to get more involved. While she was on a fast track to danger, revealing his identity to her would only put her in even more trouble. He knew Rory would do anything for him, so his love for her prevented him from saying more.

"Hey, do you want to do a joint class project this semester?" Kane offered. "I've got a section on biographies coming up for one of my English classes, and I was thinking of making them do a social studies tie-in to help them retain what they're learning. How's Hamilton sound?"

"Yes! Ooh, we could do a session on it with my U.S. History classes!" Kane was relieved that she responded so positively so quickly; the more he could monitor her, the better, even if it meant going slightly off the curriculum. "I like to watch the Broadway show with them now that you can stream it online and then make them compare and contrast the show with actual history. If you want, we can work on a more robust plan later?"

"Yeah, I'd like that," Kane said. "Are you doing anything tonight?"

Rory shook her head.

"Come on over. I'll order some takeout and we can figure it out. Maybe even light a candle or two."

Rory rolled her eyes as she pulled into her parking spot. "I'm going to hold you to that."

Kane smirked at her, then they made their way inside the school. "Come on, you gotta at least give me credit for trying."

"I'll give you credit for trying if you ever seriously ask me out on a date. How's that sound?"

Kane rose his eyebrows. Even though she often did, it always surprised him when Rory matched his energy. "Is that permission to do so?"

"Maybe it is. I guess you won't know until you try."

"Well, I can't now; it would be expected. I like to keep you on your toes." Kane winked.

"Mission accomplished on that one."

"That's what I like to hear. See you at lunch?"

"You already know it," Rory said. They parted ways at their classrooms, which were only a few doors down from one another.

As she waited for her students to filter into her class, Rory allowed herself to get lost in thought while she prepared for the day.

She often told Kane that she never knew when he was flirting with her for real or not anymore, and she still meant it. It was hard for her to discern what was Kane's typical teasing versus him actually testing the waters. As per usual, the way he spoke to her left a feeling of butterflies in her abdomen and ruddiness on her cheeks that she tried to push down. After all, Kane was Kane, and she never wanted to get her hopes up that he would decide to settle down one day.

Rory forced herself to snap out of her thoughts when Jordan entered the classroom extra early. She noticed Jordan looked lost in a daydream, but not necessarily a happy one; her eyes lacked their usual luster and her movements seemed slower.

"Good morning, Miss Miller." Jordan's tone of voice matched her glum expression.

"Good morning, Jordan. Everything okay?"

"That obvious?" Jordan sighed. "I'm, uh, having some boy trouble. That's all. It's nothing."

"Well, there's a few more minutes before anyone else will probably come in. If I can help, I'm here, okay?"

Jordan nodded and was silent for a moment. A minute or so passed as the two of them just listened to the ticking of the clock before Jordan asked, "What do you do when you can't tell if the guy that you like likes you back?"

Rory smiled, amused by their mirrored predicament.

"You know, I've been in your shoes. I've tried waiting it out and seeing if anything would happen; it just made it even harder. So, if I had to give you any advice, I would say take the first step and see what happens. Isn't winter formal coming up soon? Ask him to go with you. If he's weirded out by the idea of a date, just brush it off as a friend-date kind of thing. Crisis averted."

Rory wished she could take her own advice but was glad to at least help someone else out.

"Thanks, Miss Miller. I think I'll try that. Are you chaperoning again this year?"

Rory nodded. "I will be. If all else fails, I'll dance with you. I keep up with the trends on TikTok."

Jordan laughed. "You do?"

"Oh yeah, or at least I try to," Rory said. A few other students came into class at this point, so Rory jotted their names down for roll call. "I can't promise that I won't embarrass myself in the process, but if you can get clout out of it, then I'll take the hit."

"Thanks, Miss Miller."

Rory internally panicked; she had almost forgotten about the winter formal coming up that she and Kane agreed to chaperone in a few short weeks. She mentally cursed herself and penciled in a note for herself to make sure she still had a dress.

After their assembly last month, Rory also couldn't help but wonder if Stone Breaker would make some sort of appearance at the dance.

"Oh, and Jordan?"

"Yes?"

"That *is* how you guys are using the word 'clout,' right?"

Jordan laughed. "Yeah, Ms. Miller. It is."

CHAPTER 7

Kane, as Hematite, frowned from his perch atop one of the university's buildings. He didn't come here often anymore but still liked to make a surprise visit whenever he had the chance on a weekend. During the day, the view of the mountains was spectacular from up on the rooftops, but tonight he only saw his sister in trouble. This was the exact same spot where he had stopped Rory's stalker from hurting her all those years ago, and now Kayla and a friend were being harassed by two drunk punks wearing fraternity letters. The memories left a bad taste in his mouth.

Kayla left her blonde hair in a ponytail tonight, so Kane prepared for the men to try to use that to their advantage and grab for it. Even though she was seven years younger than Kane, people often thought they were twins with how alike in the face they looked. Kayla was tall even without heels and looked older than her years, which didn't help the twin assumptions, though Kane knew it was from the stress of growing up with drug dealers for parents.

Clearly, he thought, *the police that covered the university hadn't improved or learned their lesson.* When Rory was stalked, they didn't take any real action until the night he intervened. He wondered how many times people complained about these two students, as he shifted closer so he could attack without hurting Kayla or her friend. He didn't know her name.

"Come on, pretty girl," one of the men harassing his sister cooed. "What's wrong?" He went to reach for Kayla's long hair just as Kane predicted, but he didn't have a chance.

Kayla and her friend screamed, as Kane jumped down and slammed their attacker's head against the closest brick wall. The brick was cold beneath the man's head; the air around it even cooler. Winter was always more painful in Kane's opinion, with the air making his skin more prone to crack from dryness alongside the beatdowns. The sky was so dark that the perpetrator hadn't even seen Hematite coming.

"Run!" he shouted at the girls.

Kayla tried to follow the command, but the other guy after her—a tall yet stocky brute with sandy blonde hair and pale skin—reached out and grabbed her by the arm. Kayla started crying. In her dress and heels, she was at a disadvantage, especially with the thin layer of snow beneath their feet. Her friend wasn't in much better of a position, also dressed inadequately for a fight and fumbling for her phone in her purse.

This was precisely why Kane hated coming to the college part of town but knew he needed to. Like Rory, Kayla didn't know who Hematite actually was; she just knew that Hematite had been there for her ever since she was a little girl. He slammed the man's head into the brick wall again and then dropped him upon seeing he was unconscious.

One less asshole to worry about, Kane thought as he shifted into a boxer's stance.

Kane punched the second man in the jaw, hooking him on the side opposite his sister. The blonde man dropped Kayla's arm as he recoiled and then swung at Kane, but Kane bobbed and weaved in time to miss the hit. Kane followed up with another punch. As the man's head fell in the punch's direction, Kane used the opportunity to arch-kick him the opposite way. Kane grabbed a billy club off his belt—a weapon he relied heavily on, but for good reason—and whacked him to continue the natural momentum. The attacker spat out some blood and a few teeth from where the billy club smacked him in the face.

Once the man regained his footing, he made a lunge at Kane, but Kane grabbed the guy's sloppy punch and used the opportunity to get him into an arm bar. The man tried to struggle out of it, but Kane shoved him to the ground and hit him in the head with his billy club again. He hit his temple, and the man passed out. Kane sighed as he stood up, just glad that the fight was over with.

Kayla's friend gawked. "Oh my God, is he dead?"

"Probably not. He's just gonna take a very long nap." Kane patted the man's pockets until he found the one with his cell phone and dialed a number.

"Nine-one-one, what's your location?"

Kane wasted no time. "Two pricks tried to attack some women on campus. They're both passed out behind the dining hall by Lynx Crossing. They're alive."

"Sir, may I get your name?" the voice on the other end asked. But Kane hung up and tossed the phone on the ground next to the blonde. He looked at the two girls, who were frozen in shock.

"You again," Kayla said with a smile. She exhaled and her body slumped in relief.

"You know this guy?" her friend asked.

Kayla nodded. "He's been protecting me since I was a little kid."

"How many times do I have to tell you to stay out of trouble?"

Kayla smiled at him, picking up his teasing. She sounded out of breath but relieved. "Thank you, again. I think I owe you my life twice over at this point."

He nodded. "It's no problem. Don't think anything of it."

Kane knew his mother hadn't been using drugs when she was pregnant with Kayla, so the likelihood that Kayla had any of the abilities Kane did was slim to none. It was a large part of why Kane felt it was his duty to protect her beyond just being her older brother.

"You know, I still have that ring you gave me. The hematite one." Kayla held her hand up to show it on her pinky.

Kane grinned beneath the mask. "I'm surprised. I hear they break pretty easily."

"I guess it knows I still need it." She shifted her weight as she fidgeted with the ring, something she did out of nervous habit. "But seriously, thank you."

"Is it true that you can't die?" Kayla's friend piped up. "There's been rumors ever since you were on the news a little while ago. That's so cool."

"It's not cool," he said. He kept his rage within, not wanting to snap at a stranger. "It's a fucking curse." He looked back to Kayla and just nodded. "Take care."

Kane left at that, returning to the shadows and making a break for it before the girls could follow him. He internally groaned, as Kane understood he benefited from his powers but wished he never had them. Kane was becoming numb to the pain of it all, which in itself was something that disgusted him. But he wasn't sure if his power applied to aging or just when he was attacked. He physically felt himself getting older, and he dreaded the idea of being a decrepit immortal whose body never seemed to stop deteriorating. Worse, he wasn't sure what he would do if he had to outlive those he loved. Kane knew he couldn't fight forever, and once they were gone, he wouldn't want to anymore. The idea of outliving his sister and not getting to grow old alongside Rory was one thought he liked to try to keep out of his head.

———

About a year into Kane's foray as Hematite, he was still nameless. Everyone had just been calling him the masked vigilante, unsure of what his motives were and just speculating who he was. It amused him whenever he'd turn on the news that no one suspected he was just a teenager wearing whatever clothing he could throw together that he got at the thrift store and from the depths of his closet.

Most of what he did when he started wasn't newsworthy, beyond people noticing he was beating the cops to their jobs. Everything had changed, though, when his sister's elementary school made the headlines.

Kayla had been sick for a few days and had to stay after school to make up some tests she missed out on. Kane used the opportunity to patrol the school, resting on the rooftop in his Hematite outfit.

Thirty minutes had passed before Kane heard a helicopter flying overhead. It had approached the school quickly, and the police weren't far behind it. The sound of the helicopter blades in the air and the police sirens dominated his ears, but once they passed by—seemingly taking a lap—he tried to listen in to what was happening.

He then heard the faint pitter-patter of gunfire and a few screams on the other side of the building. Kane tried not to panic but, knowing his sister was in there, ran into the building. He wasn't worried. He was mostly positive that any bullets wouldn't kill him; he had died twice before that and lived to tell the tale after all.

Kane ran until he saw someone standing in the hallway, kicking at the doors. He was obviously too old to be a student, but too young to be a faculty member.

"Drop your gun!" Kane shouted. He didn't have his voice modifier yet, but the multiple scarves he had wrapped around his face and neck muffled his voice enough to be unrecognizable when he dropped his tone.

Kane was only sixteen and had no clue what he was doing, but it didn't stop him from charging at the other teenager. His punches were getting better than they had a few years ago, even from before he donned this mantle, but it had still been considerably sloppy. Luckily for him, his opponent wasn't much better. The shooter's knowledge of proper gun-handling had been essentially nonexistent, making it easy for Kane to disarm him.

Once the shooter was disarmed, he grabbed a knife and went for Kane's arm. Kane winced but kept moving, letting the blood slowly drip onto the linoleum of the school floors.

When Kane met his eyes, he saw that they were dazed; it was like there was nothing behind them. His eyes had been bloodshot and dilated from liquid courage, a look Kane knew all too well from his father.

Kane's jaw clenched as he grabbed the discarded gun, hit him in the head with the butt of it, and let him fall to the floor. He dropped the gun again and kicked it down the hall just in case the shooter would wake up, but from the looks of it, he would be out until the police arrived.

Kane looked up to the classroom with a fresh boot print on the door from the dirt on his shoe. He recognized it as Kayla's classroom and thought he'd faint. He grounded himself, knocked on the door, and then said, "It's safe now."

Kane heard his sister's voice through the door. "My hero!"

He smiled beneath his mask. Kayla didn't know, and since he didn't have a name, that's what she called him.

He heard her teacher call her name, but Kayla came running to the door and pushed the black paper covering the window back. Kane could see her peering through the bottom of the glass to look in.

"See!" Kayla exclaimed. "It's really him!"

The teacher glanced up at her spot from behind her desk and saw that it had been, in fact, the masked vigilante from the news.

The teacher approached the door and opened it, seeing that Kane was right: the student who brought the gun was passed out behind him.

"Thank you," the teacher said. "I already called 9-1-1. They should be here soon."

"They were checking the perimeter when I got here. I'm sure they will be too." He turned to Kayla. "You need to stop getting into trouble, alright?"

She laughed. "Trouble seems to find me, but I'm okay. You're always there."

He was planning on giving her the hematite ring in his pocket for her birthday later that week but happened to have had it with him. Despite her insisting that she was fine because he was there, Kane saw her small body trembling and her pupils blown wide, so he reached into his pocket and handed her the box.

"It's hematite," he said. "For protection. I think you need it more than I do, kid."

The attempted shooting made the news that evening. Thankfully, no one had been seriously hurt or killed. What really struck Kane, though, was the interview the stations did with Kayla. A nine-year-old's witness statement was like media gold.

"That hero came and rescued my class! And he even gave me this ring! It's made from hematite, see? Isn't it pretty?"

As the news anchors explained that hematite was a stone symbolizing protection, they all began to call him the Hematite Hero, eventually shortening it to Hematite with time.

Kane still wasn't sure what he thought of the name, but it certainly stuck.

————

The next morning, Kane felt like he could barely function. While he patrolled often, his nights out were becoming more and more frequent. Whenever Rory saw him, he'd have a cup of coffee or an energy drink handy in an attempt to stay awake. What he really needed was a full night's sleep, but Kane didn't think he could afford that anytime soon.

Juggling his usual search for answers, looking after his sister, and dealing with Stone Breaker was starting to burn him out. If Kane had to be completely honest, he didn't want to fight anymore but he knew it wouldn't be an option for a long time. He thought maybe one day in a few years, he could finally settle down and hope Rory was still single so he could make good on his promise to marry her, if she wasn't dating anyone by the time they turned thirty. He wanted to just enjoy the way the sun felt on his skin as he held her hand instead of spending all of his time out in the night. It would all be worth it, he thought, if that was what was waiting for him at the end of the super-hero tunnel.

"You okay, Kay?" Rory asked when he got in her car.

"Mhm, I'm fine," Kane grumbled as he buckled his seatbelt. Her voice had snapped him out of his daydreaming. "Late night, that's all. The usual."

"Are you sure?"

Kane nodded. He hated lying to Rory as it was but lying to her when she knew he was bullshitting her made it even worse.

————

Rory had never felt more worried about Kane. Something was going on that he wasn't telling her about, and she wasn't sure if she was more concerned or hurt that he wasn't fessing up. Rory thought Kane would tell her anything, but maybe she had been wrong. She missed her usual Kane, the one who always knew what to say to make her laugh with a crude joke in private or a wink across the room. The more she thought about it, the more she realized that Kane didn't smile as much as he used to anymore.

On their lunch break, Kane didn't seem much better than he had that morning. His eyes still looked sunken in from lack of sleep. His hair was falling out of the half-bun he kept it in so it would stay out of his face. He said little as he ate lunch, seeming to just enjoy his food and any energy it might provide.

"Come with me," Rory said once they finished eating.

"Huh?"

"Come on. We still have twenty minutes until our next classes start. Don't question it."

Kane just shrugged. "Okay." He didn't have the energy to fight, so he just followed Rory from the teacher's lounge to her history classroom. It was clear simply by looking around the room that Rory knew what kept her students' attention. One wall had a signed poster from a production of *Hamilton* that was performed in Denver. She had stitched together side-by-side photos of the characters from the show with their real-life portraits, with short bios of each historical figure.

Rory pulled a blanket out from a trunk she kept by her desk. It was fleece and had some cartoon kittens on it. When she handed it to Kane, he looked at her blankly.

"What are you doing?" Kane asked. "What's this?"

"I keep this in case any of my students don't get enough rest at home," she said. "It's clean. I just washed it last night, and no one used it today. Take a nap. You look exhausted. I'll wake you up when we gotta get back to it, okay?"

He smiled at her. Despite his smile, Rory could see the bags forming beneath his normally bright eyes. His skin seemed more pale than usual, even for the dead of winter. "I could kiss you right now, you know that, Miller?"

Rory laughed and just ruffled his long blonde hair. "You really *are* exhausted."

Kane chirped his thanks and then curled up in her desk chair. He fell asleep without a problem, despite what Rory would consider him being in an uncomfortable position.

Rory sighed as she looked on, wondering what was going on with Kane. *Surely there was more to his partying than met the eye,* she thought, and she wondered if he was more involved in the Hematite and Stone

Breaker situation than he led on. An intrusive thought suggested he could work with the other side, but then she remembered how he comforted her after Hematite rescued her and dismissed it. *There was no way,* she concluded. Rory simply made a mental note to tell Naomi that Kane was acting strangely so they could get to the bottom of it.

CHAPTER 8

Mark Stevens sighed as he scrolled through his email inbox in his cubicle. He wasn't even sure why he continued showing up to work anymore; every time he did, he just felt more and more deflated. He crafted his latest story discussing Hematite's ever-growing presence in the community—and questioning what that meant for Riverpeak—in such a way to inspire doubt in the vigilante's helpfulness.

Unfortunately for Mark, it had the opposite effect. He clicked through dozens of emails calling him a fraud. They questioned how he still had a job at *The Riverpeak Times* after consistently showing biased journalism. A few took the time to detail instances where Hematite made a personal impact on their lives, but Mark largely ignored them.

Mark knew he was on thin ice with the paper he reported for. The only reason he could get away with it so far was that his father was providing exclusive interview access to *The Riverpeak Times* on the condition that Mark was employed there.

Mark often wondered if he'd even have a job if his father's money wasn't a factor. He'd always felt like his voice had been drowned out by his father and this time was no exception. His relationship with nepotism was a complicated one: he had no issue using his father's name, status, and money to his advantage, and he was the first to admit that. But on the contrary, he wished he could make a name for himself without relying too heavily upon the Stevens family status. He desperately wanted to be accepted for who he was and what he had to say, but that reality seemed to grow further and further from his reach as the years went on.

Hematite had become a symbol of protection of sorts for the city of Riverpeak. Even many other writers and editors at *The Riverpeak Times* became wrapped up in the sensationalism of their hometown hero. Whenever they'd hear about Hematite activity on the police scanners, they'd all gather around to listen closely and rushed to send a reporter that way.

But for Mark, Hematite represented everything that made him feel bitter. Mark often still felt like the dorky boy in his grade school classes who struggled with coming into his own. He saw his inner child whenever he'd look into the mirror or saw his reflection in another late-night cup of coffee. The only difference was that the sadness in his eyes had become hollower.

He picked up his phone as it buzzed. Dougie had texted him again. Dougie was the only one in school who didn't pick on him, likely because he was also another target of the kids who were too cool for them. When Mark told him about his idea to take on the identity of Stone Breaker and try to knock out Hematite so his father's top lobbyists could stay afloat, Dougie had immediately offered to help.

Mark knew he could rely on Dougie when he told him he needed a name to go along with Stone Breaker's own identity. After all, it would be over for both his and his father's careers if the world knew what they were up to in trying to take down Hematite. Dougie's first choice was Shatterstone, something to show unity between the two of them by their similarities. Mark had never been more touched in his life.

> DOUGIE: Nothing new on Hematite. There's legit nothing on him online. I'm not sure we're going to find him.

Mark groaned internally. He was getting more frustrated with the lack of information available on Hematite. Dougie took no time to reply.

> MARK: Nothing at all? Not even on anyone he might be close to?

DOUGIE: There is that girl we saw him take into the alley. It looked like Rory Miller. Remember her from school?

> MARK: Not well. I don't think I had any classes with her. Maybe one back in elementary school? But if you think she's the one we spotted with Hematite that night before we found them, then go for it. I'm down for anything to make him suffer TBH

DOUGIE: She was real quiet in school. Let's see what she's up to these days. Don't worry, I'm on it.

Mark looked at the clock on his computer and realized it was time to head home. Whenever the clock read six, he tried to brace himself for his return to his family's house. He took his time packing his bags, trying to prolong every second until he returned home. Mark still lived with his parents, and while his father promised him a bountiful reward for going against Hematite, he had yet to see much of it beyond his usual cruelness subsiding. *Perhaps*, Mark thought, *I shouldn't ask for much more than that.*

When Mark came home, he announced his arrival with a quiet hello. Mark wished to not be perceived, but it never worked out that way. While their house was one of the nicest in all of Riverpeak on the outside, he certainly felt like there was a lot to be desired once stepping inside.

The best way Mark could describe the interior was subtle opulence. Their decor showcased his father's wealth without being tacky or too flashy. Tom Stevens was convinced that this style would give them the illusion of belonging to an old-money family. While they certainly had more privileges than others in Riverpeak, most of their money came from Tom's shady business dealings as a councilman. Elections didn't pay for themselves, Tom would always tell Mark, and the campaigns never stopped just because the season was over. If he had his way, he'd be running for mayor next.

Mark's mother's sing-song voice called from the kitchen, and he could see the back of her blonde bob from where he was standing. Overall, he had inherited her constitution. As per usual, she was the picture of the perfect housewife. "Hello, Mark sweetie! Are you joining us for dinner?"

Mark swallowed. His mother Lydia couldn't cook to save her life, but he knew what would happen if he denied her. "Of course, Mom."

His father came down the stairs at that moment, almost as if on cue. Mark could tell by the lightness of Tom's footsteps that he was in a good mood today. Mark felt his shoulders shrug back and relax at this discovery, but his voice still felt stuck in his throat.

"Hi, Dad."

"We're celebrating tonight, my boy!" Tom laughed, a boisterous sound that came straight from his gut. "You won't believe what we found out today."

"Is this that project you were telling me about?" Lydia asked Tom. Mark moved to the kitchen to help his mother set the table, as his father took his seat at the head of it.

"It is. We've been running some tests over the last few weeks. Ray did some extra testing on his boy this week and last, and to say it's been going swimmingly would be an understatement. We fed him more of the drug in his daily doses, and he's getting more control over his powers now that we found just the right amount. He can finally use a lighter now, not just a matchstick."

"That's great!" Lydia exclaimed. Mark could tell just by looking at her that she didn't understand a word of what Tom said. The only thing that rested behind her eyes was emptiness. Mark used to hate her just as much as he hated his father, but now he wondered how much she had suffered at Tom's hands alongside him.

"Hey, Dad? What is the drug, anyway? We always talk about it, but I don't even know what it is if we're being completely honest."

His father shrugged. "Oh, I don't know. It's some new thing on the market." Mark realized the irony in this, given how long they'd been in business with the drug ring, but didn't dare correct his dad. "I think they blended a bunch of things together, meth included, but I'm not sure what else. I don't keep up with it so long as it's still moving. We have supply coming in from Denver and directly here in Riverpeak, so we don't have all our eggs in one basket."

"I suppose that makes sense. Is it ready for others to use yet?"

"It will be soon, at this rate. That's great news for you and me, Mark, isn't it? If we can sell the drug as the very thing that's giving people superpowers, you know what will happen? Instant profits in Ray's hands, which means more money in our pockets."

"That's wonderful!" Lydia said with a little clap. Mark's empathy for her was waning thin.

"It is." Despite his agreement, Mark found his words to be hollow. He hoped his father didn't notice. "Dougie and I are still working on the Hematite problem."

"Good," Tom said. "Did you find him yet?"

"No, but we found someone close to him. Dougie's looking into it tonight."

"We'll take what we can get when it comes to that little punk," Tom said. "Talk about a thorn in our sides." Mark knew that "our" referred to Chief Eliza Daniels. "I can only pay her off so much before it becomes a waste. You boys are doing good work."

Mark yearned for the day when his father would acknowledge him as a man, not a boy, but he knew that today was not that day. He wasn't sure when he would earn it, but he was determined to. He picked at his lamb, trying his best to pretend it was an excellent meal but struggled to swallow it due to lack of flavor.

Once their meal was over, Mark was free for the evening. His father would succumb to his shows, and his mother would fall into a trance on her tablet, which meant that Mark didn't have to worry about their watchful eyes for once.

Mark settled into his room with the door shut as he called Dougie, who answered right away.

"Hey, man," Dougie said. "Ready?"

"I'm ready." Mark opened his web browser. "What do you have on Rory Miller?"

"She's a teacher at Riverpeak High School. I think she lives alone. I found her voter registration with her address. According to her Facebook profile, where she goes by her first and middle name instead of last, she's single. It's fairly private, but there aren't any photos of her with any guys, except for Kane Kelly."

Mark scoffed. "Kane Kelly? Fuck that guy."

"Whoa, I didn't realize you hated him."

"Shawn Jameson never left me the hell alone in school. Kane, Elijah, and Brad would just watch as I got the shit kicked out of me by Shawn. If Elijah and Kane told Shawn to stop, he just took it as a suggestion to ignore. They never actually did anything."

"Jeez, what pricks. No way she's dating him."

"No, he's not that type to be in a serious relationship, especially with someone like her. I remember in school she was too much of a goody-two-shoes. It looks like they're just coworkers who hang out sometimes. Who else does she hang out with?"

"I did find a photo of her with Kane, Elijah, Brad, and Naomi. Looks like it was at Elijah's birthday party."

"Wait, Naomi Sato? The reporter?"

"Yeah, her."

"I'm friends with her on Facebook! Let me go to her page. Maybe I can see more," Mark said and quickly opened Naomi's profile. Her cover photo gave away no details—it was just a childhood photo of her with her parents and brother standing in front of a lake by Mount Fuji —and her profile picture was an engagement picture of her and Brad.

Mark opened Naomi's photo albums and began poking around. He found one with the University of Colorado as the title, so he opted to start there. "Yup, Naomi and Rory are definitely best friends," Mark said.

"I remember them hanging out in school too," Dougie said. "Do you think Naomi's in on this?"

"I'm not sure, but she's too high-profile. She's the darling of Channel 10, and her dad is super famous locally. I doubt she'd risk her career."

"So, Naomi Sato is off the table," Dougie said. "What about Rory's family?"

"Let me see..." Mark clicked back to view all of Naomi's albums. "Oh, I found more photos from the birthday party. Let me see who else was there. Maybe the families went too."

Sure enough, there was a photo of Elijah's mom and dad standing alongside Rory's, Brad's, and Naomi's parents.

"Her parents are both tagged," Mark said. He opened both of their profiles up in new tabs. He started with Naomi's mother. "Susan Miller's page is private. I can only see her profile photo, which is a selfie she took with Rory. Doesn't help us at all." He closed out of that tab and then went to Rory's dad's page. "Ah-ha! Bingo! Dad's is public."

"Send me the link," Dougie said. "I'll work my magic and get all the info we need out of this guy."

"Already sent it to you. Looks like Dave Miller isn't super active on social media, but it should hopefully do the trick."

"I think it'll be fine," Dougie said. "Thanks, Mark. How's everything with the drug doing?"

"Not ready for us yet," Mark said. "I'm wondering when my dad will finally let me try it. I think he wants it to be safe before we try to get powers from it. But they said it worked on Ray's son; his powers are getting stronger. It took some torturing to get him there, though. I don't think the process has been pleasant."

"What do you mean?"

"You didn't know? Ray's kid wasn't born with the powers they've been testing. I thought I told you that. They just pumped him full of the drug to see what dosage may or may not work and to see if they could replicate how it happened naturally."

"Holy shit."

"My dad said they think Hematite might have been born with it. They're trying to determine who some of the other kids might be, but if they have powers, they think Hematite's the only one that's actually done anything about it. There are so many people he could be that it's pretty impossible for them to narrow it down. Lots of clients and all. But Ray's family hasn't had an easy go of it."

"Poor guy," Dougie said. "But it'll be our time soon enough."

"I hope." Mark whispered, "I'm thinking that my dad's just saying he'll let us try it, but never actually will. Especially if he gets in a bad mood. He was good today because the tests on Ray's son have been going well, but that's not the norm, you know?"

"Let's just put our trust in the process," Dougie said. "And even if he doesn't give it to us, we can always take matters into our own hands together. Right?"

Mark nodded. He wasn't sure that he'd ever have the courage to face off against his father in a situation like that, but he said, "Yeah, you're right, Dougie. I guess all we need now is to figure out what we're going to do with Rory Miller."

"I could try to kidnap her or something. She doesn't look that tough. I could probably handle it."

Mark expanded on that. "We could bring her to my dad's office in City Hall and then make a video for Hematite."

"Oh, I like your thinking! Sort of like a ransom note, but in digital form."

"And even if they aren't connected, it's a great way to lure Hematite in," Mark rationalized. "She's a high school teacher. Hematite says he wants to help the community, right? Then let's see what he does if he leaves one of its educators behind."

"I didn't even think of that! That's brilliant!"

"Do you need me with you when you make your move?"

"I don't think so," Dougie replied. "So far, what I've found beyond her address is that she's just a teacher who lives alone. She made the news in college when Hematite rescued her, so that explains her connection. But I don't think she's doing anything other than pencil-pushing for him."

"If you need backup, call me," Mark said. "I don't want to underestimate anyone involved with Hematite."

"Roger that. But it'll be fine. Just you wait. I'll get to work and see you tomorrow for Valentine's."

"See you then."

———

Mark waited for both of his parents to leave for their Valentine's Day dinner plans before he left the house. His mask was in his messenger bag, which he slung across his shoulder before he hopped onto his motorcycle.

Dougie was waiting for him at the church in front of the pond. Mark put his 3D-printed mask on, the band lightly pinching at the hairs on the back of his head, as he approached Dougie. Mark made a mental note to touch up the lightning bolt paint job on his mask since the edges were chipping again.

"Did you bring it?" Mark asked.

Dougie nodded. "I've got the ice in my trunk."

"Good," Mark said. "My parents are on their way to Denver, so we don't have to worry about them. What are yours up to tonight?"

"Same. I recommended a place out in Colorado Springs for them to try. We're clear."

"Perfect," Mark said with a grin. "Alright, let's go."

They each grabbed a bag of ice and made their way across the street. The local French restaurant, Le Petit Chateau, was the most popular in Riverpeak. Dougie's car was only about a block away, but with the weather, they weren't worried about the ice melting.

"Man, this is fucking freezing," Dougie muttered.

"It'll be better once we're not holding these bags," Mark said. "Come on, almost there."

Mark set his bag down once they were at the back door of the restaurant. He reached into his messenger bag and grabbed the hammer in the bag. He swung it down, and the door handle ripped off with a thwacking noise.

"That was too easy," Mark said as he put the hammer back in his bag and picked the ice back up. "Come on. Let's start a riot."

"I can't believe we saw this on a meme," Dougie said with a chuckle.

"Right?" Mark laughed. "It's perfect."

The first employee to spot them once they opened the door screamed. Her shout made the other employees all freeze, despite being the busiest they'd ever be all year.

"Is that Stone Breaker?"

"What are they doing here?"

They didn't speak but beelined it for the deep fryer.

"Sorry about your beignets," Stone Breaker said through his voice modifier before he and Dougie as Shatterstone chucked the ice toward the fryer from a safe distance.

Everyone ran back as quickly as they could to avoid getting burned by the splattering oil. A few people who couldn't get out of the way in time were hit with some of the backsplashes. As soon as the ice hit the boiling oil, the fryer bubbled over. Oil leaked directly into the burners, causing the fryers to go up in flames. A trail of flaming oil quickly traveled across the floor toward a rack of towels. One employee scrambled in the chaos to salvage them and prevent the spread, but they were too late.

"Let's go!"

The two of them ran out the way they came and made their way to the front of the restaurant to witness the ensuing chaos. A few patrons seated near the kitchen began running out, which caused a chain reaction of sheer panic.

"That should draw him out," Shatterstone said. "At least the fire feels nice."

"It does, doesn't it?"

The two of them watched from across the street, knowing that they were untouchable at this point. Stone Breaker tried to not laugh beneath his mask as he watched people call for help, knowing that the help wouldn't arrive, all thanks to his father.

"Hey, jerk-offs."

The two of them turned at the sound of the deep, mechanical voice. Hematite was standing behind them, still in the shadows, hands by his sides.

"Aw, look who decided to show up," Stone Breaker said. "Nice of you to join us, Hematite."

"I knew you'd be up to something tonight, but this is low, even for you. What the fuck do you think you're doing?"

"Thought we'd grab your attention with a bang," Shatterstone said.

"How'd you know we'd be here tonight?"

"Your code in the newspaper was pretty easy to crack." Hematite shrugged, to Stone Breaker's surprise at the newspaper code being uncovered. "Tell your buddy Mark I said thanks for the heads-up."

Stone Breaker swallowed. "You've got a choice to make, Hematite. Help those people or take us on."

Hematite laughed. "How do you think they all got out?"

Stone Breaker's smile dropped beneath his mask. "What?"

"You really don't notice much, do you?"

Instead of responding verbally, Stone Breaker reached for the hammer in his bag and swung. Hematite grabbed Stone Breaker's wrist before he could attack and made quick work of disarming him. Shatterstone dove for the hammer as Stone Breaker recoiled to prepare for his next move.

They both swung to attack Hematite at the same time, so he ducked. While he was lower, he elbowed Shatterstone in the stomach, to which Shatterstone doubled over and dropped the hammer.

The sudden oncoming of fire trucks nearly blinded Hematite, but he grabbed the hammer as it dropped. He aimed for Stone Breaker's knee, but Stone Breaker moved just in time. He lunged at Hematite and brought an elbow down onto his back, putting all his weight into it to make up for his overall lack of physical strength. Hematite winced, but he had been hit worse many times before. Shatterstone used the opportunity to gang up on him, as the two of them stomped at Hematite while he was down, but their kicks caused Hematite to slip out of Stone Breaker's grasp.

"That the best you got?" Hematite taunted as he got up. "What are you gonna do, kill me?"

As Hematite laughed at his own joke, Stone Breaker and Shatterstone both stopped to look at one another.

"Oh my God, we didn't think of how we'd grab him," Shatterstone mentioned out loud to Stone Breaker. "Fuck, what do we do?!"

"Just kill him! Even if he comes back, we can at least get him to your car!"

It was just enough time for Hematite to take a step back and grab both of their heads from behind. He got a good grip on their hair as he swung them both, banging their heads together. He grabbed his billy club, not wanting to use something as potentially lethal as the hammer, and whacked both of them on the way down for good measure. Before he could reach down to grab Stone Breaker's mask, police sirens interrupted his train of thought. The blue lights illuminated the night, along with the pre-existing red ones from the fire trucks that were working on Le Petit Chateau.

"Shit!" Hematite muttered to himself. If his usual detective wasn't there, he knew he'd be screwed. Instead of sticking around and unmasking Stone Breaker, he had no choice but to run off, cutting through the woods before the police could find him.

CHAPTER 9

Kane as Hematite rushed up the steps of his apartment complex, not stopping until he was inside with the door locked behind him. He rested his back against the door for a moment as he collected his breath. He was certain he lost the cops before they even caught sight of him, but close calls with law enforcement always made him anxious.

Kane tossed off his gloves and unraveled his boxing wraps as he walked over to his bedroom. He plopped the long strings of fabric in his laundry basket before he removed his cowl, balaclava, and voice modifier. He made his way over to his bathroom to wash his hands and face, taking his time with the job. Luckily, there were no fresh scars on his already bloodied knuckles, but he knew he'd be worse for the wear when he continued to undress.

Once he tossed off his fish-mouthed hoodie and shirt, he looked at himself in the mirror to check the damage. He didn't feel like any bones were broken, and there was only some mild redness on his stomach. Kane suspected at least a few of those spots would be bruised by the morning, but Stone Breaker and Shatterstone had both been fairly weak, so he knew it wouldn't be anything major. When Kane spit into his sink, he was relieved to see just saliva and no blood on the white ceramic.

Kane picked his hoodie up and quickly sniffed it. The smell of smoke still lingered from Le Petite Chateau, and he frowned at it. He was glad that he had been waiting right outside the restaurant when it caught fire so he could usher people out right away, taking some of the slack off the staff, but still wished he had caught Stone Breaker sooner. As he tossed his clothes in the laundry basket with his boxing wraps, he made a mental note to wash them right after he showered so he could get the smoke stench out.

Kane stood in the shower aimlessly for a few minutes, enjoying the feeling of the hot water against his skin. He didn't rush washing his hair, feeling meditative as he gently scrubbed the dirt, grime, melted snow, and ash off himself. There was something euphoric about a post-fight shower, like he was rinsing away the events of the evening. He looked at his hands as he bathed and wished he could wash every-thing away. He often wondered if it was all worth it or if it would amount to anything when he allowed himself to get lost in his thoughts. When that happened, his mind wandered to Kayla and Rory.

When he finished his shower and tossed his laundry in, he plopped onto his bed. He made another mental note that he'd need a new mattress soon; as much as he hated to splurge, his back needed the support more than ever.

He held his phone up in front of his face, not straying from the lock screen right away. It was a photo of him and Rory that Naomi took on Elijah's birthday. He smiled at the sight of her face, her joy at the moment clear in her expression.

He opened the contact and called her. He usually didn't call this late, but his selfishness won over as he figured it would be worth a shot.

"Hey, Kane!" Rory was a bit taken aback by his call, but she was happy to hear from him nonetheless. "What's up? I figured you'd be out by now."

"Happy Valentine's Day, pretty lady," Kane said. "Are you doing anything? Anyone?"

Rory laughed from her spot on the couch. "You too. But no, none of the above. I'm surprised you're not."

"Nah. I'm not that wild. Besides, the best place in town kinda caught on fire."

"I saw that! Thank God Hematite was there. I'm glad I stayed in tonight."

"Do you wanna maybe stay in together? I can cook if you haven't eaten yet. I promise you, you're not some last resort booty call. If I *did* have any booty calls, you'd be top of the list." If he was being honest, he hoped a relaxing evening with her would take his mind off his fight with Stone Breaker and Shatterstone. Seeing her in a normal sense would help him feel at ease.

"You know, I was just debating dinner. Is this you asking me on a proper date?" Rory felt some heat rising to her cheeks that she'd never admit to him or herself.

"It's whatever you want it to be," Kane said. He smiled, afraid of defining it despite knowing how much he needed her company. "It can be nothing serious and nothing casual all at once. Deal?"

Rory's blush instantly faded at his words. "Sure, whatever that means. Why the hell not?"

"You said I've been worrying you lately. Consider this me making it up to you."

"My place or yours?" Rory asked.

"Here's fine. I've got food to whip up. Come over whenever," Kane said, trying to hide the longing in his voice. "I'll get decent."

"Get decent?"

"Yeah. I just showered. You want a picture?"

Rory could practically hear his smirk. "Maybe another night."

"You know what? I'll take that. That's not a total dejection. See you soon?"

"I'll be right over."

Rory rushed to her closet, unsure of what to wear, but settled on jeans and a decent blouse to go along with Kane's theme of nothing serious and nothing casual. She kept her makeup simple, not wanting to make a fuss in case Kane didn't want to either, and was relieved to see him answer the door dressed similarly. He wore an old pair of jeans with a hole forming in one knee and a button-up shirt left undone over a graphic tee. His hair was still wet from his shower and slicked back, highlighting the details of his face. Rory noticed a few freckles that dotted the top of his forehead by his hairline.

"Beautiful as always," he said as he let her in. "I don't have any roses or chocolates or anything, but I make a bitchin' tofu Pad Thai."

"That's already more than I anticipated for the evening," Rory said. "It's all commercialized crap, anyway. It smells great in here."

Kane was relieved to hear her say that. He was hoping the smell of dinner would cover any lingering scents of smoke from when he returned earlier.

"I'll plate everything up. You just sit there, look pretty, and pick your favorite cheesy romance movie for us to watch over dinner in the spirit of love."

"Even if it's from Hallmark?"

"Their Christmas ones are my guilty pleasure, so go for it." It wasn't a lie, but not for the reason Rory might think. Their idyllic outline and predictable happily-ever-after formula always gave Kane some comfort and escapism from his life.

"Okay, now this is a side of you I have never seen," Rory said with a laugh as she grabbed the remote. "Even after all these years, I'd never have pegged you for the type."

"There are a lot of things you could peg me for." Kane winked.

Rory rolled her eyes, understanding what he was implying.

"But in all seriousness, you can thank Kayla. You can actually thank her for any good traits of mine."

Kane joined her at the small dining area table; since his apartment was a studio, it was easy to see the television from anywhere. Kane paid little attention to the movie, looking mostly at Rory—especially once they had moved over to his couch after eating—out of the corner of his eye. He didn't dare get caught staring at her, but he placed his arm around her shoulders as they watched. Rory relaxed into Kane's embrace and scooted to be closer to him on his couch. Kane was glancing down and smiling at her when she looked up to meet his eyes.

"What's your dream guy like?" Kane asked. He added as he pointed to the TV. "This guy doesn't seem your type. I can tell that much."

"Nah, he's not," Rory said. The question caught her off guard. "Hmm." She took a moment to contemplate her answer; the more she thought about it, the more she realized she would just be describing him. Between how he presented the evening and what he just asked her, she wasn't sure if she should be completely honest. "Someone kind who makes me laugh. That's my only criteria these days."

Kane smiled. "I like that answer. I think that's reasonable."

They enjoyed a comfortable silence together for the rest of the movie, only occasionally chiming in with commentary about the ridiculous plot. By the time the movie ended, Rory realized she didn't want to go home, even though she knew she should.

"We have to get up early for work tomorrow," she said. "It's criminal to have a holiday on a Thursday. But thanks for having me over. We should do this more often."

Kane beamed. "I'd like that. I'd like that a lot, actually. Come on, I'll walk you to your car."

They were silent on the walk down. The winter night was practically silent, save for a thin layer of snow crunching beneath their feet. When she reached her car, she asked Kane, "What was tonight?"

"Like I said, it's whatever you want it to be." He winked at Rory and leaned down to kiss her cheek. "Happy Valentine's Day, Miller."

She smiled at him, despite how puzzled she was at his crypticness. "Happy Valentine's Day, Kane."

On the ride home, she mulled over what Kane could have meant. His mixed signals from insisting the dinner was whatever to kissing her cheek had her feeling dizzy. She knew she should have been more direct with him too but also wondered what that may mean for their friendship if he really meant nothing by it and she was just overthinking it, like she had a tendency to do.

———

As Rory settled into Naomi's apartment the next evening, she said, "I'm glad you could do this with me tonight. I'm surprised you're not spending time with Brad."

"His older brothers are in town for the week, so he's on family duty. But I'm glad too. It gives us a chance to work uninterrupted. How was your night? I hope you didn't just sit at home alone watching bad romance movies like you usually do."

"You know, I did exactly that, just not alone," Rory said. "Kane invited me over."

"Wait, he did?!" Naomi jumped on the chair and crossed her legs to settle herself down. "You spent the night with Kane? Kane Kelly?"

"Yeah, what other Kane do we know?" Rory asked with a shrug. "I don't think it was anything serious. Kane doesn't take anything seriously."

"Why else would he invite you over on Valentine's Day?"

"It was just two friends hanging out, Naomi, I swear. You're making a bigger deal of this than it was. He cooked, we watched a movie, and I went home. No frills."

"He cooked for you, and you wanna call it no frills? Oh my God, you're helpless!"

"Kane's not like Brad. He's a lot more laissez-faire," Rory said. "And we've been friends for so long. If he wanted to pursue me like that, you figure he would have already."

"Maybe he's got the same fears as you. I know you've mentioned not wanting to ruin the friendship you guys have. He might feel like that too. I dunno. Come on, let's grab what we've got and get to work."

They pulled out the stacks of relevant paperwork from the files that Naomi had been keeping in her closet. They left the ones focusing only on Stone Breaker behind, pulling only what little they had on Hematite. Compared to the Stone Breaker pile, the stack was unimpressive.

"Alright," Naomi said. "I'll see if I can find any public records that give us a hint. Maybe arrest reports related to drugs if he's going after the drug rings."

"I'll check out some police reports from incidents he was involved in. Maybe someone who he helped saw something."

"Ooh, good thinking!" Naomi began typing away at her laptop.

After a few minutes, Naomi groaned from her spot on the lounge chair in her living room. Her black hair was falling out of the braid she had loosely tied it in before Rory had arrived.

"I'm not finding anything!"

"I'm not having any luck, either." Rory frowned. "I hoped that me having actually met him in person would help, but so far, it's a bust."

Rory suddenly had a revelation. She shifted the position she was sitting in from slumped to upright. Rory's sudden rapid typing on her laptop alerted Naomi to this.

"What's happening?" Naomi asked. "I'm sensing a lightbulb moment."

"He has a storage unit," Rory said. "There's gotta be some record of who bought it, right? I remember the number from when he took me there."

"Yeah, but we're not the FBI," Naomi said. "That's not gonna be public record. We'd need a warrant and a badge to pull that one off."

Rory sighed and slumped back into her previous position. "Damn it." *So much for that good idea,* she thought. "How the hell are we not finding anything? Like, anything at all?"

"He's either great with computers or has a guy that's helping him stay completely blacked out on the internet," Naomi said. "We run across that at the station sometimes. Some people just have no digital footprint. We should call Elijah for help."

"Does Brad know you're doing this?" Rory asked. Looping in Elijah would likely result in clueing Brad in, given they lived together.

"Yes … and no. He knows I'm looking into who Stone Breaker and Hematite are, but he thinks it's for work. I wasn't sure how much I should say," she said. "Brad gets it. I just don't want him to freak out, you know?"

"I'm in that boat with Kane," Rory said. "And he's been off lately. I dunno. It's hard to explain. I'm thinking he might be wrapped up in this and we don't even know it."

"You think? What do you mean by off?"

"He was so exhausted the other day that I let him take a nap in my classroom during our lunch break. And he's just made a few comments that make it sound like he knows more than he leads on. I don't know. Maybe he's just super hungover half the time. Either way, I'm worried about him."

"I'll ask Brad if he's heard anything. He tells me everything. We'll get to the bottom of it." She winked as she set her laptop down so she could redo her braid. "But I think it may be better if we don't ask for Elijah's help after all. I think Brad's chalked a lot of my stress up to wedding planning lately. And with his anxiety, I don't wanna do that to him if I don't have to."

"You don't need to justify it, Naomi," Rory said. "That's totally valid. I know how Brad can be. Good heart, would be understanding, just a nervous wreck."

"I'm glad we're doing this, though. So many people in the news industry get off to the idea of helping people. They think they're making some enormous difference, and they sell us that too. But a lot of them really aren't. A lot of them actually just make things worse." She huffed. "They don't make 'em like Cronkite anymore."

Rory smiled at her friend and reached out for her hand. She gripped it. "I'm glad we're doing this too. I don't think I could have made it this far without you. Who needs Cronkite when we've got Naomi Sato, huh? I'm proud of you."

Naomi laughed. "Thanks. The imposter syndrome is real." She took a sip of wine and then said, "I'm proud of you too. You've overcome a lot."

"Thank our therapist," Rory said with a laugh. "She acts all buddy-buddy with me and then, bam! A hard-hitting question that feels like a punch to the gut."

"I'm serious!" Naomi said. "I'm so glad you like Marissa, though. She was awesome with me and my mom when we went for therapy after the South Main Burgers fire. But you did that yourself! Healing isn't pretty, and you've really put yourself out there. Now look at us," Naomi said. "We're swimming in a sea of papers."

Rory grabbed her glass of wine from the coffee table and raised it for a toast. "To actually making a difference."

Naomi held her glass up alongside Rory's in an act of cheers. "To actually making a difference."

"Your brother would be proud of you," Rory added.

Naomi smiled at the memory of her brother. "I bet Noah would have loved to have been a part of this. I miss him so much. You know, I always thought there was more to his death than what my dad said."

"Yeah? You've never told me that."

"Mm." Naomi nodded and took a sip of her wine. "The fire he was in, the one my dad made it out of. Obviously. You know that already. But it just never sat right with me that Noah just died in a random freak fire one day. And I know that denial is part of the grieving process, but it's been years now and I've never shaken that."

"If I've learned anything lately, it's trusting my gut. Maybe you're right."

"Once we're done with this and the wedding is over, that's my next goal. Maybe this whole Hematite and Stone Breaker thing will open up a whole can of worms, and I can get to the bottom of things. Maybe we'll get some justice for Noah."

"Something tells me that this," Rory said, as she gestured at their iPads and scattered newspaper clippings, "is only the beginning of something much bigger."

CHAPTER 10

Naomi's house wasn't far from Rory's, so Rory usually just walked whenever she'd visit, if the weather was nice. The air still had a bit of a bite to it, but it finally stopped snowing, so Rory enjoyed the outdoors for the first time in months. While the cold weather wasn't her favorite, she never minded the way the chilly air hit her skin after being cooped up in the heat. It was hard to see the tops of the mountains in the distance at night, but their snowy caps were just bright enough to make out their shapes.

Halfway back to her home, she couldn't explain why but she felt her fight-or-flight response kick in. Thanks to Dr. Thornton, she was getting pretty good at identifying the racing of her heart and increased paranoia. Her instincts were telling her to run, but when she looked around, no one was around to clue her into what might have triggered her response. She tried to shrug it off as her post-traumatic stress overacting in a moment of loneliness, but she just couldn't shake off the way the hairs on the back of her neck stood up.

"Rory Miller," a voice called. It was a man's voice that Rory didn't recognize. She didn't turn around, just picked up her pace but he caught up to her. A gloved hand touched her shoulder.

Rory turned and saw a lanky, awkward man with short hair and wearing a cheap mask. Rory deduced that this must be Shatterstone, Stone Breaker's assistant. The mask looked 3D-printed, similarly to Stone Breaker's, but with less time or effort put into it, as there wasn't anything painted on the front. He wore black clothing with a red-and-yellow puffer jacket that looked brand new but scuffed up, as if he had gotten into a fight while wearing it. Rory thought his color scheme was an odd choice, given their whole point was anonymity and to stay undercover.

Rory shook his hand off her shoulder and said, "How do you know who I am?"

"We've got eyes everywhere," Shatterstone said. "You'd be surprised."

Rory tried to ignore the chill that went down her spine and her increasing nausea. "This isn't your usual spot." Rory tried to keep her voice strong, so as to not show her fear. "You really wanna do this in front of the whole suburb?"

"You really think anyone would notice? It's getting late, after all."

Shatterstone opened his mouth again to continue speaking, but Rory didn't give him a chance to start. Rory rolled her shoulders back, remembered everything she learned in her boxing classes, and threw a punch. It landed right in Shatterstone's face. She could feel the thin, 3D-printed mask crack beneath her knuckles and could hear his jaw pop along with it.

Shatterstone stumbled, so Rory hit him again. The second hit knocked him down and slid his cracked mask off his face. He was a different man now unmasked, but something about his constitution reminded Rory of her stalker all those years ago.

She didn't know what came over her, but she didn't stop punching him. All she knew was that it was her or him, and it was more important to her that he stayed down. She found herself on top of Shatterstone as she continued to land more blows, repeatedly hitting his face.

"What the hell did you think was going to happen?" Rory asked him between punches. He couldn't answer. "You think you can just fucking attack people in the middle of the goddamn road? Who gave you the right, you little punk?"

Rory was only stopped by the sudden force of someone dragging her off Shatterstone's body. Their arms moved beneath her armpits to snake around her body and yank her back.

"Hey, hey, hey!" It was Hematite. Rory huffed as he helped her stand up. "Rory, relax. What happened?"

Rory didn't answer him right away. She took a few moments to collect her breath. A few people peeked outside their windows. Hematite let go of Rory and turned her around to face him.

"Give me your hands." The words came out so fast that Rory could barely make them out. "Now."

Rory simply held her hands up in front of her, not questioning him. She couldn't tell if he sounded angry or not, thanks to the way his voice was distorted. Hematite ripped off an edge of his cowl and used it to wipe the blood that came from Shatterstone's face off her knuckles.

"Are you okay?" He spoke more gently now, keeping his gaze on her knuckles; Rory had never seen someone so focused.

Rory shrugged. "I thought it was him. He tried to attack me, and I thought it was him. I…" Rory released a shaky breath. "I don't know what came over me. It's like I blacked out or something."

Hematite knew Rory didn't like to say her stalker's name, but he knew she meant Daniel.

"Wash your hands with some antibacterial soap when you get home. But this should do the trick for now." There was a tenderness in Hematite's tone and his movements as he wiped the blood off Rory's knuckles with his cowl. Their closeness wasn't doing her any favors as she tried to calm down after the adrenaline rush.

"Will do." Her heart still felt like it was beating a million miles an hour, but she regained control of her breathing as she spoke to him. There was something about the gentle way he tended to her that helped her relax in an instant and made her feel safe. "Thanks."

"Are you hurt?" Even with his voice modifier and no way to see his facial expression, it was clear to Rory that he was genuinely concerned. If she didn't know any better, she'd say he almost sounded desperate.

When he looked up from her knuckles, their eyes met. It was the first time Rory was close enough to Hematite with proper lighting that she could make out his eye color; they were a beautiful shade of blue.

She couldn't see his eyebrows, though, as they were covered by his hood and balaclava.

Rory shook her head. "No, I'm fine. He didn't even have time to hurt me."

Hematite just nodded. "Good." He stopped wiping Rory's knuckles clean but was still holding her hands in both of his. They could both hear the sirens and lights of the police cars pulling up to the street, but at that moment, it felt like time was still between the two of them. "I'm glad you're okay. You did the right thing. I'll handle the police, okay? Just keep your hands in your pockets. It's freezing out, isn't it?"

She nodded, understanding what he was getting at. Hematite dropped her hands when the police arrived, and she shoved them in her coat before they could arrive.

"Who do you got for us, Hematite?" The cop was a short man with red, slicked-back hair and a thin mustache. He hadn't shaved in a few days and seemed more friendly than any of the other cops that Rory had encountered.

Hematite acknowledged him with a nod. "Detective McMahon. I caught Shatterstone, Stone Breaker's sidekick, attacking this woman."

"Looks like he took quite the beating," Jon McMahon said, as one of his men dragged Shatterstone's unconscious form, now handcuffed, to the car. "So much so that his mask broke."

"It's just pretty thin plastic. It was him or her, and I wasn't about to let an innocent woman get hurt. Quick decisions had to be made."

Rory chose to not say anything. Perhaps Hematite feared what may happen if she was outed as the one who attacked Shatterstone. The way they bantered told Rory that Hematite had a silent agreement with Detective McMahon, so it granted him a certain privilege they both knew that Rory could not afford. It could put her career at risk if the truth got out.

"You're on thin fuckin' ice, Hematite." McMahon's narrowed gaze conveyed seriousness, but there was a hint of playfulness in his tone as he smirked and held up a piece of the broken mask.

Hematite laughed. "Maybe, but you need me too much. Are we good here?"

"Yeah, I'd say so. Everything he said true, miss?" When Rory nodded, McMahon said, "Good enough for me."

Hematite looked at Rory and said, "I'll take you home, okay?"

Before Rory could respond, McMahon asked, "Are you alright, miss?" He made eye contact with Rory, searching her eyes to sense her comfort level with Hematite's offer. "We can bring you home if you'd prefer."

Rory nodded and forced herself to smile at McMahon; it was hard for her to feign any sort of happiness at the moment but didn't want him to fret. She could feel some tears pooling by her bottom lids, but she swallowed hard as she tried to hold them back. "I'm fine, thanks to Hematite, yeah," she said. "I'd rather go with him, but thank you, detective."

McMahon nodded. "Understood. Take care." He grabbed a business card from his wallet and handed it to her. "In case you need anything, alright?"

Rory took it and shoved it in her coat pocket. "Thank you. I'll hang on to this just in case."

After the police left, Rory and Hematite were silent on their way back to her house. They walked side by side, shoulders close enough to feel each other's warmth but not enough to touch. Hematite wanted to say something, but whenever he'd glance at Rory, he'd see that her eyes were on her shoes and deep in thought, so he opted to say nothing at all to let her process everything on her own terms.

Even though Rory had mostly calmed down thanks to Hematite's presence, the only thing she could hear was her heart thumping a mile a minute in her ears. She couldn't even hear the shuffling of their feet as they walked side by side. She was surprised that Hematite kept quiet, but his being there was enough to help her feel not so alone.

Once they reached her front step, he finally spoke. "Be sure to ice your hand too. Your knuckles might be sore tomorrow." There was a stiffness to his words, like he was holding something back, but Rory didn't think to press it.

"Thanks for the pointer. I … I'm sorry. It all happened so fast. I don't know what I was thinking. I feel like I wasn't thinking."

"Don't apologize." Hematite placed a hand on her shoulder,

making her look up and into his eyes. "It's not your fault. You did what you had to do."

Rory nodded, feeling mesmerized by the way the shades of blue seemed to swirl around his pupils. "I guess so." She swallowed. "Thanks for taking the heat for me too."

"Any time. It's better that I do than you." Rory noticed he spoke to her differently than he did to McMahon or to others, using a tone with a sweet softness that shone through his voice modifications. "I've worked with McMahon before. He lets me do my job. I won't be far in case you need me, okay? Just say the word."

Rory nodded. "Okay. I appreciate that." She smiled at him, more genuine than she had at McMahon, but Hematite noticed her smile didn't quite reach her eyes. "Good night, Hematite."

"Good night, Rory."

Once Rory closed the door, Hematite snuck up to the roof of her home. Shatterstone's arrest would certainly strike a nerve, so he didn't want to leave her alone so quickly. As he sat over the corner where her bedroom was, he could faintly hear her sobbing into her pillow.

Rory held her pillow against her chest, her knees sandwiching it between her. She wrapped a fleece blanket around herself as she wept, fully processing everything that happened to her. As she sobbed, Rory felt a sharpness in her lungs, letting the pillow muffle the sound and provide softness against her skin. She tried to blink away the images of Dougie and Daniel's faces, but as she did, they just merged into one, like a weird amalgamate from a bad sci-fi movie.

I got myself into this mess, she thought, *and there was no turning back now*. She tried to remember the words that Dr. Thornton told her in that first therapy session—"It's not your fault"—but Rory couldn't help but feel like this would have never happened had she never stuck her nose where it didn't belong.

Hematite wanted nothing more than to burst into her window and hold her. He felt a huge twinge of guilt, knowing there was nothing he could do about it as he heard her cry; it was his job to watch over the community, and he wasn't sure how Shatterstone got away with this without him knowing. Kane wanted to assure her that she was safe, even though it was a lie to do so. But he knew he couldn't.

———

The next morning, Rory called Dr. Thornton right away. The drive to Denver was feeling shorter with each visit, and Rory was just glad that Dr. Thornton could squeeze her in so quickly and on such short notice.

"Let me start off by saying that I am so glad that you're physically okay," Dr. Thornton said, after learning what happened the night before. "What exactly is going on?"

"Thanks, Marissa." Rory used the frigid February air to her advantage and wore gloves to hide a few scrapes on one of her knuckles. "It … it was a rough night. I'm not sure if I handled it better or worse than I would have a month ago."

Dr. Thornton sadly smiled at Rory as Rory recalled the night prior. "Something like this is anyone's worst nightmare, even without a history like your own. I hope you're treating yourself with kindness."

"I'm trying," Rory affirmed. "And, well, I guess I should mention why this came about." Rory paused before she confessed, "I found him."

Dr. Thornton raised her eyebrows. "You found Hematite?"

Rory nodded as she adjusted her glasses; she hated the feeling of contacts on irritated, puffy eyes. "I did. The letters for Kane and Naomi are on my phone, but I haven't had the chance to share them. It's been so busy, and the timing has felt all wrong. I never wrote one for Hematite. But I found him!"

"How did it go?" Dr. Thornton asked. "Did it meet your expectations?"

"It went great. I'd say it met most of my expectations, if not exceeded them. We've been tracking down Stone Breaker together. I just … I thought finding him would help me feel some closure," Rory said, "and so far, I still feel like something is missing."

It was the first time Rory had spoken that truth out loud. She was glad to be alongside Hematite, but there was still a hollow feeling that lingered in her chest and that kept her up at night.

"While trust should be earned and not freely given," Dr. Thornton said, "I think you need to give in to your trust more fully. Do you trust anyone? You don't have to answer right away."

Rory took a moment to think about it. She trusted Naomi and knew that without a second thought. "Definitely Naomi. She's been helping me too, with the Hematite thing."

"And what about your friend … Kane, was it? His name has come up a few times."

Rory allowed herself a moment to consider it. Normally, she would have said yes without a shadow of a doubt. She trusted Kane with her life. But lately, things had been different with him. Rory could sense that they were both hiding things from one another, despite likely fighting on the same side of the battle.

"I do," Rory said. "I do trust him. Kane's always been there for me."

"I sense you're hesitant," Dr. Thornton said. "Your next homework assignment is to evaluate your trust. Start with Kane. I think it'll help you with your feeling of something being missing. Have you told him everything?"

Rory shook her head. "Most of it, but not all of it."

"Start there. It's clear that he cherishes you based on what you've told me so far. What's the worst that could happen?"

———

Mark Stevens felt like he was going to throw up, as he watched the morning newscast with his father. He took a long sip of his coffee in hopes of not having to discuss anything with his dad, but the coffee just churned in his stomach, along with his nerves.

"Breaking news. Shatterstone, a masked figure assisting Hematite's nemesis, Stone Breaker, was arrested last night," the male anchor said.

"Riverpeak Police tell us that Hematite stopped Shatterstone from attacking a woman only steps from her home," his female counterpart reported.

"Police tell us that Douglas Doerr was the man behind the mask."

"That's your friend, right?" Tom asked. His voice was still calm, and his body was completely still on the couch next to him; Mark wasn't sure if that was a good or a bad thing.

"Yes, sir," he replied. He wasn't able to meet his father's eyes and didn't dare see what lurked beneath his calm facade.

"Let me make a call," Tom said. "Should be no problem." He stood and walked over to the other side of the living room as he waited for the phone to ring. It wasn't on speaker, which only made Mark feel like he was going to bring his coffee back up even more. "Chief Daniels! Hi. How are you doing? Good? That makes one of us," Tom said on the phone. "Listen, it's come to my attention that my son's friend was arrested last night. What's his bail? How can we work something out?"

Mark's palms felt clammy as he waited for his father to continue speaking. He kept his eyes forward, focusing on the news; they had long since moved away from the news about Dougie and were now talking about some new restaurant that had opened.

"What do you mean there's nothing we can do?" It was a question, but Tom asked it more like a statement. "You've got to be fu- are you joking?"

Tom hung up and tossed his phone on the couch. It bounced next to Mark, who grabbed it before it could fall off the edge.

"After everything I've done to build a relationship with her, and this is the fucking thanks I get." Tom looked at his son, which forced Mark to finally meet his father's gaze. Tom's brows were furrowed so much that there were extra wrinkles on his forehead. His mouth was usually in a permanent scowl when he was behind closed doors, but the frown was even deeper than usual. He pointed at Mark and said, "You better have some good ideas about how we're going to move forward. You promised me we'd take down Hematite, not the other way around. What the hell are you two doing?"

"I … I know, sir, I'm sorry." Mark winced. "Dougie told me he had it covered. He did his research. Rory just wasn't what we expected."

"She's working with a goddamn vigilante! Why the hell wouldn't you expect this?" Tom sighed, as he placed his hands on his hips and huffed. "I want both of their heads on a silver platter. You got that?"

Mark nodded. "Understood, sir. I'll make it up to you. This won't be a setback."

"Good," Tom said. "It better not be. Ray tells me they're struggling to get shipments in from Denver of materials they need because no one wants to deal with this Hematite bullshit. When his pockets hurt, our pockets hurt."

"It'll be handled." Mark had little confidence and wasn't sure what he would do next. But he said, "I promise."

Tom's phone started ringing again. "Oh, fuck me. It's Ray." He answered it as he walked to the back door and eventually outside. Mark wished he could hear their conversation but didn't dare risk following his father when he was in this type of mood. He closed his eyes, hoping something would appear to him, but the only thing that came to his mind was Rory Miller.

Mark was certain of only two things anymore. The first was that Rory Miller was a force to be reckoned with. The second was that she had some sort of personal connection to Hematite well beyond just being a big fan. If Hematite had been there to rescue her before anything could have happened, then Mark had a feeling she was the key to hitting him where it really hurt.

CHAPTER 11

R ory was relieved to see Kane looking more like himself when he arrived at her home on Saturday afternoon. He held a paper to-go bag in his hands from Jefferson's Coffee and the dark circles under his eyes finally faded. He was dressed casually in a graphic T-shirt and sweats, allowing himself to be comfortable before having to change for the school's winter formal that night.

Kane noticed right away that she was wearing her glasses but wasn't surprised.

"You look refreshed," Rory said.

"I took your advice and got a good night's sleep." Kane did actually let himself sleep in for once. While Shawn wasn't his favorite person, he had asked him to cover for him, given the increased activity in town last night while he watched over Rory. They had been working together more frequently as of late during their patrols, which Kane wasn't thrilled about, but it helped to have the extra set of eyes and someone with super-strength to scare off the members of the drug ring. "In thanks, I come bearing lunch."

"Thanks. I was getting worried about you, man."

"I could tell," Kane said. "You're the only one I listen to these days, so do with that information what you will."

Rory laughed at his teasing. "Careful! The last thing I need is a power trip."

Kane dropped his backpack in his usual spot on the floor in front of her couch. "I'd trust you with it, don't worry."

Rory swallowed the feeling of a lump in her throat. It reminded her of her conversation with her therapist from only a few hours ago.

"Speaking of trust," she said, "I have some stuff I want to talk to you about."

Kane sensed the shift of tone in her voice. "Everything okay? Come on. Over lunch. We both think more clearly on full stomachs."

Rory nodded in agreement. Over the last few weeks, she had sensed their dynamic shift as she got more and more involved with Hematite and Stone Breaker. Rory wasn't sure why, but it bothered her that she and Kane didn't see eye to eye on this beyond him just being one of her best friends.

"What's going on? Is it the Hematite stuff?"

"Yeah," she said. "Don't get me wrong; I've been honest with you. Lying to you is something I wouldn't ever dream of. I just haven't shared every detail." Rory grimaced. "Naomi and I are actively trying to find who he is now. We trust he can handle the Stone Breaker stuff, but … it's getting serious." Rory took a deep breath. "I don't know how, but I think Stone Breaker is on to me."

"He knows you're working with Hematite?" When Rory nodded, Kane asked, "Do you think he saw you when you went to go find him? That's gotta be the only way."

"Probably. Hematite told me I walked right into his territory," she said. She ran her hand over her face in exasperation. "And Shatter-stone told me the other day that they have eyes everywhere. He, uh … he came after me on Friday night."

Kane's lips formed a thin line. "What?" He already knew this, of course, but he had to play dumb. His anger from the night prior never subsided, but he had done a decent job at hiding it.

When Rory looked past some of the loose wisps of blonde hair that fell in his face, she could see a storm silently raging in his eyes. She told him what happened, then held her hand up as she paused for a bite of her sandwich. She wore Band-Aids beneath winter gloves earlier that morning when she saw her therapist, but they were on full display now for Kane to see some light bruising and scrapes by her middle knuckles.

"Oh my God," Kane said. "I'm so sorry."

"I beat the shit out of him, though. I didn't get hurt beyond, well, this." She gestured to her fists. "I iced them this morning, but they're still stiff as shit."

"Rory, what would the school think?" Kane tried to keep his voice soft, so as to not appear angry with her. "You could get fired if they found out!"

"Hematite took the heat for me, so it worked out. I guess he's buddy-buddy with some detective or something."

Kane sighed. "While I am proud of you for kicking his ass, this isn't safe. I don't think relying on Hematite is a viable, long-term strategy." He hoped that if he could sow some seeds of doubt, Rory would walk away before it was too late.

"Why not? He's proven himself to be reliable. And I think he's been looking over me personally ever since I gave him the info on Stone Breaker. He always seems to show up when I need him lately."

Kane frowned. "He can't be everywhere at once, Rory." Despite how calm he was, Rory saw his brows furrow as he picked at his nail beds, something he did when he was frustrated. "He's just one guy. I know he saved your life and I understand why you really look up to him, but he's just a man. Any single one of us could start wearing all black and kicking the shit out of the junkies on the east side of town. Don't you think now is a good time to walk away?"

"How could I walk away, Kay?"

"I am literally begging you for your own safety. It is so amazing that you and Naomi found out who Stone Breaker is and that you've been feeding Hematite what you found. I cannot understate how in awe I am at you," Kane said, "but I can't see this ending well. It's reckless."

"And who are you to lecture me on recklessness, huh? Kane, you passed out in my class the other day because you're out every night doing God knows what with Jameson like you're still twenty-one-years-old. I think you're hardly one to talk."

"You're right," Kane said with a single-shouldered shrug. "I do a lot of reckless shit. But at least I'm not risking my life."

That much is true, at least, he thought, *in a roundabout way.*

"I just want you to be safe. For everyone's sake. For yours, for mine, and for your students."

"I can't walk away, Kay," Rory reaffirmed. "My therapist recommended I open up to you about all this so I can work on building trust."

Her words hit Kane like a gut punch. He frowned and then asked, "Do you trust me?"

Rory nodded. "With my life. That's why I'm telling you everything, even if I don't like what you have to say about it." She sighed, scared of what might follow, so she added, "I want you to be honest, but please be gentle. I'm trying here."

"I trust you too." Kane grabbed a hold of her hand and gave it a light shake. "And I trust you know what you're doing. But these guys … they're unpredictable, Rory. Shit's scary out there. At least promise me you'll remember that."

"Alright. Fair."

"I just don't want to see you get hurt. Like, seriously hurt. You don't have to save everyone, you know?"

After their talk, they graded papers in silence. Instead of her usual spot by the window, Rory sat beside Kane on the floor. Some of the tension still lingered between them, but the quiet was still ultimately comfortable. When Kane glanced over at her, he wanted nothing more than to press his lips to her temple and swear that it would all be okay. He opened his mouth to speak but decided on something else.

"Hey, Rory?"

"Hmm?"

"You … You mean a lot to me. You know that, right?"

They made eye contact. Rory wasn't sure what she was seeing behind Kane's dynamic blue eyes, but there was a softness in them today that was usually masked by mischievousness. Today, he was gentler. The tempest in them from earlier had faded now, showing a beautiful sea.

"I know," Rory said. "You mean a lot to me too, Kane. I'm sorry if I've been kinda rash lately."

"I understand why you have been," Kane said. His heart felt like it was going to burst out of his chest. He desperately wanted to tell her right then and there how much she really meant to him, how he'd loved her for as long as he could remember now, but he refrained.

For Rory, she wished she could see this side of Kane more often. She smiled at him and ruffled his hair. "I've got it under control, Kane. Don't worry too much about me."

"Easier said than done," Kane said with a laugh. "I'll try to be better about being there for you through this, alright? I know it's important to you."

"Thanks."

"Besides," Kane said as he cupped her chin with his thumb and index finger. "We can't have you upset at the winter formal tonight. Those kids are going to be looking for a smiling face after they get yelled at by their math teacher for not leaving room for Jesus."

Rory laughed. "You're right. They'll be looking to us as the cool teachers that actually let them dance."

"Just no making out behind the bleachers," Kane said with a wink. "You know, I never went to any of the school dances."

"You didn't?"

"Nah. Too poor. And by the time I was old enough to get a part-time job, if I had the money, I'd just give it to Kayla so she could go to hers. Her friends were nice enough to let her borrow their old dresses."

"I didn't go, either. Naomi tried to drag me along once, but they were just never my thing. I dunno."

"What? You? Avoiding a big party? Color me shocked," Kane said with playful sarcasm. Rory nudged his shoulder as Kane said, "We should have gone together. Though I'm glad we didn't know each other back then. You'd have hated me in high school."

"Oh, I doubt that," Rory said with a laugh. "I'm shocked we never had a class together, though, after all those years."

"No, you would have seriously hated me. I was a fucking asshole who spent way too much time with Jameson."

"You still do. But I doubt you were ever an asshole."

"Suit yourself," Kane said as he shook his head. "But I'm glad I met you when I did."

"Likewise. I was too shy for my own good growing up. You've brought me out of my shell a lot, you know?"

"You're gonna make me blush. Save it for later when you wanna make out behind the bleachers, okay?"

Rory couldn't help her grin. "I'll keep that in mind."

"Wait. Does that mean you might want to make out behind the bleachers?"

The longer she looked at him, the more she thought she did. "Don't test your luck."

Rory and Kane were the first chaperones to arrive at the school for the winter formal. It was "Winter in Paris"-themed, so the gymnasium was decorated in white-and-blue-colored streamers and fabrics, with a faux-crystal chandelier hanging from the center, in a sad attempt to look somewhat sophisticated. Rory thought the only Parisian thing about it was the hors d'oeuvres if frozen foods from Costco counted.

Kane wore a simple suit and Rory wore a basic black cocktail dress and brown trench coat, not wanting to outshine the students but still fit in. They did this together every year; while they had their work cut out for them, Kane enjoyed the free food and Rory enjoyed Kane's company. They started the evening making sure their students came in sober and strait-laced, with only a handful of students having to be turned away—something Kane took note to check on the next time he went on patrol as Hematite.

"Do you think anything is going to happen tonight?" Rory asked Kane, once the crowd was mostly inside. "With all the vigilante stuff going on?"

"I hope not," Kane said. "It would blow if Stone Breaker got a bunch of kids wrapped up in it."

She did a great job of putting on a cheerful show for her students to act like nothing was wrong, taking photos with students when asked. But Kane could see the tightness in her shoulders and the way she was fidgeting with her thumbs when they'd watch the students along the gymnasium wall. To anyone not paying attention, everything was fine. But if you looked at Rory long enough, you could see the increasingly rapid rise and fall of her chest through her cocktail dress and how quickly she'd glance around the room. She was on high alert, and Kane was positive he was the only one who noticed.

"Hey," Kane whispered in her ear. "I know I'm no Hematite, but if anything happens, I've got your back, okay?"

Rory looked up at Kane and smiled. She saw no hint of joking in his expression, but that he was being dead serious for once. She nodded and said, "I know. Thanks, Kane."

The DJ interrupted them. "We've got a request from your senior class president. It's Lil Nas X!"

But Lil' Nas X didn't play. A lightning bolt sound effect rippled through the speakers. Kane saw Rory's brows furrow and lips slightly part.

"*Bon soir*, Riverpeak High School. How's your winter formal going?" The distorted voice was undoubtedly Stone Breaker's. "I believe someone here is helping Hematite. Now's your chance to give yourself up. I—."

"Sorry about that, folks," the DJ said, as he cut the message off. "I don't know how that got in my playlist. I'm making sure it's gone now. That must have been a mistake."

But Rory knew it wasn't a mistake at all. She looked up at Kane and saw that he was already looking at her. She felt a lump in her throat as she said, "We gotta get out of here."

Kane just nodded. "Come on. I'll go with you."

As Kane rushed through the crowd alongside Rory, he glanced down when he felt her take a hold of his hand. He gave hers a squeeze, letting her interlock their fingers together. Kane made eye contact with the principal from across the room and she met them halfway, blonde curls in an updo for the evening so it was easy to spot her.

"I'm taking her home," Kane said when they came together. "Stone Breaker isn't after the students. He's after her because Hematite helped her with something back when we were in college. It's a long story."

Rory was glad that Kane had taken charge of the situation. She was too busy trying to collect her thoughts and get her breathing under control without hyperventilating. All the color and warmth had long since drained from her face.

"Rory, are you okay?" The principal asked.

"I'll be fine. But if he's keeping tabs on me, I don't want any of the students to get hurt."

"Call me in the morning, okay? Not as your boss. As your friend."

"I will. Thanks, ma'am."

Kane continued to hold Rory's hand as they bolted to her car. She grabbed her keys with the other hand and only released from Kane's grip when she got to the driver's side door.

"I'm calling Elijah," Kane said as he entered the car's passenger side.

"Okay." Her hands trembled as she tossed her keys in the cupholder and hit the start button in her vehicle. She didn't realize how clammy they were until she gripped the steering wheel. Kane normally would have harped on her about letting the engine warm up before she immediately took off, but he knew now wasn't the time to pick on her about those sorts of things. As they drove by the snow-covered grasslands, she swerved to avoid a mule deer that was too close to the side of the road, but her four-wheel drive did its work and kept her in control.

She drove while Kane called Elijah.

"Hey, Elijah. Listen, dude, can I ask you to do me a favor?"

On the other line, Elijah frowned. "Are you on speaker right now?"

"No."

"A Hematite favor or a Kane favor?"

"Yes." Kane hoped Elijah would understand that he meant both.

"Got it," Elijah said. "Rory's with you, I take it? Isn't winter formal tonight?"

"Yeah, that was tonight. Here, I'll put you on so she can hear you too." Kane switched to speakerphone. "She's driving. But something weird just happened at the dance. The DJ went to go play a song request but a message from Stone Breaker played instead. The hell is that about?"

"I'm willing to bet that the DJ was set up on Bluetooth. Let me grab my keys; I'll drive over to the school and see if anyone's connected. If it is set up via Bluetooth, I'll start bluejacking and try to scare him off. I'll let you know if I find anything."

"You're the best. Thanks."

"Anytime. You okay, Rory?"

"I've been better, but I've been worse," Rory said, trying to convince herself that she was fine. She hated how a stupid message on a speaker was all it took to get her heart racing. "And I have no idea what bluejacking is, but thanks for trying in advance."

Elijah chuckled. "It's like when you AirDrop people things unsuspectedly but with an added layer of anonymity. I've got my ways. Don't worry; we'll figure something out and I've got Rick Astley bookmarked."

———

When Rory pulled up next to Kane's car in her driveway, he took hold of her hand before she could turn the car off. Rory snapped her head at him in response, unsure of what Kane might say or do next. She normally loved Kane's spontaneity, but she was too on edge for unpredictability.

"Do you want me to stay here with you for the night? Like good ol' times?"

Rory smiled at the memory and nodded, still struggling to form words as she processed everything that had happened.

"No funny business, I promise," Kane teased.

Rory wasted no time in removing her trench coat and heels when they got inside. Kane kicked his dress shoes off as Rory plopped on her couch. Kane could see the stress seeping out of her in the way she sat, with hunched shoulders and lines on her forehead. Part of him thought he should urge her to go to sleep so he could go back to the school and look for Stone Breaker, but he decided to put his trust in Elijah for the evening so he could be the friend Rory needed.

"Hey."

Rory looked up and saw Kane standing before her with both of his hands in his slack pockets. He removed his suit jacket a few moments ago, leaving him in his button-up shirt. Kane had rolled the sleeves up, showcasing his muscular forearms and a few mostly faded scars. As he removed one of his hands from his pocket and extended it out to her, Kane smirked.

"Can I have this dance?"

Rory blinked in response. "Huh?"

Kane smiled at her. "I never went to any of our school dances; neither did you. I'm all dressed up. You look beautiful, and it'd be a shame to waste that. Come on. Dance with me." She continued to stare at him, so he added, "It'll cheer you up."

Rory responded only by smiling at him and giving him her hand. Kane whisked her up and gave her a quick twirl before taking her in his arms. He held one of her hands up with his own as his other rested on the small of her back. Kane felt a warmth flutter in his abdomen as Rory's free arm wrapped around his shoulders.

Kane turned his head toward her television stand and said, "Hey Alexa, play mellow romantic songs."

Rory didn't even know the song that played, but it had a pleasant rhythm that was easy for her and Kane to sway to.

"You clean up nice, you know," Rory said.

Kane chuckled, and she felt the vibration of his laugh against her own chest. "You think so?"

"Mm. Nineties Ethan Hawke-kind of thing, remember?" She was silent again for a moment and then said, "Thank you. For everything tonight."

"Don't thank me. I'd be a pretty shitty friend if I hadn't. This was, like, the bare minimum as far as I'm concerned."

Rory appreciated his trying to brush it off. She had so much she wanted to say to Kane, but the word "friend" stuck in her mind, so she decided to just enjoy the moment as it was. "I mean it."

Kane softly kissed her hair, so gently that she almost didn't notice. Before Rory could call him on it, Kane said, "I made a promise to myself a few years ago when Naomi filled me in on what had happened to you in college. She let me into your dorm to keep an eye out so she could get some sleep. You were so distressed, and you wear your heart on your damn sleeve, so it was hard to not notice. Internally, I said I was going to make sure a girl as pretty as you would laugh at least once a day every day, so long as you knew me."

Rory felt like her heart practically melted when he said that. "You've made good on your promise, that's for sure."

"And I intend to." He thought about telling her the rest of his feelings, despite his identity, but didn't want to overwhelm her. "Between me and Hematite, you're safe, okay?"

Rory pressed her face against his chest as they continued to dance along to the song in her living room. "I know. I've always known that, Kay."

Kane said nothing else, so Rory pushed her feelings back down like she always did, not wanting to read too much into what Kane was doing and saying. She knew she should take her own advice, but so much happened that she didn't think she could take it if she was wrong.

———

When she woke up the next morning, Kane was still asleep beside her in her bed. While they had fallen asleep back-to-back, he must have shifted in his sleep because she woke up with his arm draped around her waist and his head against her neck. His breath was warm against her skin, tickling her shoulder with every slow exhale.

When she moved a bit, Kane woke up. He quickly shuffled to retract his arm. "Shit, I'm sorry. Good morning."

"It's fine," Rory said with a wave of her hand. "Thanks for staying with me. I don't think I would have gotten much sleep if I were alone."

"No way was I ditching you. Elijah texted me once you fell asleep. Stone Breaker was still there when he got there, and he followed him. Some guy left on a motorcycle after Elijah bluejacked him. He said he followed the sounds of 'Never Gonna Give You Up' to City Hall, but Elijah couldn't get much further without going in."

"It's gotta be Councilman Stevens' kid," Rory said. "I'll have to text him my thanks later. Are you staying for breakfast?"

"I have an appointment, but not until eleven. What time is it?"

"Only nine."

"I'll stay, sure."

As they sat across from each other at Rory's dining room table—
Kane in his sweatpants and T-shirt from yesterday and Rory still in her
pajamas, glasses, and hair tied back—they both just savored the
moment. Unbeknownst to the other, they both pretended that every
morning could be like this. But both knew without saying anything
that this was just the calm before the storm, leaving everything in their
minds left unsaid.

CHAPTER 12

Kane always had a weird feeling when he arrived at Potter Laboratories, and late Sunday morning was no exception. It rested on the outskirts of the town on a large, isolated plot of land. The sign showing where the property started was about a mile out from the actual building, with only the occasional moose showing face between the sign and Constance's Pond a few blocks away. Hardly anyone ever came out here, leaving Kane alone with the physician, Dr. Potter himself. The building was all slate on the outside; its interior lacked any color too, varying from shades of white to grey. The only part of it that felt real was the view of the familiar Pikes Peak in the distance.

Dr. Potter was waiting for Kane in the lobby upon his arrival. He was a lanky man whose lab coats were all a bit ill-fitting for his stature; they were either awkwardly short or strangely loose, but never both. His skin was nearly as white as his coats. Kane wasn't sure if Dr. Potter was a real medical professional, but his lab on the far reaches of town had certainly provided Kane with more answers than his own doctor.

"Mr. Kelly," Dr. Potter said, "welcome back. How has your investigation been going?"

"It's going, I suppose. I've recently received some help along the way."

"That's excellent to hear. Come, come."

Dr. Potter pushed his glasses back up his nose and led him to the usual, private room in the back of the lab. Kane could hear the light whirring of a machine in another room. Gooseflesh formed on his skin, and he wasn't sure if it was from his uneasiness or from the chill of the building.

"So, we've confirmed you can't be murdered," Dr. Potter recalled, "at least not permanently. Watching your cells regenerate was quite the show. You are aging at an appropriate rate, though, so you may not be explicitly out of the woods as far as mortality goes. Has your investigation provided any answers yet?"

"A few." Dr. Potter seemed actually relieved to hear that news. "The city government's involved. I think they're profiting off that drug that's been pumping through the west side of town. And I think that drug is why I can't be killed."

"A blood test and a quick swab should be all I need for now," Dr. Potter said. He excelled at two things: fast work and showing no emotion, which always left Kane on his toes. Dr. Potter went through the motions, swabbing Kane's cheek and pricking his finger, and then announced he'd return shortly.

Kane picked at his nail beds as he waited for Dr. Potter and the results. Dr. Potter used a lot of experimental methods that Kane couldn't explain. He tried to swallow any questionable morality that Dr. Potter may have, aware that judging Dr. Potter would make him a bit of a hypocrite himself. He was just grateful to be getting answers and to be getting them quickly; Dr. Potter's tests typically took only a few minutes.

With how small Riverpeak was, everyone knew about Dr. Potter's lab, but it seemed like no one had actually ever been inside or knew anything about him. Kane had initially gone out of an act of desperation, but so far, he was pleased. Primary care physicians didn't have the right tests, but Dr. Potter did. Kane hadn't bothered to ask how, mainly since Dr. Potter had yet to give him reason to.

As Dr. Potter returned to the room, he said, "Well, Mr. Kelly, you continue to amaze me. Once again, brilliant."

Kane forced himself to not roll his eyes. "I'm glad you find this entertaining. What is it?"

"Your theory was right about your mother. What you're experiencing can best be described as a semi-distant cousin of Neonatal Abstinence Syndrome. The main difference, though, is you're not experiencing withdrawals. It didn't show up in the blood test, but I did get it from the cell swab. That's in line with our past tests that explained the how. Now you have the why."

Kane swallowed and took a deep breath. He didn't want to get too emotional, especially in the lab. "And what about other kids who were born like me?"

The words felt strange. He always suspected it had something to do with his mother's drug addiction—the substance she used was largely a mystery to him, despite his work to eradicate it over the years, but it was still cycling around Riverpeak. However, his longtime suspicions didn't make the confirmation any less jarring. He wouldn't wish this recurring pain of immortality on anybody.

"Do you know anyone else with abilities like your own?" Dr. Potter asked.

"Not that can't be killed, no. But I do know a guy with super strength like the world's never seen. He helps me sometimes when I'm on patrol. His mom's … like mine."

"Do you think he'd be willing to undergo the same blood tests as you've undergone?" Dr. Potter asked. "I could compare your samples, see if there's any overlap and if the drugs are causing it."

"I'm warning you now, he's kind of a dick. But Shawn Jameson will come if I ask him to."

Dr. Potter grinned. "Excellent. A pleasure, as always, Mr. Kelly."

"Yeah," Kane said half-heartedly, "likewise."

Kane didn't even turn the radio on as he drove home from the lab on the west side of Riverpeak. The winding road back was lonely, especially in the dead of winter, but it allowed him to collect his thoughts as he made the trek back. The moose he sometimes saw didn't even make an appearance today, although it would have been a welcome distraction.

He felt like he was at war with himself. He and Kayla both stopped speaking to their parents the moment they moved out; given their childhood memories of drunken fights and dodging needles, their fractured relationships weren't a surprise. Part of him wanted to go back to the family's home on the east side of the city, where Stone Breaker was running amuck among the run-down homes and abandoned businesses. He yearned to sit down with his mother and father and ask them why: why he was born; why they couldn't stop using when they were expecting; and why this was the life they ended up living.

But he couldn't. He knew it would be a waste of time and energy, and that he would only leave more frustrated than he started. Kane wasn't even sure if his parents were still using or not.

He thought about driving by the house at least, hoping that looking at it would spark a revelation; he'd be there the following weekend to see his sister when she visited from college, but he was growing more and more impatient in finding answers. But instead of going out of his way to that side of the city, he just pulled into his apartment complex and sat in the parking lot, feeling numb. Kane thought he might cry, based on the lump in his throat, but he felt a void inside of him instead. The tears he desperately needed to release never came. Instead, the pressure just continued to build in the back of his throat and beneath his eyes before it eventually reached the bridge of his nose.

He rested his head against the steering wheel as he sat in silence, wondering how much longer it would take to get the answers he needed. Stone Breaker was his key, he knew that, but he felt like he was at an impasse. If Stone Breaker was, in fact, Mark Stevens, then he had a shield. If Hematite broke into a councilman's office, that would be the end of it.

But he knew for certain now that Councilman Stevens had to be at the heart of his problem. He just wasn't sure yet exactly how he would find out why Councilman Stevens was involved.

———

As excited as Kane was to see his sister the weekend after, he still dreaded every moment. Kane stared at his parents' house for a few moments from his car. He knew in the worn-down jeans, cheap shirt, and old winter coat that he'd still be cold, but it was critical to fit in on the east side of town. He felt naked without his Hematite gear, but he was here strictly for family.

Sometimes, he dreamed of what his life might look like had he been born into another family. When he did, he didn't envision a fancy home or anything extravagant. He simply envisioned something with windows that were actually properly sealed, a tablecloth on the dining room table, and an absence of mice in the winter.

In Kane's dream, his mother and father didn't scream at each other. It would be a place where he could take Rory to meet his parents. There was no clashing of beer bottles or used needles in the trash bins that he'd have to be cautious of when taking the garbage out. He wouldn't have to worry about Kayla.

The thought of his sister made him snap out of it. She was the reason he was here, after all. She had only been back in school for about a month but was home for a long weekend.

When he got out of his car, he grimaced, but he was better prepared for the way the air bit at his face than he expected. All the late nights out with only some long sleeves and some thermal undergarments made winters easier for Kane than for most people, even fellow Colorado natives.

When Kane opened the door and walked into his family home— they never locked the door—he was greeted by just Kayla. Her blonde hair, the same shade as his own, sat in a messy bun on top of her head.

"Oh, thank God you're here," Kayla said, as she all but ran to her brother. Kane could tell by the way she gripped at his shoulders in their hug that she desperately needed it.

"How many times do I have to tell you that you can stay with me instead of this dump?" Kane said with a laugh.

"It's like I always forget how bad it is when Mom says she misses me," Kayla said. "I'm crashing your couch for spring break, though."

"I'm holding you to that. How is everything? Any better?"

Kayla shook her head as she pulled away from their hug. "No. I wish. Come on, Mom and Dad are out back. I'll catch you up."

Kane knew that meant they were in the shed in the backyard, where they cooked up drugs for the local ring. "They're working again, huh?"

"Gotta make money somehow, I guess." Kayla's voice trailed off as she said it and her eyes found the tops of her shoes.

Kane shook his head. "Grab your shit. Let's get outta here."

"Won't Mom–?"

"She can yell at me later," Kane said with a shrug. "Come on. I don't feel like fighting today, and you know how Dad and I can get when he's out of sorts."

"Fair enough," Kayla agreed. "I didn't pack much. I'll be quick."

"I'll wait in my car to get the heat on."

"Thanks!"

Kayla was true to her word; she was only gone about three minutes before she was tossing her duffel bag in the backseat of Kane's car and then hopping in the passenger side.

"You're a lifesaver! When's the last time you talked to them?"

Kane sighed as he backed out of the driveway. "Is it awful that I couldn't tell you?"

"No, not at all," Kayla said. "I gotta be more like you about it. Maybe it's a mother-and-daughter thing, but I swear to God she always knows how to get in my head."

"It's not your fault. She's good at that."

"Seriously, how do you do it?"

"I realized you can't save everyone. So, I just gave up. But enough about them. What's going on?"

"I ... Do you ever just feel like you can't catch a break?"

Kane nodded. "Do I ever. What happened?"

"Maybe we're both cursed. Maybe it's genetic." Kayla laughed. "I'm doing well in my classes, and I'm on track to graduate in a few months; it's not that. But it's like, at what cost, you know? I thought I was having an existential crisis, so I figured that heading home would clear my head. That was a fucking mistake. Seriously, thanks for getting me out of that hellhole. It's like all the awful shit that happened during our childhood comes back." Kayla sighed. "Looking back … you really protected me from a lot of that."

"Somebody had to look out for us, right?" Kane said with a smile.

"I guess so. I started seeing a therapist too. Just the counseling services at school. They're nice, but I dunno, I feel like I have a lot to unpack. I haven't told any of my friends, though. I don't know what they'd think."

"You are the second person I know to start therapy this year. Maybe it's the universe saying I should too," Kane said.

"Wait, really?"

"Yeah. You know Rory. She started going last month. Said she loves it."

"Oh, I love Rory," Kayla cooed. "Speaking of her, did you ask her out yet?"

Kane grinned. "Nah. She's way out of my league." They pulled up to his apartment complex as he said that. "I'll grab your bag. I should have some extra blankets and pillows."

"I don't think I've been to your apartment."

"It's nothing special, but it's home for now."

As Kane helped Kayla get settled, she looked at her brother. "I'm really proud of you, you know? Given everything we've been through, you've really done a good job for yourself. I look up to you a lot."

"I'm proud of you too, kid," Kane said. He gently elbowed her shoulder. "Don't get too sappy on me now."

"You know, some of my friends say that you're this big-shot party guy," Kayla said. She had a cocky grin on her face, like she knew she was about to uncover some massive secret. "But that doesn't sound like you. You've never been a big-shot party guy."

"Should I be insulted?"

Kayla laughed. "No! I mean, you know. Look at where we came from. That's not really either of us, no matter how much we might try to pretend. What's really going on?"

"That is classified information," Kane said as he grabbed a can of Diet Coke® with lime—his sister's favorite—from the fridge. "It's complicated."

"Come on!" Kayla said. "I just told you my deep, dark secret that I'm going to therapy. Your turn. Why do you party?"

"I don't party."

He said it with such bluntness that Kayla froze. "Wait, what?"

"Yeah," Kane said as he sat on the couch next to her and handed her the can of soda. "I should have told you this a long time ago."

"Told me what?"

"Look around. You're smart. You'll figure it out. If you can, I'll tell you my deep, dark secret. But it stays between us. Got it?"

"Of course," Kayla said. Kane could tell that she understood the severity of it all. Her voice trailed off again as she stood from the couch and immediately wandered the apartment.

Kane propped his feet up on the coffee table as he ran his hands through his hair, pushing it out of his face. Part of him wasn't sure if this was the right move to make, but he knew he would eventually have to tell Rory. He figured practicing by letting Kayla in on it would be a good start, especially since he knew his sister well enough to know that Kayla would take that information with her to the grave.

"I'm not gonna find anything weird in your drawers or closet, will I?" Kayla asked from his bedroom.

"Depends on what you define as weird."

"Fuck's sake," Kayla mumbled. Kayla started with his bedside table, hoping she wouldn't stumble upon anything she wouldn't want to imagine her brother using. To her surprise, there wasn't much in there: just some writing utensils, a notepad, and a sheathed pocketknife. She closed it and moved on to his closet. She didn't want to invade her brother's privacy, but he made it a sort of game, so she figured all cards were on the table when she slid the door open.

There were mostly button-up shirts he wore to work and some jackets. She thumbed through a few of them until she reached the far right side of the closet. Her fingers came across what felt like a scarf, but when she pulled it out, she noticed it was more like a hooded cape. The ends were frayed and tattered as if pieces had been ripped off, both with and without purpose. She held it in one hand as she continued on until she saw the uniform pieces that she recognized as

Hematite's: the navy and black long-sleeved shirts he alternated between and the black joggers with pockets that cinched at the ankles.

"Holy shit." Kayla put the cowl back and took a step back, staring at the clothes in the open closet. She lifted her hand up so she could glance at the hematite ring that she now wore on her pinky—she once wore it on her thumb and then ring finger, but as she got older, she nearly outgrew it.

Kayla glanced to her left as she heard the shuffling sound of her brother's footsteps. He leaned against the doorframe and with half of a smile, Kane said, "I see you found it."

"It was you all along?" Kayla asked. Kane nodded. Kayla wasn't sure what else to say as she glanced back and forth between her brother and the clothes she found. She said, "Are you fucking joking with me right now?"

Kane shook his head. "I'm not. I'm serious. That's mine. It's always been me."

Kayla closed the closet door, deciding it was too much to process. "Everything makes sense, how Hematite was always there at just the right time." She glanced at her ring. "Oh my God, I fucking named you when I was nine."

Kane chuckled. "Yeah, you did. I didn't want anyone to call me anything originally, but your nickname had a nice ring to it. Pun not intended."

Kayla didn't know what else to say. She simply charged at her brother, wrapping her arms tightly around him, and burying her face in his chest. She didn't intend on crying, but she couldn't help herself.

"Didn't you die a few weeks ago?"

"Nah, you don't have to worry about that," Kane reassured her.

"I won't tell a soul, Kane. I promise."

"I know you won't. I knew I couldn't help Mom and Dad. But I knew I could help you." He patted her shoulders as he pulled away. "But I have to do something late tonight. Whatever you do, you stay here. Got it?"

Kayla wiped her tears with the back of her hand. "What are you going to do?"

"I'm going back to our parents' house," Kane said, "and I'm breaking into that fucking shed once and for all."

———

Kane tried to stick to the darker alleys as he weaved through the east side of town. His Hematite getup helped him stay disguised in the night, blending in with darker surroundings. Every time he came through the east side of the city, he felt an immense level of sadness.

Growing up, he blamed his parents for their shortcomings; he still did, to a degree. But now, as an adult, looking at the condition of his hometown, he knew there was more to it than people simply making poor life choices. Riverpeak City Council and the police department often worked but brought no real help beyond fattening their own wallets, even if it was at the cost of their constituents. Kane saw his family and the people in this part of town as the victims that they were, hoping that he could find a solution alongside the answers to his own abilities.

He slunk through the shadows to stay hidden on the way to his family's home. He was just glad that Kayla was out of there and sleeping soundly in his apartment. When he lingered by the pine tree across the street, he noticed that the lights to the house were completely out. He could see, however, that the lights to the shed in the backyard were still on. The memories from the last time he entered the shed came flooding back, but he pushed them back. He had grown a lot since then.

Kane made his way over, hoping he wouldn't have to fight his own family but bracing himself for that possibility. He opened the front door, still unlocked from earlier, and tiptoed his way through his childhood home. He paused at a picture frame that held a photo of him and his sister when Kayla was first born. The frame was cracked. Kane took the photo from it and pocketed it for himself before moving forward.

He opened the backdoor. It squeaked a bit, and he hoped it wouldn't alert anyone to his presence. There was nowhere for him to hide, so he darted for the shed and put his back against a wall by the door. He waited a moment, surprised that no one came out, and then moved to a window to peer in.

He saw both of his parents passed out on the floor. Some smoke was billowing from a burner, so Kane tried for the doorknob. It was the only one they cared enough to lock, so Kane grabbed his billy club and broke a window with it. Even with the sound of shattering glass, his parents didn't stir.

Kane propelled himself up through the window, trying to avoid the broken glass as best as he could. He first approached his parents, using his foot to roll his dad over from his stomach onto his back. His father was wearing a ventilation mask, but it clearly hadn't been enough to do the job right. When Kane found a pulse, he sighed in relief.

Kane did the same for his mother, seeing she was wearing the same type of mask as his father. Once he realized they were both alive but just unconscious, Kane moved on to the drug on the shed's counters. There were blenders, beakers, and a variety of jugs. He wasn't sure what they contained. He turned the portable burner off before grabbing a small vial from a stack of them and pouring some of the liquid inside. To make sure the temperature wouldn't break the glass, he started with a small amount before he filled and capped it.

Kane unlocked the shed door and made his way outside, using the snow to cool the vial enough to pocket comfortably. He went back into the house to cut through to the front. He moved his way back to the pine tree before he took his burner phone out to call for emergency services.

"Nine-one-one, what is your emergency?"

"My neighbors have been in their shed in the backyard for a long time, and I'm afraid they might be hurt in there. Can you send an ambulance to check on them? I'm seeing some smoke come out from there too."

"What's the address? We'll send a crew right away."

"Well, I'm at 98 Greenfield Avenue. They're the yellow house next to me."

Kane lingered by the pine tree across the street as he waited for someone to arrive. From his position, no one could see him, even with the few streetlights a few feet ahead. Only a few minutes passed before an ambulance and fire truck wailed on by, stopping right in front of his parents' home. Once he knew they'd be taken care of, he left for his apartment, not wanting to stick around any longer than he needed to.

CHAPTER 13

About two weeks had passed since Rory's encounter with Shatterstone. If it were up to her, she would still stay between home and school. She was still shaken to her core about what had happened and felt like someone was watching her every move. Rory didn't want to think of anything as a setback, but she knew in her gut that some of her progress in healing had definitely taken a few steps back. If it weren't for her picking Kane up on their way to work every morning, she would have been completely alone.

So, when Rory received an invitation to her friend Carla's birthday dinner, it provided an opportunity to be around friends rather than to carry on in isolation, something that Rory knew would ultimately make matters worse. The less she could be in her own head, the better, and Carla's party was the perfect distraction.

"Drive safely!" Carla called to Rory as Naomi walked her to her car.

"Thanks, Carla! I'll see you later, Naomi."

"Text me when you're home," Naomi said, as she got into the driver's side of her own vehicle. At that, Rory closed her car door and took off from Carla's birthday night out.

It was later than she was usually out, but it was a Friday night, and her students didn't have any homework assigned that she needed to worry about grading. Her drive home was relatively uneventful since there wasn't really anyone on the road from Denver to Riverpeak. The hour-and-a-half drive on the populated back roads always felt peaceful when it was quiet. Rory listened to an audiobook that her therapist had recommended, taking advantage of the quiet time. Even though the words often felt like ripping off tight Band-Aids, it was ultimately meditative for Rory, especially on the long ride. Her elated mood from seeing old friends helped soften the blow from the audiobook too.

When Rory hit a red light closer to town, she felt like something in her peripheral vision was out of place. She glanced over to the alley between the empty warehouses where the dumpster was normally left wide open. But tonight, she noticed the lid was down. It was odd enough that she paused her audiobook to pay closer attention.

She glanced back at the light to make sure it was still red, and when she looked over again, the light flashed. The sudden shift in light was enough to cause a flicker over the shadows along the spot where the dumpster met the wall.

Rory looked in her rearview and confirmed she was the only one on the road. She rolled the window down, grabbed her cell phone, and turned on the flashlight so she could look down the alley more clearly. No one was in the warehouses at this time of night.

"Holy shit," she whispered to herself.

It was Hematite.

Rory tossed her phone on the passenger seat and backed her car up a bit. She then pulled forward and to the left, parking her car so it was blocking the alleyway before she climbed into the backseat. When she got out of her car, she pocketed her keys and left the back door open.

"Hematite?"

He didn't answer Rory's call, and the figure before her didn't move. When Rory got closer, she held her phone with its flashlight still on over his body. She covered her mouth with her hand so she wouldn't be too loud when she saw that there was an abundance of blood pouring from his abdomen and staining the concrete beneath them.

"Fuck."

She put her phone in her other pocket and moved his limp body so she could grab him from beneath his armpits. His body felt cold and stiff. She remembered the CPR training she had when she first started teaching and checked for a pulse, breathing, or any sign of life, but had no luck.

Despite his body being stiff from the cool air, Rory dragged him down the alley. She cursed herself for wearing heels and a skirt to Carla's birthday dinner instead of something slightly more casual and practical. His body left a trail of his blood behind in thin streaks. It took her a few moments and all of her strength, but she managed to reach her car where the back door behind the driver's side was open.

She hoisted herself into the backseat and brought him with her, figuring it would be easier to rely on her own body weight for the momentum. Once Hematite was slumped in the backseat, Rory leaned over his body to close the car door, trying not to feel dirty about the whole thing. She grabbed her keys, awkwardly climbed back into the driver's seat, and then took off.

"Fuck," she muttered again. She grabbed her phone when she hit the next red light—they were all on timers, even at one in the morning —so she could plug in directions to the hospital.

Suddenly, Rory heard a familiar, gruff voice from the backseat. "Whatever you do, do not take me to the emergency room."

Rory yelped in shock. "Holy shit! Oh my God. You're alive. I thought you were dead. Are you sure?"

"I'm absolutely positive." Hematite grimaced through the pain. "They'll unmask me. I can't let that happen. Got it?"

Rory nodded as she turned the GPS off on her phone. "Right, right. I, uh, I think I have a first-aid kit at home. My friend Kane is pretty good with that stuff. I could call him—."

"No!" Hematite quickly caught himself after he interrupted her. "Don't call anyone. The less attention this draws, the better. I don't need the media going into another frenzy. If you have a first-aid kit, that's all I need."

Rory nodded. He could tell by her uneven breathing and the uncontrolled pitch in her voice that she was still panicking. "Okay, okay. Right. Okay, I'll take you to my house."

Kane thought about telling Rory the truth, but then remembered the fact that he was bleeding out in the back of her car and thought it might just worry her more. Besides, Rory already seemed determined to put herself in more danger than she needed to be, and Kane didn't want to amplify that risk. Her safety mattered more than her curiosity.

"What happened? Who did this to you?"

"I got jumped. There were five different guys, all amped up and out of their heads. I think they were sent by Stone Breaker. Whatever it is they're selling, it's getting worse. A bunch of them held me down, and then one of them introduced me to his knife."

"Can you at least explain to me how you came back to life on your own after that?" Rory asked. "I checked for a pulse, breathing, everything. You were legit dead."

"My parents did a lot of drugs, including when my mom was pregnant with me. My doctor thinks that has something to do with the fact that whenever I die, I come back within a few minutes. It's usually only ten or fifteen. It's a real pain in the ass."

"How so?" Rory asked. "Does it not heal you?"

"No … Imagine you're playing a video game," Hematite said. He found that talking to her was distracting him from the lingering pain in his abdomen where he had been stabbed. "You have two save points before a boss battle, but you forget to save at the second one. So, when you get your ass kicked, you remember everything but the character doesn't, and you have to gain some of your experience points back and whatnot. My body remembers everything; my memory is often hazy, depending on how long I'm out for."

They hit a pothole that made Hematite groan and cough. His cough caused him to spit up a little blood, but he wiped it away with his scarf.

"That and it really fucking hurts, even after I wake up."

"I'm sorry. We'll be at my place soon, okay?" She tried to hide the higher pitch of her voice but failed to mask the fact that she was freaking out. "I don't know that it totally makes sense, but I won't make you explain again. You must be exhausted. I took a shortcut, so it shouldn't be much longer."

Once they were inside, Rory rushed to help Hematite patch himself up. Kane noticed that the frenzied panic Rory was feeling in the car seemed to have melted away once it came time to help him, replaced with a steady determination. Rory was always fairly quick to take action, something that he always loved about her.

Rory started with his face, which meant Kane could keep most of his disguise on. He winced at the Neosporin® but sat still for her on her couch as she touched up a cut on his face from a knife wound just below his eye; she was careful to not remove his facial coverings entirely out of respect for his desired privacy. He kept his eyes closed, hoping she wouldn't recognize their color. The two of them were still in silence as they sat side-by-side on her couch. While it was quiet, it was still comfortable between them. Rory had a fleeting thought that it felt familiar, but she shrugged it off.

Rory was the one to break their silence first. "Why did you become a superhero?"

Hematite exhaled. "I have a sister. She's a few years younger than me. We … didn't exactly have a good home life growing up. Like I told you, my parents did a lot of drugs. They drank and fought a lot."

He paused and saw that Rory was still listening intently as she continued to adjust the balaclava and dab at his face. While Kane over the years hadn't told her a lot of the details of his and Kayla's child-hood, she knew it was rough. He figured she was in the dark enough for him to share more.

"I wanted to make sure my sister was okay. I learned how to fight from having to fend for myself against my father. Started with keeping my sister safe from bullies and our parents, and then that just snow-balled into what I'm doing now. I just don't want kids to grow up like we did."

"I really respect you, you know," Rory said. "Most people don't care enough to do anything; it's refreshing, though I'm sorry to hear that happened to you."

Hematite smiled beneath his mask. "Thank you." He glanced down at his hands as Rory took a hold of them.

"Can I take these off?" Rory asked. "I want to make sure your knuckles aren't bleeding or anything."

Hematite's heart was racing. He and Rory held hands many times, but their closeness as she tended to his wounds had him feeling like his head was spinning. So, he simply nodded his response to let her take the gloves off and unwrap his boxing wraps. Rory delicately held his hands in her own as she helped clean them up and treat the wounds on his knuckles. Bruises were already forming on some of his fingers. Hematite didn't even notice how the Neosporin® stung; this was a tender side of Rory that he had never experienced.

"Where did you get stabbed?"

"Oh, here," Hematite said, as he lifted up the bottom of his shirt. He revealed toned abs littered with different stab and gunshot scars. "I should, uh, probably invest in some protective gear. But you kinda don't care to bother when you can't die, anyway."

"Good God, they had it out for you." Rory's eyes widened at the sight. The wound by his stomach was a deep gash, but the bleeding had stopped.

"Eh, I've had worse," he said with a shrug of his shoulders. He helped her patch up the spot and once she was done, she bandaged it tightly. "Thank you for all your help." They were so close that he could see the little details of her face: the curve of her brows, the way her highlighter rested on her cheekbones, and the light mascara on her lashes. "I probably would still be over by that dumpster if it weren't for you."

Rory lightly laughed. "Don't mention it."

Their eyes met, and Hematite couldn't take it anymore. He placed a hand behind her head, fingers weaving through her hair, and quickly pulled his scarf down and balaclava up as he leaned in to kiss her.

Rory thought she was dreaming when Hematite's lips met hers. They were dry and cracked from his rough night, but she didn't even care. Rory could faintly taste iron, likely from some blood he coughed up earlier. His fingertips felt rough yet comforting against her scalp.

Rory parted her lips enough for Hematite's tongue to slip between them. Part of her brain was furious with herself. After all, she didn't know Hematite's name or what he looked like beneath the mask, hood, and scarf. But her heart knew that she didn't need to know those things. He meant more to her than she could say, not just for those times he saved her, but because of everything he stood for.

"I … I'm so sorry, Rory," Hematite said when he suddenly pulled away, quick to push his balaclava back down. He glanced down and dropped his hand. "I shouldn't have crossed that line with you. My being here and you helping me already put you in enough danger as is."

"I know you already warned me to not get too deep, but it's too late for that." Rory gently cupped his chin with her fingers and forced him to look back up at her. She could see the sadness in his eyes as she surveyed them. "You have nothing to apologize for."

Rory pushed his balaclava back up and brought their lips together that time. Hematite, to his own surprise, didn't stop her. Part of him felt relieved that she kissed him again. Rory couldn't explain it, but kissing Hematite felt as natural as breathing or eating. To avoid craning her neck any longer, Rory shifted by moving one of her legs across his lap, settling in a position where she was straddling him. Hematite's hands fell to her sides, running first down and then up her back.

Kane never imagined that he would actually be like this with Rory, especially as Hematite. He had wished for it, sure, but never thought it would be a reality, so he just soaked it all in. He admired the natural, feminine curves of her body and how plush her skin felt in his hands.

Rory had never felt so close to someone before, even without knowing his name or face. She knew there was only one place for their actions to go, and she knew that what she wanted would certainly elevate that. She mentally thanked herself for remembering to take her birth control medication that morning and then followed through with what her heart told her to do.

Rory ground her hips against Hematite's lap, feeling his erection beneath her.

Hematite thought he was going to choke. "Rory, I—."

"It's okay," she said against his lips.

He was the one to pull away completely. "Are you sure?"

"I trust you. And I promise, I'm not normally like this," she said with a nervous chuckle.

Hematite just smiled at her as his hands gently gripped her ribs. "Don't worry. I know." He swallowed a lump in his throat. "Listen, I

... do you mind if I keep the mask on? If that changes things, I'll understand."

Rory nodded and placed her hands on his shoulders. "It's okay. I get it."

That took him by surprise. "Wait. You do?"

"Yeah, to a degree. As much as I'd love to see the rest of your face ... I don't need to." She did desperately want to see who was beneath the mask, but she also trusted him, regardless of who it was. She recognized the uniqueness of their situation and wouldn't dare disrupt it.

Hematite felt his heart swell in his chest; for a moment, he thought it would creep up his throat and leap out of his mouth. Out of fear of revealing all his feelings, he opted to kiss Rory again in response. Her nonchalance about him keeping his face covered didn't shock him as much as he thought it would. He had fully expected her to ask him to remove his facial coverings, but he also knew how much Hematite meant to Rory, not just as a symbol but on a personal level.

There was a hunger in his kiss as he gripped at her body tighter, pulling her closer to him so she'd buck her hips against him once more. One of his hands fell to her thigh and slowly crept up it; it was clear to Rory that he had been holding back before but wasn't anymore. Something about his touch felt desperate and carnal,

As Rory moved her hands to undress herself, Hematite turned off his voice modifier and removed his shirt, careful to not remove his cowl. He moved the voice modifier down by his neck, disconnecting it from his balaclava, and knew he'd have to be careful without having it as a crutch. Usually, when he was unprepared, he could change his tone enough to not sound like his usual self. But he knew he couldn't get lost in his feelings and lose control.

When Hematite discarded his shirt, Rory noticed even more scars littering his torso. Unsurprisingly, he was built like a boxer with strong shoulders and well-defined abs. Her fingers gently feathered over his pale skin, tracing the slight dip between his pectoral muscles where a few scars were mostly faded. She wondered how many of these were simple injuries versus times he had died.

The fabric from Hematite's hood and scarf felt soft against her skin as he left rough kisses on her body. She glanced at his face, but his hood cast a shadow over his eyes and covered his face just enough for her to not be able to make it out entirely, especially when paired with his balaclava that still covered his hair, nose, and forehead. In fact, with the way it was bunched up, she couldn't really see his eyes and was surprised he could see much of anything.

Rory's mind was brought elsewhere, though, when Hematite's teeth gently grazed against her nipple. The fabric from his mask felt surprisingly soft against her skin as he left rough kisses against her breast. She thought she was going to go into a sensory overload as one of his thumbs ran between her legs moving in slow, intentional circles. When Rory's hand slipped beneath the waistband of his briefs to stroke Hematite, he groaned against her skin as he dipped in two fingers. Rory was already beginning to feel herself come undone; she felt more vulnerable than she had with anyone in years as she felt herself tighten around his fingers, but it was then that Hematite suddenly pulled his fingers away. Before Rory could question if he changed his mind, he adjusted how they were sitting so he could kick his bottoms to around his ankles.

Feeling desperate for her, Hematite shoved Rory's panties to the side and sat her back on his lap, this time sinking her onto him. His eyes met Rory's for a brief moment and he kissed her again, thrusting his hips upward to fill her completely. Rory matched his rhythm, the two of them finding a slow, steady rhythm that allowed them to savor the moment. The nagging voice in the back of her head telling her this was wrong had been effectively silenced when their lips connected, he removed his fingers, and their bodies united.

The rush that Hematite was experiencing had him feeling, for the first time in a long time, very much alive. He thought his heart was going to beat straight out of his chest from a combination of anticipation for Rory's next move, the nervousness of exposing his true identity, and the pleasure of the moment. The feeling of Rory pulsing around him was enough to send him into overdrive. There was so much he wanted to say as his cock twitched deep inside her, and he was half-tempted to rip his mask off, but he thought it was for the best if he just left it on at this point. The last thing he'd want to do was break her trust right after earning it so wholly.

Hematite's arms wrapped around Rory tightly to hold her close to him. His cowl nearly got in the way, and her panties bunched over to the side provided an interesting feeling of friction, but both of them felt attuned in a way that they could not compare or explain. Rory almost forgot he was wearing his mask until her hands cupped his cheeks during their embrace. As they both finished, they took a moment to soak each other in before they moved. Hematite didn't release his grip on Rory, but only slightly loosened it. She looked into his eyes again, seeing the shade of blue clearly now.

Hematite decided he'd tell her his identity eventually, but not tonight.

"If you have to go, I understand," Rory said.

Hematite cleared his throat. Rory sensed he was struggling to hide his actual voice. "I'll stay for a while. Stone Breaker is looking for you, after all. It's probably safer if I'm here for a bit."

Rory smirked; she knew he was justifying his actions, maybe more to himself than he was to her, but she didn't want to make him uncomfortable by calling that out. "Like I've said before, you're always welcome here. And you don't need an excuse to come either, you know."

He smiled at her, but only halfway. "Thank you."

That night, he held her until she fell asleep. Hematite enjoyed the moment while he could, dreaming of enjoying this every night, but he knew he couldn't. He glanced at her resting peacefully in his arms, sleeping soundly. Hematite knew Rory had been struggling with sleep lately, so to see her so comfortable touched his soul.

When Rory woke the next morning, he was gone. She wondered if the night prior had been a dream as she remembered what happened, until she saw something scribbled on a sticky note on her bedside table. She figured Hematite must have fished out from her backup stash of school supplies. It simply read:

Had to go.
    Stay in touch.
    -H

. . .

Rory smiled as she read the note over, especially when she saw the black heart scribbled in the bottom corner, but her smile faded the longer she stared at it. The realization of last night hit her like a tsunami, with no warning and all at once.

"Oh my God," she whispered to herself.

She stared at the sticky note a little while longer before grabbing her phone with her free hand and making a call.

"Hi! Dr. Thornton? Hi, sorry, I know. Marissa. Marissa. Listen, any chance in hell we can bump my next appointment up? I think I took your advice about trusting people a little too far."

"Rory, take a deep breath. You're talking really fast. What happened? Are you okay?"

Rory took a deep breath and then said, "I don't wanna give you TMI."

"Rory, I'm your therapist. As far as I'm concerned, there is no such thing as TMI, and I've probably heard worse than whatever it is you're about to tell me."

"Okay. Okay." Rory took another deep breath. "I slept with Hematite last night." Rory wasn't sure why, but she said it in a whisper. "Mask on. Didn't know his real name. Still don't. I couldn't even tell you the last time I slept with someone. Why did I do that?"

"Can I ask you something? Do you regret it?"

"Do I regret it?"

"Gut reaction. Don't think about it."

"No," Rory blurted out. "Oh, God. Is that bad?"

"Not at all. Maybe get tested just to be safe, but I'm sure you're fine. I know you know that sex is perfectly natural."

"Right, right."

"It sounds like you're self-aware and you have a history with this guy. This wasn't a stranger, and I'm not worried about this becoming a self-destructive behavior. I actually consider this good news coming from you."

"You do?"

"Hematite's been there for you. It's good that you trust him enough to be in that situation. I think it shows progress, just in a roundabout way. But we all grow differently. There's no wrong way to heal. Well, within reason. No wrong way to heal so long as you're not hurting anybody, but you get my drift."

"Thank you for talking me off the ledge."

"That's what I'm here for. Listen, if you still feel the need to come in this week, I had my Thursday lunch break slot open up. Call me on yours then, okay?"

"I will take you up on that," Rory said. "Thanks, Marissa."

As Rory hung up, she couldn't help but smile.

CHAPTER 14

A few days later, when Kane opened Rory's car door, Rory expected the morning air to be much more frigid. But she was met with a pleasant surprise by the warm breeze. March's end approaching meant that spring was coming too, though the snow still wasn't letting up and wouldn't any time soon.

"How was Carla's birthday party? That was this weekend, right?" Kane already knew the answer but was curious about how much Rory would say.

Rory nodded. "Yeah. It was good! It was nice to get out of the house again."

She paused, and the excitement in her voice naturally faded when she did. She wasn't sure if she should tell Kane that she found Hematite and brought him home. Kane didn't need to know all the details, but she also wanted to be transparent with her closest friend.

Kane immediately noticed her mood drop but tried not to take it personally. "Rory? You okay?"

Rory glanced over at Kane at the red light. Their gaze met and when she looked Kane in the eyes, she could have sworn she was gazing into Hematite's eyes again. They were that same striking blue, like the sky on a clear day holding back storms.

"Rory?"

"Yeah, I'm okay," she said with a gentle shake of her head. The green light prompted her to keep driving and gave her an excuse to look away from Kane. Their eyes were definitely the same, of that much she was certain.

"I can tell something is up. What happened? You know you can tell me anything."

"I'm, uh, just a bit shaken up still, that's all."

She was still taken aback by the fact that she had been intimate with Hematite. She couldn't help but wonder if she'd completely ruined her working relationship with him after that, but she told Kane only half of the truth.

"I found Hematite dead last night. I got him in my car, and he came back to life in the backseat before I could take him to a hospital. If you look back there, you'll probably find some blood stains. I tried to do a deep clean this morning but was running later than I wanted to."

Her therapist wouldn't be happy about her omission after working on some trust exercises, but Rory felt it was a necessary step back.

"Holy shit." Kane once again feigned his surprise; he wasn't sure where his acting abilities came from, but he was especially grateful for them lately. "I mean, I guess it's a good thing you found him and not someone else."

"It was still kinda freaky. At the moment, I was so pumped with adrenaline from just trying to get him out of there. But looking back … it was pretty intense."

Kane reached for one of Rory's hands and held it. It was large enough to engulf her own, both in size and warmth. "That must have been. I'm surprised you didn't call out today."

"He's okay; that's ultimately all that matters," Rory said with a shrug. She glanced at his knuckles and mentally compared them to Hematite's; there was some discoloration in the same spots that Hematite's were bloodied or bruised the other night. "I might have nightmares for the rest of the week about it, but I guess I find some comfort in knowing that he can't die so easily."

"There you go." Kane gave her hand a gentle squeeze, and she turned to smile at her friend. She couldn't help but think how much

Kane's eyes reminded her of Hematite's. Rory tried to shake the feeling in both her heart and her gut, but there was no other plausible explanation.

It has to be coincidental, Rory thought. Kane and Hematite were so fundamentally different as far as their personalities went that she thought it couldn't be Kane.

"Also, Stone Breaker made a video about me," Rory said. "Naomi sent it to me this morning, hence me running later than I wanted to."

"I saw it when I was getting ready this morning. I wasn't sure if I should bring it up."

"I think you're right. He must have seen me with Hematite when I went to go drop that evidence off. It's especially concerning given that Naomi and I are ninety-nine percent positive that it's Mark Stevens. He's a reporter, which means he has easy access to anything he wants to know about me."

"I think he's too much of a chump to actually do anything for now," Kane said. "But don't worry, Rory. I got your back. Why haven't you guys reported him to the police?"

"We don't have any hard proof. What we have is just theory and speculation based on what we both know, plus some cryptic messages in newspaper articles that Mark wrote. And given his father hooked up with the police chief ... I'd say our chances of getting a warrant are slim." She frowned. "I could barely get the police to take me seriously when I reported the guy stalking me in college, and there wasn't even some weird connection going on there. Naomi and I both went together, but I think they saw two college girls and just laughed. We have to leave this one to Hematite."

"Yeah, that's true. You're right. Unfortunately, looks like a lot of crime in this town has to be left to him."

The corruption of their local police department never escaped Kane; the fact that he was still able to perform his vigilante duties for the last twelve years was a testament to that. But he suspected a much bigger picture than the police liked to paint. Detective McMahon always worked his cases lately, and Kane was certain that it was intentional.

Kane had a revelation. "Here's something you and Naomi can look up," he said. "Look into his father. See where he gets his money from. Who his lobbyists are should tell you a lot."

Rory smiled. "That's brilliant. Thanks, Kane."

Kane grinned. "I told you I'd come around eventually to help in my own way, right?"

———

Rory stood before her class with her hands clasped in front of her. "Alright, you guys, are you ready for some current events? We'll start with Jordan, as we usually do."

Jordan, who sat in the front row in the left corner of the classroom, unfolded her newspaper clipping. "I brought an article about Stone Breaker. I don't exactly have much commentary on it, but I thought you should see it anyway, Ms. Miller. Is that okay?"

"Yeah. I've seen it." Rory leaned back against her desk, barely sitting on it, as she sighed. She hoped her casual body language would put her students at ease. "Go ahead, Jordan."

"Stone Breaker released a new video Sunday night threatening a Riverpeak High School teacher," Jordan read. "Stone Breaker spoke directly to Rory Miller in the video uploaded to his YouTube channel Stone Breaker Rises." Jordan paused before she said, "Hey, Ms. Miller?"

"Yes, Jordan?"

"Are you okay?"

The question stopped Rory in her tracks. She tried to hide her surprise to not further alarm her students, but as she looked at the crowd of twenty faces before her, she could already tell they were all thinking the same thing.

"I'm okay, Jordan," Rory said with a smile. "Thank you. You guys don't need to worry about me, okay? Nor do you need to worry about yourselves."

"Ms. Miller, we're not kids. Don't lie to us," Jordan said.

They are kids, she thought; *they're only fifteen.*

Another girl asked, "Stone Breaker isn't gonna come to the school, is he? My parents are getting nervous."

"Stone Breaker isn't coming to this school, and he will not hurt me," Rory insisted. "That isn't a lie, nor is it just wishful thinking."

"Then why did he upload that video addressing you last night?"

"Because I have ... a friend that Stone Breaker wants to hurt," Rory said. She chose her words carefully and didn't want to get the students too riled up. "And no, I don't know who Hematite is. So don't even ask."

"Is that your friend?" one of the boys asked. "What can we do?"

"Nothing," Rory said. "You will all make me very happy by not worrying and not getting involved. You're safe as is. Let's keep it that way, okay?"

Rory swallowed back her genuine feelings, something her therapist would frown upon, but she had to stay strong in front of her students. She let their class move on without further ruckus, but when Kane joined her in her classroom for their lunch break, Rory's bottled-up emotions were on the brink of spilling over.

Kane could tell just by looking at Rory that everything had caught up to her. She was maintaining her composure well enough to the naked eye, but he could see the worry in her face in a way that only someone who had known her for a decade would recognize.

"We'll stay in here," Kane suggested. "Let's talk."

Once Kane locked the door behind him, Rory burst into tears. Kane rushed to grab a tissue from where she kept them on her desk and pulled one of the student's chairs up so he could sit beside her. His hand ran gently up and down her back.

"Hey, hey," Kane whispered. "I'm here. I got you. What's really going on, Rory?"

"They're just fucking kids," she managed between her sobs. "They shouldn't have to worry about this."

Kane knew she hosted current events as part of her curriculum every Monday. The Stone Breaker video, which was posted late Sunday night, must have been a hot topic.

"But what about you?" Kane stressed. "What's going on in that pretty head of yours, huh?"

Rory gave herself a moment to take a few deep breaths. Kane let her take them without judgment and just continued to rub her back.

"I know I ran into this on my own," Rory said, "but I feel like I can't ever catch a break, you know?"

Kane nodded. "Rory, it's not your fault. Stone Breaker being a piece of shit is not your fault." He leaned in to kiss her temple, so softly that Rory almost didn't feel it. "And you're right. It's bad enough for someone to be stalked once. I can't even imagine going through it twice." Kane paused before he added, "You're the strongest person I know, you know that?"

Rory released a nervous chuckle through her tears. "I don't feel very strong. I feel like I'm holding on by a thread."

"Yeah, but you're still holding on."

Rory looked up into Kane's eyes and was met by Hematite's once again. When she looked at Kane, she felt everything she had when she and Hematite first embraced. The coincidences would explain everything: why he was acting strange, his sudden increased exhaustion and nights out, and his resistance to getting involved.

"Kane, you trust me, right?" Rory asked.

"Of course, you know that."

They never broke eye contact. Rory gave herself another moment to catch her breath after her breakdown and then asked, "Are you Hematite?"

Kane felt like his heart sank into his stomach. "What?" he asked, trying to play dumb and cool.

"Please don't lie to me," Rory said. She held eye contact with him. Kane was too afraid to break it in fear of revealing himself.

"Rory, why would you think that?" Kane asked. He was trying desperately to skirt around the issue; lying to her always ate at him, but he wouldn't be able to live with himself if he lied to her now.

Rory shook her head. "I dunno," she said. "Just a hunch."

"I wish I were as cool as he was."

"Maybe I'm just delusional right now," she said, recognizing that her emotions were running high. On top of it all, she was seeing Kane in a new light. A part of her wondered if she was just desperate for him to be Hematite after the weekend's events. She shook her head and grabbed a new tissue. "Forget it."

Kane internally relaxed, but not entirely. The gig would be up soon, he thought, and he needed to do something about it—he just wasn't sure if that meant upping the ante or finally coming clean.

———

When Kane suited up in his Hematite disguise that night, he beelined it for Rory's house. Even if her safety wasn't hanging in the balance, he was deeply concerned for her to the point where it was making him nauseous.

Hematite scaled her single-story home to get a 360-degree view of her property. After Shatterstone had already stopped her on her way home, he wasn't sure what Stone Breaker would do next. Kane took out both his cell phone and a burner phone. He used his phone to pull up Rory's contact information and plugged her number into the burner.

When Rory heard her cell phone buzz against the coffee table, she set her tea down to look at it. She didn't recognize the number, but the text message was reassuring.

> UNKNOWN: A little birdy told me you need some extra help this evening. I'm camped out for the night. Sleep well and let me know if you need anything. -H

Rory smiled. She wondered if it was Kane's doing.

> RORY: Do you want to come in? It's like 35 degrees out there.

Outside, Hematite smiled as he pocketed his cell phone and kept the burner in hand.

> HEMATITE: I can see everything from my spot. Don't worry; I'm plenty warm enough.

> RORY: The second step by the front door has a loose brick. Spare key's in there. Come in if you change your mind.

> HEMATITE: I'll take note of that. Thank you.

Only a few minutes later, Hematite heard Rory's front door open. He shifted to glance over and saw Rory stepping outside. She had a stainless-steel mug with a lid in her hand. She wore her winter coat over her pajamas, unprepared for the cold but still smiling.

Rory heard the sounds of shuffling on her roof and looked up toward it. She waved as she saw Hematite perched there. If she didn't know to look for him, she wouldn't have spotted him, since his outfit blended in with the night sky.

"There's this local tea shop up in Denver that my therapist got me hooked on," Rory called up. "They made this blend; it's kind of like an English breakfast, but with lavender and honey. I hope you like it."

Kane tried not to laugh. *Leave it to Rory*, he thought.

He shifted to the edge to jump off her roof, made sure his voice modifier was turned on, and met her by the doorway. "Thank you." He accepted the mug. "That's very thoughtful of you."

"I don't think I'll be able to sleep if I know you're freezing your ass off out here all night. It's the least I could do."

"I'll head in if it gets too cold. First, I want to be sure of a few things. I promise."

"I'll hold you to it." She smiled at him as she went back in. As the night went on, she tried to stay awake in case he changed his mind but sleep eventually won that battle.

When she woke up the following morning, the only sign of Hematite was the cleaned mug resting on her dining room table. Rory held the mug in her hands and brought it to her chest, using it to feel close to Hematite for a moment as her drowsiness subsided.

She pondered her situation as she drove to Kane's house on the way to the school. She still had so many unanswered questions, but she knew she was sure of a few things now that helped narrow her search for Stone Breaker.

The first was that Mark Stevens was Stone Breaker; there was no other explanation. She also was sure that Hematite's theory about the Stevens family profiting off of the drugs would turn out to be correct.

The second was that Kane was involved with Hematite and not telling her the full truth. She still wasn't convinced, despite their conversation the day prior, that Hematite and Kane weren't one and the same. But even if Kane wasn't Hematite, after last night, she knew Kane had some sort of connection to the masked vigilante.

It simultaneously made sense to her and made no sense at all. Hematite always seemed so stoic and stern, despite his heroic acts of helping people in need throughout Riverpeak and other towns near Denver. Kane, however, was usually joking around and didn't take much of anything seriously.

But Kane's late nights and bright blue eyes would make so much sense. How Hematite knew to look after her last night would be explained instantaneously if it were Kane.

Just as she pulled up to Kane's apartment, she received a text from Naomi.

> NAOMI: Let's meet up this weekend. I have four candidates for Hematite.

> RORY: Add a fifth. I'm still not sure of it but add Kane Kelly to our list.

CHAPTER 15

Rory wasn't sure how to feel when she got the text from her mom inviting her over for dinner and to catch up, but she still found herself at their front door. Rory's parents' home looked no different than how it did during her childhood. They, like everyone else in Riverpeak, set their roots there and let them grow deep enough to be permanent. As a child, she didn't understand the appeal of the small town, despite its general suburban safety. As an adult, she valued and appreciated it deeply.

She wasn't in the door for more than a few seconds when her father, Dave, embraced her. His skin, only a shade or so lighter than her own, was dry. Rory made a mental note to get him a nice moisturizer for Christmas.

"We saw the news. We've been so worried, Rory."

She offered her parents a sad smile. "Thanks, Dad. I'm okay, I promise."

"Come on, dinner's ready," her mother, Susan, said as she pulled Rory in for a hug. "You know you can talk to us about these things, right, honey?"

Rory just smiled. "I know." It was a lie. In truth, she didn't think she could. She knew thanks to a few therapy sessions that her parents meant well but didn't know how to process their daughter's trauma. Rory mentally reminded herself that it wasn't her fault as she sat down at her parents' dinner table. As her parents talked about the YouTube video where Stone Breaker mentioned her by name, Rory just blankly stared at her meal. She spun her spoon in the small bowl of butternut squash soup for a minute before finally taking a small slurp. She hardly tasted it in her trance.

Her father's change of inflection as he asked a question made her snap out of it. "I mean, why does this Stone Breaker guy even want to go after you?"

Rory took another sip of soup as she composed herself. "Because I know who he is and told Hematite."

The only sound was Rory's father's fork dropping. She took another sip of soup, finally tasting it now. It was perfect: the flavors of butternut squash, salt, and cream all completely balanced, just like everything else in her family's life.

"You what?" her mother asked in nearly a whisper. There was no anger in her voice, but simply pure shock.

"Yeah, I've been working directly with Hematite. Surprise, I know."

Her father asked, "Does your boss know?"

Rory shrugged. "She doesn't need to."

Her mother gasped. "Rory!"

"What? She doesn't," Rory said. She surprised herself with her calmness; *maybe the therapy was working*, she thought. "I haven't broken any laws, and I'm not in violation of my contract. I simply found evidence to support the identity of an attempted murderer and told his victim."

"And not the police?"

"Yeah, Dad, because that's worked out well before." Rory shot her father a glance, and he nodded his head, remembering her past. "I know this is alarming. But I meant it when I said you didn't need to worry about me. I'm an adult. I'm capable of making my own decisions."

"The last thing we want is for you to get hurt or fired," her mother said. Rory could tell that her mother was attempting to be empathetic; it was mostly working. "But this ... I find this extremely concerning."

Rory met her mother's eyes. Her conviction came from her mom's side of the family, which anyone could tell simply by looking at them both in a room together.

"You taught me to fight for what I thought was right, no matter what the stakes," Rory said, without breaking her mother's eye contact. "This is me doing just that, whether you like it or not."

Her mother sighed and nodded. "Please tell me you know what you're doing."

Rory grinned. "I do. And I'm not alone."

"Let me guess, Naomi too?" her father said. "You two were always thick as thieves."

Rory just nodded. The rest of their dinner was quiet, save for the sounds of silverware. Rory couldn't tell what her father was thinking, as his posture was oddly stiff. Her mother, however, seemed to be deep in thought. Rory was both grateful for the silence and unnerved by it.

"I'll help with the dishes," she said when they finished. Her mother stood side by side with her by the dishwasher as her father took care of putting away leftovers.

"Rory," her mother suddenly said, as she passed her a rinsed dish. "I'm proud of you. You know that?"

Rory stopped to look at her mother. "Thanks."

"Seriously, I'm really proud of you. I know when you were deeply hurting a few years ago, it wasn't easy. This can't be, either. But I hope you give them hell."

Rory blinked. She saw her own face in her mother's, but a bit more hardened.

Her mother continued. "We moved to Riverpeak before you were born because we were told this town was safe. And it is. But what's been happening lately has been out of control." Susan sighed. "But I have faith in our next generation knowing that you're the one teaching them."

Rory swallowed back some tears that built up. "I think that's the nicest thing anyone's ever said to me. Thanks, Mom."

"I will always worry about you. I'm your mother. But I trust you are doing what you know is best in this ... unusual situation."

Rory couldn't help her smile. She wasn't exactly sure what her mother was thinking, but she knew that Susan's strong sense of justice mirrored her own. "That means more to me than I can even say."

Rory left her parents' home feeling renewed. She wasn't sure what had changed over the years, but it threw her for a loop as she made the short drive back to her own home. She decided to not think about it too much and to just be grateful for the fact her parents at least partially understood.

As she drove through the suburbs, she noticed taillights behind her the whole way. Before she reached her street, she took a random left turn to see if they'd follow. She took three more, feeling increasingly uneasy as the taillights maintained their distance and knew she was being followed once she made the complete square.

She grabbed her cell phone and quickly scrolled in her contacts to the phone number that Hematite had texted her from. It rang a few times before she heard his altered voice on the other end.

"Rory?" Hematite was surprised she had called. "What's going on?"

"Yeah, hi," she said. She forced herself to slow down her breathing before it could get too out of control. "I'm driving home right now, and I'm being followed. I confirmed that after taking four left turns. Think it's Stone Breaker? It's not his usual Harley, but I'd be willing to bet he borrowed one of Daddy's nice cars."

"I'd bet on it too." He shifted his stance, so he was no longer sitting on the edge of the library's rooftop but crouched to be more alert and ready to move. "Where are you?"

Rory glanced at the street signs as she drove by. Her foot put a bit more pressure on the gas pedal. "Driving on South Street. Just passed River Road heading toward downtown."

"I'm not far. I'm on my way from Main Street. Head toward Jefferson's Coffee, and I'll meet you there."

"Got it. See you there soon."

"Stay on with me just in case," he said. He waved his hand at

Shawn, who was sitting with him, to tell him to follow. Shawn got up and did as instructed. "You said it's another car?"

"Yeah, I see two headlights." She looked in the rearview mirror again. "It's too dark for me to see what kind of car, though."

"That's alright. We'll know it's you."

"We? Who is 'we'?"

"I have a strong friend," Hematite said. "Very strong."

"What does that even mean? Since when do you have friends?"

"I take offense to that. I have friends."

"No, you don't, dude," Shawn said from behind him.

Hematite rolled his eyes.

"Alright, I'm almost at Jefferson's. I can see it."

"Make a sharp turn into the parking lot. Jefferson has cameras. We've got you covered." He turned to Shawn and said, "Go ahead, dude."

Rory pulled into the parking lot. The car behind her didn't make the turn in time. Rory heard it screech, as it made a quick turn in a doughnut shape. As Stone Breaker's car swung into the parking lot, a large body jumped on top of the roof. Rory jumped a bit in her seat as she heard the crushing noise. The person on top of the car had a wide frame with muscular arms and a strong back. Their build reminded her of a powerlifter in a Strongman competition. They punched above the driver's seat where they were standing and it made another loud, crunching sound.

"Don't leave your car," Hematite said to her on the phone. "You're safer in the car." At that, he hung up.

Hematite followed suit, leaping on top of the car to join his companion. Even though Hematite himself was mostly muscle, he was significantly leaner than his friend, who made him look even smaller. Something about the larger one's silhouette looked familiar to Rory, but with his face covered in the dark, she couldn't say why.

The car backed out of the parking lot and swerved, likely in an attempt to shake Hematite and the second hero off. Rory wasn't sure who he was, but she sensed he was like Hematite, in that he was born differently than his peers.

"Get the window!" Hematite suggested to Shawn. "I can get in!"

Shawn nodded and leaned over to punch the window on the passenger side. Rory could hear the glass shatter even from her spot in the parking lot.

Hematite used his legs to slip into the car through the broken window. He could feel the shattered glass beneath him as he tried to weasel his way in. He was greeted by Stone Breaker behind the wheel. Stone Breaker tried to reach for something in the center console, but Hematite didn't waste any time. He threw a punch at Stone Breaker's face, feeling the ABS plastic beneath his cloth-covered fist; unfortunately for Hematite, this mask was much thicker than Shatterstone's had been. It gave Stone Breaker just enough protection to not completely lose control, but his swerving got worse.

"Crash the car, dude!" Shawn shouted from above. "I'm good up here!"

Kane grabbed the wheel and gave it a hard turn. The car spun out and eventually crashed into a pole, the back end taking the brunt of the impact. Shawn jumped off just in time and broke his fall with a roll, using his momentum to his advantage.

The airbags prevented Hematite from seeing much in the car, but he reached for Stone Breaker and grabbed his shirt. "Leave Rory Miller out of this," he said. "Do you understand me?"

"You think I'll listen to you?" Stone Breaker coughed. "Tough shit, asshole."

The passenger side door opened. Hematite glanced back and saw Shawn standing there. They nodded at each other, and Hematite grabbed at Stone Breaker, trying to pull him out of the car with him. Once Hematite was out, Shawn took over, grabbing a firm hold of Stone Breaker and giving him a light toss with only one hand. Stone Breaker rolled a few feet away from them and eventually made an impact with the asphalt beneath him.

Beneath his mask, Mark as Stone Breaker could taste some blood. He lifted his mask just enough to spit it out on the road without revealing his face. As he adjusted it and rolled onto his side, hoping for a moment to recover, he looked up to see Hematite approaching. Hematite's black pants cinched at the ankles, highlighting the shape of his long, muscular legs. Stone Breaker saw Hematite reach for the billy club that gently swung from his belt and detach the clip. Stone Breaker grimaced as the billy club made contact with his arm.

Stone Breaker realized that he made a big mistake in trying to follow Rory home. He waited for the second thwack of a billy club, but it never came. When he looked up, he saw both Hematite and the newcomer staring down at him.

"Bet you weren't expecting him, huh?" Hematite said, as he nodded his head toward the larger fellow.

Stone Breaker couldn't respond. He coughed again. A bit more blood spilled out.

Hematite crouched down, resting his elbows on his knees. He was still holding the billy club.

"What the fuck did I ever do to you?" Hematite asked.

Stone Breaker didn't have an answer ready. He knew that if Hematite uncovered the truth, it would be detrimental to his father's campaign and personal funding. But Stone Breaker knew that wasn't a sufficient answer for two reasons: it wasn't something that Hematite did to him personally, and it would say far too much.

"Go to hell," Stone Breaker said as he coughed again. The second guy kicked him in the stomach. With that, Stone Breaker's coughs became uncontrollable.

"Ease up," Hematite said to his friend. "I'd like to have a heart-to-heart with this asshole here."

Hematite's accomplice scoffed. "Suit yourself. Not my style, but it's your mortal enemy, not mine."

Hematite rolled his eyes. "You know, someone's probably calling the police right about now. What did you think was going to happen tonight?"

Stone Breaker tried to force himself to get up. He slipped on his hands a bit.

Shawn got his foot ready again, but Hematite held a hand up to stop him. Stone Breaker noticed that despite being physically stronger, Hematite held the authority over this other super-powered man.

"You can't know the truth," Stone Breaker settled on. "No matter what."

"And why's that? Who will pay the price if I know what they're up to?"

Stone Breaker shook his head. "I'm not a fucking idiot, Hematite. You won't get me to talk so easily."

"Oh, Jesus. You sure you don't want me to just knock him out?" Shawn asked Hematite.

Hematite exhaled through his nose and could feel the tension in his clenched jaw as he faced Stone Breaker.

"You wanna know what happens when the police come?" Stone Breaker laughed, as he realized the reality of the situation. "There's a good chance they're in on it. Do you even know how deep this goes?"

"He's probably full of shit," Shawn chimed in.

"How deep?" Hematite asked.

"They're getting paid." Stone Breaker smirked beneath his mask. "Very well, at that."

Hematite could feel his patience growing thinner by the second. "Who is paying them?"

Stone Breaker kept laughing. "You can't know the truth," he repeated, but this time with more confidence. Most of the police force was aware of the situation, thanks to his father's connections with Chief Daniels. "Money really does buy happiness, don't you think?"

———

Naomi was surprised to see the call from Rory come through on her work phone. Rory had the number, but only ever called it in the event of an emergency.

"Rory? What's wrong?"

"What are people saying on the scanners? Did you hear anything about Stone Breaker or Hematite by Jefferson's Coffee?"

"Whoa, whoa, slow down. What's happening?"

"I was just followed by Stone Breaker. Hematite got him."

"Police were just dispatched," Naomi said. "They're on their way. I think someone nearby called. Hold on." Naomi paused to listen to what they were saying. "They want Hematite. Someone just said they're tired of him. You said Stone Breaker is there? They haven't even mentioned him on the scanners."

"Fuck! Listen, I don't trust the police. I mean, you already knew that, but I really don't trust them now. Something weird is going on with Stone Breaker, Councilman Stevens, and Chief Daniels. That affair Stevens had with Chief Daniels is probably still ongoing if I had to guess. Plus Kane mentioned to me the other day that we should look into their lobbying records, so I think that he was on to something. Thanks!"

"Rory!"

But all Naomi heard on the other end was silence as Rory hung up. She frowned and turned to her computer, and, in the search bar of her browser, she typed in Councilman Stevens' name.

———

Rory tossed her phone in the cupholder and, with shaky hands, began driving. Hematite and his friend needed to get out of there, and they needed to get away quickly. Rory made the short drive down the road where they were, maybe only a mile away, and stopped at the pole where the car had crashed into.

She rolled the window down and stuck her head out.

"Hey!" All three faces turned to look at her. "Hematite and ... whoever you are! Get in here!"

"And just leave him?" Hematite retorted.

"No way!" The other man agreed.

"It's useless!" Rory said. "The cops won't help you. He's," she pointed at Stone Breaker, "with Daniels and Stevens, and the cops know that!"

"Shit!" Hematite exclaimed. He stood from his spot by Stone Breaker and retracted his billy club. He looked at Shawn and said, "Fuck it. Do your best."

Shawn chuckled. He knew Hematite would be furious if he killed Stone Breaker. He opted to give him a light kick to the head to knock him unconscious—or at least light by Jameson's standards. The two of them then ran to Rory's car just as the police lights came into their field of vision. Their sirens were off.

"They're after you," Rory said as the two got into the car. "Come on, we can get out of here before they spot me." She made the first turn she could and felt instant relief once she realized the police weren't following her. They likely stopped to help Stone Breaker.

"Thanks for the getaway car," Hematite said from the passenger seat. "You didn't have to stick around."

"Of course," she said. "We're a team. Friends, even."

Hematite laughed, remembering their conversation from only a few minutes ago. "That's one way to put it."

"Jesus Christ, please make out somewhere else," Shawn said from the backseat. Like Hematite, his voice was also modified, but he used a high-tech face mask to do so.

"Ignore him," Hematite said without hesitation.

"It's fine." Rory glanced at his friend in the rearview mirror. He was wearing a gray shirt with a puffy maroon jacket over it to keep warm. A black scarf wrapped around his neck and kept the black voice-changing mask on over his face. Rory asked him, "So, who are you?"

"I'm Brick Beast, thank you for asking." He tugged at the black-and-red beanie that was covering his hair and his ears. "No one ever does."

"Thank you for your help tonight," Rory said. "I really appreciate it."

"Don't inflate his ego any more," Hematite warned. Rory couldn't tell if he was being playful or serious.

Shawn laughed from the backseat. "Jealous your girlfriend is giving me attention, Hematite?"

"Can it." Hematite shifted uncomfortably in the passenger seat.

"I'm calling Naomi," Rory said to change the subject. "I didn't call the cops since I don't trust those fuckers. But she checked the scanners for me. They, uh, they said they were looking for you, not Stone Breaker. Like, to arrest you."

She put Naomi on her car's Bluetooth® speaker. Naomi answered after only one ring.

"Are you okay?" Naomi said upon answering. "You scared the shit out of me!"

"I'm sorry, I'm sorry," Rory said. "I'm fine. I have Hematite and Brick Beast in the car, and I'm getting them the hell away from there. Listen, did you hear anything else on the scanners?"

"They just said they picked up 'his' son. I'm not sure who 'his' is. Probably Councilman Stevens. Who's Brick Beast?"

"A friend of Hematite's, I guess."

"I have super strength," Shawn piped in from the backseat. Hematite groaned in annoyance.

"That and a lot of pride," Rory said.

Hematite spoke next. "Naomi Sato, right? You've been helping Rory."

Naomi nodded subconsciously on the other end. She tried to keep her excitement internalized. "Hi. Yeah, I have."

"Listen, Stone Breaker told me tonight that the police are getting paid off. We need to find out who is paying them off. Is that something you can look up?"

"I'm already looking into Councilman Stevens' financial history. Lobbying records have to be public, after all," she said. "I'll let you know what I can find. He's most likely getting paid by someone to keep everything quiet. I'm sure that money is what's going toward the police department, especially given his special history with Chief Daniels."

"Thank you. I think you're on the right track. Keep up the good work."

"Of course," Naomi said. "I'll let Rory know of anything that I come up with, and she can pass it along to you. Sound good?"

"Yes. If there's anything locked down, send it to her too. I know someone who can break into just about anything if it's online."

"Noted," Naomi said. "We'll figure it out. Oh, and by the way, the scanners just mentioned they're bringing 'his son' back to the station. They're headed back. Just avoid the station and you should be clear."

"You're the best, Naomi. I'll catch you later." Once they hung up, Rory asked Hematite, "Where should I take you?"

"Just go home," Hematite said. "We can head out from there. I want to know you're there safe."

"Aw, how sweet," Brick Beast commented from the backseat.

"You okay? For real?" Hematite asked as she pulled into her driveway, speaking in a whisper since he didn't want Shawn to hear. Rory was still surprised by the tenderness in his voice, despite their history. It never sounded like it belonged to him in that outfit.

She nodded. "I am. Thank you."

When she went inside, she locked the door before heading to the window. She peered out of the blinds to see where they would go off to, but they were already gone. Rory couldn't shake the feeling that she knew both of them more than they let on.

CHAPTER 16

Detective McMahon was surprised to see his personal cell phone ringing in the middle of the night. He groaned as he rolled over in bed and reached for his phone, while gently shushing his wife to coax her back to sleep.

"Who the hell is calling you?"

"I dunno; it better not be work," he said. "Get some rest, honey; you need it." His first instinct was to hang up on them before he even answered, especially since the number showed up as Unknown, but his thumb slipped and he took it. Even though it wasn't on speaker, he still heard the voice loud and clear on the other end.

"Detective, are you there?"

At that, Detective McMahon was wide awake. He'd know that voice anywhere. He leaped out of bed as he answered. "Hematite? What's going on? How did you get my number?"

"Rory Miller gave it to me. Listen closely. There's something going on at your station, and I thought you should know about it. The officers are getting paid off to help Stone Breaker. I understand I'm not exactly everyone's favorite guy with the law, but you don't strike me as the type of person to throw stones from a glass house. Do you understand what I'm saying?"

"What?" he asked. "Who is getting paid off?"

"Are you?"

"No, absolutely not. I would never."

"I fear you may be the only one. You have given me no reason to not trust you so far. I hope you don't intend to change that. We coexist well, don't you think?"

"I'd agree, yes," Detective McMahon said. "How do you know this?"

"Councilman Tom Stevens is definitely connected to Stone Breaker, who told us he could get away with whatever he wanted because the police were paid to side with him. Naomi Sato with Channel 10 News confirmed this with the chatter she picked up on the police scanners at the station. We have some loose evidence showing Stone Breaker is Tom's adult son, Mark. The arrest of Mark's friend Douglas Doerr for his activity as Shatterstone also confirms this, as far as I'm concerned."

"You know the only reason they couldn't bust that little twerp out is that I had to convince them to not grant him bail? I had to bust my ass for that. No wonder."

"I hope you're as angry as I am," Hematite said. "What do you say?"

"I've been helping you because I think you're ultimately doing a good thing for this city. I don't like your methods. But I'll be damned before I try to say they don't work. I enjoy coexisting with you, Hematite, and I don't intend to change that. So yes, I'm pretty angry."

"I'm glad you and I are on the same page," Hematite said. "If I hear anything, I'll make you aware if you promise to let me do what I need to do over the next few weeks. Do we have a deal?"

"What do you need to do?" Detective McMahon asked.

"I'm not completely sure yet. But I'm not going to kill anyone, if that's what you're wondering."

"No, I know that's not your style."

Hematite chuckled. "That's one way to put it. Do we have a deal?"

Detective McMahon glanced back at his bedroom, where his wife had fallen back asleep, and nodded. "We do."

————

Naomi's house had fewer papers scattered about compared to Rory's last few visits, but it still looked like a sea of documents in the living room. There weren't as many newspaper articles this time, but more photos and personal records on the floor.

"Like I said, I've narrowed it down to five people, including Kane," Naomi said; if she had any personal thoughts on the matter, she didn't show it. Naomi was talking strictly business. "I've got their photos all lined up here." She gestured to the coffee table. The five of them were spread out, almost like a row of mugshots, but with social media profile photos.

"It's definitely not this guy," Rory said as she pointed to the first photo. "Hematite has blue eyes, not brown." She looked at the second picture. "And it's not this guy, either." She discarded a photo of a man with brown hair. "His lips are too thin."

Naomi's brows furrowed. "Whoa, whoa, whoa. Hold on. You've seen Hematite close up enough to know? And doesn't he always keep his mouth covered?"

"He usually does. I haven't seen all of his face, but I have seen his mouth and chin."

"When exactly was this? I thought we couldn't unmask him."

"We can't. I … You can't tell anyone." Rory wasn't sure why she was speaking in a whisper, given that she and Naomi were alone in Naomi's home. "This stays between us."

Naomi nodded. "I promise to keep this a secret, but I'd be lying if I said you weren't making me nervous."

Rory exhaled and said, "I may have slept with Hematite a few weeks ago."

Naomi's eyes widened in shock. "You what?!"

"I know, I know!" Rory held her hands up in defense. "On the way back from Carla's birthday dinner, I found him when I was at a red light. He was dead in an alleyway, Naomi. I couldn't just leave him there."

"Oh my God," Naomi said. She pinched the bridge of her nose, a habit she picked up from Brad. "I can't believe what I'm hearing."

"I patched him up at my house. He begged me to not take him to the ER. And then everything just sort of happened," Rory explained with a shrug.

"It 'just sort of happened?'" Naomi asked with one eyebrow raised. "So that's how you saw some of his face? Did he take his mask off?"

"Well, no. He pulled part of it up to kiss me, but then asked if he could keep it on, so I let him." Rory realized how it sounded once she said it and grimaced, anticipating Naomi's response.

"Oh my God, Rory! You let him?!"

"He's a fucking vigilante, Naomi; of course I let him!" Rory said. "I didn't want to break his trust or scare him off after everything we've been through!"

"You know what? I'm gonna pretend I don't know this," Naomi said. "Just look at the rest of the lineup and tell me who you think has the closest lips and jawline."

"Fair enough," Rory said. She turned her attention to the remaining photos on Naomi's coffee table. The longer Rory stared at the three photos, the more she couldn't deny it. She lingered over the first two for a moment, really taking in their features to make sure she wasn't mistaken. "Who are these guys, anyway?"

"I had a few different criteria. First, I went off of their age. We know that Hematite started around, what, twelve years ago? But based on what we know, he had to have been a teenager when he started. So, I picked men close to our age. Then, I looked at where they lived and made sure they were in Riverpeak, plus their occupation. If they had a job that keeps them only during the day, then they have the time to live a double life at night. And finally, I tried to see if they'd have a motive. The drug problem on the east side of town isn't exactly small anymore."

Rory then reached for Kane's photo and stared at it. The longer she examined his face, the more she knew that Hematite had to have been Kane. Rory had thought their eyes were identical for a while now, but their lips and jawline were also the same now that she really paid attention.

"Kane insists it's not him, but I just have this gut feeling," Rory said. "I can see it in his eyes, Naomi. These other guys, they look too different. But with Kane … it adds up."

"What are the odds that Stone Breaker has come to the same conclusion?"

Rory frowned. "I don't know. It depends on how much he knows. My guess, though, is that he doesn't, and that's why he's laser-focused on me."

"Can I ask you an honest question without you getting mad at me?"

"Sure."

"I only ask because I know that it's not your style," Naomi cushioned.

"Just spit it out."

"Do you genuinely think that Hematite is Kane? Or are you just hoping that he's Kane after hooking up with a masked vigilante without knowing his name?"

"That's a valid question," Rory said; it was so valid, in fact, that she couldn't even be mad at her friend. "Hematite told me about his history, how it all started as a way for him to protect his sister on the down low since they had a really crappy childhood. Kane is very protective of his sister, Kayla."

"True."

"That and earlier this week, he showed up to watch over my house late at night after I had a mental breakdown at school. Kane comforted me on my lunch break and had to talk me down from it. The same night, I get a text from a random number telling me that somebody told him I needed him there. I've thought for a while Kane has been involved, but now I am positive that he is him."

"Oh, wow," Naomi said, as she ran her hand through her straight black hair. "In that case, then I think you're right."

Their attention was diverted by the sound of the doorbell ringing. They both glanced at the front door and then at each other, unsure of who it could be.

"Brad has a key," Naomi said. "It's not him." She reached for her phone and pulled up an app. "Let's check the cameras."

Rory looked over Naomi's shoulder to check the security camera footage from the front of the house. Her heart felt like it stopped entirely as she watched Stone Breaker, wearing his mask, leaving a note at the door before leaving right away. He didn't stay long enough to leave much of a trace beyond the piece of paper he taped to the front door.

"Let's get it," Rory said. She was trying to be brave: she tried to emulate Hematite, wondered how he'd respond to this, and rolled her shoulders back to handle the situation. It didn't change the fact that her heart was now racing at what felt like a million miles an hour. "Come on."

Rory went to the front door before Naomi could even protest. She glanced around to make sure no one was still standing outside before she grabbed the letter and then closed the door again.

"What's it say? Do we even want to know?"

"Yes," Rory said. She unfolded the paper and scanned the typed letters once before reading the note out loud. "It's an invitation."

"What?"

"He wants to meet me downtown," Rory said. "Here, read it."

Naomi grabbed it as Rory processed the words on the page. She wasn't sure if she felt like screaming or throwing up but refrained from both in an attempt to think rationally. The letter read:

Rory Miller,

I am quite tired of playing cat and mouse with you. I'm sure you are too. If you seek answers, I have some—and I'd be willing to provide them on the condition that we learn to coexist peacefully.

If you will let me do my work, then I will tell you anything you want about Hematite. I have the secret to his immortality and may be able to provide you with your own powers too.

If you agree, come alone to City Hall on Main Street. I'll be waiting for you next Saturday night at eleven.

-SB

"Provide you with your own powers? What the hell is that supposed to mean?" Naomi asked. "Does he seriously think you'll fall for this?"

"It's obviously a trap, yeah," Rory agreed. "We have about a week to think about it."

"Think about it? No. No, no, no."

Rory nodded as she grabbed the letter. "Yeah. I'll fill Hematite in tomorrow. I want to sleep on it first. We could use this to our advantage."

"Rory, you shouldn't put yourself in danger over this," Naomi said. "You've already toed the line enough."

"And I haven't come this far just to leave an opportunity like this behind. We could sneak up on him. Have Hematite in the wings. You ready to film the whole thing with a news crew. I just gotta work out the logistics."

Naomi nodded, but she seemed hesitant. "Yeah, okay, I can see your point. At least stay here tonight. He might still be outside. You can borrow some of my pajamas."

Rory didn't like that Stone Breaker was still following her every move, but she tried to not think about it too much. She didn't have the energy for another mental breakdown. "Thanks, Naomi."

"In the meantime, though, I'm taking a photo of this," she said, referencing the letter. "I think we know what our 'Breaking at Eleven' story will be next weekend."

Rory hoped that a Saturday morning boxing class would ease her worries, but her grip on the steering wheel was so tight that her knuckles were almost white. The drive to her boxing gym wasn't far, but any distance in her paranoid state felt like it was moving in slow motion.

When it came time for drills, Rory hit the punching bag so hard that the rest of her class stopped to look at her. The chain that suspended the bag in the air rattled as the bag swayed back and forth. She became suddenly aware of the thin film of sweat that covered her body and the way her knuckles were trembling beneath her boxing gloves. Her breathing was heavy and labored as she dropped her hands by her sides.

"Miller," her boxing coach called out. "You okay?"

Rory looked at him and then looked around. The class was still looking at her, waiting for an answer.

Rory shook her head, but still said, "I'll be fine." That didn't seem to satisfy her coach, so she added, "It's … complicated."

When the class ended, she reclined her car's seat back as far as she could. She focused on her breathing, a technique that Marissa taught her, as she looked around her and tried to identify different objects that were white or rectangular. It helped a bit, but her heart rate didn't completely become stable, despite her workout ending.

Rory could feel another good cry impending, so she took out her phone to open up the feelings diary app she downloaded. She answered the little prompts about how she was feeling and what categories were impacting her mood, but she froze when the prompt with a text box appeared.

I often do this when I feel out of control…

Rory stared at the prompt for a few moments as she debated her answer. She looked back, trying to identify her behaviors and come to terms with herself. She remembered Kane once told her she didn't have to save everyone. Now she understood what he meant by that.

Rory simply typed in a superhero emoji, but she customized it to look like herself instead of the standard yellow. She then switched over to her phone's contacts to pull up Hematite's burner phone. She wasn't sure how quickly he cycled through them, so she hoped the number was still his when she tapped the call button.

Kane spit his toothpaste out as he went to search for his ringing phone. His cell phone was by his side, but the burner was going off in the other room. He quickly rummaged for his voice modifier before he answered just in time for the last ring.

"Rory? Are you okay?"

"Hi," Rory said breathlessly on the other line.

Kane frowned; she didn't sound like her usual peppy self, but meek. He immediately asked, "What's wrong?"

"That obvious, huh?" Rory released a nervous chuckle, and a sob almost came out with it. "I, uh, got a letter from Stone Breaker. He wants to meet me. I think it's a trap. It's pretty obvious actually, but I think we can work with this."

Kane swallowed his anger. The moment she said those words, he felt like he was suffocating. "He what?"

"Yeah, he clearly didn't learn his lesson from the other day." The more she spoke, the more Kane could hear her confidence return, but it didn't stop his scowl. "He gave me a week from today. I think he's planning something."

Kane unclenched his fist to run his hand through his hair as Rory read him the letter. He subconsciously paced through his apartment. "And what are you thinking?"

"I'm thinking we plan our own next steps in the meantime. He gave me a time and place. Naomi said she's going to get a news crew together so they can have cameras and live coverage."

"Live coverage of what?" No matter how hard he tried, he couldn't unclench his jaw. The news of Stone Breaker sending a letter to Rory and trying to negotiate with her had his head spinning with frustration. On the one hand, he knew Rory was right; they'd be foolish to not take advantage of this opportunity, and the still rationally functioning part of his brain knew that. But on the other end, the idea of Rory using herself as bait nearly drove him over the edge.

"Whatever happens. Hopefully an arrest," she said. "We'd need to get Detective McMahon involved. I think he's the only one not wrapped up in this whole mess."

Kane nodded. "I wouldn't say I trust him, but we could rely on him, sure."

"That's good enough for me," Rory said. "Can I meet up with you? Maybe at your storage unit?"

Kane swallowed. "Meet me there Monday night. We'll discuss it then. That should give us time to gather anything we might need."

Rory grinned. "Perfect."

Once Kane was off the phone with Rory, he released a loud groan to get the aggravation off his chest. He gave himself a moment to collect his thoughts before he decided, rubbing his temples before plopping on his couch and resting his head in his hands. Kane's biggest fear, the very thing he had been trying to prevent for the last eight years, was coming to fruition.

Kane eventually stood to grab his laptop and started looking for maps of the city council offices. He figured there had to be something available, whether it be a blueprint or a fire escape route. As he got to researching, he grabbed his cell phone and called Elijah.

"Hey man, what's up?" Elijah answered.

"Are you busy?" Kane asked. "I need your help."

"I'm at Jefferson's Coffee," he said. Kane heard Elijah say, "Hey, Aaron? Can you make that two? Sorry, sorry, you're the best. No, keep the change." Elijah then said, "I'll be there in a few. What happened?"

"Stone Breaker made an offer to Rory," Kane said. "She wants to use herself as bait. As much as I want to tell her abso-fucking-lutely not, she's ... she's onto something. I have to trust her." He sighed.

"How much time do we have?" Elijah asked. He then said, "Thanks, Aaron! Okay, I'm on my way."

"A week," Kane said. "I'll fill you in more once you get here."

"Have you told her yet?" Elijah asked. "Does she know you're Hematite? Please tell me she knows."

"I almost don't want to answer that question," Kane said.

Elijah laughed, the kind that came from irony rather than amusement. "You haven't told her a damn thing, have you?"

"I think she's onto me. She asked me at school the other day if I was Hematite. I brushed it off, but I'm not sure she's entirely convinced I was being honest with her."

"I know I don't know Rory quite as well as you and Naomi do," Elijah said, "but I do know her well enough to say that I don't think she'd put her life on the line and re-traumatize herself if she didn't think it was you behind the Hematite getup."

Kane furrowed his brows. "What do you mean?"

"C'mon, dude. Brad, Jameson, and I have bets on when you two will finally get together and on who will crack first. I think I speak for all of us when I say we're pretty tired of your whining about pining for her when we all go out together and you get tipsy."

Kane sighed. "Unbelievable. I'm never drinking with you guys again."

Elijah bore a shit-eating grin, and Kane could hear the playfulness in Elijah's tone as he said, "Oh, please. My bet is on you cracking first, so don't disappoint me. I'll owe Brad twenty bucks if I'm wrong," Elijah added. "No pressure or anything, though."

"Yeah, yeah," Kane said to dismiss the conversation. "You almost here?"

"Pulling up to your complex now. Let's see what we can do."

CHAPTER 17

The snow felt soft against Kane's face as he stood outside of Rory's house. He hadn't dressed completely prepared for it but was warm enough. Even if he hadn't, his conviction was burning inside of him enough to make up for it.

Kane stared at Rory's door for a few moments. He wasn't entirely sure what possessed him to act on the bundle of nerves rumbling around his stomach, but he felt like he was going to implode if he continued to hold this in much longer. The light was on downstairs and her car was in the driveway, so he knew she was home as he stood there. Once he knocked, he realized that there was no turning back now. While he waited for her to answer, he ran through how the conversation could go in his head. He wasn't expecting Rory to respond to his protests, but he decided that no matter what happened, this wasn't Hematite speaking. This was simply Kane going into protective big brother-mode like he often did for Kayla.

But Rory wasn't Kayla. As he waited for her to answer, he felt like he was waiting for an eternity. When he exhaled, feeling at war with himself and trying to release some of his internal tension, he could faintly see some of his breath before him.

Meanwhile inside, Rory put her half-cleaned bowl in the sink at the sound of the doorbell. She wasn't expecting anyone, so she approached softly so as to not raise any potential indication about where she was in the house. She stood on her tiptoes to peer through the peephole in the front door and sighed in relief at the sight of Kane.

She opened the door to see him standing there with his hands shoved in his coat pockets. A few snowflakes had peppered across his blonde hair. Rory could practically see the anguish in Kane's face, but she did not know what could bother him this much.

"Hey! What brings you here?"

"I ... Can I talk to you?" Kane asked. Rory had never heard him sound so nervous.

Rory nodded. "Of course, Kay. You always can, you know that. Come on in."

Kane was quick to kick his boots off, not wanting to tread snow through her house. He said nothing at first, still trying to pick the right words to speak so he wouldn't reveal himself. He knew she was suspicious, so he had to be even more careful than usual, but his emotions felt like they were going to physically expunge themselves from his body.

Rory kept her eyes on Kane's face, noticing the way his eyes looked. She sensed she was seeing a side of Kane he rarely showed, if ever at all. His vibrant eyes that normally held such life looked like there was an immense sadness behind them.

"Do you want to sit down?" Rory asked.

Kane didn't even answer. He just stood there, looking as anxious as she'd ever seen him.

"Hey, what's going on?" Rory asked gently. "I can tell something's up. Talk to me." She swallowed, took a step forward to be closer to him, and placed her hand on his shoulder. It forced him to look into her eyes. "I know we haven't been as open with each other as we usually are, and I'm sorry for that. But you can talk to me, Kane. Please do."

Kane just nodded. It was such a slight movement that had she not been focusing on him, she might not have noticed. "Listen, Rory. I ... I've been really worried about you." Although he practiced the conversation a thousand times over in his head, he wasn't sure what was going to come out of his mouth as he continued to speak. "All of this Stone Breaker stuff is getting really out of hand. I know you and Hematite have been working together, and I know he's got your back, but I'm still completely fucking terrified." He closed his eyes for a moment as he said, "I don't know what I would do if I lost you."

"Hey, hey, it'll be alright." Rory took one of his hands in her own to comfort him. "We're so close. Hematite and I have a plan. It'll be fine, Kay."

"And what if it's not fine?" Kane asked. That sadness in his expression was more prevalent than ever, as he opened his eyes again and made eye contact with her. "Then what? You … you could die. And you wouldn't come back like Hematite does. I love you, Rory, and I'm scared, and I can't just sit here and watch you walk into a death trap!"

Kane realized what he said the moment he said it; that hadn't been a part of his plan.

"What?" Rory asked in almost a whisper, feeling like time had completely stopped. She was both confused and enlightened all at once. Rory had more questions than answers, but it all added up and made sense in her head.

"I love you, Rory," Kane repeated. He couldn't take it back, he thought, and there was no use in hiding it anymore. He realized the right moment he was always waiting for would never come. His bright blue eyes never left her dark ones as he said, "I have loved you every single day of my life for the last eight years. It's about damn time I told you."

"I never thought you'd say that," Rory said. She didn't realize it, but she was smiling. When she looked inside herself, she understood in hindsight that she had felt this way all along, no matter how desperately she tried to pretend otherwise for the sake of their friendship. Maybe Naomi had been right about her hoping that he was Hematite for this very reason. Rory felt, for the first time, as if she could finally trust someone in earnest.

Kane let go of Rory's hand so he could kiss her properly, this time as his full self instead of hiding behind a mask. Rory felt completely immersed by Kane the moment his hands cupped her face and his lips were on hers. His calloused fingertips felt rough against her cheeks, but their familiarity brought her comfort. One of Rory's hands fell on Kane's ribs and the other found its way to the back of his head, tangling in his shaggy blonde hair.

Kane moved one of Rory's hands off her face to wrap his arm around her waist and pull her body closer to his. Rory could tell by the way Kane's lips moved with hers and the way his arms held her that he was, in fact, her Hematite.

"I love you so much, Rory," Kane said against her lips between kisses. "I have always loved you."

Now that she knew the truth, both about Kane and herself, Rory knew she could say with confidence, "I love you too, Kane."

Kane wasn't sure how he'd feel if Rory were ever to say those words and now that she had, he was dumbfounded. As he looked at Rory, as if she were the only other person in the world, all of his fears came bubbling back up to the surface.

"It's late," Kane blurted out. He thought about how he needed to go grab his uniform so he could keep patrol over her home to watch over her. "I should let you rest."

"Don't go," Rory pleaded. There was no hesitation in her voice. "You're worried about my safety, right? Then stay the night."

Kane froze. He blinked a few times as he stared at her, unsure of if this was really happening. This surprised him more than it did when he was disguised as Hematite. "Rory..?"

Rory smiled at him and nodded.

They both went in for the second kiss. Kane's lips were soft against Rory's, and she immediately noticed how slow and gentle he was, which was unexpected but pleasant. Rory felt as if Kane were acting like she was made of porcelain as they kissed, but the passion from eight years of repressed feelings remained.

It felt different for him now that he wasn't disguised as Hematite, like he was finally able to truly express himself to her. Finally, he could indulge in his deepest desire. One of Kane's hands softly cupped her chin, and the other ran up her side, from her hip to her ribcage, just beneath her chest. As Kane's hand rested there, the kiss deepened but remained slow and sweet. It was a different type of sweetness than he was used to, but still good.

As Kane deepened the kiss and as his grip on her side tightened, Rory moved the kiss forward by guiding Kane to her bedroom and then slowly lowering him back onto her bed. Kane was surprised that Rory was telling him it was okay to advance. He thought his heart was going to beat out of his chest when Rory brought her lips back to his, only for them to detach to head for his jawline. She kissed and dragged her lips against Kane's skin there and down his neck. Kane's breathing hitched when she kissed a certain spot, so she lingered there for a moment as he unraveled. When he moaned beneath her, he felt his pants grow tighter as arousal grew in his lower abdomen.

Kane enjoyed each sensation as he guided one hand up to Rory's breast, which caused her to tug her shirt off in a quick movement between neck kisses, but he was also terrified. He couldn't remember the last time he had ever been in a serious relationship, nor could he remember the last time he hooked up with someone—with the exception, of course, being his romp with her as Hematite. He wanted things to work with Rory, but his fears still lingered.

But Rory was different from just anyone, and Kane couldn't help but think that as he pulled his own shirt off and continued to touch her.

What Kane didn't know was that Rory was terrified too, despite her willingness, as Kane's fingers fumbled with her bra clasp and released it. As she continued onward, she worried about what this meant for their friendship. Part of her knew, though, that it would all work out, as she glanced at the faint scars littering his torso, including a fresher one along his stomach in the same spot where she had bandaged Hematite.

As one of her hands slipped underneath his briefs, which caused Kane to moan her name and rest his head against the pillow behind him, her anxiety settled in. She feared him rejecting her after all of this if it was just his emotions running high. But all at once, it felt right to her, and it was liberating. The way Kane would breathe and moan beneath her felt like a rush. Both of them felt a sense of intimate trust with the other now that they were vulnerable, literally and metaphorically, and knew each other's secrets.

Kane leaned back up to kiss her breasts, snapping her out of her internal struggle. As Kane worked his way up Rory's body, he lingered at her lips before doing anything else. "The second you want me to stop, I will."

"I don't want you to stop," Rory said.

"You're on birth control, right? I didn't exactly expect this to happen," Kane admitted with a nervous chuckle.

Rory nodded. "Yeah. You're fine, Kay."

Because their first time intimate together happened with him as Hematite, Kane felt like he was experiencing this now for the first time. He wasn't in a rush or worried about hiding anything and thus had every intention of taking his time with Rory. He didn't need to ravage her like a man starved this time but could appreciate the finer details. Before he could take the lead, Rory kissed down his body, pausing at each scar to place her lips there, too. When she reached his erection, Kane's hands rested in her hair and gently tugged.

Rory wants me too, he thought, until it morphed into just her name playing over and over again like a broken record. As she lowered her lips further and further down his shaft, he wasn't sure how much of it was just in his head or was actually verbalized. Before she could make him come, Kane gently urged Rory off him so he could roll her over onto her back. As her curls splayed behind her. He kissed down her body until he found the spot between her legs and worked there, kissing and sucking and making her come undone underneath him, returning the favor from earlier to make her feel how she deserved to feel.

Everything about Kane was so undoubtedly familiar to Rory, not just from years of friendship and flirtatious banter, but from her time with Hematite too. Rory tried to silence her thoughts so she could just enjoy the moment, which wasn't difficult with the way Kane seemed to know her body like he was an expert on the subject.

When he pulled back up and finally entered her, Kane kissed her again with an intensity that matched his earlier confession.

"No more secrets," Rory said against his lips.

Kane just nodded. He knew what she meant, despite the two-fold layers of it. "No more secrets."

As he entered her, that was all the confirmation Rory needed.

———

When Kane woke up on Sunday morning, he felt disoriented. He had no idea where he was until his eyes adjusted to the light peeking through the blinds. A quick glance around and the feeling of a satin pillowcase beneath his head told him he was in Rory's bedroom.

So, it wasn't a dream, after all, he thought.

Rory was still asleep beside him. Both of them were still naked, her comforter providing a decent amount of warmth despite the early morning chill. Rory stirred in her sleep, so Kane pulled her closer to him and kissed the top of her head. His heart thumped against his chest when she nuzzled into his body. Kane never thought that this could be his reality.

Kane also thought it couldn't be after this morning. He didn't want to hurt her, and he wagered that trying to brush this off as a one-time thing would hurt her less than potentially getting killed. Before he could get too lost in his own thoughts, Rory woke up. She stretched a bit like a cat in Kane's arms.

"Good morning, pretty lady," Kane said. His voice was hoarse with sleep.

"Good morning, Kay. I can never tell when you're flirting with me for real anymore."

Kane laughed and kissed her forehead. "For real. All the time. I've been too much of a coward to tell you for real, though."

When Rory leaned her head up to kiss Kane on the lips, any thought he had in his mind about telling Rory that they couldn't be like this disappeared. He simply tightened his grip on her body, enjoying the way she felt in his arms, and ignored his nagging doubts. Threats on her life aside, Kane was convinced that he wasn't enough for her. But she loved him too, and maybe that was enough after all.

"Is there anything else you'd like to tell me?" Rory asked, a hint of mischief in her voice.

Kane swallowed. He trailed his fingers up and down her spine as he held her. "Like what?"

"Kane, I'm not stupid," Rory said. "I know you're Hematite. I'd bet everything on it." She added with a pout, "And besides, no more secrets, remember?"

Kane couldn't fight her, not here and not now. So, he simply nodded, resigning to the fact that she had him figured out. "What makes you so sure?"

"Your eyes. The way you look at me. The way you kissed me was the same." Just when he thought she was done presenting her evidence, she said, "And the scar on your stomach from when you got stabbed that's still fresh sealed the deal. It's only been about, what, two weeks since then? It's barely faded, Kay. You think I'd forget something like that?"

Kane laughed. "Busted." His smile turned into a frown. "Yep, uh, all my nights of drinking and partying were actually nights I was watching over Riverpeak or a nearby city. If you hate me for lying to you for all these years, then I'd understand," Kane said. "You're well within your right to tell me to go fuck myself."

"Kane, don't be ridiculous." To Kane's surprise, she kissed him again. He had never seen her smile so brightly. "I'm so glad it's you. Not just because I was right, but because it's you."

"I've just been trying to protect you," Kane said. "If I were found out or if anyone were to see you with me, that would put a huge target on your back. But you seemed pretty hell-bent on throwing yourself right into the fire anyhow." He gently ran his hand through her hair, letting the loose coils wrap around his index finger. "But know that everything I told you as Hematite … that's all true. And everything I told you last night was true too."

"You're worth the risk to me, Kay. Don't deny yourself what you want because you're scared, okay?"

Kane's heart sunk; Rory suspected, somehow, what he had been thinking earlier. Her words continued to enable his heart to act over his head.

"Stone Breaker is too close for comfort right now. We'll have to keep things kind of on the down low for now, okay? Just in case. Once he's gone, though, fair game."

Rory nodded. "Okay. I can work with that." She shifted her position so her legs straddled Kane's waist. She traced her hands up his well-defined stomach, absorbing the hardness of each muscle and noticing the many scars of varying shapes and sizes across his torso. When her hands reached his chest, she said, "Thank you for saving my life all those years ago, Kane."

He smiled up at her. "I don't need thanks. But I'm glad I was there for you."

"You always have been," Rory said. "Costume or not."

"I think the word you're looking for is uniform."

"It's a fucking costume, Kay. A cool one, but still a costume."

Kane laughed. Rory had never seen him smile more genuinely as he said, "Fair enough." He pulled her body closer to his to kiss her cheek a few times before he kissed her lips. "You have no clue how long I've wanted this," he said in a whisper, almost as if he was too afraid that speaking the words out loud would jinx it.

"I understand why you hid all this from me, but I still wish you had told me sooner. I get why you didn't, though. To be honest, I probably would have done the same thing, so I can't really be mad at you."

"You're too good for me; I don't deserve this."

"Nonsense."

"How long have you suspected it was me?"

"A while now. You'd been acting weird, you know that? But after that night..." Her voice trailed off and Kane knew what she was referencing. "I was really sure of it. I was getting suspicious, and I had really hoped it was you, which probably is what helped me see it through."

She leaned down to press her lips to Kane's. He met her halfway there. As Rory kissed him, she brushed her fingers through his blonde hair to comb it out of his face. Kane smiled into the kiss and his expression remained when they pulled away. Rory surprised him by turning over onto her back and bringing him with her, so now his head was using her chest as a pillow, with her arms wrapped firmly around him.

"What are you doing?"

"Holding you," she said matter-of-factly. "I can tell you need it right now, so just let me do this, okay? You'll feel better."

Kane nodded. "Can't believe I'm falling for a cheesy line like that one."

She had been right, so he wouldn't deny her this. Hearing and feeling the rise and fall of Rory's chest and her slow, steady heartbeat made him feel more at ease. His hands ran up and down her arms before reaching her sides. Kane let her hold him like this for a few minutes before capturing her face with his hands to pull her in for a final, deep kiss.

"We should probably get up, huh?"

"Unfortunately. Come on, I'll make breakfast."

Kane could tell that Rory's mind was racing as he helped her cook. She was so laser-focused on making the perfect eggs that he could tell she was disassociating a bit. Kane placed his hand on her shoulder and kissed her cheek to help snap her out of it.

As they sat down, Kane said, "You probably have a ton of questions."

Rory sat at the spot right beside him. "That's the understatement of the century."

"Ask away, sweetheart." He nudged her elbow with his own. "While I still feel guilty for my sins."

Rory nearly snorted. "Okay, first up." She sipped her coffee. "Were you ever planning on telling me?"

"Not at first. I wrestled with the idea a lot, though. But I decided a few weeks ago that I'd eventually fess up sooner rather than later; you just beat me to it." He shrugged as he took a bite of his toast. "My anxiety attack last night helped push everything along too."

"I'm sorry that I didn't consider how this might affect you too," Rory said with a nervous chuckle. "Talk about tunnel vision."

"You don't have to apologize. Worked out, didn't it?" He winked before he added, "No, for real though, this has been a big deal for you. I get that." He leaned over from his seat next to her to kiss her temple to show that he meant it. "What else you got? Nothing is off limits."

Rory pondered for a moment before she asked, "How did you find out that you can't die?"

Kane took a long sip of coffee before he answered. "The hard way. My parents actually saw it all happen."

"Oh my God. Shit, I probably shouldn't have asked that."

"No, no, it's fine." Kane waved a hand as he took another sip of coffee. "I told you nothing was off limits. Hm, let's see. I think I was fourteen, fifteen maybe? That's when I started doing all of this, but I didn't know about the whole 'can't be murdered' thing yet. I tried to take on this guy who was selling drugs; my parents just made the stuff from time to time for the drug ring, and this was their usual dealer. I got my shit rocked, and he stabbed me right in the side."

Kane lifted his shirt up a bit to point to the spot between his ribs. The scar had faded enough over the years that the naked eye could not see it, but now that she knew to look for it, Rory could spot it clearly.

Kane continued, "I was so scared. Never been more scared in my whole life. My parents didn't wanna get busted, and I didn't want Kayla to see anything, since she was still pretty little. So, I ended up just crawling to the back corner of their shed, thinking about all my life choices. No one called for help." Kane frowned at the memory and his lips made a light smacking sound. "I blacked out after bleeding out. Then I was really confused when I woke up about fifteen minutes later. My parents thought it was just a really awful trip and didn't even realize what happened." Kane lightly scoffed. "They left me on my own to figure it out with my doctor. I took myself, and they weren't really any help either, so that's why I go to Dr. Potter now. He's a weird little fucker who probably orders his groceries from Omega Mart, but he gets the job done, at least, and he doesn't ask me any questions that he knows I won't want to answer."

"Jesus, Kane. I'm so sorry."

"I gotta admit, as nervous as I was about telling the truth, it's nice to not feel so alone with it anymore," he said. "It was a lot for one person to carry on top of everything else, ya know?"

"I can only imagine." Rory grabbed his hand. "And don't worry; I'm not mad. Really."

Kane grinned as he chewed his food. "I really thought you were gonna be beyond pissed. Thanks for understanding."

"That's what I'm here for, isn't it? Wait, one more question. So, how are you changing your voice?" Rory asked. "When you're in your costume, that is."

"Oh, easy. Elijah built some tech into a mask for me. It took us a few tries to get it right, but it's pretty cool. It goes under my balaclava and just has a switch. Only thing is that it has a tiny battery so I gotta recharge it every day."

Kane hid it well in the way he spoke, but he was just as terrified now as he was the first time he died. His fear this morning had been that Rory might consider leaving him for knowing the truth, but that intrusive thought had long since passed; her nonchalance simultaneously did and did not shock him. But he knew Stone Breaker could seriously hurt her and succeed at using her as bait. If their plan went wrong, then it could be all over in a flash. His worst fears were unfolding in front of his eyes, and he felt powerless to stop it, but he knew that this could be their only chance to get Stone Breaker right where they wanted him.

He went to express these fears, but he stopped himself because he knew that now was not the time. Instead, he simplified his thoughts and said, "I'm worried about you, Rory."

"Don't be fooled. I'm freaking out too," Rory said. "I'm trying to not think of what could happen if things go wrong. But I trust you, and I trust Naomi."

"Let's get everyone together today. You can call Naomi. I'll call Elijah. He, uh, he's been helping me for a while now."

"Wait, really?"

"When I first started, I offered him protection for secrecy and tech work. He knows now, though," Kane explained. "I filled him in on the letter last night. Let's have everyone meet at the storage unit this morning."

Rory nodded. "Deal."

CHAPTER 18

As Rory brewed another pot of coffee downstairs, still on a high from the bliss of the night prior, she set her phone on the counter and put it on speaker. As she waited for Naomi to answer, she grabbed two mugs and hummed to herself. She glanced out the window, noticing that the sky was clear for the day. She welcomed the reprieve from the snow and the way the sun streamed through the window.

"Good morning," Naomi said. "What's up?"

"I have…" Rory pondered the right word, "news. I have a lot of news."

"What kind of news?" Naomi asked. "Hematite news?"

"Yeah. Hematite is here now. Like, right now. He actually has been since last night."

"Did you…?" Naomi sighed. "Again?"

"I mean, yes, but it's not like you're thinking. Just … just hear me out. It's Kane. Kane is Hematite. He told me this morning."

"Rory, Rory, slow down," Naomi said. "What the hell happened?"

"Kane came over last night. He's buggin' out, Naomi. I've never seen Kane so scared in my life. Long story short, he owned up to it when I called him on it. I think it would have been kind of hard to not, given the circumstances, though."

"About damn time," Naomi said. "Well, I'm glad we narrowed that down. So, what's next? Are we still going through with the plan?"

"Even better. This is my other news. Are you free a little later this morning?"

"Yeah, I'm grabbing dinner with Brad and his family tonight, but otherwise, I don't have anything going on."

"Good. Meet me at the storage facility at eleven o'clock. Don't ask questions. Don't bring anyone. Just show up."

"Deal," Naomi said. "I'll see you there. I'm assuming you're bringing Kane?"

"That's correct. We'll get more into it there, okay?"

———

Meanwhile, Kane was sitting on the edge of Rory's bed, still in nothing but his briefs and a long-sleeved T-shirt. He was grateful that Rory let him borrow her toothbrush so he didn't have to feel dirty in his clothes from the night before.

Elijah was quick to answer. "Hey, dude. You're up awfully early for a weekend."

"Yeah, yeah," Kane said. "Sorry if I'm interrupting your family's Shabbat thing."

"You're fine. I could step away. My mom keeps it pretty low-key since it's just us. What's going on?"

"For starters, Rory knows. Don't panic. I told her. I, uh … I told her everything."

"Wait. Everything as in everything?" Elijah laughed. "I'm proud of you, man. What happened?"

"To spare you the gory details, Brad owes you twenty bucks."

"Sweet. I take it that's not all you called to tell me, though."

"You're as sharp as ever. Listen, Rory and I have a plan. Naomi's involved too. We're about to let her in. She's willing to keep helping us. Are you able to meet me at the storage unit in about two hours?"

"Yeah, done deal. I should be out of here by then."

"You sure I'm not interrupting Shabbat?"

"Nah. I think God'll give me a free pass for this. I'll see you later."

———

As Rory hung up her phone call, Kane announced his presence by wrapping his arms around her waist from behind. He rested his chin on her shoulder.

"Is this okay?" Kane asked, indicating this display of affection.

Rory nodded. "More than okay."

Kane nuzzled his face into her neck before he planted a kiss there. "Good, 'cause I'm not going anywhere."

"I know you're not. But I wouldn't have it any other way."

"I'm kicking myself for not saying anything sooner."

"We've got all the time in the world, Kay," Rory said.

Kane was silent in response. He just nodded and kissed her jaw, feeling unable to get enough of her and like he had to make up for the lost time. He gave himself a moment to soak in the moment before he broke the silence. "Thanks for the coffee." He grabbed his cup. "Naomi's in?"

"She'll be there. Elijah too?"

Kane nodded as he took a sip. He smiled; the coffee was just the way he liked it, a testament to how well she knew him.

"Good. I know Mark is physically weak, but we'll need all the help we can get. Persistent little roach."

"You're really sure it's him, huh?" Kane said. "I think you guys are right, but I never like to be too sure of anything right out the gate."

"We're positive," Rory said. "Though I think there's more than just him waiting behind the curtain."

"One asshole at a time."

Rory brought Kane back to his place before they went to the storage unit so he could get some clean clothes and freshen up. Kane led Rory into his bedroom as he took a quick shower. He swung his closet door open and said, "In case you didn't believe me, feel free to take a look."

Rory did just that as he bathed. The fish-mouthed hoodie from the night she found him on the east side of town was the first thing she saw hanging up. Behind it was a row of black and navy long-sleeved shirts and a few pairs of black tactical utility joggers, all more or less the same pair.

When Kane got out of the shower, he saw Rory still standing in front of the closet. He said nothing at first, wanting to observe her in the trance she seemed to be in. She found the hanger where his cowl was lazily hanging, and her fingers were running slowly over the fabric.

"Don't you still have that piece I ripped off for you all those years ago?" Kane asked.

Rory was a bit startled when he broke the silence; she was so focused that she hadn't even noticed the water in the shower stopped running. "Yeah, I do. I'd never dare get rid of it."

"I remember that night like it was yesterday," Kane said. "Brad told me that Naomi mentioned some guy was creeping you out, so I started keeping a closer eye on you. I was surprised to see you still holding onto that scrap piece when I went to your dorm after changing faster than I ever had in my life."

Rory laughed at the mental image. "This is more than I ever would have imagined."

"I thought about telling you for a long time." Kane stood beside her to grab some clothes. Their shoulders touched as he put on his pants and Rory could smell the subtle sweetness of his body wash. "About this. About how much I liked you. But I kept waiting for the right time. I had every intention of some romantic gesture or something for when I'd tell you I liked you, and I was hoping I could tell you about this just naturally in conversation without springing it on you. But those perfect moments never seemed to come up."

"I both never would have guessed it was you, but always hoped it would be," Rory said. "When Naomi and I started first looking into it, I wasn't sure if I could even trust myself when I thought it could be you."

Kane smiled and kissed her cheek before he put a clean shirt on. "I'm glad I didn't disappoint."

Rory laughed. "You could never."

"Even after all the lying?"

Rory nodded. She could sense that this was the first time Kane truly showed his feelings for her without hiding behind a joke. "I told you, I get it. Kay, I am not walking away from this. I'm not walking away from you."

When Kane held her face with both of his hands and kissed her in response, Rory could tell he put every bit of himself into it. Kane's emotions were still running high from the night before and if he had to be completely honest with himself, he was more frightened than he could vocalize. So instead, he opted to just enjoy the way Rory's lips felt on his own while everything still felt so uncertain.

When they reached the storage unit at 10:45 in the morning, Naomi was already there and still sitting in her car. They parked alongside her, and she got out of the car once they did. They were just waiting on Elijah to break away from his mother's Shabbat brunch to join them.

"I can't believe it," Naomi said. "I won't get too into it until we're in a more private spot, but holy shit, Kane."

Kane made a jazz hands motion. "Surprise!"

It wasn't much longer until Elijah arrived. Once the four of them were together, Kane walked them to the storage unit where he took Rory when she first found him nearly two months ago now. He opened the door with ease and, with an extended arm, let his friends go in first before he closed the door behind them. The storage unit was exactly how Rory remembered it, but Naomi took a moment to look around.

"You've been working out of this?" Naomi asked. Kane nodded. Naomi looked at Elijah. "Have you been here or am I the only new one?"

"I have, but it's been a while," Elijah said. "We usually work out of my office these days."

"Wait, your office? Like, your home office? Does Brad know?" Naomi asked.

"No. You know how heavy of a sleeper he is. So, what's the plan?"

"Right now, it's for me to take Stone Breaker's bait," Rory said. "I figured Kane can follow me in secret, and Naomi can be ready to break the story so that way no one can pay their way out of it."

"Exclusive eyewitness reports," Naomi said with a wink. "No one will ever know it's you, Kane."

"Just the way I like it."

"Why don't we hook you up with a tracker, Rory?" Elijah suggested. "I've got something we can use that gets real specific. Think GPS but on steroids. We'll know exactly where you are in the building. You can just keep it in your pocket so it's inconspicuous."

"I like that idea," Kane said. "That'll make me feel better if we can keep tabs on her in case anything goes wrong." He sat in the folding chair and opened the laptop. "Now all that's left is to figure out how I'm going to get into the building. Can't exactly waltz right in the front door."

"If we're tracking Rory, you can stay outside until we know where she is. Then, you can enter from the closest entrance. Might need to break a window."

Kane grinned at Elijah. "I'm not above property damage."

"What about security cameras?" Rory asked.

"I can jam them," Elijah said. "Easy peasy."

"Whoa, whoa, let's slow down for a second," Naomi interrupted. "This is great and believe me, I am all for this. But I need something from Tom before we start breaking and entering. I don't know if it's possible, but it might be worth a shot to try before Rory gets in there."

"What do you need?" Elijah asked.

"I've been trying to find out who his connection to the drug ring is. I looked into his campaign donors and who is funding his campaign, but nothing struck me as out of the ordinary. Lots of small business owners. I think someone is covering something up, but I don't know who. Elijah, how far are you willing to go?"

"I think I've already broken a few laws and gotten away with it. It's whatever. Are you thinking what I'm thinking?"

"If we could get into Tom's computer, it might uncover this whole thing," Naomi said. "I just don't know how locked down a city government server is going to be. It might be a lot of work for you."

"A lot of work? Please, Naomi. That's kindergarten shit. You'd be surprised at how easy it is to get into government-run servers. I swear, it's like they haven't updated a thing since the nineties. I just need you to do something for me to make this work. You should be able to do this yourself, even during the day."

"What's that?"

"There are ways to figure out passwords or what someone is typing just from their keyboard strokes," Elijah said. "If you can plant something in there to get me a steady audio stream, I could get all the info we need to get in there. I'm sure they have a VPN in case any of the employees have to work from home or while traveling."

"Brilliant!" Naomi said. "I'm sure I can come up with a reason I need some quotes for an interview. I can leave something in there for you."

"I have some audio bugs. They're wireless and should do the trick. Next time you swing by to see Brad, I'll get it to you when he's in the bathroom or something."

They were all interrupted by Kane's burner phone ringing. "Hold on guys," Kane said. "I'm sorry. I gotta take this." He answered with a brief hello.

"Mr. Kelly," Dr. Potter greeted. "Are you alone, my friend?"

Kane rolled his eyes; he'd hardly consider Dr. Potter a friend. "No, but I'm with people I trust. Is that good enough?"

Rory, Elijah, and Naomi all looked at each other, hoping to understand. All they found was mirrored confusion on each other's faces.

Dr. Potter said, "Yes, yes, that'll do. I have some results from the sample you brought me. Now, you know I don't do results for things like this over the phone, but I'm available throughout the day if you'd like to swing by. No one else is due to come in except for your friend Shawn Jameson, though I've been calling him for the last three days now."

"Yeah, he beats to his own drum, that's for sure."

"You're more than welcome to bring the people you trust," Dr. Potter said. "I don't care if you come alone or not."

"Solid. Thanks. I'll be there soon." Kane hung up and then looked at his friends. "That was my doctor. I don't know if he's actually a doctor, but that's a whole other story. He runs that lab on the west side of town. I have to head over there. You don't have to come if you don't want to, but it's okay if you do."

"I'm going," Rory said with no hesitation.

"Me too," Elijah said.

"We're here to help, Kane," Naomi said. "You don't have to do this alone anymore."

"Thanks, guys. I'll explain on the way."

"Should we take one car?" Rory asked. "I'll drive."

"Good idea," Kane agreed.

"So, what's going on?" Naomi asked.

"I broke into my parents' shed a few weeks ago," Kane admitted, "when Kayla was in town. I'm assuming all of you know what I mean by that. Anyway, I grabbed a sample to see if we can find out what the hell it is. My hopes aren't really high because their shed nearly caught on fire after they passed out from the fumes, but I figured it was worth a shot."

Kane spent the car ride filling them in on what they may need to know going into their fight with Stone Breaker. As nervous as he was, part of him felt like a weight was lifted now that the burden wasn't only his to bear. He hated putting that onto others, but he tried to allow himself to enjoy the selfishness of it all.

As they made their way down the winding road to Potter Laboratories, Elijah said, "You know, I've always been curious about what was in here. Kinda looks like Convergence Station."

"Potter's morally questionable at best, but ultimately harmless," Kane said. The moose wasn't there, but a few marmots made an appearance now that the temperatures were slowly rising. "I guess I can't judge."

After they entered the building, Kane led his friends down the familiar stretch of hallway before they reached the lobby, where Dr. Potter was waiting in his white coat.

"Well, Mr. Kelly, I have to admit," Dr. Potter said, "it's a relief to see you have friends. I was getting a tad concerned about your lonely soul."

"Whatever. What do you have for me?"

"Come, I'll show you." Dr. Potter began to walk down a corridor without waiting for them. "Now who do we have here? Miss Sato, I recognize you from Channel 10. I'm delighted to see you without any cameras. And you must be Miss Miller from that Stone Breaker video. Who else do we have?"

"I'm Elijah. I'm the IT support."

"Ah, splendid. A pleasure, Elijah. Well, I'll start with the bad news, per se," Dr. Potter said once they reached one of the testing rooms. The blinding white fluorescent lights and spotless stainless steel were cold and intimidating, giving everyone a slight sense of unease. Rows of test tubes, burners, and various tools that Rory only recognized from the chemistry classrooms at the school lined the walls. "The drug was unfortunately rather burnt off and thus not entirely conclusive, but I did want to test one thing before we call this a wash. The good news is I detected traces of methamphetamines, and I think it may still give us some answers."

"What are we testing?"

"If this reacts to your cells. I want to see what happens. Can you spit in this tube for me? Halfway should suffice."

Kane glanced at his friends as he took the vial. "Sorry, you guys. This might be gross."

Once Dr. Potter had the saliva, he put it in a Petri dish and then added a drop of the liquid that Kane brought. Dr. Potter watched the substances through a microscope and smiled in wonder.

"Well, Mr. Kelly, we have at least one answer. This is definitely the drug that was used to give you your powers in utero. I'd be interested in testing Mr. Jameson's as well."

"Wait, Jameson?" Elijah piped up. "Like, Shawn Jameson?"

"Ah, forgive me," Dr. Potter said with a light chuckle. "Well, I suppose now they know."

"Shawn's been helping me," Kane briefly explained. He looked at Rory and added, "Brick Beast. That's the secret identity he gave himself."

"I honestly should have guessed that it was Jameson with a name like that," Rory replied.

"Your results did look very similar, by the way," Dr. Potter said. "I won't say much else for Mr. Jameson's privacy, but I figured you'd want to know after bringing him here."

"Thanks," Kane said. "Was this all?"

"It was for now. Thank you for coming out, Mr. Kelly and friends," Dr. Potter said. "I'll walk you out."

When they got back in the car, Elijah asked, "Should we get Jameson involved? I kinda hate the guy, but super strength could work to our benefit."

"No," Kane said. "I don't want this to be a huge production."

"Fair enough. Should we at least have him on speed dial?"

"We won't need it, but if it'll make you feel better, sure," Kane settled on. "He's not the most reliable. When he's there, he's often a great help. But it's always a 50/50 shot on if he feels like showing up, and another 50/50 shot on if he'll help because he genuinely cares or because he wants to make a name for himself."

"That sounds like Jameson, yeah," Elijah said.

Rory dropped Naomi and Elijah off at the storage unit before she drove Kane back home. When she pulled up to Kane's apartment, they glanced over at one another. Kane reached for Rory's face and caressed her jaw in his hand. "How are you feeling about all of this?"

"A little scared, but I trust you," she said. "I think this will work."

Kane nodded. "I'm glad at least one of us is hopeful."

"I have to be. I think I'd go insane otherwise. Besides, it's for the greater good."

"Not if it means you get hurt. But I'm proud of you."

Rory smiled. She moved her hand to the back of Kane's neck and brought their faces together, so their foreheads touched. "I couldn't have done this without you."

"Nah." Kane smirked. "I know you've always had this in you. You'd be just fine without me." He ran his thumb slowly along her jaw as he pressed his lips to hers. The feeling sent shockwaves down his spine, and he hoped Rory felt the same as he did. "Just please don't do anything rash."

She kissed Kane's nose. "I won't do anything too stupid without you. Don't worry."

"Good."

CHAPTER 19

Rory took a deep breath as she looked up at Riverpeak City Hall on Main Street, the moon shining brightly above it, as if to guide her way. She glanced at her watch, seeing that there were only two minutes until eleven o'clock. She swallowed, unsure whether Stone Breaker would be true to his word and actually show up. As she waited, she hugged her coat closer to herself to generate even a bit more warmth. Even though spring would be there soon, the evening still brought quite the chill. She tried to avoid the voice in her head rattling off everything that might go wrong.

"Rory Miller."

Rory looked up and saw Stone Breaker standing at the top of the city hall steps. He was wearing his 3D-printed mask, but Rory wondered why he even bothered anymore. She decided to not say anything about his identity, wanting to save that for Naomi or Kane in case they needed it.

"Did you think I wouldn't come?" Rory asked as she stepped forward, feeling a fire in her chest that she tried to hide by acting cool and casual. She made her way up the steps. Stone Breaker flinched as she did, clearly on his guard. He crossed his arms over his chest to stabilize himself and hide his fear. Rory added, "You think I don't want to just end this crap?"

"I wasn't sure if you would," Stone Breaker said. Now that Rory was close to him, she could see the wire of the small microphone. It ran up his shirt and was clipped to the collar; Rory realized that it must be connected to whatever device changed his voice. "Follow me."

Rory just nodded as she followed Stone Breaker. A chill shot up her spine, and she checked over her shoulder every few steps, not wanting to lose her way or be off guard. This was undoubtedly a trap, and she wasn't totally sure what she was walking into. She cracked her knuckles out of nervous habit as they walked out, and the popping noise from them echoed off of the dark, empty city council hallways. Riverpeak City Hall was small, about a quarter of the size of Denver's, so it made it easy for Rory to see where they'd be going.

As they reached the office labeled with Tom Stevens' name, Stone Breaker held the door open for Rory. "After you."

Rory knew he would make his move now, but she continued to play the part of the unsuspecting victim. The minute Stone Breaker was behind her, she felt him grabbing her hands and tying a rope around her wrists. She shuffled a bit to feign a struggle but had fully expected this to happen.

"I'm surprised you came alone. I doubted you'd have the courage to," Stone Breaker said, "but it's making this all too easy for me." Once her hands were tied, he grabbed her by her shoulders, spun her around, and pushed her backward. Rory stumbled a bit but regained her footing before she could fall; she thanked her boxing classes for that. She glanced behind her and saw that there was a chair there, which was likely where he had been aiming.

"Is there a reason for this?" Rory asked, referencing the ropes around her wrists. "I really don't think this is necessary."

"After what you did to Shatterstone? Oh, it's absolutely necessary," Stone Breaker said. He reached into his pocket and pulled out a handgun. He didn't point it at Rory but simply made her aware of its existence. "Your cooperation is appreciated. Can you sit down for me, Rory?"

It was clear to Rory, even through the mask, that Stone Breaker was serious now. She could feel her heart rate speed up at the sight of the gun, but not wanting to end the operation before it had even started, she took a seat in the chair.

"Thank you."

"Can I ask why you wanted me here if it wasn't for negotiations?"

"You're far too naïve. Haven't you ever seen a superhero movie?" Stone Breaker asked, as he kneeled down by her feet. He pocketed his gun so he could grab the rope with both hands, tying her by her ankles to the legs of the chair. "The superhero always comes and saves the day. I figured you'd have him tailing you right about now. But it looks like you never learn, do you?"

Rory frowned; she knew what he was referencing. "Forgive me for being an optimist, I guess."

"Your optimism has made this easier than I expected," Stone Breaker said, as he grabbed a ring light and shifted it. The sudden addition of a bright light nearly blinded Rory for a moment, the fluo-rescence of it giving her an instant headache.

"Don't I get to ask you some questions? Wasn't that part of the deal?" Rory asked. "You promised me answers."

"Sure. I suppose I could entertain you while I make sure we have the perfect shot," Stone Breaker said. "What's your first question?"

"You said you know why Hematite can't die. Is that true?" Rory already knew the answer to this question after having gone to Potter Laboratories with Kane, but Stone Breaker didn't know that. She hoped he could give some additional context.

"It's that drug that's popular on the east side of town," Stone Breaker said. "I don't know the exact compounds of it, but it affects women who are pregnant. Gives their babies powers. We're not exactly sure why."

"So why try to cover that up and protect that? Wouldn't that put politicians and leaders in compromising positions if someone like Hematite used their powers for bad?"

"That's where you're playing checkers and we're playing chess," Stone Breaker said. Rory noticed his use of "we" as he spoke. "We're already seeing how we can replicate it in living people. Give the people in power even more power, if you know what I'm saying. We're already ahead of the curve."

Rory swallowed at this revelation. "So have you taken it, then?"

Stone Breaker paused; Rory took that as a no.

"You haven't, have you? They won't give it to you."

"You get one last question before I turn the camera on."

"Sure. Why are you doing this?"

"Do you know what it's like to be bullied, Miss Miller? To feel alone?" Stone Breaker said. He paced the office.

Rory tried not to laugh. "Come on, dude. Look at me and take a wild guess."

Stone Breaker seemed to ignore her, which didn't surprise her. "Everyone around me has always been popular. Influential. Powerful. I go to the news thinking I can finally have my voice heard, and what do you know? Nothing. No one cared. It was always Hematite this, Hematite that."

Rory rolled her eyes when his back was turned.

"I'm still surprised Hematite isn't with you now," he said.

"Well, no one else was doing anything about you," Rory said. "And even Hematite can't do everything by himself."

"This is it for you, Miss Miller," Stone Breaker said. He reached into her jacket pocket, pulled out the tracker, and stepped on it. The crushing noise rang loudly in Rory's ears. "Yeah, I noticed this. This will all get paid off. No one will be any the wiser about what happened to you by the time we're finished."

Rory forced herself to stop for a moment and gather her thoughts. She recognized her mind was going back into dark places and internally thanked Marissa for all the help she had received so far.

Rory wasn't safe now. She knew that her grounding exercises wouldn't work here, but she'd be damned if she didn't try to save herself, regardless. She remembered how Marissa told her it wasn't her fault and how she was stronger than she thought.

She tapped into her fight-or-flight, trying to spin some sort of silver lining for herself. Rory hoped she would one day walk away completely healed but realized that she likely would live with this forever in some way, so she might as well try to make the best of it.

Rory said, "I don't let people treat me like this anymore." She wasn't sure where her courage came from, but she trusted Kane would still pull through despite the tracker being broken. She took a moment to take in her surroundings and saw the bug that Naomi had planted earlier in the week. It was still stuck on the bottom of the desk. She grinned.

"And what's that supposed to mean?" Stone Breaker asked.

"Come closer and find out," Rory taunted.

"Oh, no. I like you right where you are, and I like me right where I am," Stone Breaker said. "I'm sure Hematite will see that your little tracker is broken and come running to the rescue. Then I'll have him right where I want him too."

Rory just laughed. "You never learn, do you?"

Rory couldn't see it beneath Stone Breaker's mask, but his brows furrowed. He knew she was now using his own words against him. "What do you mean by that?"

"I swear to God, you are the densest person I've ever met," Rory said. "You think you can get away with all this just because Daddy is rich, and you feel entitled to your power? Do you think you're actually going to win here? Have you learned anything? Haven't you ever seen a superhero movie?"

Stone Breaker's frown deepened. "What the hell are you talking about?"

Rory felt a sense of accomplishment from his response. He was clearly getting riled up now, and she hoped it would buy both her and Kane some time. "You're just a scared, little boy. That's why you've got me tied up, isn't it?"

"Watch it or I'll tape your mouth shut," Stone Breaker barked.

"Do you even realize how bad of a look this is for you? White dude in a mask ties up female Riverpeak teacher as a hostage in a government building?"

"You're awfully sure you'll come out of here ahead. Now watch it or else."

Rory grinned again, but wider this time. "Or else what?"

Stone Breaker stopped to think instead of answering her right away. He took a step back and paced again. He realized she was right: if anyone found her like this, it would immediately be a public relations nightmare for him and his father. "Fuck!" he said it beneath his breath, but his voice-changer made it loud enough for Rory to hear.

The sound of shattering glass was enough to distract Stone Breaker. Both he and Rory looked toward the source of the noise and saw Hematite leap into the office from the now-open window.

"Hope I'm not late to the party," Hematite said.

"You think I didn't think this would happen?" Stone Breaker laughed and pulled the gun back out from his pocket and pointed it at Hematite's chest. "I came prepared for you this time."

But Hematite was not phased. He made quick work of disarming Stone Breaker; *to call it a fight would hardly be accurate*, Rory thought.

"Cute." Hematite moved to where Rory was sitting and, using a pocketknife, cut the rope holding her wrists together. As he cut the ropes holding her ankles to the chair, he handed her the gun. "You know how to use this?"

Rory nodded. "I know enough." She was reminded of the last time he turned over a gun to her all those years ago when he first rescued her.

"Then I'll let you hold on to this." He made eye contact with Rory to ensure she was okay before he turned to Stone Breaker. "That shit won't work on me, Stevens. You should know that by now."

"You know my name," Stone Breaker said softly.

"Yeah, I do. And I warned you, didn't I? You can't just kill me so easily, and you should have just left Rory Miller out of this. Remember?"

"How long have you known?" It was clear in Stone Breaker's voice, based on the way it shook, that he was panicking.

"A while now. You were pretty easy to figure out. You left all sorts of hints in your articles and then some extra digging from some friends of mine just confirmed the whole thing."

Stone Breaker reached behind him for something on his father's desk. He grabbed the letter opener and unsheathed it, revealing the sharp tip, then quickly threw it at Hematite. He dodged just in time, the opener just missing his arm and instead wedging itself into the wall. Stone Breaker then quickly charged at Hematite, pushing him into the wall with his elbow up against his chest.

"Why won't you die?" Stone Breaker shouted in his face, despite knowing the answer. His frustration had effectively taken over, and Rory's earlier goading hadn't helped his mental state.

Hematite shrugged. "I guess it's just not my time."

Hematite laughed at his own joke as he elbowed Stone Breaker to push him off, but then grabbed Stone Breaker's shirt to gain control. Stone Breaker nearly fell as Hematite ripped the 3D-printed mask off of his face. It made a hollow sound as it slid across the floor before eventually joining the pile of broken glass.

Right when Mark stood up, Hematite front-kicked him in the sternum. Mark flew back into the door before falling down to the ground, and Hematite opened the door to shove Mark down the hallway. As he did, he turned to face Rory.

"Get the hell out of here! I'll take it from here!"

Rory glanced at the broken window as Hematite resumed his fist-fight with Mark. With Rory getting to safety, Hematite could fight dirty without worrying as much about Rory getting hurt. Hematite swung again at Mark, who continued to stumble backward from the hit.

Mark knew if he were to stand a chance, he needed to think and to think quickly. As he took another blow from Hematite, he glanced around the dark hallway to see where he could get the upper hand. He recognized the secretary's office and quickly tried the door handle. It was locked. Mark cursed under his breath and quickly kicked the door down. The wood shattered beneath his foot as he kicked it a few more times. Once Hematite was closer to him, he weaseled his way through the hole.

"Where the hell do you think you're going?" Hematite followed Mark into the room and once he was inside, Mark threw a paperweight at the light above. Part of the cheap panel came crashing down, but Hematite moved out of the way just in time to avoid it. He looked at Mark and saw him rummaging for something in a drawer in the secretary's desk.

Mark pocketed something and then grabbed a stapler. He chucked that at Hematite, who held his arm up to block it but still got whacked in the head. Hematite picked it back up and tossed it aside, wanting it out of the way as he continued to approach Mark. He ran toward Mark, ready to punch him again, but Mark grabbed the punch and pulled Hematite toward him. He placed his arm down on a paper cutter, right by the large blade. Had Mark been stronger, it may have worked, but Hematite kicked him off and moved his arm away before Mark could use it.

The two of them exchanged blows as Hematite tried to lure Mark outside. If Naomi was set up, he wanted everyone to see Stone Breaker for who he really was. As they made their way back down the hallway, Hematite kicked Mark in the stomach. Mark reeled back into the wall hard enough to break the glass on where the fire extinguisher was resting. Mark quickly grabbed it, hoping to have a one-up, and threw the tank at Hematite. Kane caught it and tossed it aside; Mark used the distraction to his advantage by approaching Hematite. He swung a punch before Hematite grabbed him, now taking the lead. Hematite regained control for a moment with a few hits, but Mark was picking up on his movements. Hematite glanced behind him, seeing that they were still heading in the general direction that he wanted them to go toward the entrance. Mark kicked Hematite, which brought him up against the wall at the end of the hallway.

Before Hematite could make another move, Mark charged at him. He grabbed the item out of his pocket and held the letter opener he grabbed from the secretary's desk up to Hematite's neck. He had placed it beneath the thick layers of fabric. The blade felt cool against Hematite's skin.

"Got you, you fucking asshole." Mark used his other arm to keep Hematite in place.

Hematite was backed into a corner and knew if Mark bested him, he'd come back in a few minutes. He didn't care about dying, even if a dull blade to the throat would sting like hell. But he worried about Rory and Naomi. He knew Naomi was waiting outside with the news van, and he wasn't sure how far out Rory made it.

"Go ahead." Hematite suspected Mark wouldn't actually slit his throat, which was the only reason he didn't fear calling him on his bluff. "I can't die, anyway. You already know that."

"Unfortunately, the drugs are the only thing keeping me from completely killing you," Mark said, as he pressed the letter opener deeper into Kane's neck. Kane could feel his pulse rapidly against the spot where the blade applied pressure. "I wonder what'll happen if I can bring you to the rest of them, though."

"To who?"

"My father knows all about it," Mark said, as he made eye contact with Hematite. "Why do you think no one in this town ever gets sober? The real guys in charge make sure of that with their wallets. But you'd never guess who runs the show. Just give up."

Before Hematite could respond, Mark sharply gasped. Mark slowly looked down to his right side and saw a large shard of glass sticking out of the side of his abdomen. Hematite glanced at the piece of glass, wondering where it came from. The blood was already quickly soaking Mark's shirt, but the shard sticking there was blocking it from completely releasing.

Mark stumbled backward. It was just enough to give Hematite a chance to grab his billy club and whack Mark down, causing him to fall unconscious. Hematite took a second to collect his breath and whacked Mark one last time with the club to be sure that he was down.

Hematite looked up to see Rory standing before him. Rory's breathing was labored, and a thin sheen of sweat coated her face, likely from nerves. Her hand had a strip of blood cutting across it from how tightly she gripped the glass shard before plunging it into Mark's side. There were too many thoughts swirling in her brain for her to vocalize. Despite her red palm's sharp pains, she felt more in control than she had in a long time. Even though Stone Breaker had not been her battle to fight, she still felt a vindication that she hadn't known she was longing for over the last eight years.

Hematite said nothing as he quickly took the few steps needed to embrace her. As he did, he buried his face in her hair, holding on to her tightly. "I thought I told you to get out of here," he said.

Rory smirked. Her lips felt dry, and she felt them crack a bit as she smiled at him. "And just leave you here to fend for yourself? Absolutely not."

Kane kissed the top of her head. Rory wasn't sure he'd ever let her go.

"Do you still have the gun? Please tell me you still have the gun."

"I do. Should we give it to McMahon? I already called him for you. I had his business card on me and used the office phone. He should be here any minute now."

"You did the right thing. Bring it to the station with you later, okay? Now let's get the hell out of here."

Rory nodded. "Okay. But we should grab something from Stevens' office first. Elijah might need it and even if he doesn't, I don't think we'll want it there when the cops show up. I spotted it when I was waiting for you in there."

They power-walked back to where Rory had been held. Rory grabbed the bug that was beneath Tom's desk, ripped it off, and pocketed it where her tracker once was. "Elijah should have everything he needs, by the way."

"Perfect. You ready to go?"

Rory nodded. "Yeah, come on."

The two of them snuck out the window that Hematite broke into so they could dodge any reporters waiting out in the building's front. As they moved through the town to walk back to Rory's car and determined the coast was clear, she called Naomi.

"Are you okay?" Naomi immediately asked. "I hear police sirens. They've gotta be close. I think they're on the way. Was that you?"

"Yeah. I called Detective McMahon. We're out of there. Don't worry," Rory said. "It was Mark, after all. He's unmasked. The mask should still be on the floor of his dad's office, in case McMahon asks."

"Roger that. Stay safe, okay?"

"You too. Call us if you need anything."

"Got it. We're live in ten. I'll text you when we're done."

When they reached Rory's car, Hematite said, "Let's go to Elijah's. They won't think to look for you there, and every reporter in town is going to want an interview."

"Good thinking," Rory said. "How do you feel now that this is finally over?"

Hematite shook his head as he got into the passenger seat. "Part of me is relieved that Stone Breaker's taken care of." He frowned as he remembered what Mark had told him. "But I have the feeling that I have a lot more work cut out for me. This is only the beginning."

CHAPTER 20

The roads were so dark that Rory felt like her headlights were barely helping, but she didn't dare draw attention to herself with her high beams as she drove to Elijah and Brad's home. Kane still kept his balaclava, cowl, and hood on for an added layer of anonymity, but there was no one else on the road going the same direction, as their car and the streetlights were few and far between. A few news trucks passed by them, heading toward City Hall to report on what had happened.

"You sure you're okay?" Kane asked. He had turned his voice modifier off to preserve the battery. Rory felt at ease hearing his real voice under there, finding comfort in knowing without a doubt that it had been Kane all along.

"I'm sure," Rory said. "I might need an extra appointment with Marissa, but I'm fine." For the first time in a long time, she felt at peace internally. It was so striking to her now, after constantly feeling like she was on pins and needles for all those years. She felt as if a weight had been lifted off her chest that she hadn't even known was there to begin with.

Kane chuckled lightly. "I was really nervous about what might happen if I died."

"What do you mean? I thought you can't be killed."

"I can't," Kane said. "But I wasn't worried about me. I wasn't sure what he might do if he got to me, and you hadn't made it out of there in time." Kane released a long exhale. "I rarely have anyone to live for in a life-or-death situation like that."

She slowed down once she reached the suburbs, grateful for the extra visibility that the streetlamps brought but nervous about being detected, especially with Kane. She was taken out of her thoughts by her phone ringing, which started as soon as she got to her neighborhood.

"Shit," she said. "It's McMahon. I have to take this." She answered him on her car's speaker, connected to the Bluetooth® so Kane could hear too.

"Miss Miller, where the hell did you go?" Detective McMahon asked. "I'm arriving on the scene with a handful of officers I can trust, and the reporter here tells me you're nowhere to be found."

"I was not about to wait around and see if Stone Breaker would wake up," Rory said. "Am I in trouble or under arrest?"

Detective McMahon was silent for a moment. Rory heard him take a deep breath through his nose. "Are you with Hematite right now?"

Rory swallowed. Kane nodded at her, confirming that it was alright to tell the truth. "I am. He's the one who got me out of there safely."

"No, you're not in trouble," Detective McMahon said, remembering his promise to Hematite from a few nights ago. "And I'm not arresting you tonight, Miss Miller. Hematite was the only one to fight with Stone Breaker, right? Right?"

Rory understood what he was getting at. "That's correct, detective."

"I'll get a full statement later but just so I can do my due diligence while I'm here, can you give me a brief rundown of what Stone Breaker did to you?"

"I was tied with rope to a chair. You can see the cut ropes in Tom Stevens' office still."

"We'll have to check tapes too, but knowing Hematite, I will probably have to take your word for this," Detective McMahon said. "Something tells me he had those turned off like he usually does. You aren't in trouble, Miss Miller. You're a victim. Though I will need you to come down to make your statement, eventually."

Rory faintly heard a reporter—not Naomi, but an unfamiliar voice —asking Detective McMahon if he'd be willing to make a comment.

"We'll call the PIO and let you know when we're going to host a presser. No comment for now . . . Sorry about that, Miss Miller. If you'd like to wait until the media frenzy dies down, you have my permission to do so. I don't know that my boss will like that, but I can imagine you are very shaken up, especially after being stalked and kidnapped."

"Yeah, definitely. I can swing by later tonight. I will take you up on your offer, though."

"I'll be stuck at the station pretty late. Something like this is gonna require a lot of paperwork, that's for sure. This number is my cell. Just shoot me a text before you come, alright?"

"Thank you, sir." Kane nodded, so Rory said, "Hematite sends his thanks too."

Detective McMahon chuckled. "I appreciate your time. Have a good night, Miss Miller. I look forward to seeing you later."

When they hung up, Rory took a deep breath. She asked Kane, "Can you do me a favor?"

Kane nodded. "Sure. What is it?"

"You don't have to tell her you're Hematite. But can you just text my mom as yourself and let her know that you're with me? And that no matter what she and my dad see on the news over the next couple of days, it's been taken care of? They have been following the story without me really telling them what's going on, and I think they're kind of freaked out."

Kane nodded and grabbed his personal cell phone. "Of course." Kane did so and chuckled to himself when he saw the response from her mom.

"Oh God, what did she say?"

"She said thank you and that if you don't ask me out soon, then she might do so herself. Permission to tell her she doesn't have to worry about that?"

Rory smiled. "Permission granted."

"So, it's not too late for me to ask you on a proper date once and for all?"

She laughed. "I mean, shit, we're both alive. It went as well as either of us could have asked. I think a proper date would be an appropriate means of celebration."

Rory glanced over at him, and she could see his smile reach his eyes.

"I totally fucking freaked when your tracker turned off and Elijah couldn't spot you anymore," Kane said. "Elijah tried to calm me down but, uh, busting through the window, it was. I don't think I've hung up on someone faster. So much for laying out a map of the place to find a discreet entrance."

"I'm okay," Rory assured him. "Your timing actually couldn't have been any better. Mark was rambling about how horrible his life has been."

"Ooh, ouch. That alone had to have been torture."

"Worse than the ropes, that's for sure," Rory said with a laugh. "Seriously, Kay. I'm okay. I, uh, got a little mouthy with him in there. You'd have been proud. Speaking of Elijah, does he know we're on our way to his house?"

"He does. He told me to come here after if we needed. We'll just have to go in through the back, though. I can't exactly hang out on the front steps of someone's house looking like this."

"Fair point."

Rory parked her car in Elijah's driveway on the side furthest from the streetlight to give them some extra cover from the dark. As she looked up at his home, she realized just how intensely she had put her trust in not only Kane and her friends but her own instincts. She wasn't sure if she'd taken the same steps a few months ago, but she was just glad she had now.

"He said the gate to the backyard should be unlocked." Kane tried it and it worked. "Let's go."

Rory followed Kane in before he closed the fence's door and latched it. Rory felt a sense of relief the moment she was on Elijah's property, grateful for the chance to breathe.

They didn't have to wait long for Elijah once they knocked on the back door. Elijah was wearing jeans and a hoodie, having expected their arrival.

"Come on in. Relax," Elijah said. "Let me just double-check that all the blinds are closed upstairs in case you need to get up there. You know the drill, Kane."

"Thanks, dude," Kane said, as they came in through Elijah's kitchen. As Elijah moved back upstairs, Kane and Rory took a seat on the couch in his living room. They both released a deep breath, feeling an intense sense of relief, even though they both knew that it would only be temporary. Kane lowered his hood and removed his balaclava now that he was in the privacy of Elijah's house. His cheeks were still flushed from his fight with Mark earlier, but he was otherwise pale from his anxieties.

Kane reached for Rory's hand and gripped it tight. She couldn't tell if he was trying to comfort her or himself. They glanced at one another on the couch. His eyes were wide as he processed the evening's events, and Rory was sure she didn't look much better off than he did.

Rory brushed some of Kane's hair out of his face from where it had fallen out of his ponytail. Her thumb ghosted over a light bruise that had already formed on his forehead.

"You okay?" Only Kane could hear her.

Kane nodded. "Piece of shit threw a stapler at me. I may need your help hiding that with makeup for work. I don't think my hair will totally cover that one."

"I'll grab some in your shade tomorrow morning."

Elijah came back downstairs at that. "Coast is clear, and all the blinds are accounted for. You guys are safe here, and I don't think anyone will think to look here. If they go anywhere, it'll be your place, Rory."

"Thank you, Elijah," Kane said. "I can bring Rory home later. Just want to avoid talking to the media."

Rory nodded. "Seriously, Elijah. Thanks."

"Yeah, no problem. I'm just glad I can help. We've always had each other's backs. That won't change. Here, let me get you some ice for your forehead. That spot looks pretty gnarly."

"Where's Brad?" Kane asked.

"He had to run to his parents' house after work. I don't know when he'll be back," Elijah said from the kitchen. "I can text him, but I don't know if he'll respond. But congrats on finally getting him, you two. Hometown heroes over here!"

"I don't know about that," Kane said with a nervous chuckle, as he leaned back on the couch. He accepted the ice pack from Elijah and used his free hand to hold it up to the forming bruise. His gloves and boxing wraps prevented his hands from feeling the chill. "Sometimes I wonder if there's a better way of going about all of this than just beating the shit out of people. Doesn't feel like there's any heroism there."

"Well, I appreciate you beating the shit out of people when I haven't been able to," Rory said. "I'm sure Kayla does too. And Naomi. And everyone else you've helped."

"Believe me, that thought runs through my head too." Kane squeezed her hand again. "Changes nothing, though."

"Don't beat yourself up, man. Rory's right."

Kane leaned his head against Rory's shoulder, letting his shoulder slouch a bit as he did. "God, I'm fucking tired." Both Elijah and Rory could tell from his tone of voice that he meant both physically and emotionally.

"Let's see if Naomi's up yet," Rory said. "It's only 11:30. Their newscast should still be on. I think they wrap right around midnight."

When they turned on Channel 10, they saw Naomi standing in front of City Hall. Behind her, Stone Breaker was being taken out of the building. The red-and-blue lights from a police car off-camera faintly illuminated Naomi's face.

"Breaking news. Stone Breaker has been caught by the masked vigilante Hematite. Police here on the scene tell me that Stone Breaker's mask was found inside Councilman Tom Stevens' office. They tell me his son Mark was the one behind the mask. Mark is now under arrest on multiple charges, including kidnapping a local woman. Eyewitness reports exclusive to Channel 10 tell me that Stone Breaker brought a Riverpeak High School teacher here to bring out Hematite."

"Thank God," Elijah said.

"I grabbed your bug, by the way," Rory said. "How did that go?"

"Thanks! I got into their server. It took me a few tries, but I have one of my computers set up with their VPN and logged in to Tom's account. I unencrypted the files too." He glanced at Kane. "We can have you gift them to the police tonight if you're taking Rory for her statement. I already made a copy for us to hang on to."

"Good thinking. I'll bring her over later when she's ready. If it comes from me, McMahon won't mind, and chances are he'll let me get away like he usually does. Anything incriminating on there?"

"Oh, yeah," Elijah said with a clap of his hands. "There were so many emails detailing bribes he accepted. Seriously, this dude did not think twice about leaving a digital trail. Typical boomer behavior, I guess." He rolled his eyes with a grin. "Basically, he was being bribed to vote in favor of the guys selling and pushing all these drugs." Elijah paused and blew a raspberry in exasperation. His smile had completely dropped. "I just haven't wanted to say anything to Naomi because it's looking kinda bad for her dad."

"What do you mean?" Rory asked.

"We can't tell her yet," Elijah said. "I'm not totally sure. And regardless, it's looking nasty for Stevens, which is really all I'm concerned about for the time being. But all the dirty drug money is coming from some guys that own franchises of South Main Burgers."

"The restaurant he started?" Rory asked. "I mean, it checks out. He's always lobbied for Stevens. Naomi always tried to convince him otherwise, but her dad never gave in."

"I want to do some more digging first before we say anything to her," Elijah said. "I want to be completely positive. No sense in freaking her out if it's just a coincidence, you know?"

"We have to find out how he's involved," Kane said. "I don't think it's a coincidence. Stone Breaker told me it's not his dad behind all of this, just that he was profiting off it. I don't think he had any direct involvement other than turning a blind eye in exchange for the right price. Plus, Jameson said he saw some suspicious activity by the South Main Burgers in Denver, but he never got with me about if he figured out why."

"Wait, for real?"

"Yeah. He mentioned that all he really got a glimpse of was a ton of traffic in and out of there really late one night. It was well after closing. But you're right in that we shouldn't say anything to her yet, just in case."

"How long has this stuff been going around, anyway?" The more they talked about it and processed it, the more Rory realized how deep this was. "How has this never been on anyone's radar except yours?"

"At least since I was born, and we're all pushing thirty. I'm guessing well before that, though." Kane frowned. "Money's one hell of a drug too, isn't it?"

Rory frowned. "This is so fucked."

"Yeah. What's even more fucked is I think a lot more people are using this here in Riverpeak than we even realize. Potter ran some extra tests on that sample I gave him. He said even if it wasn't burned to hell, it doesn't look like it's very shelf-stable, which tells me it's probably being delivered only around Denver and some other surrounding cities."

"And if it can't go far, they can't make a profit if they don't have a high local demand," Elijah realized with a sigh.

"There's probably a lot of people who use it, but just aren't addicted," Kane said. "It gets people hyped up. How many people use it to get through a shitty workday, and then the addicted ones get recruited to help them? Just look at my parents, for starters. They've been exploited by those assholes for years."

Rory glanced up and saw a photo of Brad and Naomi from their engagement photoshoot and froze. She remembered her conversation with Naomi a few weeks ago, her words about being suspicious of Noah's death ringing in her head as clear as day.

"Do you think this has anything to do with Noah's death?" Rory asked. Both Elijah and Kane looked at Rory, surprised to hear it. Rory explained, "Naomi told me she wasn't totally sold on her brother's death just being a fire caused by a freak accident, especially since their dad got out but Noah didn't. She said she wanted to look more into it once the wedding was over and she had the time to, but what if this is why?"

"No way," Elijah said, but not like he entirely believed his own words. "Noah was too good of a guy to be tangled up in all this."

"I think you're on to something, Rory. I know Noah was like an older brother for all of us, Elijah, but think about it. Look at what happened to my parents' shed the other day. They cooked it for too long, passed out from the fumes, and the whole thing nearly went up in flames."

Elijah exhaled. "Shit."

"Especially if it looks like there's a definitive connection to South Main Burgers," Rory said. She shook her head. "Wasn't he working with his dad to help pay off his master's degree?"

"Yeah," Elijah said. "I don't want you two to be right. But Noah's death could be a good place for us to look if we keep going."

They all glanced at the front door as Brad suddenly entered, still in his scrubs from a late work night at the emergency clinic. Brad was a bit of a gentle giant, smaller than Shawn, but still towering above most of his friends. He had been his high school quarterback and was still built like he was, even years later; he had thinned out a bit and his stomach had softened but was still square-framed and wide-shouldered. Since he worked with animals, he kept his dark hair short. Despite his size, he wasn't a threatening guy to look at, the softness in his golden-brown eyes revealing his kindness with nothing more than a quick look.

"Hey, Elijah!"

Brad didn't even notice Rory and Kane at first, going through his usual motions for his after-work routine. It wasn't until the door was locked and his jacket was hung on the coat hanger that he noticed an unmasked Hematite and Rory sitting on the couch.

Brad just stared at them with a blank expression, trying to comprehend what he was seeing before him. As far as Brad was concerned, nothing ever happened in Riverpeak, and his life was a series of routines he was quite fond of. Brad blinked a few times and then rubbed his eyes as if he were imagining things, but Rory and Kane never disappeared from the couch.

"Hey, Brad," Rory said sheepishly to break the silence.

"Hi," he said, clearly feeling lost. "What's…" He pointed at Kane and Rory on the couch and at Elijah standing by them. "What's going on here?"

"I can explain," Kane said. He stood to walk over to his friend, lingering to drop Rory's hand. "Brad, I'm sorry I didn't tell you sooner. But please know that I didn't tell literally anyone until now. Not Elijah, not Rory. It has nothing to do with my trust in you."

Brad scoffed lightly in disbelief. "What, man, are you legitimately Hematite?"

Kane nodded in silence.

Elijah said, "I've been helping him. I didn't know until about two or three months ago, and neither did Rory. She found out after me. A bunch of reporters are desperate for an interview after Stevens' arrest, so I'm letting them hide out here until it's late so they can head home without being bothered. You don't mind, do you?"

"No, of course I don't mind." He sounded like he was in a daze. "Wait, like Councilman Stevens?" Brad asked, the inflection of his voice indicating how truly out of the loop he was. "What happened?"

Kane glanced back at Rory, who spoke up. "His son was Stone Breaker. He kinda kidnapped me tonight." Rory waved her hand toward him in a beckoning motion. "Come on, Naomi's reporting on it now."

Brad looked at the three of them in disbelief. "Wait, for real?"

"Yeah, man," Elijah said.

"Wait, so does Naomi know too?"

"As of a few days ago, yeah," Rory said. "This was the big work project that she told you about. She was sworn to secrecy once we told her it was Kane. I'm sure she'd be apologizing profusely if she were here right now and not on the clock."

"Kane?" Brad asked with a slackened jaw. He wanted to hear it from Kane for himself. "This is really for real? You're not joking right now?"

Kane nodded. "Yeah. It's always been me."

Brad ran his fingers through his hair, then over his face. He pinched his nose as he said, "Holy shit, dude."

TO BE NORMAL

RIVERPEAK HEROES
BOOK 2

JESSICA SALINA

To the cycle-breakers:
I'm your family now.

CONTENT WARNINGS

To Be Normal is an adult superhero romance that contains drug use, physical violence, gun violence, murder, blood, and consensual sex scenes.

CHAPTER 1

E lijah Baron avoided East Riverpeak whenever he could, and there was no wondering why either. If you asked him, the east side redefined desolate after a failed attempt by the local government at expanding their small Colorado town. He knew the government attempted to gentrify it a few decades ago, but a handful of empty homeless camps and cars with missing parts scattered the road instead. Some buildings looked like they had the potential to be nice but never completed construction. A handful of homes were mixed between the empty shops, but they also seemed empty besides the melting snow.

With his friend Brad leading the way, they came across the abandoned burger joint that still resembled its past life as a former fast-food chain. A sign reading South Main Burgers hung over the door but had long since faded and desperately needed a power washing, much like the rest of the building. Graffitied wood planks covered the windows; someone smashed them in years ago, and the boards covered the open space left behind. On one plank, someone spray-painted the words "STONE BREAKER WAS RIGHT" in red graffiti. Blue spray paint crossed the last two words out, and the word "SCREW" was above

Stone Breaker's name. The door to the restaurant used to be dead bolted, but someone had broken it open with pliers.

Brad pinched his nose with his fingers in annoyance. "Oh, for God's sake. Please tell me they didn't go in again." He was still in his scrubs, having rushed here from the Riverpeak Veterinary Clinic. Some dog fur still coated his broad shoulders and thighs.

Elijah sighed. "You already know the answer to that."

Brad tugged at the door, which opened with surprising ease. He peeked through the crack before opening it all the way. "Okay, no one's here. Kane and Jameson must be in the back."

A thin layer of dust coated everything in the restaurant; just being in the place gave Elijah the urge to take a shower. He instinctively pulled his beanie down in an attempt to cover his head from sight, in case anyone was watching them. His friends always gave him a hard time for being paranoid, but lately, that feeling came in handy. The restaurant booths and tables were long abandoned, some with graffiti on them that matched the boarded-up windows. Brad and Elijah hopped the counter, its dust coating Elijah's khakis, and made their way to the back, hoping to only find their friends.

They found an office where they discovered their friends Kane Kelly and Shawn Jameson inside, who both looked up at the sound of footsteps. The two were going through some desk drawers, and Kane sighed in relief when he saw it was just them. Kane was Shawn's polar opposite, as his blond hair had grown out and looked shaggy. He was wearing a pair of loose-fitting joggers with a matching black T-shirt, scarf, and navy hoodie. His balaclava was in his hands, which were covered by his boxing wraps and some gloves. His lean frame hinted at muscularity, but it was subtle—like he wasn't intentionally working out but still got into a street fight from time to time.

Next to him, Shawn towered over Kane. Elijah got the sense that Shawn came here after a sales meeting. He'd gelled his short, brown hair into a comb-over and was still wearing a button-up pinstripe shirt, tie, and blazer.

"Well, I had to see it to believe it," Elijah said. The agitation was clear in his voice. "Really, guys? In broad daylight? I thought we knew better than this."

"What the hell are you two doing here?" Brad asked. "It's one o'clock on a Friday."

"Oh, hey Brad, Elijah. What's going on?" Shawn asked with his usual nonchalance, acting like nothing was unusual to avoid Elijah's typical scolding.

"Seriously, what the hell?" Brad reiterated. "I think I speak for both of us when I say this was not how I anticipated spending my lunch break."

"Don't look at me; it was Kane's idea," Shawn said, his hands shooting up by his head in defense.

Elijah sighed, feeling his chest deflate beneath his flannel. "Kane, can you please explain why you called?"

"With Mark and Tom Stevens both in jail, the drug ring's lost some of their political power and their rug that they could sweep shit under. Jameson and I were doing some investigating to figure out their next move, and I'm using spring break to my advantage, here."

"Do Rory and Amy know you two are out here?"

Kane replied yes at the same time Shawn said no. Elijah couldn't hide his scowl, mainly directed at Shawn.

"Rory helped us narrow it down to here," Kane said. "If they're working here at night, then we thought coming during the day might be best. You know, just in case."

"Did you find anything, at least?" Brad asked. "And are we free to get out of here?"

"We did. I was hoping you two could hold on to what we found; that's why I called."

Shawn nodded. "If anyone will get busted today, it's either me or Kane. So, we thought this info would be safer with you."

"Oh, Jesus Christ. Naomi's taking this wedding really seriously, guys. If my groomsmen get arrested, she'll freak."

Kane grinned, his confidence showing through. "Calm down, man. Here, let's split this stuff up. Elijah, I'm giving you this." He grabbed a handful of thumb drives in a plastic sandwich bag from the desk. "And Brad, did you bring your backpack like I asked?"

Brad nodded.

"Then take these, and let's get the hell out of here."

Brad accepted the stack of papers Kane handed him and shoved them in his backpack. Kane put his balaclava back on as they made their way out of the restaurant, pulling his scarf up over his face and wrapping it around his head to hide his hair, but a few loose strands still stuck out. Shawn pulled a plain black mask out of his briefcase and used that to similarly conceal his identity. Elijah wished he and Brad had enough time to grab something similar along the way. He fidgeted with his beanie again, hoping it would suffice, even though he knew it wouldn't against his auburn curls.

When they reached the front of the restaurant, Shawn swung the door open and ushered Elijah, Brad, and Kane out. He stood behind them as the other three stared in front of them at the slowing car in the road as it crept to a halt. It was a vintage vehicle, too pristine and expensive to belong in the east side of town. Its clean, white exterior stood out against the drabness of the rest of the city, and it popped set against the concrete and a few small patches of snow.

"Holy shit," Elijah said.

"Mr. Sato?" Brad asked, but too softly for the man in the car to hear.

The man in the backseat was undeniably Naomi's father, Reiji Sato, and the owner of the abandoned restaurant, with many of the same facial features as his daughter. His cheekbones were higher and more prominent than Naomi's, but still the same shape as hers. Next to Naomi's father sat a man they'd never seen before, with slicked-back gray hair and large sunglasses that concealed most of his face. He said something to Mr. Sato and then to the driver.

With his eyes wide and mouth gaped open, Brad was in a state of shock. Shawn's booming voice snapped Elijah and Kane out of their own surprise.

"Come on, dude, we gotta bail!"

"I'm inclined to think he's right," Elijah said, as he took off with Shawn and Kane. Elijah glanced back and saw that Brad was still standing there frozen, staring at his soon-to-be father-in-law in the vehicle.

"Come on!" Elijah called back. "Jameson! We need assistance!"

"God damn it!" Shawn groaned as he turned around. He easily

lifted Brad over his shoulder and then took off, catching up to Elijah and Kane.

Elijah glanced behind him and saw the vehicle was trailing a safe distance behind them, but still within range. "Uh, guys? We have a problem. I'm pretty sure they're following us."

"Cut through that alley on your right," Kane said. He turned his voice modifier on. "If you go through the next few, it's a shortcut to the storage place on the edge of downtown."

"Got it! Thanks, man!"

Kane and Elijah moved down the alley and heard Shawn not far behind them. Before Shawn made the turn, they heard a gunshot followed by Shawn shouting.

"Fucking asshole!"

Meanwhile, Elijah and Kane ducked behind a dumpster in the alley to wait for Shawn and take cover.

"Are you okay?"

Kane nodded. "Yeah, of course. Are you?"

"I'm good."

Shawn entered the alleyway, with Brad still slumped over his shoulder fireman-style. "Okay, let's go!"

"Are you guys alright?" Elijah asked.

"Fine," Shawn said. "Thankfully, Mr. Sato's friend is a shitty shot, at least when he's in a moving vehicle. I think Brad's brain is broken from the attempted murder, but no gunshot wounds."

"You guys go ahead," Kane said. "I'll stall him."

"What?" Elijah asked. "Are you sure?"

"Yes," Kane said. He adjusted his hood over his head and cracked his neck. "I'll be fine. Can't die, remember?"

"Dude!" Brad went to protest, while still on Shawn's shoulder, but Shawn cut him off.

"Not to sound like an asshole, but there's no time! Come on!"

Elijah hated to admit it, but Shawn was right. He glanced at Brad and could tell from the quiver in his lip that it pained him to leave Kane behind.

"He'll be okay, Brad."

"I know, but still."

They ran through the last few alleys, careful to check before they crossed roads, to reach the storage facility Kane often worked out of.

"I know that we typically just handle this shit on our own with Kane, but given what just happened, shouldn't we call the police?" Elijah asked.

Shawn just laughed. "Call the police. That's funny. You're cute sometimes, Baron."

"I hate you, god damn it."

"Unfortunately, McMahon's on vacation this week. He took one after all this Stone Breaker bullshit. He told Rory, who told Kane, who told me."

"Crap. So, what do we do?"

"Wait for Kane to give us the next steps."

"I can't believe it, dude." Brad seemed like he was still in a trance. "What am I gonna tell Naomi?"

"You're not gonna tell Naomi a fuckin' thing, buddy," Shawn said. Once they made it to the storage facility, he put Brad down and removed his mask but Elijah didn't stop moving.

"We should keep moving. If they follow us to Kane's unit, it's game over."

Brad was finally walking again, no longer completely frozen, but his movements were comparable to a zombie's. They slowed their pace, not seeing any vintage or unusual cars, and felt more relaxed once they were in the crowd of Main Street's shopping strip. Here, where brick buildings intermingled with false fronts against the backdrop of the mountains, it was easy to blend in with the rest of their town.

Shawn slapped Brad between his shoulder blades. Brad lurched a bit as Shawn told him, "Naomi is balls deep in wedding planning. This will not go over well."

"No. You have to tell her," Elijah said. "It'll be better if you're honest, and you'll have to tell her eventually."

"No, he won't. We can just play dumb about the whole thing."

"I dunno," Brad said. He rubbed his eyes, feeling like his two friends were the angel on one shoulder and the devil on the other. He wasn't sure who he was more inclined to listen to.

"She'll probably figure it out on her own. This is *her father* we're talking about."

"Can we eat?" Brad asked as they passed by the diner; he had always been a stress eater. The diner was wedged between an old music shop and a tattoo studio. The soft jazz coming from the diner clashed with an acoustic guitar playing from the music shop, likely someone's lesson from the sound of inexperienced riffs.

"Yeah, man. We should have time. Come on," Elijah said as he held the door open. "We'll wait for Kane here. He'll know to look for us."

"What if Naomi's dad looks for us there too?" Shawn asked. "Kane will probably only be able to stall him for so long."

"Then we figure it out. They probably won't want a scene in public, and I haven't seen their car. Was that Mr. Sato's?"

Brad shook his head. "It must have been that other guy's, whoever he was."

A group of teenagers dressed in all black sat in a booth in the diner's corner, but it was otherwise empty. The diner's wood trim and red walls gave it a homey feel, but something about it was still unsettling. Elijah attributed it to the decor on the walls, which was nothing short of random: paintings of the Rocky Mountains by local artists, old photos of random people from the 1800s, vintage skis, an old sign from Pike National Forest, and a large rainbow trout made from metal. None of it matched, but somehow it all made sense here.

"Three of you?" said the diner's hostess without bothering to look up from the podium she stood behind.

"We might have a fourth later," Shawn said.

"Oh, it's you. Come on, I'll get you your usual booth."

The hostess led the group to a booth on the opposite side of the diner as the teenagers, who were picking at a single lunch entree split among the three of them. Part of the ceiling looked like it wanted to cave in, but it wasn't over their booth so Elijah paid little attention to it. The hostess blew a bubble with her gum and popped it. Elijah sat opposite Shawn and Brad.

"Kane not with you today?"

"He's stuck at work," Elijah said and hoped she didn't realize it was spring break.

"Right, right. Coffee for everyone?"

"Please and thank you."

"Let's see those papers," Shawn said once she left. "Kane and I didn't get much of a chance to look through them."

"Yeah, sure," Brad said. He took the papers out of his backpack and plopped them on the table. "It looks like a lot of accounting and inspection records, plus some tax returns. Why the hell did Kane give me a bunch of accounting records?"

Shawn went to say something, but the waitress cut them off with her arrival. She wasn't the hostess who sat them, but a high schooler feigning her tone of voice to sound more enthusiastic.

"Here's your coffee," she said. "Oh, what's all this?"

The men glanced at each other, unsure of what to say. Elijah cleared his throat and said, "My company might use the software that Shawn sells. He wanted to pass over some of the paperwork to me, since my work email was down."

"Oh, got it," the waitress said with a nod, promptly dropping the subject now that it bored her. "Anything to eat?"

Once they ordered and the waitress was gone, Shawn spoke up.

"I just got a text from Kane. He's following the car, so we'll catch him later. Looks like he passed right by the diner. They must have just missed us."

"We're way in over our heads." Elijah nervously laughed. He still felt guilty about the lie to the waitress, despite it being necessary. "Including you and Kane."

Shawn scoffed. "Kane'll live."

"That's beside the point."

Brad pulled a flask out of his backpack and poured some of it into his mug. He chugged his spiked coffee and then asked, "What the fuck am I gonna do?"

"Why don't we get all of the information together before you decide if you should tell Naomi?" Shawn's glance moved from Brad and then to Elijah. "Can we all agree to compromise there?"

Elijah crossed his arms as he leaned back in the booth. "I hate that I'm agreeing with you."

"Twice in one day? I think this is some sort of record."

"Don't get too excited. I just think it'll be better to have as much intel as we can going into it." Elijah sighed. "I mean, we knew something was gonna come out of South Main Burgers from this. But I was not expecting Naomi's dad, of all people, to be directly involved."

"I wonder what's on those flash drives," Brad said.

"Probably more financial records, but I'll look into them this weekend," Elijah said. "Whatever it is, I have my work cut out for me."

"Given he was shooting first, asking no questions at all, I think it's safe to say that there's more than financial records on there," Shawn said.

"What did Rory find to point you guys there, anyway?" Brad asked. "I still feel so out of the loop on this stuff."

"Just some clues from Mark in his old news reports. Kinda like the ones he used to leave to hint at his own next moves. We're going *way* back on some of these," Shawn said. "Little bitch thought he was the Riddler or something."

"Well, his screw-up is probably gonna be a huge help," Elijah said. Their food arrived, causing them to fall into silence, all three of them feeling stiff and awkward to avoid looking suspicious as the waitress handed them their plates. Elijah bid her a quiet thanks as she left.

"I just hope none of this gets in the way of the wedding," Brad said, as he took a bite of his burger. Elijah tried not to wince as his friend spoke with his mouth full. "I think with her role at the news station, Naomi feels like all eyes are on her right now, y'know?"

"Do you have a date to the wedding yet, Baron?" Shawn asked. Shawn's taunting smirk indicated he already expected the answer.

Elijah shook his head. "No, but it's looking like that may be for the best. There's already so much going on, and I can't even imagine juggling that right now."

"He'll meet someone when the time is right." Brad flashed Elijah a sympathetic smile.

"I'm not worried about it," Elijah said dismissively, even though it was a bit of a lie. He didn't care about not having a date for the wedding, but when Brad moved out, he wasn't sure he could afford the lease on their house anymore. He shook it off, wanting to think about the matters at hand more than his living situation. "What's next, Jameson?"

"Kane's been taking over here, and I've been keeping watch in Denver. Work has me out there more often than not these days, so it's easy for me to keep the cover from Amy. Though it seems like the action is more concentrated here now." He took a bite of his burger and proceeded to speak with his mouth full. "We used to see a good deal of movement up in the cities, but my theory?" He held up a French fry and pointed it at Elijah. "Our pal Reiji wants to make sure that he maintains control, and that starts at the local level. I think Stevens was a big, local hookup for him, especially since Stevens was also his key to the police here in town."

"We need solid proof," Elijah said.

Shawn scoffed. "I'd say being shot at is solid proof."

"Paper trail proof." Elijah rolled his eyes. "Obviously." He patted Brad's shoulder next to him. "We'll get this sorted before your wedding day, Brad. Don't worry."

"I *am* worried. I'm even more worried about Naomi finding out before we're ready to tell her."

"I'll loop in Kane, and he can loop in Rory. It'll be okay."

Elijah knew those three words—"it'll be okay"—were a lie too. He had been doing more of that lately and he wasn't sure he was okay with it, but if it meant Brad kept his cool, he supposed it was fine.

"So, let's assume the worst here," Shawn said. The three of them all remained silent as the waitress returned to refill their drinks. "Let's say this doesn't get resolved by the wedding day. Then what?"

"Then we figure it out after," Elijah said. "We'll figure it out, regardless."

"Listen, I do not want anyone getting hurt on the wedding day."

"They won't," Elijah said without hesitation.

"What makes you so sure, Baron?"

"Well, Jameson, unlike *you*, some people actually care about appearances. Mr. Sato included. You think he's going to throw his decades of hard work away at an event as public for him as his daughter's wedding?"

"He could if he wanted to assert dominance," Shawn said. It was a valid counterpoint, but Elijah didn't want to admit that he agreed with Shawn for the third time in one day. "No room for a power vacuum, if you get what I'm saying."

"Don't worry, Brad. We'll handle it," Elijah said.

Based on his frown, Brad didn't look convinced. "You don't care if I smoke after work tonight, do you?"

"After that?" Elijah shook his head. "Of course I don't. I'll even join you."

"Ok, good. Ugh, I think I'm gonna be sick."

Elijah sensed he'd be busier than ever in the coming months, but he bit back his anxieties with his lunch. "Just trust us, okay?"

CHAPTER 2

The difference in Elijah's Friday afternoon and night gave him whiplash; it didn't even feel like the same day. He welcomed the routine of helping his mother set the table, hoping he could use the motions to clear his head from what happened at the restaurant.

But nothing helped.

He knew he was supposed to be relaxing and decompressing for Shabbat, but the more he tried, the more the realization of his afternoon snuck up on him. There his mother Lena was, bringing out her favorite Judaica for their party of three, as if Elijah hadn't evaded gunfire just a few hours earlier. He could never tell her or his father, nor did he have any desire to, but he struggled with biting back how rattled he truly was.

Despite everything else Lena cooked, the smell of fresh bread overwhelmed his senses. It was too much food for three people, but Elijah knew his mother would force him into taking home leftovers, and he certainly wasn't about to complain about that. Normally, it evoked a warm, inviting feeling through his chest that reminded him of the simpler days of his youth. But as Lena said the prayers over the challah, the Hebrew went in one ear and out the other to Elijah.

"You okay, sweetheart?"

His mother's voice snapped him out of his thoughts. Elijah smiled at her and nodded. "Yeah, *Ima*, I'm fine. Just a lot going on, that's all."

"Oh, I bet. I saw that the Millers' daughter recently got kidnapped. How awful." She offered him a sad, sympathetic smile. "She's one of your friends, yeah?"

"Yeah. She's Kane's girlfriend." He took a bite of his fish to shut himself up. Despite being an active member in it, Kane's world as Hematite felt incredibly separate from Elijah's own life. He often felt like he was just an outsider looking in at all of it, even when his fingers made their way across his keyboard on Kane's behalf. "Apparently that YouTube weirdo had been stalking her for a while since she found out who he was. I guess she was trying to find Hematite and ended up finding him instead, so he got pretty pissed."

"Oh, I can't believe it! Are they alright?"

"I think they're okay, all things considered. Kane actually brought her by the other night. Brad and I let them crash after she escaped. She was pretty shaken up." Elijah didn't say anymore out of fear of saying too much. He didn't dare.

"Does she know who Hematite is?"

"If she does, she's tight-lipped." Lying on Shabbat made him feel dirty, but he was sure God would understand.

"You guys did the right thing," his father, Rueben, said. "I'm glad that little fucker got arrested."

Lena glared at her husband over her glass and laughed in shock. "Rue!"

"What?" He shrugged. "Kid had it coming!"

Elijah hid his smile with a sip of his wine. Lena just rolled her eyes.

"Did you know him from school?"

Elijah nodded. "Jameson used to beat the crap out of him when we were little."

Rueben held back a laugh. "I probably would have too."

Lena smacked his arm with her napkin. "Rue, don't say that! Goodness gracious." She sighed and took a long sip of wine. "I'm just glad Rory's okay. You know, some girl went missing last week. Rory could have just as easily if it weren't for Hematite finding her when she got kidnapped."

Elijah frowned. "Someone went missing?"

"Yeah, didn't you hear? I guess not. You're so busy lately helping Brad plan for his wedding. It was on the news. Poor girl, she was working at the Hooters just outside of East Riverpeak. Apparently, she never showed up for one of her shifts. Her coworkers were on the news, and they're hoping a customer didn't do anything to her. They found a bunch of drugs in her car, but everyone she knows swears up and down that she never used."

"That's awful." Elijah made a mental note to bring this up to Kane. If there were drugs in her car, he wondered if this had anything to do with the same drug ring behind Kane's powers.

"Ugh, it is. I know you're all grown up now, sweetheart, but if your friends ever need a place to come, I hope they know they can always come here."

Elijah smiled. "They do, *Ima*, and they appreciate it."

That much was true, at least. Lena Baron always had an open-door policy for Elijah and his friends that hadn't gone unnoticed. It was why he and Kane were so close; there were still signs of their friendship in the old guest room, in the form of childhood photographs taken on Polaroids and old game consoles. Their friendship developed over late nights after Kane got into a fight with his father and brought his sister over for safety's sake. In hindsight, Elijah thought, he should have guessed sooner that Kane and Hematite were one and the same.

"Good," Lena said, snapping Elijah out of his own thoughts once more. "I worry about you guys. This town's going crazy."

Elijah nodded with a nervous laugh. "Yeah, that's for sure."

If she only knew, he thought.

———

Elijah did a double take on the five minute walk back home from his parents. The green house down the street no longer had the FOR RENT sign in the front yard, which had been up for close to a year. It took him a second to realize the sign was missing; no one thought anyone new would move to town, and everyone else was pretty settled in either their childhood homes or renting with friends. Elijah tucked a dark red curl trying to poke out of his beanie back beneath it to keep it out of his eyes before moving on.

When he entered his own home, he saw Brad in the kitchen, quickly putting some food away just out of Elijah's view.

"Smells good, man." Elijah ditched his jacket on their coat hanger.

"It's that kugel recipe your mom gave me a few months ago. I'm sending her a picture 'cause I don't think it's right, but Naomi still liked it."

Elijah chuckled. "She'll be thrilled, regardless."

"Hey, did you see that a girl moved into the house down the road?"

"I saw the sign got taken down." He put his wallet and sunglasses in their usual spot in a side-table drawer. "Why? Did you see who moved in?"

"I only got a glimpse as she was bringing some of her boxes in. Carla told Naomi that it was some famous author or something. I dunno, dude. You know I don't read much. Naomi was all abuzz about it tonight."

Elijah stifled a laugh. "Did she say which author?"

Brad stopped what he was doing to recall. "Hannah Cohen, I think? I think she writes these pretty big fantasy romance novels and streams on Twitch. She looked pretty cute. You should find out if she's single."

Elijah rolled his eyes; Brad had been encouraging him to find a girlfriend for ages now. "I'll keep an eye out for her," he said, hoping to shut him up.

It wouldn't be hard to spot her; even though he didn't know what she looked like, everyone knew everyone in Riverpeak so a new face would stick out like a sore thumb. The name sounded familiar too, but he couldn't place where he had heard it right away. He was sure that the next time he went to his childhood home for Shabbat, he'd see the name along his mother's bookshelf.

"Good," Brad said. "Naomi keeps saying we need to double date with someone other than Kane and Rory. I don't want her trying to play matchmaker. Last time that happened, it was a fucking disaster."

Elijah internally cringed at the memory of their double date, where

Naomi tried setting him up with her friend Carla when they were in high school. Carla had been nice enough, but they were so incompatible that Naomi stopped trying after their short-lived stint.

"Yeah, that's one way of putting it," Elijah said.

"Seriously, though. When are you gonna start taking chances? Getting out more?"

"Huh?" Elijah rose his thick brows, taken aback.

"I mean, even Kane finally got together with Rory. And turns out he's a superhero or something. What's your excuse?"

"I am not making excuses!"

Brad winked as Elijah scoffed at him. "Keep telling yourself that."

Elijah knew he couldn't live with Brad for much longer; once Brad and Naomi got married, Elijah wouldn't be able (or willing) to be the third wheel. Moving back in with his parents was definitely not an option, especially as a single twenty-seven-year-old. Now and then, he'd check the housing market, but nothing became available that was suitable for one person. Even the house the new girl moved into was huge for just one person; Elijah figured she must have been pretty desperate to move if she was by herself and moving into a three-bedroom home.

"I gotta call Kane back," Elijah said. "Naomi's not staying the night?"

"Nah, they changed her work schedule, so she's trying to get adjusted. This way, she doesn't pass out at the wedding reception from exhaustion." Brad gestured to Elijah's phone. "Hematite business?"

"Most likely."

"Let me know if I can help, okay?"

"Dude, you're fine. You've got a wedding to prepare for." Elijah smiled at his friend before he made his way upstairs to his office, dialing Kane's number along the way. Kane answered by the time Elijah was sitting at his desk, his attention on his personal laptop in the corner.

"Yo. You free?"

"Yeah, I just got home. Listen, have you heard about that girl who went missing on the east side of town?"

"I did. I tried tracking her down. Couldn't find her." Kane sighed.

"The drugs in her car … it was the same one. I brought a sample to Dr. Potter, and he said he'd never seen a stronger dosage of *anything* before, let alone that."

"Shit." Elijah ran his hand over his face. "You think someone planted it?"

"No. Worse. I think someone drugged her and *then* planted it. Anyway, that's not why I called. Can I come over tomorrow?"

"Sure, I don't have anything planned. Why? What's worse than missing people?"

"There's something I want us to look into together. Well, someone is more like it."

"Okay," Elijah said, his voice trailing off. "Too big of a job for Rory?"

"Yeah, I want to really get into this one, and I think it's out of Rory's scope. It's suspicious, that's all. May or may not be connected to the missing people, but I'm not sure yet. I'll explain more tomorrow. I gotta patrol in a minute."

Elijah frowned, unsure of what Kane had up his sleeve. "Okay. If you insist. Must be pretty big if you can't say so over the phone. Swing by whenever, dude."

"Thanks, man. Maybe Dr. Potter's rubbing off on me. And while I've got you, can you check if there are any security cameras set up near Third Street South in East Riverpeak?"

Elijah half-expected that question to come. "Let me guess, that's where they found the girl's car?"

"Yeah. I wonder if we can see who grabbed her. I'm heading there right now in case they returned to the scene of the crime."

"Got it," Elijah said. He pulled some security camera feeds up, having gained access to all of them long ago by less-than-legal methods. He scanned them all quickly, looking for any signs that they were in that part of town. "Were there any landmarks near there?"

"That old gas station should be across the street from where she lived. It was at her house."

Elijah pulled it up, biting his thumbnail in anticipation as he went through the files and scrolled back to last week. "Do you know what day she went missing? I didn't catch the news report, but my mom filled me in a bit."

"Same night that Rory got kidnapped last week."

"Hmm. No way that's a coincidence. They knew you'd be busy."

"That's what I think too. Now that we know what we know, it makes sense. I can't help but wonder if all of that crap with Stevens was a diversion."

"I dunno about that," Elijah said. "I think Stevens was just an idiot with his own agenda that happened to sort of go along with the crime ring's own interests."

"Either way, they're a total thorn in my side. Any luck on the cameras?"

"They're grainy as hell. You can see someone coming in, but the footage isn't great, and it's from far away at night." Elijah frowned. The footage was in black and white since it took place overnight, which didn't help with the clarity either. "Zooming in makes it worse. Sorry, but these are as good as useless. Must be cheap cameras."

"Shit. Well, thanks for looking anyway. I'll see you tomorrow, okay?"

"Of course. I'm gonna try digging a little deeper here. See you, dude."

Elijah opened his software and tried to pull up everything he could downtown. Even if there wasn't any luck on Third Street South, he hoped maybe there was another camera that would show the events leading up to the girl going missing. Whoever was responsible was careful; Elijah couldn't see anyone and in the one other instance where the kidnapper made an appearance, his back was facing the camera, offering no identifiable features.

Then, Elijah tried a different approach by searching for the victim online. The news report shared her first and last name, so Elijah used that to find her Facebook profile and other social media handles. Her email address was available on her Instagram profile, so he made quick work of logging in to her Facebook account, hoping there might be some conversation history that gave a clue.

Elijah laughed to himself when Facebook asked if he'd like to turn on multifactor authentication. He supposed it was good news for him that she had it off, but it was something that never got old.

There were about fifteen unread messages—he was careful to not open those so to avoid giving anyone false hope from a read receipt—and a ton of comments on her last post expressing concern. Elijah went back through the old messages that didn't have anything new in them, hoping to find something but she was squeaky clean.

Elijah slumped back into his chair, pulled his beanie off his head, and sighed—he hated this feeling. He rarely came up empty, and even though he knew logically that he shouldn't, he always blamed himself when he did. Between catching Stone Breaker and luring out the rest of the drug ring, Elijah had hoped for a bit of a break, but with people going missing, he wouldn't have a chance to properly help Brad plan for his wedding due to searching for clues. He hoped whatever Kane had to say tomorrow would get them in the right direction.

When his mind wandered to thoughts of Brad's wedding and everything that needed to be done, it reminded him of his own ticking clock to either find a new place to live or find a secondary source of income. Elijah moved through his bedtime routine with a painful awareness of how rapidly his future was approaching but tried not to think about it too much once he laid in bed. He had a wonderful family, as small as it was, and his friends were the definition of reliable, so he knew he shouldn't feel alone.

But as they all got married and kept growing up, he felt stuck in perpetuity, a feeling he drowned out with his game console. With headphones plugged in, he played the latest *Pokémon* game to distract himself from the crippling reality of his situation before eventually falling asleep. It would be tomorrow's problem—at least that was what he kept telling himself anyway.

CHAPTER 3

Elijah slung his laptop bag over his shoulder as he got out of his car. He gave a quick glance around the parking lot and found the tan Honda Prelude. The car was about as old as he was, making it a dead giveaway that Kane was already there.

Elijah made his way to the back of the storage facility, weaving through the rows of identical units, and knocked three times on the door for Kane. It slid up not long after his knock, revealing Kane in an old pair of jeans and a T-shirt. The storage unit looked more or less the same as the last time Elijah visited. The papers that Kane used to have hanging up about Stone Breaker now lived in a file cabinet in the corner, which was a recent addition to the space. Now, there were some photos of Reiji Sato and various South Main Burgers locations with sticky notes pasted over them. Each of the sticky notes had information scribbled on them, some in Kane's handwriting and others in Rory's.

"Looks like you've been busy."

"Yeah, you could say that. Only reason I sleep these days is because Rory shares her melatonin gummies with me."

Elijah noticed a large bruise on Kane's collarbone with a fresh scar.

"You should pick up some with CBD in them too; it'll help with the inflammation. You okay?"

"Eh, it hurt like a bitch, but I've had worse." Kane shrugged. "Though that's probably not a bad idea."

"So, what did you find when you went after Mr. Sato?"

"He called someone but I couldn't make out who. Sounded like he was going off in Japanese."

Elijah blinked as he waited for Kane to continue speaking. "That was it?"

"Well, they shot at me a ton too." Kane rolled his eyes as he ushered Elijah over to his desk. "Just as I finally heard Sato talking, his friend that was in the backseat with him got me. But that's not what we're here to talk about."

"Alright, alright. Forget I asked. What did you call me for?"

"This," Kane said, as he sat in the metal folding chair and slid his phone across the desk. The phone's web browser was open to a rental listing online that had recently been taken off the market.

"The place a few houses down from mine?" Elijah's bottom lip found its way between his teeth, as he picked the phone up and tried to understand what Kane was getting at. He squatted next to Kane to be closer to his eye-level. "What's the big deal?"

"I want to look into the girl who moved in," Kane said. "Well, I sort of already started. Rory's been helping me. But we need your help too."

Elijah set the phone down on the desk. "Why? You know her?"

"Well, no. That's the thing. Nobody does." Kane rose an eyebrow. "That's weird, right?"

Elijah thumbed through the photos of the listing. "Why is that weird? People move all the time. That house has been up for rent for, like, a year now. I'm surprised they didn't just sell it."

Kane's eyes shifted from the phone screen to Elijah. "That's part of why I think it's so weird. The people who lived there before were pretty well-to-do. Maybe they were in on whatever Reiji's got going on."

"What makes you think so?"

"Nothing in particular. There are just very few people I trust these days to not do anything weird. You know everyone on that list." Kane brushed some of his hair back with his hand before throwing it up in a messy bun. Elijah noticed Kane's hands lightly trembling as he then reached back for his phone, a telltale sign of his nerves. "Anyway, we found out who moved in. Her name is Hannah Cohen."

"So I've heard."

"Great! Then I don't need to explain. I'll send you everything we've already dug up about her. But do you think you could do a deeper dive?"

"Sure, yeah," Elijah said. His email dinged as Kane sent it. The file was so large that it ended up sending via Google Drive. "Man, this feels dirty," Elijah said with a shudder. "And not for nothing, but we gotta get this off of Drive. Now." Elijah reached into a desk drawer and grabbed a few thumb drives. "Next time, pull a Reiji and put them on here."

"Right. Anyway, this is all public info, so don't feel bad about it or anything. Naomi and Rory did way worse damage to Mark and look at how much good that brought us."

Elijah sighed. "Yeah, but that doesn't mean I like it. At least with Mark, they had good reason to think that Mark was up to no good. This girl is a complete stranger."

"A complete stranger who moves here at the same time as all this drug ring drama and girls start going missing? Yeah, totally not suspicious," Kane said. "You're not a little bugged out by it?"

"I mean I am, but it's a fifty-fifty shot as far as I'm concerned."

"Well, let's make sure we know."

"Yeah, yeah."

"Just find out whatever you can about her. Even if it means you have to meet her yourself in person."

Elijah's hands fell to his hips, as he sharply looked at Kane. "Whoa, whoa, whoa. Wait. What? What are you saying?"

"I'm saying go make a new friend," Kane said, sarcasm all but dripping from his voice. "I don't trust the timing of this. You're single. Go take her on a date or something."

Elijah gawked at him, unsure of what to think. "Excuse you!"

"You haven't gotten any in years, man. At worst, you break her heart and I get to send her to McMahon. At best, you get some. You can thank me in advance," Kane said with such ease that Elijah could barely believe it.

"Now this feels *really* dirty."

"Come on. We need this, and there's no one better fit for this job than you."

"I'm the computer guy, not the James Bond type. You and Jameson are much better suited for the theatrics, thank you."

"Can you imagine Jameson doing this, though?" Kane raised an eyebrow at Elijah and then said, "That's what I thought."

Elijah exhaled his frustrations, hating that Kane had a valid point. "You're a sick asshole, you know that?"

"Why thank you." Kane winked. "Where would I be without you?"

Elijah rolled his eyes, not blind to how thick Kane was trying to lay it on now. "Dead in a ditch somewhere, probably."

"Oh, ouch." Kane clutched his chest. "That hurt more than getting shot."

"Now you're just being extra on purpose."

"You'll do it though, right?"

Elijah realized he'd been picking at one of his nail beds with his thumb. He wasn't sure how long he had been doing that for. "Fine. But only because I don't want any more people to go missing, and I think your cause of concern is at least a little valid."

"Thank you!" Kane clasped his hands together. "I seriously owe you one, Elijah. Which reminds me … I may have gotten the ball rolling on this for you."

"Say what now?"

"Well, Rory and I did a bit of preliminary investigation. Hannah Cohen is Jewish. She's new in town, so she'll probably be looking to meet people. There's not exactly a synagogue anywhere between here and Denver, so we may have taken the liberty to sign you up for this dating app we found."

"You *what*?!" Elijah couldn't believe what he was hearing, but he could believe the casualness with which Kane told him this.

"Yeah. It's like Tinder, but just for Jewish people. We thought she might be on there and if she's not, well, maybe you'll find a date for the wedding or something."

"Ah, yes. A date for the wedding with a stranger who lives all the way out in Denver."

"I mean, an hour and a half or so isn't really that long distance, is it? And that's assuming things with Hannah don't work out."

Elijah groaned. "How did you even make this for me?"

"I created an email address for you, and then Rory just pulled some of your pictures from Facebook. You're Reform and keep kosher, right? I thought you were but wasn't totally sure."

"Yes. Oh my God, why am I even answering you?"

"Just give me your phone."

Elijah begrudgingly handed his phone over to Kane, who downloaded the app onto Elijah's phone and logged him in. He faced a light blue screen featuring a girl's photo, name, age, and a brief description.

"So, what do I do?"

"If you think she's cute, swipe to the right. Swipe left if you aren't interested."

Elijah leered at Kane. "This feels antisemitic." He was only half joking and Kane knew it.

"And I thought you said that I was the dramatic one."

"I'm going to swipe left on everyone to spite you," Elijah said, making quick work of it just to prove a point.

"Then don't come crying to me when you're moving back in with your parents."

"Wait, dude," Elijah said. He froze, forcing himself to stop his thumb from moving. "What did you say that girl's name was again? Hannah, right?"

"Yeah, Cohen."

Elijah stared at his phone's screen. The profile listed was for a woman named Hannah who was less than a quarter mile away. Her photo was casually inviting, with an outfit that was modest yet chic. It must have been from a professional photo shoot, likely from when she had taken headshots for her author photo in her book's jacket sleeve. Her dirty blonde hair reached her shoulders and was lightly blowing in the breeze. Elijah couldn't tell where she was based on the background of the photo but based on the palm tree that was out of focus, it certainly wasn't Colorado. If she was working for a drug ring, she was perfect for the job; she'd be the last person anyone would suspect.

"Did you guys find her social media pages or anything like that when you did your … how did you word it, 'preliminary investigation'?"

Kane nodded. "Don't tell me you already found her."

"Does this photo look familiar?" He held his phone out so Kane could see more easily.

"Dude, that's her!"

"So, what if we don't match?"

"Then we figure out a way to stage a meet cute."

Elijah rolled his eyes. "I'm not a character in your students' books."

"Well, get ready to be." Kane patted Elijah on the shoulder. "What's her bio say?"

Elijah read it out loud. "*New York Times*-bestselling author, Florida transplant, she/her. Combating writer's block by speed running *Breath of the Wild* on Twitch. Reform Jew, mostly kosher."

"Swipe right. Let's see what happens."

Elijah took a deep breath and swiped to the right. A neon blue Star of David flashed onto the screen with three words written in the center: *It's A Match!*

Elijah immediately panicked. He hadn't expected to actually find Hannah on this app that Kane set him up on, never mind match with her so soon.

"Message her already!" Kane exclaimed. "What are you waiting for?"

Brad's words ran through his mind too. His friends were right: he needed to start taking chances, and Kane needed his help. Part of him hoped that Kane and Rory's fears were for nothing and that Hannah would make for a nice plus one to Brad and Naomi's wedding. He suddenly noticed his own heart pounding in his chest, then tried to shake the feeling. His brain told him that there was no point in getting excited.

"What do I even say?" Elijah asked.

"Just be casual," Kane said. "I dunno. I'm not exactly the best person to ask for relationship advice."

"I mean, you got together with Rory after pining for God knows how long."

"We don't have eight years to dick around and drag this out, Elijah."

"Touché."

Elijah sighed and stared at his phone. He glanced over her profile once more and then decided on something he hoped wouldn't be too cheesy.

> ELIJAH: Alright, I gotta ask: what's your speed run record so far?

His phone immediately dinged with her response.

> HANNAH: I've got it down to forty-five minutes. Trying to break forty though. Any pointers?

> ELIJAH: Maybe my moral support can give you an extra boost, lol

> HANNAH: Hey, I'll take what I can get.

She added the emoji sticking its tongue out to her reply.

> ELIJAH: Are you new in town?

Elijah knew the answer already, but Hannah didn't need to know that.

> HANNAH: Just moved in! You from around here?

> ELIJAH: Yup, lived here my whole life. So what brought you to Riverpeak, of all places?

> HANNAH: I wanted to see if Jack Nicholson had the right idea with The Shining

> ELIJAH: I'm not gonna find you frozen in the ice someday, am I?

Hannah led with the emoji that was crying from laughter.

> HANNAH: No, no. Hopefully not, anyway. I have made approximately zero progress toward my next book and my deadline will be here before I know it.
>
> HANNAH: Figured a change of scenery could spark some inspiration before it sneaks up on me, y'know?

Elijah showed Kane the messages. "I'm not sure if we should buy this or not."

Kane frowned. "I didn't even know people knew Riverpeak existed outside of here. Keep pressing."

Elijah nodded and responded to her message on the app.

> ELIJAH: How did you even find this place? I didn't even think it was on the map.

> HANNAH: I know someone who used to live here. She loved it but had to move for work. And it's waaay cheaper here than in Denver.
>
> HANNAH: My advances and royalties are decent, but they're not that decent, hahaha

Elijah turned to Kane. "I wonder who she used to know. I don't want to press too much so I don't sound like a serial killer."

"Keep it light," Kane advised, "and then offer to take her out."

Elijah nodded. "Right, right." He exhaled, feeling a bundle of nerves bubble up in his chest. He couldn't quite place why he was nervous, and he felt that twinge of anxiety so often these days that he almost felt immune to it now—almost.

He turned back to his phone.

ELIJAH: Well, you picked a good place. I think haunted hotels are the least of your worries.

HANNAH: Maybe you can tell me more about the town over dinner?

Elijah's eyes widened. "Wow, she's forward."

"Bingo," Kane said. "Let me know how it goes, dude."

"What else are we doing to check into this?" Elijah asked, as he replied to Hannah with his affirmations. "How do I know this isn't just a setup?"

"Okay, maybe it *is* a kind of setup, but it's killing two birds with one stone," Kane admitted. "Rory's combing through her books to see if she can find any deeper symbolism that could tip us off and is pulling some background info with Naomi. She didn't tell Naomi that the drug ring is connected to her dad, but she told her she thinks Hannah might be in it."

"How far do you want me to take this?"

"I trust you to do whatever you feel you need to."

Elijah groaned again. "This is so fucked up."

Kane laughed and leaned back in his chair. "Welcome to my life."

———

Elijah still felt nauseous over the whole thing the following morning. To his relief, he and Hannah sent a few texts back and forth, having moved off of the dating app. It did not convince him that this was helping at all, but he rolled with it. At the very least, it boosted his confidence, and Kane hadn't been wrong yet.

Naomi spent the night with Brad at their house, so Elijah made a point of quickly and quietly getting up, brushing his teeth, and throwing on some clothes so he could get out and try to take his mind off of everything for a few minutes. Elijah did little to tame his tight auburn curls beyond throwing his usual beanie over it. Even in the late spring, Riverpeak was always cold enough for one.

Elijah had a car, but the town was so small that he seldom used it in the warmer months. He genuinely liked the constant state of snow that

Riverpeak was in, but he cherished days like today when the sun shone, and the sky was clear. Hoping the briskness in the air and a fresh cup of coffee would wake him up, he opted to walk down to Jefferson's Coffee.

Elijah passed by the green house on his way downtown from the suburbs. He couldn't help but glance at it as he walked by, but he tried to not let it stop him despite his slight envy. Trying to find a one-bedroom place to live in a town where no one ever moved was proving to be a near impossible task, even with the decent enough living that he made. He had inquired at Kane's apartment complex, but even they weren't accepting new applicants this year.

The mom-and-pop stores lined the streets as he approached downtown Riverpeak. They were all in their neat, little row, slightly different shapes and sizes but creating the picture of a perfect small town. The grass was finally peeking through the snow, its color returning to it after a long winter, but the mountains in the near distance still wore their snow caps. The smell of Jefferson's Coffee lured Elijah in like it did every Sunday morning, the strong and fresh notes of mocha mixing with the faint scent of spruce from the nearby woods.

But Elijah snapped right out of his thoughts when he saw an unfamiliar blonde in line in front of him. Her hair was the same length as Hannah's was in her profile photo on the dating app, but it wasn't until Mr. Jefferson at the counter took her name that he confirmed it was her.

His mind raced again. *What are the odds?* In a small town like Riverpeak, admittedly the odds were pretty great for something like this happening, but he'd hoped that it wouldn't be today of all mornings. As he rattled off his drink order to Aaron Jefferson, Elijah saw her standing by the other end of the counter, sending a text to someone on her phone. He wondered if she was talking to anyone else on the dating app. If she kept her options limited to the Riverpeak area, he'd be the only one—after all, he was the only Jewish guy in town besides his father. Her seeing other people might put a hiccup in his plan.

"Hannah?"

She looked up to face him with large, dark eyes like a doe. The bright lights above caught on her simple, silver Hamsa necklace that rested against her black turtleneck, bringing it to Elijah's attention as if to further confirm that this was, in fact, her. A few buttons adorned her denim jacket, including one from NaNoWriMo, an anime character, and some Zelda symbols. She was significantly shorter than him, almost comically so, forcing Elijah to have to look down at her. Elijah cursed himself for wearing an old pair of joggers and a hoodie, but deciding that he needed to cement himself in her life now or never, even with the promise of a first date coming up.

He hated that she was even prettier in person; a genuine attraction would only make things more complicated. She flashed him a smile, and he reciprocated, hoping time wasn't actually moving as slowly as he felt it was. His brain felt like static on an old television set and his heart pounded against his chest, even though all she did was look at him. He could have sworn his heart dropped into his stomach. All he'd said was her name, but he still felt as if everything was happening too fast, and he couldn't get the wires uncrossed in his brain. It was unnatural, and he knew it, but he didn't have time to think about it too much. He needed to roll with it, whether or not he liked it.

No matter what, he reminded himself he needed to stick to the plan. At least this way he could get it over with.

CHAPTER 4

Hannah had never seen somebody so effortlessly handsome until she laid eyes on the man behind her in line, making her all the more grateful that she swiped right. Light freckles dotted his cheeks and prominent nose, perfectly highlighting the structure of his face and his cheekbones. His eyes were a brilliant shade of green that Hannah had never seen before, like a deep forest that was vibrant with life, yet cautious enough to stand strong. They rested beneath full eyebrows that suited him well and matched the soft, dark auburn curls sticking out beneath his knit beanie.

She recognized him right away.

"Elijah! Hi!" She smiled at him, feeling like this was an interesting twist of fate. "You are so tall, holy shit."

Elijah laughed. "I guess I left that out of my profile."

"Either that or I'm just horribly short. Maybe both are true. Probably both. Is this your usual coffee joint?"

"It's the only one in town, but even if it wasn't, the coffee's fantastic."

Her cheeks ruddied. "Right. Small town, Makes sense. What brought you to the app?"

"My best friend is getting married later this year, and they're all tired of me being single. I think they were hoping I could find a date."

"Well, I'm glad they did. It's nice to meet you in the flesh."

"Yeah, you too," he said, as he shifted his weight from one foot to the other. "I wish I had known I'd see you here. I'd have paid for your coffee."

"Don't worry; I don't require bribery for friendship."

As Hannah said it, a voice in the back of her head said she was a naïve fool. *Maybe I am being naïve,* she thought, *or maybe I was in the coffee shop at the right place at the right time.* If she was going to make it in Riverpeak for the next year, she needed friends. If they happened to be easy on the eyes, it was just a bonus.

So instead of listening to that voice, Hannah focused on Elijah in front of her. She felt Elijah's nerves radiating off of him and hoped they were butterflies, the kind that fluttered from the stomach and scattered in the chest. She felt them herself as she stared at him, in part because she was excited to finally make a friend and also because he was even better looking in person.

Elijah went to say something but stopped himself when Hannah's drink slid across the counter.

"Order for Hannah! Here you go. You new here?"

"Yeah, why?"

Aaron faked a grimace. "Explains a lot, that's all."

Hannah swirled her coffee a bit in her hand. "Is it that obvious?"

"You look like you're ready for a snowstorm."

Elijah laughed. "Aaron's not wrong."

"Oh, please! I think you're both being dramatic."

"Here you go, 'Lij,'" Aaron said as he grabbed an iced coffee. He pointed at it and then said to Hannah, "That's the sign of a local."

"Whatever. I'll get back at both of you in the summer when you're complaining about the heat."

"Sure, sure. Well, I'm Aaron. Let me know when you're ready to drink like you live here."

"Yeah, yeah. Will do. Nice meeting you." She looked at Elijah, who moved in sync alongside her as they made their way out of the cafe. "What are you up to today?"

He shrugged. "I don't have anything planned. Do you?"

"I was going to scope out some cool places to write for when I feel like getting out of the house. Anywhere come to mind?"

"Actually, yeah. I can think of a few spots. Want me to show you around?"

"I'd love that! Thanks. You said you grew up here?"

Elijah nodded.

"What made you stay?"

"A few things. My parents are here and they're kind of all I have, besides my brother in Denver, so I didn't want to move super far from them. I work from home, and my friend Brad needed a roommate, so we moved in together. He's the one getting married, so I'll have to figure something out if I don't want to move back in with my parents."

"It's nice that you're close with them. I wish I could say the same."

Elijah made a mental note of that. "I definitely got lucky, that's for sure." He scratched the back of his neck. "All of my friends ended up back here, actually. I dunno. I guess it's just a Riverpeak thing."

Hannah nodded. "My old hometown was like that. Tiny, little suburb in New England. We moved to Orlando when I was in middle school. There's something to be said for it, I guess."

"I suppose." He wasn't sure what to say, so he took a sip of his coffee.

"I like your rings."

Elijah glanced down at his hand. "Oh, these?" There were two, one on his right ring finger and another on his thumb. "Thanks. They're old family heirlooms. I'm surprised you even noticed."

"Eh, I've been told I'm quite observant."

Hannah looked him up and down. Elijah seemed nice enough, but something about him was so stiff. Typically, she'd find this off-putting enough to shrug off and move on, but it perplexed her. Hannah could tell he was receptive to her but sensed something troubled behind his eyes and in his posture. *Maybe that's where those nerves stem from,* she thought.

"We're coming up on the end of the main strip now. This'll take us straight to Constance's Pond. It's a pretty walk."

"A pond, huh? Is it nice?"

"Yeah, it's got a little park and some benches. Anything striking your fancy along the way for a writing spot? First impressions, perhaps?"

"Hmm." Hannah took a moment to think about her answer. There was so much she could say but didn't want to info-dump on him. Hannah noticed that Riverpeak's sole defining feature was that it had none. The town was relatively small—only a few hundred people lived in Riverpeak based on census data she found online, which seemed accurate based on her stroll through—but the majesty of the snow-capped Rocky Mountains along the trail to the park was as refreshing as the drink in her hand. Perhaps it was because it was so foreign, but something about the mountain air hitting her skin felt exhilarating.

Hannah could feel the difference already, in that she felt freer now that she was several thousand miles away from home. *The difference in altitude probably has something to do with it too*, she thought, especially when combined with the residual nerves from Elijah beside her.

"I'm not sure yet because it's so quiet. Like, freakishly quiet. But I think I like that about it here so far." She didn't want to directly call him out on his stiffness, in case he was just awkward around new people, so she said, "I feel like I'm missing something, you know? I'm glad I ran into you so you could show me around."

When Elijah blushed, he surprised himself. He tried to remember what brought him here in the first place so his head could rule over his heart.

"Anytime," he said as nonchalantly as he could, and then realized he had to work harder to get her to like him if he was going to earn her trust. Dizziness accompanied the thought and he tried to shake it off; it felt unfamiliar, but he thought maybe he was still nervous and tried to shake it off. "I'm glad my friends convinced me to join that app."

Hannah nodded with a soft smile in agreement. "So, is there anything I should know about Riverpeak? Like maybe why everyone's so obsessed with Bigfoot? I've seen signs everywhere."

"Ha! Nothing too crazy. I would just steer clear of anything east of city hall. Not because of Sasquatch. I'm not sure if you've watched the news or anything since moving here, but there's kind of a drug problem that operates outta there." He was curious how she'd react to this news, so he used his iced coffee to hide his expression as he took another sip and watched her closely in his peripheral. "It looks like a city from a quick glance, but it's just a very failed past attempt at bringing businesses out to bumfuck nowhere."

"I heard about that, yeah. Can't be worse than Florida men on bath salts, but I'll keep that in mind."

Elijah wasn't sure if Hannah's overall lack of reaction was noteworthy or not. Her dismissal of it caught his attention, but it was too early to know if her trying to lighten the mood was intentional or just something she always did.

"I dunno. It's weird. It stays pretty concentrated. I think whoever is in charge is pretty territorial."

"Think they'll ever catch 'em? I saw that guy's arraignment hearing last night when I was trying to learn more about it here. Stevens, right?"

"Yeah, he was on the city council. Not sure how much will actually change, though."

"Time will tell, I guess."

Elijah nodded; she was right. Time would tell him what he thought of her too.

They slowed their pace as they approached Constance's Pond, which rested in front of a small grassland. The grass was tall and yellowed, but low compared to the skyline of the Rockies. Some frost still coated the top of the grass, preventing it from fully coming to life.

"Here we are."

Hannah couldn't help but smile to herself as she looked across the mountains' reflection in the water, looking like every Instagrammer's dream come true. "This is so beautiful. God, I can't get over the mountains. There's like, no one here, either."

"Just wait 'til summer. Everyone'll bring their kids fishing or fly kites once it thaws out a bit more. Just watch for moose. They come through now and then."

"Oh, are they mean?"

"I mean, no, but they're not exactly friendly either."

"Aw, too bad. They're cute. Do you come here a lot?"

Elijah wasn't sure why he was caught off guard by the question, but it still made him clear his throat. "I used to come here a lot with my friends when we were kids. I don't so much anymore, though."

"Where do you like to hang out, then?"

Elijah internally panicked, despite how innocent of a question it was; he couldn't answer honestly. He released a nervous chuckle and passed it off with, "You know, I'm realizing that I don't have much of a social life these days."

"Well, we'll have to change that then, won't we?" She grinned at him as he fought back the ruddiness that once again threatened to overcome his cheeks. Hannah sensed some hesitation in the way his free hand suddenly shoved in his pockets, and it stayed there until they returned to Main Street.

On their way back through town, Elijah took care to point out a few spots in downtown Riverpeak that they missed. Most of the boutique shops were open for the day, but they strictly stayed on the sidewalks, too wrapped up in conversation to even window shop.

As they reached the suburbs, Elijah said, "If you ever need anything, I'm only a few doors down."

"Thanks." Their street was so close to the small downtown area that it hadn't taken them long. Hannah debated letting him into her house but didn't want to give the wrong impression, especially after only having just met him. She could tell that Elijah was nervous enough for whatever reason and feared the idea may throw him over the edge. "Same to you. Thanks for giving me the lay of the land."

"Yeah, yeah. So, we're still on for dinner Friday night?"

"Yeah, looking forward to it. Give me your phone."

Elijah grabbed it from his pocket and passed it to her. Hannah pulled up her Facebook profile.

"Here. In case you want it."

"This prevents me from having to look like a creep by trying to find you on there, so thank you." They both laughed as he sent the friend request. "I'll see you Friday."

———

Once Hannah was inside, she pulled out her own cell to accept his friend request, eager to learn more about him. His profile photo was from his grad school commencement ceremony, black gown open to reveal his button-up and slacks beneath. His cap and diploma were both in hand. Elijah didn't have a blurb beneath his name, but his information checked out compared to what he'd told her so far:

Systems Engineer at Western Mountain Technologies.

Studied Computer and Information Sciences at University of Colorado Denver.

Single.

That last confirmation is a relief, she thought.

Hannah couldn't help her smile as she tapped to see Elijah's about info, especially now that she was confident he was exactly who he said he was. His birthday was on May 27, only about a month and a half away, and his parents and brother were both listed under the section with family members.

Hannah moved on to his photo albums and got lost in some pictures, even though there weren't a ton. Most of them were photos or videos someone tagged him in versus uploaded himself. She scrolled through past parties, college memories, and an assortment of photographs taken over the years. She even went as far back as his younger brother's bar mitzvah.

As she scrolled through his page, she couldn't help but feel like there was something more to him. Hannah understood that not everyone was super active on social media, but with the way he spoke about Riverpeak, she suspected he'd bitten his tongue. Hannah continued looking through his Facebook for any clues about him as she moved to her office and reached absently for her compression gloves (advertised as being perfect for arthritis or carpal tunnel, making them her saving grace).

She paused to glance out the cracked open window behind her desk, which had a pleasant view of the mountains beyond the other rooftops. If she felt like snooping, her next-door neighbor's yard was also directly in her line of sight. Their dog played in the backyard, occasionally barking at the teenager next door. When the breeze came through the window, she could faintly smell someone cooking brunch.

Her phone buzzed with a text from her friend Michele, snapping her out of a trance.

> MICHELE: Stuck on the runway in La Guardia FML. How's your new town?

> HANNAH: It's in the middle of nowhere OMG. Literally perfect.

> HANNAH: It also has IRL superheroes, soooo that's a thing.

Hannah tacked on the side-eyes emoji before hitting send.

> MICHELE: Wait, for real?!

> HANNAH: Lol yeah, there's this vigilante who wears a mask and fights crime lords or some shit. Pretty sure he can't die?

> MICHELE: What do you mean by can't die?

> HANNAH: Like literally cannot die. Immortal. Has a subscription to life that cannot be canceled.

> MICHELE: Immortality arc in your next book then??

> HANNAH: That's what I'm sayin!

> MICHELE: Ok but how do I join cuz...

> HANNAH: Don't worry, I'll let you know if I figure it out. You know, for book immortality arc research, ofc.

Hannah added the emoji that was winking and had its tongue sticking out before she hit send and then turned to Google, trying to learn what she could about the local vigilante's gifts. She wondered how much Elijah knew, but she didn't want to press him too much in one day. If she couldn't find it out now, she figured she'd get it out of him eventually; after all, she had at least a full year. She was in no rush if it meant she got answers.

Her phone ringing broke her concentration. When Hannah saw the name on the caller ID, her mood instantly soured. As much as she didn't want to, she begrudgingly took it.

———

Kane took his phone out the second he heard Hannah answer her own. The vibrations of the phone against the desk alerted him from his position on her rooftop, but he wasn't sure if she'd answer or if it was just a spam call. He opened the audio recording app that Naomi shared with him and pressed play, hoping for some sort of clue. There was no hello or introduction from Hannah.

"Yeah?"

There was a long silence on Hannah's end. Kane wasn't sure if she hung up or if the person on the other end was just long-winded. He couldn't make out what was being said on the other line; if it hadn't been for her cracked window, he wouldn't be hearing anything at all.

"Listen, I really don't want to talk about it."

A brief pause.

"No, no. Please, for the love of God, just stop."

To say she sounded exasperated would be an understatement. Kane was dying to know who she was talking to, as he waited for the bits of conversation he could hear.

"No, it's really not that simple." Her irritation grew firmer, morphing into full-blown annoyance. "No, it's not. I don't care if you think it is. It is a lot more complicated."

Kane heard Hannah blow a raspberry as she set something down; it sounded like an elbow hitting a desk as she switched positions.

"Listen, listen. God, do you stop talking?"

She'd snapped. She wasn't at the point of yelling, but Kane could tell from the bite in her tone that she was applying a great deal of restraint.

"You wanna say they did nothing wrong? Then where the hell is my ten grand, huh? Because I certainly don't have it, and I would love to know where it is."

Kane was half-tempted to barge in through the window right then and there but had the sense not to.

Hannah laughed but clearly didn't think whatever the person on the other line said to her was funny. "Believe me, that's not even scratching the surface of how badly they fucked this up. I'm gonna ask you again: where's my ten grand?"

A pause.

"Please, don't give me any excuses."

Another pause, longer this time, but still brief.

"What do I want? The respect that I've more than earned. And the ten grand would be nice, like I said."

Hannah's groan broke the silence that followed the phone call. Kane gave it a few more minutes to see if anything else would happen, then hit the end recording button and sent the file straight to Elijah.

> KANE For our records.

> KANE: And idk about you but $10k sounds a lot like drug money to me.

CHAPTER 5

The sushi restaurant felt alive with the patrons and staff running through the place, especially when paired with the sound of Japanese city pop playing softly over the speakers. It was a small hole in the wall wedged between two smaller shops on the main stretch of downtown Riverpeak. A few red paper lanterns hung from the ceiling, guiding the way to the oak sushi bar. The walls of the restaurant matched the bar, though a variety of artwork covered most of the wood: some vintage promos for Sapporo and Kirin beers, reprints of Edo-period art, an old *King Kong vs. Godzilla* poster, lucky cats of various sizes, and a collage near the bathroom that had different scenes from different manga or anime from the sixties through nineties. With the sushi chefs at work for everyone to see, it was almost a sensory overload given the small space but it still felt homey.

The woman at the front had mousy brown hair thrown up in a bun. She looked like she was the same age as Hannah's mother, maybe younger. Her faintly bloodshot eyes crinkled in the corners when she beamed at Elijah.

"Elijah, sweetie! Just two of you today?" She was already reaching for two menus.

"Hey, Mrs. Jameson. Yup, just two."

"Come on, I'll get you a table. Who's your friend?"

"This is Hannah. She just moved here. Hannah, this is my friend Shawn's mom." It physically pained Elijah to refer to Shawn as a friend, but at the end of the day, that's what he and Shawn were, whether they liked it or not. He also couldn't bring himself to say otherwise in front of Shawn's own mother.

"Oh! Well, welcome to Riverpeak. Can I get you two anything to drink while you look over the menu? Ladies first!"

"I'll have a green tea."

"Same."

"Great! I'll be back."

"This is probably one of the best places to eat here if you want something casual," Elijah said. "And also one of the only places. The French place down the road is kinda fancy, but they burned down a few weeks ago and are still cleaning up."

"Oh, shit."

"Yeah. It was that Stone Breaker guy."

"What a prick. I heard about the drug thing with that vigilante or whatever you wanna call him ... Hematite, was it?"

Elijah nodded. "Yeah. The east side of town is really volatile right now."

"I can imagine. I went down the rabbit hole for that on Google the other night after you warned me about it. What's his deal?"

Elijah swallowed. He knew he couldn't say much and was curious about what Hannah might say, so he'd need to tread the waters of this conversation carefully.

"Hematite doesn't view his powers as a blessing. I personally think it would be nice. But I've heard he hates it. Rumor also has it that he didn't have the best childhood, thanks to those drugs. So, I think he's trying to just make a better future for the town's kids."

"You seem to know a lot about him."

"He's been around since I was in high school." Elijah shrugged, trying to play it off. "You hear things over time. Small town, you know? Everyone knows everybody's shit. But Hematite ... he's the one mystery that no one's been able to crack, I guess."

Hannah still got the sense that Elijah knew more than he was leading on, but she dropped it for now. "I saw there's a little diner near here too. Any good?"

"Yeah, they're alright. Standard diner stuff. Jameson's mom works there sometimes too, though she's usually there in the mornings and here at night. I hope you never meet him, to be honest."

Hannah laughed. "I thought you said he was your friend?"

"Ever since elementary school, it was always me, Brad, Kane, and Shawn. I don't think anyone really likes Shawn, but he kind of never left. We've all been through so much shit, though."

"Like what?"

Elijah looked up and saw Hannah glancing at him from over the large menu. Their eyes met, which compelled Elijah to tell the truth, but he swallowed it back. He reminded himself that he was the one here to figure out what she was up to, not the other way around. He could have easily chalked her questions up to her being curious about her new town, but he couldn't help but wonder if she somehow knew.

Their gaze only broke when Mrs. Jameson arrived with their tea. She set the two cups down and rested the pot in the middle of them. They both thanked her in sync.

"Of course! The usual to start?"

"Do you like gyoza?" Elijah asked. Hannah nodded. "Yes, please. Thanks, Mrs. Jameson."

"Veggie, right?"

"You got it."

Once she was off again, Elijah caught Hannah looking at him expectantly. Her light hair looked a shade darker in the dim lighting of the restaurant, and he could see the reflection of one of the lit-up paper lanterns in her eyes. He'd hoped she would have forgotten her question and cursed himself for having said too much already.

This was backfiring.

"Kane and Shawn have never had it easy." *Simple would be best*, he thought as he prayed that this could work to his benefit. Elijah whispered, "This isn't the only job she has. Jameson and Kane are both from the east side."

Hannah nodded in understanding. She suspected there was more to it, especially in how Elijah's eyes darted away from her own.

"And you?"

"Me?"

"Yeah, you." There was a twitchiness in how Elijah looked away that hinted he wanted to say more, so much more, and Hannah would take any crumbs she could get. "Not that I'm implying you had anything to do with that, but you know. Do any mysterious secrets await me?"

Hannah smiled, and Elijah felt a pull to her. Something was physically drawing him closer to Hannah, prompting his elbows to prop up on the table as his chin found its way to his hand as he spoke. His eyes never left Hannah's, as the sensation caused a warmth to pulse out from his chest.

Part of his brain tried to fight back; it wasn't like him to feel strongly about *anyone* this early on, romantic or otherwise. He never believed in love at first sight, but something supernatural took over and Elijah let it, as the smell of jasmine and green tea leaves wafted toward him.

"Nah, I'm pretty run-of-the-mill."

"Oh, don't sell yourself short. Didn't you just say you and your friends have been through some shit?"

Elijah laughed as he mentally cursed himself out. "Yeah, but nothing crazy. Let's not pretend that I'm the only mysterious one here," Elijah said. Relief washed over him when Hannah didn't press further. "What's it like being a big-shot author?"

"Please. My genre is niche enough that I don't know I'd call myself a big shot, but I wouldn't trade it for the world. I get to essentially spend my time in a fantasy world for a living. But when you hit a creative block, it's rough, so I like to try to keep my head down."

Elijah noted her phrasing. "Truth be told, I think the whole town already knows that you're here, head down or not."

"Yeah?"

"Yeah. Shabbat these days is just praying over challah and then town gossip about the new author in town once my mom's downed a glass of wine, in that order."

"And does she know we met on a dating app?"

"No, no. I haven't said anything. Don't worry, I'm good at keeping secrets if need be."

Hannah raised an eyebrow at him. Now *that* was what she was looking for from him, wondering what secrets Elijah kept close to his chest. Before she could think about it too much, her phone vibrated in her pocket and the screen of her smart watch lit up. She gave it a quick glance before rejecting the call.

"Sorry about that. Well, I'm trying to be a bit more of an open book. Pun not intended. I don't need to be kept a secret."

"Is that so?"

"Mhm. I'm trying to live more in the moment, you know?" She took a sip of tea, enjoying the earthiness on her tongue, and Elijah mirrored the action. Her phone vibrated again, and she tapped the reject button on her watch faster this time. Hannah took a second sip of tea to wash down her aggravation and then continued as if it wasn't happening. "It wouldn't shock me if the leasing agent was the one who spilled the beans. When I met her to get the key, she wouldn't stop talking. Apparently, she's part of some local book club that read one of my books."

"Oh, yeah, I think my friend's girlfriends are in that. Do I know her?"

"Probably? I think her name was Carla."

"Oh, yeah." Elijah rose his brows as he took another sip of tea in order to bite his tongue. "Doesn't shock me. She's friends with my roommate's fiancé. We're both in the wedding." He hoped bringing that up would ease some suspicions that she may have about Hematite; if Hannah suspected him as the vigilante, she might not if she thought he was too busy with a wedding.

"You sound thrilled," Hannah said, with a hint of sarcasm and a smirk. She paused when another server brought the gyoza over without a word, running a variety of plates to different tables in their row. They each grabbed a pair of chopsticks as Mrs. Jameson returned to take their sushi order.

Once they were alone again, Elijah asked, "Did you tell anyone you were moving to Colorado?"

"Just my best friend Michele. And my publisher too, what with taxes and all. I guess I have a track record for just up and going somewhere when I feel like it. This would be three-for-three, though this is my first time going somewhere for more than a week on a whim."

"No shit? Where to?"

"First trip was to London. You know those flight deals that are stupid cheap because someone goofed and listed it for, like, $50? I found one of those and just went for a few days."

"You'll have to show me how to find those."

"There are so many apps for that now. Oh, and then I hijacked Michele's family trip to Poland once. She was my little sister in my sorority back in college, and her parents felt bad because mine weren't the traveling type. My mother's way too anxious to ever get on a plane or drive further than a few hours, so they let me tag along. Again, told no one. Got to see where my great-grandparents were from before the family scattered in the forties, so that was cool."

"That is nice."

Hannah nodded as she took a bite of gyoza. "I promise I'm not a flight risk."

Elijah nodded. "Living in the moment."

"See? You get it."

He smirked. "I think your next book should be a memoir."

"I'm waiting until I'm older for that one," Hannah said. Elijah waited for the explanation as she took another bite of gyoza. Her phone went off a third time. "Oh my God, I'm so sorry. Some people can't take a hint. Let me just turn this off real quick."

She took her phone out to do as she said and then re-pocketed it. Given they called three times and she didn't seem worried, Elijah couldn't help but wonder who it was.

"Anyway. What was I saying? Oh yeah! Memoirs. Once a few people die, my likelihood of getting sued for defamation will go way down."

"Am I allowed to laugh at that?"

"Please do. I cope with humor."

"Valid."

"So, when do I get to learn more about your mysterious life, huh?"

An airy laugh passed through the smile that came over his face. Internally, though, he felt like he was going to combust. "It's really not *that* mysterious. You are considerably more interesting than I am."

"Says the guy who grew up with a superhero in his hometown! You must constantly feel like you're living in the next Hollywood blockbuster."

"Sometimes, admittedly, yeah," Elijah said. He pondered what he could say that wouldn't give too much away. The stakes were two-fold: he both couldn't say anything that gave away Kane's identity or involvement, especially with how tense everything was in light of Mark and Tom Stevens' arrests, and he also didn't want to scare away the woman across the table from him. Elijah wagered the only reason she was this interested in him was because he was the first person she met in a new town and was trying to find some inspiration for a new story. That was assuming she was innocent, but Elijah wasn't sure if he was convinced yet.

Hannah waited to see if he'd say anything else, but he simply averted his gaze from her to his tea. She knew she'd need to poke and prod a bit more to get some answers out of him, so she started with something simple. "So, tell me about your friends. Who else might I meet?"

"Well, there's Brad and Naomi, for starters."

"That's your roommate and his fiancé, right?"

"Yeah. Brad works at the vet clinic, and Naomi's a reporter for Channel 10. They're both super nice and have been together for practically forever. Then there's Rory, her best friend. She's dating our good friend, Kane. They both teach at the high school. Rory's quick as a whip, and Kane's always been the life of any party."

"Kane and Rory, got it."

"And of course, there's Jameson. I already told you about him. I know he and his girlfriend, Amy, have been going through some rough patches. It's pretty bad. I won't say much else since I don't want to kill the mood."

"Gotcha." Hannah nodded. "Anyone else?"

"That's it. They're an overall pretty chill group. It's typically pretty low-key when we get together."

It is a total lie, Elijah thought; nothing was low-key anymore. Their latest excursions included running from Mr. Sato's drug ring, trapping a supervillain with his own trap, and Elijah hacking into security cameras or Bluetooth systems. He normally wasn't the type to lie, but he wasn't even sure where it came from. It just fell from his mouth in an act of preservation for both him and his friends.

Elijah wondered if this was how Kane felt during all those years that he lied to Rory about his identity. He made a mental note to apologize for chastising him so much about it. *Now*, Elijah thought, *I understand*. Keeping it a secret from his parents or the other people he knew wasn't a problem; it was easy enough to just act like everything was normal when someone already had a preconceived notion of what his life looked like.

But presenting his life to a total stranger was a whole other challenge, especially when he found everything else about himself so ordinary when compared to her whirlwind of a life. He wondered how he could compare with impromptu trips abroad and penning the next great, modern fantasy romance. He wasn't even the superhero of his town—just the IT guy with twelve years' worth of secrets to keep and no powers of his own.

"You learn a lot about a person by their friends."

Elijah took a bite of gyoza to hide his expression, a trick Kane taught him. "Yeah?"

"Yeah. I think who we choose to spend our time with says a lot about us."

Their sushi's arrival interrupted them. They both quickly glanced at Mrs. Jameson to say their thanks before their eyes moved back to one another, locking in a silence that was equal parts comfortable and tense.

Elijah glanced away from Hannah as he took a bite. When he glanced back up, he noticed her eyes were still on him as she chewed. He rose an eyebrow to communicate, hoping the message of "Everything okay?" would be received despite the silence.

Hannah seemed to understand. Once her mouth wasn't full, she said, "I'm still trying to figure you out, Elijah Baron." She experimented with how his full name felt on her tongue and decided that despite them having only known each other briefly, it felt hauntingly familiar. "You don't talk about yourself much."

Hannah hoped her statement would put him on the spot. She noticed the way his eyes would dart away whenever she brought Hematite up, and that he'd talk more about his friends than he would about his own life. She was certain now that he was hiding something, and she couldn't help but wonder what it might be.

"Not much to say." Elijah shrugged a shoulder. He felt like his stomach did a flip, but not from the sushi.

"Even though there's never a dull moment in Riverpeak?"

Elijah internally cursed himself again. "You got me there."

"Alright then, let's start there. What's the craziest thing you've ever done?"

Elijah pondered on it. Bugging a government official's office so he could hack into their server and expose their dirty money was the first thing that came to mind. His first instinct was to keep that off the table, but it was just crazy enough that Hannah probably wouldn't believe it.

"Hacked the local government. Don't repeat that too loud."

"Is my FBI webcam agent gonna lose their shit right now?"

"Oh yeah. Big scale operation."

Hannah leaned back in the booth. "You're joshin' me."

"Do you doubt my skill?"

Hannah rose a brow. "No but come on. Don't get me all excited about something that's not true. That's all you got? No crazy escapades during Birthright?"

He couldn't help the smile. Why did she have to have such good comedic timing? "I'm not a big party guy or anything, and my mom never let us go on a Birthright trip, which I'm admittedly glad for, given, y'know, everything."

"Alright, fair. Same. Okay, I'm listening."

"Unfortunately, I don't have any crazy stories. Like I said, I'm pretty run-of-the-mill."

Even though he said it with such causality, Hannah sensed something beneath it.

"Well, maybe I like run-of-the-mill. So, what do you like to do, then?"

"I do like hiking. There are so many great places to hike around here too."

"You'll have to show me your favorite spots." Hannah took a bite of sushi, but the glimmer of her smirk never left her eyes.

"Would that be a date?"

"Would you be upset if it was?"

She was so cool and collected that it threw him for a loop. He nodded his head at an angle, as if he were considering it. "I'd only be upset that you haven't given me a proper chance to ask you out yet." The words fell out of his lips so fast, it surprised him that he even said them. Usually not one for such brazen confidence, but he felt at ease around Hannah in a way that was unlike him.

She laughed. "Then yes. It would be a date." Hannah's smile grew as she took a mental snapshot of this moment: the easily flustered Elijah Baron with a dusting of pink growing across his cheeks.

Before he could say anything in response, Mrs. Jameson arrived with the check. Elijah held one hand out to Hannah, as he reached into his pocket with the other. "Don't you even think about it."

As they left the restaurant, they each grabbed a mint from the dish on their way out.

"So, what do you think of Riverpeak so far?" Elijah asked. They walked side by side on their walk back to the suburbs. There wasn't much traffic on the roads, but the streetlights lit the way plenty enough. Elijah tried to not let himself feel too comfortable, as he reminded himself once more why he was really here.

"I've gotten more words down in the last week than I have in months. The mountains are certainly inspiring. Plus, there are a few mysteries here that I'm determined to crack. Yourself included."

"Me?" Elijah pointed to himself. "Nah! I'm telling you, I'm just a boring IT guy."

"See, I don't believe you," she said, half-accusation and half-joke. "I don't think you're boring. But I'll get you to crack one of these days."

Elijah swallowed and hoped she didn't notice the tension he felt developing in his shoulders. He awkwardly shoved his hands in his pockets, unsure of what to do with them now that he was hyperaware of his body language. "Is that so?"

"Mhm." Hannah felt a sudden rush of nervousness as a knot formed in her neck. A quick look at Elijah told her where the feeling came from, and she hoped her casual tone would help him relax. "I'm making it my personal mission in life. Writing deadlines be damned."

Elijah picked up on her teasing, but he still couldn't help but feel a bit of a chill shoot down his spine, as he wondered why she cared so much. "What do you think the craziest thing I've done is, then? Let's hear it, Sherlock."

Hannah pondered it for a moment. Elijah tried to shake the thought that her facial expression while deep in thought was cute. "I bet you've done some shit like Neo in *The Matrix*."

"Eh, it's a living," Elijah said with a shrug. They both laughed, and Elijah was just glad that Hannah played it off as a joke. The more he thought about it, the more he realized she was almost right. "So would that make you Trinity?"

"Oh God, no. I can't fight to save my life. If we're talking Keanu, even Bill and Ted could kick my ass."

They reached her house too soon for Elijah's liking. He wanted more time; their date went well, but he knew just as much going into it as he did going out. Elijah walked her to the doorstep, unsure of what to say next. It had been years since he had been on a date, and the idea of this being all for show muddied his brain. He wasn't sure if he morally should, but he asked her, "Is it okay if I kiss you goodnight?"

As Hannah nodded, Elijah brushed some of her hair behind her ear. He leaned down, and she met him part of the way by lifting up on her tiptoes so Elijah could gently capture Hannah's lips with his own. He thought the tension would release from his body when he did, but it only bubbled up more.

Hannah relished in the feeling of how soft his lips felt on her own, unsure of whether a kiss had ever made her feel so dizzy before. There was a trepidation there, both of them experimenting with one another, but neither of them felt in a rush to stop it. They smiled at each other when they pulled away, only to bring each other back in for a second kiss, equally sweet as the first. It remained closed lipped, but this time Elijah's thumb acted on its own accord and traced Hannah's chin.

"Good night, Hannah," he said, his nose nuzzling against hers as he mentally swore at himself. *I shouldn't have taken it this far,* he thought, but he felt like he was being pulled closer and closer to her. He wasn't any closer to figuring out what she was actually doing in Riverpeak, but instead found himself enjoying his evening a little too much. As his mind raced, he couldn't put his finger on why he was doing this, and he was already internally chastising himself for getting lost in the moment. He had more questions than answers, but perhaps that would come with time.

But when she smiled at him and said, "Good night, Elijah," he felt his heart leap in his chest. He finally understood what people meant when they said they felt like they were on cloud nine.

With a third, final fleeting kiss to try to shut his emotions up, he departed. Hannah waved at him from the door as she went inside, but once she was in, she felt like she was in a daze. The feeling of butterflies lingered in her stomach, and it only made her panic. She took a deep breath as she reclaimed her thoughts and took out her phone to text Michele. It would be late back on the East Coast, but Michele was a night owl anyway and Hannah knew she'd be up. The only thing Hannah *was* certain of was that she needed some advice from a trusted friend who wouldn't judge her, because catching feelings had not been part of the plan.

As Elijah walked away from her house, he felt an internal shift, like a tightrope snapping. A fog dissipated in his head that he hadn't even realized was there until it faded, like a spell losing its magic after its caster walked away.

There was only one thing he thought to do: grab his cell and call Kane's burner phone.

"Elijah? What's up?"

"I just had my date with Hannah."

"And?"

"Something wasn't right. It's like I forgot why I was there in the first place."

"I think that's just called having a nice night. Don't worry, I won't get mad. Besides, I don't expect you to get all the dirt on her in one date."

"No, dude. Like some Professor X shit or something." Elijah rubbed his eyes with his free hand, feeling the soft sleeve of his flannel against his cheek as he did. "I didn't even realize it right away, but my head was all messed up. Something's weird."

"Are you saying what I think you're saying?"

"That I think she's like you and Jameson? Yeah, I think she has powers."

CHAPTER 6

O f all the places Kane could have asked Elijah to meet up with him, he'd been hoping for anywhere but the abandoned South Main Burgers on the eastern edge of Riverpeak again. But there he was, wearing gloves that felt a bit too tight for him as he typed away on the computer to hack into it. The dust floated around them, lingering in the air like it was stuck in limbo. Elijah fought the urge to sneeze.

"Any luck?" Kane was dressed in his full Hematite attire, but the voice modifier was turned off since it was just the two of them.

"Just got in," Elijah said as the login window vanished, revealing the desktop. "Reiji is predictable, to say the least. Give me a few to pop around."

"You rock. I'll stay on guard."

As Elijah combed through the files, he sighed. "Nothing I haven't already seen. There's actually less here than there is on the thumb drives. I think Reiji cleaned house."

"Well, thanks for trying."

Elijah went to open one last folder, but a sudden acrid scent overwhelmed his nostrils. "Do you smell that?"

Kane lowered his scarves and sniffed, not moving the balaclava. "Smells like burning plastic."

Elijah stood from the chair, abandoning the computer and grabbing his backpack. "We gotta get out of here. Like, now."

Kane grabbed an old brick and hurled it at the window, shattering the glass so they could easily escape. The smell only grew stronger as they moved out, and once they were outside, they spotted the source: the garbage and recycling bins in front of the building were engulfed by slow flames.

"Someone on Reiji's team has a thing for fire, huh?" Kane asked, as he turned his voice modifier back on.

An unknown man called out, "Where do you think you're going?"

They didn't see whoever spoke. The male's voice sounded vaguely familiar, but neither of them had time to ponder over it. Kane and Elijah bolted, running for the nearest stretch of alleyways. Elijah pulled his beanie down over his head more, hoping to conceal any loose curls. The buildings they passed caught fire too, each one in slow succession. When Elijah glanced back, he saw that the South Main Burgers remained untouched, except for the trash and some exterior signs.

"How are the flames spreading this fast?"

"That's a question for another time!" Kane barked back.

As they ducked into an alley, Elijah pulled out his cell phone.

"What are you doing?"

"Texting Rory our location so we can get the hell out of here."

"Here, I know a safe spot we can hide out."

Kane grabbed Elijah's wrist and pulled him down an alleyway. There was a gap between two of the dumpsters in the alley that was just long enough for both of them to fit, if they sat facing each other. They sat in silence, listening for the sound of footsteps or crackling embers, but neither came. The smell of the garbage surrounding them took over Elijah's senses, especially with the fire burning in the near distance, making him wish he had something to cover his nose as Kane did. He had to stop himself from gagging when the breeze picked up.

When headlights passed and a car stopped, blocking the alleyway, they both peered around the edge of the dumpster to see who it was: thankfully, it was just Rory. They both scrambled to get out of the alleyway and into her car. Kane climbed into the front to sit next to Rory as Elijah slid into the back, quickly buckling his seatbelt so Rory could take off as soon as possible. They passed a few fire trucks on the way, sirens blaring as they sped in the opposite direction.

"Please tell me you didn't start those fires."

"No, no. I had Elijah hack into the computer at the old South Main Burgers. We were hoping for more information, but it's nothing that wasn't already on the thumb drives Shawn and I grabbed earlier."

"Who started them, then?"

"Not sure. We didn't get a glimpse of him."

"Shit. Sorry, guys. Where to?"

"The storage unit, if you don't mind."

"Of course not."

"Thanks." Kane leaned over to kiss her cheek. "Appreciate you."

"Please let Elijah stay home from now on. Poor thing looks like he's seen a ghost."

"I'm right here, you know."

Rory laughed. "Come on. I know you've taken worse roasts than that."

"I'm not even giving you the satisfaction of a response," Elijah said with a smile and not a trace of malice.

"Seriously, though, are you both okay?"

"Unscratched," Kane said. "Elijah caught a whiff of it just in time for us to bail."

When they reached the storage unit, Elijah left the car first with thanks while Kane stayed behind for a moment to chat with Rory privately. Elijah didn't mind waiting outside the car if it meant not feeling like a third wheel. He saw them kiss before Kane emerged from the vehicle, and they waited for her to leave before slinking off.

"There's usually no one here right now," Kane said. "We should be all clear."

"Good. I didn't see anyone follow us, either."

When they finally reached Kane's storage unit, Elijah took in the unit's changes as he set his bag down on the desk. Most of the newspaper clippings from Mark Stevens were back up but moved to another part of the walls to take up less space. Now, all the financial records Kane gave Brad for safekeeping hung up on the walls alongside them. There were also articles detailing South Main Burgers, anything featuring Reiji Sato—mostly business owner spotlights for Asian-American and Pacific Islander Heritage Month from the local newspapers—and more articles covering Noah's death, which were hung up at Rory's urging. They hung on the wall in rows, so Kane knew exactly what he was looking at and so that everything flowed in chronological order; he was surprisingly organized. Sometimes Elijah forgot Kane was a teacher, but it showed in moments like this.

"So, here's what I found," Elijah said. He'd reorganized the thumb drives into three smaller, labeled containers, which now took residence on the desk. "This one is just more financial records. Looks like they used the restaurant as a front since it's super easy to cover that much cash coming in and out. Most people would chalk this up to normal restaurant funds, and it makes it really easy to sweep shit under the rug." He set the second box down on Kane's table by his laptop. "These were all password-protected, but they had a bunch of the paperwork from that fire that killed Noah."

"Wait, for real? In the restaurant?"

"Yeah. I wasn't expecting to see it either. At least not from there. My guess is Reiji was hiding this from his wife."

"What was it?"

"I thought it might be something about his death records. But the more I dug into it, the weirder it got. The paperwork just doesn't make a whole lot of sense when you look at it closely. From a glance, you wouldn't question anything. But the info just doesn't add up. Some reports say they found a body; others don't. The only thing that's consistent is the time of death. It's bizarre."

Kane sighed. "So, what's next?"

"I found Reiji's secretary on LinkedIn. She had her email on there, so I sent her a phishing one with a link that'll download this Trojan on her computer and give me access. Now I just gotta wait for her to click on it. She looks like the type that would fall for that kinda crap."

"Do you think Reiji killed his own son?" Kane asked.

"I dunno, dude. Why would he do that? But that brings me to this."

Elijah picked up the third bin of USB drives. "This is the blackmail box. Mostly blackmail against Stevens."

"What do you mean by blackmail?"

"I wish I hadn't opened it, to be honest." Elijah grimaced as he remembered the evidence, which was burned in his brain against his will. "Tons of details about Stevens' affair with Chief Daniels. Text messages. Video. I was eating lunch when I went through this stack. I don't recommend you do the same."

Kane's nose scrunched when he frowned. "That is unfortunate."

"I don't think I can ever look at either of them the same again." Elijah shuddered. "There's also this with Brad's dad. Look." Elijah grabbed a thumb drive, plugged it into the computer, and opened a video file. "There's some security camera footage with him showing up right before the fire goes off and leaving right before he can get caught in it. He's also on a seller's list."

"Shit. I knew his dad was a hot mess but didn't realize he was my parents' coworker."

"I don't think anyone knew. His mom's pretty strait-laced. But I think it's a setup. I wouldn't be shocked if they called him there to make it look like someone else started the fire. But I'd be willing to bet that everything is internal."

"That tracks. I could see that. What else?"

"I also couldn't find anything tied to Hannah Cohen. But after taking her out to dinner the other night and texting her every day, I'm still not sure what to think."

"Oh?"

"There's a complete lack of paper or digital trial. Her phone rang a few times during our dinner, but she never took it. She just sent 'em straight to voicemail."

"Maybe the person who has her ten thousand dollars? I'm still convinced that's drug money. What else would that be?"

"Maybe, maybe not. I dunno. Like I said, she never took the call. If I was waiting for a payment that big, especially if it was dirty, I'd be taking that call no matter what. She just as easily could have snuck into the bathroom or something, but she didn't."

Kane raised a finger as he made his counterpoint. "Unless she's on to us."

"Which is a very real possibility. I didn't say anything—you know I would never—but I think Hannah suspects I know a lot more than I was leading on. And when I tell you I had some sort of weird brain fog, it was unlike anything I'd ever experienced. Like she always knew what I was thinking and could amplify it, if that makes sense. It's hard to describe."

"Do you think she's involved in whatever is going on with the missing girls? Maybe manipulating their trust and sense of ease?"

"Could be. I mean, I think that's definitely connected to Reiji some-how. Maybe it's Hannah, maybe it's him, but I'm leaning more toward him. But I want to look more into it before we say so for sure."

"I'll reach out to Potter. Maybe we can get Hannah over there. I'll see what his availability is to run some tests, if you can bring her in. What's your theory about the missing girls?"

"It's either a careless employee or intentional messaging. I'm gonna take a deeper dive into some of the files I copied over to save for myself. Between this and Noah's death records, I got a lot to hyper-analyze."

"Good. I want every T crossed and I dotted. I'll get Rory on it too. She's good at spotting shit I don't even think of. But thanks for all this, man."

"Of course. Here." Elijah handed Kane a thumb drive as he removed the other from the laptop. "This has a copy of everything. You can share it with Rory. More than one person looking at this kinda stuff is always helpful. It's easy to go cross-eyed after a while."

Kane's phone buzzed. "Speaking of Rory," he said. He picked it up and checked the text from her. "Holy shit. One of our students just went missing."

––––––––

Hannah relished in the low humidity levels as she typed away, overlooking Constance's Pond. A few kids were playing on the other side, their voices barely a whisper from the bench where Hannah sat. The mountains and sunset reflected in the small pond and the grass swayed gently in the breeze, but as the sky grew increasingly pink and brilliant, she packed up her laptop so she could head home before dark.

As she left, she kept an ear out. She'd come to this spot more often than not for her writing sessions, and the last time she did, she overheard a few men speaking in both English and Japanese. She hadn't made out the full conversation, but she picked up some words that were less than kind, if she remembered her half-hearted attempt at Duolingo lessons correctly. Even if she didn't know the occasional word in the mix, it was clear that the Japanese speaker was furious. It left her constantly wondering if they'd return and say more. The nosy side of her, however, was left disappointed.

When she cut through downtown, she felt a hand wrap around her forearm. She didn't have time to see where it came from as they jerked her into the nearest alleyway. The only light illuminating her path was from a pink neon sign coming from inside the tattoo parlor, visible from one of its windows, and a streetlight out in front of a closed boutique. Before she could say anything, the figure before her held a finger up to her lips. She glanced down at the finger, completely perplexed, before evaluating the man before her.

"Be quiet," he said. His voice sounded modified, and his attire was fairly simple: black pants, a navy hoodie, and boxing wraps woven around his hands. He wore a black, tattered cowl around his neck, which—when paired with his balaclava—completely covered his face, except for his eyes. Hannah could barely make his eye color out, despite their proximity.

"You're that Hematite guy, right?" Hannah said in a whisper. She shuffled a bit to try to wiggle out of his grasp.

"I need to talk to you." He stepped away from her, respecting her desire to be let go. If Hannah bolted, he was confident he could keep up, and keeping her at least somewhat comfortable would likely result in a more successful interrogation.

"About what?"

"About why you're really here."

Hannah frowned. "What is that supposed to mean?"

"How much did Reiji Sato pay you to move here?"

She blinked at him. "Huh?"

He repeated the question, harsher this time, and added, "Don't play dumb."

"I don't even know who that is," Hannah said. She couldn't help the way she blurted it all out. "Am I supposed to know who that is?"

Hematite stared at her for a few moments, but it felt like an eternity. Hannah's heart was pounding, which only worsened when she noticed he kept a hand where his billy club attached to his belt. The air felt thick between them. She wished Elijah was there to vouch for her character, but she only had herself to rely on.

Hannah started rambling. She mentally cursed herself the second she started but knew she could not stop now that her mouth was open. "Listen, Hematite, I think you're really cool. I can't fight to save my life. I don't know who Reiji Sato is, and I came here to run away from my problems at home and so far, it's working really nicely, and I'd like to keep it that way."

"What problems?" Hematite asked. Even though she couldn't see his face, and he had a voice modification system, she could tell he asked her through gritted teeth from his tone alone. His grip on the billy club tightened. Hannah mentally cursed again; she could have worded that better. "Did Reiji Sato offer you a way out of those problems? Does he have anything to do with the $10,000 you're owed?"

"What? No. My mom's fucking crazy." Hannah held her hands up, hoping he'd lay off. "Like, so crazy that it was preventing me from doing my job. You are one of, like, three people who know that." She took a breath, desperately needing fresh air in her lungs. "Wait a second. How did you know about the ten grand?"

Hematite scoffed at her. "Must be nice to just up and go instead of facing your issues."

"Believe me, it is nice," she agreed, feeling more desperate by the second, "but I definitely tried to face it. And it is not what you're thinking." She placed her hands on her hips as she sighed. "I totally fucked this up, huh? I swear, I have nothing to do with whatever the hell is going on. If anything, I've been eager to see what's up myself."

"Why? What's it matter to you?"

"At the risk of sounding like an insensitive asshole?" She'd phrased it like a question to soften the blow. "It doesn't matter to me, really. But, you know, writer's block and all. I'll take whatever crumbs of inspiration I can get at this point."

He continued to glare at Hannah, as she continued rambling in self-defense.

"It's really not that unusual. I think any author would tell you that their FBI webcam agent is a little concerned sometimes." She gulped down some bubbling nausea. "I'm not helping my case, am I?"

Hematite sighed. "No, you're fine. I can tell you're nervous."

"I talk a lot when I'm in situations like this, so sorry about that little, mini-trauma dump."

He let go of the billy club. Hannah released a breath, as her hands on her hips slid to her thighs. Each breath stung her lungs a bit, so she focused on her breathing.

"I do know who Naomi Sato is, though, so can I safely assume that she's related to Reiji?" Hannah looked up at Hematite and then stood up straight again, finally feeling balanced. "Well, I haven't met her, but I know of her and know some of her friends."

"It's her father. I'm investigating him." He only told her in case she was lying to him. It would serve as a warning in that event.

Hannah had a realization. "I think I can help you, actually. I heard a part of a conversation that I don't think I was supposed to hear."

Hematite's head tilted. "I'm listening."

"I was writing by Constance's Pond the other day, right? I don't think they spotted me on the bench, but I overheard a Japanese guy speaking to these two men outside. One guy he was with called him Ray. Now that you mention it, I'm assuming that's short for Reiji.

"Unfortunately, I don't know Japanese beyond some basic vocab. But some of it was in English."

"What did you hear?"

"If my anime-watcher brain recalls correctly, I heard a phrase that can mean 'I'll kill you.' He was talking to these two white guys. One man looked like he could be any thirty-something with brown hair that he slicked back. There wasn't anything noteworthy about him. The other guy looked like he was only a little older than me, but his hair was gray, you know? Hard to say how old he is with that, especially from a distance. They all went in and out of Japanese and English. They were talking a lot about business in English, specifically referencing a restaurant, but he never said which one."

"He owns a burger chain. Why didn't you tell anyone sooner?"

"Who would I have told?" Hannah was calmer than she expected in her response. "There isn't exactly a Hematite hotline. And I don't think the police do much with 'he said, she said' types of situations."

Hematite groaned; it was a mechanical sound with his voice modifier. He shook his head before he looked back at Hannah. "Touché. Thank you."

Hannah nodded, unable to say anything. She wanted to, but the lump in her throat was too suffocating.

"Don't think I won't still keep my eye on you."

"I don't know if that's threatening or reassuring."

"I don't know yet, either."

"You never told me how you knew about the ten thousand dollars."

He leaped up onto a nearby fire escape and was gone without another word. Hannah looked up to see him already halfway up the building. "Great," she said to herself with an exasperated sigh. As she continued her walk back home, she thought about what he asked her.

She thought over how she could have told someone sooner and why he'd think to ask that. Hematite hadn't seemed to have an answer for her either. *The only way*, she thought, *is if Hematite is someone I know.* She recalled how Elijah always seemed to look the other way when Hematite came up in conversation. Hematite was shorter than Elijah, so she knew it wasn't him, but that didn't leave his friends out of the question.

When Hannah got home, she went back down to the Google rabbit hole of Hematite. She tried more unconventional sources; when Reddit threads offered no help, she even signed up for a Nextdoor account and dove into the section of her security camera app that shared posts from neighbors. There were a few sightings listed, but no one had any clue what Hematite's identity could be. In fact, the more she looked, the more she realized that a lot of Riverpeak and surrounding Denver suburbs thought Hematite was older than Hannah deduced.

If he was one of Elijah's friends, he'd be in his late twenties, but some people theorized he was in his late thirties, since he started being a vigilante around twelve years ago. No wonder he could keep his identity under wraps so easily—no one was suspecting a twenty-seven or twenty-eight-year-old. Hannah blew a raspberry, feeling defeated.

The only thing she was certain of now was that she'd have to ask Elijah, but the real question was how she'd get him to actually tell her the truth.

CHAPTER 7

Elijah struggled with the button on his shirt's sleeve as he rolled it up. Even though it had been a few weeks since he and Hannah started talking, his hands still trembled. His clammy palms weren't helping his case, but even with his lightweight chinos, he'd be damned if he left the house in July with his sleeves down. Summer was in full swing, meaning the nights were temperate, yet still dry. He was glad Brad was already out with Naomi to celebrate Fourth of July with her and her friends; otherwise, he'd never live this down.

His anxiety stemmed from two places: he wanted to continue to make a good impression on Hannah, whom he was seeing tonight, but that was the lesser of his worries. What concerned him more was the rising threat of whoever was looming over Riverpeak. With Stone Breaker, they had clues hidden in Mark Stevens's newspaper articles, showing when his next move might be. But Reiji stopped relying on his lackeys and was taking the reins from his seat of power, moving swiftly and quietly, and there were still so many unknowns about the silver-haired man in the car with him.

All Elijah wanted was a normal night out with the woman he hoped to call his girlfriend, assuming all went well rather than to shit.

He knew that was probably asking for too much, but he hadn't realized how lonely he felt until recently. He suspected he *always* knew he felt this way but denied it time and time again until forced to face it headfirst. He reckoned it was why he enjoyed Hannah's company a little too much for someone who was dating her on assignment rather than organically. He poked at some of his dark auburn curls as he gave himself a once- over in the mirror but then sighed, gave up, and threw his usual beanie on.

No matter what Kane thought, one thing was certain: Elijah liked Hannah. He liked her a lot more than he should.

Later, when he knocked on Hannah's door, Elijah hoped he didn't look as nervous as he felt. If she was nervous too, she didn't show it. They greeted each other with a hug, which turned into a quick kiss. Elijah still couldn't believe it, even as Hannah laced her fingers through his own as they began the short walk downtown for the Independence Day festivities. Her hand was so much smaller than his and even though he knew he probably wouldn't last long in a fight like Kane, it still gave him the feeling that he could protect her if she was on Hematite's side. The feeling felt foreign; he hadn't felt about anyone like that ever before. He couldn't help but wonder if she even needed his protection or if someone on Reiji Sato's team already filled that position.

"You look deep in thought."

Hannah had snapped him out of it, as Elijah realized he was staring at her.

"Everything okay?"

He nodded. "Yeah. You look really nice." It was true—her red-and-white floral maxi dress flowed in the breeze beneath her denim jacket —so he hoped it would be enough to hide the real cause of his nerves.

"Thanks! You do too. Though I doubt that's the only thing on your mind." Hannah gently nudged his elbow without removing her hand from his.

"You're right, admittedly. How'd you know?"

"I guess I'm good at reading you is all. I'm quite observant, remember? Though I often find myself trying to crack your case, I am getting better at it."

Elijah grinned. "And what makes you so determined to crack my case, anyway?"

"I dunno," she said playfully. "Maybe I have a crush on you."

He laughed. She was always making him laugh, and he hated that. It was just making his heart tug away from his brain even harder, like a rubber band that would inevitably snap.

"There's something behind your eyes that I can't quite place," she said, more serious than before. "And I am nothing if not persistent. You put up a good wall. That, and I think you're a super nice guy. Can you blame me for wanting to dive deeper into that?"

Her smile only grew when she saw the blush overcome him. She meant it, but she also secretly hoped that if she pulled at his heartstrings enough, he'd spill. She felt like a harpist, delicately plucking away to learn the melody of his mind without any sheet music, all while making sure the notes didn't go too sharp or too flat.

Elijah decided that somewhere between a lie and the truth was his best bet. "Before you got here, that Stone Breaker guy had a tendency to attack during holidays. I know it's been a few months now, but I guess since the drug ring is ramping into high gear, I'm still on edge."

It was only part of the truth, but she didn't need to know that.

"That's understandable. For what it's worth, based on what I've been seeing in the news, it sounds like they're going for a more low-key approach."

"That just makes me even more nervous." Elijah released a breath that almost formed a laugh with his confession. "At least with Stone Breaker, his loud mouth meant we came to know what to expect. But now?" He deflated as he sighed, and his voice dropped to nearly a whisper. "The unknown freaks me out. You must be nervous too, what with all these girls going missing."

"A bit, but I try not to think about it too much. I saw on the news that another one went missing this morning. I figure if it was you, you would have kidnapped me already."

"It's not me. But I'm glad I don't have to clear my name or anything. This is, what, the fourth one?"

"I think so. It was another high school student. They wouldn't say her name because she's a minor. The other one's mom posted on Nextdoor, though. I hope they find them okay."

"Fuck," Elijah said. "Keeps getting worse."

"Yeah. And the craziest shit happened. I met Hematite the other day. I meant to tell you, but it totally slipped my mind since we've both been so busy."

Elijah felt his heart rate increase, but not from their walk. "Wait, seriously?"

"Yeah! He flagged me down on my way home from Constance's Pond. I was there writing, minding my own business, and then the next thing I know, he's dragging me into an alley to ask me what I'm really doing here."

Elijah was surprised, despite knowing that Kane had planned to figure out her deal. This sort of open interrogation wasn't like him, but Elijah chalked it up to tensions being high after the whole Stone Breaker incident.

"I hope he didn't give you any trouble. You don't strike me as the secretive type." It was yet another lie, but he hoped saying that would get Hannah to open up more in the event she was hiding something from him. A light breeze passed by them, a welcome sensation that cooled his face.

"It's fine. I don't think it took him too long to learn that I'm a total wimp." Hannah wanted to say more—she had so many questions and so many suspicions—but didn't want to darken the mood any further. She opted to change the subject. "So, how all out does Riverpeak usually go for this?"

Elijah smiled but noticed how she wasn't saying any more about it. He couldn't help but wonder if there was more to it. "They go all out, but it's still pretty casual. You'll see what I mean."

As they approached Main Street, the smell of food trucks lining the road grew stronger. Red, white, and blue-striped banners hung from most of the shops, with flags hanging from the streetlamps. A few families had taken their spots already on picnic blankets, ready for the fireworks to set off, even though they still had an hour to wait. Elijah grabbed them both some drinks from one of the food trucks, but Hannah's meeting with Hematite continued to run through his mind.

He couldn't help but wonder if Kane found something out about her that he didn't pick up on. Elijah couldn't shake the feeling but tried to remind himself that if Kane *had* broken down Hannah, then he would have known about it by now. No news was good news.

They took their seats on the sidewalk. The benches and park were already occupied, but the roads were closed, and there was plenty of room along the curbs. Their shoulders touched and, as old classmates and acquaintances passed by, Elijah took time to introduce Hannah briefly before they continued on their way. With time, his drink made its way into only one of his hands and the other moved behind Hannah on the sidewalk. Hannah leaned into Elijah when it did, feeling the warmth of his body radiating onto her. Despite everything that happened recently, like this, she felt secure.

By the time they settled in and sipped half of their drinks, the first firework went off with a screech and a pop over city hall. The rest followed suit, appearing to line the tops of the row of shops in downtown Riverpeak. It was too dark to see the mountains behind them, except for a few valleys closer to town, their silhouettes illuminated by the bright lights of the display. As the fireworks boomed overhead, Hannah and Elijah glanced at one another, and they could each see the reflection of the colorful sparks in the other's eyes. As her heart skipped a beat, Hannah leaned over to kiss Elijah, taking advantage of the fact that she was closer to eye level with him from their spot on the curb, compared to when they stood. She could taste a hint of his beer on his tongue, the orange notes standing out above the malt.

Elijah felt the sudden urge to pull Hannah closer to him and never let her go, but he also didn't want to spook her. So, he settled for letting her hold his face while he kept his arm around her waist, savoring the way they naturally blended.

But the moment didn't last long. The two broke their kiss when they heard some sort of commotion faintly around them, unsure of the source. The sound of some cell phone camera shutters competed with the booming of the fireworks.

It was Hematite.

Hematite stopped directly in front of them, then nodded his head at Elijah and continued to move back through the alleys behind them. He powered through the crowd, waiting for no one, despite the hands and cell phones reaching out for him.

"Shit," Elijah muttered under his breath as he stood.

"Was I imagining things, or was he talking to you?"

"Yeah. I, uh … well, shit. I can explain later, okay?" Elijah held two hands up as he trailed after Hematite, using the excited crowd to his advantage so he could blend in and disappear without a trace. "Listen, I'm sorry, but I gotta go. I'll call you, okay?"

"Whoa, whoa, whoa, hold on!" Hannah stood and chased after him, not letting him get too far ahead of her. "I'm going with you!"

It surprised Elijah to see Hannah following him. She had to take two steps for each of his long strides, but she kept up with his pace.

"Hannah, this is dangerous. You probably shouldn't."

"My date just up and goes off to help a masked vigilante, and you expect me to just keep watching the fireworks? I don't think so! Explain. Now."

Hannah had a point; he'd give her that. "Are you mad?"

"Depends on how you answer."

Elijah swallowed. He expected Hannah might find out eventually, but this was not how he was hoping it would happen. "Long story short, I'm Hematite's IT guy. I can't say much else than that. Does that suffice?"

"How long have you been Hematite's IT guy?"

Elijah grimaced. "Since high school."

Her eyes widened as her jaw slackened. "For ten fucking years?!"

"More like twelve, actually. But I've only known who he was for a few weeks now. I found out who he really was right before you moved here. He was trying to make sure he could keep his identity under wraps and needed help. I would have told you sooner. It's just not my story to tell, and I didn't want to break Hematite's trust either."

Hannah exhaled. "Alright, you know what? That's fair. I can't be mad at that."

"Wait, seriously?"

"Yes. You're lucky we're in a situation where I don't have much more time to process this. Where is he leading us?"

A voice in the back of his head told him any sane person would be furious. But his heart fought back, despite his brain trying to get him to think logically, reminding him that Rory never got mad at Kane. Maybe it wasn't so unusual after all.

"I'm not sure. But if he's having me follow him in public like this, it must be an emergency."

They followed him through the crowd before Hematite scaled a shop and leaped over it. Elijah took Hannah down a thin alley between two of the stores to meet up with him in the back.

"I just hope you don't think I'm some sort of magnet for trouble," Elijah said.

"No, no, not your fault."

"Thanks." He smiled. "I can't promise how this will go. Just be ready for anything."

When they made it to the back of the shop, Hematite was waiting, with his back against a wall. He looked around before he spoke to Elijah and Hannah.

"You brought a friend. Sorry for crashing your date."

"It's fine," they both said at the same time.

"How much do you know?" Hematite asked Hannah.

"He just told me on the way here that he does IT for you. I don't know anything else."

"Your secret's safe with me, I swear," Elijah added.

Hematite nodded. "I believe you. We can make this work. Three sets of eyes are probably better than two right now."

"What's going on?" Elijah asked.

"A fire broke out on the east side. Very similar to the one that killed Noah Sato a few years ago. I need you to see if any of the surrounding shops have surveillance camera footage of who set it. Plus, I'm not convinced that this has nothing to do with that latest missing girl. Can I meet you at your house when I'm done?"

Elijah nodded. "We'll head there now. Brad's with Naomi for the night."

"Perfect. I'll call you when I'm ready." He paused and then looked at Hannah. "Can I trust you?"

"I'll prove it to you tonight, okay?"

"You better."

———

Once they were back in the suburbs, and out of earshot from anyone, Hannah said, "I can't believe you're a superhero's sidekick!"

"Sometimes I can't either," Elijah said with a nervous laugh. Hannah barely heard it through the booming of the fireworks in the near distance. "Do you think we were spotted?"

"Probably not. What with all that commotion? I don't think anyone thought anything of it. Do you have any powers?"

Elijah shook his head. "No. I'm completely ordinary. Which sounds bad, but I guess it's a good thing considering how he got his powers."

Hannah rose a brow. "Which is..?"

Elijah was relieved; he could tell by her tone that her shock was genuine and that she didn't have a clue. Even if he was wrong, he figured she'd already know the answer if she was working with Reiji. "Drugs. Not that he took. Hematite doesn't do drugs. His mom was addicted to this drug that's going around town and has been for decades. I guess if you're addicted and pregnant, your babies get superpowers."

"Oh, shit. That's … that's rough."

"Yeah. That fire he mentioned? Noah was Naomi's brother. It was some freak accident at one of the South Main Burgers restaurants. No one knows how it happened, but if you ask people living on the east side of town, they'll tell you drugs were involved."

"Like a cover-up?"

"Probably. C'mon," Elijah said, once they reached his front door. He was quick to close it behind Hannah and lead her upstairs, where he flipped open his laptop.

Hannah leaned against his desk as she looked around his office and soaked everything in. Degrees from the University of Colorado and certifications hung behind him on either side of the window. His office's dark tones were warm and inviting rather than dull and gloomy. To Hannah's left was a large bookshelf with a variety of knickknacks that further told Elijah's life story. There were photos of him with his family and with Brad, Shawn, and Kane. A few IT books rested on some lower shelves—their spines hinted that Elijah read them all the way through—and assorted tchotchkes from tech conferences filled the empty spaces. Some trophies from high school basketball and football broke up the photos and ornaments.

Those explain the muscular arms, she thought. There were a handful of anime figurines on the shelves too, one of them matching the sticker on his laptop.

Elijah's phone lit up. Before it could even ring, he picked it up and put it on speaker.

"Hey. You're on speaker, FYI. Hannah's here too."

"Thanks," Hematite said.

"What's across from the fire?"

"That abandoned office building; you know the one. I think it's by the South Main Burgers location we raided a few weeks ago."

"Got it," Elijah said. After a few keystrokes and clicks, he pulled up their cameras. "Probably trying to wipe away any extra evidence. I've got the feed."

"Damn, you're fast," Hannah said under her breath.

"I basically have all of these saved for ease of reference at this point." Elijah quickly scanned his monitors and then said to Hematite, "Reiji Sato left the building right before the fire. Looks like it's contained to the back room where the computer was and not spreading. It's already dying down, actually."

"That's exactly what I needed. I'm going inside."

Elijah downloaded some footage and then pulled up an additional window. He frowned as he saw Reiji from another angle, on the phone with someone as he left the building just moments before the back room burst into flames. Elijah clicked into other security cameras around the area, trying to find some semblance of whoever might have been the one to start the fire.

"I'm in," Hematite said. "Fire's out, but Jesus Christ, it's smoky in here. Any sign of anyone?"

"I'm looking now. It's really hard to tell. Hannah, can you take control of this monitor?"

"Got it." She took over his personal laptop so he could focus on Hematite's position.

"If you want to take a crack at some of those documents on my desktop too, be my guest. I've put the ones I'm still working on in a TBD folder."

"Luckily, I am the CEO of multitasking," Hannah said. She kept the cameras open in one window, which she minimized to take up half the screen, and opened the folder on the other. She clicked on the first file on the list, which was a death record.

"How did they extinguish it so fast?" Elijah asked Hematite. "Didn't it *just* break out?"

"Yeah. No fire crews have made it out here or anything. I'm not sure."

"Speaking of fire," Hannah said, "this report doesn't look right." She pointed to some notes in the document. "That's not how it works when you burn a body."

Elijah rose a brow. *Have I been wrong to not suspect her?* He tried to shrug the thought away so he could focus on his tasks at hand, but given everything going on, it tugged at his internal doubts. "You know about body decomposition after dying a fiery death?"

"I write a fantasy series with dragons in it," she said with a nonchalance that hit Elijah like a freight train. "Of course I do. Don't look so surprised."

Solid point, he thought. He hadn't read her books all the way through yet but picked up a copy of the first in the series after their first date and skimmed through it. Hannah's dragons would kill people on demand for their owners, so it made perfect sense that she'd have previously researched anything and everything to do with fire and burning alive. Logic told him not to worry about it, while anxiety told him it was yet another convenient coincidence that had to be something more, perhaps even something Reiji scouted her for.

"Hey."

Her voice snapped him out of it.

"Yeah?"

"It's going to be okay, alright?"

At those words, Elijah felt some of his anxieties fall to the wayside, as if warm water washed over them and rinsed them down his body until they shook off at his feet. "Thanks."

As Elijah clicked through feeds on his other two screens, trying to reroute his focus back to the house break-in, Hannah nudged his arm. "Hey, look here. There's someone inside by a window."

Elijah glanced over and felt his blood run cold. "Dude, get the hell out of there," he warned Hematite. "I know they can't kill you, but I think you might be about to meet someone who is more than willing to try for the hell of it."

"Who? Reiji?" Hematite asked.

"Worse."

Hannah studied Elijah's expression. The color completely drained from his face and his jaw was as tight as humanly possible, the tension visible through the thin skin of his face. She reverted her gaze back to his screen and saw who he zoomed in on. A man who looked like a younger version of Reiji was still on the screen, but his hair was longer —reaching where his neck met his shoulders—and slicked back. Traditional Japanese tattoos covered one of his arms from shoulder to wrist, but he was too far away to discern what they were of, especially with some lingering smoke in the frame. The skin on his other arm was severely burned, now essentially a giant skin graft from a past incident.

"What do you mean?"

"Get out of there!" Elijah heard his heart beating in his ears, pounding like a drum that only grew faster as it began to crescendo. "We need to talk through this more, and I don't want you getting found out!"

Suddenly, Hematite was silent. Hannah and Elijah looked at each other as they waited to hear anything other than Hematite's slowed breathing. After a moment, they heard his footsteps.

"Did you see him too?" Hematite asked after a few minutes.

"I did," Elijah said. "I think he started the fire. He was at the restaurant?"

"He was in the office behind the kitchen, behind the gray-haired guy. Well, what's left of it, anyway. It's mostly burned now. I don't think they saw me, but I'm out of there. Is this for fucking real?"

Hannah chewed at her lip. "Using my new-girl-in-town ignorance to my advantage here, who was that, and why are we freaking out?"

"That's Noah Sato," Elijah said. "He died six years ago."

CHAPTER 8

Hannah checked her starting word count for the day and sunk back into the bench in relief. She was much further along in her story than she thought, putting her in a favorable position for meeting her deadline if she maintained the pace. The words came much more effortlessly to the page again, reminding her of her early days as a writer when she could write an entire book in a month. She wasn't quite that nimble-fingered this round, but that excited feeling in her chest returned. Her usual routine of finding places around town to write and people-watch had proven effective, so she found herself at Constance's Pond once again. The smell of pine and the wildflowers in the breeze grounded her.

Her phone's notification chime broke her rhythm, letting her know that more time had passed than she realized. Hannah saw the text from Elijah first come through on her laptop, so she opened the message in a new window.

Elijah's phone partially covered his face in the photo he sent, but that wasn't the focal point of the picture, anyway. His beanie was off for once, revealing his messy curls that looked brighter in the fluorescent lighting of the changing room he stood in. He wore a four-piece suit with a black jacket and pants, white button-up, and emerald green bowtie and vest. A handkerchief in the jacket pocket matched the accessories. The text accompanying it was just one word.

ELIJAH: Thoughts?

As she looked at the photo on her laptop, she couldn't control the smile that tugged at her lips.

HANNAH: Look at you! So handsome!

She tacked on a heart-eyed emoji before hitting send.

Elijah took a few minutes longer than he usually did to respond. Hannah chalked it up to him being busy with the other groomsmen and thought nothing of it until she saw the text come through.

ELIJAH: All I'm missing is you on my arm. Care to be my +1?

Her smile grew. His delayed response made perfect sense now; knowing Elijah, the pause was likely because of a combination of his perfectionism and his nerves that he often tried (and failed) to hide.

HANNAH: I would be honored.

She included the smiling emoji surrounded by small hearts.

Hannah glanced up from the laptop; something moving a few feet away caught her attention in her peripheral. Using her computer as a cover for what she was really doing, Hannah continued to peer from her spot on the bench and noticed that the two men looked familiar: one Japanese, the other a white brunette in his thirties. It was the same two men as before that she'd seen and alerted Hematite to. The silver-haired one was with them sometimes, but he was absent today.

Now that she knew Elijah worked with Hematite, Hannah quickly picked up her phone. She snuck a photo of the two men, who were too far away to see her, and hoped Elijah would answer more quickly than their last exchange mere seconds ago, now texting him with her phone now.

> HANNAH: Hematite question! Do they look familiar?

ELIJAH: Looks like Reiji from here, I think? Pretty sure he wore that suit to Brad and Naomi's engagement party.

When Hannah looked back up, she saw Reiji and the brunette leave.

> HANNAH: They're on the move. I'm following them, lol

ELIJAH: What do you mean, lol??

ELIJAH: Hey, be careful. It could be dangerous if they spot you!

> HANNAH: Yeah yeah ik ik. Don't worry, I'll be fine. Promise.

She added a winking kissy-face emoji to ease his concerns and then tossed her laptop in her bag, monitoring Reiji and his associate when she was sure they weren't looking at her. Hannah casually placed the strap over one of her shoulders, letting it rest across her body so she wouldn't have to worry about it sliding off as she followed them. Once they were a few paces away, she got up to follow as discretely as she could.

As the two men made their way through the suburbs, the homes grew exponentially in size and in grandeur. As they kept going down a few blocks, Hannah noted the two- and three-story mini-mansions with perfectly cut lawns. Even the mailboxes exuded class, a detail that felt excessive. Hannah thought of the people living on the east side of town and wondered what their mailboxes looked like.

Probably not like this.

When they made a turn up some steps, Hannah texted Elijah.

HANNAH: They're about to head inside. Do you know where the Satos live?

ELIJAH: Close to Naomi. Same street, I think.

HANNAH: Lol, idk where that is. Can you FaceTime me, maybe with your screen recording on? It'll be less suspicious than me taking pictures in case they see me. Especially out here. I bet everyone has a security cam.

After only a few seconds, the FaceTime call came through. Hannah answered, holding her phone up to eye level but quickly tapping so the camera would switch to the one in the back.

"You're still dressed up? What a treat!" It was true; Hannah wished she had a moment longer to admire him. "You should wear a tux more often."

"You think so?"

"I do! You know, the green looks lovely." It had a double meaning that she prayed Elijah picked up on. While he wore a green tie, Reiji and his associate entered a large house with a green door and matching shutters. Hannah panned the camera in the slightest.

Meanwhile, Elijah beckoned Kane over. Kane had his own phone handy, fingers moving a mile a minute as he jotted down notes while looking over Elijah's shoulder.

"How's your Hebrew?" Elijah asked, almost in a whisper.

"Mostly out of practice. But if you talk to me like I'm a second-grader, I'll manage."

In Hebrew, he asked for the house number. As Hannah passed, she took a glance and rattled it off back in Hebrew to him. That much she could manage, at least. Elijah set his phone down on an end table in the dressing room, grabbed Kane's phone from him, and wrote it down. He didn't want to risk anyone hearing it on Hannah's end.

"What street?"

"Prescott Road, or something like that? I remember walking down this way with you when you showed me around town that one day. The houses here are something else. Wow."

"Hey, Brad?"

Brad entered the frame, his tux different from Kane's and Elijah's. His tie was white instead of the same green that the other men wore.

"What's up?"

"Do you know who lives here? It's not Naomi's parents, right?"

Brad looked at the address on Kane's phone and shook his head. "No, it's not. That's close to Naomi's place, though. Only a few houses down."

"I can pull up some real estate listings once I'm home," Hannah offered. She tried to see if she could spot anyone in the windows now that the two men were inside, but the blinds were all drawn. Not so much as a silhouette shone through. "Maybe that'll provide some insight."

"I'll do the same. Good idea." Elijah wondered if he could still access Carla's MLS database; she shared a password with him once for some IT troubles back when they briefly dated, and he sensed she wasn't bright enough to change it. "Thanks, Hannah. This was super helpful."

"Yeah, anytime. You know I got you."

Elijah's heart fluttered.

Powers or not, maybe he was right to trust her after all.

When Elijah sat down with his laptop that night, he cracked his knuckles and stretched his neck before he turned his microphone on. All three of his computer monitors were set up, with his attention primarily being on the one in the middle. Security camera feeds rolled on one screen to show him Kane's exact location. In the dark, it was difficult to spot the vigilante on camera, but Elijah was so used to looking for him at this point that it didn't take him long to notice the shape of his cowl and hood in the night, no matter how grainy the footage.

"Alright, testing. You good, Kane?"

"I'm good. Man, this new earpiece is awesome. We should have thought of this sooner," Kane said, as he turned on his voice modifier. "Do you have the cameras up?"

"Ready and rolling. While you're here, I'm running a program to see if I can get remote access to Reiji's computer, so hopefully, we can get some answers between the two of us. Luckily, his secretary was as gullible as I thought." Elijah enlarged the windows on his screen, showing the front and back doors. "There's someone going in and out of the back. I'd stick to the front."

Elijah could hear the smirk in Kane's tone that was undoubtedly also on his face. "That's what the dark outfit is for."

"Be careful. If you end up dead, who knows where you'll wake up if they catch you."

"I mean, are we sure that's an awful idea?"

"Kane!"

"Sorry, sorry."

"They're probably already suspicious as is. Let's not just give them what they want on a silver platter, please."

"Yeah, you're right."

Elijah rolled his eyes as he continued to comb through some of the stolen thumb drive files. He started with the ones involving Brad's father. There was security camera footage from the restaurant showing Mr. Evans stumbling up and banging on the doors, but the audio was missing. Elijah skimmed through, having already seen this and knowing how it ended—with Brad's father leaving the restaurant, only to run once it burst into flames.

He tried searching once again for another angle, hoping he'd simply missed it before, but found nothing. Elijah went back to the original, zooming in on Brad's father, hoping to get a better look despite how pixelated it was. He glanced over to check on the cameras he had up on his other screen, making sure Kane was okay.

On his third monitor, he saw an alert pop up: Reiji Sato's computer was as good as his. Elijah mentally thanked his software as he took advantage of the open ports and vulnerabilities now at his fingertips, and his monitor transformed into Reiji's with his new remote access. Desperate for solutions to the loose ends, he began digging for extra documentation that may support whatever Reiji ditched on the thumb drives.

"No fucking way," Elijah whispered to himself as he clicked into a folder. There was an entire folder dedicated to Noah, specifically the forged death records. Elijah saw them all in their original form, unlike the changed versions he found on the USB drives. He dug deeper, finding a Notes app entry with a list of passwords on it and smiled.

This is too easy, he thought, *but leave it to boomers.*

He went to work trying a few of the passwords, getting into Reiji's bank account on the second try. A prompt to set up multi-factor authentication popped up, and Elijah laughed—that never got old. He found statements going back to Noah's death date and got to printing them, wanting paper copies just to be safe. As he scanned them, he saw a charge for a doctor's office; it was the same one that filled out the paperwork he'd seen before.

Elijah leaned back in his seat as he took in the information. He suspected something was off but hadn't expected the whole thing to be forged in its entirety. That only confirmed the man they saw on the Fourth of July was, in fact, Noah Sato.

Now seeking information about the house, Elijah went back to Reiji's desktop. He glanced back, checking the cameras again, and relaxed. The people by both the front and back doors were on the ground and as still as a board, likely thanks to Kane. Elijah's phone pinged: the message was from Kane's burner. Photos came through of what looked like the basement. Heavy-duty storage containers lined the walls, and a few tables broke up the space with different vials and test tubes on top. Whoever was working out of there with Reiji was no doubt manufacturing in the basement; that was further confirmed by the vents on the walls near the small windows.

Elijah then dove further into Reiji's bank statements. Wanting to cross-reference the monthly rent with any withdrawals, he pulled up the address where Kane currently was in another tab. Sure enough, it added up.

"The house is a cover," Elijah said to Kane. "Is anyone else there?"

"The two guards outside are down for the count. I haven't seen anyone inside."

"I'm not convinced you're alone. I know I've already said it, but be careful, dude. Maybe Noah lives there. I found the paper trail of his forged death record."

"I didn't go upstairs, but the first floor looked pretty plain. Just looked like some home staging, like any realtor would set up."

"Check the fridge. If you see leftovers, make a run for it."

Elijah went back to the security footage from the night of Noah's death. He kept the zoomed-in image of Brad's father up on one of his monitors while he used the other to peruse more of Reiji's files. The more he poked around, the more unsettled he felt. He was certain of one thing: Reiji was in many people's pockets to keep his operation under wraps.

He eventually found the original Word document with the list of reliable sellers, opening it to see if it was different than the one he'd found on the USB drives. This one looked more recent. Kane's parents were both on the top of the list, followed closely by Shawn's mom, Carol. Elijah felt nauseous when he saw the three Xs lined up next to Carol's name; he didn't want to imagine how many people got their fix from her in *that* way. He did a quick scan for his own family members and sighed in relief when he didn't see any of their names—not that he thought they'd be on there, but he couldn't handle another surprise today—but then saw Brad's father toward the bottom of the list. A question mark was next to his name.

"You're right," Kane said. "Leftovers in the fridge. I'm bailing."

"Good call." He texted Brad to ask him if he was still awake but didn't get a response. Instead, the door to his office opened. Brad stood in the doorway, bags under his eyes.

"I'm up. Can't sleep. What's up? What are you doing?"

"I, uh…" Elijah ran his hand through his hair. "It's hard to explain. Hematite business?"

Brad pinched the bridge of his nose and came in. "What's going on?"

"I wanted to show this to you." Elijah scooted his chair over so Brad could get a better look. "So, no gentle way to put this, but I think they framed your dad for Noah's death."

"What?"

"I found a security camera video in a folder called Blackmail that showed your dad leaving the restaurant where Noah died. This was right before the place caught fire. So, I looked more into it, and I found your dad on this list of sellers for Reiji. For, you know ... the drugs."

"I'm not shocked." Brad's frown deepened as he released a sigh.

"But get this: Noah's death certificate is a total fake. Reiji paid some doctor to sign off on this and everything. There are all sorts of inconsistencies if you look close enough, and we've got enough of a paper trail to stitch it all together."

"So, why are you telling me this?"

"Because I'd rather you hear this from me than from someone else. Someone like Reiji. After all, you *are* about to be his son-in-law. And I wanted you to know this so that way if he tries to say anything to you, you're well-equipped to handle it."

"Makes sense," Brad said, though his voice quivered. "I appreciate it. What else did you find?"

"Noah lives there; Kane saw leftovers in the fridge just now. There are withdrawals from Reiji's bank account every month that are the same price as the rent. He must be hiding it from his wife or something. It's a front for both their home base *and* for Noah to stay hidden in plain sight."

Kane's voice interrupted their conversation. "Cutting the call. I'll be okay."

"What happened?" Elijah asked, but there was no response. "Fuck!" He scrambled to expand the window with the security cameras on Reiji's house, desperate to see more.

"I have a morbid question," Brad posed. "Is there any sort of way that Kane can actually die? Like, what if he gets decapitated or something?"

Elijah frowned. "I don't know. I hope not." He flipped through the cameras until he found a feed of the backyard. Kane was backed into a fence with a leather jacket-clad arm propped up against his throat.

"Do these have audio?"

"Yeah, here," Elijah said. "Hopefully we can hear it, and it's not too far."

"Thought I smelled a rat," the man said, as the audio came through. Elijah and Brad knew that voice anywhere; it was undoubtedly Noah.

"Too much of a coward to show your face, Hematite? Or is your brain made of rocks too?"

What Kane did next surprised Brad, Elijah, and even Noah: he head-butted Noah, hard enough to make him stumble and release his grip. As Kane made a run for it, Noah flicked on a lighter and tossed it toward Kane. The lighter landed on Kane's back, and the flame quickly spread up his cowl, as if it had a life of its own. Kane fought the ever-increasing heat as he yanked the cowl off, face still covered by his balaclava, and made quick work of hopping the fence. Elijah heard Kane swear as he tried to drop the cowl and stomp on it, but the fire only grew, refusing to extinguish. Once the door to the back gate opened, Kane grabbed his cowl and sprinted out, into the night.

"Can you see him?" Brad asked.

"No. Shit."

After what felt like an eternity, Kane's voice came through the other end. "Elijah, you there?"

"Dude, what happened?!"

"He saw me from the window and came down to say hello. That fire was weird as shit, I'm telling you. Something's up with that lighter."

"Or with him, if he has a soft spot for arson."

Elijah heard a splashing sound. "Oh, thank fuck. Perfectly placed puddle. My shirt sleeve is toast."

"Why didn't you ditch the cape or whatever the fuck? That would have been the smart thing to do."

"Because God forbid one of my hairs or something was on there!"

"Is that not the point of your balaclava, beyond hiding your face?"

"Yes, but I can never be too careful."

"Alright, alright, enough," Brad interjected. "We're both glad you're okay, Kane."

"I think he's like you," Elijah said. "The fake death records, framing Brad's dad but doing nothing with it, the multiple instances of fire. They gotta be covering up more than his livelihood, you know? Think he has powers?"

"There's no way," Kane said. "He'd have to have been born with it. Naomi's parents would never."

"I mean, we thought they'd never be behind a crime ring peddling drugs through the suburbs, now didn't we?"

"They're not using, and I don't think they ever have. That much I can tell," Brad said. "Especially not enough to pass on powers."

"Then how?"

"Hell if I know!" But then, Brad had a realization. "I bet the missing girls would know, though. Noah's gotta be behind all that too, you think? He was always great with women."

"I know who to ask," Kane said. "He has a full sleeve, right? It's time we pay Jolene a visit at her tattoo studio."

CHAPTER 9

Reiji scowled when he reached the white-and-green house a few blocks from his own home, one of the many rental properties he had in their county. He made enough to keep this one as his own to run their primary operation, and when he was away, his wife May thought he was doing on-site visits to the restaurants.

The house looked normal on all accounts but was empty upon entry, save for a few pieces of staged furniture and the light coating of dust that covered them. After wiping some dust off an end table, he made his way straight to the basement; with the help of Dr. Potter, he set the ventilation system up perfectly so as to not raise the suspicions of any neighbors, while also keeping everyone downstairs safe. The smell always made him scrunch his nose, but he was grateful for the pack of stray cats that lived in the backyard that took the blame for it. From the unfinished basement, he couldn't hear them meowing.

"Welcome home," Noah said. He was leaning against one of the long metal tables with an unlit cigarette in his mouth. Reiji snatched it from him and pocketed it in his suit jacket.

"You know that's a fire hazard we can't afford."

"Lighten up, *oyaji*. I know what I'm doing." Noah stuck his hands in the pockets of his black bomber jacket.

Reiji narrowed his gaze at his son. He'd encouraged Noah to speak with a bit more respect in the past but had long since given up, especially now that Noah was in his early thirties. He barely even recognized Noah anymore, and not just because of the tattoos and scars that littered his arms and chest. "Do you?"

"Do I? Have the last few rounds of tests not proven how in control I am?" Noah looked his father up and down in judgment. "You strip my life from me, and this is the thanks I get?"

Reiji sighed, trying to not let his aggravation get the best of him. Now more than ever, he needed to keep his cool in front of everyone. A few employees were at the worktables behind him that filled the room, and he could lightly hear some glass clanking against metal as they worked. "Your sacrifices have not gone unnoticed."

Noah scoffed. "I'm still stable. Potter ran all those tests you asked me to get from him. Freaky rat bastard."

"You know better than to underestimate said 'rat bastard.'" Reiji looked at the storage containers to his left and pushed one in against the wall, making it sit flush with the others. "What did he say?"

"No one can replicate Hematite. Powers will vary from person to person. But I am alive and well, thank you. Just don't ask if I have a fever. Answer'll always be yes."

"Good. Anything else?"

"He's as tight-lipped as ever, but I think we're clear for mass distribution. That should bring in some funds."

Reiji shook his head. "Not yet."

Noah visibly scowled. "Why the hell not?"

"I know Tom liked your ambitious ideas, but he had no idea how this all works. He was entirely out of touch. It's not that simple. We have survived this long by staying under the radar and by paying people off. As you know, we recently lost many of those connections, either directly or indirectly, so now we have to be extra careful."

"And when will we get to finally sell this shit to the masses, huh?" His father was silent, so Noah asked, "Does Mom get to know yet?"

"No. I actually need you to scale back the Hematite attacks until after your sister's wedding. I'd like to recruit Naomi's fiancé, which means I'll need you to lie low for me. If Naomi finds out, our entire operation is over."

"Oh, so after everything you did to me, I get tossed to the curb like trash until I'm convenient for you again?" Noah frowned and rolled his eyes. "You seriously think sweet, little Bradley's not gonna tell her everything?"

Reiji's jaw clenched. "I have my methods of keeping him quiet."

"Give me a fucking break." Noah pushed off from the table and walked across the basement, weaving through workstations and not bothering to glance back to his father.

Reiji groaned as he walked the other way, making his way toward a group of his employees. Normally, he'd never tolerate this attitude from his own son. However, he needed Noah too much, and he was already volatile as is. The rope he was balancing on was becoming increasingly thinner and tauter.

Carter, his most trusted confidant, spoke up first. Carter had combed back his brown hair, modeled after the way that Sterling often slicked his back. "How's Noah doing?"

Reiji shook his head. "Impatient, as always."

"He'll see. It'll all pay off."

"What's the status on the Kellys?"

"They've got a lot of eyes on them right now since they're pretty fresh out of the hospital. We better leave them be for a while."

Reiji's silence spoke volumes. The Kellys were some of the best sellers for the last few decades. Them being out of commission, coupled with Stevens's arrest, was making the operation a lot more complicated.

"Are their children visiting them?"

Carter whistled lowly. "No. My understanding is that both of their children couldn't care less about them."

"A pity." Reiji actually meant it, feeling partially responsible.

"The news, on the other hand…"

"Understood. And what about Carol Jameson?"

"A viable option, last I checked."

"Good. Call her. We could use her help selling."

"I thought you didn't like her methods."

"I don't. But I also like keeping Sterling happy and being able to have a steady cash flow to report. They froze all of Stevens's assets, and Eliza will probably never regain her role as chief of police, no matter how hard she tries." Reiji gripped the table in front of him. "Besides, the Jameson boy might have powers similar to Hematite. We'll see if he steps into the limelight when his mother is back under pressure."

"I like your way of thinking, Ray."

"Take care of her, and I'll handle our newest recruit. My daughter does not know, but she doesn't need to."

Noah laughed from across the room and sauntered back over toward his father. He said, in a sing-song tone, "Bradley's gonna blab."

"Let him, then," Reiji said. His grip on the table tightened, as he tried to keep his composure. He wouldn't let his son get a rise out of him and he wouldn't crack under pressure; he couldn't, not now. "Perhaps he will lead Hematite right to us. We made you to handle Hematite, did we not?"

Noah bit his tongue. The bitterness in his father's voice was not lost on him. "Potter tells me I can't kill him. I can knock his ass out, sure, but he's not dying." Noah grinned. "But he's connected to Rory Miller. That's Naomi's best friend and Kane Kelly's girlfriend. I think that speaks for itself."

"Hematite has helped more women than just Rory Miller," Reiji said. "I would advise against obsessing over her as Mark Stevens and his little friend did. Look where it got them."

But Noah continued, as if Reiji hadn't said anything. "Not to mention the girl that followed you here the other day has been going out with Elijah Baron. Isn't he Brad's best man?"

The room fell silent; even the clanking beakers and vials stilled at the revelation. All eyes were either on Reiji or Noah. Reiji felt his ears grow warm as he stared at his son. "What?"

"You didn't see that girl ... what's her name? Hannah? New in town? She followed you and Carter here the other day. Looked like she was filming and everything." Noah leaned against the table, positioning himself right next to his father. "Don't tell me you've gotten so comfortable that you don't bother to look over your shoulder anymore."

"When was this?"

"'Bout a week ago."

"You said nothing sooner?"

"You didn't notice." Noah laughed. "You know, I'm worried that you're cracking under the pressure."

Everyone in the room all glanced to the stairs at the sound of a new arrival. "Don't worry. No one's cracking under pressure."

His footsteps were light against the steps on his way down. His gray hair was loose today, not gelled back how it usually was, and his black suit jacket was tossed over his shoulder, held there with one hand. In the other was a book. He wore a black disposable face mask to hide some of his face, but everyone knew who he was.

"Sterling." Reiji straightened.

"Sorry I'm late. I had to run some errands." He waved his hand, showing the book he was holding. "Hannah Cohen's debut. Can you believe it? I didn't think they'd have a copy anywhere. Had to go all the way out to this little, used bookstore in Colorado Springs."

"Doesn't Amazon have it?" Noah asked.

"They do. But I'd much rather have something that looks a little more loved. You two aren't the only ones with tricks up your sleeves."

"You knew about Hannah Cohen too?" Reiji asked.

"Of course. I have been keeping a very close eye on her since she arrived here in Riverpeak. No one moves in without my knowing." Sterling tossed his jacket over the railing and then tucked the paperback beneath his arm. "Go on, continue with what you were saying. Pretend I'm not here."

"Sterling, I..."

"Ray, relax. It's fine. I heard most of it on my way downstairs. You're not in trouble. Your daughter's getting married, after all! I'm sure there's a lot on your mind."

Sterling said it as smooth as honey and with a genuineness that couldn't be feigned, but Reiji knew there was a warning beneath the surface that didn't need to be said. He wasn't in trouble—not yet anyway.

"Listen, Noah. I don't need Hematite dead," Reiji said. "I just need him *here.*"

Noah opened his mouth to speak, but Reiji held a hand up. He whispered the rest to his son, trying to not cause a scene, especially in front of Sterling. Sterling leaned back against the newel post, thumbing through the used book he'd purchased that morning.

"I already know what you're going to say. My answer is still no. Not one of your little experiments has been successful. All but one has died. We can't draw that kind of attention to ourselves, so I recommend you stop while you're ahead."

"We're collecting data while weeding out the weak," Noah said.

"We?" Reiji took a deep breath, exhaling through his nose. "There is no 'we' in this crusade of yours, Noah. I am trying to provide for our family. Plain and simple."

"Our family, huh?" Noah reached into his father's jacket pocket to take his cigarette back. He placed it between his lips and, with a roll of his eyes, walked away. "I'm taking a smoke break. Don't worry, I'll go outside."

"You shouldn't be buying those."

"Relax." Noah waved his hand in dismissal as he made the trek up the stairs. "How much worse off can I get?"

"Disgusting," Reiji muttered under his breath. He thought back to the day that Noah died, wondering if that was truly when this shift in his son began or if it was something else entirely.

———

Noah grabbed his sunglasses from the counter and some deli meat from the refrigerator as he made his way outside, stepping out into the fenced backyard. One of the feral cats meowed at him knowingly, prancing over to see a familiar face before he could make it far from the back door. Noah crouched down to scratch the black cat between its ears, causing it to purr and nudge against his skin. He had grown used to the ammonia-like smell that leaked out from the basement vents by now. Once the cat had its fill of affection, it snatched the deli meat from his hand and trotted off into the corner of the yard to eat it in peace. As per usual, it would leave no scraps.

Once the cat was a safe distance away, Noah grabbed the cigarette from between his lips and tossed it across the yard. It landed in the grass about midway through, which he was grateful for; now the fence wouldn't be at risk. He reached for his lighter and turned it on, staring at the fire for a moment. He focused on the flame and grinned when it shot directly toward the cigarette, which blew up in a billow of orange light. Before the grass could follow suit, he brought his attention to that and, with the extension of his hand, extinguished the flames.

He turned his head at the sound of the door behind him opening and closing. Reiji approached him and stood by his side. He wasted no time in asking, "Do you hate me?"

Noah didn't answer right away. He cast his gaze on the cat, finishing its pieces of deli meat before any of the other strays could make their way back to the yard. "Depends on how you'd define hate."

Reiji sighed. "I'll take what I can get."

There was another pause between them. Reiji pondered what to say next as he and his son watched the stray cat lick its claws. He wasn't sure how to get Noah to fully understand him, but he hoped that seeming to level with his son would get him what he wanted.

"You know Sterling has been watching you closely, correct?"

"Of course I know. We've been spending more time together these days. Not that you've noticed."

Reiji nodded once. "He reminds me a lot of you, in some ways. Very headstrong. Put into a destiny that he could not entirely resist."

Noah scoffed. "Destiny's what we're calling it now, huh? Not you strapping me to a chair in the back of a shitty fast-food joint and injecting me with so much of that meth cocktail that I couldn't even feel anything?" He glanced at his burned arm. "Maybe it's better that I didn't feel any of it."

"It was Sterling's idea to find a test subject. You already know that he wants powers for himself too. But we needed to know we could have someone take care of Hematite before he did that to himself. We have his father and Dr. Potter to thank for this gift. Were you aware of that?"

Noah finally looked at his father. "Wait, you're telling me that this was all Sterling's idea?"

"It was. He is the one in charge around here, after all. Everyone answers to someone, Noah. Remember that. No matter how high up you go, there's always a bigger fish lurking in the weeds, ready to strike."

"Since when are you the analogy type?"

"He asked me to take charge when his father passed. 'He's too young,' he said. Didn't think any of his father's men would take him seriously, since they'd known him since he was in diapers. I needed to provide for your mother and grandmother, to pay them back adequately for everything they've done for me. The restaurant didn't start off strong. This changed everything."

"*Sobo* always did say that money goes where money is."

"And Sterling was always a bright boy. He knew when to step back and let others take the lead." Reiji took a deep breath. "His father seemed to have a Midas touch about him. He could spot an opportunity a mile away, and he always knew how to make the most of it. South Main Burgers was no exception. He taught me everything I know."

"Let me guess, not just about the best type of meat locker to use, either?"

"That is correct. Sterling was at the restaurant a lot growing up; I'm sure you remember. His father homeschooled him and had him study a lot from there. Said it would be a good way to show him real-world experience. One day, when what we have now was still in development, a competitor of ours tried to rob the location we had on the east side. Sterling was the only other person in the restaurant at the time besides the employees and myself. He took a moment to evaluate the situation, and he bludgeoned the man with one of his textbooks."

Noah had a hard time picturing Sterling, who was lanky enough to put Slender Man to shame, bludgeoning anyone with a textbook, but he didn't question that. "Why are you telling me this?"

"Because I think you're on his level, if not above it now with your enhancements."

"Enhancements?"

"I just hope you know that anything I've pushed you to do was because I truly believed in you."

Noah felt a strange sensation in his throat. He wasn't sure if he felt like he was going to scream or throw up. "You saying there were alternatives?"

"You were made to defeat Hematite and to make sure Sterling wouldn't die. I knew your body could handle what they were creating. I feared that testing on anyone else would lead to senseless deaths. Do you understand where I come from now?"

Noah shrugged. He still didn't agree with it, but after his father's attempt at bonding, he didn't want to completely scorn him. "Sure, I guess. So, what's this got to do with me now?"

"He's watching your every move. All of your successes. All your failures too. I know you think this drug is ready for the masses, but it's not. But he is willing to try." Reiji cleared his throat. The cat was gone; he wasn't sure where it had run off to. "Be careful with those girls, you hear?"

As Reiji turned to go back inside, Noah spoke up. "Hey. Not so fast. How did you know I wouldn't die, huh?"

Another pause. In the reflection of the glass on the back door, Reiji could see his son looking back at him from his spot on the back patio. He saw so much of his younger self in his son's face, but so little of his spirit at the same time.

"Just a hunch."

"A hunch?"

"Yes. There's no way I could have known for certain. But you've always been strong."

Noah laughed as he asked, "Are you for real?"

But Reiji didn't answer any further, instead opting to head back inside. Noah remained in the yard and just kept laughing in disbelief. When the breeze picked up, he was hit with the smell of the fumes from the basement, the torched cigarette, and the dead grass beneath it. It was enough to snap him out of it.

The black cat emerged from the fence's corner, where it had gone to eat the last of its meat in peace. It gave Noah an expectant meow, but Noah just scratched it between the ears again.

"Un-fucking-believable," he said, unsure if it was to himself or to the cat, "am I right?"

CHAPTER 10

That evening, Brad swallowed as he followed Reiji through his home. No one else was inside; Naomi's grandmother was sitting on the back porch, and Brad wasn't sure where Naomi's mother was. It left Reiji and Brad alone, as they moved past the *butsudan* and into the study. Brad wondered how Reiji could bring himself to look at it every day, knowing that his son was actually alive. He could have sworn that the eyes in the photo of Noah on it were following him, but knew it was just his general uneasiness about the whole situation.

Reiji's study was nothing short of sophisticated. His desk rested in front of a wall covered entirely by bookshelves. The wall to the side of it directly in the back of the room had a large window overlooking the backyard, giving Reiji a clear view of his mother-in-law in case she needed something. The rich pink and orange hues of dawn flooded the room, giving it an even warmer tone. Reiji moved to a drink cart in the corner and grabbed two glasses. The leather of the chairs by his desk matched the rich mahogany of the bookshelves, and Reiji silently gestured to one of the two seats for Brad to sit in.

Brad broke the silence. Neither of them had said anything since his arrival, the air between them thick with discomfort. "You wanted to see me, Mr. Sato?" He'd received the invitation on his lunch break that morning to swing by on his way home, and Brad didn't feel like he was in a position to decline the request.

"Can I interest you in a drink, Brad?"

Brad just smiled as he shifted in his seat. He was sure his smile looked as awkward as he felt. He tried to hide his reluctance, as he accepted the drink and took a short sip to be polite but didn't care to touch it further.

"You've taken such good care of my little girl over the years. So, I'd like to extend that thoughtfulness back to you. I think we can come to a little agreement, so your friends don't get hurt," Reiji said. "Don't you agree?"

"What do you mean?"

Brad remembered what Kane advised him before he left to play dumb. It would be crucial to his survival today. He knew when he got the call from Reiji that afternoon that it would be serious business, not just a casual chat about the wedding, but he still wasn't sure to what extent. They hadn't spoken since Reiji caught them breaking into the South Main Burgers a few months prior, so Brad had been dreading this inevitable moment.

"I want my daughter to be happy. Isn't that something we have in common?"

"Of course." Brad nodded, having fully expected Naomi's name to come up like this. He knew Naomi was Reiji's pride and joy, but Reiji still wasn't above using her name to manipulate Brad's feelings.

"If Naomi knew what I knew, it would simply devastate her." Reiji's casual tone made Brad even more nervous than he already was.

"What are you getting at?"

"Patience." Reiji rose a brow and paused, the air as stiff as it was when Brad arrived. "I also want to do my work in peace. I've done so for the last thirty years, and I'm not about to let some punk in a mask ruin my life's work. One of your friends is Hematite. Am I correct in that assumption?"

Brad froze in his panic.

Reiji laughed. "Ah, of course, you'd be sworn to secrecy. Don't worry; I'm not sure which one of you it is, but I do know it is either you or your friends. Maybe all of you take turns wearing the mask. I won't make you prove it to me, at least not today. You can relax."

Brad did not relax.

"That's not all I know, though." Reiji leaned forward, his elbows on his desk. He set his drink down and clasped his hands together. As he spoke, he cracked his knuckles one by one. "Do you know how my son died, Brad?"

"Of course. He died in a fire." Brad maintained a casual tone, hoping he wouldn't expose his inner panic. He heard his heartbeat in his ears as clearly as he heard Reiji speaking to him. "It was a freak accident."

"Let me rephrase that. Do you know how my son really died?"

Brad blinked intentionally, adding to the effect of his playing dumb. "Is that not what happened?"

"I have kept this to myself for the last six years, for my daughter's sake. The fire was an accident, yes. But it was entirely preventable. He and I were working late at the restaurant together. We were alone. We would have been fine had your father not come."

Brad's brows furrowed. "My father? What the hell was my dad doing?"

Brad knew the answer—it had all been a setup—but he also knew that he needed to act like he didn't know that. Luckily, feigning ignorance was easy enough for him, especially since he knew Reiji wasn't his biggest fan in the first place. No one would ever be good enough for Naomi to him; Brad had accepted that long ago and was at peace with it.

"I still ask myself that question," Reiji said with a tut of his tongue. "He came to the back of the restaurant asking for help. He was clearly out of sorts, if you understand what I'm saying."

"Yeah, unfortunately, I do." Brad knew Reiji had planned this encounter already, but the presentation didn't do his nerves any favors. Reiji played all his cards incredibly carefully, a fact that Brad was well aware of. It seemed like this common knowledge was what Reiji banked on, and if that were truly the case, he had a solid argument, no matter what.

"I've done a careful job of making sure no one else has to get hurt.

In truth, this business makes me sick, but I do what I have to do for my family. So, I'd like to make you an offer so we can all continue to be happy."

Even though Brad had a feeling he knew what Reiji was going to offer, he still felt sick to his stomach.

CHAPTER 11

Nobody had ever interrupted Hannah while she was writing at the pond until that night. When they first called for her, she was so focused on the manuscript that she didn't even notice right away. Part of her was grateful he had; she'd been so focused on writing, she'd lost track of time again, and it would be dark soon.

"Excuse me. My apologies. You're Hannah Cohen, right?"

The man asking was slender and everything about him was strikingly long: long legs, long fingers wrapped around a briefcase handle, and a narrow face. The sunset bounced off the small, gold designer logo on the black frame of his sunglasses. It clashed with his silver hair, which he'd slicked back and was cut at his chin. Even without the sunglasses, Hannah could sense one thing about him by the way he carried himself and dressed.

She knew old money when she saw it.

"In the flesh. I'm sorry, have we met?"

"No, no, forgive me. Just a fan of your work." He smiled, revealing flawless teeth and a smile to match. "I've been catching up to your fantasy series, but your debut about the haunted house? A modern classic in the horror genre." He sat beside her on the bench, opened his briefcase, and pulled out a well-worn paperback. "I must have re-read this thing a hundred times between work meetings. Mind if I snag your signature?"

"Oh! Of course." She rummaged in her bag for a marker. She could have sworn she'd seen him before but couldn't place where. "I didn't know anyone still read this ol' thing."

"I can see the Stephen King influences. Extraordinarily done."

"Aw, thanks! Yeah, I love his work. Who should I sign it to? I didn't catch your name."

"Ah, my apologies. It's Sterling."

"Spelled like the silver?"

"Yeah, like the silver." He ran a hand over his hair. "Ironically enough, I know."

"Don't sweat it. Luckily for you, Emilia Clarke made it trendy a few years back." Hannah wasn't a fan of sitting in silence when signing book copies, so she opted for small talk. She hoped it would help jog her memory too. "I haven't seen you here before. Are you from around here?"

"I am. Work beckons, though, so I don't get out too much. Lived here my whole life. Though I suspect most people here could say the same thing."

"So I've heard." Hannah capped the marker and handed him the book back. "There you have it."

"Thanks a bunch. Means a lot. Hey, you're dating that IT engineer, right?" He pointed a finger at her and then brought it to his chin. "What's his name ... Elijah?"

Hannah paused; she'd expected him to leave, not pry into her personal life, never mind know about it. "Says who?"

Sterling shrugged a shoulder with a casualty Hannah disliked from him. "Small town. Everyone knows everything around here."

"Mm. Right." Hannah crossed her legs so she could discretely shift on the bench; she didn't want to be obvious about how she was trying to distance herself from him.

"Anyway, you should watch yourself with him."

Hannah blinked. "With Elijah? How do you figure?"

"I overheard him chatting with his friends about some dating app."

"Oh, yeah. That's how we met." Relief washed over Hannah's chest, despite the lingering discomfort from the man's prying. "Thanks for your concern, though. That's kind of you."

"No, no, not like that. How do I put this?"

Sterling took a sharp breath as he glanced at the lake, and then his eyes met Hannah's. When they did, Hannah realized it right away: she'd seen this man from a distance with Reiji Sato.

"I think he's using you. I'm not sure how, but be careful, alright?"

Hannah shifted again under his gaze, feeling scrutinized. "Oh, okay. Not sure what to make of that, but thanks, I guess." She didn't know what else to say; all that Hannah knew was that she wanted him to leave.

"Right. Thanks again for signing this. Enjoy the rest of your day."

"Of course. Have a good one."

He stood, nodded, and went on his way. Hannah followed him with her eyes as he left, confirming he was gone before grabbing her belongings and scrambling home. Her mind raced with thoughts of what Sterling could have meant—if she should even listen to him at all.

As far as Hannah was concerned, there were four possibilities.

The first was that Sterling was an obsessive fan, desperate for attention and perhaps a little jealous. But that didn't feel plausible. Sterling all but oozed confidence in the kind of way that only someone with extreme generational wealth could. She'd never seen a more well-fitted suit, a sharper sense of style that was timeless and crisp. Had they met in any other circumstances, Hannah would have thought him to be rather suave. Hannah couldn't think of a good reason why he'd be jealous of Elijah, even if he *was* a crazed reader.

The second was an offshoot of the first, and rather than jealousy, Sterling just had a thing against Jewish people. Hannah was all too familiar with the insults hurled at people like her and being sneaky was no exception. But her brain still couldn't accept it, given that Sterling claimed to be a huge fan. *With a last name like Cohen, there is no way he hasn't connected the dots*, Hannah thought, *so that rules out anti-semitism.*

The third was that he knew about her involvement with Elijah and Hematite. This could have simply been a warning.

But it was the fourth possibility that Hannah couldn't shake. As much as Hannah didn't want to admit it, there was a chance that Sterling was telling the truth. The critical voice that sometimes spoke in the back of her mind grew, telling Hannah this was what she got for being so trusting and willing to leave the comforts of home.

Hannah reached into her bag, grabbed her phone, and called Michele.

"You usually just text me. What's going on?"

"I just had the weirdest fucking encounter of my entire career." She gave Michele the recap. "I didn't make a mistake moving here, did I?"

"Fuck, no! As much as I miss you, you needed this! How's your writing?"

"It's been good. I'll probably hit my deadline."

"Ok, and your Twitch streams?"

"I'm streaming less out of writer's block and more out of fun, and my sub count has gotten pretty high. I just got into their Partner program."

"Sounds like you're in a better place since you moved. I know your mom was a neurotic control freak with too many opinions, but you don't have to worry about that anymore."

"I swear, whenever something goes wrong, I hear her voice in my head. I'm so sick of it. Though it's been progressively less. This was just so bizarre, though."

"No, yeah, that dude sounds like a total creep. Do *you* think Elijah is using you?"

"I mean, I don't think so. But he's so reserved! I think that's why my brain even went there."

"This is gonna sound random, but I promise it's not. Have you guys hooked up yet?"

"We haven't. We go out a fair deal, so it's not like we aren't going on dates or anything."

"Let me guess. Superhero business eats at his time?"

"Yeah. Precisely. Plus, I get the vibe that he's really self-conscious."

"Get the pole out of his ass and then see what happens. Maybe he'll relax then, and you'll get your answers."

"You think so?"

"Babe, you're the queen of dragon smut. Of *course* I think so."

CHAPTER 12

When Elijah logged in to Twitch for the first time, he didn't understand the appeal of watching someone else play a video game. But there was something relaxing about watching Hannah perform trick shots that he couldn't be bothered to attempt himself. He almost forgot why he was watching—to search for any hidden signs or secrets in her live streams. Despite everything, he wanted to leave no stone unturned.

But it was completely normal. Hannah was streaming a playthrough of *Breath of the Wild,* as per usual. He didn't catch what this exact speed run was for, but there was nothing out of the ordinary.

"Chat, can I ask you a favor? I feel super old for even asking this." Hannah paused for dramatic effect, leaning back in her pink gaming chair. The chair matched some neon pink mood lighting that illuminated her room, her cat ear headphones, and the pastel-colored art prints that Elijah couldn't fully make out behind her. "But can someone please tell me what poggers means?"

The chat exploded with responses. Hannah cracked up and adjusted her cat ear headphones as they all came in.

"I know, I know. I should know better by now. But you guys kept saying it, and I didn't have the guts to ask. I'm twenty-seven years old, and none of my friends in real life use Twitch. Like, I just got them all on TikTok with me. We're trying to keep up, you know?"

With no warning, Brad threw open the door to the office, making Elijah nearly jump from his chair.

"Dude, I'm freaking out!" Brad's breaths were short and fast. As Elijah stood from his chair, he didn't even need to ask Brad what was going on. "Reiji wants me to work for him. He told me I don't have to answer him right away and that I can think about it, but I don't think I have a choice. I knew he'd want to say something after he tried to kill us, but I was not expecting that!"

"Slow down, dude." He placed a hand on Brad's shoulder, grounding his friend. "You already know that it's not your dad's fault."

"Can't you just delete all of that stuff?!"

Elijah frowned. "If I delete something off of his desktop, then he'll be really suspicious."

"Come on, Elijah. Can you please just delete it?" The desperation was clear in Brad's voice and paired with tears welling in his eyes. Whatever Reiji offered him had him more spooked than Elijah had ever seen him.

Elijah sighed. "I still have access to his desktop. Let's just hope he doesn't notice."

"Thank you. I appreciate you trying to be the voice of reason right now, I really do. We know it's not my dad's fault, and that Reiji framed him in case this exact scenario happened. We know that. But he's not just a few steps ahead of us. He's years ahead. What will Naomi think?"

"Naomi will probably understand whenever you get around to telling her." He tried to bite his tongue, but only could so much. "Though sooner will probably be better than later at this point."

"I know. Don't remind me."

Elijah pursed his lips, as the realization dawned on him. "You have to say yes."

"What?!" Brad's already pale skin lightened, as the color drained from his face.

"You do! You can't tell him no! God knows what he'd do if you said no beyond just sharing the blackmail. And then he'd *really* realize that I deleted it. Don't give him a reason to look for it. You said it yourself; you don't really have a choice."

"Oh, god damn it. God damn it, you're right." Brad paced. "Dude, I don't want to be a drug dealer!"

"I know, I know. Hey, hey, listen. Listen. We'll get together with Kane and maybe Jameson, and then we'll work through a plan, okay? You don't have to become a drug dealer. Naomi doesn't have to think your dad killed Noah, and your dad doesn't have to go to jail."

"I think he knows, Elijah," Brad said with a shaky voice. "He said he knows one of my friends is Hematite."

"Wait, what?" It was Elijah's turn to feel shocked. Part of him wondered why Brad didn't bring that up sooner, but Brad was known to be too flustered to think straight when stressed. Elijah allowed himself a moment to catch his breath and found himself hyper-aware of the throbbing feeling that appeared in his forehead. "Did he say who he thought it was?"

"No, but he said he knew it was one of us, or maybe we all took turns. I don't know, maybe he was bluffing. But given everything that's been going on, I kinda believe him."

Elijah remembered their South Main Burgers raid. "He saw us with Kane in some of his gear. He's gotta know it's him; it can't be hard to deduce that much. We should have been more careful."

"He specifically said he wasn't sure which one it was or if it was all of us. I'm not sure what he's going off of beyond that day."

"Hmm. Weird." Elijah glanced at his laptop and saw Kane finally enter the screen. He muted the other window with Hannah's Twitch stream. "Come on, Kane's about to talk to Jolene at her tattoo studio. I've got him rigged with a camera. Wanna sit with me and listen in?"

"Yeah, that'll probably help me clear my head. Let me go grab a chair. I'll be right back."

"I'll be here watching." Elijah felt like that was all he did. He wished he could be more useful, wished he had some sort of power or ability other than texting someone, hoping they'd slip up and say the wrong thing. Brad's return brought him out of his thoughts.

"Do you think we should just suck it up and call the cops? It's not like Chief Daniels is there anymore."

"Absolutely not. We still can't trust them, at least not until we know for sure where this new police chief lies."

"We should at least call McMahon," Brad said. "That's his name, right? I mean, I literally got a confession!"

"I wish it was that simple, dude. Really, I do. But we're working kind of outside the law here. If you went to McMahon, he'd probably have to still bring you in too."

"But isn't he close with Hematite?"

"They've only more recently started working together, and even then, that's pretty rare. McMahon knows he needs him to try and figure out what's going on with all these missing women, and they helped each other a lot with all that Stone Breaker shit, so they're sort of co-existing. I wouldn't call them close, though."

"Oh. Shit. I guess you're right. Oh, look, I think he's going inside."

The lighting inside the tattoo shop was too dim for Elijah to get a perfect look at what was going on through the surveillance camera, especially with a lack of natural light after nightfall. The back wall had a painted mural of magical girls from various anime, eyes sparkling and wide. Black-and-white manga pages covered another wall, but the shop logo was spray-painted in the middle of it in bright pink. In the corner, Elijah could see some shelving that housed pre-packaged snacks, some water bottles, and an array of figurines.

High-energy, peppy Japanese music blared over the sound system, sounding as if heavy metal and kawaii culture had a love child. It mostly drowned out the sound of mechanical buzzing, as someone in the back had the last spots of color filled in to new ink. The music grew quieter as the door chimed, making the sounds of the tattoo machine seem louder.

Jolene changed tremendously in the ten years since they last saw her, but in a way that suited her. She'd dyed her formerly blonde hair half hot pink, half green, and there was hardly an inch of skin visible beneath the tattoos on her arms. She wore a black T-shirt with a yellow-and- red-haired anime character tucked into red plaid pants. Hematite didn't recognize the character but figured Elijah would.

"Sorry, superhero, but I'll need an ID and an appointment to get you some ink." Jolene quickly glanced up from her tablet, which rested on the check-in counter of the shop, to look at Hematite, but she didn't stop working on her sketch. "And I swear to God, if you ask me for Pike's Peak, I'm gonna lose my shit."

Hematite scoffed, the sound distorted by his mask and voice modifier. "I'm not here for a tattoo. And if I was, it wouldn't be of Pike's Peak; don't worry."

Jolene laughed. "Thank God for that. How can I help you?"

"I actually have some questions, if you don't mind."

Jolene rose an eyebrow but returned her gaze to the outline for her next client. "I'm not in trouble, am I?"

"Do you have any reason to be?"

She shook her head. "Don't think so. I mind my own business." Her nonchalance matched her words.

"Then no, you're not. I have some questions about a potential client of yours."

"What is this, some sort of police questioning?"

"Consider it more of a private investigation."

"Hm. Okay. Fire away."

"Have you tattooed a man recently with a full Japanese sleeve?"

"Yeah, some guy came in here about eight, nine months ago looking for that. I was stoked because I don't get to do those too often. Most of my clients just want anime characters or manga panels."

"What was his name?"

She puckered her lips. "Can I ask why you're asking?"

"I suspect he's the reason all those women have gone missing here in Riverpeak. Did he say anything weird to you?"

As Jolene pondered it, her stylus found its way to her bottom lip. "Huh. You know, there actually was, now that you mention it." She gestured to a chair across from the counter, pointing at it with the stylus. "You can sit if you want. This might take a bit."

"I prefer to stand."

"Suit yourself. Well, normally I'm a bit more confidential about my client base, but you *are* Hematite, so I guess I can trust you. His name was Noah Sato."

"His ID checked out?"

"Yeah. Why?"

"You know he died a few years ago, right?"

"What? When was this?" Her surprise was genuine as she asked in a sort of whisper, even though it was just them at the front of the shop. The tattoo artist and client behind them likely couldn't hear their conversation over the machines and music.

"Six years ago or so."

"Oh. That's when I was working as an apprentice at a shop up in Denver. I didn't stay super up-to-date on what was going on down here. Was too busy trying to focus on my work and grow my socials."

"Right." Hematite nodded. "What was he like?"

"Noah? He was very charming. Was a total blast to talk to, even though he was kinda weird. Said he was reconnecting with his heritage, though he didn't sound too serious when he said it. But he knew where the line was between fun and inappropriate, you know? Never outright flirted with me or anything, but the conversation was mostly good."

Hematite knew what she meant; he toed that line with Rory before, his own sense of humor a bit influenced by Noah himself. "But it took a weird turn?"

"Yeah. He mentioned that he was hoping to get some people together for a project he was working on. He asked me if I'd be interested in learning more, but I told him I really couldn't dedicate much of my time to anything outside of the shop. Even when I'm technically off, I'm still managing the logistics of this place, posting on social, and working on stuff for clients. I'm a total workaholic but I love it, you know?"

"Did he say what kind of project?"

"No. Once I told him that I didn't really have time for anything else, he dropped it. Sorry I can't be more specific."

"It's fine. What was his tattoo about? Did it have any meaning?"

"Oh, yeah. Pretty much all traditional Japanese pieces do. Well, they should, anyway. That's, like, the whole point, so they're all typically pretty symbolic. Sometimes it's a social status thing; sometimes it's a religious thing."

"What did he get?"

"A snake and a kitsune surrounded by cherry blossoms."

"Meaning…?"

"I'm not sure exactly what it means to him. But we've got our snake, which is often used sort of like a phoenix, right?" Jolene set the tablet down and grabbed a binder from the countertop. She flipped through the portfolio until she reached the page with a photo of Noah's tattoo and used her stylus to point out the sections she was talking about. "Snakes shed their skin, so it's all about rebirth or change. Kind of similarly, cherry blossoms are all about how time passes and how life is short."

Pretty ironic, Elijah thought as he watched, *given Kane's power.*

"And what's a kitsune?"

"They're trickster foxes. Different colors can mean different things, but I'd say they're pretty straightforward."

"This has been surprisingly helpful." He thought about what Hannah said earlier about a Hematite hotline and debated giving Jolene the number to his burner phone to contact him if she saw Noah again but decided against it. "Use a fox emoji in an Instagram caption or story if you see him. I'll be watching."

"Ooh, a secret message! I'm in," Jolene said.

"Any other weird clients?"

"No, not that I can think of. Anything else I can help you with?"

"We should be good here. Thank you, Jolene."

"Yeah, anytime."

As Hematite left, he spoke into his earpiece. "Did you get all that?"

"I did," Elijah confirmed. "He's clearly not hiding."

"No, and if he is, he doesn't want to be."

CHAPTER 13

As the temperatures dropped day by day, the leaves transformed into shades of orange and red, making a beautiful foreground for the green-and-brown mountains in the distance. Hannah couldn't help but snap a photo and send it to Michele as the brisk, early evening air caused goose flesh to spread across her mostly bare skin. She was used to Florida's never-ending summer, but she just reminded herself where she was heading and what she hoped to do. If she was successful, the discomfort her Halloween costume brought her in the cold would be well worth it.

> HANNAH: How pretty is this place in the fall!!

Four heart-eye emojis accompanied the text. Michele was quick to reply, ever the night owl. After sending some starry eyes emojis, she sent a follow-up question.

> MICHELE: Are you going to Elijah's?

> HANNAH: Yeah, lol when am I not these days?

MICHELE: Have you locked that shit down yet?? I have been stalking your Facebook for status updates for MONTHS, and you know I hate that app.

HANNAH: I mean, we talk all the time, and we go on dates like every other weekend. I'm into hiking now! Idk I think we're just having fun??

MICHELE: omfg ... how's that pole up his ass doing?

HANNAH: tbh, I think it is wedged firmly in there, and I kinda wanna see how long it takes for him to yeet it out...

MICHELE: Do I need to fly out to Denver to whack some sense into him?

It ended with the raised eyebrow emoji.

HANNAH: No no no!!! Definitely just his anxiety or something, lmao. Like I said he's very self-conscious.

MICHELE: Ok good ... but know that I will.

HANNAH: Lol, I'm here now so I'll keep you posted!

Hannah added the side-eyes emoji and then pocketed her phone in her purse.

When the doorbell rang, Elijah had his candy bowl at the ready but smiled at the sight of Hannah. While he wore a Spider-Man suit, she was donning a much more revealing look. The yellow shorts hung loosely from her hips, held in place by suspenders connected to a matching crop top. When paired with a red cardigan hanging loosely off her shoulders and some purple temporary hair dye in her short blonde hair, Elijah would recognize the look anywhere.

It is almost ironic, he thought, *that Hannah dressed as Faye Valentine.* He couldn't decide if it was sheer coincidence or a sign that she was operating right under their noses. But the way the sheer, thigh-high stockings ran up her legs clouded his thoughts too much for him to make a decision.

Elijah's brain was effectively as good as putty.

"Wow." Pink already dusted his cheeks. The sight of her dressed in the costume alone was enough to make him self-conscious about how he looked in his superhero suit—specifically, if she could tell just how much he enjoyed her look. "You look great."

"Thanks! So do you," she said, admiring the way the skin-tight suit clung to his frame, "but what else is new."

"Oh, please." He greeted her with a quick kiss as he closed the door behind her, swallowing back his arousal with little luck. "We get a ton of kids every year. Hope you're ready."

"Hell yeah. I was born ready," Hannah said. "You should see the crowds back in Orlando. Especially with the warm weather, they never seem to stop out there."

"I always feel bad for the kids when it's extra cold, but it's not supposed to be too bad this year. I'll never forget once when we were kids, the guys and I went as the four Ninja Turtles. We had to wear hoodies over our outfits. Shawn denies it, but he cried about it all night. It got us extra candy."

Hannah laughed. "My hometown was like that too. Five-year-old Hannah was absolutely gutted that she had to wear gray sweats beneath her Anastasia dress one year."

"That is unfortunate, but thanks for coming by. Brad ditched me for Naomi, as per usual."

"Any excuse to hang out with you." Hannah's nose scrunched as she smiled at him, and Elijah felt winded. "I'm just glad you're not too old to dress up."

"Nah, never." Elijah tossed her a piece of candy, and she caught it. "Do you have a favorite Halloween movie you like to watch? I can put something on while we wait for the kids."

"Nothing too gory. I can only handle that when it's animated."

"Noted."

"I'll grab us some drinks," Hannah said, as she moved her way to the kitchen. "What do you want?"

"There are some local IPAs in the fridge that are pretty good. Wine too, if you're into that. Whichever you're in the mood for works for me."

As Hannah grabbed two beer bottles, Elijah swallowed the lump in his throat and took a silent, deep breath, hoping she wouldn't notice. Normally, he could compose himself, especially since he'd been seeing Hannah for the last six months now. He knew what Hannah looked like. He knew what Hannah's body looked like. But now, he felt powerless.

As he contemplated if this was the power he suspected she had at work, he blurted out, "Do you want to stay the night?"

Elijah realized how it sounded after he said it and visibly winced. From the kitchen, Hannah turned to face him as she shut the fridge with her hip. Her eyes were wide, but she didn't look upset. Instead, she was smirking.

"I swear to God, I'm not just trying to get in your pants. I just ... I don't know if you're staying in Riverpeak once your lease is up, so our time is potentially limited together, you know? So, I want to spend as much of it with you as we can." His speech sped up as he continued to voice his concerns, another sign of his anxieties. "And I know long distance is a thing, so we can cross that bridge when we get there if you do decide to leave Riverpeak. But that doesn't make me any less anxious."

Hannah walked back over to the couch and set their drinks down on the coffee table in front of them. Elijah didn't take his eyes off her as she approached. She leaned down to cup his cheeks with her hands, forcing eye contact now.

"I know my life is sort of in flux right now, but no matter where I go, I want you to be a part of it. You don't have to be worried about anything, okay?"

There was so much more Hannah wanted to say, including how she had no plans to leave, but wasn't sure how much of it she should— especially if his uncertainty would finally push Elijah to act in the way she wanted.

His eyes widened. "You mean that?"

"Mhm, I do. And for what it's worth, I would love to stay the night."

Elijah moved one of his hands behind her head so he could bring her in for a kiss. He wrapped an arm around her waist and shifted so he could pull Hannah closer to him until her legs rested over the tops of his thighs.

Normally, Elijah's nerves got the best of him, so he played it safe. But tonight, his impatience was winning his internal battle. When he clutched Hannah's thighs, as if he'd never touched them before, Hannah kissed him deeper to egg him on. His lips made their way to Hannah's jaw and neck, and she gripped his bicep, where she could feel the tension in the muscle beneath the polyester. Desperate for more, his hand on her hip raised to meet her waist.

Hannah wasn't about to complain or stop Elijah now that he'd shared this side of himself. It couldn't have been any more different from the chaste kisses they'd shared, prompting Hannah to make a mental note to text Michele that the metaphorical pole had finally been removed. The fabric on his arms was smooth to the touch, but no comparison to his clean-shaven face.

Elijah's phone ringing interrupted them, and he pulled away at the sound of the ringtone he set specifically for Kane's burner phone. Hannah's brows furrowed in confusion.

"I'm so sorry," he said. His cheeks were a bright shade of pink again. "It's Hematite. This is his burner."

"Oh, by all means," Hannah said. Elijah kept his arm wrapped around her waist to keep her against him, not wanting to lose what they'd started. As he put his phone on speaker, he set it down next to them on the couch. His now-free hand slowly ran up and down her leg.

"Hey, dude," Elijah greeted. "What's going on?"

"Are you home?"

"Yeah, why?"

"Just checking. See you soon!"

"Whoa, whoa, wait!"

But it was too late—Kane already hung up.

Elijah mentally cursed, half-tempted to call Kane, but he knew it would most likely be fruitless. He turned his attention back toward Hannah. The more he thought about her, the more he realized how desperately he cared for her against his better judgment. There was still so much he didn't know, but he envied her carefree spirit and wished to keep her close for it. "I'm sorry we got interrupted. I hope you're not upset."

"Why would I be upset? It sounds important, whatever it is."

"I can't wait for this wedding to be over. Don't get me wrong. I'm so happy for Brad and Naomi, I really am. It's just a lot to juggle right now, you know?"

Hannah nodded. "Given everything, yeah. It is. I'm here for you, though, okay?"

"Thanks. If I'm this stressed, I can't even imagine how Rory's handling it as maid of honor with all of this," he said, gesturing vaguely with one hand, "going on."

The doorbell rang shortly after that. Elijah offered to get it, leaving Hannah to refill the candy bowl in the kitchen. When Elijah opened the door, Kane, with Rory, said, "Trick or treat!"

"Hey, guys." Elijah's cheeks were still ruddied from a few moments prior; he hated that he could feel the heat on his face. "For the record, I'm not here alone. Hannah's here. Is that okay?"

"Do you trust her?" Kane asked quietly enough so only Elijah and Rory could hear him.

"I do."

Kane noticed how Elijah didn't hesitate.

"Then we're coming in. Come on, Rory."

Rory trailed behind Kane as they passed the mezuzah on the front door and entered Elijah's house. Hannah waved at them from the kitchen before striding in. Kane hadn't bothered with a costume, wearing just a plain hoodie with some jeans. Rory was wearing all black and purple, with her makeup hinting that she had ditched a witch hat before leaving her house.

"Kane, Rory, this is Hannah. Hannah, these are my friends, Kane and Rory."

"Nice to finally meet you guys," Hannah said. She studied Kane, remembering that Elijah said Hematite called—not Kane—and compared his stature to Hematite's in her memory. "I've heard great things about you."

"We've actually met before, Hannah," Kane said. "I'm sorry that I suspected you. But if Elijah trusts you, so do I. He's an excellent judge of character."

Hannah blinked a few times at him before she put the pieces together. "You're Hematite, aren't you?"

"Bingo."

"That explains a lot, actually. I'm surprised I didn't see it sooner."

"That's because I'm damn good at what I do," Elijah said. Hannah never heard him sound so confident.

"I'm gonna cut to the chase. We have concrete evidence that Reiji Sato is the head of the drug ring now. Between everything you've reviewed and collected and some surveys I've done, we have all the proof we need."

"And does Naomi know?" Elijah asked.

The silence that followed spoke volumes.

After a few beats, Rory said, "I feel like such a fucking shitty friend." She sat at the dining room table and, with an exasperated sigh, she lowered her head onto it. Her forehead hit its cool surface with a soft thud, causing her curls to billow around her.

"We still haven't told her," Kane said. "Much to your chagrin, I know."

"I'm actually so glad you're here, Hannah," Rory said, muffled against the table. "I feel so lost because this is all so close to home. And he knows where all of us live and knows so much about all of our families. It's tripping me up."

Kane nodded. "An outsider's perspective could be nice."

Elijah's phone rang again. "It's Brad. Let me make sure he's okay. Excuse me, guys." He stepped out back to take the call, leaving Hannah alone with Kane and Rory.

Rory lifted her head and flipped her hair out of her face. "You've been spending a lot of time with him, right?"

"Yeah. Quite a lot, actually."

"What do you think of him?"

"I mean obviously she likes him," Kane said matter-of-factly.

"You know what I mean, smartass," Rory replied with a smirk and mischievousness in her tone. Kane just stuck the tip of his tongue out in response.

Hannah wasn't sure how much she should say. Out of respect for Elijah and his privacy, Hannah simply answered, "I think he's really great. Really, *really* great. He doesn't give himself enough credit."

"Oh, yeah! That's nothing new," Kane said.

Rory added, "He doesn't really date much, so it's nice to see him finally opening up to someone."

"What do you mean?"

"Oh, you know, he's had a few girlfriends here and there, but it'd never last long."

"A lot of people didn't even show an interest in Elijah until they found out he was going to work some tech gig. They just saw dollar signs," Rory said with an eye roll. "So, I can't blame him for just focusing on his career."

"I haven't dated in a long time either, so I get what you're saying."

Rory's eyebrows raised. "Really?"

"I gave up a while ago, but my friend encouraged me to try this dating app when I moved here so I could meet people. But a lot of guys see that I write fantasy novel sex scenes and lose any remaining dignity. You should see my Instagram DMs."

"I don't even want to imagine," Kane said with a frown.

"Yeah. It's bad. And any that didn't care ... well, my family did a pretty good job at sabotaging those relationships." She exhaled and quickly explained. "Long story short, my mother was a narcissist who wanted me all to herself."

"Was?" Rory asked. "Oh, I'm so sorry. Did she...?"

But Kane already guessed the answer and stifled his laugh.

"Oh, no. She's alive. She's just vile," Hannah said without a care in the world. "I don't talk to her anymore."

"Nice! Welcome to the self-orphaned club. You can join my sister and me," Kane said. "Luckily for you, Elijah's mother is probably the sweetest woman in Riverpeak. Whenever Kayla and I needed to bail for the night when we were kids, she'd always let us stay there. No questions asked."

"I love Lena. You're in for a treat if Elijah ever introduces you two."

"Our boy is all grown up. When did you cut your parents out, if you don't mind me asking?"

"When I moved here, actually. It's something I'd wanted to do but hadn't had the balls to for years. But enough is eventually enough, as it sounds like you know."

"Good for you. You hangin' in there okay?"

"Every now and then, the voice in the back of my head tells me I'm a terrible person, but I'm managing. Praying a lot but managing."

"It gets easier. It'll probably help that you're so far away. Whatever it was, just know that you did what you had to do. Forgiveness works great for some people. But for others, you gotta just walk away. Like I told Rory and my sister, you can't save everyone."

Hannah smiled. "Yeah, you're right."

They all hushed when Elijah came back in. He glanced at his friends, getting the sense that they had been talking about him but shrugged it off. "Bad news. Naomi just got called in for work. I guess they need all hands on deck since the cops found a bunch of people overdosed on the east side tonight. It's bad."

"They're making the dosages stronger," Kane said. "They've also been outright killing people. This might just be their most recent way of doing so discreetly. I think the fire back in July ended up getting too much attention."

"But the good news is that they found Jordan Jefferson," Elijah added. "She's home now. They say she won't really talk, but they're hopeful she'll open up eventually, maybe with a trauma therapist."

"Oh, thank God," Rory said. "I was so worried about her. She's such a good kid."

"They found her completely alone in a garage on the east side somewhere. All she'd say was that it didn't work. She won't say what 'it' is, though."

Rory frowned. "We need to find out what they're doing and why. Do you think we can bug his house like we did Tom Stevens's office?"

"Stevens's office was easy. Naomi was able to plant it." Elijah sighed. "I think her dad's gonna be smarter than that. How are we gonna get it in there without him noticing?"

"I'll break in," Kane said. "I can be sneaky about it."

"Or, better yet, we have Brad play double agent. He *did* get an offer to work for Reiji, after all."

"Do you think we can pull that off?" Rory asked.

"The earbuds have worked really well for Kane and me so far," Elijah said. "We can get him set up with one and go from there. Reiji's already suspicious that it's one of us, so maybe this will help clear our names if Brad enthusiastically helps."

"Have you talked to him about this?" Kane asked. "About what this means?"

"He knows."

Almost as if on cue, Brad returned home, still in his scrubs. The light bags forming under his eyes made him look more exhausted than Elijah had ever seen him, thanks to the situation with his future in-laws weighing on him.

"Hey, everyone. I take it I'm just in time?"

"Yeah," Kane said. "We were just talking about the offer Reiji made you."

"I'm taking it," Brad said. "It fucking sucks, but I can't tell him no. At least I can help you guys that way."

"I'll have eyes on you at every move, dude," Elijah promised. "You'll be okay."

"Did Reiji ever say anything to you about the girls?" Hannah asked. "Did he give you any indicators of what that may be about?"

Brad shook his head. "Nothing about them."

"See if you can find anything out next time you're there," Kane said, "and let me know before you go. If it's a weekend or weeknight, I can be there on the down low, if it makes you feel better."

"I'd like that, yeah," Brad said with a nod. "Between that and Elijah's surveillance, I'd feel pretty good." He sighed. "Never thought I'd say I'd want Big Brother watching, but, well."

"Say, Hannah," Rory chimed in. "What do you think of all this?"

Elijah sensed that everything Rory said was a front to test the waters. If Hannah noticed that, she didn't show it.

"I think this is the best route," she said. "No better way to find out what he wants than by earning his trust, right?"

Kane and Rory glanced at each other. Hannah sensed a stiffness between them but couldn't place it. She wondered if Kane still doubted her.

"Rory and I should get going. East side calls."

"Be safe out there," Elijah said. "Need anything from me?"

"I should be good. Thanks, though."

As they left, Brad announced he was going to bed. They bid Brad their good nights and made their way upstairs not long after him, Hannah heading to the bathroom to change out of her costume. As Elijah unzipped his Spider-Man suit and pulled his arms out of the skin-tight fabric, he got a text from Kane.

> KANE: So, she's definitely not directly responsible. But still, keep an eye out.

Elijah had little time to respond, so he just sent the thumbs-up emoji. When Hannah joined Elijah in his room, comfortably dressed in an oversized *Cowboy Bebop* shirt and thin leggings she'd packed in her purse, in case she'd gotten too cold, he set his phone on the bedside table.

"I only have my bed, if you're okay with sharing."

Hannah could have sworn Elijah's voice cracked a bit. While he'd unzipped his suit and pulled this top half off, the torso and arms dangled from his waist, revealing an abdomen as lightly toned as she'd suspected. She nodded her head and said, "Yeah, I don't mind. I don't think it's a big deal."

"Yeah, you're right. Didn't want to make you uncomfortable."

"Why would it? After all this, Elijah, and you're worried about sharing a bed?"

Her teasing paired with her grin made him feel weak in the knees. "Excuse me for being a gentleman," he said with a nervous laugh, joining Hannah in getting ready for the night. "You sure you don't mind this?"

"I'm absolutely sure. Are *you* okay with sharing a bed? I don't want my lack of giving a shit to influence you, either."

"No, no, it's not that. I'm fine," Elijah insisted. He was scared she got the wrong idea now and mentally cursed himself for what felt like the millionth time that night.

Hannah smiled. "Okay." She felt the butterflies in her stomach, a feeling she wasn't used to. Being able to care for someone uninterrupted felt like a luxury.

Meanwhile, Elijah was not used to being in situations like this and wasn't even sure how he ended up here, especially after their earlier conversation. They looked at each other awkwardly before he said, "I can sleep in my costume or in jeans or something if you want—"

"Don't you dare," Hannah interrupted. "Get comfy. This is your house. Stop *kvetching*."

"Right, yeah." He pulled the Spider-Man suit off his legs and quickly grabbed a new pair of briefs from a drawer before he made his way to the walk-in closet to change. "Just making sure you're okay, that's all."

"I appreciate that, but seriously, you're fine."

She climbed into his bed and when he returned, he wore a matching shirt.

"Alright, space cowboy, I see what you did there."

"Couldn't resist."

The silence between them as they tried and failed to fall asleep was awkward, deafening, and entirely unlike anything they had experienced with one another until this point. The air felt stiff, and after tossing and turning for a few minutes, Elijah and Hannah looked over at one another at the same time. Unbeknownst to the other, both of them felt something unravel within them. The last thread for the evening snapped.

Elijah was the first to break. "Please tell me I can do more than just kiss you."

"I was starting to think you'd never ask."

In an instant, Elijah brought his lips to hers and shifted so he was on top of her, supporting himself with his arms. Hannah smiled into their kiss as she ran her hands up his biceps; she noticed how tense they were for the second time that night. Even after all these months, she could sense that something was still bothering him, but she brushed it off; clearly, it wasn't bothering him enough to stop him from proceeding.

A voice in Elijah's head told him to pause, as their clothes made their way to the bedside floor, but he ignored it. He kept going, succumbing to his loneliness and his attraction to her. Elijah could hardly taste the beer and candy from earlier, lost in the heat of Hannah's mouth. As he reached his fingers down, tracing her ribs before dipping to her hips and then beneath the thin fabric, Hannah bucked her hips up to reach his fingers faster. Unable to help it, Elijah moaned into the kiss in response as his tongue slipped past her lips.

Egging him on, Hannah reached up for Elijah's curls, weaving her fingers through them and giving them a tug. It broke their kiss, and Elijah could only curse as he gasped in pleasure. His gasps turned into pants as Hannah began to stroke him, looking up at him with lust-blown brown eyes.

To think that he was the object of her desires sent him over the edge, leaving his mind empty as he finally entered her. Elijah took his time to savor the moment, and from the look on her face, Hannah didn't mind. As he glanced down at her, his auburn curls starting to obstruct the top of his vision, he picked up the pace with each call of his name which sounded more and more like a moan as the night went on. As Hannah tightened around him, her nails ran down his back, sending Elijah into sensory overload and triggering his own release.

And *that* triggered the return of his thoughts.

So many questions of *what if* ran through his head, especially as he contemplated if this meant that Hannah had him right where she wanted him—that all of this had been part of some larger scheme, not unlike the one he was supposed to be doing—but eventually, he found them being drowned out by how good everything felt. *I might hate myself in the morning*, he thought.

But that is tomorrow morning's problem.

CHAPTER 14

E lijah sighed as he picked up his phone to check the time and cursed himself when he realized it was one-thirty in the morning. This wasn't the first time in the weeks since Halloween that he'd stayed up too late without even realizing it. The change in music in his headphones to a suddenly rapid piano tune alerted him to a villain in the game he was playing on his Switch, so he fast traveled out of the spot, hit save, and then turned off the console. Once he set it down, he thumbed through Instagram, accidentally tapped into some Stories, and scrolled through them to try to fall asleep.

No matter how many books he read or games he played before bed, he couldn't take his mind off his guilt. It didn't help that he'd been reading Hannah's fantasy series and watching her Twitch streams and that, as a result, it inspired him to do a rerun of *Breath of the Wild*. She'd found a way to occupy every corner of his mind, especially since she learned his secret: that he was "Hematite's sidekick," as she so naturally put it. But the guilt of their circumstances was eating at him, especially after Halloween night. He was certain now that she had nothing to do with the drug ring, and that everything had been a matter of sheer coincidence. Even still, they'd shared a bed and been intimate, all in the name of finding out the truth about her. He felt dirty in a way that he couldn't come clean from and wished he'd never lied.

Elijah stopped in his tracks when her Instagram Stories popped up. It was a photo of her writing desk by a window that overlooked the mountains behind Riverpeak, clearly brightened up to better highlight their snowcapped tips. Only a few words were overlaid, reading,

"Late night writing sessions just hit different."

A cup of tea was on her desk and the timestamp in the top left corner by Hannah's username was only from twelve minutes ago.

The next Instagram Story was a close-up selfie of her, clearly meant to be silly based on the angle being just below her nose—positioned just above her nostrils—with the text overwritten saying, "someone tell me to go TF to sleep lmaoooo" from four minutes ago. The only light in the photo was from her laptop in front of her.

Elijah's fingers moved to her contact on his phone without a thought. He debated reaching out for a moment, not wanting to interrupt her writing, but the voice screaming at him to tell her everything took over. The next thing he knew, his phone was ringing with her name on the screen.

"Hey, Elijah! What are you doing up?"

"I saw your Instagram Story. It's still technically Shabbat. Shouldn't you, you know, not be working?"

Hannah laughed. "Ooh, busted. Forgive me, Rabbi, for I have sinned."

He stifled a laugh of his own. "Please. I'd make a terrible rabbi."

"I don't think you called me to discuss a career shift in theology. What's up?"

"Can't sleep. I mean, obviously. I was thinking of going for a late-night stroll, maybe just around the pond to clear my head. Seems like you're in a similar predicament."

"That I am. Got about a thousand words in tonight and then? Crickets."

"Want to join me? Maybe we can clear our heads together?"

"Sure! I don't see why not."

"I'll pick you up. I'm not gonna make you walk there this late. See you soon."

The entire ride to her house and then to Constance's Pond, Elijah's head continued racing. *It is now or never*, he thought, but he wasn't sure how to tell her the entire truth. The pond was eerily peaceful, as it grew closer to two in the morning. Elijah glanced over to Hannah, who was walking on his right side, closer to the pond than he was. She had a sort of carefree nonchalance about her, despite everything going on around them. The moonlight suited her, illuminating her hair and face. The late fall night brought a gentle breeze that made her lift her face to the sky with a gentle smile.

Elijah wished he could be so carefree. He asked, "You aren't worried?"

At that, she looked at him with wide eyes. "About what?"

"Well, you know." He gestured aimlessly in front of him. "Everything."

Her smile lingered for a brief moment before falling into a more neutral expression. "No. I used to be, though. Not about you or what's happening here. Just about everything in general. I have horrible anxiety, but it's getting better."

Elijah blinked at her. Hannah and anxiety didn't feel like two words that belonged in a sentence together in his mind, not after everything she'd told him about herself. "I would have never guessed that."

"I decided to just start doing whatever the hell I wanted. Guess I was tired of being held back." She shrugged a shoulder as they walked, feet gently digging into the soft dirt and sand beneath them with every step. "My anxiety … it's not fully my own. It's worse when I'm with my mother. She's, well, she's something else. Let's just say there's a reason I don't talk to her anymore. Myriad of reasons, actually."

"Oh," Elijah said. "I'm sorry to hear that."

"Don't be." Hannah smiled up at him reassuringly. "Walking away from her was a tough decision. It ate at me for a long time. But finally going no contact was the best thing I could have done for myself."

Elijah felt like a complete idiot. She mentioned not being close with her family before, but he hadn't known it was to this extent. It explained nearly everything. "When did you go no contact?"

Her smile fell into a neutral expression again. "A week before I moved here."

"Is that why you moved to Riverpeak? Like, why you really moved? I mean, I get you were suffering from writer's block. But I always thought moving somewhere for just that was a bit extreme." He quickly added, "I hope that didn't offend you. I've just been thinking about your time here and was curious."

Hannah nodded. "That was a part of it. I did come here for a change of scenery and pace, since I had writer's block like the world's probably never seen. But honestly, you could probably better categorize it as a depressive episode. I realized my mother's incessant negativity was why; it really weighed on me."

Her neutral expression now turned into a frown. As Hannah spoke, her expressions became more animated and relaxed, like the weight of her secret had finally been released.

"I'm sorry I didn't tell you sooner. You're a big family man, so I wasn't sure if you'd get it. I just … I never know how to bring it up, you know? It's such a buzzkill! And a lot of people don't get it until they hear everything she's done, which is, well, a lot."

"Do you want to talk about it?"

"If you don't mind hearing me gab about it, I'm more than happy to share."

"I'm all ears."

"Long story short, the last straw was when I realized she opened a credit card in my name and then racked up $10,000 in debt with it. That's why I started Twitch streaming. A writer's advance isn't enough to cover the bills and a surprise debt like that, even when your books get as big as mine. But just as I get it paid off and go to close the card, I see a charge for her utility bill on it. Mind you, she had plenty of money for her country club's fees so she could golf every weekend. It's not like my parents were poor and needed help. If they were, I would have lent them some cash in a heartbeat without a second thought. But they were just entitled. I never saw a penny of that back, either."

Elijah felt like facepalming but refrained. "Is that who was calling you nonstop when I took you to dinner that one night?"

"Sort of. It was my mom's cousin trying to play messenger pigeon.

I ended up blocking her completely once I got home. I didn't want to have to block my entire family, but they kinda didn't give me a choice."

Elijah felt his heart drop into his stomach. Her cousin must have been the one on the other line in that phone recording Kane sent him too. It all added up, with none of the pieces pointing back to the crime ring.

"You know, the weirdest thing happened a few weeks ago," she said. "At first, I thought nothing of it, so I didn't bother to say anything."

"What was it?"

"Some stranger told me you were using me."

Elijah's brows rose. "What? Really?"

"Yeah. Said he was a fan. He flagged me down to sign a book."

"Aren't most of the guys who read your work just horny weirdoes?"

"No, no, not this one; it wasn't that series. My first novel was a paranormal thriller. It did okay, but it's kind of niche. He had me sign that one."

"Weird."

"Yeah. It was so bizarre that I haven't been able to shake it."

"Well, you don't have to be worried."

"No, but it feels like you sure are."

Elijah gulped as the fuzzy feeling returned to his head.

"Are you lying to me, Elijah?"

His brain was buzzing to the point of making him dizzy, and he couldn't stop the words from spilling out of his mouth. "I wouldn't call it a lie."

"Holy shit, he was right?"

"Well, er, no. I can explain, alright? I owe you an apology. Like, an enormous one."

The feeling of betrayal and confusion was as clear as day on Hannah's face, which made Elijah feel even worse about what he was about to say.

"I ... I have to be honest with you. You've proven yourself to me, and I think the guilt is what's keeping me up at night." Elijah sighed.

"When I first started talking to you … Kane was half-convinced that you might have something to do with this drug ring bullshit. And in his defense, it *was* really suspicious, you know? A power vacuum nearly opened up with Tom Stevens's arrest. And then you show up out of nowhere. And I don't think you get it … no one moves *here*. I don't think anyone's moved here since the eighties."

Hannah stopped walking. She reached for Elijah's shoulder to signal this to him in case he continued along the pond. When he turned to face her, he saw her brows had furrowed and her lips were slightly parted. It was a cross between shock and anger.

"What?"

"I know. Hannah, I'm so sorry. I … I didn't even create my profile on that app; Kane and Rory did. They were hoping you'd be on it, and then you were." He couldn't stop the word vomit now. "Everything happened so fast. It was shitty of me, and I'm so sorry."

Hannah scoffed, went to say something, and then bit her tongue. She averted her gaze to the pond, letting her vision defocus on the moon's reflection in the dark waters. "You know, I knew something was off when I first met Hematite." She finally looked at Elijah again. "You know what he said to me? When I told him I saw Reiji Sato going off on some guy in Japanese one day, he asked me why I didn't tell anyone sooner. Who would I have told then?"

"We didn't know much about what was going on then. We were desperate, Kane especially. I tried telling him it was probably nothing, but he's been so spooked."

"My whole life, I've felt held back, and I saw this house for rent for dirt cheap and thought, 'You know what? This is a sign. Fuck it.' No drug rings or crime bosses involved." Hannah shook her head. "I never even heard of Reiji Sato or this drug until I met you. If anyone should have been suspicious, it should have been me!"

"You're right." Elijah ran both of his hands over his face before they plopped onto his thighs. "I feel like such an asshole."

"Do you even like me? Or am I just invited to the wedding to make sure I don't do anything while you're all away for the weekend?"

Elijah's expression completely dropped. "I invited you because I want you there." He felt his heart beating rapidly; Hannah could tell too, thanks to the sudden quick rise and fall of his chest. Elijah reached for her and was relieved when she didn't flinch away from his touch. His hand cupped her cheek, and the other fell to the top of her shoulder, as he forced her to meet his eyes. "Despite how it started, Hannah, I..." The words felt foreign on his tongue. He thought about saying them but held back. He didn't want to unload too much on her at once. "I have never felt like this about anyone before. Literally ever."

Hannah closed her eyes for a moment as she took a deep breath. When she opened them, the tears were still welling, only partially blinked back. Elijah wiped the bottoms of her eyes, removing any that threatened to fall further.

"You're mad," Elijah acknowledged.

Hannah nodded.

"You have every right to be. I'd be pretty pissed too."

"Why are you even bothering to tell me this?" Her voice cracked, as her emotions threatened to take over.

"Because I'm too fucking honest for my own good. The only secret I've ever been able to keep in my life is Kane's, and that's because no one asked. I justified my playing dumb by telling myself it counted as a life-saving lie under God." Elijah wiped another tear from her eyes. "I've always sucked at lying, but I especially can't bring myself to lie to you." Elijah moved his hand on her shoulder to the other side of her face so he could pull her in closer and kiss her forehead. "Please let me make it up to you."

"I don't even know what to say to you right now."

In truth, she thought, *I am too far deep into this whole situation to walk away now.* And despite her anger, she knew Elijah was just trying to do right by his friends. Even though Hannah wasn't about to totally let him off the hook, she knew she'd do the same if the roles were reversed.

But her mind wandered. The voice in her head wasn't her own but her mother's, pulling her back to what she knew: back to Florida, away from the mountains, away from superheroes and Elijah Baron, and away from everything she'd grown to know and love over the last few months. In Florida, the only thing that changed was the direction of the breeze that the palm trees swayed in and how high the tide was as it washed up on the beach in a never-ending summer. There were no changing seasons, no snow to reveal the paths of superheroes with their footsteps imprinted in the white powder, no unpredictability.

"Hannah?"

Anger aside, Hannah melted into him, trying to quiet her mind as she pulled him in for a hug. She was in desperate need of something to ground her. Elijah was quick to pick up on the oncoming anxiety attack and wrapped his arms around her. The grip he had around her waist was enough to show that he meant every word he said.

Had this happened a year ago, Hannah thought, *I may have been more furious.* But she was too mentally tired to be that viscerally angry anymore. Hannah tried to release it with some tears that leaked onto his shirt, and when she pulled away to wipe her eyes, she caught a glimmer of something unnatural sparkling in the water.

"Do you see that?" Hannah pointed in its direction and stepped away, trying to identify the mystery object. Elijah nodded and followed Hannah as she approached it. When she kneeled to get a closer look, she immediately covered her mouth with her hand.

"What is it?" Elijah asked. Hannah stood and took a step back.

"I think it's a body; it looked like a girl's hand. There were still rings on her fingers."

"Let me call Kane. He'll call McMahon."

While they waited, Elijah and Hannah sat a few feet back, so as to not lose their spot, but also not have the body wash up on their feet. Elijah kept an arm around Hannah's shoulders, where she lightly trembled in his grip from everything but the breeze.

Detective McMahon was the first to get to Constance's Pond, his arrival indicated by flashing lights and sirens from two cop cars. He brought a small group with him, ready to investigate the scene. Ever since the Stone Breaker case, McMahon had been assigned all things Hematite-related in addition to his usual detective work. His red hair was a mess on his head, and he was in need of a shave.

"I take it you're Hematite's friends?"

Hannah and Elijah stood as Elijah nodded and introduced themselves.

"You found the body?"

"We were going for a walk when I saw something shiny in the water that didn't look usual," Hannah said. She pointed behind them with her thumb. "I went to take a closer look and saw a hand."

"We'll investigate. Hematite show up?"

Elijah glanced over McMahon's shoulder. "Looks like he's here now."

McMahon turned and saw Hematite, wearing his full winter gear. It was still considerably thin for a late fall Colorado night, but McMahon didn't question it.

"You okay?" Hematite asked Elijah and Hannah. When they both nodded, he turned to McMahon. "I'm here if you need me."

"You think the perp might show up?"

"Wasn't it you who told me they like to return to their crime scenes?"

"Fair point."

A responder by the water looked up and shouted to McMahon, "This looks like the waitress who went missing! No sign of the rest of the body, but her uniform's washed up!"

Hannah and Elijah looked at each other, then at Hematite and McMahon.

"Go home," McMahon said to Hannah and Elijah. "We can take it from here. You both shouldn't have to see any more of this. We'll call you if we have any questions. I take it Hematite has your numbers?"

"He has mine, yeah," Elijah said.

"Stick together in case I need you both. But for now, go get some rest, okay?" He turned to Hematite. "You have my clearance to scope the perimeter and do your thing."

Hematite nodded and was off, slinking into the shadows. Hannah and Elijah took that as their cue.

"My place or yours?" Elijah asked.

"We can go to mine. I'd hate to wake Brad up."

"Right, yeah."

They drove to her house in relative silence, letting the music on the radio play to fill the void, but the volume was still low. Elijah reached over and grabbed Hannah's hand, hoping she wouldn't pull away. He sighed in relief when she laced their fingers together.

When they got to her house and into her bedroom, she patted the spot next to her, once she was in bed; it was an invitation for Elijah to take the space. He joined her slowly, trying to not seem too eager. He was more shaken up than he'd like to admit, and he imagined Hannah wasn't much better off. She was doing a good job of hiding it overall, but when he looked into her eyes, he could see it lingering behind her expression. When Hannah glanced at him, he held an arm out in an offering. A sad smile overcame his face, some hope glimmering behind his eyes.

"Truce?"

Hannah accepted the invitation into his arms, resting against his torso. His warmth instantly overtook her, causing her to easily rest with him as her head fell back onto his shoulder. "Truce."

He softly hummed in satisfaction. His fingers ghosted through her hair. "You okay after everything?"

Hannah nodded. "I will be."

"I'm surprised you've been so calm. I mean, I'm not complaining. It's helping me stay calm. But holy shit."

She shrugged a shoulder. "I'm used to pushing my emotions back. Crazy mother, remember? It's why I write," she said. "But I think I can use this to our advantage."

"How so?"

"So, I did some digging into the town drama when I moved here, and even more so after the Fourth of July. If we think these missing girls are connected to the Sato family, then wouldn't the former police chief know?"

"I mean, she might, but I doubt she'd tell us anything."

"Ah, but she might tell *me* something if I went to her as the new girl who is completely alone and scared out of her fucking mind."

"What are you saying?"

"I'm saying I want to help, and I think I can get her to talk. Woman to woman, you know?"

"It's worth a shot," Elijah said. "You think she will?"

"I think she's a scorned lover who lost what was fueling her narcissism and will open up to a frightened young lady in an act of self-importance. Of *course* I think she'll talk."

"I can get you set up with some recording devices. She'd never know. Let's get Kane up to speed in the morning, but I think you're on to something."

"Sounds like a plan. We should probably try to stay up in case McMahon calls, huh?"

He nodded. "Want me to grab your remote? I can reach it from here. We can put something on to take our minds off everything."

"Yeah, that'd be great. Your pick."

After three episodes' worth of making conversation, Elijah glanced at Hannah for a response, only to find she'd dozed off. He didn't bother to wake her; if McMahon needed them tonight, he'd have called already. Elijah wasn't sure what he did to deserve this but mentally thanked God for it anyway. As he unwillingly fell asleep, he thought about how his confession went too smoothly and all felt too good to be true.

It was.

CHAPTER 15

A s Hannah brewed a pot of coffee the next morning, Elijah frowned at his phone. He wasn't sure if the text from Kane could have come at a better or worse time than now.

KANE: Dr. Potter's ready.

Elijah knew there was no other way. His stomach churned as he choked back the dread that overcame him. It wasn't his proudest moment, but his desire for answers progressively settled the nerves in his core. *This is the lowest I've gone,* he thought, even though he'd done much worse in the name of justice.

God, Elijah thought, speaking to no one in particular, *I really hope you understand.*

"It's not Jefferson's, but it's the best imitation latte I could do."

"Thanks. Hey, wanna go for a drive this morning?"

"A drive?"

"Yeah. Just want to clear my head and check something out with you, if you don't mind."

"Sure, yeah. No biggie. It snowed overnight. Are the roads clear?"

"Should be. Town's pretty good about keeping up with it."

"I've got some travel tumblers we can bring if you wanna take these to go."

"Sounds good."

Elijah offered his car, the stiffness from walking the night prior still thick. If he was being honest with himself, his head felt clear this morning, though he wasn't sure what prevented him from telling Hannah where he was driving her. Lying came more naturally to him these days than he felt comfortable with, and he made a mental note to himself to work on that.

They were silent for the first ten minutes, just drinking their coffee. Hannah was still waking up, a self-proclaimed night owl rather than a morning person, but watched as the surrounding fields seemed to go on forever. Stubborn brown tufts had broken through the snow and ice, accompanied only by a lone lark fluttering from branch to branch. The suburbs of Riverpeak were almost out of reach, now a speck in the rearview mirror.

"Elijah? Where are you taking me again, exactly?" Hannah forced herself to look at him instead of the empty grasslands out the window. "Why are you so nervous?"

"Who says I'm nervous?"

"The crack in your voice, for starters. But I just get that vibe, I dunno. You're really easy to read."

"Well, there's someone I want you to meet, that's all."

"In the middle of nowhere?"

"It'll make sense when we get there."

"What the hell is that supposed to mean?"

"I'm sorry. I don't want to worry you. I can guess how this looks, but I promise, I'd literally rather die than put you in harm's way."

Hannah said nothing.

"If it makes you feel better, text your friend Michele. It's okay if she knows we're here."

It helped. "Great, but where is here?"

"Potter Laboratories."

"Why is there a lab out in the sticks?"

"Dr. Potter's kind of a private guy. But he's helped Kane a lot. I think he can help you."

"Help me with what?"

"Hannah, I … I think you have powers."

Hannah blinked at him; he'd said it so fast that it didn't register right away. "What?"

"There's a chance you might have powers, and I think it can't hurt to have a professional check."

"Are you fucking joking me right now?"

"My timing is shit, I know, but no. I wouldn't be bringing you here if I wasn't serious."

Hannah took a sip of coffee to force herself to think before speaking. It was the last sip, hardly enough to warrant any reflection. "You couldn't have told me this sooner?"

"I mean, I've been running on personal anecdotal theories here. And I thought you might say no."

"This is not like you."

"You're right. I'm sorry. It's shitty. But we can turn around if you want."

Hannah was silent for a moment. Her gaze moved back out the window as they passed by the sign, which was guarded by a yellow-bellied marmot.

"Why do you think I have powers?"

"You'd describe yourself as an empath, right?"

"Sure, yeah."

"So, um, well, at the risk of sounding batshit crazy, I think that's your power."

Hannah scoffed. "I mean, lots of people are empathetic."

"Yes, but you're on a whole other level. You always know exactly how I'm feeling and sometimes, you can even change how I'm feeling. And it's not just because I enjoy your company. It's like my brain gets all foggy and something shifts in there. I don't know how to explain it better."

"Are you saying I'm controlling how you feel?"

"I'm not sure. That's what I think, anyway."

"Oh."

Hannah sounded so dejected that it instantly sent a pang through his chest. That fuzzy feeling was absent from his mind, so he figured it was genuine.

"I don't think you're doing it on purpose, for what it's worth."

"Great, yeah. It's just a lot to process."

"It's a long shot. Especially since you're not from here, you know? We don't have any proof that the drug ever left Colorado. I just think we need to be sure."

A sob came out, but it sounded more like a hiccup.

"I'm so sorry. I know I've said that a lot this morning, but I'm going to keep saying it."

Hannah was silent for a moment before she said, "Is it okay if I trauma-dump for a moment?"

"Yeah, go ahead. I'm here for you. Even if I am part of the problem."

"I just ... it's a lot, you know? And the more that I think about it, the more I think you're right, and now I'm questioning everything in my life that's ever happened to me."

Hannah hiccuped again.

"Can I hold your hand?"

"Of course you can, Elijah, for fuck's sake. You're not part of the problem. This isn't your fault."

Elijah reached his hand across the center console to grab hers. As he did, Hannah's breathing slowed. He parked in the laboratory lot but made no moves to unbuckle his seatbelt.

"My whole life, all I ever wanted was to be normal," Hannah said. She leaned back in the passenger seat, an invisible weight lifted off her chest at the confession. "I knew when I was a little kid that something was off. And just when I finally leave home, hoping to escape the crap that I told you about yesterday and just enjoy being normal, there's ... this."

After wishing he had powers of his own, he couldn't help but feel guilty about his initial jealousy. All he could say was, "That sucks. I'm sorry."

"I wish you wouldn't apologize." Hannah shook her head. "I'm glad you told me."

"Sorry. Ah, shit."

Hannah managed a breathy chuckle. "You are the closest thing to normal I've felt in a long time. Do you know how much that means to me?" Hannah used her free hand to wipe her eyes. "I've never told anyone this before, but I love you, Elijah, and it's pissing me off because I'm mad at you. But I love you and how normal you make me feel."

Elijah squeezed her hand, feeling frozen at the moment. He opened his mouth to speak, but Hannah continued.

"You don't have to say it back. I'm sure you are trying to sort out what's real versus what I've somehow manufactured, assuming these tests turn up positive. It's gotta be hard on you too."

"No! I love you too. There's no weird fuzz in my head right now, so I can say that much with confidence."

Hannah swiped at more of her tears. "You don't have to say it just because I'm a wreck. There's a lot of baggage here and as much as I'm trying to leave it behind, it looks like it's caught up to me."

"Hey, hey, hey." Elijah released her hand so he could unbuckle his seatbelt and cup her face. "We've all got our shit, alright?" He leaned over the center console to kiss her, putting everything he had in it so she could tell he meant it. "I've done so much that would warrant you never speaking to me again, but you have shown me nothing but grace and compassion, and fuck, I'd be such an idiot if I let you go because of something you can't control."

She sniffled. "You mean it?"

"With every fiber of my being and a clear head. I hope you never leave this god-forsaken town."

"Who said I was planning on it?"

He smiled. "It'll be okay. I promise you. Look, I know I don't have any powers to reassure you, but I'll put this brain of mine to work."

Hannah nodded. "Let's go see this Potter guy. I want to know what the hell is up with me."

———

"Ah, the IT support is here. I see you've brought your partner."

After introductions, Dr. Potter brought Elijah and Hannah to a room so sterile that it made them feel dirty just walking into it. They could see their own reflections in the floors and the metal countertops, and when Hannah saw her own as Dr. Potter took a blood sample with the delicacy of a flower, she didn't recognize herself. It was her expression that she didn't recognize, perhaps because she'd gone so long faking a smile that she forgot what a blank slate looked like.

"You okay?"

Dr. Potter wasn't in the room anymore when Elijah asked. As Hannah looked around, she realized she must have zoned out during the process.

"I'm not sure."

"Need anything?"

"No, I don't think so. I just ... thanks."

"For what?"

"Well, for letting me just go through the motions as I process it all."

"You don't need to thank me for that, Hannah."

Before they could say anything else, the door swung open, marking Dr. Potter's return. He held a few papers out to Hannah.

"For your records, Ms. Cohen. Your bloodwork is in line with Mr. Kelly's and Mr. Jameson's. I don't believe you told me what it was you suspect your abilities are. Mind if I ask?"

"I'm extremely empathetic, apparently. So much so that I can control people's emotions, except I don't know how I manage that."

Dr. Potter silently moved to the corner of the room. He stuck a patch on his temple, which was connected to a machine via wire. Elijah remembered this from Kane's stories; it was some sort of brain scan. Elijah wondered why Dr. Potter attached it to himself, as he attached a second to Hannah's temple.

"Well then, Ms. Cohen." Dr. Potter grabbed a scalpel. "Only one way to find out."

Hannah nearly jumped in her chair at the sight of the scalpel, her heart leaping in fear with her. "Whoa, whoa, what are you doing?!"

Elijah's whole body tensed. "We didn't agree to anything weird, Potter."

"Oh, fascinating!" Dr. Potter set the scalpel down. "Tell me, IT support, have you experienced the effects of her power?"

"A few times. I felt like I short-circuited or something."

"Like static on an old television set."

"Yeah, exactly."

"When did this happen? Was it also during a period of stress?"

"No, quite the opposite. On dates."

"Truly fascinating." Potter clasped his hands together. "Ms. Cohen, I think that answers your question. With this, I believe it's your body's response to stress, whether it be good or bad. I will review this," Potter said, as he pointed to the brain scanner and then removed the patches, "and please do let me know if this happens again. I'd love to test this theory."

"Sure, yeah. Thanks." She didn't sound like she meant it.

"Oh, and one more thing, Ms. Cohen. You're not from here, are you?"

"Yeah. I know about the supercharged meth or whatever the hell it is, though."

"Is there any way your mother was in Colorado during her pregnancy?"

"No. She's never done drugs, either. I know her well enough to know she'd never touch the stuff. My dad was pretty clean too and has been since he met her. Only good thing she's done for anybody, I'd wager."

"Then how is this possible?" Elijah asked. He looked at Potter. "Is there another way?"

"We don't have enough research to suggest there isn't another way, so there are other possibilities, I'd wager. Anything coming to mind, Ms. Cohen?"

When Elijah looked back at her, he saw that her eyes had blown wide. Hannah's skin had gone a ghostly white, almost matching the bright room around them.

"Can it come from fathers too? Or does it have to be the mother while she's pregnant?" She swallowed. "What about before she's pregnant?"

Potter rose an eyebrow, making it visible above his glasses' frames. "What are you suggesting?"

"Do you have any DNA tests?"

"Most certainly. I'll retrieve one for you."

As Potter left, Hannah keeled over, clutching at her hips as she bent at the waist. "I think I'm gonna be sick."

Elijah placed a hand on Hannah's back to comfort her. "What's your theory?"

"When I was in high school, my dad caught my mom cheating on him. But looking back, I remember this other time and I'm starting to think it was ... well, something. My mom had a client that traveled a lot for business between Boston and Denver. And when I was in the third grade, maybe? I was home sick, and he called the house phone. He panicked and hung up when I answered, and my mom told me not to tell my dad. Said he wouldn't get it and assume the worst. But what if it *was* the worst?"

Elijah understood the implication, feeling almost as startled by the realization as she did. "Oh no. Hannah, that's awful."

"Don't you have a list of all of their dealers?"

"I do. Do you want me to check if his name is on it?"

"Please."

When Potter returned with the DNA test, Hannah went through the motions in a daze. She remembered spitting into a tube and not much else until Potter announced he'd call Hannah when the results were ready. The biting cold when they left the lab brought Hannah back to a normal headspace.

"God, my head is spinning."

"Information overload?"

"Yeah. Just with everything that's happened the last few days. I don't even know which feelings are mine or someone else's anymore," Hannah said, as she pointed to her temple, "and there's just so much going on up in here."

"Do you want to do something I don't usually do but will probably help you get out of your own head?"

Hannah cocked an eyebrow at him as she stood by the passenger side door. Elijah stood opposite on the driver's side.

"Completely legal, I promise."

"I'm listening."

"Do you want to get a little high?" He pinched two fingers together.

"Kane won't be around to listen in on a drop-in with Eliza until tomorrow anyway, so we can just relax today."

"I've never smoked."

"We don't have to if you don't want to."

"No, no, I'm open to it. First for everything, I guess."

"We'll grab some on the way home. I promise that I won't let you get stoned off your ass."

———

Elijah was true to his word, as he cracked a window open in Hannah's bedroom. Hannah sat with him on the bed, nestled between his long legs with her back against his chest. He held her spare Switch controller loosely in his hands as they shared a joint. Even with the breeze coming, the subtle smell—equal parts pine and lemon—lingered in the room.

"I am so bad at Smash Brothers, so you're probably gonna win," Hannah said.

He kissed her temple, feeling his shoulders relax already. He could see the shift in Hannah too, with the way she leaned back against him with an elbow propped up on his thigh.

"It's been a while since I've played, so we're probably evenly matched."

"I call dibs on Byleth."

"Fuck it. I'm going in as Isabelle."

Hannah laughed as he made the selection and felt a warm calm work its way through her body. She felt it coming off Elijah too, wrapping around her like the smoke that passed their lips and amplifying the soothing sensation for a fleeting moment before it passed.

For the first time in years, Hannah had nothing on her mind. Her thoughts remained only on the game in front of them and Elijah behind her, and even then, it was fairly minimal and straightforward. Even her hands, which normally ached between constant typing and then gaming on a live stream, felt less inflamed.

"Thanks for this. I needed a chill night."

"Least I could do to atone. Maybe I'll even let you win too."

"That would put you further along the proper path to forgiveness."

"Yeah? I'm glad to know I'm already on it."

"Mhm. This was a good start." Hannah grabbed the joint from between his lips for another puff. "I don't wanna talk about it too much. But just know that even though I might be kinda mad about it for a while, I also don't want to lose you. If you hadn't been suspicious of me, I'd have gone my whole life never knowing this."

"I'd say you don't even know how relieved I am to hear that, but you probably do."

"Actually, no, I don't. It's funny. When we first got it going, I felt, like, twice as chill as I did now. I think I was picking up on your relaxation. But now? Just nothingness. I've never felt nothingness. This is *so* fucking nice."

"When everything settles down, we should do this more often, then. I'd be an idiot to not take advantage of my second chance here."

"I know why you did what you did. Don't worry about it. Okay, well, maybe a little. At least enough to give me a few sympathy wins."

"Only a few."

Elijah kissed her and then kissed her between every round, regardless of who won or lost. After their joint was nothing but smoke, and they'd gone through more rounds than they cared to count, their hands dropped the controllers and moved to each other.

CHAPTER 16

The next morning, Hannah took a deep breath as she stared at Eliza's home from the driver's seat of her car. She couldn't remember the last time she actually drove and hadn't realized how much walking she had been doing since moving to Riverpeak until now. The wealthier part of the suburbs was still fairly close, but far enough to justify driving in case there was a need for a quick getaway. She wasn't sure what to expect from Eliza, but ultimately, Hannah was hopeful. If she knew anything, it was how people with narcissistic personalities worked and, based on the exterior of the home alone, Eliza fit that bill.

Hannah felt bad to be casting judgment based on her house and news articles she read online, but the signs were already clear. From what Hannah knew about Eliza Daniels, she lived here alone with her husband; her adult daughter moved away from Riverpeak. The home, however, was three stories tall and far too large for a couple whose child flew the nest. Hannah wondered if Eliza could even afford the house, or if she was in debt over it. If Hannah's hunch was right, it would be the latter.

"Okay," Elijah said into her earpiece, "can you hear me?"

"Loud and clear," Hannah said. It was the same setup that Elijah used with Hematite. The piece was so small that her hair hid it well enough and even if it didn't, it just looked like a hearing aid. "Can you hear me?"

"I can. Don't turn your mic off. Everything's recording on my end."

"Okay." Hannah got out of her car. "This thing's pretty badass. I feel like I'm in a spy movie. Anyway, I'm heading to her door now."

"Good luck. I'll be on mute unless I need anything from you, okay?"

"Got it."

At that, Elijah hit the mute button on his end. Kane stood beside him, with his hands placed on the edge of the desk as he looked over Elijah's shoulder.

"This was her idea?"

"Yeah. When we got back from Constance's Pond, she brought it up."

"How did you even end up there the other night?" Kane asked. "It was, like, two in the morning."

"I couldn't sleep. Then I saw she was online, and I called her. Couldn't help myself."

Kane chuckled. "You're down bad, bro."

"Yeah, I know," Elijah said with a huff. His mind wandered to the morning after they found the body; they had fallen asleep in each other's arms after realizing McMahon wasn't going to call, something they hadn't fully realized until they woke up. It wasn't unlike last night, where they'd enjoyed a deep sleep thanks to the flower they'd smoked. "It's gonna be the death of me. Damn my guilty conscience."

"You told her everything?"

"Everything. I felt like shit, Kane. I still feel like shit, and I think the fact that she's even still talking to me, never mind helping us right now, is proof that God has my back."

"Either that or she just thinks you lay really good pipe."

"Dude, shut the fuck up."

"Oh, come on, Elijah. Get the pole out of your ass. Unless…?"

Elijah rolled his eyes. "You *would* say that."

"I mean, am I wrong? It's gotta be good if you're simping this hard."

"We only have twice, for the record. Not all of us think with our dicks, Kane."

"I just like to see you blush, baby," Kane teased. He cupped Elijah's face with one hand and shook it, making Elijah's lips pucker against his will. Elijah swatted Kane's hand away and glared at him. "I'm surprised only twice. It's been a few months already."

"We haven't been in any rush, especially given the circumstances. I think Hannah had a bit of an existential crisis after visiting Potter, so we got high and played Smash last night."

"And then proceeded to smash?"

Before Elijah could scold Kane for the on-the-nose joke, they stopped to listen to the sound of a door opening from Hannah's microphone, followed by Eliza Daniels's voice through Hannah's earpiece.

———

"Miss Cohen."

"Hi! I see that we can skip introductions."

"Word travels fast around here. To what do I owe the pleasure?"

"I wanted to ask you a few things about Riverpeak." Hannah picked at her nail beds and diverted her gaze to her fingers, then back to Eliza. "It's been so hard, you know, being new here." Kane and Elijah could hear her voice quiver, sounding like she was about to cry.

"Oh, you poor thing." Eliza ushered Hannah inside the home. "It must be scary moving to a new place as a single woman."

"You can say that again," Hannah agreed with a breathy laugh. "All of this vigilante talk and girls going missing just … it all has me so nervous. I figured you'd be a good person to ask."

Eliza sighed, as she grabbed her mug of tea. "I wish I still was. Do you want a cup? The kettle's still warm."

"Sure, thanks."

Kane looked at Elijah. "Damn, she's a great actor."

He nodded. "Yeah, she is."

"You know that I'm not the police chief anymore, right?"

"I know, but that office is so … testosterone-heavy, you know? Men don't get it. They'll probably all just think I'm being hysterical since I found that poor girl's body by the pond."

Eliza smiled at her softly as she handed her the mug. "I know, honey. Men are awful. Come, sit. I've got the fireplace going."

Hannah took a seat on the deep red couch across from Eliza, who sat in a chair that looked practically lived in from frequent use. The stone fireplace provided a gentle background noise as it crackled and popped from time to time. The smell of the burning wood overpowered any scents wafting from the tea. Very few photos adorned the walls; none of them featured any family members but one collage, where the photos were all old in their black-and-white or sepia-toned glory.

"You have such a beautiful home." Hannah didn't mean the compliment; even with the fireplace, the house felt cold and empty, but she sensed Eliza was like her own mother and knew exactly how to manipulate that to her own advantage. "Reminds me of my house growing up."

"Oh, thank you. I can't bring myself to leave, as much as I probably should." Eliza sighed with the hint of a regret she'd never admit. "It's far too big for me now."

"It is?"

Eliza nodded. "I live alone now. I haven't told anyone this, but my husband left and my daughter ... well, she won't speak to me. It's nice having you here. I'm glad someone feels like they can still turn to me."

Hannah nodded in understanding. Her thoughts wandered to her own mother. "I guess we all like to feel needed, huh?"

With a sip of her tea, Eliza's moment of vulnerability faded. "But I love it here. I love this city. No matter what people say about me, they're mistaken."

Hannah tried not to laugh. She opted for a smile, forcing it to look genuine, as she did her best to mean what she said and tap into her stress. If there was ever a time to practice her power, it was now. "I've been terrified, what with these girls going missing. I guess I'm not sure how I can protect myself."

"Oh, honey," Eliza reached out a hand to Hannah, placing it on her forearm. "I wouldn't worry about it if I were you. He's not going after girls who he thinks would be missed. You've made such a name for yourself! You should be proud. Hold your head up high."

Bingo, Hannah thought. She took a long sip of her tea as she soaked in what Eliza said. "He?"

"Oh, I've said too much," Eliza said with a careless laugh. As she loosened up, she spoke with her hands. "But woman to woman, I think you need to know. You know, you remind me so much of my daughter. You're such a sweet girl, Miss Cohen, and so accomplished."

"Thank you."

"It's that Sato boy. The one who died. Did you hear about that? I suppose not; that was long before you moved here. You know that reporter, Naomi Sato?"

"Yeah, I've seen her on TV a few times."

"It's her brother. I thought he was dead myself. He was helping his dad with the restaurant that he runs so he could try to pay his way through grad school. His father offered to pay for it, but Noah insisted he do it himself. Said he didn't want to get by just on his father's merit. A foolish move if you ask me. Anyway," Eliza said, pausing for a small sip of tea. "There was this massive fire at one of the restaurant locations. His father Reiji made it out just fine, but Noah wasn't with him. We did a thorough investigation, but my people came up with nothing. But then Tom told me that Noah was actually alive and well."

"How is that possible?"

"That's what I said! Tom convinced me to keep my mouth shut, but that son of a bitch is the reason I'm out of a job, and I trust that you'll keep quiet. Woman to woman, right?"

"Of course," Hannah said. Everything was going exactly as planned.

Kane laughed. "Wow. Talk about lack of accountability."

Eliza took a deep breath. "They paid them all off. One thing that most people don't know about this town is that everybody works for Reiji Sato. Hell, even I did, and I didn't even realize it." She scoffed. "That piece of shit was using me to keep me on his side. Tom worked closely with Reiji, you see. And here I thought he actually liked me!" Eliza laughed, even though she clearly didn't think it was funny.

"I'm so sorry. That's awful," Hannah said. "Talk about a breach of trust."

"Thank you!" Eliza said. "Here I was, thinking that this man gave half a shit about me. And it was easy to believe! My husband's a total asshole and Tom's wife, Linda? God love her, but she's got to be the dumbest woman I've ever met. And as a councilman, Tom and I worked together quite a bit; it wasn't out of the picture."

"Ask her how she knows that it's Noah," Elijah said.

"Did he say that Noah would do this? Or why?" Hannah asked. "I know you said I shouldn't worry, but my anxiety tends to get the best of me."

"Something to do with that drug. What the hell is it called? Ah, whatever. You know the one I'm talking about?"

"I think so. The one on the east side that they talk about on the news?"

"That one. Stay away from there and you'll be fine, honey. Tom told me it all has to do with that. As long as it keeps moving, they're happy. I guess Noah's doing his own thing, though. I wish I could tell you more. Oh, I hope that bastard is rotting in his cell."

"Me too, for your sake," Hannah said, as her phone started to ring. The name Amanda flashed across the screen, but there was no photo; that was her cue to leave. "Excuse me, this is my literary agent. I should probably go take this. Thank you for the tea. I'm feeling a lot better now."

"Of course, honey. Come by any time," Eliza said. "Are you staying in Riverpeak much longer?"

"At least through the year," Hannah said. She set the mug back in the kitchen and quickly made her way to the door. "Thank you again, Mrs. Daniels." Not wanting to seem suspicious, Hannah answered the phone before she was out of the door. "Amanda! Hey!"

"You're good to turn the mic off now," Kane said into the phone; Hannah did just that. "Are you still in earshot?"

"Yeah, almost done with the manuscript," Hannah said. "I should have the first draft fully revised by the end of the week. Did you want to look it over before I go into hardcore editing mode?"

"Understood," Kane said. He heard a door shut behind her.

"Okay, we're all clear." Hannah quickly made her way down the street. "Did you guys get all that?"

"Affirmative," Elijah said. "Nice work in there."

"Thanks. Happy to help. I suspected she might talk, but I didn't think she'd talk *that* much."

"Yeah. That was … wow," Elijah said. "Sounds like she was happy to just get it off her chest."

"Narcissists like to feel important. Any other leads?"

"Jordan won't talk," Kane said, referring to the girl who was rescued. His phone vibrated as he spoke. "McMahon's been keeping me updated. We've both tried talking to her, and then I tried talking to her at school and so has Rory. She told Rory that she can't say anything."

"I'm not totally surprised. Poor kid's probably traumatized," Hannah said. "Anyway, I'll be at your place soon."

Kane showed Elijah his phone.

"Good timing. Brad's about to head to Reiji's now," Elijah said. "Just text me when you're here. We'll be switching to his earpiece in a minute so we can record everything. Oh, and Hannah?"

"Yeah?"

Elijah had more he wanted to say, but with Kane beside him and their time cut short, he kept it simple. "Thank you. For everything."

———

The only reason Brad didn't faint was that he knew Elijah was listening in. The earpiece gave Elijah a direct feed and was small enough to blend right in with his skin. He hadn't cut his hair in a while, having been too busy with getting everything together with the wedding for Naomi, so the dark strands just covered any pieces that might be obvious.

He felt like he was in a trance going through the rental house. It was the same one Hannah showed him, Kane, and Elijah on FaceTime, but seeing it in person made it feel even more real. What threw him off the most was seeing Noah Sato leaning against a table, directing a few men as they worked on measuring some batches. Brad knew Noah was still alive, but he still hadn't been prepared to see him face to face. His scarring looked even worse in person; his flesh was discolored and wrinkled, painting his arm in uneven, raised shades of maroon and gray.

Noah turned his head as Brad and his father approached. He grinned. "Hey, Brad. Long time no see."

Brad knew he was a terrible actor. He also knew that Noah had a way of seeing right through anyone and everyone, so he kept it simple and decided to pose everything as a question. "Noah?"

"Surprise, surprise, right?" Noah laughed. "Sorry, Pops; I just couldn't help myself. The man is marrying my sister, after all. How is Naomi?"

Reiji's jaw visibly clenched. "Noah. I told you to wait upstairs."

"Oh, what? You think I'm the worst thing he's gonna see today? Please." Noah slung his tattooed arm around Brad's shoulder. "Come on. We're about to be brothers! Don't be so damn stiff."

"Naomi's good," Brad said, as he forced himself to look at Noah next to him. Locking eyes with him was like making eye contact with a ghost. "We're saving a seat for you, you know. At the wedding."

Noah placed his free hand over his heart; the scarring extended to his palms but stopped at his fingers. "I'm touched. I think that's the nicest thing anyone's ever done for me in years."

"Noah was generous enough to let me test on him," Reiji said. "I knew he could be strong enough to withstand what we're trying to do."

"Is that pride I hear in your voice?" Noah grinned. "That's a rare treat."

"Yes, I am proud of you," Reiji said. "But we have a certain way we need to operate. Isn't that right, Brad?"

Brad ignored the way his heart pounded in his chest. "I guess that makes sense, sure."

"Let's catch up later, yeah?" Noah dropped his arm from Brad's shoulders. "I'll let my dad have you back." He winked at the two of them before he slipped his way upstairs. Brad desperately wanted to follow after him to see what he was hiding but needed to stay in the basement for now.

"May I ask what happened to him?"

Reiji's jaw was still tight. "Secret's out, I suppose. The fire at the restaurant was when my son was reborn."

"So, my dad had nothing to do with it?"

"No, no. But Naomi doesn't know that, remember?"

Brad nodded. "Don't worry, I won't say anything."

"You're a good boy, Brad. I know you won't. Come along now. I'll show you how they cook. Someone about to join my family shouldn't need to get their hands dirty, but I need more eyes here to make sure everything goes smoothly. I need to prioritize networking again, and it's hard to do so when I'm stuck here. Quality is the only thing keeping us afloat right now. If we lose that, we lose our customers."

"Right."

Brad took in everything that Reiji showed him, doing his best to say as little as possible so he wouldn't slip up. Kane and Elijah coached him through it when he needed to, with Hannah checking on the recording status of the audio files to make sure nothing was corrupted or had otherwise stopped working once she'd joined them. After he'd introduced everyone, Reiji brought Brad back upstairs.

"Don't leave without catching up with Noah," Elijah said into Brad's ear. "The more we can get out of him, the better."

"Is it okay if I see Noah?" Brad asked Reiji, as they reached the front door. "I won't let him affect my job. Don't worry; it's just been a long time, you know?"

"I suppose that's only natural. Just remember: Naomi cannot know about anything under this roof. Is that clear?"

"Yes, sir. Goes without saying."

"Good. I have to attend to some business. Thank you, Brad, for being so understanding."

Brad wondered if the business was with the silver-haired man from the car. "Yeah, of course. We're about to be family, after all."

Brad offered Reiji a genuine smile, but the weight of his words was not lost on either of them. Brad then made his way up the stairs; because the house bore the same layout as the house he shared with Elijah, it was easy enough to get around. He took a quick glance around and noticed cameras in the hallway. As he knocked on the only closed door, he looked away from them to not draw any suspicion.

Noah opened it and smiled from ear to ear. "Glad you came. Let's chat, shall we?"

"Yeah. I've missed you, dude. We all have."

Noah plopped into a desk chair and leaned back in it. It tilted a bit but bounced back. "It's been rough, man. I'm not going to lie. Well, don't just stand there. Take a seat wherever."

Noah chuckled as Brad did just that on the edge of the bed. He could sense Brad's discomfort a mile away.

"You know, it crushed me when he told me you guys got engaged. Not because it's you. Our dad fucking hates you, but you know I've got your back." Noah spun in the chair. "But because I wanted nothing more than to see my little sister that day."

"I bet," Brad said. A nervous laugh followed beyond his control. "I know you two were close."

"She'd hate who I've become," Noah said. The way his voice trailed off made it seem as if he hated who he'd become too. "Where's the wedding, anyway?"

"Up in Aspen." Brad felt too scared to lie. If he did, he'd be caught in a heartbeat. *Short and sweet,* he reminded himself.

"Let me guess." Noah held a finger up and then pointed it at Brad. "Elijah's your best man? Or is it Kane?"

Elijah and Kane looked at each other. Elijah muted himself and then asked Kane, "Is it just me, or is he asking something entirely different?"

Kane nodded. His mouth formed a thin line. "He knows. I'm sure of it."

"Good guess. They're both in the wedding. Your tattoo is cool," Brad said to change the subject. "I didn't know you were into those."

"Once I got the burns, my other side felt naked, you know?" Noah reached for a frame on his desk and held it up. "I wouldn't go back, though."

"No?"

"I have a real chance to make a change here. And I'm so fucking close," Noah said. "He's totally against it, you know, but after everything he did to me? It's my God-given right to use this."

He set the frame back down so Brad could see the photo now. It was one of him and Naomi from one of their trips to Japan; thousands of red torii gates stood behind them, and Noah had a kitsune mask propped up on the side of his head that was too big for him. They both looked so young in that photo, smiling widely for the camera in their yukata. With how much had changed since then, it might as well have been a lifetime ago.

"You know, Brad, you could help me on the down low," Noah said. "What's he got you up to?"

"Supervising production, mostly," Brad said. "Why?"

"I want everyone to be more empowered," Noah said. "Shitty police. Shitty politicians. An abandoned financial district. I mean, Jesus Christ, my old man and his boss got half of this town on some puppet strings. If people just woke up and realized their full potential, imagine how great Riverpeak could be." He leaned forward in his chair. "Do you get what I'm going for here, Brad?"

"I think I do. You think more people can get powers?"

"Yes! See, I always knew you were smarter than you even gave yourself credit for."

"I mean, I'm just supervising. How can I help?"

"I need samples. Strong samples. I got one that almost made it. The first three were total busts, but I don't think anyone's missing them. Looks like the search party's already ended."

It immediately clicked for Brad, Elijah, Hannah, and Kane. Kane exclaimed a curse.

Elijah rushed to turn his mic back on. "Ask him about Jordan." He muted himself again.

"Well, at least everything Eliza told me today was true," Hannah said. She sighed. "Why just women?"

"If you knew Noah, you'd already know why," Elijah said. "I'm glad he didn't get to you. He was very good with women. Like, *very* good. But I doubt he was hitting on a teenager, so I'm hoping we can get Brad to dig deeper."

Brad cleared his throat. "Like that girl they just found? Jordan Jefferson, right?"

"Ah, yeah. I didn't initially want to work with her, but she stumbled upon me working with her friend's older sister. I couldn't just let her run home and tattle on me, now could I? Kid was way too much of a goody two-shoes for me to not."

"I think I'm gonna be sick," Hannah said.

Brad pressed for more. "What happened?"

"I overdosed her, thinking she'd die like the others. Shocked the shit out of me when she took well to it, but not enough to have the desired effect." He sighed. "I don't think she could have handled more, and then the news went fucking crazy. I didn't realize who she was. Daughter of a cafe owner? Fuck me, right?"

"Jeez."

"Yeah," Noah said with a sigh. "But at least I got some research out of her. Good to know that it was the girls that were the problem, not me. Anyway, you down? If we get strong enough samples and enough of them, we could start really helping people, you know? They just gotta be able to handle it."

"I mean, yeah, sure, dude," Brad said. He was already planning on what he'd be drinking straight from the bottle when he got home, so he could at least look at himself in the mirror later. "Especially if your dad's going to eventually leave me alone. It should be easy enough."

"Good. I knew I could count on you. Oh, and if you mention any of this to Naomi or, worse, to Hematite?" Noah smirked. His tone dropped. "I'm going to burn you to a fucking crisp."

"Right, yeah," Brad said with a nod.

"Anyway, you should probably get going," Noah said. "Stick around too long and people might wonder where you are."

Elijah exhaled. "Oh my God."

"If he knows it's one of us, why the hell is he being so open with Brad?" Kane paced. "What the hell is going on? Are we in the fucking Twilight Zone?"

"It's a threat, obviously. Brad's always been mild-mannered. They're taking advantage of that."

"It's almost like he *wants* to be found," Hannah said. "Why else would he leave the hand behind?"

"Huh?" It came from both Kane and Elijah simultaneously.

"I mean, think about it. They never found the rest of that girl's body, but we did find her hand and her uniform. He's being completely transparent with Brad, and he flexed to you when you nearly got caught, Kane. Seems like he's pretty confident and I think he wants the fight. Maybe he wants to be sure who Hematite is, *and* he wants to get the hell out of that house. That's my character analysis, anyway."

"Luckily, Brad won't need to put up with this for too long," Elijah said. "Thanksgiving and the holidays are coming up, and then it's time for the wedding. He's going to be too busy to be there too often. Reiji's gotta know that."

"I don't think Reiji cares," Kane said.

"I guess we'll find out," Hannah said. "Something tells me it's only going to get a whole lot worse from here."

CHAPTER 17

Elijah's phone rang as he revisited the files on Reiji's thumb drives, making sure he didn't miss anything in the weeks since Brad started working undercover for Reiji. His work for the day was bordering on obsessive and manic, so he was grateful to be snapped out of it. His mother's name flashed on the screen, alongside a photo of the two of them together.

"Hey, *Ima*."

"Hey, sweetheart. Just making sure you're joining us for Thanksgiving. I wasn't sure what time your annual friends thing was gonna be."

"Oh, yeah, that's not until Friday. I'm all yours on Thursday. Say, do you mind if I invite someone to join us?"

"I don't mind at all! Who is it?"

"Please don't be mad at me for not telling you sooner." Elijah leaned back in his chair as he braced himself for impact. "But I'm seeing someone, and I don't think she has anywhere to be."

"You have a girlfriend, and you didn't tell me?"

"We've sort of been seeing each other the last few months, yeah," Elijah said, the confession spilling from his lips as swiftly as he could say it. He knew his mom wouldn't be mad, but he didn't like the extra attention. "She doesn't have any family here or anything, and I'd just hate for her to be alone, you know?"

"Honey, that's wonderful! Of course you can bring her over! Is she Jewish?" She then added, "Just curious. It's okay if she's not. You know I don't care either way."

"Yeah, she's Jewish."

"Is she real?" Rueben asked over the phone. Elijah groaned when he realized he must have been on speaker.

"Yes, she's real! She's the one who just moved to town a few months ago a few houses down from me."

"Ignore your father," Lena said. "We can't wait to meet her."

––––––

Hannah felt more nervous than she cared to admit as she moved through the Baron family home. Family functions never went well for her back home, but she reminded herself that her family functions weren't normal. This was Elijah, after all, and Kane had spoken extremely highly of the Baron family. It was hard to imagine anything going off the rails.

A few photos lined the cream-colored walls, where a large frame held multiple small pictures directly across from the front door. There were two different baby photos: one with thick auburn hair, and another with thinner brown strands, making it obvious which one was Elijah and which was his brother. The rest of the photos were of them both at different ages, primarily in elementary school, but a photo in the middle showed them both as adults at Elijah's college graduation. Hannah spotted a bookshelf in her peripheral vision, standing tall in the living room with all her books in one of the rows. She hoped her makeup hid her natural blush.

"Your home is beautiful, Mrs. Baron."

"Oh, thank you. Please, call me Lena. This is my husband, Rueben. How rude of me to not introduce you two sooner."

Hannah noticed how Elijah favored his mother as far as his appearance went. Their hair was the same reddish shade and their eyes matched in color, as did the way their skin crinkled at the corners of their eyes when they smiled. Elijah inherited her prominent, straight nose and plump lips, though his thick brows and long face came from his father, who exclaimed, "She's real pretty, 'Lij!"

"You are too kind," Hannah said.

The front door opened after that, revealing Elijah's brother. He was considerably shorter than Elijah, closer in height to Lena than to anyone else. Elijah ruffled his brown hair, making him playfully scowl a bit.

"Will you ever stop doing that?"

"Nah. Lou, meet Hannah. Hannah, this is my brother Louis."

"Hey! Nice to finally meet you. I've heard a lot about you."

Hannah raised a brow. "You have?"

"You have?" Lena parroted.

"We text every now and then," Elijah said with a shrug.

"I mean, that's nice, but I can't believe Lou knew before us."

The oven beeped, taking everyone out of their conversation. Hannah reflected as she helped them bring the food out, unable to help the train of thought that passed through her mind. The lack of passive aggression in the air stuck out like a sore thumb as she sat at the table with the Barons. She felt more comfortable than she ever had with her own family and didn't realize there could be a family gathering without someone screaming or fighting. It took everything in her to hold back tears out of fear of embarrassment; after all, the last thing she wanted to do was spoil the mood by sharing all the miserable parts of her life story. Once she returned to the table, Hannah swallowed her feelings back with a small sip of her wine and made a mental note to journal it out later. *I'll write a memoir one of these days*, she thought.

Rueben broke the silence and ultimately brought Hannah back from inside her own head. "Elijah, I think this is the first time you've brought a girl home."

Louis nearly choked on his food as he tried not to laugh.

"*Abba*," Elijah said through gritted teeth, like he was embarrassed but trying to hide it. Hannah noticed his cheeks turned a bit pink. Elijah glanced at her to see how she was reacting, only to find her smiling at him. Hannah shot him a wink as she stifled her laugh.

"How long have you two been dating?" Rueben asked. He had a smirk on his face, as if he knew he was torturing his son.

"A few months now, yeah?" Hannah said, as she looked at Elijah.

Elijah felt relaxed as he looked at her and smiled. He mentally thanked God that she rolled with his father's punches with such ease. "Yeah, depending on how technical you wanted to get."

"Alright then, I gotta ask," Rueben said. He spoke with his hands but was still cautious to not point his utensils at anyone. "Everyone's been saying you're this massive author. Is it true?"

Hannah nodded as she sipped her wine. "I wish I was as much of a big deal as everyone thinks I am, but sure."

"I've got everything on the shelf, Rue. Didn't you notice?" Lena turned to Hannah. "You're too humble. I love your work, sweetheart. How do you come up with all that?"

"Thank you."

Hannah could feel all their eyes on her, something she wasn't used to but wasn't entirely uncomfortable with thanks to her recent endeavors on Twitch—but even then, the virtual eyes weren't visible and were much easier to tune out. She felt Elijah's hand on her knee, which prompted a reflexive smile.

"Truth be told, I was pretty lonely growing up, and I kinda still was until I moved here. My imagination wandered a lot as a kid, so I guess the idea of my story just never left. So, I wrote it down one day, joined a writing challenge to get it all on paper, and here we are."

"Good for you for making something out of it," Lena said, sincerity dripping out like warm honey. "You should be very proud."

"Thanks," Hannah said, taking another sip of wine to hide her blush. Elijah gave her knee a knowing squeeze.

"My girlfriend got into your books after we started watching your streams," Louis added. "We'll have to grab a selfie later for her."

"Yeah, of course."

"Hell yeah. Sweet."

Rueben turned to his eldest son. "How'd you snatch this one up, huh, 'Lij?"

"Kane signed me up for a dating app against my will."

"My friend Michele encouraged me to try one so I could meet new people when I moved here. Elijah was the only guy I bothered to match with."

"You should have introduced her sooner, Elijah!" Lena scolded, but there wasn't any malice in it. "Poor thing's probably been keeping Shabbat all by herself. Start coming over on Friday nights, okay, sweetheart?"

"I'd love that."

"I hope you haven't been too lonely."

"Nah, he's been keeping me company," Hannah said. "Did you know he's quite handy? Last month, he helped me build my sukkah and everything."

"So *that's* why you couldn't make it!" Rueben pointed an accusatory fork at his eldest son. "The truth comes out!"

Elijah's hands shot up defensively. "I mean, I never lied!"

"No, no, it's fine," Rueben said, with sarcasm so thick it could be cut with one of the butter knives on the table. "I knew the day would come soon when we'd be replaced. First Louis, now Elijah."

Lena smacked her husband's arm with her napkin. "Oh, for goodness sake, Rue. The dramatics."

Elijah sat back and watched as Hannah conversed with his parents. The way she fit right in with his family was tearing him apart—the more time he spent with her, the more he pictured a future with her, only to remember that she was here for work and there was a chance she wouldn't renew her lease.

But the seriousness of this wasn't lost on him, either. Even if Hannah moved back to Florida after her lease was up, she was sitting at his family's dinner table. His father was right—this was the first time he brought a partner home ever, if he excluded the rare high school girlfriend for study dates. If Hannah moved, their relationship wouldn't end but just face a new hurdle. But seeing this had him envisioning diamond rings and hearing shattering glass to the point where he had to subtly double-check that no one dropped their wine.

He soaked it all in while he could. *Hannah is a natural,* he thought; if he hadn't known about her past, he would have never guessed it. Elijah forgot what it felt like to not have someone to text at any hour of the day or night and wondered how he went so long without someone by his side, especially with the way Hannah seemed to fit perfectly into his own family. It must have been obvious that he was lost in thought because, at one point, Hannah looked at him and whispered, "You okay?"

He nodded. "Yeah. More than okay." It was just loud enough for her to hear. He left a quick kiss on her temple and made a point of being more active in the conversation through the rest of the evening. Despite that, he still felt very much stuck in his own head on their walk home later that night. Once again, Hannah was the one to snap him out of it.

"It was really nice to meet your family."

"You think so?"

"Of course! They were really sweet. I like them a lot. Besides, I got to see your baby photos." Hannah laughed as he turned a shade of pink again. "Come on, Elijah, don't be embarrassed."

"If you were anybody else, you'd be getting a very different reaction from me," he teased. Elijah didn't want to bring anything up that would kill the mood, and it made sense to him why she enjoyed herself as much as she did. This was likely a first for her.

"That was really, really nice. I can see why you like it here so much, you know."

He softened. "What do you mean?"

She shrugged, not wanting to get too emotional but he could still hear the change in her voice. It almost cracked. "Just, you know. Nice town. Nice people. You have a great family. Do you work tomorrow?"

"Unfortunately, I have to before Friendsgiving, yeah. But if you wanted to stay the night, I shouldn't be too busy during the day, since all of our clients are off."

Hannah grinned. "Count me in."

———

When Elijah got dressed for work the following morning, Hannah couldn't help but watch him from her spot on his bed. His green dress shirt showed his toned frame in the warmth of his home; he'd rolled the sleeves up to his elbows, revealing freckles along his forearms that matched the ones that dotted his nose. His actions were enough to motivate her to get ready for the day. When she finally got out of bed, Hannah also ditched the cardigan she brought with her for the day. The heater helped, but she felt mostly adjusted to Colorado life.

"I think Rory and Kane are getting here early," Brad announced when they made their way downstairs. "So, we can talk."

"Good. That's good." Elijah quickly got to work on heating up some pre-prepared side dishes, making the house smell like the rosemary and thyme seasoning on the potatoes, as Hannah helped Brad get the table ready.

It wasn't long until Kane and Rory arrived, carrying some pieces Kane cooked himself—fresh cornbread was in the mix based on the smell wafting in from the containers. After they made their rounds of greetings, Kane cut right to the chase.

"With the wedding getting closer, I'm getting really worried about this whole situation. It just feels like a golden opportunity, especially if they suspect it might be one of us."

"Does she know yet?" Hannah asked. "Like, you've told Naomi by now, right?"

Brad, Kane, and Rory looked at each other and said nothing. Their silence answered for them.

"When the fuck are you gonna tell her?" Elijah asked, as he ran a hand over his head. It had been almost a year now, and he was out of patience on Naomi's behalf. "Why is she not in the loop yet?"

"We don't know *how* to tell her," Brad said, holding his arms out. "How the hell am I supposed to tell her, dude? I'm being serious!"

Elijah scoffed. "You just tell her!" He said it like it was the most obvious thing in the world. "Is it so hard for you to just be honest with her? She's gonna be your wife soon, dude! Your wife!"

"I can't, okay?" Brad pinched the bridge of his nose as he groaned. "This has all gotten so out of control."

"She's gonna seriously hate us," Rory said with a sigh. "We royally screwed up here, you guys. I don't even know if she'll believe it."

"We have evidence."

"Yeah, Elijah, but still. This isn't just some theory anymore ... she loves her dad. They've always been close. Same with Noah. This will really fuck her up."

"I can tell her," Hannah said. Suddenly, all eyes were on her. "Listen, she doesn't know me from a hole in the wall, and I really don't care if she gets mad at me. I can take the heat. And not for nothing, but personal biases aside, I agree with Elijah. It would be better if she heard it from us instead of through work."

"What if we just didn't tell her at all?" Brad asked.

"She's going to find out eventually," Elijah said. "Whether it be through her job or at her wedding if something happens. Like Kane said, that's the perfect stage for some shit to go down."

The door opened, meaning that their time was up. Naomi came in, bearing a bottle of wine that she brought to the counter after hugging everyone. Brad grabbed the side dishes stacked in a bag hanging off her arm to help her carry everything in, promptly bringing everything to the kitchen.

"You guys look like you were talking about something major," Naomi said. "What's going on?"

Everyone looked at each other. Hannah placed her hand on Naomi's back and guided her to the other side of the living room. "Come on. I'll fill you in."

"What about Bra—"

"He knows."

Hannah brought Naomi to the couch in the living room.

"You'll wanna be sitting down for this one."

"Oh, God. What, did someone die or something?"

"Well, sort of the opposite," Hannah said. She blew a raspberry and decided to keep things to the point but was careful to not sound too harsh. "Your friends love you a lot, and they have been wanting to tell you this. But they're scared you'll get mad, which is why I'm here: I barely know you. At the risk of sounding like Dark Helmet, you're my new boyfriend's roommate's fiancée. So, if you get mad at me for telling you, then quite frankly, I won't really give a shit. No offense: it just is what it is."

"Right, right, makes sense," Naomi said. "But why would I be mad?"

Hannah swallowed and ripped the metaphorical Band-Aid off. "We can say with absolute certainty that your father is involved with the crime ring here in Riverpeak. I don't think he's directly involved in manufacturing, but he provides a front for them and helps with funding."

Naomi's eyes widened as she felt her skin grow cold. "What?"

"I'm so sorry, Naomi. This is probably a lot to take in. Kane and Shawn found a ton of records tying everything back to your dad and have even run into him in person."

As Hannah explained everything, Naomi looked at her in complete silence. She kept her composure, the only indication of her surprise being the expression in her eyes.

"And there's one more thing you should know," Hannah said. "It's about your brother Noah."

"What about him?" Naomi asked, sounding defeated.

"Elijah saw security camera footage of a man who looks a whole hell of a lot like him. Plus, Kane ran into him, and, despite some … updates to his personal style, it seems like him. So, he's still alive. The bad news is that it also looks like he's helping your dad."

Naomi glanced at her hands, which were now shaking. "Noah's alive?"

"Yeah, I think he is," Hannah said. "Like I said, from what Elijah and Kane have told me, he looks a little different than he did before. But it is him. It looks like he's responsible for all those fires that have been popping up since that Stone Breaker guy got arrested and for the missing girls."

"I knew something weird was going on, but this?" Tears began to well in Naomi's eyes. "Why the hell didn't anyone tell me?"

"They wanted to be sure, and they didn't want you to be upset. This was done with a whole lot of care, Naomi, I promise." Hannah remembered her power and tried to focus on helping Naomi feel more at peace, while still giving her the space to process the news.

Naomi's lips formed a thin line as she glanced away, giving herself a moment to collect her thoughts. "How long have they known?"

"From what I could gather, they found out about your dad when they dug into that councilman's records that Elijah swiped. The first time they saw Noah was on the Fourth of July."

"They've known my brother is alive for four, almost five months and didn't bother to tell me?" Naomi scoffed. "Unbelievable. I'm … I'm not mad at you. Don't take it that way. But what the fuck?"

"I gotta agree with you. It's shitty all around," Hannah said with a nervous chuckle.

Naomi surprised Hannah when she pulled her in for a hug on the couch. Hannah returned the embrace, letting Naomi cry and feel it out. She shot Elijah a glance from across the room and grimaced, hoping he'd understand the expression. Hannah was unsure of what this all meant but hoped it was a good thing.

"Thank you for telling me," Naomi said after a few minutes. She took a deep breath as she pulled away from the hug, wiped her eyes, and then walked over to the kitchen. She grabbed the bottle of wine she brought, popped the cork off in one swift motion, and put the mouth of the bottle straight to her lips. After taking a few gulps, she set the bottle down by her spot at the table. "I already know I'm gonna need all of this, so I figured it's better than wasting a glass." She plopped down in the chair, her typically perfect posture overcome with dejection.

"Oh," Brad said, "and we should probably mention that your dad recruited me to help him. I've been going undercover for Kane."

Naomi grabbed the bottle of wine and took another swig of it. Some of her lipstick smeared on the mouth of the bottle, staining it a dark red. "Are you okay?"

Brad shrugged. "I mean, I'm still alive."

"So, how do we stop my family?"

CHAPTER 18

As Hannah wrapped up writing a chapter, a text from Elijah pinged through. She was surprised he wasn't enjoying the bachelor party weekend but wasn't about to kvetch about hearing from him.

> ELIJAH: Remind me to take you to this hotel for a weekend trip. It's totally more suited for a romantic getaway than it is for bachelor parties. I may have fucked up in picking this place haha

> HANNAH: Aw I'd love to join you! What's it look like?? Is it boutiquey??

Elijah sent her a photo of the room to show the brick accents on the walls and the stylish, classy decor.

> ELIJAH: Nice, huh? We each got our own. Brad snores, Kane sleeps naked even if it's freezing outside, and Jameson's just an asshole. I don't think any of us were willing to take our chances lol

> HANNAH: Does that leave you as the blanket snatcher, or do you have another bedtime fatal flaw that I should know about?

> ELIJAH: Probably. You'll have to let me know.

Hannah felt her heart flutter when she opened the latest text from Elijah. She read over it twice and set her laptop down on her bedside table, deciding that Elijah was in need of her full attention. She wasn't sure if Elijah meant his last message sexually or innocently, so she decided to test the waters.

> HANNAH: As long as you promise to keep me warm, I won't mind if you hog all the blankets! My fatal flaw is I get cold very easily but can't be bothered with real pajamas.

> ELIJAH: Ok, now I'm wondering… what do you wear to bed, then?

Hannah opted to show, not tell. She stood up and moved to the wall mirror that hung behind her door so she could snap a full-body picture for Elijah. She was wearing nothing more than an oversized old *Trigun* T-shirt and some cheeky panties that weren't really visible beneath her shirt. She posed with her hand on her ribcage to help accentuate her figure.

Hannah sent Elijah the photo, feeling bold and hoping that it would be well received.

> HANNAH: Usually just something like this…

His nonchalant reply threw her off guard.

> ELIJAH: Guilty as charged, too! We have the same shirt on haha. Except it looks way better on you than it does me.

He'd added the winking kissy-face emoji, but Hannah paid more attention to the attached photo. Elijah's His legs were lean, yet strong, with notable thigh muscles. His auburn curls were even more unruly than usual with his bedhead, making him look even more effortlessly sexy than usual. That was only amplified by the very visible shape of the rest of his body through his boxer briefs.

> HANNAH: I guess one of us is gonna have to change, then! But I'm still not used to the Colorado cold...

> ELIJAH: If only you were here, I'd keep you warm.

> HANNAH: And how would you do that?

She could feel the excitement growing between her legs as she watched the three dots pop up as he replied.

> ELIJAH: I'd hold you close to me as I run my hands slowly up and down your body to give you some friction. Would that help?

As Hannah sighed in contentment, settled into her spot in her bed, and began to let her hand roam over herself, she wondered if Elijah was doing the same.

> HANNAH: It would! You know, you're tempting me to just show up at your hotel.

> ELIJAH: I wish you would. I can't stop thinking about you, you know...

> HANNAH: You're always on my mind, too. What are you thinking about right now?

> ELIJAH: Forgive me if this is too blunt, but if I'm being perfectly honest... I'm thinking about how good it would feel have my face buried between your legs.

Hannah let her head fall back to her pillow. "Fuck."

> HANNAH: Please don't ever apologize for that bluntness ever again

HANNAH: I guess for now I'll have to just pretend my fingers are your tongue. Would you prefer me riding your face or strapped down to your mattress?

ELIJAH Why not both? You really think I'd only want to do that once?

As she fingered herself, feeling her climax build from the anticipation alone, she thought now would be a good time to tease him back; after all, she was quite enjoying this bolder side of him.

HANNAH I'm always down to switch things up. If I ride your face, I'd love to lean over and take care of you, too.

ELIJAH: Just the idea of those pretty lips around me has me so turned on.

HANNAH: If you've got me this wet now, I wonder how wet I'll be when you're back from Denver.

She wasn't lying: she was beyond aroused, so much so that she couldn't ever recall feeling this sexually driven before moving to Riverpeak. Part of the thought scared her since she knew rationally that she only had known Elijah for a few short months, which was still fairly soon. But Hannah also knew her connection to Elijah was real, and everything they'd been through together only strengthened that bond.

ELIJAH: I cannot wait to feel for myself. I'm getting so close. Do you mind if I think of you while I cum?

"Fuck!" Hannah repeated. Leave it to Elijah to make consent sensual. She pictured him fisting his cock, alone in his hotel room, and moaning her name.

HANNAH: I'd have it no other way. So long as you don't mind me doing the same for you.

ELIJAH: Please do.

And just like that, she felt the wave of pleasure crash through her body as she imagined him experiencing the same.

———

Elijah was in the mood for anything other than a bachelor party. While his unexpected sexting session with Hannah the night prior helped ease some of his stress, it didn't stop him from feeling on edge tonight.

The bar in Denver was dim with just some Edison lights hanging overhead, which made the rows of bottles behind the bartender glisten. The exposed brick walls and low, deep booths with couches along the perimeter emitted the vibe of an old speakeasy. Chatter was low and hard to hear over some jazz music playing Christmas melodies overhead.

"This place is cool," Brad said.

Elijah nudged his friend with his elbow. "Thought you'd like it."

They took their spot at a high table. Elijah's feet were still firmly planted on the ground, even on the tall stool, so he struggled to get comfortable. He glanced around, trying to wonder why he felt so uneasy. Maybe it was just his physical discomfort in a chair too short for him, though that was nothing out of the ordinary.

As their drinks arrived at the table—a beer for Brad, Kane, and Shawn, but just a diet soda for Elijah as the designated driver—Elijah monitored his surroundings. The crowd mostly comprised of couples enjoying a quiet moment, but another group of men sitting in a booth in the back caught his eye.

Kane tapped Elijah's left leg with his foot to get his attention. Elijah looked to his blond friend and rose a brow at him.

"Everything good?" Kane asked in a low whisper. Some story that Shawn was telling distracted Brad, and Elijah hadn't paid attention to a word of it. "You're reminding me of Rory."

Elijah lifted his glass to his lips and ever-so-slightly tipped it toward where he was looking. "Don't stare but tell me if they look familiar." He took a sip.

Kane pretended to crack his neck before he answered. "The one in the brown jacket hangs out in East Riverpeak a lot. I think Hematite knocked him out once."

Elijah nodded. "Anyone else? I could swear I've seen some of them somewhere. Probably on cameras."

"The two men he's talking to look familiar too. They don't know us, though. We'll be fine. We'll just lie low."

Elijah nodded.

"I'll be right back, you guys," Shawn said as he stood. "I gotta take a leak."

"Shawn," Kane said. He grabbed Shawn's forearm.

"What, dude?"

"Don't talk to anyone. Keep your head down." Brad couldn't hear Kane's whispered warning. "Got it?"

"Yeah, whatever." Shawn shrugged Kane off and made his way over to the restrooms.

Kane sighed. "Fuck."

Elijah nervously took another sip of soda, waiting for the inevitable as the bubbles flattened on his tongue.

After a few seconds that felt like hours, Kane asked, "What do you wanna bet there's gonna be an issue?"

Elijah checked his watch, curious about how long Shawn had been in the bathroom for. Before he could answer, the sound of shattering porcelain caught their attention, followed by a string of profanities from multiple men.

"Well," Elijah said, "there's your answer."

"Big problem, you guys!" As Shawn scurried out of the bathroom in a frenzy, Kane, Brad, and Elijah all turned to look at him. A few other patrons turned to look at Shawn as he made his way through the high tables, barely spaced out enough for him to weave through without running into someone. His eyes were wide. Fear was not an expression Shawn often showed, so it caught all their attention right away. "We gotta go! Let's get the fuck outta here!"

"Shawn, what's happening?" Brad asked. Elijah and Kane already had an idea as they feared the worst. Elijah fumbled for his wallet to quickly pay their server, slapping a fifty-dollar bill on the table in hopes that it would act as an apology for bailing.

"Come on, we're good," Elijah said. He pocketed his wallet and turned his car on remotely with his smartwatch. "Jameson, explain on the way to the car."

"We gotta rush. It's that guy we saw with Naomi's dad," Shawn said. "The one from the car that day. A bunch of dudes were with him, and I think they recognized me, so we're in deep shit if we don't get the fuck out of here."

"He's here?" Kane asked, as they made their way outside. "What the hell is he doing *here*?"

"Drug deals in the bathroom, apparently. I thought I could take them real quick, no problem, but slam one guy into a urinal and next thing you know, his friends are drawing guns on you."

"Dude!" Brad smacked the back of Shawn's head. "Didn't Kane tell you to lay low?"

Right as they reached the front door of the bar, Kane glanced back and saw the silver-haired man heading through the kitchen. He wore a black trench coat over his dress pants and moved in a blur too fast to discern his exact next move.

"He's heading out back," Kane said. "Wouldn't shock me if someone else is joining him."

The man that followed was a tall brunette in a business suit, similar to the silver-haired man's but noticeably cheaper. He reached into his pocket for something.

"Come on, let's move!" Kane pushed his friends toward the door. As they made a dash for it, they heard a gun fire. The bullet shattered a vase holding fake flowers that was near Shawn's head. A few people screamed as the staff scrambled to find a phone to call for help.

"Car's on!" Elijah swung open the door as he slid into the driver's side seat. Another bullet crashed through a window and hit the car next to them. Once everyone was inside, Elijah didn't even wait for them to all buckle up, focusing instead on taking off. They heard a few more gunshots as they hit the street but were greeted by silence after a few minutes.

From the back seat, Brad looked behind them and saw another vehicle catching up. "We're about to have company. I think they're right behind us."

Another gunshot confirmed that. Elijah swerved out of the way just in time to dodge it and groaned as his car's lane keep assist beeped at him.

"Not now, damn it." He smacked the steering wheel before fumbling with the buttons to turn it off.

"Elijah, they're getting closer," Brad said. "You might wanna step on it."

"Buckle in if you haven't already, everyone." Elijah pushed further on his gas pedal, abandoning his usual safe driving tactics to adopt a lead foot. "What's going on back there?"

Kane unfastened his seatbelt and turned to Brad. "Switch with me. If they're still shooting, I stand a better chance than you."

"Not about to fight you on that!"

Kane climbed into the back seat over the center console with little trouble given he was leaner than Brad, who had a harder time climbing over into the passenger seat as Elijah sped off. The road ahead was a long stretch through the grasslands, which were coated in a light sheen of snow. Elijah took the first turn he could and slowed down so Brad could settle in more comfortably and catch his breath. More bullets fired, so Elijah picked up the pace again until he couldn't see their headlights anymore.

"Dude, what are we gonna do?" Brad asked. "He knows where we all live!"

"I'm gonna take a detour into town," Elijah said. "Let me make a call."

Everyone waited for the call to answer with bated breath. The phone didn't ring for long, which made Elijah sigh in relief.

"Hey Elijah!" Hannah's greeting was as peppy as ever; Elijah would have killed for her ignorance right about now. "Shouldn't you be at the bachelor party?"

"Hey. Just a head's up, you're on my car's speaker. I'm heading back with the guys. We're ... in a bit of trouble."

Brad looked at his friend next to him with wide eyes. "'A bit' is the understatement of the century."

"What kind of trouble? Are you okay?"

"Elijah, go faster," Kane commanded from the back. "Their lights are showing up behind us again."

"Is someone following you?" Hannah asked.

"Well, yeah," Elijah said. "We were barhopping downtown and when Jameson went to the bathroom, he stumbled upon a drug deal or something."

"What can I do right now?"

Shawn snorted. "Where'd you find this one, Baron? Mail order?"

"Watch your mouth, asshole!"

"How much you paying her?"

Before Elijah could get into an argument, Hannah quipped, "More than you could afford."

"Hey!"

Elijah stifled a laugh.

"Anyway, now is not the time for that. How can I help you guys?"

"I'm trying to lose them now. I think we'll pull it off," Elijah said. "But uh ... well, let's just say these guys all know us and where we live, thanks to Naomi's dad. Once we get into town, we'll have to hide out for the night. If we ditch my car elsewhere, do you mind if we crash at your place? Just for tonight."

"Yeah, come on by. I'm home. I'll be around, and I've got the room. Can I meet you anywhere with my car?"

"Go to the hospital. I'll meet you in the ER's parking lot in about forty minutes."

"Alright, I'll be on my way."

"Thanks. I really owe you one."

"Buy me dinner some night and I'll call us even. Stay safe."

Despite the stakes, Elijah smiled. "You too."

———

Hannah rushed to grab some extra blankets and pillows from her closets. She didn't have any extra mattresses but gathered what she did have at record speed, then tossed them in the mostly barren spare rooms. She had some time to spare before she had to get to the hospital, so she swung by the first open store on the way to pick up some toiletries and air mattresses. The guys could fend for themselves in inflating them, she figured.

When she pulled into the hospital parking lot, there was still no sign of Elijah and his friends. Ready for them, Hannah waited in her car with the doors unlocked, then sighed in relief when they pulled up to her with no one behind them.

"Glad to see you're okay and alone."

"There was a cop at a speed trap," Elijah said, as he joined her in the front seat. "We slowed down just in time, but our followers weren't so lucky. Thanks again for this."

"Yeah, of course." Once everyone was in the car, Hannah wasted no time hitting the road. "I grabbed some air mattresses and cheap toothbrushes on the way so you guys won't have to sleep on the floor. They only had two, though. Someone will have to fight for the couch."

"You sure you're not paying her, Baron?" Shawn asked from the backseat.

"Seriously dude, shut the fuck up." Elijah turned to Hannah and took on a much gentler demeanor. "Please ignore him."

Hannah shook her head as they pulled up to the house. "Well, you guys should be safe here for the night. I've got the extra rooms, so if you need a hideout, I've got your backs."

"Seriously, thank you," Elijah said. Brad echoed the sentiment as Kane and Shawn grabbed the air mattresses and pharmacy bags from the trunk.

Kane offered to take the couch, claiming it to be more comfortable than his own bed, and stepped outside to call Rory and let her know what happened. As he did, Brad and Shawn went upstairs to manage their air mattresses in the mostly empty spare bedroom. As they did, Elijah found himself in Hannah's room.

"Seems like we have a habit of sharing a bed after a traumatic event."

Elijah laughed. "Seems like it." He kissed the top of her head. "We'll have to change that. Not … not like that. Well, unless you want to!" He sighed. "You know what I mean."

"You overthink too much. Come on."

They went through the motions of getting ready for bed together in the primary bathroom, almost as if they'd been in step with each other for decades. They didn't say much; Hannah was too nervous to say the wrong thing as Elijah decompressed from the night's events. She could tell from the look in his eyes that he was still processing everything around him, so when they laid beside one another in the bed, Hannah simply asked, "You okay?"

Elijah glanced over to meet her gaze, finally feeling brave enough to do so. He nodded. "Yeah, I think so. For the most part, anyway." He let his head drop back into the pillow. "Didn't realize dodging shootouts was part of wedding planning."

There was so much Hannah wanted to know, but his distress radiated off him. Hannah tried not to absorb it, especially now that she was aware of her own empathy. If she was stressed too, it wouldn't do him any favors.

"I have a lot of questions. But you don't have to answer them now. I'm just glad you guys are all okay."

"I appreciate that," Elijah said with a nervous laugh. His hands found her cheeks and, once they did, he pulled Hannah in for a kiss. His lips felt warm against hers, a pleasant contrast to the chill of the toothpaste they recently shared. There was a sort of seriousness in the way he held her face, despite his touch remaining gentle.

"Can I get you anything?"

"Maybe, actually. Can you practice on me?"

"How do you mean?"

"The adrenaline's bound to wear off, and I'm not sure if that's a good or a bad thing."

"Sure, come here." Hannah wrapped her arms around his waist and focused on Elijah's heartbeat, pressing her ear against his chest. "You're safe now. We're okay."

They sat in silence for a few moments, and Hannah heard his heart rate return to a more standard rhythm. His muscles slackened around her, and he released a sigh that sounded as if it had lifted a weight from his chest.

"Much better already. And hey, no fuzzy feeling this time."

"Glad to hear that. I've been pretty self-aware, so I'm glad that it's working."

"I'm really grateful for you, you know that? Not many other people would just go with the flow like this."

"I think that's the adrenaline talking."

He chuckled and kissed the top of her head. "Maybe, but I mean it. Sweet dreams."

"You too. Good night."

CHAPTER 19

Elijah was the first to wake up the next morning. As he blinked his eyes open, adjusting to the light streaming in through the crack in the blinds, he winced; there was a pain in his upper back he couldn't quite place. He wasn't sure if it was from the position he slept in or from some borderline reckless driving the day before. Hannah's hair tickled his neck, the strands just long enough now to reach him from her spot on the bed. When he stirred, she came out of her own slumber with a bit of a stretch. He heard her joints crack a few times as she turned to him.

"G'morning. You okay after yesterday?"

Elijah pulled her closer to him. After everything, he needed something to help him feel more grounded. The softness of her mattress and her skin doubly helped him as his brain remembered everything from the night prior. "All things considered, I can't say no."

Hannah smiled when he kissed her. It was sloppy in his early morning stupor but still sweet.

"Thank you again for helping us last night. I was really banking on you picking up. I don't know what we would have done without you."

"I wasn't gonna leave you guys stranded, Elijah. Don't be ridiculous."

"Still! I guess I owe you dinner."

Hannah laughed. "Take me out after the wedding, space cowboy."

He lightly chuckled at the reference to both *Cowboy Bebop* and the night prior. "I would anyway." He wrapped his arms around her tighter and pulled her in for a closer embrace. "You've been surprisingly cool with all of this."

Hannah shrugged. Her fingers trailed along Elijah's chest, where she traced some of his light freckles. "Why wouldn't I be?"

"Huh?"

"I think it's cool, what you do. I mean, it's not cool that armed drug dealers were chasing you yesterday. But my personal bullshit from a few weeks ago aside, I think it's cool that you're helping people."

"I mean, I'd say Kane is more than me."

"Don't discredit yourself! You're doing something pretty amazing, Elijah."

He smiled. "You're too nice to me."

"Well, somebody has to hype you up." Hannah leaned up to kiss his jaw. It made him blush; she learned in the past that it was an instant way to practically turn Elijah into putty.

"Should we go check on everyone?"

Hannah pretended to think about it as she left a few more slow kisses along his jaw. His hold around her body tightened. "Hmm." She glanced at the clock on her bedside table. "I bet they're not even awake yet. Besides, I want you to myself for just a little while longer."

Elijah hummed in pleasure as Hannah's lips moved to his. His hands ran up her bare back, savoring the moment for as long as he could. He wanted to give her what she wanted; he wasn't sure when their last time may be, so he savored every second. "You don't have to twist my arm very hard."

———

When they finally made their way downstairs, Kane was the only one up. He waved to them from Hannah's kitchen, whipping up some eggs.

"Morning! Hope you don't mind that I raided your fridge to feed everyone."

"No, not at all," Hannah said with a dismissive wave of her hand. "I would have offered if you hadn't beaten me to it."

"Did Elijah catch you up to speed yet?"

Elijah nodded. "I did when we were getting ready." He gave her the rundown when they were in the shower, but Kane didn't need to know that detail in particular.

"Good." He shifted the pan of scrambled eggs off the burner. Whatever Kane had seasoned them with permeated the kitchen with its savory scent. "I figured we could figure out what's next once Brad and Jameson wake up."

"Yeah, sounds good."

"We won't be in your hair for too long, Hannah, I promise," Kane said.

"Stay as long as you need," Hannah said. "I'd rather you guys be safe than sorry."

Brad and Shawn weren't asleep much longer. Hannah stood by the kitchen island as the four men sat around the dining room table. Elijah insisted on giving up his spot, but Hannah refused for the sake of being a good hostess.

"So now what?" Brad asked. "We have to be at a rehearsal with Mr. Sato tomorrow."

Hannah asked, "Have you guys come up with any way to potentially stop him?"

"Not yet. We've been trying, but we keep coming up blank," Shawn said.

Kane chimed in. "The violence on the east side is worse than ever. They're really kicking it into high gear. I've had to spend almost every night there lately."

"Denver hasn't been much better, either," Shawn said. "I've been taking over Kane's usual spots there. Let's just say these kids will have some serious withdrawals if they go home for winter break."

Hannah made a mental note to check on Rory. If she was worried about Elijah, she could only imagine how Rory must feel knowing Kane was out there, even given his special circumstances.

"You don't think he's gonna try anything at the wedding, do you?"

All four of them looked at Hannah. No longer was she just an outsider looking in, even if she felt like it while she was leaning against the counter as they all sat together.

"No, he wouldn't," Brad said, like he didn't believe himself.

"Would he, though?" Kane frowned. "What better time than when we're all in the same room together?"

"Listen, he might be an asshole, but he loves Naomi more than anything." It was the most conviction that Hannah ever heard come from Brad. It seemed to startle the other three just as much as it surprised her. "He will be on his best behavior. He cannot risk an incident at the wedding. I also get the vibe that his mysterious business associate is more high class than that. I haven't even met the guy."

"I think Brad's right," Shawn said. "He's gonna be more worried about his reputation. Especially if he doesn't know that Naomi knows."

Elijah's head tilted to the side in thought. "I think it can't hurt to be cautious."

"I think you just like disagreeing with me, Baron."

"Will you seriously shut the fuck up?" Elijah rubbed his eyes. "Not everything is a competition. Kane might be safe from death, but that's something the rest of us will have a harder time avoiding if we aren't careful."

Hannah hid her chortle with a sip of coffee. The more Shawn spoke, the more she understood why Elijah didn't get along with him. She wondered why Brad and Kane still tolerated him, if not for his super strength.

"What would you do?" Kane asked Hannah, looking directly at her. All eyes were on her again. "You haven't been in it as long as we have. I'm curious what your approach would be."

"Leave the wedding off limits, but expect the worst going in," Hannah said. "If he's going to strike, it'll be silently. Maybe he won't do it, but he'd frame someone. Like how he framed your dad, Brad."

"Who would he even frame this time?" Brad asked.

"I dunno," Hannah said with a shrug. "It seems like a lot of people work for him, though. Could be anyone."

"Let's meet after the wedding," Kane decided. "Hannah's right, and I don't want all of us to walk into a potential trap. There isn't anything we can actively do until it's over, anyway. It'll be suspicious if we do."

"Want me to hide some cameras in the venue and record everything?" Elijah asked.

"You're the man, dude," Kane said. "That'd be great."

"I'll grab some on the way."

————

Once they all cleared out, walking home in their own separate ways, it left just Elijah and Hannah. The news was on the television in her living room, repeating the story throughout the newscasts: Denver bar gunmen caught at a traffic light heading into Riverpeak. The news showed a few mugshots, but none of them were Sterling's. Elijah and Hannah weren't alone together for more than a minute before his phone started vibrating in his pocket, making him jump like a startled animal. Hannah raised an eyebrow as he recovered and grabbed his phone out of his pocket.

"You good?"

"Yeah, yeah. I think I'm still on edge. I'm sorry; it's my mom. She probably saw the news."

"Go ahead. I'll make us some fresh coffee."

"Thanks." He answered the phone. "Hey, *Ima*."

There was a brief pause on Elijah's end, but Hannah could hear her voice through the phone, even from the next room in her home's open floor plan.

Elijah cut her off gently. "*Ima, Ima, Ima.* Calm down. Everything's okay, I promise. *Ani beseder.*"

He ran his hand upward over his face and then through his hair, where he left it.

"No, I did not get shot. Yes, I was sober when I drove. No one followed us home. Some cops caught them in a speed trap." He exhaled through his nose as his mother spoke. "It's complicated, *Ima*. But I promise you, I am not doing anything illegal or shady." He grimaced as he said it, knowing it was technically a lie. "No, I'm not alone right now."

There was a longer pause.

"Don't worry. We're all back in Riverpeak. I'm with Hannah right now. She let me and the guys stay at her place, just in case."

He looked at Hannah in the kitchen with a nervous look on his face. Hannah just nodded at him and tried not to laugh as Elijah's whole body relaxed.

"I know, *Ima*. Yeah, she knows what happened. She actually helped us out last night when we were trying to get away. We might be in an awful predicament if it wasn't for her." Another pause. "I promise I'm okay. The guys are fine too. They went home this morning."

Elijah looked back up at Hannah and mouthed his thanks, as she set down two cups of fresh coffee on the table. She placed a reassuring hand on his shoulder.

"Yeah, yeah, I'll swing by tomorrow morning. *Ani ohev otach*. Bye." Elijah sighed as he set the phone down on the table. He replaced it with his cup of coffee for a quick sip. "Thank you."

Once he set the mug down, he grabbed Hannah's from her hand, placed it next to his cup, and then pulled her into his lap. He rested his head against her shoulder.

Hannah ran her fingers through his curls, keeping her nails close to his scalp. She closed her eyes and took a deep breath, hoping to soothe him. He hummed softly beneath her touch.

"I think I get my anxiety from her."

Hannah chuckled. "Can't say I blame her for freaking out. If I hadn't known, I'd probably be in the same boat."

"I haven't told her anything, so she's completely in the dark. It's getting harder to keep this all to myself. It kills me to lie to her."

"It's necessary," Hannah said. "But I get it. Do you want me to go with you to see your mom?"

Elijah nodded. "It'll be easier for me to keep up the lie if I have some backup. We can just go on our way to the venue." He leaned up from his spot at the table to kiss her cheek. "I appreciate you."

Hannah shifted to sit in the chair next to him. "What a whirlwind."

"Bet you weren't expecting this when you moved here, huh?"

"No, not at all. But I wouldn't trade it for anything. I'm glad I stuck it out."

"Me too. I don't even want to think of what might have happened had you not answered the phone. I still feel like shit about everything."

"Don't. I'm over it, I promise," Hannah said with a reassuring smile that reflected in her eyes. "I've been doing this thing where I try not to hang on to shit anymore, you know?"

"You'd have every right to."

"I know, but I've got a stomach that's as Jewish as I am. Last thing I need is to give myself an ulcer. Better to just roll shit off."

He laughed. "That's one way of looking at it."

"I'd do anything for my friends too, so I can't really blame you for that. And besides, I doubt you'd have taken me to meet your parents if none of this was real."

"If it were up to my father, he'd convince you I'm a total dweeb."

"I mean, I don't need him to convince me of that, but it takes one to know one."

Her smirk was contagious, spreading across both of their faces. "I guess I set myself up for that one. Come on, we should get ready for this mini-road trip."

"You think everything will be okay?" Hannah asked.

Elijah sighed. "Honestly? Not at all."

CHAPTER 20

The three-hour drive from Riverpeak to Aspen was unlike any stretch of road Hannah had experienced. She was in the passenger seat, staring out the window so she could take in the scenery. Both her and Elijah's formalwear hung up behind them on the grab handles as he drove them to the wedding venue out in the mountains. As they spoke about anything and everything except for their worries, Hannah continued to take in the wide expanses of peaks and valleys on either side of them. The mountains seemed to connect in front of them at some unknown point ahead of the road, which would occasionally fall out of their field of vision when they went uphill.

"This is literally breathtaking."

Elijah smiled. Hannah took photos the entire way, unable to help herself, no matter how many times she put her phone back down. She stopped resisting her urges about an hour ago.

Once they got past the grasslands, which had mostly been dead in the middle of winter, the sights transformed around them and captivated Hannah the most. The leaves on the birch trees lining either side of the road were long gone, revealing the creeks and mountains they concealed in the warmer months. The ice gave the tops of the water a glossy shine that made it look like crystals when the sun caught the snow on the mountains, which reflected on the surface.

"Seriously, Elijah. I hope you guys never take this for granted."

"It's easy to when you live here, but I try not to. You ever been skiing?"

"Never."

"Wait, what? I thought you grew up in New England! It snows out there."

"Yeah, but my mother was the type of person where if she didn't like something, then no one liked it. She didn't like the snow, and she wasn't an athletic person, so, yeah. Never skied."

"Do *you* like the snow?"

"Is it crazy to say that I wasn't sure until now? My mom was so vocal about how awful she thought the snow was, so I don't think I actually formed my own opinion growing up. I liked how Florida was never cold, but … I dunno. Something about this is so beautiful. So, I think I do?"

"I'm totally taking you skiing, then."

Hannah looked at him as he pulled into a long stretch of road leading into the parking lot. "Yeah?"

He nodded. "I promise."

Hannah continued staring out the window as they pulled up to the wedding venue. It looked like something out of a fairy tale, with snow covering the ski resort in a thick blanket. It looked more like an Alpine village than it did a hotel, with exposed brick foundations and wood panels against white walls. Hannah could see the three-mile-long stretch of gondolas and ski lifts running behind the building, a teaser for tomorrow's access to the ceremony venue. The snow flurrying outside was thin and light, just enough to set the mood without completely turning the sky grey, as they stepped outside to grab their bags.

Their room was a step above a standard hotel, but from the looks of the resort, Hannah and Elijah shouldn't have expected any less. It was exceptionally modern, with gray carpet, white walls, and matching furniture—quite the contrast from the exterior, but still matching the glamorous ambiance. The room even had a mini bar in the corner and a gas log fireplace across from a couch.

"Well, this is certainly fancy," Hannah said. As she peeked out the window, she saw some elk grazing in the grass.

"We all splurged on the suites. Naomi and Brad had the longest engagement known to mankind, so we all had plenty of time to save. Not that I'm complaining; I couldn't tell you the last time I took a vacation."

"We'll have to change that! We gotta get you out more."

"Yeah, yeah. I know, I know. Maybe I'll let you force me away from my computer."

As she took a photo on her phone of the elk from the window, she said, "You did promise me a ski trip, like, an hour ago."

"I did, and I will honor that. But for now, we have a wedding to get ready for. And I," he said as he rummaged in his bag, only to take out a small box, "have some cameras to hide before tomorrow. It's a big place. Care to join me?"

———

Once Elijah took his place beside Brad at the podium the next day, he found Hannah in the crowd. The white folding chairs were still filling up with guests making their way to the outdoor terrace on the mountaintop, but given her spot close to the front, it was easy to find her. She shot him a wink, and he smiled in return.

He appreciated the show of support; he didn't enjoy having all eyes on him, and he was looking forward to Naomi and Brad stealing the show. But as they waited for the bridesmaids to begin their walk, all eyes were on Brad, Elijah, Kane, and Shawn. The lingering fear of a crime ring member causing a scene didn't help, either. Elijah doubted they would do so out in Aspen; they were among the mountaintops with nowhere to run or hide if caught, and it was a long way down. *While it would be nothing short of risky*, he thought, *I've seen stranger things over the last few months.*

But Hannah was there, so Elijah just focused on her and the light music coming from a harpist seated at the edge of the platform. It was all he could do to stop himself from having a complete anxiety attack in front of well over a hundred people, and it wasn't even his own wedding. He was grateful for the reprieve when the music kicked in louder and Naomi's bridesmaids made their way to join them down the aisle, where a white runner and rose petals prevented their heels from digging into the grass beneath. Their green dresses were all slightly different to best suit their bodies and personal style preferences, but their colors all perfectly matched each other and the grooms-men's ties. He focused on his breathing and hoped he didn't look as tense as he felt. As he took a silent, deep breath, he got an overwhelming whiff of spruce and the flowers behind them that would frame Brad and Naomi.

The music shifted and everyone turned to look behind them, waiting anxiously for Naomi to walk down the aisle. Reiji was by her side, arm in arm with his daughter, looking content. Hannah sensed he was putting everything aside for the night, so it could truly be all about Naomi, as it should be. It was obvious from the way he looked at her and the tears misting his eyes.

Naomi fit the role of the bride like she was born for that level of elegance. Hannah had never seen anyone glow like her. The long sleeves and illusion neckline covered in filigree matched the pattern that extended across the top of her stark white gown, reaching halfway down the large A-line skirt. The layers of fabric flared out just enough to give her the illusion of being a princess; an actual ball gown would have dominated her smaller frame, but this shape was perfect for her size, glittering like the snow on the mountains in the sun. A handful of her aunts snuck out their cell phones to grab photos once Naomi reached the floral archway Brad stood under but luckily had the sense to not be obnoxious about it, given the photographer's earlier announcement of an unplugged ceremony.

Everything about the ceremony looked like it was straight out of a movie. Hannah thought that the Elk Mountains behind them didn't look real and would have believed it if someone told her they were a painting, especially with the sun starting its descent and coloring the sky pink and orange. If it wasn't for the minor headache and nausea, she might not believe the horizon was real at all. After the last few months in Colorado, she thought she'd have been better equipped for the altitude by now, but at over 11,000 feet, she supposed it didn't matter much.

When the officiant made the official call for the crowd to speak now or forever hold their peace, Hannah glanced around with only her eyes, not daring to turn her head but desperate to know what may happen. If Noah or someone else were to make a scene, then now would be the perfect time to do so with a dramatic flair.

Thankfully, they were met with silence. Hannah didn't spot anyone so much as stir from her view of the crowd over the floral decorations hanging from the chairs. The officiant proceeded, and they moved on to their vows shortly after. They were short, traditional, and only had the smallest personal touch. Hannah still felt like her head was spinning but wasn't sure if it was from the altitude or the adrenaline anymore.

Luckily, her symptoms subsided once she—along with the rest of the guests after the ceremony—made her way to the outdoor space just outside of the reception hall. The slightly lower altitude was much more manageable for her body, which allowed her to feel more in focus as she glanced around. She saw the wedding party taking photos in the distance and watched them as she leaned against the balcony, using it to steady herself as her headache and nausea finally passed.

As she watched them pose against the backdrop of the mountains, not bothering to tune in to any of the dozens of conversations happening around her, she forgot momentarily about all her struggles at hand. Her mind couldn't help but wonder what her own future wedding might look like. When Brad was told he could now kiss his bride, Hannah and Elijah's eyes met. She wondered if he had been looking at her the entire time and what he was thinking if he had.

Hannah snapped out of her trance at the feeling of a hand on her shoulder. The voice beside her was feminine and familiar. "Sweetheart, how are you?"

"Mrs. Baron! Hi! Don't mind me. You'd think with all the hiking Elijah and I did over the summer, the altitude wouldn't hit me so hard. You look gorgeous!"

"Oh, thank you. You're stunning, as always." Lena rested her forearms on the railing, her pose matching Hannah's. "Where did you get this?"

"What, this?" Hannah glanced down at the simple, faux-velvet jumpsuit she was wearing, a deep blue color. The pant legs flared out enough to give the illusion of it being a skirt. The sleeves cinched at her wrists, but the deep V-neck prevented it from feeling like too much fabric. "It's just a rental. I didn't bring a lot with me when I moved. I gotta mail it back by Tuesday."

"How much longer is your lease? It must be getting close, no?"

"Only about three more months. Can you believe it? I just wrapped up the first round of edits on my book too. Felt like that would never happen."

"Congratulations! I'm so proud of you, honey," Lena said. "Getting up and moving across the country for work all on your own. That was very brave of you."

Hannah smiled. She wasn't exactly sure why, but Lena's words made her feel especially touched. She sensed it was because she craved conversation like this with her own family but knew better than to expect it.

"Thank you, Lena," Hannah said. "That ... It really means a lot."

Lena smiled back at Hannah and took a hold of her hand. "I'm not sure if you're planning on staying here or not come next spring, but you're always welcome in our home. I hope you know that."

Hannah just nodded and swallowed; her makeup was too expensive for her to cry it all off. "I do. Coming here has been life-changing, that's for sure. You know, I feel like I've finally found my people."

"Does that mean you have something up your sleeve? Maybe something shaped like house keys?" Lena asked. She rose an eyebrow, and Hannah could immediately see where Elijah got that facial expression from.

"Nothing finalized yet. I'd hate to jinx it."

"I can live with that answer. I like the sound of it. Wherever you end up next, though, you better let me get you to sign my copy of your new book."

Hannah laughed. "I will personally see to it that you'll be the first one to get a copy."

———

The sound of Hannah's laughter trailing across the yard caught Elijah's attention. The guys weren't completely in the clear yet but had a quick break, as the photographer captured a few shots of Naomi with the bridesmaids. Elijah saw Hannah and Lena chatting, nudging shoulders like they were old friends.

A bittersweet feeling overcame him at that moment: sweetness because his mother and the woman he loved got along so swimmingly, but bitterness in that he still didn't know if Hannah was renewing her lease or not. It was everything he could have ever dreamed of, and it was there in his grasp, but he feared it would slip away sooner rather than later. Nothing had ever gone this well for him, and even if they kept everything up, their dynamic could shift in ways he couldn't even predict. Just as he was getting used to dating someone without having some ulterior motive, that could all change. He hoped it wouldn't but tried not to get his hopes up too much.

———

"You know, I actually based the heroine off of Esther," Hannah told Lena.

"Really? You know, I thought she reminded me of her, but everyone told me I was reading too much into it. Oh, I can't wait to tell my book club."

Hannah nodded. "Yeah, Esther is my favorite. I've always turned to her story when I was feeling down on myself."

"You remind me of myself when I was younger."

"Do I?"

"Yeah, yeah. You know, Rueben and I moved out here when I got pregnant with Elijah. We knew we wanted our family to have a quiet life. This was the perfect place to do it."

"It is, isn't it?" She didn't want to get too emotional, but she could feel happy tears threatening to build up again. She took a sip of her drink to swallow them back. "Your family has been so kind to me since I moved here. I really appreciate it."

"Oh, sweetheart. Don't even mention it." She wrapped an arm around Hannah, who returned the gesture. "I'm sure this won't be the last we see of you. Elijah told me about what happened with your parents. We're here for you, okay? I know it can't be easy. But I'm a call away if you ever need anything. Doesn't matter what it is. You know, I was telling him," she pointed to Elijah in the crowd, "that Hannah Baron has such a nice ring to it. I hope you don't mind me saying so. But he knows I hope it's your turn next."

Hannah laughed. "You're not wrong. And no, I don't mind."

"Good, because I'm already calling you that behind his back," Lena said with a wink.

"Calling her what behind my back?"

Lena and Hannah glanced behind them to see Elijah towering over them. His hands moved to rest on each of their shoulders.

"Oh, nothing bad, I promise," Lena said. "You look so handsome, 'Lij."

"Thanks, *Ima*. She's not making fun of you, is she, Hannah?"

"Your mother would never!" Hannah said, fake-offended on Lena's behalf. "I quite like her secret nickname for me." Hannah winked at Lena.

"Eh, I'll figure it out, eventually."

"Oh!" Hannah reached over to the table on the other side of her. "I snagged these for you. I had to convince the server that I wasn't just a *nosher*, but I figured you'd be hungry."

Elijah took the tray of h'ors 'oeuvres and left a kiss on Hannah's forehead. "Thank you. We've barely had a chance to eat today. You're the best." The three of them shifted their stances so they could stand around the high-top table together as Elijah took his first bite. The cool weather had chilled the food, especially since it wasn't fresh out of the kitchen anymore, but he was so famished that he barely noticed.

"Everything going okay?" Hannah asked.

Elijah nodded. "It's been going pretty smoothly." He made eye contact with Hannah, communicating non-verbally what he couldn't say in front of his mother: no issues yet. "The day-of coordinator is pretty on top of things and there hasn't been much drama, especially since we got all the kinks worked out at the rehearsal yesterday. I think

Jameson got into a fight with Amy this morning since she'll barely speak to him, but what else is new?"

"Oh, that poor girl," Lena said. "Don't worry, honey. I'll try to steal her away for a moment later."

"She'd probably appreciate that. I can't tell you how many times I've tried to tell her to dump him."

"Naomi doing okay, at least?"

"They did a first look with her dad," Elijah said. "He ugly cried, and then she almost started crying but stopped herself before her makeup could get ruined. I didn't even know the man had tear ducts."

Hannah tried not to laugh as she took a sip of mulled cider. The sweet notes of apple and spices warmed her up as the music changed from some softer tones to a louder, jazzy number. Elijah scarfed down the last of his food, then gave both Hannah and his mother a quick kiss on their cheeks.

"That's my cue. I'll see you guys in there."

Hannah and Lena gave him a wave as he was off, joining the rest of the wedding party as they shuffled their way inside for their grand entrances to the reception. As they wrapped up their drinks before finding their way to their seats, knowing they'd be told to head inside soon, Hannah's eyes followed Reiji Sato as he moved inside. She subtly scanned the crowd once he was gone and didn't see anyone who looked like they shouldn't be there or anyone with silver, slicked-back hair, but she wasn't entirely convinced that was the case.

Everything was going too smoothly.

CHAPTER 21

As Hannah grabbed the place card with her name on it, she did a quick evaluation of the reception hall. She hoped now that she was closer to the other guests, it would be easier to gauge someone who didn't belong, but no one's face stuck out. She was at her table alone for now, scanning the crowd for silver hair on someone seemingly too young for it, but Amy joined her soon after she was seated. Amy's freckles matched her light red hair, which was pin-straight and reached her mid-back. Her bangs parted in the center and just hit the top of her large, round glasses.

"You're Hannah, right?"

"Yeah! Amy, isn't it?"

"Nice to meet you. Shawn told me about you."

"Pleasure's all mine." Even in the slightly dimmed lighting of the room, anyone could see that Amy's eyes were bloodshot behind her glasses. There was a tense silence between them for a moment before Hannah said, "Let me know if you need anything tonight, okay?"

"Damn, word spreads fast." Amy chuckled, trying to brush it off. "Thanks."

"My friends in college all used to joke that I have the bladder of a hamster, so if you ever need to sneak away to the bathroom, just say the word. No one will think it's weird."

That got a genuine laugh out of Amy. They were soon silenced, though, as the DJ spoke into the microphone. He began by acknowledging the grandparents present, who stood or waved from their seats. Brad's parents were then announced and came dancing in; Brad's dad already had some liquid courage coursing through his veins. Reiji and May were next, followed by Shawn and one of Naomi's friends, who Hannah hadn't heard of, then Kane and Rory.

Hannah zoomed her phone camera in as Elijah and Carla both came dancing in, following Kane and Rory's suit. Elijah's moves resembled the choreography from the end credits of *Jujutsu Kaisen*, which got a laugh out of a handful of others in the crowd who got the reference. They took their spots along the wall with the rest of the wedding party, waiting for it to be Brad and Naomi's turn, but Hannah's attention was elsewhere. From a quick look at the wedding party and their nervous glances around the room, it was clear they felt the same distractions weighing on their shoulders. Thankfully, Brad and Naomi were swept into their first dance with no interruptions.

After the dance, everyone was called to the buffet to give Brad and Naomi a moment to eat before they had to make their rounds. It was the perfect opportunity to evaluate the crowd again, but still, nothing stood out. Hannah thought she was going crazy, playing a game that was impossible to win because she was the mouse when she thought she was the cat. When everyone made their way back to their tables, Elijah planted a gentle kiss on Hannah's forehead as he sat down. His brief public display of affection lingered longer than usual, but Hannah wasn't about to complain.

As Hannah took a sip of her drink, Elijah whispered, "Please don't leave my side for the rest of the party."

Hannah grinned at the desperation in his voice. "Naomi's aunt was that bad, huh?"

"Oh yeah. She's laying it on thick and has been since the rehearsal. Naomi tells me her ex-husband was Jewish, so I must be her type."

"I will have you know that I have no dignity. I could really scare her off if you wanted, but it may not be appropriate."

"What were you thinking?"

"I could start loudly discussing the intricacies of writing high fantasy porn."

Elijah smirked, entertaining wherever this conversation may lead. "And what do those intricacies include, dare I ask?"

As Elijah took a sip of his beer, Hannah said, "Well, for starters, I could talk about if my writing about humans having sex with elves is kosher or not."

Elijah nearly spat his drink out, causing him to choke a bit. He cleared his throat and held a hand up to the table to show he was okay. A few eyes glanced their way, curious what the ruckus was about from a few tables over.

"Well?" Elijah asked when he collected his breath. "Is it?"

"Believe it or not, it checks out."

He whispered even lower but rose an eyebrow. "Would you like to me get a pair of fake ears, then?"

They laughed together. Hannah poked his nose. "Please don't."

"Sorry, was that too far?"

"Nah. I had it coming. Not that I mind."

"Hmm. Noted."

When Hannah looked into his eyes, lit up by his smile, she still saw the deep forest like she had when she first met him. She wondered if she'd ever learn the trees well enough to call the forest home.

Shawn was the one to speak up, breaking them out of their bubble. "So, Hannah. How much did Elijah pay you for this outing? I imagine weddings are a premium service."

Elijah set his fork down. "What's your problem, man?" His response caught everyone off guard. He wasn't hostile; Hannah could tell he was as mentally exhausted as he sounded.

Shawn scowled at him and took a bite of his chicken. "What?"

"What is your problem? Like, would it kill you to not be an asshole to me for five whole minutes? You think Brad and Naomi wanna worry about us fighting right now?" He sighed. "We've been through so much shit together, Jameson. Cut it out already."

Shawn laughed. "Whoa, someone's hypersensitive."

Kane chimed in, not to Elijah's surprise but certainly to Shawn's. "He's right, dude. Don't be a dick."

"Besides, I'm still out of your budget."

Amy stifled a laugh at Hannah's quip but quickly pretended like she was choking on her wine when Shawn glared at her. The DJ interrupted them, calling up Brad's mother and Naomi's father for their respective speeches. Elijah and Hannah paid extra close attention to Reiji, curious to see if anything would slip. He was a few drinks in and, for once, emotional. Now would be the time, if ever at all.

"Brad, I know you would do anything for my daughter. I know she is in good hands with you, and it makes me proud to unite our families. Naomi, I love you dearly. To watch you grow into the woman you are has been an honor."

"Weird," Rory whispered. "I thought Reiji couldn't stand Brad."

Reiji cleared his throat as if he wanted to say more, but simply stepped away to hug them both. There was some applause in the crowd as he did, essentially muting whatever he said to his daughter or to Brad when they embraced.

"This is so sweet. Thank you so much, Mr. Sato. And next up is our best man, Elijah Baron!"

Reiji didn't make eye contact with Elijah when he passed off the microphone. Kane whooped to encourage Elijah, who gave an awkward wave to the crowd as the noise died down.

"I think Brad picked me as his best man because I'm the responsible one, so rest assured there won't be any embarrassing stories coming out of my mouth."

This earned a laugh from the crowd, easing the tension after Reiji's emotional moment.

"We all knew this day was coming since we were four. At least I did. But it doesn't make it any less special, and I'm so glad to be here, you guys. You two bring out the best in each other and you always have. I already know the two of you are going to have a lifetime of happiness and of keeping each other on your toes in the best way possible. Congrats, both of you."

Rory was next, their microphone passover happening between more applause. Elijah smoothed his jacket out with his palms as he sat back down, and then rested a hand on Hannah's knee beneath the table while they listened to Rory's speech. While she spoke and then when Naomi and Brad cut their wedding cake, delicately swiping a bit of frosting on each other's noses instead of going for a full-blown cake smash, Hannah and Elijah kept their eyes on the crowd. The table where Reiji sat with his wife and Brad's parents was right between their own and the bride and groom's, but Reiji wasn't who they were worried about anymore. As the cake was served, Hannah pretended to stretch her back and neck to glance around the room.

"Anything?"

"No."

"I mean, I guess that's a good thing, right?"

"Do you think Noah is showing up? It feels so fifty-fifty to me," Hannah said, stopping only to let the catering staff serve them their dessert. They leaned closer to each other once they were gone, noses close enough to just ghost over one another. "Part of me feels like he'd have just taken a seat right in the one they left for him at the ceremony, but part of me also feels like he wouldn't want to ruin this day for Naomi, you know? Sounds like he really cared about her."

When Elijah spoke, Hannah could smell the mint on his breath that the day-of coordinator had practically shoved in his mouth earlier that night. "He did. From what Brad said, he still does. But I dunno. You're right, and something's weird."

Shawn interrupted them. "Care to share with the rest of the table, lovebirds?"

As they parted, Elijah frowned and said, "Later. Now's not the time."

Amy tucked some hair behind her ear as she looked at Hannah. "Everything okay?"

Hannah nodded and smiled at her. "Yeah, yeah. No biggie."

Rory texted something on her phone and, beneath the table, placed it on Hannah's thigh. Hannah glanced down to read it.

NOAH?

Hannah picked it up with one hand, keeping it low, and discretely replied in the Notes app.

WONDERING IF HE'LL SHOW?

She placed it back on Rory's lap as she took a bite of the cake. The vanilla frosting was so sweet that it was almost gritty, strong enough to dominate her entire palette. As Hannah tried to mellow it out with her drink, the DJ called the bride and groom back up for their bouquet and garter tosses, expertly timed as to get people back on the dance floor quickly.

"All right, all my unmarried shes, theys, and gays! Come on up to the dance floor! If you know someone who is trying to sit this one out, then call them out. Don't worry. I do not mind making a scene."

Naomi pointed at her eyes with two of her fingers and then pointed to the table with Amy, Rory, and Hannah. The three women made their way over, joined by a handful of the other women in the crowd—mainly Carla, Naomi's other friends, and some cousins from both families. When Naomi tossed the bouquet, she didn't fling it far enough, so Hannah, who was in the front row with Rory, reached for it as a gut reaction so it wouldn't fall to the floor.

"Alright, miss in the blue jumper! Come on over and wait for your partner! Fellas, it's your turn! Come on up!"

Hannah and Elijah locked eyes as he moved up with the rest of the crowd, laughing a bit at the predicament. When Brad tossed the garter, it flew directly in Kane's direction. His instincts kicked in, forcing him to catch it, even though he didn't exactly care to. Before all eyes could look at him, Kane moved his hand right to Elijah's chest as he relaxed his grip. "Oops," he said sarcastically and winked at Elijah. He then moved his hand behind Elijah and clapped him on the back. "Go get 'em, tiger."

Elijah couldn't bring himself to look at Kane. "Please never say that again."

Kane mimicked a growl. Elijah shook his head at his friend before he made his way to where Hannah was waiting for him. He placed a hand on her shoulder.

"My parents are here. I think I'm gonna throw up."

Hannah laughed more loudly than she should have and then

stopped herself. "I'll wear it right above the knee so this doesn't get too awkward."

"I owe you one."

As he crouched on his knees in front of her, his fingers shyly ghosted on the skin of her legs. Elijah moved his eyes to Hannah and then felt a flush of embarrassment, so he trained his eyes on her shoes, not daring to look out into the crowd that expectantly stared at them. His cheeks were nearly as red as his hair, but he was relieved once it was over. The crowd cheered once the garter was in his hands and off Hannah's leg. He helped Hannah up from the chair, feeling terribly stiff in the shoulders as he did.

"You know," he whispered to her, as they returned to their seats to drop off the bouquet and garter, "that's kinda creepy, if you think about it."

Hannah just laughed at him again. "It is quite the show, isn't it?"

A romantic slow song came on after that, with the DJ encouraging everyone to grab their loved ones to dance close. Elijah offered his hand to Hannah, and they returned to the dance floor, just happy to not have all eyes on them for the moment. Neither of them was convinced that nothing would happen as the night grew closer to its end, but they decided to enjoy the moment while they could. Elijah treasured the opportunity to hold Hannah close as they swayed to the slow song, feeling as if it were only the two of them as they danced; anything would feel more private after that public display of intimacy.

Despite everything, Hannah allowed herself to feel secure in Elijah's arms as they slow-danced. Her head rested comfortably against his chest with how much taller he was than her, even in high heels.

"It's been one hell of a ride, huh?" Elijah said, as if he could read Hannah's mind. Hannah thought that at this point in their relation-ship, they must have somehow been sharing a handful of brain cells.

"Yeah, this last year has certainly been something. Not to get too sappy or anything, but I'm really glad I met you."

Elijah could feel his heart rate quicken and wondered if Hannah could hear it over the music. He mentally reminded himself to keep his pace slow, so he tried to tune in to nothing but the rhythm of the song and her voice to steady himself. "Really?"

Hannah nodded. "My time here could have been very different. We've had our ups and downs, but I'm grateful for you."

Elijah's eyebrows raised as his jaw slightly slackened; he was unsure of what else to say. He moved one of his hands to gently cup her jaw, then stopped to capture her lips in his, not caring if they missed a moment they shouldn't. It was a risk, sure, but it wasn't anything he couldn't calculate. He felt like this moment was too good to be true and that the shoe would drop at any second, but maybe, just maybe, Reiji would make sure nothing spoiled his daughter's day. Maybe, Elijah hoped, that luck truly was on his side for once.

Their kiss was only interrupted by the change of music from the DJ. "Gangnam Style," despite being a tad outdated now, played.

"Remind me to tell you something later," Hannah said. That smirk of hers that he had grown to know and love graced her face, like she had some big secret that he didn't know about. Before he could ask what it was right then and there, Brad and Kane came over to Elijah, each with a beer in tow. Their free hands found their way to Elijah's shoulders.

"Come on, dude!" Brad's speech was not quite slurred, but his inhibitions were on their way out the door.

Elijah glanced at Hannah, but she winked at him and patted his chest. "I gotta pee anyway. Tear it up." Hannah waved her fist in a small circle above her head like the dance on her way out of the ballroom. Amy stepped in stride with her.

"Mind if I join you in the bathroom?" Hannah glanced over Amy's shoulder and saw that Shawn wasn't too far behind her. Amy continued, "I need help with my dress. These straps are a total pain in the ass."

"I don't mind at all." The straps on Amy's gown looked simple enough, crossing once in the back. "They look it, but worth it. I can't get over this color on you."

"Thank you." Amy's whisper had been barely audible over the Korean music bumping through the speakers, but the sound was nearly muted the moment Hannah and Amy went to the bathroom.

Hannah didn't realize how loud it had been until the door closed behind them. The bathroom lights made her wince from how bright they were compared to the dim lighting of the ballroom.

"Oh my God, he's driving me fucking crazy," Amy said the moment the door closed. She leaned against the bathroom sink as Hannah made her way into a stall. Her words lacked enunciation, the wine relaxing her enough to open up. "I don't even know what to do anymore."

Once Hannah joined her at the sink and washed her hands, she used the opportunity to dab her nose and forehead with a tissue to reduce oil without messing up her makeup. "Do you need a ride home?"

"No, no." Amy sighed. "It's like whiplash. When we first got together, he was so doting and sweet. Now I can't do anything right. God, it's fucking warm in here."

As Amy shrugged her shawl off, Hannah's eyes darted to Amy's arm. The freckles on Amy's face trailed down her shoulders and arms, but a bright green-and-yellow blemish popped against the pale skin.

"Did he give you that bruise?"

"Oh, this? It's like a week old now. Says he doesn't know his own strength, but I'm calling bullshit on that."

Hannah frowned and held her hand out, palm facing the ceiling. "Give me your phone."

"What?"

"Just give me your phone. You have it with you, right?"

Amy nodded and reached into her bra, where she had kept her phone tucked away. "Here. Why?"

"I'm putting my number in here. You need *anything*, you let me know right away, alright?"

Amy tried to smile, but it looked more like a thin line as her lips retreated into her mouth. "Thanks."

"I know it can be scary walking away from toxic people," Hannah said. "It sucks. So when you're ready, you just call me."

"I appreciate it."

"Don't even mention it."

"Come on, we should head back before people wonder what's taking us so long," Amy said.

"Yeah, you're right." Hannah opened the door, eager to rejoin the party, but stopped once the additional source of light from the bathroom illuminated the hallway. Something caught their peripheral vision, so she turned to see what she spotted in the window, still on high alert. The door slowly swung closed behind her as Hannah approached the window, unsure of what she'd find.

"You good?"

"Yeah, yeah. Go ahead, I'll be right there. Thought I saw something, but it's probably nothing."

Sure enough, there was a foot sticking up from the ground. When she was close enough, she saw the rest of the body that it belonged to. Hannah immediately put her hand over her mouth to prevent herself from screaming. A string of profanities escaped her lips, muffled against her palm.

Outside the window was none other than Reiji Sato. He was on the ground, looking paler than usual, with blood pouring out from a stab wound in his chest.

CHAPTER 22

Hannah ran down the hallway, her heels being the only noise until she reached the reception hall. She surveyed the room and pushed through the crowd until she spotted Elijah, his curls standing tall among the sea of people.

"Hey! There you are!" Elijah exclaimed as she joined him on the dance floor. He was dancing with Brad while Naomi danced with Rory. His smile turned into a frown the moment he saw her face. "Hannah? What's wrong? You look like you saw a ghost."

"Everything okay?" Brad asked.

"I'm stealing your best man," Hannah said. "When this song ends, go kiss your wife. Kiss her so hard you think you're going to bruise your mouth. Do you understand me?"

"What?" Brad's brows furrowed, forming a deep crease between them.

"Kiss your wife. Kiss her for so long that the crowd cheers." Hannah grabbed Elijah's hand. "Come with me. I need help."

Elijah let Hannah guide him through the reception hall, the two of them weaving through the tables where only a few people still picked at dinner. Hannah grabbed a random glass and knife to clank it, getting the few others who were seated to do the same to urge Brad and Naomi to kiss. As they passed, they saw Kane at the bar, just about to grab a drink for himself and Rory, but Hannah used her free hand to grab his arm and drag him along with them. Kane exhaled in surprise at the sudden jerkiness but followed along, quick to pick up that something was amiss.

Once they were in the lobby, Elijah asked, "What's going on?"

"I'm gonna call 911 in a second. But I need you both to help me make sure that no matter what happens, Naomi or her family do not come this way. I don't care how bad they have to pee."

"What the hell happened?"

Hannah looked around and stopped once they reached the top of the hallway where the bathrooms were. "It's Naomi's dad. He's dead."

Elijah blinked. "What?"

"God, just saying it makes me think I'm gonna be sick. Someone killed him. I saw him outside through the window. Looks like someone stabbed him in the heart."

"Holy shit," Elijah said. "For real?"

Hannah nodded as she grabbed her phone from her skirt pocket. "I'm gonna call for help. I just don't want Naomi or her mom to see this. It's … it's bad."

"Fuck," Kane said with a deep exhale.

"People are gonna think it was Hematite if this all gets out," Elijah realized.

"That's why I brought you too, Kane," Hannah said. "You needed to know."

Kane looked like he was lost in thought as he mulled over the impossible decision he had to make: stay or get suited and leave. "Who the hell would kill him?"

"Someone who wants power and someone who wants Hematite gone for good," Elijah said. "This was a setup."

"They are probably going to question everyone here," Hannah said. "Whoever did this must know that Hematite is here."

"What do you mean?" Kane asked.

"Well, look at the position you're in," Hannah said. "Both you and Hematite can't have an alibi, right? And if you just mysteriously dip out of here, it's gonna look really weird."

"I can figure something out," Elijah said. He placed a hand on Kane's shoulder. "Go back to get Rory that drink. Take her, Brad, and Naomi aside to tell them what happened, and once the police get here, we can offer to help bring the Sato family home. Got it?"

Kane nodded. "Right. Once we're out of here, I can get changed. I brought my suit just in case."

"We can figure something out. I'm not sure how yet, but we'll make something work. Go. I'll help Hannah."

With a nod, Kane left.

Elijah sighed and muttered, "I'm gonna have my work cut out for me later, that's for sure." He brushed some loose strands of hair behind Hannah's ear. "You okay?"

Hannah shook her head. "I'm barely keeping it together. That was the last thing I was expecting to see when I left the bathroom." She reached into her pants pocket, her hands shaking as she grabbed her phone. Elijah wrapped an arm around her and used it to pull her closer to him.

"I'm here, okay? You're okay."

As Hannah dialed 911, she glanced up at him. He offered her a smile, and his eyes looked as steady as ever, but she could tell from the tightness in his jaw that he was doing his best to keep his composure too.

As Hannah rattled off the information to the 911 dispatcher, the faint sound of music coming from the reception hall came to a stop. The silence that commenced caught Elijah's attention as he gently ran his fingers over Hannah's shoulder, trying to comfort her as the world stopped around them. As he looked back down at her, he noticed a few stray tears fall out of the corners of her eyes. He reached for the handkerchief in his suit jacket pocket so he could quickly dab them away for her. Some of her eye makeup was smeared, leaving a hint of a gray streak where the tears fell.

"Thanks. They said to stay here and that they're on their way."

The only sound that followed was that of a few heels clicking down the tile halls. It was Naomi, holding up the skirt of her wedding gown, walking side by side with her mother. Even from across the hall, Elijah and Hannah could both see the tension in their faces. Brad,

Rory, and Kane were right behind them, encouraging them to slow down.

They only stopped when they reached Hannah and Elijah. Naomi's mother's words were biting, her anger misplaced. "What happened?"

"Unfortunately, I don't know. I'm just the one who saw him when I was coming out of the bathroom. I'm so sorry."

"This can't be true," Naomi said. "Please tell me this isn't true."

Naomi met Hannah's eyes and saw her tear-stained cheeks. Hannah couldn't stop her lip from quivering. "I'm so sorry," she repeated. "Please, don't go down there. You shouldn't have to see."

Kane and Rory joined Hannah and Elijah, forming a barricade to prevent anyone from storming through. Naomi's mother tried to push past, but Rory was the one to stop her with a gentle, familiar hand.

"Mrs. Sato, I don't think you should see this," Rory said. Her voice was soft, as if she couldn't quite believe it either and was stuck in a nightmarish trance. "Help is on the way, okay?"

But she pushed through anyhow, not letting anyone stop her until she reached the end of the hall by the window. The wail she released upon seeing her husband's corpse was loud enough for all of Aspen to hear, ringing in everyone's ears as most of the guests moved out into the hallway. The sound of her cries as she collapsed to her knees nearly drowned out that of the police sirens as they came blaring up the road.

———

As Rory paced the hotel room on the phone, Naomi slid down the wall until she fell to the floor. The skirt of her gown made a poof sound as it billowed around her. Hannah sat beside her, careful to not sit on the skirt out of fear of tearing the delicate fabric. Naomi reached over and grabbed one of Hannah's hands.

"Thank you, by the way."

The two women looked at each other.

Naomi continued. "You handled that really well. I appreciate that." She swallowed and then said, "First dead body?"

Hannah blinked. "What?"

"Was this your first time seeing a dead body?"

Hannah shrugged. "Second, if you count a severed hand."

"Ah, that's right. You found that girl with Elijah. You know what's really fucked up?" Naomi was looking at Hannah still, but her gaze almost seemed like it was elsewhere. "I've seen maybe a dozen or so for work. So, when I see my own father like that? I'm just ... I'm numb." A sound escaped past Naomi's lips. Hannah couldn't tell if it was a chuckle or a sob. "I should cry like my mother, not feel completely desensitized."

"There's no right way to process something like this. You should do whatever comes naturally. Be kind to yourself."

Naomi nodded. "Yeah, you're right." There were no hints of tears to come. "I'm sure it'll hit me later. When I'm at work, it usually does. You know, everyone thinks I live this glamorous life. I'm sure you get it."

Hannah nodded. "You got that right." She didn't add much else to let Naomi say her piece.

"Do you know how many people email me at work asking who my makeup artist is? Half the time it's complimenting them, even though it's me, and the other half is telling me I look like Bozo the clown and that I should fire them. I work fucked-up hours, I see fucked-up shit, and this is what I get for it. Makeup insults and just complete numbness." Naomi sighed. "I should call Marissa."

"Marissa?"

"My therapist. Rory sees her too."

"Do you have her card?"

"I can text you her info later, yeah."

"Thanks."

"Sorry for dumping that on you."

"You don't have to apologize for a single thing today," Hannah said. "I know we haven't known each other long, but for what it's worth, I like you a lot. I'm here for you."

That made Naomi smile for a moment. "Thanks. I wonder if my mom knew. I don't think my grandmother did. But my mom..." Her voice trailed off as she pondered the idea, her gaze now looking somewhere distant. "Even if he didn't tell her, she's so sharp, you know?"

"Do you think you'll ask her?"

Naomi shook her head. "I dunno. At least not anytime soon. How can I without exposing myself?"

Hannah blew a raspberry. "Fair point."

Rory crossed the hotel room to join them, phone still in hand. "We're clear to go home. This place is effectively a crime scene. Brad, Kane, and Elijah are on their way up."

Naomi sighed in relief. "Thank God."

Hannah stood and offered Naomi a hand so she could join her. It was difficult with her dress, but she managed.

"Brad's going to grab your mom and grandmother on your way out so I can sneak Kane out of here," Rory said. She had so many questions she wanted to ask, but now was far from the appropriate time. "We'll figure it all out later."

Naomi nodded. She still felt incredibly hollow; it showed in the way she carried herself with slouched shoulders and glazed-over eyes. It was impacting her more than she realized at that moment, the physical response kicking in before the mental.

Brad didn't hesitate to pull Naomi in for a tight embrace the moment he arrived. Elijah and Kane weren't far behind him but couldn't make their way into the room where Brad was holding her; the skirt of Naomi's gown took up what was left of the doorway. The moment she was in Brad's arms, the tears started freely flowing. His grip on her body tightened before he pulled away to wipe her tears. They said nothing to one another but moved in a sort of rhythm that only a couple who had been together as long as they had could fall into.

After a moment, Brad broke the silence. "Come on. Let's get your mom and grandma, okay?"

Naomi just nodded, incapable of words now. The reality sunk in now that the shock had worn off.

Rory and Kane gave each other a nod as they followed suit, heading down to the stairs at the other end of the hallway instead of toward the elevators. Elijah and Hannah met each other halfway in the room, alone now.

"Silver lining on this grey cloud was that I knew one of the cops from my childhood summer camp, so I was able to sweet-talk him a bit." Elijah sighed. "We should wait a moment. It'll look weird if we all bail at the same time, especially if Rory and Kane are trying to sneak away."

Hannah nodded. "Do they know who did it?"

Elijah shook his head. "No clue. I'm gonna be honest ... I don't know if Kane is going to pull this off. Riverpeak's not exactly close, and it's not like Denver is much better either."

"He's never killed anybody though, right? Isn't that, like, his whole thing?"

"It would thrill enough people to believe that this happened that it wouldn't matter," Elijah said. "Mark Stevens might have been a complete idiot, but he had quite the following online. I don't know how many of them were actually from Colorado, let alone Riverpeak, but he'd get at least a few thousand views whenever he'd upload something."

Hannah finally asked the question she'd been thinking since she found Reiji's body. "Do you think it was Noah?"

"Fuck." Elijah ran a hand over his face. "I don't know. The Noah I knew wouldn't have it in him, but it's hard to say."

"Does this place have security cameras?"

"The cops are going to want those," Elijah said.

"Any way *you* can get them first?"

"What are you suggesting?"

"I'm a niche micro-celebrity and the one who found the body. Makes for a decent distraction to slip into a security office, no?"

A smile slowly crept onto Elijah's face as he pulled Hannah in for a quick kiss. "You're brilliant, you know that?"

She grinned. "Yeah, I know. We'll go out the main way so I can run into an officer and offer to help."

"Where have you been all my life?"

She grabbed two bobby pins out of her hair. "On my way, I think. Here, you'll need this if the door is locked. You ever lock-picked before?"

He shook his head.

"Okay, crash course time." Hannah adjusted the pins so that way, they were ready for Elijah to use. "You'll use this one like it's a sort of lever that gets held like you would a key. Then this one is what you'll use to feel around the pins."

"It sounds like you've done this a few times."

Hannah shrugged. "My friends and I were stupid in college. You learn how to do this pretty quick when you have a habit of locking yourself out of your dorm."

His smile only grew, but he wiped it off his face by the time they made their way back to the venue. As they returned to the lobby, it didn't take long for Elijah to spot the security office. He and Hannah looked at each other before splitting up, Elijah heading toward the back wall as Hannah approached a few officers standing by. Through the window, Hannah could see that Reiji's body was already covered with a sheet, where some of the blood stained the area over his chest.

"Um, excuse me?" Hannah said. The two officers turned to her. "I know you gave us the okay to go home, but I just wanted to make sure there wasn't any other way I could help."

Hannah positioned herself perfectly. All the officers now had their backs to Elijah, so he could sneak down the hallway toward the security office. He peered in each of the windows, coming up with excuses for why he was there in his head just in case he ran into anybody. He found no one. The security office door had frosted glass on the front, but no light was coming from behind it or through the space between the door and its frame.

He took a deep breath as he picked the lock of the door with the hairpins Hannah gave him. There was still a chance that someone was inside, but it seemed unlikely. It took him a few tries, and he kept checking over his shoulder to make sure no one was coming, but he turned the knob. He hesitated, knowing that if he got arrested, he probably couldn't get one of his friends to afford his bail, but then took the leap.

When no one else was in there, he sighed in relief and rushed to close the door behind him. He didn't dare to turn the light on, instead heading straight for the computer. He needed to guess the password protection, and without his usual gear at home, he'd have to rely on only his own smarts so he used the light of his phone to scan the room for clues. Hannah could only hold a conversation with the cops for so long before things seemed suspicious, so he knew his time was limited.

"Alright," he said to himself. "Big brain time."

Elijah spotted a few things that could be of use. On the desk, there was a photo of a family in a small frame taken at a child's birthday party. There was another picture of a golden retriever next to the family photo. Children, spouses, and pets were common passwords, so he knew he was in luck if he could figure out what their names were. Elijah did another quick scan of the room and found a criminal justice degree hanging on the wall. He opened a private browser on his phone and then started looking up her name in the browser, hoping a LinkedIn or Facebook profile would show up.

The correct Facebook profile was the first result. It was undoubtedly hers, since the profile photo was the same as the one framed on her desk. Her page was mostly private, but he scrolled through the old profile pictures to see if he could find any hints in the captions. Luckily, she mentioned her children's names in one of them, and a friend had commented on a photo of their dog mentioning his name too. He kept scrolling, hoping for anything else, and grinned when he hit a photo taken from her kid's birthday. From the looks of it, they were twins, and she had uploaded the photo on their actual birthday last year.

Elijah started by using a combination of the birthday numbers with the dog's name. On his third attempt, the screen opened up to her desktop: it worked. He poked around to find the security camera feeds and pulled up the ones from that evening. He rapidly clicked through, trying to find the feeds from outside, and found one pointing toward the front door. Hoping for a better angle, he opened those feeds in a new tab and then kept clicking through until he found two others that could be promising.

In one, he caught a glimpse of a figure approaching, wearing all black. They wore baggy black pants, a black hoodie with the hood pulled up, and a black face mask. The perpetrator didn't look like Hematite, but they were seemingly trying to emulate his appearance. Elijah had nothing to save the tapes on, so he started recording the screen on his phone so he could save a copy without leaving any trace that he'd been there. He contemplated deleting them outright but figured it would ultimately look too suspicious. Then, Elijah popped through to make sure no one could see him break into the office, deleted any incriminating evidence from both the software and its trash bins, and temporarily disabled the cameras in his path for just long enough to sneak back out of there. It would simply look like it glitched out.

On his way out, he detoured into the reception hall. His wireless cameras were exactly where he'd left them, hidden among the centerpieces. He snatched the thumbnail-sized cameras, shoved them in his pocket, and then made his way back to Hannah.

When he returned, Hannah was still chatting with the two officers. At a glance, it almost looked like they were old friends. One of the two looked a bit more bored than the other, who was soaking up every word that Hannah had to say. She saw him in her peripheral and gave a slight nod, so subtle that it looked like it was part of the conversation she was in, but enough for Elijah to understand. He made his way back down the hallway, waiting for her to wrap it up and move on. She wasn't much longer before she joined him.

"That was easier than I thought. Their cousin owns a local bookstore up here. I think I accidentally just signed myself up for a meet-and-greet. Got everything you need?"

"As good as I could get, yeah. Grabbed my cameras that we hid too. I couldn't see their face, but they definitely modeled their style after Hematite's typical look, that's for sure. I'll show you in the car, but we should call Kane and Rory on the way."

"I'm impressed. You pulled that off pretty quickly, all things considered."

He flashed her a smile. "Thanks. I appreciate the bobby pin tip; it came in handy."

"Hey, I'm just glad me and my friends being certified dumbasses in college came in handy."

"What we need to do is make it look like Hematite was somewhere else. I'm not sure how we're going to do that. Maybe a fake report?"

"That could work. Even if he doesn't show up on a camera for a while, at least there'd be someone verbally saying they saw him."

Wasting no time as they made their way back to Riverpeak, Elijah dialed Kane's number the moment they were in the car. Kane was quick to answer.

"You guys outta there?"

"Yeah. Hannah and I have a potential plan. Do you?"

"We've bounced a few ideas around."

Rory chimed in. "What's yours? We'll start there."

"Hannah helped me sneak into the security office. I filmed the camera footage on my phone from the moments leading to Reiji's death. You can't totally see the guy, but Hannah and I think it could be Noah. He tried to dress like you, so I thought maybe a fake report of a Hematite sighting could be beneficial. We're three, four hours out from all your usual spots, so no way we'd get you somewhere in time."

"Say something about me being on the east side of town. That's the most believable. It'll be a few hours, but me being out until two, three in the morning isn't totally out of the ordinary," Kane said. "We can make it work."

"What about GPS and stuff? Isn't that trackable if we call something in?" Hannah asked.

"That's what I'm here for," Elijah said. "I'll talk you through the best steps. Calling it in won't be the way to go. We'll want to post something somewhere online on a fake account."

"Oh! I know," Hannah said. "I've got it. Leave it to me, guys."

"Keep us posted," Kane said. "We'll let you know when we're in Riverpeak."

"Sounds good, dude," Elijah said. "Drive safe." Once they hung up, Hannah started making a call. "Who are you calling at this hour?"

But the other end picked up before she could answer him. "Michele! Oh, thank God you have a fucked-up sleep schedule. Listen, I need you to do me a major favor."

"What's up?"

"Promise you won't ask any questions?"

"...I guess?"

"Can you create a fake Nextdoor account? Pick a random street in Riverpeak. I'll send you my address in case you want to just use that to grab a neighborhood. Long story short, a friend of mine was just framed for murder. The guy who did it knows we're all out of town, so I can't just go on Nextdoor and hook him up with an alibi myself."

"Holy shit. But yeah, of course. I got you."

"You are the best! I'll send you everything now and what to say. Thank you, thank you! I owe you!" Hannah smiled when she hung up. "Bingo."

"Just tell her to sign up on her computer and to use a VPN if she can," Elijah said. "No one can trace back the location if shit hits the fan."

"Got it. Michele's trustworthy, don't worry. She doesn't know Kane's identity or anything, but we can count on her for this."

"I swear, you always pull through," Elijah said. "Thank you."

CHAPTER 23

I t couldn't have been a worse day for a funeral.

The wind whipped as snow threatened to fall for the second time that day, causing Hannah to button her black pea coat shut in hopes of some reprieve. Her scarf wasn't providing much protection either, and the cold nipped at her skin until it felt numb. She could only assume that Reiji would call one of the mausoleums home, given how hard the earth felt beneath her feet—though her seldom-worn dress shoes probably weren't helping.

"Thought we'd never find a place to park," Elijah said. His ears were a bit pink from the cold biting at them without his usual beanie to hide his head, left at home to show some respect for the dead. The lot was near full, its only saving grace being the large, grassy field directly beside it.

"Me neither. You ready for this?"

"As ready as I can be. It feels weird, I dunno. I'm sure you get it."

"No, I know. It is weird."

Elijah was grateful for that; Hannah always seemed to read perfectly between the lines. It felt bizarre heading into the funeral knowing everything that transpired when most of the guests were without a clue. They couldn't help but wonder who would be in attendance.

"At least he'll have a pretty resting place," Elijah said, trying desperately to find a positive spin for the sake of his own sanity. He wasn't wrong. The mountains created a perfect backdrop behind the funeral parlor and cemetery behind it, and while the trees were all devoid of their leaves now, it was easy to imagine how lovely it would look in the spring and summer.

"Do you think Noah will show up?"

"I'm not sure. Reiji will draw a crowd, and I think they made this public on purpose. When it's this high profile, I doubt he'll show face."

"Eh, true. I wonder if Naomi ever found out if her mom knew what was up."

"I don't think so. I haven't heard anything from Kane or Rory, and they would have told me."

The Satos had a private event earlier in the day for just the remaining family members in town, but now the doors were wide open. Hannah and Elijah could barely move through the building, immediately feeling the stiffness of body heat when the door closed behind them. They squeezed their way over to the table with the guest book, which was surrounded by two small vases of dark-colored flowers and fake candles. It was all set on top of an ornate runner to set the mood, though the mustard yellow wallpaper made everything feel cheap. Reiji's name was written in a frame in cursive that stood behind the guest book, waiting to be signed as an act of finality. As Hannah passed the pen to Elijah, she spotted Kane and Rory in the crowd. Rory saw them first.

"You guys just get here too?"

"Yeah. Didn't think there'd be such a big turnout," Elijah said. "I knew Reiji was popular, but wow."

"I'm hoping we can weasel our way in there soon," Rory said with a frown. "Naomi's been texting me from her smartwatch. From what I can make out through the typos, she really needs a break. I hope I can steal her away."

"We can go through with you," Hannah said. "Strength in numbers."

Elijah turned to Kane. "Everything good, dude?"

"So far, at least. It's so crowded in here that I don't think anyone could pull a fast one." He patted Elijah on the shoulder. "We're fine, man. Try not to sweat it today, okay?"

The four of them felt like they were stuck swimming upstream as they moved through the lobby, but thankfully, a few people recognized them from the wedding. They gave them the occasional place to cut through the unintentional barricade before they eventually hit another tight squeeze that required nothing faster than a slow shuffle. If the halls were crowded, the viewing room was even more condensed, and the worn-down blue pews didn't help. They were sure that a third of the crowd knew Reiji professionally and another third knew him illegally, but from a quick glance around the packed room, everyone seemed to be on their best behavior.

"Watch your step on your left," Elijah warned. "Photos and flowers. Kind of hard to see through the crowd."

"I can't see it at all from down here, so thank you, giant man," Hannah whispered back. "Oh shit, I should watch my mouth. I forget not everyone copes through humor."

He chuckled. "You're fine, *h'aim sheli*."

Hannah's head snapped toward Elijah. "*H'aim sheli*? This is new."

"Oh. Uh, it just kinda rolled off the tongue."

"At a funeral?"

Elijah shrugged his shoulders. "First for everything."

"I mean, I like it. Just threw me for a loop."

Elijah offered her a smile, so small that only she could see it, as if it were a secret between them. Before they knew it, they were at the front by the casket, where the Satos stood near the body. The smell of the flowers only partially covered the scent of embalming fluid that the entire building faintly reeked of.

"Oh, thank goodness it's a closed casket. I still have nightmares about what he looked like. I don't think I could stomach seeing him again after that."

"I bet." Elijah placed his hand between her shoulder blades. "If anyone asks you anything weird, just walk away, okay? I got your back."

"Thanks. I can't even imagine how Naomi is handling all this."

"Me neither." Elijah took one last look at the casket. "Well, may his memory be a blessing."

As Hannah looked around, she felt more tethered to the surrounding people than she did to her own blood, despite all the strangers filling in the gaps. Just as Hannah wondered if she truly was the heartless monster her mother always claimed her to be, she shook it off. If her mother had been right, then she wouldn't feel the sympathy she did for Naomi and her family—even Reiji himself, despite his involvement.

The realization dawned on her when it was their turn in the lineup. She hadn't even thought of her mother in months. The only exception was when prompted with a question about family, notably when Kane reaffirmed her decision with his own life experiences. Her eyes trailed up to follow Naomi's movements, as Rory pulled her in for a tight hug and shared a memory of her father. It snapped Hannah out of her own train of thought, bringing her back to the moment.

"I should have known," Naomi said. She was speaking softly so her mother beside her couldn't hear. Hannah and Elijah barely could over the soft piano music playing over the speakers. "I'll never forget how weird he was acting when we were setting up the butsudan for Noah. Mom and I were bawling our eyes out, and my dad was just silent. We thought it was just his own way of grieving, but … he knew. I should have guessed."

"There's nothing you could have done," Rory reassured her. "He loved you so much, Naomi. That's all that matters at the end of the day."

"Can you run to the bathroom with me?"

"Yeah, come on." Rory gave Naomi's mom a hug, and then let her know that she'd be right back with her daughter. Kane, Elijah, Brad, and Hannah blocked the path in front so she could sneak away uninterrupted from the other side of the room. Once she was gone, they made their way down the procession line without incident.

"I overheard some people talking," Kane said. "Seems like no one's really sure if that vigilante was up to this or not."

"I saw on the news that he was in Riverpeak that night," Hannah said to play along. "So, there's no way. Right?"

"Lots of rumors, anyway." Kane shrugged.

"I hope they catch the guy," Elijah said. "I wonder if they'll find out why."

"I'm sure the cops are looking into it." Kane winked at Elijah, hinting that he was working with McMahon on this or about to be. "They'll get the answers they need, eventually. Always do in a small town like this."

It wasn't long before Naomi and Rory returned. Naomi's makeup looked fresh, though her eyes were still red and puffy from all the crying. Brad reached an arm out to bring her close to his side.

"There's a room in the back that we can duck into. Can we head that way?"

"Of course. Come on, hon," Brad said. "Let's go, guys."

Naomi looked at her mother and received a nod in response. As they stepped away, they saw a man making his way out of the room, who fell in step with them.

"Naomi Sato, right? I'm so sorry for your loss," he said. His silver hair was slicked back, and his coat reached his knees. Based on his cufflinks, he knew Reiji professionally somehow, but he seemed far too young to be a business associate.

Hannah recognized him right away. Her heart felt caught in her throat, but she knew she couldn't do or say anything right now. Now was not the time or the place, despite this being Sterling's obvious flex.

"Thank you," Naomi said. She didn't stop walking. "Have we met?"

"I don't believe so, but your father always spoke so highly of you. He and my father both worked in the restaurant industry. Sterling Harrison." He held out a hand.

"Oh." Naomi shook his hand. "Well, thank you for coming, Sterling."

"Of course. Mr. Sato taught me a lot over the years about entrepreneurship. He was a good man." He continued his path toward the exit. "Take care, now."

As they went into the small room reserved for the family, Naomi released a groan. "Who the hell was that?"

"I see we're all thinking the same thing," Kane said. "Naomi, don't worry about it for now. It's the last thing you need."

"Was that a threat?" Her eyes went wide.

"Hey, hey." Rory approached her and held her face. "Deep breaths. With me, okay?"

As the two took a few together, Hannah and Elijah shared a glance with Brad and Kane.

Kane said what they were all thinking. "That's our guy."

"He didn't look much older than us." Elijah caught himself about to chew on the inside of his lip.

"Do you know anything about him?"

"No, but I'm about to once I get back to my computer," Elijah said. "When one door closes, another opens."

"Wait, you know him?" Hannah asked. "Remember how I told you someone said you were using me?"

Elijah blinked. "Wait, what? That was him?"

"Yeah. How do you know him?"

Elijah recalled running from the South Main Burgers a few months back. "Do I have a story for you…"

———

The air seemed to bite outside, even for Noah. He thought that getting off the motorcycle would help, though it was just one of those miserable days where it was best spent indoors. But he had some business to attend to and wanted to take his new toy out for a spin; it was now or never.

He left the bike on the edge of the parking lot, which thankfully didn't arise any suspicion since it was so crowded. Instead of approaching the building, Noah made his way up a hill to stand by a tree overlooking the parlor. Before he could even have a moment to think for himself, he saw someone leave the funeral parlor and approach him. He felt an increased warmth in his chest as he tensed, shifting his weight so he could disembark but eased and fell back against the tree once he could more clearly make the man's silhouette out.

"I thought I might find you here."

Noah waved once he realized it was Sterling. Sterling looked sharp, largely thanks to the inheritance he received from his father's death. Noah couldn't even fathom how much the black coat he was wearing cost; he wished he could have asked Naomi which designer it was. She would have known.

"They bringing the old bastard out back now?"

"Oh, come on. Don't talk about Ray like that. He was a good partner." Sterling ran his hand through his already-graying hair, slicked back with gel that had long since dried. He fished a cigarette out of his jacket pocket. "Got a light?"

Noah laughed. "Good one. Want the lighter or a party trick?"

"I'll spare you. I'm sure it gets old."

"You can say that again."

Sterling held out the cigarette carton. "Want one?"

Noah accepted the offer, lit both of their cigarettes, and the two men took a drag in synchronization.

"You're not freezing your ass off out here?"

Noah shook his head. "I'm a human furnace these days. Maybe that'll be my superhero name when I face off against the great Hematite."

A laugh audibly bubbled up in Sterling's throat. "You didn't strike me as the type to use a call sign."

"You got that right. Shit's fucking stupid. The hell are we doing, playing Batman on the playground?" Noah took a quick puff of the cigarette. It was something he rarely enjoyed since acquiring his powers, but he figured his father's funeral was a special enough occasion. The tobacco tasted worse than he remembered, the bitterness lingering on his tongue.

"I met your sister just now."

Noah's back stiffened. "How's she doing?"

"She's a goddamn train wreck if I've ever seen one. Can't say I blame her, though." He took a drag. "Though I do agree with your assessment about her friends. Which one is that Kane Kelly fella you spoke of?"

"The blond. He checks all the boxes."

Sterling nodded. "Good to know. Are you in the headspace to talk shop for a few?"

Noah shrugged and kicked a nearby pebble. "Now's as good a time as ever."

"How old are you now, again? My age, right?"

"Yeah. Freshly thirty-two."

The piece of hair that Sterling pushed back already fell into his face again, covering his left eye in a stiff strip from the gel. His eyes were so dark that Noah could barely differentiate the difference between his pupils and irises. "At least one of us is aging gracefully."

"Oh, give me a break. Women see my arm and think I'm Leatherface or some shit. At least you can get hair dye if you're so insecure."

"Ha, fair point. I'm waiting to see if it grows on me. Maybe people will take me more seriously if I just let it go, you know?"

Noah nodded. He normally hated small talk, but he never minded entertaining Sterling. Their interactions had been few and far between over the years, but they always picked up right wherever they left off. "You always did have a total baby face."

"Listen, your dad was great with the guys. He managed the business really well on my behalf when I needed him to and kept up the front spectacularly. He and my father got along before the old man croaked, so I knew I could count on him. I was too young for this shit, y'know?"

Noah nodded along. "Now's your time to shine. Congratulations on your new solo career."

"No, not yet," Sterling corrected. "I want you to take over for now."

Noah looked away from the funeral parlor to gauge Sterling's expression. "Excuse me, what?"

Sterling bore a small smile that told Noah he wasn't joking. "I don't have shit for powers yet. You, however … you are a fucking marvel." Sterling took another drag of his cigarette, longer this time than the last. "I mean it. I'd love to get to your level, but God knows what power I'll be gifted with. Watch it, like, just give me a tail or something dumb."

They both laughed for a moment before Sterling became serious again.

"And I understand that transformation is rather uncomfortable."

Noah rolled his eyes. "Tch. That's putting it lightly."

"Take over. They all respect you. I can get on board with your vision, Noah. If you can pull this off, I think Riverpeak will be better than ever."

That caught Noah's attention. After years of wanting nothing more than to reintegrate into society, Noah was relieved to hear someone say they supported his plan. He knew, though, that Sterling wasn't doing this from the bottom of his heart and knew him well enough to know how analytical he was. "And let me guess: you need me to help you?"

"You're sharp. I've always liked that about you."

"Do I have much of a choice?"

"Of course you do. I'm smart enough to know that gunfire isn't anything compared to your literal fire. You could burn me to a crisp." Sterling nudged him with his elbow. "The power imbalance is more in your favor than you think, Noah. Don't worry."

"Oh, that I do know. Quality of life is a consideration too, though."

For starters, he wasn't sure what would become of the house now that his father was dead, but he was sure that wasn't something a little money couldn't fix. While the official inheritance would go to Naomi and his mother, Reiji left a safe behind in Noah's room at the house that he could access. Additionally, leading the crime ring wasn't the life he envisioned for himself. Ideally, he thought, everyone would be equal—and this was just perpetuating the very thing that made his blood boil.

"If you're worried about having a place to live, I bought the house. Don't worry, I won't be posting an eviction notice or anything like that."

"I appreciate that, but that was only one part of what I was thinking about."

Sterling furrowed his brows. "Are you not happy?"

Noah's head rolled back as he laughed. "Fuck no. You think I'm happy about any of this? But the way I see it, my options are to either take your offer or be on the run for the rest of my life. I don't think so."

"Congratulations on your promotion, then," Sterling said. He patted his free hand down on Noah's shoulder. "This is what you wanted, isn't it?"

Sterling winked at Noah and put out his cigarette in the snow, which crunched beneath his feet, as he made his way back to the funeral parlor. Noah watched after him before lighting out his own and then set the two on fire, leaving no trace of them behind beyond some mixed ash in a puddle of melted snow.

As Noah's eyes wandered over the building's exterior, he saw a black vehicle enter the parking lot. A man with red hair in his forties stepped out of it. Noah recognized him right away; McMahon wasn't there to pay his respects to Reiji, he wagered, but to see if Noah was there. Noah stepped away and once McMahon was inside, hopped back on his motorcycle to head home and figure out what his next move would be.

CHAPTER 24

lijah slumped back into his chair in his office. "Any luck from the third camera?"

Hannah shook her head. "Nope. I'm switching to camera five now. Any luck on your end?"

"Nothing at all." Elijah chewed on his bottom lip. After a few weeks, they still had no luck in finding the killer's face on camera. "How did we set up so many cameras and have a videographer at the wedding and not get a damn thing?"

"I mean, at least we stole the security footage."

"Yeah, but still. I mean … how is there nothing?"

"I think that was Noah's idea." Hannah paused the recording from the fifth hidden camera and turned to look at Elijah. "So, my amped-up empathy aside, I get the vibe that something else is bothering you. What's up?"

"You are not wrong." He spun in his chair so he could face her directly. "Your lease is up in, what, two or three months now?"

"Something like that."

"Are you renewing it?"

"No."

He frowned and before Hannah could elaborate, he said, "Then let me say this: I'm really, really going to miss you. But I love you, and I know we can make long-distance work. Guess I'll have to take you skiing before the season's up."

"Elijah, you can take me skiing whenever the hell you want."

He blinked at her. There was a hint of mischief in her eyes that matched her growing smirk he couldn't understand. Before she said anything else, Hannah kissed him with a gusto he wasn't expecting; it was as good of a response as he could have asked for. Elijah was taken by surprise but surrendered to the warm, gentle feeling of her lips on his. Everything about Hannah, at least to him, was gentle in that way, despite her free spirit. Elijah liked that she had that dichotomy about her.

When she pulled away, she cupped his face with her hands to force eye contact.

"Remember how I never got to tell you that little something-something at the wedding? This is it. I'm not renewing my lease because I bought the house."

"Oh. Oh!"

She laughed as the realization dawned on him, feeling the way the relief coursed through his veins.

"Oh, I feel like a moron. I shouldn't have cut you off. I'm sorry."

"It's fine. I won't lie; I enjoyed that little, sappy confession."

"Okay, now you're just embarrassing me."

"Teasing aside, I have a proposition for you."

"Only if it's also met with a sappy confession, so I feel less like an idiot."

"Okay, fair." Hannah pondered on it for a moment before she continued. "I used to spend way too much time caring about what other people think—people who I thought mattered but who ultimately didn't matter at all. Since moving here, I have never felt more mentally clear, and I know now that I have to live my life for myself," Hannah said. "It looked so perfect from the outside, but really, I was just so hollow until I moved here, and I met you. And I know that we have only known each other for about a year, but I was wondering if you would want to move in with me. Brad's already out, and your lease here is up at the end of the month, no?"

Elijah blinked at her a few times. His heart was beating faster than ever before. Even though he was completely still, he felt dizzy. "Are you serious right now?"

"More serious than ever. There's enough room for both of us to have a home office and everything. If I'm wrong in my feelings, then just say so. It's fine, but ... what do you say?"

Despite everything, the smile she gave him was crooked and nervous, unsure of what his answer might be.

"Hannah, I would love to," Elijah blurted, not worried about sounding too eager. A wave of relief washed over him: that she was staying, that he wasn't moving back into his childhood bedroom, over her admission of the impact he'd had on her. He never thought someone would feel like that because of him, but there she was, bearing it all.

Hannah's grin was infectious. "Good. You're stuck with me, space cowboy."

He rested his own hands on her cheeks to bring their lips together again. No matter how many times they kissed, it sent shockwaves down Hannah's spine. She felt a warmth in her heart from his words, wishing she could stay with him like this forever before she remembered that now she practically could.

———

Elijah moving in was a simple process. They consolidated most of their belongings and sold a good chunk of random items on Facebook Marketplace and Nextdoor along the way, since Brad and Naomi had gotten a ton of new appliances as wedding gifts. The walls became less sparse once it became their house, not just Hannah's. New photos joined older ones, some from Elijah's old space and others that were taken of them together at the wedding.

Now, the photographs were joined by balloons and a birthday banner from the surprise party Elijah put together for Hannah. As the clock struck midnight, Hannah looked around. Brad, Naomi, Rory, and Kane remained after everyone else left. A comfortable silence overtook them as they gathered in a circle in the living room. Elijah's arm dangled around Hannah's shoulders, keeping her warm as the temperature outside dipped before their heater could catch the memo.

"I'm surprised Jameson didn't come," Kane said. They were sitting around the coffee table, with Elijah and Hannah on the floor using the couch as a backrest, Kane and Rory behind them on the sofa, and Naomi and Brad sharing a large chair. Some party streamers and balloons were still strewn about, but much less meticulous than they were when they first arrived.

"I think he and Amy are fighting again," Naomi said with a sigh. "She called me crying this morning saying she couldn't make it. Said she wasn't feeling well and also claimed she wasn't crying, but I could hear her sniffles. It was pretty obvious that she didn't have a cold."

"When is she gonna break up with that asshole already?" Elijah asked. His legs stretched out in front of him and beneath the coffee table as Hannah sat between his legs, their go-to cuddle position. She was short enough that even when seated, Elijah could still see his friends in his field of vision over her head.

"I've been asking her that for years now."

"Same," Rory said. "He treats her like shit."

"He treats everyone like shit," Elijah said. "I hate how we can't shake him."

"I know you'd probably kill him if you legally could, Elijah," Brad piped in, "but he has been there for us when shit gets tough."

"Yeah, so he can hang it over our heads later." Elijah lifted a hand off the floor to lazily twirl his finger around some of Hannah's hair. "I vote we officially replace him in our circle with Hannah."

Rory nearly snorted with her laugh.

"Aren't you two sweet," Kane teased.

Rory's brows raised as she brought her drink to her lips. "I mean, he's got the right idea."

"It doesn't sound like the bar is very high, but thank you, I guess," Hannah said. "But I get it. I think a lot of people have that one friend."

"Who is it for you?" Naomi asked.

She shrugged. "Used to be this one girl, but I haven't talked to her since college. My friend circle's always been pretty small, come to think of it."

It was from a combination of being the only Jewish kid in her predominantly Roman- and Irish-Catholic neighborhood growing up and also her mother's strictness, but her friends in Riverpeak didn't need to know that. The mood already dropped at the mention of Shawn, and she didn't want to contribute to that any further.

"Well, consider it expanded," Rory declared. "Elijah, you did good. I like her. Especially a lot more than Shawn."

"You're just sucking up because you want to be in her next book," Kane said.

"I mean, hey, if that's the perk of having an author friend, then so be it!"

"Hey, Kane, I've been meaning to ask," Brad spoke up. "Did everything turn out okay? Or as okay as it can be, I guess."

He nodded. "Barely, but yeah, thanks to that Nextdoor post from Hannah's friend. I think we're in the clear."

"There are still people who wonder, though," Rory said. "There are a few theories going around in my classroom: if it was Hematite, if it was a copycat trying to frame him, if it was just totally random." Rory glanced at Naomi. "You alright?"

Naomi nodded. "I think I'm still too shocked to fully grasp everything. I'll be okay. We'll have a second to breathe, eventually."

As Brad kissed Naomi's head to comfort her, a knock at the door interrupted them. Hannah reached for her phone in her pocket to pull up the app for their security camera; Elijah looked over her shoulder to view the feed with her.

"No fucking way," Elijah said under his breath.

"Who is it?" Brad asked.

"Looks like Noah."

In that instant, Naomi stood. "I'm answering it."

"Are you sure that's a good idea?"

"He's my brother. I don't care if it's a good idea."

No one said anything else; Naomi would stop at nothing, nor did anyone feel it was their place to stop her. She opened the door with fervor, keeping one hand on the handle as she faced Noah.

It was undoubtedly him. Their faces were strikingly similar, with their plush lips and straight noses. Naomi looked her brother up and down, taking in the sight of him for the first time in six years. He wore a black bomber jacket, a white T-shirt, and black jeans to hide his skin, but she caught a glimpse of some burn marks creeping up near his neck. As he leaned against the door frame once it was open, Noah fidgeted with a lighter.

"Hey, sis. Thought I might find you here tonight."

———

Noah and Hematite face off in PLAY WITH FIRE.

PLAY WITH FIRE

RIVERPEAK HEROES
BOOK 3

JESSICA SALINA

To anyone who has been hurt and did not behave like the "perfect victim."
Give 'em hell.

CONTENT WARNINGS & DISCLAIMER

Play With Fire is a supervillain romance that features drug abuse, torture, murder, physical violence, and consensual sexual content. There are also references (but no on-page depictions) to past domestic assault and implied past sexual assault (not inflicted by the love interest; he would *never*).

If you or a loved one are in an abusive relationship, you can contact the National Domestic Violence Hotline by visiting TheHotline.org, calling 1-800-799-SAFE (7233), or texting START to 88788. It's free and confidential, 24/7.

CHAPTER 1

Since gaining the ability to manipulate fire, Noah loved nothing more than the feeling of the cold mountain air on his skin, especially during or after snowfall. In the distant skyline, the mountains were coated in white, their steep sides and pointed tips showing the promise of a winter wonderland. One of the side effects of Noah's power was he always ran a high temperature, and nothing soothed his permanent fever quite like an alpine night after a snowy day.

It was why he stole Mark Stevens's old Harley Davidson in the first place; it wasn't like Mark would be using it, since he got caught as Stone Breaker last year and wouldn't be leaving his jail cell any time soon. The feeling of the breeze on his face and the smell of pine that permeated Riverpeak, their small town in Colorado, almost made him forget about his powers.

Almost, anyway.

The burns on his arm and shoulder would never let him truly forget.

Those burns were the reason why Noah always wore a jacket, even though he wanted nothing more than to crack the ice on top of Constance's Pond and dive in to cool off. He hated them, not only how they looked but what they reminded him of. Covering them up allowed him to almost forget about them, plus they gave him a layer of anonymity that he once cared about.

He didn't care anymore, though. His father was dead, by his own hand at that, and he'd gotten away with it. But it didn't matter.

None of it mattered.

It was why he was driving to his sister's house on Mark Stevens's motorcycle in the first place.

What did it matter?

What the hell? Fuck it.

From the information that his boss, Sterling Harrison, had gathered, his sister Naomi and her friends were at Hannah Cohen's house —*Hannah Cohen and Elijah Baron's house now,* he reminded himself. Noah wasn't sure how Sterling always knew where everyone was, the whisper network spanning far larger than even Noah realized, but he was just glad that he was on Sterling's good side. He figured he had a permanent position on that list, given everything he'd been through, but that didn't stop him from only trusting Sterling about as far as he could throw him. After all, those burns he almost forgot about were there so Sterling wouldn't have to wear them.

Noah shook the thought from his head as he pulled into Hannah and Elijah's driveway. It was packed, but he was able to fit the bike in sideways on the end. No one was parked on the street, and he recognized all of the cars; it was everyone he hoped it would be. He saw his sister Naomi and her friend Rory's cars, so he wagered Brad and Kane were there too, but there was no sign of Shawn Jameson. *The majority of them will do,* he thought. *Shawn will find out soon enough through the grapevine.*

Noah bounded his way up the stairs and eyed the security camera as he knocked on the door. As he waited for a response, he pulled out his lighter and twirled it between his fingers, feeling bored with only the camera and a mezuzah to look at. After all, his boredom was why he was here in the first place, and he didn't need to hide anymore. No one was there to say no to him or tell him that he was wrong for paying his sister a visit. He had no intention of staying long but just wanted to say hello and pass along a little warning.

Their father might have been oblivious to who Hematite was, but with Noah's monotonous routine from being holed up in the house, he became observant. Paying attention to everything around him was the only thing he could do to stop himself from going completely off the deep end, though he suspected he already had a foot off the ledge anyway.

Naomi answered the door, to his delight. He'd been hoping for either her or Kane to answer, since he was positive that Kane was the one behind the Hematite moniker. Noah had been suspicious of Kane ever since Shatterstone's arrest; Mark and Dougie's obsession with Rory Miller made it easy for him to put the pieces together.

Naomi hadn't changed much in the last six and a half years since he saw her, save for the engagement and wedding bands on her left ring finger now. He leaned against the doorframe as he took in his sister's expression, reading her body language with ease as he continued to fidget with his lighter. She was tense and nervous, but hope glimmered behind her sad eyes.

He almost felt bad about squashing it.

Almost.

"Hey, sis. Thought I might find you here tonight."

———

As Naomi stared at her brother on the other side of the doorway, she felt frozen in time. It took everything in her body not to burst into tears, but she didn't want to break so easily. She wondered how Noah knew to find her here; she and her friends were still at Hannah and Elijah's house, which none of them shared online yet. Rory had a rule about not posting where she was until after events, not during, since being stalked—something all of them respected and followed for her sake.

But Noah's arrival turned the celebration sour. Hannah warned her before her wedding that Noah was dangerous now, that he was part of her father's string of secrets. However, Naomi saw her face in his own —and their recently deceased father's face—despite how much Noah had changed.

The Noah she once knew was a sweet boy in a sweater who carried psychology textbooks to their father's restaurant, trying to pick up whatever shifts he could to pay his own way instead of relying on their family's money. The Noah that Naomi remembered would carry her on his shoulders when she got tired after hiking through shrines, when they'd visit their grandparents overseas, and would be in bed by ten o'clock.

This Noah felt like a new man who happened to be wearing her brother's face. He'd been burned, literally and metaphorically, and it showed in the way he carried himself and the red skin creeping up his neck, past his shirt and undoubtedly beneath his jacket.

But that didn't stop him from being her brother.

"Noah?" Her free hand shook and the one holding the doorknob tightened, her knuckles going white from her death grip.

"In the flesh."

"How are you alive?" Naomi already knew the answer was tied up alongside forged documents in a web of lies, but it didn't mean seeing him really standing before her felt like any less of a gut punch.

"I don't know that I'd say I'm alive, per se." He scoffed. "Definitely more so than Dad, though."

Naomi shook her head, unsure of how to respond to his crass joke. The tears building up unleashed from her eyes, flowing freely down her face now that she'd heard his voice. She released her grip on the doorknob and wrapped her arms around his waist, face buried into his chest, as she held her brother for the first time in over six years. The warmth radiating off Noah's body was the only thing grounding her at the moment, reminding her that he was, in fact, alive. If she wasn't so choked up, she'd ask him if he was running a fever.

"You're home, Noah. You're home."

Noah placed his hands on Naomi's shoulders. His lighter remained between his middle and index finger. He allowed his sister a moment to weep and let it out of her system, not minding that her tears were staining his T-shirt.

"Naomi."

Noah used his hands on her shoulders to gently push her away from him. Naomi looked back to his face, still weeping, and met Noah's eyes.

His eyes, unlike the rest of his body, were cold.

"This isn't why I came here."

Naomi sniffled. "What?"

He lit up the lighter he'd been fidgeting with and kept his focus on the fire. Naomi's eyes widened, as its flame grew three times its size before he snapped it shut. It happened so quickly that she almost didn't have time to register it.

"I just wanted to pay my condolences." His speech was slow, each word holding an exorbitant amount of weight. He moved his gaze up from the lighter to his own sister's eyes. "It's too bad someone had to go and stab Daddy Dearest right in the heart."

Naomi took a step back. "Wait a minute. How did you know that? That wasn't public."

In the living room behind them, Kane shifted as if to stand from the sofa behind Hannah and Elijah, but Rory placed a hand on his thigh to ground him. If Noah was there playing with flames on a lighter and hinting at what they all thought he was implying, then he already knew Kane's secret.

Naomi wasn't sure why he was there at all; this was no family reunion.

Noah tutted his tongue. "A shame, really." His grin never left his face as he turned and walked away, leaving his sister in a daze. As he reached the road for the motorcycle, he pocketed his lighter. Naomi blankly watched him straddle the Harley Davidson, which he patted. "Pretty nice, huh?" he called up to Naomi, who was still standing in Elijah and Hannah's doorway. "I swiped it off of that Stevens brat after he got thrown in jail." He waved and, with no genuine sincerity, said, "*Goshuushousama desu*, little sis."

At that point, Brad stood up and crossed the living room to join Naomi, who was still staring down at the spot where Noah drove away. As he led her back into Elijah and Hannah's living room, Brad closed the door while she stood still. He slowly rubbed her back when he returned to her but knew that she was too shell-shocked to respond, still processing Noah's words.

"He has powers." Tears welled in her eyes and her lips quivered, but she seemed to refuse to cry. "What else was my father hiding from me?"

Kane and Elijah looked at each other.

"What did you see?" Kane asked.

"He was holding a lighter. The flame ... it was frickin' massive. That was a warning." She exhaled a shaky breath. "Hannah, can you toss me a pillow?"

Hannah reached behind her and did as Naomi requested. Naomi pressed her face into the pillow and, still standing, screamed into it. Her yell soon turned into full-on sobs, as her emotional dam continued to overflow. Brad just kept rubbing her back, hoping it would make her feel better. Hannah stood up from her spot to grab Naomi a fresh glass of water and some tissues.

It was muffled by the pillow, but Naomi asked, "Brad, did you know?"

Brad blinked in surprise. "About Noah?"

"Yeah. Did you know?"

"Only a little bit, but not the full extent. Your dad wanted to keep him a secret from me. I don't think he wanted you to know."

"I saw him, Naomi," Kane confessed. "He threw a lighter at me, and I nearly caught on fire within an instant. That's how fast it took over my cowl."

"We wasted a lot of time looking into Hannah when we shouldn't have," Elijah said. "I think Noah took advantage of that. We could have been better prepared to face him otherwise."

"I was paranoid as fuck," Kane said in agreement. "Sorry again, Hannah."

"This can't be real," Naomi said through her tears. She lifted her face from the pillow and hiccupped as she sat down on the floor. When Brad joined her there, she leaned into him, instinct taking over. "Hannah, can you..?"

"Yeah, I got you." Hannah offered Naomi a sad smile, as she settled back into her spot against Elijah's side. "I'm still practicing having more control, but you should start to feel a bit calmer soon." Hannah prepared herself to change Naomi's mood with her abilities.

"Thanks. How the hell did this happen?"

"Dr. Potter said the drugs he found in that girl's car were the strongest dosage he'd ever seen of anything, right?" Rory asked. Kane nodded. She continued, "I think your dad found a dosage that they can use on living people. Not just unborn babies."

"Yeah, but why would Noah want to spread that around?" Naomi asked. "That doesn't make any sense. Noah never thought like that; he wanted to help people. That's why he went to school for psychology. Nearly ruined his relationship with our parents over it. He had a rougher time of life than I did, and I think he wanted to fix other people's problems instead of his own." When she said it, her eyes widened as she answered her own question. "Oh. *Oh.*"

"Curse of the firstborn," Kane said. "That's what he told me once, many moons ago."

"Noah would want other people to feel empowered." Naomi blew her nose with a tissue from the box Hannah handed her. "But yet again, I'm pretty sure that the Noah I used to know is long gone. Maybe his methods of empowerment have become increasingly fucked up."

Everyone knew what Naomi wanted to say next, but she couldn't bring herself to say it. Noah's sarcasm had not been lost on anyone hearing their conversation from the other room when he spoke of his father's death. All of them received the message loud and clear: Noah Sato had the blood of three women and his father on his hands, and he likely was not stopping there.

"It'll be okay, Naomi," Kane said. He tried to sound reassuring and tried, but failed, to smile genuinely. "We'll take care of him."

"He's my brother. I should be the one to deal with him. If I can just talk some sense into him, maybe he'll listen to me. Has he said anything to you? Maybe when you were fighting?"

"No. I haven't been burned to a crisp before and didn't care to find out what would happen if I did. Just because I come back doesn't mean it doesn't hurt."

"We also don't know what he's going to do now that your dad's gone," Elijah said. "I want to watch him very closely from here on out. He's too unpredictable."

"Not to me he's not. Fucked up or not, I know my brother inside and out. Dad was devastated when Noah said he wanted to be a psychologist because he hoped Noah would take over South Main Burgers one day. Whatever our dad was after, Noah is probably going for the opposite."

"You don't need to theorize; I already know," Brad said, hinting at Naomi's father's side business. "Noah wants to mass distribute. Your dad was more subtle about things, but Noah asked for my help in getting him samples behind your dad's back. Something about helping people reach their full potential. 'Potential' meaning superpowers, I'm assuming."

Naomi turned to Kane. "I had a feeling. What are you gonna do now?"

"You have to keep going," Kane said. "He's on to us, but we need him at arm's length."

Brad frowned. "Should we run this by McMahon?"

Kane sighed. "Probably. I don't want you getting busted. I'll let him know that you're helping me with something and are going under-cover. That's all he needs to know."

"We need to find out who my brother is going after next," Naomi said. "We know he's targeting exclusively women."

"If he's showing up here, I think he's done testing," Kane said. "Noah's not playing around anymore."

"Should we follow him?" Hannah asked.

Kane shook his head. "I don't wanna give him a reason to be even more suspicious than he probably already is of me."

"Should I go check on all the security cameras in town?" Elijah offered. "If we all take a different monitor, then we can really check them all at once."

"I want to see where he goes," Naomi said. "How long does it take you to get set up?"

"Not long. Come on."

Everyone followed Elijah upstairs to his office. A few moving boxes still scattered the edges of the room, but he was mostly set up so he could work between unpacking. He hopped into his computer chair and opened all the security feeds as quickly as he could. His friends formed a semi-circle behind him, anxious to see what they would find on his screens.

"If anyone spots that bike, speak up."

It took a few minutes, but it was ultimately Naomi who spotted him. "There!" She pointed to the third monitor, and Elijah clicked into the feed.

The camera overlooked the full parking lot of a bar on the outskirts of the east side of town. Naomi caught it just as Noah pulled into the last parking space and disembarked the bike, adjusting his jacket before making his way inside.

Naomi frowned. "What the hell is he doing there?"

Even though she'd asked the question out loud, Naomi wasn't sure if she wanted to know the answer.

CHAPTER 2

Amy Brewer flinched at the sound of a glass breaking. *He didn't mean to,* she told herself. *He didn't mean to drop the glass like that, and he didn't mean to scare me.*

Did he?

Shawn Jameson looked at her with disgust in his eyes, which looked a bit too small for his head. She never noticed that about him until right now. His broad shoulders were tense—they practically met his ears— as his thin lips formed a frown below his flushed cheeks, a telltale sign of his anger. Even with her long legs, he still towered over her, as his frame made his natural-born strength visible to anyone who looked at him.

"What was that for?" To her dismay, her voice shook as she spoke. It made her sound weak and afraid, which would only give him even more ammunition.

"It was an accident." He said it with such venom that she was certain it was a lie.

"Bullshit, 'it was an accident!' Is breaking my stuff really necessary?"

He scoffed. "God forbid anyone makes a mistake around here."

"Oh, you're one to talk. And you know it wasn't a mistake! You're just trying to prove a point and be the bigger, louder one, and my stuff has to pay the price for it."

Shawn shook his head as he crossed his arms, puffing his chest out in the process. "Amy, what are you doing?"

"No." She wasn't sure where her voice came from, but she decided to roll with it while she had this momentum. "No, Shawn, you are not going to talk to me like that."

"Like what?"

Amy balked at him, as she gestured to the room around them. "Like this! Like I'm fucking crazy or something!"

"I mean, come on." Shawn kept his cool. He was so good at keeping his cool that sometimes, she thought he was right and that she *was* absolutely insane, like he always either said or implied. "You're the only one screaming. Just look around, Amy."

Her eyes darted around the room as she observed their surroundings. Her apartment was a complete mess. The glass Shawn dropped had shattered all over the fake hardwood floors, splaying in every direction. One of the couch pillows made its way down the hall from when she threw it at Shawn earlier after the small dining table she had was split in half, right down the middle; that was from Shawn—more specifically, his fist slamming down on it.

Typical of him to cause a scene and then blame me, she thought. Amy knew if she didn't do this now, then she may never muster up the courage again. She was acting purely on impulse, something that was new for her as she was used to acting out of fear or complicity.

Not anymore.

"I am so sick of this!"

"Yeah, yeah, you always say that. God, everything is so all or nothing with you." He waved his hand dismissively and grabbed his coat. As he made his way out the door, he said, "I'll see you tomorrow."

Amy groaned. "No, you won't!" she said with a shout. That made Shawn stop in the doorway. The wind whipped through the hallway of the apartment complex, howling loud enough to give her pause. Shawn had drowned her voice out enough over the last few years; she didn't need the weather doing that to her, too, especially now. "I don't want you to see me ever again!"

Shawn turned back and placed a hand on her shoulder. "Chill out. You want the whole apartment complex to hear you?"

She grunted as she pushed his hand off her. The biting air from the wind gusts brought in light flakes of snow, too small to discern their shape. "That's your only response? Get lost, Shawn."

"Remind me: how many times have we been through this again?"

"I'm serious. If you come here again, I'm calling the police."

Shawn laughed. "Yeah, because Riverpeak PD is known for being the pinnacle of law enforcement." The sarcasm practically dripped from his voice.

He wasn't wrong about that—the Riverpeak Police Department was good at being useless, and just about everybody knew it—and Amy hated that he was right. The crime ring pedaling the drugs responsible for Shawn's superhuman strength wouldn't be successful if the cops actually did their jobs instead of falling to bribery and corruption. Amy knew, too, that it wasn't the police that helped Rory Miller in her hour of need, but Hematite.

Twice.

That left Amy alone if she needed help. If Shawn really did want to come back to her apartment, nothing would stop him. It was why she put up with his behavior for as long as she already had. Fear wracked her body, making her shake, but tonight she was filled with something she usually wasn't: adrenaline. Shawn worked with Hematite, whoever that was, which meant that Amy would have to fend for herself in this fight.

At this rate, she thought, *I'm done for either way.*

So, what the hell?

"I'm serious! We're done! Goodbye, have a nice life, go fuck yourself!"

At that, Amy slammed the door behind him. The sound of it made her flinch, even though she was the one who slammed it. She could hear Shawn's footsteps shuffle away, confirming he left, and once there was nothing but silence on the other end, her tears finally came. When she looked at her hands, even though her vision was blurred from her tears, she could see that she was shaking. One of her long, black acrylics broke off in the foray. She wasn't sure when or where it fell, but she figured the bottom of her bare foot would find it eventually.

I should have known better, she thought. *I should have known that it would come to this.*

When Amy first started dating Shawn Jameson, when she told people, they'd scowl and ask, "Really? *Him*?" They'd call him every name in the book: selfish, an asshole, heartless.

But that wasn't what Amy saw. The Shawn she met and started dating was generous, always bringing her flowers or jewelry. He complimented her beauty, something she wasn't used to, and nights of passion were frequent. Her initial judgment of his character was only solidified by the fact that he secretly fought in the name of vigilante justice, helping the more famously anonymous Hematite where the cops often failed in their small mountain town. Amy wasn't sure who Hematite was, but Shawn confessed one day that he was Brick Beast. She hated the name, but never dared tell him; it was the thought that counted, anyway.

But with time, the gifts stopped coming. She was lucky if he'd remember her birthday. The comments of how stunning her red hair and freckles were shifted to jokes relating her to Carrot Top or Ron Howard, and if she was upset, he'd tell her to stop being so sensitive. Their nights of passion became exhausting, and what she wanted never mattered when it came to anything. The Brick Beast stunt turned out to be nothing more than a grab for fame, something that always seemed just out of his reach. He was no Hematite, no matter how hard he tried. She suspected that was where a lot of his anger came from.

The understanding of everything he'd done to her hit her all at once. The sudden realization hurt just as bad as the acts themselves. She thought about calling someone, but she wasn't sure who. Hannah Cohen shared her phone number at Brad and Naomi's wedding a few weeks ago, but what would Hannah be able to do? The other thought that crossed Amy's mind was a hotline, but her fingers never made it to the screen of her cell phone. She felt too much like a wounded animal with its tail tucked between its legs to even think straight.

Amy couldn't even remember how the fight started, even though it was only a few minutes ago. Since all of their fights, more or less, began the exact same way, she supposed it didn't matter. Shawn would say something she found needlessly mean or casually cruel; she would be visibly hurt, no matter how hard she tried to hide it; and Shawn would be upset that she was upset. It was a self-fulfilling prophecy and an endless cycle.

Amy couldn't help but think of everyone who told her Shawn was a rotten, no-good piece of shit. She hated to say it, but they were right. Amy defended him behind his back for the last two years, but it got her nothing but physical and emotional bruises from him.

She only stopped crying because, after a few minutes, her tear ducts went dry. She felt completely spent and at some point, during her emotional breakdown, she made it onto the floor. Amy wasn't sure how long she sat there for or when she crawled into the fetal position, wrapping her arms around her knees as she gently rocked back and forth. She squeezed her eyes shut, trying to feel anything other than the overwhelming pain that stemmed from her chest.

Her phone in her pocket pinged. The vibration made her jump, and she slumped her head against the wall behind her. It was just from Hannah.

> HANNAH: Hey Amy! Missed you tonight. Girls' night soon?

Amy didn't bother responding. As much as she appreciated the sentiment, she wasn't in the headspace to carry on a conversation with anyone right now. All she wanted to do was wake up from whatever nightmare it was that she felt like she was living in.

The fact that Amy felt like she didn't have anyone to turn to that truly understood her didn't help her despair. As kind as Hannah seemed, she was as good as a stranger to her. Anyone that would understand had long since exited Amy's life, and all thanks to Shawn. No one wanted to spend time with him—not even his own friends, let alone hers. And when she did have the opportunity to slip away for a night with her friends without him, the guilt trips were underway, pulling her further and further from her social circle.

Now, it left her with no one.

Amy contemplated typing this all out as a message to Hannah but then thought better of it. It was Hannah's birthday, and she was celebrating tonight, so Amy didn't want to be the buzzkill.

When Amy tried to stand again, her legs felt wobbly beneath her. She relied on the wall behind to get her footing, and once she did, she tip-toed around the shattered glass. Hoping the task would help calm her mind, she focused on cleaning it up, but it didn't do much for her worries. Once the glass was safely discarded, she opened the fridge and found it empty. When she looked down, she screamed and leaped at the sight of a spider crawling across. She clutched her chest as she realized what it was, grabbed a sheet of paper towel from the cabinet, and then squashed it.

Can't catch a break.

All of the possibilities overwhelmed her. The worst-case scenarios came to her mind first. She heard enough horror stories and watched enough true crime on television to know what often happened to women like her. With Shawn's super strength, he could very easily make it look like an accident. Amy hoped that the breakup would be met with silence, but all her past attempts went the same way: she would tell Shawn to get lost, then he would be back at her doorstep the next day on his knees, crying and begging for forgiveness, only to never change his behavior.

One day at a time, she reminded herself. *Just survive the night and then worry about tomorrow in the morning.*

Survive.

She moved to her bedroom, rummaging through her clean laundry pile that she'd yet to put away for some active wear. As much as she didn't want to work out, she knew that the endorphins would help her clear her head. Luckily, at this late hour, the twenty-four-hour gym at her apartment complex was empty.

Once at the gym and her over-ear headphones were on, she zoned out. Poppy hits trending on TikTok gave her the extra boost she needed for her heavier lifts, songs that Shawn would have teased her for but, now, she didn't care. He wasn't there to judge her anymore.

Twenty minutes into her weight-training session, as she was checking her pump in the mirror—*better, but not strong enough*—the door swung open. Amy glanced in the mirror to see one of her neighbors come in; she recognized him, someone from the first floor of her building. He wore a too-large T-shirt that said "DAD" on it and had Mickey Mouse ears.

DAD waved and said something, but Amy couldn't hear him.

She lifted up one of her headphones. "I'm sorry?"

He nodded and smiled, the kind that suburban white dads were practically known for: lips pushed in, pressing wide across his face, as if to say, "Hello, I am acknowledging your existence."

He moved to the weight rack she was at. "Hey there, how are ya?"

"Fine, thanks." She put her headphones back on, not in the mood to talk.

DAD was probably trying to squeeze a workout in when he could, but his presence alone annoyed her. He picked up a weight too heavy for himself, stumbled back before recovering, and used it for bicep curls. Amy watched him in the mirror with a scowl, tempted to correct his poor form and half-lifts but didn't trust herself to not bite his head off. DAD must have picked up on this; he left after only two Taylor Swift songs. Amy sighed in relief as she wrapped up her workout, glad to be alone again as her anger subsided.

When she returned to her apartment, unfortunately, she didn't feel any different than she had before—her workout had been a nice distraction, but her apartment brought her back to reality and forced her to face her emotions again. Now instead of feeling depressed, she was just depressed and sweaty. As her hair fell out of her small ponytail, she remembered how the fight began: she'd cut her hair recently, and Shawn was mad she didn't consult him first.

Amy grabbed her phone, feeling desperate now. She stared at the text message from Hannah again for a moment. As much as she wanted to call her, Hannah was with Elijah, who was part of the very same social circle as Shawn. Maybe Hannah meant her words at the wedding, but a few months had passed since then, so there was no telling if the offer still stood.

Instead, she moved to her Internet browser, searched for a number, and then tapped on it to dial. Her hands shook as the automated voice spoke on the other end.

"You have reached the National Suicide Prevention Lifeline, also servicing the veterans' service line. If you are in emotional distress or suicidal crisis, or are concerned about someone who might be, we're here to help. Please remain on the line while we route your call to the nearest crisis center in our network."

Once she was connected, she didn't know what to say. Amy pulled the phone away from her ear and just stared at it, frozen in time. Words failed her, stuck in her throat as she came to terms with everything that unfolded over the last two years.

Whenever the world "abuse" crept up to the tip of her tongue, it rolled back and lodged itself in her throat. It left her gasping for air and needing to say it with a desperation she'd never felt before—but no matter how badly she wanted to scream, no sound came out. Acknowledging the hurt and her victimhood was a tough pill to swallow.

"Are you still with me?"

She pulled the phone back up to her ear. "Hi, sorry. Yes. Um, it's been a night. I have to go. I'll be fine."

She hung up as she spoke the lie and then made her way back to the refrigerator, hoping something would magically appear that she hadn't noticed before, but she was still disappointed. Amy decided that if she was going to survive the night, she needed something stronger than water.

CHAPTER 3

The bar, tucked away where east and downtown Riverpeak intersected, was seedier than Amy would like, but it was open despite the late-night hour and had booze. That was all she cared about as she approached the entrance, the last building in a strip of wooden buildings with front facades.

Amy's eyes darted around the room out of habit once she entered. While the exterior looked like it hadn't changed since the days of the Wild West, the interior was more modern. The wall behind the bar consisted of exposed brick, but it was the only nice part of the whole place; from the looks of the brick, it was a newer addition to the building. There was a stain on the floor that she couldn't quite identify; it looked like it had been there for so long, nobody probably knew what it was.

The budget must have gone to the brick wall, she thought.

The wallpaper wrapping around the rest of the interior was a dark maroon color to emulate wine but just made the place feel drabber than it already was. Her hair stuck to her neck, mostly dry from the air conditioning in her car from her drive there, but the sections underneath were still damp from her workout. It didn't help with her overall discomfort. At least her joggers and an oversized hoodie made her feel equal parts cozy and protected, hiding her from the world around her. She shoved her hands in the sweatshirt's pockets, retreating into them as well.

Amy didn't like being out when she was vulnerable like this. She usually put on a front of being stronger than she was, something she picked up on after years of being told she was "too sensitive" and "just needed to chill out." When she wasn't outwardly calm, she felt out of control, and the idea of anyone else taking that to twist as they saw fit made her want to hurl. But the thought of being alone and sober with her thoughts for the rest of the night felt worse.

When she reached the bar, she slid up on one of the stools. There was only one other person down on the opposite end, as most patrons gathered at the tables behind her. To her surprise, no one lurched about in a stupor; everyone seemed even more put together than she felt, making her feel guilty for her harsh judgment of the place. Amy recognized a few of the patrons from serving them at the theater her family ran downtown, but most of them were unfamiliar to her.

The bartender—Carter, according to his name tag—was a tall brown-haired man in a brown jacket who seemed nice enough. She almost didn't hear him over the live acoustic guitarist.

"Can I get you anything?"

Amy cleared her throat, which felt dry after crying for so long and screaming at Shawn earlier. "Do you have vodka cranberry?"

"Sure do. It'll be right up."

She zoned out as she watched him make her drink. As much as she wanted to down it as soon as he slid it across the bar to her, she thought better of acting on that urge and nursed it. Her eyes stayed trained on her drink, not wanting to spark any conversation with the bartender or any patrons who might see her. Her eyes felt sore from crying and based on her reflection in her drink, they were still puffy. Amy wanted to cry all over again, as she almost did in the car on the way to the bar but didn't have it in her. She'd cried so much her skin felt dry, drained, and spent.

As the night went on, Amy stayed at the bar, keeping her back to the door and the rowdy patrons at the tables. She knew she should have kept a closer eye out, but her ability to care had more or less dwindled. *Things couldn't get any worse,* she thought, *so what the hell?*

"I haven't seen you here before."

Amy averted her gaze from her empty glass to the man now sitting next to her. He had to be at least ten or fifteen years her senior, and while he wasn't unattractive, something about him beyond his age gave her the creeps. Even though they were of completely different statures, his energy reminded her too much of Shawn's.

"Yeah, this isn't my usual joint." She didn't realize how hoarse she sounded and wondered for just how long she'd stared at her empty glass.

"Can I get you a refill?"

She offered a polite smile as she shook her head. "No thanks. Trying to pace myself."

"You sure, sweetheart?"

"I'm sure."

Amy shot Carter a glance, hoping he'd get the silent cry for help. Carter met her eyes, nodded, and then looked away. She found it weird that he said nothing, but maybe he was keeping an eye on her in some other way. As she moved her eyes to her glass again, hoping the man would get the hint, she caught Carter nodding at someone in the distance.

Maybe help is coming after all.

That would be a first.

The man next to her didn't seem to pick up on these subtle transactions. "So, sweetheart, you got a name? I don't think you mentioned it."

Before Amy could protest again or tell him to buzz off, a second man approached the bar. He wore a loose-fitting purple button-up, which was half tucked into his black jeans, and a black jacket was draped over his shoulder. From the way the shirt shined, it must have been silk. The top three buttons were undone, hinting at a strong chest and some tattoos beneath the surface. He rolled his sleeves up as he spoke, revealing where the tattoos led down his left arm. All Amy could make out in the bar's darkness were some cherry blossoms on a branch on his forearm. The right arm was covered in old third-degree burns; Amy couldn't bring herself to look at them for too long.

His dark hair—which just reached the base of his neck—was slicked back, accentuating his long face; he boasted prominent cheekbones that rested high above a strong jawline. What really caught Amy's attention were his honey-colored eyes, which looked first at her and then at the man sitting next to her as he quickly evaluated the situation. He faintly smelled of cigarette smoke, which Amy assumed could be blamed on the lighter he held between his teeth as he rolled up his sleeves.

"Hey, buddy." The lighter between his teeth partially muffled his voice, which had a natural gruffness to it. "Do me a favor, will you?"

"You talkin' to me?" the older man turned around and asked.

He rolled his eyes. He wasn't very tall, maybe only an inch taller than her, but still had a commanding presence. "Who else would I be talking to?"

"Alright. What do you want? I'm grabbing a drink with this lady here."

"Are you? I mean, look at her," he said, swiping the lighter from his teeth now that his sleeves were up. He gestured at Amy and then grabbed his jacket from its spot over his shoulder. "What do you notice? Do you see her eyes?"

The man beside her stopped to look but said nothing. Amy wished she had powers similar to Hematite and Brick Beast so she could shrink herself but couldn't. Her eyes felt dry and swollen, but she hadn't bothered to check how bloodshot they might be since leaving her house. She wasn't even wearing eye makeup, something she usually didn't go without, since she knew she was at a high crying risk presently.

Now, as Amy stared at her rescuer, she wished she was. *The most attractive man I've ever seen in my life*, she thought, *and I look like I just crawled out of a sewer.*

"She clearly spent the last twenty minutes crying. My guess would be either in the bathroom or her car, but maybe into her last drink for all I know. Do you really think she wants to be talking to you right now? Dealing with your shit?" He laughed and flicked the lighter on for a split second, just long enough to get the point across. In a much lower and deeper voice, he said, "Get the fuck out of my face."

The man didn't think twice. He gave Amy one last, bewildered look and then scurried off.

She was surprised when the man with the lighter asked her, "What do you like to drink?" The rougher edges of his voice softened, sounding airier as he spoke to her and pocketed the lighter.

She shrugged. "Whatever."

"No, not whatever." When she looked at him, he was grinning with his bangs falling into his eyes. "Let me ask you one more time." He pushed his hair back with his hand. "What do you like to drink, miss?"

"Um," she said, as her finger slowly traced the rim of her empty glass, "Vodka cranberry, I guess. That's sort of my go-to."

As he sat at the now-empty barstool next to her, placing his jacket in his lap, he flashed two fingers to Carter. "You heard her."

The bartender nodded. "Thanks for the assist."

"Yeah, happy to help, man. Looks like I got here at just the right time." As Carter got to work on their drinks, the dark-haired man said to her, "Who told you that you can't get what you really want, huh?"

Amy bit back a scoff. "What are you, a psychologist or something?"

He shrugged his shoulder. "You're not far off. I got my degree in it but never got to use it. That's what makes me a great pseudo-bouncer." He winked. "It's admittedly fun to scare sick bastards like that off."

"Why not?" She wasn't sure she cared, but she had nothing better to do than talk to him, and he *did* just rescue her. "Why didn't you get to use your degree, I mean?"

"Well, I *am* legally dead."

If she hadn't cared before, now she did. Her eyes widened, curious to hear the story in hopes of it distracting her. "What? Like the IRS fucked up or something?"

"Heh. Something like that, yeah." His eyes scanned her, as the tip of his tongue darted out to lick his bottom lip. "You never answered my question."

"My ex-boyfriend." Amy wiped some new tears that pooled in her eyes; just when she thought she was empty, they threatened to show her vulnerability once again. "Everyone thinks he's some sort of hero or something because he hangs out with Hematite. But he's not." She sighed. "He's the biggest fucking asshole to walk the face of the earth."

He let out a low whistle as he brushed back some of his hair again. As his bangs moved out of his face, Amy noted how handsome he was; despite his demeanor and overall appearance, he had a sweet face. "Wow. That is quite the title. You said he hangs out with Hematite?"

"He's not as famous, though I'm sure he wishes he were. Ever hear of Brick Beast?"

"That name sounds vaguely familiar. That's your ex, huh?"

"Yeah. His real name is Shawn Jameson. He's..." She sighed. "He's truly awful."

As soon as she said the words, the part of her that felt the need to protect Shawn screamed inside her own head. But then she remembered that she didn't need to defend him anymore. Shawn never did that for her, so it was about time that she started protecting herself instead of him. If he suffered in the process, then so be it. After all, someone like him shouldn't be allowed to call themselves a hero.

The man beside her gave her a gentle nudge with his elbow. "Well, I'm sorry for his loss."

Carter slid them their drinks, and the man beside her tilted his glass toward her. Amy clanked his glass with her own before she said, "Well, that's one way of looking at it. Cheers."

As they both took a sip, Amy watched him, trying to get a good read on him. He was attractive, that much was certain, but something unidentifiable about his easy-going smile drew her in, along with the subtle, cryptic manner of his words that made her desire to learn more about him. There was a message in everything he said, she was sure of it, and it was probably why he was so good at getting her to open up to him, even though she didn't even know his name.

"You're a beautiful woman. I'm sure you deserve better than to be crying over him in a shithole like this." He glanced at the bartender and said, "No offense, Carter."

As Carter waved a hand in dismissal, Amy chuckled. "Thanks, I suppose. You know, I left him earlier tonight."

His eyes widened and eyebrows raised in surprise. "Earlier tonight?"

"That's correct."

"No shit."

"Yeah. I still can't believe it myself. It was a long time coming, I think."

"Hey, you know what? I'll drink to that. That explains what you're doing here."

"Mhm. I guess I didn't have anywhere else to go." She held her drink with both hands but couldn't take her eyes off him. No one had ever captivated her so quickly before with such a natural draw that she couldn't help it, and he didn't seem to mind her lingering gaze. "So why are you here, especially if you think it's a shithole?"

His grin returned, taking over his entire face as it crinkled his eyes and lifted his cheeks. "I guess you could say I didn't have anywhere else to go, either." His tongue darted out to quickly swipe his bottom lip again. "I didn't catch your name."

She normally would make up something and retreat, but something about the way he smiled at her so casually compelled her to answer honestly. "I'm Amy. I don't think I got yours, either."

"Noah. It's a pleasure to meet you, Amy."

"Pleasure's all mine."

As he took another sip of his drink, Amy looked him up and down against her better judgment. The very same judgment led her astray with Shawn, so she wondered if she should even bother listening to it. Noah caught her checking him out, eyes darting across his frame, and he smiled wide as he set his drink down.

"All things considered, how are you feeling?"

Amy shrugged. "Fine, I guess. This is helping take the edge off," she lifted the glass to gesture to it, "but I thankfully still have my wits about me."

"Then forgive me if I'm misreading, but I'd be happy to get you the hell out of here if you'd like to distract yourself elsewhere."

Amy blinked, surprised at his offer but pleasantly so. It was a reminder that Shawn wasn't the end-all, be-all of her life, and the idea of moving forward—no matter how—appealed to her. The fact that he didn't seem phased by her baggy clothes and lack of makeup wasn't lost on her, either. Cute or classy outfits and a flawless complexion were necessities her mother insisted every self-respecting woman needed, further enforced by Shawn's notable attitude shift when she was fresh-faced.

But here Noah was, buying her drinks and looking at her from the corner of his eye. She'd never seen someone give her a look so sultry before. There was a saying she heard once in college that the best way to get over someone was to get under someone else. At the time, she laughed it off, but now, she understood.

Before Noah could change his mind and rescind the offer, she downed the last of her drink and then said, "I would love to."

CHAPTER 4

While Amy wasn't sure of much anymore, there was one fact she could say with confidence: Noah's kiss was intoxicating.

It started the minute they walked in the front door of his house, pausing for him to lift her over his shoulder to carry her up the stairs. It made her yelp with delight and giggle until he shut her up with another kiss, the two of them ditching clothing as they moved to his bedroom. The kiss only ended once her back was on his bed, a thin quilt the only thing separating her from the sheets and mattress. He supported himself with his hands as he hovered over her, eyes scanning her nude body.

"I'm gonna have to start working out with you."

She laughed. "You're welcome to but you look pretty fit yourself."

Now that his shirt was off and they were in the light of his room, Amy could better make out the tattoo on his right arm. The kitsune was dancing—or maybe fighting—with the snake that coiled around his arm and up over his elbow. The fox's nine tails splayed over his shoulder to form a perfect, large fiery circle, whereas the snake wound primarily down his forearm, its scales resembling flat emeralds. The cherry blossoms Amy saw earlier filled in some of the gaps with a burst of pink, contrasting against the black around it.

Noah's left side, however, was worse than she thought. The skin was damaged not just on his arm, but over his shoulder and part of his chest. The flesh looked purple in some spots and red in others that had been just out of view with his unbuttoned shirt at the bar. He chuckled when Amy's eyes fluttered over the grafts.

"Is it absolutely hideous?" As he leaned his face closer to her own, she glanced up to meet those captivating, honey-colored eyes of his and felt herself melt into the mattress. "I see you checking out my arm."

"No, no, it's not too bad."

"You can be honest. I won't be offended." He couldn't help his smirk; if Amy didn't know better, she'd say he got off to the thrill of it. "It's pretty awful, right?"

Amy shook her head. "I think you're pretty good-looking either way."

Noah laughed. "You're so fucking polite. It's cute." He tugged at her bottom lip with his teeth and then rolled over onto his back in a sudden, swift motion. He placed his hands beneath his head with such a casualty that it practically gave her whiplash. "I have an idea."

Amy's brows furrowed. "What's that?" She propped herself up on her side to look at him, pushing some red locks out of her face that fell when she shifted.

"I would love nothing more than to see you just let it all out. Why don't we see what you can do, yeah?" There was a beat of silence before he added, "However you wanna get yourself off. Show me what you got, sweetheart."

––––––

Amy was certain she'd dreamt everything: the bar, the handsome stranger scaring people off and charming her into bed, having sex with him. Never had she been in charge before like that, so it would only be natural for it to all be a dream.

But when she rolled over in bed the next morning, she was still in Noah's room. It wasn't a dream, not in the slightest, further proved by the fact that Noah was still beside her. He was reading on his phone but bookmarked it and set it down when he saw she was awake.

"Morning. Didn't wanna wake ya. How'd you sleep?"

"Great, thanks. You don't have to stop reading on my account."

"Come on, what do you take me for?" Noah rolled onto his side so he could face her. He reached out for her with his tattooed arm, hand brushing some of her hair out of her face. "Why would I wanna pay attention to a book when I've got a beautiful woman in my bed?"

Amy blushed as he pulled her in for a kiss, his hand behind her head now. Before she knew it, Noah rolled over so he was on top of her, his kiss growing deeper and more intentional. After everything she'd been through, it was easy to unravel beneath Noah. It only took him one night to learn all the right places to kiss and touch, something she hadn't experienced in years, even with Shawn.

So, this is what sex was supposed to feel like.

Noah moved his mouth from her lips down to her jaw. His voice and hot breath against her skin snapped her out of her thoughts. "Sorry. Just can't get enough of ya."

"Please don't apologize for that."

He chuckled against her skin. "Well, then in that case..." He proceeded with his kisses, nonverbally promising a morning filled with as much pleasure as the night before. "You can back out now if you're completely disgusted. I know it's pretty unsightly, especially in the daylight."

"Maybe I think your red-and-purple skin is a turn-on," she said, with only a hint of sarcasm.

He laughed. "Good."

Noah's lips made their way to her neck as he caressed her skin with calloused fingers. He sucked with force near Amy's collarbone, which caused her to let out a little yelp; that would definitely leave a mark, which she was sure he intended to do.

"I thought you said purple skin was a turn-on?" Noah teased as he then kissed where he left a hickey.

As he proceeded, she still wasn't convinced that she was awake and not dreaming.

After they got ready for the day ahead, as she walked downstairs, she realized her alcohol consumption the night prior must have masked the acidic smell of the house. All in all, the home was fairly barren; if she didn't know any better, she'd thought no one lived there. While it was lovely, with decent furniture and arrangements, none of it seemed used. It looked more like a real estate listing photo than it did a lived-in home.

As Amy joined Noah in the kitchen, where he started preparing coffee, she leaned against a counter and asked, "Do you have cats?"

"Ehh, sort of. We get a bunch of strays that I just can't help but feed. They're so damn cute, you know? I'm hoping they'll trust me enough to bring to the vet to spay and neuter 'em."

"Ah, so that's what that smell is. That's actually really sweet."

Noah chuckled. "Sorry. I usually light a candle but had a few other priorities last night." He winked, which made her blush.

"It's fine. Really. I love cats, so I'd probably fall victim to their cuteness, too."

Noah looked behind him at the back door and brushed the blind aside. When he released it, it swung back with minimal force. Amy had fully expected to flinch at the sound, but it was gentle enough that she didn't.

"They're not there now, but next time they come around, I'll send you some pictures."

Her eyes lit up. "Really?"

"Yeah, of course. You sound so surprised."

"Oh. Sorry."

"What are you apologizing for?" He looked at her over his shoulder as he set two mugs down on the counter. As the coffee brewed, the sound of steam gently fizzing, and the smell blending with that of the cats, he turned around to lean against the counter opposite her. "You don't have to apologize to me for a fucking thing."

She went to apologize again but caught herself. "I'll try to remember that."

"Old habits die hard, I know. You in a rush out of here?"

"Not exactly. I don't have to work until later this afternoon. My family runs the theater downtown, and even though there aren't any shows now, they still like to have someone at the box office during the lunch rush."

Noah nodded. "As long as I get your number before you leave here, I don't give a shit where you go after this."

Amy laughed, surprised by his request. She hadn't expected him to even be there when she woke up, never mind making her coffee and getting her number. "Yeah, that can be arranged. You really had my back last night. And this morning, literally."

He smiled as the coffee pot dinged and turned to pour them both a cup. "You take anything in your coffee?"

"No, black is fine."

"Really? I would have guessed the whole works."

"What makes you say that?"

"Just something about you."

"In truth, I used to, but my New Year's Resolution last year was to cut back. I used an embarrassing amount." Embarrassing, she remembered, because Shawn used to make fun of her for how sweet she liked it. But now, she was used to black.

"Well, I won't judge you," Noah said with a shrug, as he took a sip of his own while handing her the other mug.

"Wait, wait, hold on. I am judging you. Is that not scalding?"

"Nah. Nothing is too hot for me," he said with a wink. "Just how I like it."

Amy watched him as she took her own sip of coffee but withdrew to let it cool down. Everything about the morning felt unusual, causing mixed signals to swirl between her brain and heart. *Something is off,* she thought *it has to be.* Part of her thought the barely touched home was a red flag, but it was also possible that he just kept a clean house and had nice things. How much he made working as a "pseudo-bouncer" was beyond her, but maybe there was more to that story that was ultimately harmless.

She knew better. This was too good to be true—the sex, the considerate conversation over morning coffee, him asking for her number.

He'd identified her insecurities within seconds of meeting, another possible red flag, but after dealing with how insensitive Shawn was, it was a strange sort of relief.

There was a missing puzzle piece, however, and Amy wanted to stick around to find it. After all, the likelihood of everyone in her life being terrible had to be low. She'd been through enough—surely her bad luck was out, and it was time for things to swing in her favor.

Either the other shoe would drop, or it wouldn't. She couldn't know if she ran.

"This coffee is really good, by the way." It was—she'd never had something so smooth.

"Admittedly, I'm a bit of a coffee snob." He spoke with his hands, pinching two fingers for emphasis. "I order it from this local farm out in Hawai'i. Can't drink anything else."

Maybe there is more to him than just being a bar bouncer.

"Ah, so it's Kona. No wonder it's so nice. Your whole house is really nice, actually."

Noah shrugged his shoulder. "Former rich kid. Can you tell?"

That explained the furniture. "Former?"

"Inheritance. Enough to do as I please, more or less."

"Oh, I'm sorry for your loss."

"Don't sweat it."

Amy tried to analyze him similarly to how he analyzed her the night prior. Based on how nonchalant he seemed, she figured the death must have been a long time ago, and she didn't think much else of it.

"Well, for what it's worth, you don't act like you used to be a rich kid. God, those are the worst."

Noah chortled. "You're telling me." He took another sip of coffee and studied her. "You look like you have so much you want to say. Go ahead, spit it out."

Amy blushed, feeling the pressure. "Oh. I mean, I sort of do, I guess. This is new for me. My ex and I were together for a few years, and I hadn't dated much before him or anything, so, I guess I'm just taking it all in."

"Don't worry, Amy. This can be as casual as you want it, got it?"

She nodded. "Cool. Here, let me get you my number before I forget."

They swapped phones and exchanged contact information. Amy noticed that he only put his first name in, opting to use a fire emoji instead of his surname. Like the rest of the morning, she felt conflicted about this—not wanting to look too deep or find only the worst in people, but there was a mystery about Noah she couldn't deny. It would be easy to only see the worst after everything she'd been through, but she didn't want to go there. Maybe she should, but she refused to become too jaded. Her whole life, she was chastised for having a pity party for herself, so now was her chance to prove everyone wrong.

"Any time you want to distract yourself from life, just let me know. I'd much rather you come to me than spend time at that sketchy-ass bar."

"I will definitely be taking you up on that. You are a way better option than that weirdo you rescued me from."

Noah laughed. "I'd certainly hope so!"

"Yeah, that bar is actually really low."

She laughed with him, relishing the moment. The coffee was finally the perfect temperature, something she could savor for a few minutes longer before she would be on her way. Despite the circumstances, Amy sensed this wouldn't be the last time she saw Noah.

———

After a few women died in his care and only one managed to survive, Noah thought he had a good grasp on if someone would be a viable candidate for his experiment or not.

But Amy was a walking bag of contradictions.

Physically, he sensed she could handle it. Amy was tall, standing at almost the same height as him, with a naturally lean frame. She was rather toned, clearly having spent a lot of time in the gym—likely to try to keep up with Shawn. A strong frame meant she'd likely withstand the painful effects of the drug and transformation.

But mentally, Amy was broken. Whenever she spoke, she immediately went into explaining herself, which he figured had to do with why she apologized so much. Her emotional fortitude might not be up to par and could make her snap under the pressure, but it wasn't anything he couldn't fix.

Noah couldn't blame Carter for scoping Amy out, especially if this time, it actually helped him sell the lie that he worked at the bar. It was the same way they found the waitress and the other women, though Amy was the first time Noah actually took one of his test subjections home.

That was just to make a point. Sleeping with one of Hematite's sidekick's ex-girlfriends would give him leverage, he figured, and an easy way to make her trust him into spilling more information. While Hematite was his target, Brick Beast was a stepping stone he didn't realize was there before. Using Rory Miller would be too obvious, and Rory packed more of a punch than she seemed, so turning to another member of their social circle was a viable option. The fact that Shawn Jameson also happened to have superpowers from the drug made it even more worthwhile.

And then there was Naomi. Noah wondered if Amy even realized she was his sister. He remembered Naomi mentioning her a few times when she was in school, but not half as much as Rory or Carla. Had Amy known, she'd have likely said something. From what he could tell, his sister was ignorant of the abuse her husband's friend was inflicting on people while claiming to be a hero.

He wondered if Hematite knew. Part of him hoped he didn't, just so he could see the look on his face when the news inevitably broke.

How delicious would it be to break Hematite's worldview like that?

That thought alone fueled Noah enough to push forward. Even if Amy couldn't handle it, their new partnership was undoubtedly worth it. The information she'd provided in one short night and morning was already worth its weight in gold. While he'd originally planned to lure her in after a few outings just to make her an offer, he decided to change his approach.

First, he'd have to get Amy's trust. So far, that was on track. If he helped her get revenge on Shawn, then they could expose his behavior and rile up Riverpeak. An angry populace would lure out Hematite, which would allow Noah to gain some closure after everything that happened to him and empower the people to stand up for themselves. After all, Hematite enabled Brick Beast, and a true hero would never let someone like that get away with what they did.

To create a super-powered town, all he had to do was find a way to distribute the drug en masse. He wasn't sure how, but something told him that Amy would be his ticket to that, too.

CHAPTER 5

Noah made good on his promise of sending cat photos to Amy's phone the following afternoon and almost every day after for the following two weeks. Some of the cat photos were clear close-ups, beautiful portraits that highlighted mangled fur against beautiful eyes begging for tuna cans. Others looked like Bigfoot photos, blurry and chaotic as they zoomed by in the backyard. The latest was of a black cat nuzzling against his hand, demanding to be pet, so Amy sent some heart emojis in response to it as she walked to work.

The Riverpeak Theater had been a local staple for generations, owned and operated by Amy's family for as far back as she could trace her ancestors in Colorado. The fact that none of them ever left since settling there in the 1850s was why Amy's parents were as stiff as they were. Appearances mattered more than feelings, something Amy remembered every time she walked into the theater so she could put on her own one-woman show.

It was easy to tell, even without reading the historic marker plaque, that the theater was built in the 1920s, the art deco influences maintained throughout the years. The only thing they'd changed was the carpet in the lobby, which didn't help in making it feel less gaudy, and they'd added signed cast posters from the various stage plays and musicals in the halls. As much as she disliked the fake gold arches embossed on mint wallpaper, she was fond of the way the ceiling drew her eye down the halls toward the back of the theater. When she grew bored, she'd often count how many lines were on the ceiling and wallpaper while humming along to whatever song a performer in the show was singing. She was doing just that from behind the box office counter when a low whistle caught her attention.

"Well, isn't this nice."

Amy's eyes lit up at the sight of Noah. His hair was slicked back, the ends reaching just beneath his ears. A few strands hung over one eye. He was wearing the same jacket he wore the night they met and a blue button-up shirt.

"What a pleasant surprise!"

"I was passing by and figured I'd say hi. Is now a good time?"

"Yeah, yeah. I'm bored out of my mind right now. There's still a while until intermission down in the black box."

"Looks like perfect timing on my part, then. How are you holding up?"

"Good. Every day gets a little easier and harder all at once. That probably sounds ridiculous."

"No, not at all. I know the feeling." He reached over to tuck a loose strand of hair behind her ear. His fingertips trailed down her jaw to her chin before he dropped his hand, sending sparks down Amy's spine. "It's normal."

When their eyes met, Amy had to restrain herself—she was working, after all, and was sure her parents wouldn't be thrilled if they checked the security cameras to see her kissing a seemingly random man in the lobby.

"Can I ask a stupid question?"

"There are no stupid questions," Noah stated.

"You barely know me. Why are you so nice to me?"

Noah shrugged. "Why wouldn't I be nice to you?"

He was so nonchalant that Amy felt as if she were in a dream again. She blushed, more easily than she'd care to admit, and adjusted her name tag so she would have something to do with her hands.

"I guess I'm just not used to it."

Noah grinned as he leaned across the counter, elbows propped up. "You are so cute when you get all flustered, you know that?"

Amy felt her breath catch in her throat when Noah leaned in to kiss her but, instead, tugged at her bottom lip with his teeth. What started as an excuse to forget about her past by cleansing herself with someone new turned into something much more complicated.

"Right now? Really?"

"Oh, come on. No one's here. What are they gonna do? Fire you?" His smirk grew cockier. "Doubt it."

"Yeah, but that doesn't mean I shouldn't maintain some semblance of professionalism."

"Professionalism? I can be professional."

"Yeah?"

"Mm." He winked. "No, I don't have a professional bone in my body. Do you even like doing this, anyway?"

"Eh, yes and no. I love musicals. Like, love them. I know they're cheesy but it's just so fun, and seeing a show is always so relaxing. Like pre-scheduled escapism. That and live music is always nice."

Noah smiled as Amy justified her love of theater. "When I was a kid, my mom took us all up to New York once just so we could see *Cats*. It scared the shit out of my sister."

"No way! Please tell me that's not the last show you saw, at least."

"Unfortunately, it was. What's your favorite?"

It took Amy a second to process Noah's question; she wasn't used to anyone caring, at least not genuinely. Every now and then, a guest would ask her if a show was good or not, but it was to gauge if they should shell out the money for tickets rather than actually valuing her opinion.

Noah must have sensed this from her pause because, to lighten the air, he said, "Please tell me it's not *Cats*."

Amy laughed. "No, it's not *Cats*. I'd probably have to say *Hadestown*. You'd like it."

"I'll have to keep an eye out for tickets, then. Speaking of which, how much longer until intermission?"

Amy glanced at a television screen in the lobby that showed the performance. "It's just a rehearsal, but they're wrapping up the end of the first act now."

"I'll let you get back to it before my unprofessionalism rubs off on you, then." Noah winked, leaned in to kiss her cheek, and then spun on his heel to head out the door.

She spent the rest of her day and her walk home hoping that her parents wouldn't check the security cameras like they sometimes did when they were bored. She was only snapped out of that thought when, upon reaching her front doorstep, her phone pinged. It was Noah.

> NOAH: Can I treat you to dinner?

> AMY: I mean, I won't say no.

Part of her wondered if keeping this up was a good idea. Jumping into something new felt dangerous, especially as her heart was still healing. But the thought of not spending time with someone who made her feel so seen was more upsetting than a possible worst-case scenario, so she texted him her address.

> NOAH: Wear your favorite outfit. See you in an hour.

> AMY: Favorite fancy outfit or favorite casual outfit?

> NOAH: Fancy.

––––––

Amy swung her closet door open, unsure of what to pull out. Her dress from Naomi and Brad's wedding caught her eye, and after thumbing through everything in her closet, she determined it wasn't too fancy for whatever Noah had up his sleeve.

She hadn't felt this exhilarated in years, so much so that her hands trembled as she did her best to draw a straight line on her eyelid over her eyeshadow. When she heard the knocking on her door, she slid her

glasses on in hopes that the massive frames would cover any imperfec-
tions in her makeup.

Noah stood at her doorway, dressed similarly to how he was
earlier. He'd swapped his jacket for something more formal, and his
dress shoes shined in the light of her apartment's lighting when she
opened the door. As he held his hand out to her, Amy realized that
whenever he did this, he used his tattooed arm, not the burned one.

"Shall we?"

Amy grabbed her purse from the coat hanger by the door and
accepted his offering, fingers wrapping around his own as she locked
the door behind her, and they moved out of her apartment complex.
When they reached his motorcycle, he offered her the helmet, opting to
go without one.

"You sure?"

"Yeah, I'll be careful. Promise."

The helmet barely fit around her glasses but was comfortable
enough. As she put it on, her eyes scanned the parking lot, looking for
any signs of Shawn or someone she wouldn't want to see. The only
vehicle she recognized was Kane Kelly's old Honda, but the Prelude
never left the parking lot, and Amy wasn't sure that Kane was even
aware of the fact that they lived in the same complex. She had to hike
her dress up to properly straddle the bike behind Noah, wrapping her
arms tightly around him.

When they arrived outside Le Petit Chateau, Amy was relieved.
While Noah seemed to run warmer than most, it was only a buffer
between her skin and the sharp breeze of a winter evening. She was
just glad that it wasn't snowing for once.

Amy shook off her shiver as she disembarked the motorcycle.
Noah wrapped an arm around her and pulled her flush against his
side.

"Oh, you're so warm."

"So I've been told." Noah held the door open for her. "After you."

Le Petit Chateau wasn't always this upscale; it used to have a
small-town charm to it, but after the fire Stone Breaker caused last year,
they used the opportunity to renovate. A small chandelier hung from
the center of the ceiling, while the light from its fake candles bounced

off the crystals and created a warm atmosphere. Some soft jazz music played overhead.

After they were seated, their conversation consisted mostly of small talk until their food arrived, leaving them with a bit more privacy now that they were less likely to be interrupted by their server. There were still a few warm slices of baguette between them, which Amy enjoyed without guilt. Whereas Shawn would have some snarky comment for every little thing she did, Noah didn't seem to care at all what she ate.

"Thanks for taking me out tonight," Amy said. "This was a nice surprise."

"Sure, yeah. I know we've been doing things kind of backwards, so I figured this was only right. Besides, I've been wanting to take you out properly."

She looked down at her plate as she failed to stop her smile. "You know, Noah, I've gotta say, I don't think anyone has swept me off my feet like this."

"Personally, I think you deserve it. I mean, come on, look at you." He pointed at her with his fork. "This strappy blue number is nice."

She hoped the warm lighting of the restaurant would hide her blush. "Thanks. I'm actually really glad I got to wear it again."

"That so?"

"Yeah. I only got to wear it once for a wedding, but the whole thing went to hell. Believe it or not, the bride's father got murdered during the reception, and we all had to leave early."

Noah swallowed. "No shit."

"Yeah. But enough about that. Total buzzkill, sorry."

"What are you sorry for?"

"Oh, um, for bringing up a sad topic?"

Noah waved a hand dismissively. "One of these days, I'll get you to stop apologizing for everything."

Amy leaned forward, her elbows resting on the table in front of her as she studied his face. Now that she thought about it, he looked familiar. "Wait a second. What did you say your last name was?"

He cleared his throat. "I didn't say, actually. But it's Sato."

"Noah Sato. O-oh! Oh my God! You're," Amy dropped her voice to a whisper, "you're Noah Sato! Didn't you die a few years ago?"

"I mean, I *did* tell you I was legally dead."

Amy ran a hand through her hair as she slumped back in her chair. "Here I am gabbing about your dad's death in relation to my fucking dress."

Noah laughed. "It's fine, Ames, seriously. As shitty as it sounds, I'm, uh, not exactly upset about his passing, to be completely honest. Besides, I like hearing you gab about your dress."

"I'm sorry, I'm just going to need a few minutes to process that information."

They laughed together, shaking off the awkwardness that washed over the dinner table. It explained everything to Amy: the nice house, the inheritance money, and everything she'd been wondering about for the last few weeks. But those answers left her with even more questions.

Part of her was hesitant to ask, but she decided to anyway. *I survived Shawn,* she thought, *so I can survive anything.*

"What have you been up to for the last … what has it been? Five, six years?"

"Six or so, yeah. Going on seven, I think. To be honest, the time has gotten away from me."

"Holy shit."

His gaze moved to his hands as he smiled, tongue running across one of his teeth as he thought over what he was going to say next. "It's a really long story. Maybe I'll tell you one day. But for now, what's important is that I almost died, and my dad covered it up."

"What about your mom and sister?"

"Things were too messy, so I've stayed away."

"Noah, I'm so—."

"Don't say you're sorry. I'm fine, really." He looked up at her through his lashes as his thoughts trailed to Naomi. "Shit sucked, but now we're here, so it all worked out."

————

Whereas most of the boys in his kindergarten class thought the idea of having a baby sister was gross, Noah couldn't have been prouder to be a big brother.

As his mother cradled Naomi's small form, wrapped in blankets, his father asked him to pledge the very first promise he'd ever make in his life: to be her protector and look out for her, always.

Noah took that title of protector seriously, even though Naomi never really needed him to be. She was popular enough, friends with both Carla's merry band of extroverts and the quiet bookworm Rory. Brad loved her the moment he laid eyes on her in kindergarten, so the two came to a truce.

But then, when he was in his mid-twenties and got a phone call from his sister in the middle of the night, he felt like he'd failed. She was only in her sophomore year of college, and he was too busy juggling the illegal work his father had him running and his graduate program to have even realized anything was wrong until he picked up the phone.

"Wait, what do you mean Rory's been stalked? Are you with her?"

"Yes, I was."

"Was? Are you safe?"

He wondered how much of this happened right under his nose without him realizing it. They were on the same campus, after all, and while students pursuing a Master's degree didn't often encounter the undergrads, there was still no excuse.

As Naomi assured him that she was, in fact, safe, his jaw clenched. The pencil in his hand snapped, and he scrambled to salvage the pointed half by adding an eraser cap to the jagged edge. He'd sharpen the part with the original eraser later.

"But you wouldn't believe this. Hematite stopped that Daniel kid. Hematite! We actually saw him!"

"That vigilante from back home? What the hell's he doing here?"

"I'm not sure. Maybe he's a student. You'd like him; he was just as badass as you theorized he'd be."

Noah chuckled and tried to swallow back the feeling of failure. "Well, if I ever see the bastard, I'll have to tell him I owe him one for having your back."

———

After noticing the tone of their dinner shift, Amy took a deep breath as subtly as she could, hiding it behind a sip of her wine, but Noah still must have caught on. The action took him away from memory lane and back to the present moment.

"Hey. Look at me."

Amy did as he instructed.

"It's okay. I'm not mad at you." He offered her a crooked smile. "I'd swear on my father's grave, but I hated the bastard, so that's off the table, I guess."

That made her laugh, even though she felt bad about it.

"There's that smile. Believe me now?"

Amy nodded. Her heart still raced in her chest, but she meant it when she said, "Yeah, I do."

"Good. Here, you gotta try this." Noah stabbed some of the food on his plate with his fork and held it up for Amy. "Come on. Open up."

She entertained him, letting him feed her a sample of his escargot. As the garlic and butter flavors melted on her tongue, and as Noah expertly changed the subject, she wondered if this was too much too soon. She'd been so sure that he'd be livid, forgetting for a moment that everyone wasn't as explosive as Shawn or cold as her parents. It had been an accident and a natural follow-up question, but Noah didn't fault her for it. If his biggest red flag was that he was a bit private, then she'd take it if it meant not having to fear making simple mistakes anymore.

That train of thought was what prompted her to invite him in when he brought her back home. Maybe it was because he was the polar opposite of Shawn, but he was so easy for her to get enraptured in, and tonight was no different. As Amy set her purse down on the coat hanger in its usual spot, he stepped behind her and his hands roamed down her shoulders.

"What would you like tonight, sweetheart? Hmm?" He kissed the spot behind her ear, a spot he learned sent shivers down her spine when they'd first met.

"You know, you always let me lead, which is nice, but I'd like to see you take charge for once."

Noah raised an eyebrow. "That's what you want?"

She nodded, turning to face him now. "Yeah. Prove you're not mad at me from earlier. That's not too tall of an order, is it?"

Noah kissed her and pulled her with him to her living room. "Not at all."

As he kissed slowly down her body, his hands roamed, gripping her biceps, ribs, and hips. Amy squirmed beneath his touch, delighted by the feeling but still not expecting it. Despite his burns, the pads of his fingertips were as gentle as the sighs that passed his lips.

"I'm sorry. It's just that you're so soft," he complimented. "You sure you want me to ravage you?"

"Now it's my turn to tell you not to apologize."

Noah's hands found Amy's face—she realized how cold she was when he touched her, his warmth spreading through her body—as he backed her up against a wall in the living room, kissing her with unrivaled intensity. Her back gently met the structure with a soft thud, not hard enough to hurt but just enough to thrill. A few weeks ago, she would have gone into a panic attack, but now, the action held a new, less frightening context for her—one of the main differences now being that she actually knew what an orgasm felt like.

Noah pulled away from the kiss with her bottom lip between his teeth, leaving her nearly breathless; his kiss at the theater must have been a teaser for tonight. "And what about for that? Should I apologize for that?"

"Only if you don't continue," she said. Something about the way he kissed her felt right. She hadn't expected him to be in the mood after their conversation briefly turned to his father's death, but clearly, he meant it when he said he wasn't upset by it.

Noah's smirk from earlier returned as he kissed Amy again. After a few moments, his tongue encroached on her mouth. One of his hands lingered by her hip, keeping a tight grip there, but the other hiked up the skirt of her dress and slipped beneath the hem to rest on her hip bone.

"And what about this?" Noah asked as he paused for a breath. "Should I stop and say sorry, or do you want me to keep touching you?"

He wasn't going to hurt her—this was just dirty talk. She knew that. "Touch me wherever the hell you want. Just keep going."

When his hand continued its trajectory up the front of her body from its place beneath her dress, she shrugged his jacket off his shoulders. He only removed his hand to discard it, but then found his place on her ribs again.

"Do you trust me?" Noah asked.

"I don't trust anyone."

He laughed as he took off his shirt, tossing it on the floor behind him to reunite with his jacket. "Good answer. I can respect your honesty."

"But I'm not going to stop you, if that's what you're wondering."

"Good enough for me." Despite how thin he was, he was surprisingly strong and used his strength to lift her against the wall. As he teased at one of her nipples with calloused fingers, his mouth moved to her neck, teeth dragging until he reached Amy's collarbone.

He sucked with a sudden force, making Amy yelp in surprise; that would definitely leave a mark, which she was sure he intended to do. He repeated the action down her body, alternating between teasing with his teeth and covering her with red and purple splotches, some more visible than others. He left the final two on her hip and inner thigh before he knelt before her and buried his tongue beneath her legs. Amy could feel him grin against her as he discovered just how aroused she already was, and he took his time exploring her with his mouth as if to torture her.

But even still, Noah's tongue was as sharp with sarcasm as it was between her legs, so it didn't take long to feel release. Once Amy felt herself tipping over the precipice, Noah pulled away.

"Now, doll, did I say you could come yet?"

Amy groaned and leaned her head back against the wall as Noah stood, but it turned into a gasp as he lifted her up higher against the wall and filled her in one swift motion. It was insanity meets lust, and maybe because her mental state was just as cracked as his own was, Amy never felt more understood and turned on simultaneously in her life. Her judgment was right—Noah *was* dangerous, but by God, did she love this thrill.

CHAPTER 6

N ow that she knew the truth about him, Amy felt incapable of getting Noah off her mind. The fact that he was technically a dead man didn't stop her from inviting him back home after the dinner where he confessed he was a Sato. It also didn't stop her from enjoying the rest of their night and the following morning together. But when he left, she was alone with her thoughts, which roamed in an unexpected direction, leaving her at war with herself.

He was too mysterious, as much as she loved that he had that air about him, and she couldn't quite place what else it was that he hid from her. But on the other hand, she was convinced Noah would never hurt her; she wagered he would have already done that if he really wanted to.

They fell into a rhythm over the next couple of weeks: Noah would visit her at work unexpectedly or text her when she was at home to let her know he was right outside, ready to pick her up on his Harley. Nights bled into mornings and days bled into weeks, as their time together only increased. When Valentine's Day rolled around, red roses were delivered straight to her door without a note, but she didn't need one to know who they were from. Had she still been with Shawn, they would've never arrived.

As she sat bored behind the ticket window at the theater one day, she texted Noah.

> AMY: Happy Valentine's Day! Thanks for the roses. They're beautiful.

> NOAH: Glad you got them. What time do you get off work?

> AMY: Late. I'm on clean-up duty. Rain check?

> NOAH: No problem.

The text was followed by the emoji that was winking and blowing a kiss.

Her workday was relatively uneventful, with only a few people coming up to buy tickets as last-minute gifts for their partners for future shows. As she made her way home in the freezing rain, she cursed herself for not bringing an umbrella or raincoat. Amy rushed to shower when she got to her apartment, hoping to beat the inevitable lightning; she was inexplicably paranoid about it traveling through her piping. As she emerged from her bedroom, comfortable now in her pajamas and waiting on her tea kettle to brew a cup, a knock on her door startled her. It was too soft to be considered banging, but she sensed an urgency. Her mind went to two places: it was either Shawn, hoping to use the bad weather to manipulate her into letting him in, or a surprise visit from Noah.

When she looked out the peephole of the door, she sighed in relief and immediately opened the door. Amy opened it and found Noah standing there, eyebrows knitted together in worry and looking a bit pathetic. He smiled when he saw her, but it didn't reach his eyes. Amy had never seen him look distraught before, so the expression seemed unnatural on his face.

This didn't feel like the rain check she requested.

Before she could say anything, he said, "I need your help."

"Are you okay? Come on in."

She stepped aside to let him into her apartment, moving back to the kitchen to finish making her tea. She grabbed an extra mug as Noah smiled at her in a way that sent a chill down her spine. She hadn't seen this smile before, not on his face and not on anyone else's. Despite his distress, his confidence seemed to leak out of him, and she hoped by being here with him, she would soak it all in like a sponge.

"I'm fine but thank you for asking."

"Are you sure? It seems like something is bothering you."

"I'm sure, but you're awfully perceptive. There's a secret I should share before I ask for your help, that's all. But first, mind if I ditch these somewhere so I don't soak your apartment?"

"Oh! Of course, I don't mind. I don't have any men's clothing lying around, but you can get out of your wet clothes and bundle up in some blankets or something if you want."

He gave her a soft smile and took a sip of tea. "Thanks. I'll leave these wet rags in your bathroom to dry."

"No worries. I gotta do some laundry anyway if you wanted to throw 'em in the machine."

He seemed strangely melancholy as he moved through the small apartment; not that it was strange for him to be feeling like that, but strange that he was allowing it to consume him for the evening in this way. Amy leaned against the counter as he changed, waiting for him to return. When he emerged, he was naked and holding nothing but a cell phone and a lighter.

Amy crossed the room toward the couch and handed him the blanket draped across the couch. Noah looked hesitant but then she said, "I use a free and clear detergent. It shouldn't bother your skin."

He took it, immediately enveloping himself in it, and then plopped down on one of the cushions. Amy smiled as Noah relished the feeling of it and brought over the two cups of tea to join him on the couch.

"This is really nice," he said, as if he were lost in a trance. "Not too warm."

"It doesn't get much use this time of year, since it's my favorite for spring and summer, but you usually run hot, so I thought you might like it." She moved back to the kitchen to grab the two cups of tea. "I've dubbed it the comfort blanket."

"I can see why." He took a sip of the tea and instantly recognized the nutty, earthy tones. "Did you get genmaicha after I said I liked it?"

He remembered texting her once about it, some small talk to fill conversations as he worked his way into her heart to gain her trust.

"Maybe." She smiled. "I didn't even know they made teas with rice, and it sounded interesting, so, yes, I did. Took me a few times to figure out how to make it right. You would have gagged at my first attempt."

He chuckled as he stared at the yellow liquid and the light steam still rising from it. "Y'know, I gotta admit. This is … almost touching."

"What about it?"

"Oh, you know. The detergent you use. My favorite tea. This," he said as he lifted a hand, blanket clutched in his fist.

Amy shrugged. "It's nothing. You sound surprised by it, though."

"I stopped giving a shit if people cared about me ages ago. But it's still nice in a way, I guess."

Truly, he felt strange internally. On the one hand, he only accepted Amy because he saw a great use that he could get out of her. But on the other hand, there was more to it that Noah couldn't place; these were feelings he buried a long time ago. He wasn't sure if this would interfere with his plans or help them.

"You make it sound so easy," Amy said. He turned his head to look at her. "I envy that."

He went to say something but was interrupted by a particularly loud crack of lightning. A low, rolling thunder followed it as the rain picked up even heavier outside.

"So, what brought you out this way?" she asked.

"Work," he said, "plus, I wanted to bring you this and talk to you about something." He handed her the flip phone. "I got you this so we can contact each other about official business, assuming you accept my offer. I was over on this side of town and then the storm started." As if he was sensing her next question, he said, "I'm not in a rush, though."

"You can stay as long as you please," Amy said. "And like I said before, you can come by whenever."

"Thanks. For the hospitality, I guess."

"Yeah, of course," she said. Amy wondered if the phone was stolen but was still grateful for it regardless. "But what's this official business you keep referencing? Why do I need a burner phone for that?"

Noah sighed as he set his mug down. "Ready for my secret that I said I had?"

"As ready as I'll ever be."

Noah held up the lighter, but then got a whiff of something strong: sweet notes of vanilla blended with lavender. He glanced around the room until he saw the lit candle on her coffee table. He pointed to it, directing Amy's gaze there. She looked at him before diverting her full attention to the candle, and he smiled. There was a glimmer in his eyes and a curve to his lip that toed the line between confident and cocky.

"Go on. Look."

She gasped when the flame on the candle wick grew, dancing up to the sky. Before it could flirt with her ceiling, it blew out as quickly as it had grown. The smoke billowed around them, and Amy wondered if maybe she was more like a moth attracted to the flame.

At least she would be warm.

"How did you do that?"

Noah shrugged his shoulders, as if what he had just done was completely ordinary. "I'm kind of like Hematite and … Brick Beast, was it? Sorry, I can't help but physically cringe whenever I say it."

Amy's breathing became rapid. *Another super-powered person?*

"Main difference is that I wasn't born like them. My old man, he ran a bunch of tests on me before he croaked. Now, I need your help, and I admittedly felt a little guilty because I probably should've told you this sooner. Especially given your history, I would understand if this puts you on edge."

Amy thought about it for a moment. On the one hand, it *did* make her feel on edge, just as he said. But at the same time, she knew that with Noah, it was different. It wouldn't be fair for her to hold him to the same standard that she held Shawn. No matter what he was about to say next, Noah had already proven himself to be a better man.

"It's fine. You're fine. You were saying?"

Noah's lips curled up on one side. He posted his next statement as a question. "Hematite's trying to stop it from spreading but imagine how empowering it would be to give people the strength they need?"

"What are you getting at?"

"I'm saying it's time to distribute. Just look at me: I'm living proof that these natural-born powers can be replicated." He placed his hands on her shoulders, forcing eye contact. As the rain slowed, Amy saw a conviction in Noah's honey-colored eyes, looking more like amber as the sun set outside and streamed its magnificent shades of red and orange through her window, breaking past the storm clouds. "Imagine if you could get back at that piece of shit? Properly fight back?"

"Are you saying I can?"

Noah pursed his lips and sighed. His gaze softened, the conviction she saw a mere twinkle now. "I'm saying you maybe can."

"What does that mean?"

"That means I think I've perfected the dosage. Keyword being 'think.' I've been working on this for a little over a year now, but I just need a large sampling size to confirm it."

The idea of vengeance wrapped in justice appealed to her and had her mind racing with ideas. "The theater."

"What about it?"

"Th-the theater. The spring musical kicks off in a few weeks. What if we put whatever it is you're distributing in the drinks at the bar?"

"Could be an option. You serve on tap?"

"It's where most of our profits come from. If it can be put into a liquid, it should be easy enough for me to spike the drinks."

Noah grinned. "Are you saying you're in before I've even formally asked?"

Amy nodded. "I don't have anything to lose at this point, so yeah. Fuck it. What do you say we get the ultimate revenge on my shitty ex-boyfriend, huh?"

Almost as if on cue, her cell phone chimed and buzzed twice, indicating a new text message. Amy stood and crossed the room to the kitchen counter. When she picked her phone up, she froze. It was a text from Shawn, the push notification flashing across the top of her screen like a warning sign.

SHAWN: Missed you on Valentine's.]

Her phone pinged again with another text.

SHAWN: You over it yet?

She wanted to reply to the effect of, "Go fuck yourself," but Amy stopped herself when she felt a lump form in her throat, the telltale sign that she was about to cry. She promised herself that she wouldn't cry over Shawn anymore, and she didn't want to get this emotional with Noah, at least not yet. She was afraid—of what, she wasn't completely positive. Amy wasn't sure if it was of looking weak, unstable, or something else entirely, despite how they met.

Then the memory came flooding back as she tried to bite back the tears. The first time Shawn laid a hand on her, it was for this very reason. Verbal insults got under her skin easier than she'd like, and she was always the type to cry at everything—from depressive episodes to elation to frustration, earning her the title of crybaby from her parents at a young age and later from Shawn. Just remembering how he shoved her against the wall as he told her to get a hold of herself made her spine ache all over again. Her anxieties told her to curl into a ball and find a safe corner to hide, but to her surprise, Noah didn't bite back. He softened.

Amy felt rough skin wipe away the tears that fell. She looked up; Noah had left the couch to join her, but the blanket was still wrapped around his shoulders. At that moment, she was grateful that they were close to the same height so he could be on her level. As she looked at him, she saw a gentleness in his expression that hadn't been there before.

"It's okay to cry," Noah said, the words falling from his lips out of habit. Noah got the sense that even before Shawn, Amy had a hard time regulating her emotions. The sight of her choking up and holding back tears transported him back to when he'd comforted his sister after a bad day. Those words were what he used to tell Naomi whenever she was upset when they were children. He shook the thought from his head. "Let it all out, Ames."

"Sorry. I thought I blocked him. I guess in my breakdown that night I forgot to."

"You don't owe me an explanation; it's fine. Do whatever you gotta do, alright?" Noah pressed his lips to her forehead as her phone pinged again. "Him again?"

Amy checked. "Yeah."

"Give me your phone."

"Huh?"

Noah held his hand out, palm facing up. "Give it."

Amy put her phone in his hand. "What are you going to do?"

"Get him off your back." Noah grinned. "Permission to send whatever?"

She shrugged. "Sure. I don't really care at this point."

Noah read over the third message from Shawn.

> SHAWN: You can't be pissed at me forever.
> Just chill out.

"Wow, the nerve of this guy," Noah muttered as he typed away.

> AMY: Sorry, but I think you have the wrong number.

> SHAWN: Don't fuck around with me like that, Amy.

Noah opened the camera app on her phone and let the blanket drape from his shoulders, revealing that he was shirtless. He took a selfie with his middle finger up, burned skin creeping up to the bottom knuckle, and then took a screenshot of the image so their location data wouldn't transfer over. He sent the photo to Shawn.

> AMY: Who's Amy?

Before Shawn could reply, Noah blocked the number and then handed the phone back to Amy. "He's blocked now. Probably sent him into a little panic beforehand, though."

"You don't think this will put a target on our backs?"

"I've fought Hematite already. He ran like a dog with its tail between its legs and he's immortal. I also happen to know that Shawn answers to Hematite. So no, I'm not too concerned." Noah placed his hands on her shoulders again. "From now on, we're gonna be spending a lot of time together, you and me. And if that piece of shit so much as even thinks of laying another hand on you, I'll know about it. Our circle? We know everything that happens in this town. Eyes and ears everywhere." He smiled. "I would take great pleasure in setting that motherfucker on fire for you. Got it?"

She nodded as she wiped her eyes with the back of her hand. "Got it."

"Good. You're safe now, Amy. I'm glad we found each other."

CHAPTER 7

As the days passed, so too did the cold weather, which occasionally returned only to vanish as quickly as it had reappeared. Noah already missed it, and it wasn't even offi-cially spring yet. The black cat curled around his leg as he sat on the back porch. He scratched between its ears, enjoying the sound and feel of the cat's purring.

"You like that, Tuna Breath, don't you?"

The cat looked up at him and meowed, a scraggly sound that made Noah laugh.

"Where are all your friends, huh?"

It meowed again. If Noah didn't know any better, he'd say they were having a conversation.

As the cat slinked away, Noah stared at his phone on the porch beside him, debating on if he should text Amy or not. She'd occupied his thoughts more than he'd ever admit. There was something about finding a girl completely emotionally destroyed at a shitty bar and making her smile that gave him a rush. Every time they spoke, she'd open up more, loosen up more, and let him in more.

His old self was at war with his present self. This was supposed to be an easy job: Carter, one of Sterling's men who'd once worked under

Reiji and now under Noah, spotted distressed women at the bar, had Noah play bouncer, and then charm them into being test subjects. The equation was simple.

But then Amy dropped that her ex-boyfriend was Brick Beast, and he found himself enjoying her tangled between his sheets more than anticipated. Even though she'd offered to help, this wasn't his plan. Everything had gone to hell, but at least he was in control of the flames.

He'd barely opened up to her himself, but still shared more than he would have with anyone else. If he shared some carefully curated details about himself with her, then there would be more of a mutual connection instead of blatant give and take. Something was oddly comforting about confiding in her, though, and handing over the little pieces of his life he'd been forced to conceal for the last six and a half years.

When he stood up and grabbed his phone, the cat meowed again.

"I gotta check on everyone downstairs, buddy. Sorry." He pocketed his phone as he made his way inside and went to the basement. Only Carter was left, throwing the last of the small bags into a briefcase.

"How was your smoke break?"

Noah shrugged his shoulder. "That black cat came back. Sweet thing."

"As long as it does, we still have a cover. You're doing a good job, you know," Carter said. "Leading everyone."

"You think?"

"I know. Everyone respects you. You've been strong after your father's passing."

If only they knew why, Noah thought. "Well, business doesn't stop just because he pissed a few people off."

"Ever find out who did it?"

Noah shook his head. "They say he was dressed like a Wish-dot-com version of Hematite. Probably some wannabe hero."

"You think it's the Kelly kid?"

"Who, Hematite or the killer?"

"Both."

"I think he's Hematite, but I don't think Hematite killed my father, though. Like I said, he had his fair share of enemies." He swallowed. "Did Brad show up when I stepped out?"

Carter shook his head. "He hasn't since Ray's funeral."

"Figures. I had a feeling he was a double-crossing asshole."

"So did Ray. I think he wanted to scare him."

"You say that like it's hard. Brad's afraid of his own shadow."

Carter chuckled as he closed the briefcase. "Well, that's everything. I'm off. Stay well, my man."

"You too. Take care."

Carter patted Noah's shoulder as he made his way upstairs. Noah lingered in the basement, cleaning up whatever the rest of his father's employees—*his* employees—forgot to put away or discard. He'd fallen into a routine of tidying up before he took a cold shower and called it a night, with either a book from the Riverpeak Library he'd checked out using a stolen card or a movie. Something about the basement always made him want to scrub himself clean, both externally and internally, in a way only a mind-numbingly bad movie could provide.

His decision to message Amy or not was made for him when he saw a Snapchat message from her waiting for him when he emerged from the shower. When he plopped onto his bed in nothing but a towel around his waist, he opened it to a selfie of her behind the bar at the theater.

> AMY: Sooooo bored. There's like four drunk dads and no one else to serve at this theater camp student show.

A crying emoji was at the end of the sentence. Noah used his burned hand to take the photo so his tattoo would show, not the reddish flesh on his other arm.

> NOAH: I think you should come over tonight.

He added a kissing emoji and then moved the text bar so it covered his nipples. Her response was immediate, just a standard selfie with her eyebrow raised.

AMY Why's that?

And a wink emoji. She was making him spell it out.

Noah placed his free hand just above his groin and made sure the photo didn't extend past his fingertips.

NOAH: I'm hungry.

She sent him a photo of the drink menu, which had a small selection of snacks.

AMY: Whatchya want?

Noah laughed. He knew that she knew, likely just to see if he actually would take it that far. He took a selfie of just his face now. As he posed, he covered his nose, mouth, and jaw with his hand, but stuck his tongue out between his middle and index fingers. He winked and hit send without bothering to add any text.

———

When Amy arrived at his house after work, Noah got his wish. He had every intention of telling her the full story, but when she kissed him the moment he opened the door, his plan went out the window. He opted instead for carrying her upstairs and then positioning her over his face on the stairs, not even bothering to take her all the way to his bedroom. The security cameras probably picked up on them, but now that he was the only one to check the feeds, it didn't matter much. *If Shawn texts her again*, he thought, *maybe I could send a little video to further illustrate that she's moved on.*

Maybe it was because the two of them were alone and broken in a way that only they could understand. All of the prior candidates didn't have any special stories—sob stories, but nothing Noah hadn't heard a million times before. But Amy had been hurt by the very people who claimed to be heroes that he was up against, and something about that made the way she tasted extra sweet to him. They'd both been damaged by the very same system, an unlikely bond he'd never intended to make.

"Stay the night," he said after they were done.

He hated how those words slipped out when she was there, but he couldn't stop himself.

"Sure." Amy smiled at him. She looked deep in thought, like she was studying his expression just as much as he was studying hers, as they moved from the stairs to his bedroom. For as much as he tried to hide what he truly felt on any given day, Amy managed to knock one of his walls down. "Something's on your mind."

Noah shook his head and smiled at her. "It's nothing. Nothing important, anyway."

"Noah, come on," she said, almost in a sing-song voice. "I'm not dumb."

"I never said you were."

She playfully flicked his shoulder on his tattooed side. "My point is even if it's not important, you can tell me."

He wasn't sure what to tell her. As much as he wanted to keep their momentum going and further build her trust, he also knew better than to reveal too much too soon—or at all.

"I know, sweetheart. But seriously, it's nothing. Just overthinking, that's all."

"You? Overthinking?"

He nodded. "My brain never shuts off, believe it or not. Don't worry about it. Just get some rest."

As he kissed her goodnight, Noah knew that this was beyond self-indulgent now, far past the point of no return. But now that he'd enjoyed a taste of freedom, he couldn't get enough of Amy, to the point where it plagued his mind as he tried to sleep until eventually, he dreamed of the man he was before.

———

Noah bit his bottom lip to hold back tears. The pain felt like a hot iron branding his whole body at once, but there was no crying in drug labs, so he grit his teeth and took another deep breath. The leather straps on the chair held him down by his ankles, wrists, and chest, forcing him to stare at his father as Dr. Potter injected him with another syringe; they usually distributed a crystal form, but their secret would be out if Noah had meth teeth, and results showed faster when shooting up. The only reason the restraints weren't suffo-catingly tight anymore was because his sweat coated the space between the leather and his skin. It dripped from his forehead and saturated his clothing, and he wanted nothing more than a cold shower to rinse it off.

Reiji frowned as Noah squirmed and hissed. "Come on, son."

Noah wanted nothing more than to bite back at his father, but it took everything in him not to scream from the burning pain. He'd been through this for years now, but it never got better. The pain only ever worsened, growing hotter and more intense with every test run they performed on him.

So far, this dose was the strongest they'd tried, testing how much his body could handle before some miracle happened. As his head throbbed, Noah wondered if what his father and Dr. Potter were trying was even possible.

Reiji huffed. "Why isn't it working?"

Dr. Potter gave Noah a closed-lipped smile, the kind where his lips pursed in an act of silent sympathy. He then turned to Reiji and said, "He's showing progress. For babies in the womb, they have a more prolonged exposure at extremely high doses, high enough to risk miscarriage in any other circum-stance. Therefore, it's not a perfect one-to-one replication, nor will it be."

"We can't keep doing this."

Finally, something Noah and his father agreed on.

"Shall we cease for the day?"

"No, not yet."

"We've been going at it for years. My professional advice? Let him rest, just for the rest of the week."

"After all this time?" Reiji approached Dr. Potter, close enough now for Noah to smell his father's cologne: cardamom, bergamot, musk, expensive. A fourth scent, though, still overpowered the rest, but Noah wasn't sure where the sulfur came from. He was too focused on trying to regain his breath that he couldn't be bothered to care.

"Let me compare his blood against Hematite's again. We will evaluate from there."

Reiji exhaled through his nostrils, slow and heavy. "Fine."

As Dr. Potter prepared a new needle and syringe, he turned to Noah and softened. "How are you feeling, Noah? Well enough for a status report?"

Noah wasn't sure if the doctor's sudden gentle speech made him feel grateful or annoyed. He felt like death was wrapping its long fingers around his neck, cutting off the supply of oxygen to his lungs, but when he tried to open his mouth, his stomach churned. He stilled for a moment in hopes it would settle, but when the feeling persisted, he sputtered out, "Do you have a bucket?"

Dr. Potter set the needle down and grabbed what Noah requested, holding it in front of his face. Reiji groaned and looked away as Noah lurched into the bucket while Dr. Potter held the rim for him. The contents tasted like burnt charcoal as they came up, the flavor lingering in his mouth and burning his throat; and it didn't look much better in the bucket. As Noah looked at the black sludge before Dr. Potter yanked the bucket away, he was certain he was going to die. He almost wished he would so this torment and the heat coursing through his veins would all be over.

"I'm still running the blood test, but he needs rest," Dr. Potter said, as he set the bucket down with a harrowing thud. Noah had never heard anyone speak so firmly to his father, and he wasn't entirely convinced he hadn't hallucinated it. Dr. Potter grabbed a handkerchief from one of his lab coat pockets and used it to dab Noah's chin clean. "He cannot proceed like this."

"My son is strong. He'll be fine."

"That may be true, but I will not risk his life over this when it is so clearly apparent that he is unwell. With all due respect, Mr. Sato, this is unwise and irresponsible, even by my standards."

"And what if the next dose is the one?"

"Even so, these are not suitable conditions. We will need to change our approach moving forward."

Reiji sighed once more, long and deep—his signature when he was wrong but refused to admit it. "Just take his blood, and then we'll go. I'm expecting a payment at the restaurant, and we need to be going. Share the results with me in the morning."

Dr. Potter nodded. "Just one last prick, Noah. There, there."

Noah didn't even feel it. His chest hurt too much, his heart felt like it would emerge from his body like a bad science fiction movie, and his breathing *felt extra labored after vomiting up the lava-like substance. The room seemed to spin around him, despite being stationary.*

"Doc, I…"

Noah didn't finish his sentence. Instead, he gasped for a breath that felt as sharp as knives as a pins-and-needles feeling overwhelmed his legs. He wasn't sure if steam was coming off his skin or if his vision was going blurry. Given what they were doing to him, perhaps both were true.

Dr. Potter sucked his teeth and pulled something else out of his lab coat. "Here. Take this." He unwrapped it and shoved it into Noah's mouth. It was black but tasted like a strawberry hard candy with an earthy, smoky taste that didn't naturally belong. "I've added activated charcoal to this, as well as my own personal touches, patent pending. That should help."

Noah couldn't tell if Dr. Potter was joking or not. He wanted to lunge for him and then his father, but that was what the leather straps were for. He hadn't always felt this angry, but he didn't blame it on the methamphetamines like his father did.

His anger wasn't because of the drugs; enhanced, maybe, but not the cause.

It was just because of his father.

———

Noah woke in a cold sweat, and his worries from the previous day remained that morning. He looked down at his arms and plopped his head back against his pillow, giving himself a moment to breathe. Between his burn and his tattoo sleeve, the marks on his arms from repeated needle injections were gone, having disappeared beneath altered skin—just the way he intended.

Even after six years, the memories of the experiments haunted him. He'd been so close to a normal life, to finishing grad school and getting out of Riverpeak, but that one day robbed him of that. His father robbed him of it. Instead, he could still taste the lava he'd puked up that day nearly seven years prior.

As he turned over and sat up, he ran a hand over his hair, pushing some of it out of his face. He swung his legs over the edge of the bed, needing a moment to think, but it was hard to clear his head with Amy in his bed. The sun streaming on Amy's face made her glow, illuminating her red hair and highlighting her freckles. Part of him—his old self—wanted to reach out to her, brush some hair out of her eyes, and protect her from what would come. But he couldn't do this alone, and his desire to prove a point triumphed.

Focus was paramount, and he was forcing himself to not fall off schedule. The ache in his burned arm snapped him out of his focus on Amy, reaching with his other to grab the moisturizing ointment he kept on his bedside table to ease the taut skin's stiffness. He was stalling, distracting himself from Amy beside him, knowing it was only a matter of time before she woke up.

When she did, he wasn't sure if he should cook her breakfast or kick her out the door.

CHAPTER 8

When Amy woke up, she felt more refreshed than she had in years. She hadn't realized how little true rest she'd gotten when she was with Shawn, but now, she found sleep came easier. While she wasn't sure how much of that could be attributed to time with Noah or away from Shawn, she was just relieved to feel at peace. She was still nude from the night prior, as was Noah, as he applied a moisturizing, odorless ointment to his skin. From the looks of the bottle, it wasn't cheap.

"Sorry if I woke you," he said, deadpan as he focused on applying his ointment while in bed. She couldn't decipher what he was feeling. Knowing him, Amy wondered if he even could.

"It's fine," she said, as she rubbed her eyes. "You didn't."

Before she could continue, Noah interrupted, "Everything out of your system now?"

Her brows furrowed as she stretched her arms out and cracked her neck. "Excuse me?"

"Come on, Amy," Noah said, as he turned to face her. "You and I both know that you don't know what you're getting yourself into." He sighed. "I'm surprised you're even still here. I half expected you to sneak out in the middle of the night to avoid anyone seeing you."

She shifted to sit up. "If you think I was here just to get laid, then you're mistaken." She was almost offended at the idea but also knew the circumstances were bizarre.

Noah scoffed. "If you're going through your rebellious rebound phase now, then trust me. That's exactly what you have been doing for the last few weeks. But now that you've seen the truth, I've gotta admit, I was expecting you to bolt."

"I'm serious," she said, standing her ground. Amy's sudden sternness caught his attention. "I decided enough was enough, Noah. Sure, maybe this started as just a hook-up, and I can understand you being hesitant now that I know everything. But you and I … we have the same endgame, here. Where is this coming from?"

"There is a pretty high likelihood that no happy ending can come from this. I'm just trying to make sure your expectations are clear."

"I gave up on the idea of a happy ending a long time ago," Amy assured him. "I just want justice for both of us at this point. Doesn't matter what that looks like."

Noah ran a hand back through his hair and finally looked at her. "You know that this is it, right? If you proceed with me today, then you can't change your mind about this anymore. This is a rabbit hole you can't easily climb out of."

"I know." She sighed. "Let me guess—this is a test."

"Abso-fucking-lutely it is."

"I'm committed, Noah. There's no sense in trying to push me away."

"Fine. Then let's set some ground rules before I take you downstairs and give you the rundown. You work with me. You don't work for Sterling or Carter or any of them in the drug ring. It's just you and me."

"Let me guess again—the drug ring cannot know this," Amy said.

Noah grinned. "Good girl." He was relieved. *I don't know if I have it in me to tell her to scram*, he thought, even if he wasn't totally sure why he felt that way.

"I want to help you. However you need it, let me know."

"What are you expecting in return?" Noah didn't think she'd just let him use her so easily.

"I'm not," Amy said honestly. "I'm sure you're used to nothing being free, but the idea of revenge gives me peace of mind."

He frowned. "He really fucked you up, huh?"

"I mean, yeah," she said with a shrug. "Him, my friends who basically abandoned me because of him, my parents. The only reason I still speak to them is because I work for them. But we've never seen eye to eye."

"That sounds familiar. So, what's your endgame now?"

"Make sure that the wrong people don't get put up on pedestals."

"Well then, sweetheart, you came to the right man." Noah winked at her. "It's getting too dangerous out there, and you're too valuable of an asset to risk. You'd do best behind the scenes."

"Sure, yeah. And if you ever need anywhere to go that's not here, you can always come to my apartment."

"That's probably better than here. You're too high profile to be seen around here anymore than I'm sure you already have been."

"Says the guy who gave me a hickey. Am I not too high profile for that?"

"Nah," he teased with a wink. "I take pleasure in people wondering who marked up the Brewers' precious little daughter like a schoolgirl behind the bleachers."

She rolled her eyes. "If you're that desperate for that fantasy, Noah, I've got some old Halloween costumes."

He barked a laugh and leaned across the bed to give Amy a kiss on her lips. It left her feeling dazed as he said, "You and me, we gotta look out for each other."

She nodded. "Yeah. We do, so no more of this trying to push me away bullshit."

"If you're ready for this, I can show you everything. But once you go down there, that's it. You're in. It's not so easy getting out."

"I know. Like I said, I'm in. When I say I have nothing to lose, I mean it."

"Alright then. Shall we?"

———

As they moved downstairs to the living room, the bareness of it all made so much more sense to Amy. She saw everything in a new light, finally understanding why he kept it looking like a model home, untouched and without flaw. It hid a deeper secret both below and above: Noah's existence and the drug with a chokehold on their town. They stopped at a door between the living room and the kitchen.

"It's just behind here," Noah said. He grabbed a key from a side table and used it to unlock the door, putting the key back in its place. He did so like it was a routine he'd done a thousand times before, acting solely on muscle memory. Noah opened the door to the basement steps and waited for Amy to grab it before he proceeded, leading the way down. It was so dark that Amy had to stay close to him until they reached the bottom, where Noah flipped on the light.

"This is what I've been hiding from you. Behold, the basement!"

Noah held his arms out as he turned on his heel to draw her attention to all corners of the room, making himself look like the ringmaster of a drug-funded circus. There were rows of tables with different science equipment and other tools: beakers, portable stovetops that she'd seen people use for camping, food scales to measure weight, vials, syringes, and small plastic bags. As Amy took everything in, Noah leaned against one of the tables.

"I wanted to show you before everyone shows up later tonight for work."

Amy approached a table with a few full bags. They were filled with an amber-colored crystal. "So, this is the stuff, huh?"

"In the flesh, and I the fruit of its labor. This is what I've been doing for the last few years. My father hid me from my family because of all this."

"So that explains why someone killed him."

"When you're in this business, you make a lot of enemies," Noah said. "But you don't have much to worry about, especially with me. No one will expect someone as squeaky clean as you to pedal all this."

"Except Shawn, now that you've texted him."

To Amy's surprise, Noah smiled. It wasn't the reaction she was expecting. She recognized it before, somewhere between confident and cocky. Toeing the line seemed to be a pattern with him.

"Let him think that. If he comes crawling to us, then he'll be right where we want him. But until then, I'm going to enjoy keeping you my little secret."

"This looks like a pretty big operation, so I'm not going to fight you on that." Amy looked around the room, taking it all in. She was in over her head, that much she knew, but if she was to work exclusively with Noah, then she thought it couldn't be so bad. After all, he'd been there for her when no one else was, providing both a distraction and, now, a unique opportunity. Amy held her own hands, fidgeting with her fingers. "So, before we get started, I have a few questions I'd like to ask, if you don't mind."

"Not at all." He shrugged, his tone matching his nonchalant body language as he shifted his weight. "Fire away."

"I always knew there was a drug problem over on the east side, but this is ... a lot. How widespread is this?" She gestured at the room as she asked and leaned against a table with nothing on it.

"We've got a pretty popular market up in Denver, what with all the colleges up there, and there's some demand in Colorado Springs. But the money? It's in all these small towns between here and there."

"Wait, really?"

"I mean, you figure, small town, not much to do, so they try it to get through their boring days. Gives them energy, you know? That's the meth in there working. But that crash?" He let out a low whistle. "They hate it. Sterling's father developed this over at Potter Laboratories. It started as just meth, but they had the doctor out there make some tweaks. I'm not sure exactly what he did or how he did it, but now we're here."

"So that's how they get powers. From whatever that doctor did to it."

Noah nodded. "More or less. It's a bit more complicated than that. There were a few pregnant women who couldn't quite shake their addictions. One of those was Hematite's mother; another was your ex-boyfriend's. Their babies came out as super-powered, little freaks of nature."

"Huh. So, what inspired you to do this, anyway? I mean, I get the general gist of everything. My life probably would have been incredibly different had I been able to properly fight back, but is there more to it?"

Noah licked his lips. "Hmm. How do I explain it?" He picked at his thumbnail with his teeth. "You know, it's weird. When Hematite saved Rory Miller in college, my sister was with her. The way Naomi explained it to me, he saved their lives. Said Rory's stalker was some crazy piece of shit who felt entitled to women." He sighed. "So, it feels weird now that Hematite is trying to shut down our whole operation. Man saved my sister's life, and now I gotta take him out. And I can't help but wonder how different things might have been if my sister or Rory had a fair chance to take that guy down themselves."

"Wait, for real? I didn't know Naomi was with her."

"I think it screwed Rory up more than it did my sister. And while I don't think that guy had powers, imagine if he did. Then what, you know? People would think twice before they tried any shit, that's what, and people who have been kicked down can finally get back up. Just … this whole thing is fucked. It's time we level the playing field."

"Do you think you'll reunite with her? It sounds like you care about her."

Noah shook his head. "Once upon a time, sure. But things are different now. We can't, not in the way she hopes. I'm at peace with that." He picked at his nail again, but then caught himself. "Sorry. Bad habit that I do when I can't smoke. I'm trying to ween off."

"It's fine. Can I ask one last question?"

"You can ask more than one if you really want."

"Do you know who Hematite is?"

"I think I do. I have a pretty good theory in the works. Why, do you?"

Amy shook her head. "No. I asked, but Shawn refused to tell me. The bastard never shuts his mouth so I thought for sure he'd spill, but Hematite must have something on him or something. I've never known Shawn to be loyal without good reason."

Her phone vibrated twice in her back pocket, shaking the table behind her. They both ignored it.

"It's pretty easy to figure out if you look at this whole interconnected web of people," Noah said. "Hematite sure did spend a lot of time with Rory Miller last year, didn't he?"

Her phone vibrated again, two more quick pulses.

"Wait, hold up. You think it's Kane Kelly?"

"All I need to do is yank that stupid mask off his face to be completely sure, but I'd put money on it, yeah."

Another vibration indicated another text message.

"He lives in my apartment complex."

"Small world, then, huh?" Her phone buzzed once more. "Sorry, but who the fuck is texting you so much?"

"I have no idea. Let me check. I'm so sorry."

"I'm not upset with you, sweetheart. Shit, my bad. I could have worded that better." Noah crossed the room to stand beside her, resting his chin on her shoulder. "Just wondering what's so urgent."

Amy felt the tension leave her body right away; her shoulders relaxed, cracking in the process. "Thanks. I don't know this number, but I'm pretty sure it's Shawn. My guess is a burner."

Noah grabbed her phone. "Don't even give this asshole the time of day."

He scanned over the messages, quickly reading them in silence.

> SHAWN: This has gone on long enough.
>
> SHAWN: You know that being Sato's whore won't fix your problems, right?
>
> SHAWN: Didn't realize a dead man could still get it up. Is it cold when he goes in?

Amy tried to peer over to the side where he held her phone to read the texts, but Noah snatched it to his chest before she could. "What's he saying?"

"Nothing you should worry about." Noah kissed the top of her head and then stepped away. He pulled out his own phone, took a photo of hers to keep a record of the texts, and then deleted Shawn's messages from her phone. The video he had of them on the stairs crossed his mind, but he decided against sending it, feeling too protective over Amy. "I don't want you looking at that."

"Yet you're taking photos of it. Can I ask why?"

"Evidence. Just in case. One of us should keep records of this, but you don't need this shit, and it won't do your mental health any favors."

Her gaze softened as she smiled. "Your inner therapist is coming out."

There it was again—his old self wrestling for dominance within his mind. She brought out that side of him more and more, and Noah wasn't sure if it would help or hurt him in the long run. He decided to play dumb. "My inner therapist?"

She giggled. "You do this thing sometimes where you get a little analytical when it comes to emotions. But it's sweet."

"Guess I can't help myself." Noah winked.

Amy blushed before her expression faltered, remembering what was on her phone. "I just wish we could say the same about everyone else."

"Well, hey, if he wants to start talking shit, guess what?" Noah looked as confident as ever, his usual smile taking over his face. "Two can play that game."

Her eyes narrowed, but his smile was contagious. "What do you have in mind?"

"You've seen how many followers Mark had. Let's take over the YouTube channel. Give them something to watch."

CHAPTER 9

Walking through the security scanner of the local prison was not something Amy ever thought she'd do in her life. Even though she was only a visitor, she still felt guilty of something for just being there. Amy's breath felt stuck in her chest, only released once they moved on. She had nothing to hide from the security guards, but it didn't make her feel any less uneasy. Noah, however, maintained his usual confidence. Maybe that was his secret—to fake it until he made it, even in front of the police.

One of the guards stepped to be in stride with them. "Follow me."

"Are we not going to the visitation room?" Amy asked. "That's the other way."

The guard laughed. "Visitation? No. This little shit's lucky that he gets visitors at all." Amy couldn't quite place his accent; her guess was Boston, if not New York. "But he won't see outside of his cell. He's too violent."

Noah's eyes widened. "Since when? Kid's a twerp."

"That's what we thought, too, until he beat up two guards. Guess he's toughened up since being here."

"Ha! No fuckin' way."

"That's what I said when I found out."

As the men laughed, Amy swallowed, suddenly unsure if this was a good idea.

Once they were alone with the guard, still moving through the halls, he said in a lower tone of voice, "You ask me? It's too bad he didn't start acting like this until he got thrown in the can, you know what I mean? Maybe the little shit wouldn't have lost to Hematite and his little girlfriend. Wicked fuckin' loser."

Boston, Amy thought. *Definitely Boston.*

Noah said, "Yeah, you're tellin' me. Silver lining is that at least he finally grew a spine, though, right?"

As the guard took them down a long, dark hallway, he said, "Silver indeed."

The hall was damp enough for the moisture to linger on Amy's skin, building up with some nervous sweat. Noah couldn't look any less bothered by their surroundings, and Amy felt like there was an inside joke she wasn't in on.

"Last one at the end. Since this town's pretty boring, he's the only one down here. Have at it." The guard turned around and left them alone in the hall of empty cells, leaving only the sound of his footsteps behind.

Noah whistled as they walked the rest of the way. The sound echoed off the halls alongside a leaky pipe dripping at a tantalizing slow rate, and Amy was pretty sure it was a way for him to taunt Mark. If it was, it worked.

When they reached the last cell, they saw Mark sitting in a chair facing the bars. His blond hair grew out in the last year and he hadn't bothered to shave his face, leaving him with an unkempt beard and scorn in his blue eyes.

"Nice of you to show up."

"Oh, hi Mark. How's it going, huh, buddy?" Noah flashed Mark a smile, but Mark didn't return the expression. "This is Amy. We're … colleagues, so to speak."

Mark's dead stare bore right through Amy. "We're acquainted."

"Hey, Mark." Amy waved at him and licked her lips out of nerves. "Sorry to see you like this."

"Yeah, it sucks."

"Oh, you two know each other?" Noah asked.

"We had classes together in high school. What do you want, Sato?"

Noah kept his hands in his pockets. His gaze was at his feet, as if he couldn't care less that Mark was here. "You don't seem too thrilled to see us, so I will cut right to the chase. I would love nothing more than to bring Stone Breaker back."

Mark rolled his eyes. "And how do you suppose we'll do that?"

"Oh, not we." Noah gestured to himself and Mark with his pinky and thumb, then turned his hand so he was pointing at himself and Amy. "Just me and Amy."

Mark laughed loud enough for it to echo.

"What's so funny?"

"Wait, hold on. Let me get this straight. So, you want to bring Stone Breaker back but without Stone Breaker?"

Noah smiled. "See, you get it!"

"No, I don't fucking get it! How the hell does that work?"

Amy shifted her weight, needing to release some pent-up energy. Time away from his father must have given Mark a new fortitude. Amy always remembered him as timid and meek, not unlike herself. But time changes people, as she felt it changing her, and Mark was no different.

"Well," Noah said, "the way that I see it is that Stone Breaker is a moniker, not a man. How many different Robins did Batman go through, you know?"

Mark leaned back in his chair and crossed his arms. "Think about the implication for a minute, there."

"I'm well aware of the implication," Noah said. "I know you're pissed off because you're here now, but let's face it. You were a pawn. And before you blow up at me for that, I was also a pawn. Unfortunately, not every pawn survives the chessboard. We're all just here trying to protect the king."

"So, what does that make you now? Sterling's little queen?"

"It may look like that, but I'm still just a pawn, too."

Mark frowned. "Alright, alright. So how do you propose we'll bring Stone Breaker back?"

"Can you get us the login for your YouTube channel?" The blow should have been devastating, but Noah delivered it with such charm that Mark didn't even realize it hit him. "Amy and I understand that you're limited. Can't exactly create YouTube videos from here. But we want to get back at Hematite just as bad as you do. If it works, I can even make it worth your while."

"How do you reckon?"

Noah finally looked up at Mark. "I could get you the hell out of here."

Mark's eyes narrowed in annoyance. "I don't exactly have the option to be bailed out. Detective McMahon fought tooth and nail for that and won."

"I wasn't talking about bail." Noah winked. "I won't say much more. You get my drift, right? So how about we get those login credentials?"

Mark didn't say much else. He rattled them off, which Amy jotted down on her phone the second they left the building.

"Too fucking easy," Noah said. "Kid's grown some balls since we last saw him, though, huh?"

"For real. He used to be so mild-mannered."

"I think his father scared the shit out of him, but now? Now that's a concern of the past. Heard his dad's mistress is doing alright, though."

"Speaking of which, what's the deal with the new chief? Have you heard anything about him?"

"Boss is already on it. Even though we lost the connection with Eliza, there are still a few other departments that Sterling has a shoe in with."

"So more or less under your crew's control?"

Noah shrugged his shoulder. "Almost, anyway."

As they got in the car, Amy asked, "Are you seriously going to stage a prison break?"

Noah laughed. "Yeah, right. What do you think I am, stupid? No fuckin' way. He can rot in there for all I give a shit."

———

Once they returned to Noah's house, they got to work logging into Mark's Google account. He'd created a separate one for Stone Breaker in a half-baked attempt at making it harder to track him. Luckily, he didn't have multi-factor authentication on—also so anyone couldn't trace a phone number back to him.

"And we're in," Noah said from the chair in front of his desk, where his laptop was flipped open.

Amy looked over his shoulder. "How many subscribers does he have?"

Noah grinned like he just won the lottery. "Three thousand."

"Three thousand? That's it? That's nothing."

Noah looked from the computer screen up to Amy. The glow of the laptop illuminated his face as the sun set behind the mountains out the window, darkening the room. "Maybe online, yeah. But imagine if we got three thousand people in a room. Even if we only got three hundred of them. Shit, even thirty would be helpful."

Amy understood what he was getting at. "You want to reach out to them? Can we do that?"

"YouTube won't show you who is subscribed, but we can make a video asking for help. What do you say?" Noah stood up and moved to his closet, beginning to rummage in a box on the floor of it.

"What are you looking for?"

"This." He stood back up and returned with a neon mask. "Can't show your face, after all."

"Wait." She pointed at herself. "My face?"

"I mean, yeah. It's *your* ex-boyfriend." Noah passed her the mask. "Figured I'd let you do the honors."

Amy held the mask in her hands. When she flipped it on, the three vertical, neon lines were where her eyes should be lit up to a bright red, as did the mouth. When Amy looked up, she saw the childhood photo on Noah's desk. A kitsune mask was tilted on his head in the photo; from the looks of it, he and his sister were at a festival. She wondered how many different masks he had.

"I dunno."

"Come on, Ames, I know you can do it. It'll feel cathartic."

She nodded reluctantly, only because she knew he was right. "Where did you get this?"

"Online. I don't have a 3D printer, but either way, the neon is cooler than whatever dumb paint job Mark did to his."

"Touché."

"All in favor of killing his shitty lightning motif?"

Amy nearly snorted. "You don't have to twist my arm for that. Are you going to wear a mask, too?"

"Me?" He shook his head. "No, I don't need one."

"Why not?" Amy was surprised to hear that. "Shawn and Hematite wear them. So did Stone Breaker and his little sidekick, I don't remember his name. So, shouldn't you?

"Mark was an incompetent man-child who couldn't get the job done well enough to not rely on a mask, so let's not compare ourselves to him. Apples to oranges. Me? I don't have anything to hide. Not anymore. You, however, I want to protect."

Amy's surprise turned into something more sentimental. "Oh, wow."

"Wow?"

"It's just that I don't think anyone's ever said something like that to me before."

Noah grabbed her face and kissed her forehead, sending butterflies through her body that stemmed in her solar plexus. "Well, get used to it. And hey, if you want to change your clothes before we film, I've got enough without logos or anything."

"What do you think? All black?"

"That will probably be easiest to hide." Noah moved back to his closet and thumbed through. "They'll probably be a little baggy on you, but that'll help hide who you are even more."

"Good thinking." As Noah picked some plain pieces, she removed her jeans and sweater, replacing them as he handed her the black hoodie and pants. "God, I'm gonna look like Hematite in this."

Noah laughed. "You know so did the guy who killed my dad. Maybe they'll really freak out after this. Could work in our favor." Noah took his computer chair, slid it out to the center of his bedroom, and then grabbed a few books, piling them up as Amy changed. "I'll film."

Amy took a deep breath as she slid the mask over her face and sat in the chair. Noah stood next to his phone, which he'd set up on the stack of books to act as a makeshift tripod. Once she sat, he flipped the lights off and then drew the blinds. The only light in the room came from Amy's neon mask, which provided a faint red glow. She could barely see from it but could make out Noah well enough through the mesh over the eyeholes.

"How's the lighting?"

"Pitch black," he said. "They'll never know where we are, so don't worry."

"Okay. And what about my voice? Should we just edit it in post?"

"Yeah. Mark did that, too. Are you stalling?"

She was glad she had the mask to hide her blush of embarrassment. "Maybe."

"You got this, Ames. I believe in you. And besides, if you fuck up, we can always just film another take. I got all day."

She took another deep breath. "Right, right." Amy straightened her posture, which made her upper back audibly crack as her shoulders rolled back, and then she spoke to the camera. "Stone Breaker is back … sort of. He's still in jail, but that hasn't stopped us from moving forward. After all, he was never operating alone."

Amy stopped, unsure of how much to say. The sudden urge to crack her neck arose, but she ignored it and continued, "While Stone Breaker's arrest set us back, Hematite has won only that battle. With your help, we can win the war."

When she paused to take a deep breath, she made a mental note to edit it out later. At the reminder that anything she wasn't happy with could simply be cut, she felt some tension in her jaw release with a light crack. She continued, "Stone Breaker wanted to take down Hematite, but I think we need to dream bigger. I think we need to stop this hero society that we've created here in Colorado and let everyone feel more empowered. We need to put these heroes in their place, one by one."

Amy rolled her shoulders back, feeling more confident. The mask gave her a boost, but she found herself in a rhythm the more she spoke. This kind of confidence didn't come easily to her, but after a few weeks with Noah, she felt like she'd been deprogrammed from a cult.

"Let me turn your attention to Brick Beast. Brick Beast does not care about you. He does not care about Riverpeak or Denver or Colorado Springs. He doesn't even care about Hematite! Can you believe it? Brick Beast only cares about one thing: himself."

As she said those words, it felt like a weight was lifted off her chest. The burden of keeping Shawn's secrets and protecting him was no longer hers to bear, and she knew that if it came down to it, Shawn wouldn't do the same for her—but Noah?

Noah would.

"Heroes like this, who chase the fame Hematite got, have no place in this world. We happen to know everything you need to know about Brick Beast, and we're willing to drop the details once we hit 100,000 views. But until then, give 'em hell, and let us know if you spot either of them."

When she was done, Noah asked, "Why 100,000?"

Amy shrugged as she took the mask off and stood to stretch her legs. She hadn't realized how hot she'd been under it until it was off her face. "I figured we might as well monetize it."

"Hm. I like the way you think."

"Should we film the second video so we can have it ready?"

"Sure, if you want."

"I'm in a groove now. Might as well ride the wave while I still can."

Amy put the mask back on and settled back into her seat. As she did, Noah said, "I'm real proud of you, Ames."

"You are?"

With a warm smile that reached his honey eyes, he nodded. "Yeah, I am. You've come a long way already. Ready?"

"That means a lot, especially coming from you. Thanks. Ready."

"We're rolling."

"We are here today to expose the false hero Brick Beast. Let me introduce you to Shawn Jameson. Shawn Jameson is your stereotypical greasy salesman who doesn't care about others around him. Brick Beast is taking advantage of the crime in this city to give himself a spotlight rather than genuinely wanting to help those in need. Have you noticed how much worse crime has gotten in Riverpeak, not better? He abuses his friends and partners with no remorse."

She smiled. This felt good.

It felt *too* good.

When she looked at Noah, he was smiling; that was all the approval she needed.

"And unlike Hematite, he bleeds like the rest of us."

CHAPTER 10

When Amy took the mask off for the second time, she gave Noah a smile unlike any he'd seen from her. Her expression would put a Cheshire Cat to shame. Noah recognized that glimmer in her eyes from his own reflection, particularly from the night he killed his father. That meant only one thing: Amy was getting revenge, and she was loving it.

Noah leaned back in his chair. "Felt good, didn't it?"

She exhaled and felt some pressure leave her body. "Even better than I thought. I wasn't sure if I'd be able to pull that off since I'm not typically the video type, you know? But holy shit! Let's get these on to your computer so I can edit them before I start doubting myself."

"Fair enough." He sent them to himself, then set his phone on the desk where he sat. "Want to unpack that?"

"What, my self-doubt?"

"Yeah."

"This is just really new for me. I don't know, I guess it's because I've never stepped out of line before." She stood up from the chair she was in and removed his clothing, draping the articles across the back of it while she changed. "Typical of me to hop from one extreme to the other."

"That so?"

"Does that surprise you?"

He shook his head. "Honestly? No, I can see that."

"I bet you're also wondering why I didn't leave him sooner."

"How long were you together? Two years, right?"

"About that."

"Well, regardless, no, I wasn't thinking that. I was almost a psychiatrist, remember? So I get it. Walking away from something like that can be fucking terrifying, even if you don't factor in the literal superhuman strength. You're not beating yourself up for that, are you?"

"You know," she said, as she sat on his lap, "no matter how many times you do it, it never ceases to amaze me how you can just see right through me."

Noah kissed her cheek. "You're lucky you're cute, or else I'd start chargin'."

That made her laugh. *Good,* he thought.

"That so?"

"Mhm. But I can think of some alternative forms of acceptable payment."

Another laugh.

Good. More.

"Alright, there. Cool it with the porno plot."

She was still laughing as he kissed her, and it sent a vibration through Noah's chest as he wrapped his arms around her. It had been years since he felt joy like this, a kind of warmth that even he couldn't produce.

I could get used to this, Noah thought, *especially once I reach my goal.*

When Noah broke away from the kiss, he glanced at his phone on the desk as it buzzed and lit up. Sterling's name flashed across the screen.

"Sorry, sweetheart. Gotta take this." Noah kissed her cheek as he grabbed his phone. She shifted off his lap so he could step out of the room for privacy. He wasn't sure why Sterling was calling and while he trusted Amy enough, his gut told him this call should be private. Noah answered as he slid down the railing to reach the ground floor.

"Sterling! How's it going?"

"Good, good, thanks for asking." Sterling spoke slowly and with purpose, every word holding a deeper meaning. Noah knew him well enough to know that. "Are you alone?"

"Depends on how you'd define alone."

"Is anyone in the room with you?"

"No, not in the room."

"Okay, great. I can speak candidly then."

"I'd be disappointed if you didn't speak candidly with me."

"Heh. Listen, I have a question for you. I noticed you're spending a lot of time with Amy Brewer. Is that correct?"

Noah leaned against the arm of the couch. "And so what if I am?" His tone was light, not wanting to provoke Sterling but also wanting to stand his ground. How Noah worked was no one's business but his own—including Sterling's.

"What are you doing with her?"

Noah shrugged a shoulder, even though Sterling couldn't see it. "We're just having fun."

Sterling replied with a hint of a chuckle. "Fun? Is that what you're calling it, then?"

"Yeah. We're having fun." It wasn't a lie, but Sterling didn't need to know how much Noah stretched the truth.

"So it'll be no problem using her as the next test."

Noah swallowed. "Unfortunately, not so simple. In the spirit of speaking candidly, I don't know if she can handle it."

"Hm. Yet she's still here. You sure it's just fun, Noah?"

"I'm sure." That was a lie, but Noah justified it by following it with another truth. "There are other ways she's useful until she's strong enough."

"Relax, relax. I'm just making sure your emotions don't get the best of you. Doesn't her family run the community theater?"

"They do."

"Be careful. I don't like messing with anybody too high profile."

"From what I gather, she's got no real friends, and her family couldn't give half a shit about her. There's a fat chance they'd even notice if she went missing. I'm not worried."

"Still, be on your guard."

"No need to sound like my old man."

Sterling laughed. "No, no. I certainly don't want to end up like him, either. Don't mind me. Just checking in, that's all. Say, while I've got you, have you heard from," Sterling tutted his tongue, "Potter, was it? The doctor you lovingly call a rat bastard."

"Heh, yeah. He's got enough from Kane Kelly to confirm my suspicions. I've got him mixing some of Kelly's shit with the dosage we found for you."

"Not his literal shit, I hope."

"Yeah, actually. No, of course not."

Sterling laughed again. "Excellent. I'm happy to hear it. Keep me posted, will you?"

"Sure, sure."

Before Noah could say anything else, Sterling hung up. Noah pulled the phone away from his ear and stared at the blank screen for a moment, digesting the vague threat.

Amy and the theater were his key. Noah knew that; he'd just have to prove it.

He bounded up the stairs, anxious to return to his room and Amy. The other women had been mere test subjects, but she was shaping up to be a valuable partner. Noah saw his own desire for revenge reflected in her eyes whenever he looked at her and the same disdain for the so-called community around them. *Perhaps*, he figured, *it's why we work so well together*.

When he re-entered his room, he said, "Just a check-in from Sterling. Nothing urgent. All good."

Amy glanced away from the computer to look at him. "Sterling?"

"Big boss man. See, everyone thought that Stone Breaker was the scary one. But when Sterling gets involved? Ooh, he's cold."

Noah didn't want to dive too far into that with Amy so he wouldn't scare her away; he'd watched Sterling kill men for getting caught by Hematite before without so much as batting an eye.

To change the subject, Noah asked, "How's the video?" He leaned over her, propping his chin on her shoulder to see. "Oh, cool edits. You're good at this." His phone alarm beeped, causing an initial wave of annoyance to wash over him until he saw it was just a reminder on his screen. "Sorry, don't mind me."

Noah shrugged off his jacket and tossed it behind them. It landed on the edge of his bed. His shirt followed, joining the jacket as he reached inside the desk drawer and pulled out a bottle of moisturizer. Amy didn't recognize the brand, but she could tell by the bottle that it was expensive and the same one he'd used the last time she saw him lotion up. Noah applied the gel to his burned shoulder and then worked his way down the arm.

"If I do this too close to going to bed, I feel all slimy and can't sleep. Hence the alarm; otherwise, I forget."

"No worries. Do you need a hand?"

"Oh, no, I've more or less got it down. Sometimes I miss a spot here or there, but it's usually close enough."

When he finished applying, Amy got up, squeezed a pea-sized amount out, and rubbed it into the back of his shoulder. "Here. Missed a spot."

Noah's lips twitched as he fought a smile. He lost that fight. "Thanks. Appreciated."

"How did you get burned, anyway?"

Noah glanced at Amy over his shoulder. Her eyes widened beneath his gaze.

"Sorry, should I have not asked that?"

"No, no, I don't care. Just surprised you asked."

"Oh, thank God. I got kinda nervous for a second."

"You're fine, sweetheart." Noah kissed her temple. "So, my dad pumped me full of the stuff, right? You know that already. And this one day, they pushed me to the brink. I had to take something for my overdose. It kicks in, and I'm finally not feeling totally ill, so he brings me to the back of one of the restaurants so we can chat privately and pick up a payment from one of his sellers. He asks if I'd felt any changes and I said no, not besides how sick I felt. We start fighting, but I walk away because all of a sudden, I'm sweating bullets again."

"Oh, wow." She was facing him now, eyes on his as he spoke.

"He makes a call and a few minutes later, the seller he was waiting for shows up. He stumbles to the back. My dad hands him something,

I didn't catch what, and then the guy leaves. He starts yelling at me again, telling me how time is ticking, and I start to feel real sick. But it's different this time. I'm feverish, I'm still sweating, and all I can smell is sulfur. When I ask, he says he doesn't smell it, but now he's pissed that I've changed the subject. You see, he thinks I'm faking it at this point. I tell him that if this is what my future holds, then I want out. I point like this," Noah said, as he gestured with his burnt arm, "and then next thing I know, the fryer beneath my arm lights up. My whole fucking arm catches fire. My dad tries to help me put it out, and once my arm is mostly clear, we try to get the thing under control. But it wouldn't stop. Whole building caught fire next. So, I told him to leave."

"You didn't go too?"

"Nah, I hoped I'd die." Noah sighed and ran his fingers through Amy's hair. "I really hoped it would've killed me. As my anger started to turn into acceptance, I noticed the flame start to dwindle down. I realized it was me." He sighed. "The smoke alarms went off before the place completely burned to a crisp, so he tells me to just run to the rental and stay there. Says he'll clean it up. Next thing I know, I'm legally dead and can't even talk to my family anymore."

"I'm so sorry, Noah. That couldn't have been easy."

"It wasn't. I'm not going to sit here and say it was." He swallowed. "You know, sometimes I barely recognize myself."

"How so? Beyond the obvious, I mean."

Something in his chest made him want to reach for Amy. *She cares.* It felt foreign and unusual to him. He'd gone years without so much as a sympathetic remark, and while he hadn't felt he needed it, it didn't stop him from wanting to cling to her. After everything she'd been through, she still cared for those around her.

How noble, he thought. *Please don't stop.*

"Just ... I wonder how different my life might have been. If it was all a waste. Only reason I got wrapped up in this shit was for the cash. But I usually stop myself before I can go too far down that rabbit hole, you know? No point in dwelling on what-if questions."

"Well, I don't think it was a waste," she said. "After all, you've helped me a lot. You still are."

He smiled, more genuinely than he had in ages. "Is that so?"

When she nodded, he grabbed her waist and kissed her. Noah loved the way she melted right into him, somewhere between trust and desire. Her lips felt like they were meant to kiss his and only his, but he stopped himself from going there before the thought could continue.

He was getting soft; that was dangerous.

But by God, does she help me forget.

As they kissed, Noah unbuttoned Amy's shirt and tossed it aside with his feelings. He didn't have time for his emotions, no matter how much they tried to bubble back up.

How pathetic that all it took for me to break was for someone to care.

Noah quickly undressed her before whisking her to his bed, all but tossing her back on the mattress. He stalked over her, trying to gain some semblance of himself back. Indulging himself in her allowed him to narrow his focus and reset his brain, bringing her to the brink so he could remind himself who he was. He wondered if Amy caught on to this, but she seemed to be encouraging him with her moans and the way she'd grasp his hair. So if she did, then it must not have bothered her enough to be worth saying anything.

Noah's hand splayed across her stomach and ran up her sternum, bypassing her chest and heading straight for her throat. His fingers wrapped around her neck, forcing her to look up at him. While he applied no pressure, the feeling of leather-like burnt flesh encasing her skin was enough to have Amy gasping.

"I love it when you look at me," Noah said. "Yeah. Just like that, sweetheart."

Amy didn't know she could feel this much pleasure, and Noah always seemed to push that line every time they spent time together. Never had she felt the shaking of her thighs like this or the way her heart thrummed against her chest. Everything Noah did was for her satisfaction, and she was convinced he did so because he knew it always made the wires in her brain cross. All she could manage was to stutter out his name.

He tutted his tongue. "Come on, I know I can make you say my name louder than that. How about this? I promise that I'll make sure you do before the clock strikes midnight."

"Is that so?"

"It is. Be a good girl for me and I'll make it worth your while."

Noah kept one hand on her throat, never pressing, but letting his fingers linger along her windpipe. Her heart raced from the thrill of it all, and she was hyperaware of the rapid rise and fall of her chest as her breathing quickened. Noah's other hand slowly caressed her body, knuckles tracing over the slight curve of her breasts. He splayed his hand out over one of them, gripping it tight before letting the rough pads of his fingers drag over her nipple. Amy's breath hitched as his mouth lowered to trace where his knuckles had just been, all the while keeping his other hand on its spot around her neck.

"Noah, fuck," Amy muttered. As she felt the heat build in her body, spreading lower, she instinctively bucked her hips up, but his hands moved to her hip bones and pushed them down. Like a cat stalking its prey, Noah slunk down to the space between her legs.

"I told you to be a good girl for me, sweetheart. Don't you even dare think about moving." As he began to kiss up one of her thighs, his hand trailed up the other, slightly ahead of his mouth. When he reached her underwear, he pushed them aside to kiss her clit. Amy whimpered, struggling to obey his command of staying still.

"Noah, *please.*"

He looked up at her through his eyelashes as he inched her panties down off her legs. The look alone had her body feeling shockwaves. "Come on, Ames. I know we can do better than that. Let's see if I can have you saying my name a little louder before I even properly fuck you, shall we?"

Noah kneeled before Amy, his tongue as sharp with sarcasm as it was between her legs. One of her hands shot up to reach for the sheets above her head, needing something to hold on to, as Noah's teeth grazed her clit. Before she could process the sensation, he all but buried his tongue in her and took his time exploring her. An expert in Amy's mind and body, it didn't take Noah long before he felt the tell-tale sign of her clenching around his tongue. His name passed her lips in a breathy moan.

"Come on, sweetheart, we're gonna have to get a little louder than that," he said, antagonizing her between licks and nips at her clit. As he sucked, Noah inserted two fingers to slowly pump in and out of Amy.

Noah once more looked up with those warm, honey-colored eyes of his—blown with lust, a power trip, and something else Amy couldn't quite put a finger on—and she came again a second time not long after with a louder moan she couldn't control.

"I don't think you're understanding. I want the fuckin' neighbors to hear you," Noah said as moved to crawl on top of her. "Don't hold back. You're already past the point of no return."

"You want me to scream?" Amy asked, feeling bold. For as much as Noah was trying to take the reins, Amy knew he enjoyed the challenge, a game of cat and mouse that she didn't mind losing. "I wonder if you can make me."

Noah accepted the challenge by slamming his cock into her, but found himself groaning again. Normally he had more control of himself, but it felt so good to be inside of her, and she was so wet that it was already driving him crazy. He didn't realize he paused until all of a sudden, Amy flipped him onto his back without ever withdrawing from him. Noah's head rolled back into the pillow as she began to ride him, setting a quick pace with deep thrusts. His hand playfully smacked and then gripped at her ass as she rolled her hips into his.

"I am *so* going to punish you for this."

With a grin cocky enough to rival his own smirk, she said, "Whatever it is, I'm sure will be well worth it."

Noah allowed himself to bask in the pleasure for a moment, including the feeling of her release around him. But once she came, Noah turned Amy to her side and took control once more. He lifted one of her legs up over his hips so he could continue his ministrations, and as he did, he reached over to rub her clit with his middle and index finger. From this angle, Amy could feel him—*really* feel him—and her orgasms started to flow more freely with the increased pace of his hips.

"Fuck, Noah!" It was louder than Amy intended, but she couldn't help the intensity with which she found her release once more. He nipped at her ear and didn't let up, but rather just continued exactly what he was doing. Just when she thought he was going to stop, Noah kept going, leaving her overstimulated. "Fuck, *please*."

"Please what, doll?" Noah whispered into her ear. "You want me to come with you, is that it?" He moved his fingers from her clit, licked one of them clean, and then shoved the middle into her mouth. "See how much you already have?"

"Noah—"

He just chuckled. "Don't worry, I'm not far behind you. You feel so fucking good, Ames."

Noah had stayed true to his word, to the point where he felt lost in her. Something about how she opened up and trusted him when she was on top of or beneath him aroused him on its own. He wasn't sure he'd call it power, since he often willingly handed that over to her the moment they were alone together in his bedroom, but his influence showed as she grew more and more daring. He was liberating her, and he loved it as much as she enjoyed going on her revenge tour. Noah wagered he wasn't entirely bad if he was helping Amy. Even if he had an ulterior motive, the ends justified the means—and if she enjoyed his means just as much as he did, then maybe she'd thank him at the end of the day.

CHAPTER 11

Noah took no pleasure in visiting Potter Laboratories, but sometimes, a house call was necessary. When he walked in the front door a few days after filming videos with Amy, he was met by Dr. Potter working on a computer at the front desk.

"Well, you were easy to find for once," Noah said as he entered the building.

Dr. Potter leaped in his chair. Upon seeing Noah, his shoulders instantly slouched, while his hand reached for the back of his head. "Ah! I was not expecting to see you today."

Noah shrugged as he leaned across the front desk. "The boss has been asking some questions, so I just want to make sure we're all on track. I was running some errands today, so I figured I'd stop by."

Dr. Potter adjusted his lab coat as he stood from his chair. "Naturally. Shall we?"

Noah let Dr. Potter lead him through the laboratory halls, but he practically knew this place like the back of his hand by now. The white and silver rooms and hallways were so sanitary that something about them felt empty. The entire facility was devoid of life, and Dr. Potter's unsettling demeanor didn't help. When Noah first met him before he obtained his fire powers, Dr. Potter always seemed to hold his head high. But now, Noah couldn't recall the last time he'd seen Dr. Potter confident like that.

Noah knew he made the doctor nervous. After all the successful tests resulting in Noah being the super-powered man he was today, it was no wonder why. He hadn't exactly been shy about how he really felt, airing his grievances any chance he got to remind those around him that the one holding the real power was not happy about it. Especially now that his father was out of the picture, it meant Noah essentially got what he wanted—and after more than thirty years of bending to everyone else's wills, he figured it was about time they bent to his.

And bend they did. Noah would be lying if he said he didn't enjoy the power trip.

Dr. Potter held a door open for Noah, revealing the room they usually went to for his exams. Two beakers displayed on a table were connected with some tubes, where two fluids blended together through the tubing.

"And here it is, as you and Mr. Harrison requested," Dr. Potter said. "Cell and blood samples from Kane Kelly combined with the latest dosage."

"How's it working?"

"We won't know until we try," Dr. Potter said. "But fortunately, everything seems to be stable. I'm going to monitor it for the next few weeks and try to replicate this response to check its stability in repeat trials." Dr. Potter swallowed. "We can't be too sure. And ideally, I'd have a more recent sample, but Mr. Kelly hasn't visited in quite some time."

Noah nodded. "Right. Not a bad idea to keep testing, and I can try to get what you need. Last thing we want is blood on our hands, right?"

Dr. Potter chuckled nervously.

Noah nudged him with his elbow, which made Dr. Potter jump. "Come on, Doc. Lighten up."

"Of course, Mr. Sato."

"Mr. Sato? Who do I look like to you, my father?" Noah scoffed. "You know what? Don't answer that question."

"My apologies, Noah."

"Should we test this on anyone?"

"With Kane Kelly's..?"

"Nah, nah. Maybe with a different person's sample so we don't have a bunch of immortals running around here? I think if someone else got their hands on this, Sterling would find a way to kill them over it."

"Ah, I'm sure he would. Was there a test subject you had in mind?"

"I'm sure Sterling wouldn't mind if you gave yourself a little some-thin'-somethin', you know? Given all you've done for him and his old man."

"Oh, I couldn't possibly." Dr. Potter adjusted his glasses as he looked down at his polished dress shoes. Noah could see the doctor's reflection in them.

"Why not?"

"Allow me to assure you, I am not the hero. I am simply a man of science."

"Alright, if you insist." Noah smacked his lips. "I'll let that thought marinate for a while and get back to you. And hey, I've got another question for you. Do you happen to have anything on Shawn Jameson?"

"The Brick Beast? I do. Kane Kelly brought him here once. I used him to confirm the pattern of those affected in utero. He possesses strength unlike any other."

"He got a weakness?"

"Not that I am currently aware of. I also am not sure if Hematite does. As far as I know, Kane's cells are regenerative in nature. I would imagine Shawn's cells operate similarly, especially considering how muscle cells work to strengthen."

"Theory or confirmed?"

"Only a theory, unfortunately. Speaking of which, there is one I'd like to bring to your attention. It is something I would prefer to discuss with you privately before we share this information with Mr. Harrison."

"What's that?"

"Why you have developed your exact power and why we cannot

replicate Kane's ability exactly. This is assuming combining it with some of his cell samples won't work."

Noah rose a brow. "I'm listening."

"I suspect powers are granted based on what you need. How this is determined in utero, I am still unsure. It requires much more study. But I have noticed a trend, if you will. You needed to survive a fire. Kane needed to survive numerous attempted murders. And Shawn Jameson was born to a single mother who barely provided for him, needing strength to rely on himself."

Dr. Potter looked like he wanted to say something else, but he smiled instead. But there was an unease in his expression Noah would have spotted from a mile away, which made him examine the doctor more closely. The fact that Dr. Potter wouldn't meet Noah's eyes only added to his suspicions.

"Who else?" Noah asked.

"I beg your pardon?"

"Who else has powers that you noticed this trend in?"

Dr. Potter's eyes almost widened, but he stopped himself. Noah caught it just in time to notice. "No one. My mind nearly wandered. It makes me curious as to what Mr. Harrison's power will be. After all, what could you possibly need when you want for nothing?"

———

The itching wouldn't stop, but there was nothing Noah could do about it. Strapped into his usual chair with leather restraints around his chest, wrists, and ankles, all he could think about was breaking free of them so he could scratch through to his bones.

But with all the drugs, he couldn't. The progress he made in the gym when he was in college, trying to work off the stress of his graduate program, had been thrown away. When he wasn't forcibly high, he tried to keep up with his gym routine and eat mostly protein; it was the only reason he hadn't completely thinned out.

Reiji crouched in front of him and struck a match. "Ready, Noah?"

Noah knew the drill so well that when his father struck a match, it was an immediate response. Noah did his best to hold his head up and focus on the flame, which expanded to four times its size. He was tempted to blow it back into his father's face, but he restrained himself.

"All right," Reiji said, "now snuff it out."

Noah did just that. The flame disappeared as quickly as it'd been stricken into existence.

"Good." *Reiji looked toward Carter.* "Hit him with another."

Noah groaned. "Fucker."

Carter tried to smile, but it just made his face look mangled from how uncomfortable he was. "Sorry, Noah. Come on, buddy, chin up."

As Carter injected him with another dose, Noah looked from him and then back to his father. "You're all trying to kill me, aren't you?"

"No, son, no one is trying to kill you."

He whined. "Then why are we still doing this?"

When he agreed to help his father with his drug project, he hadn't quite expected this. Noah initially thought he'd be helping around the restaurant, whether it be hands-on work or managing operations from home. But then, his father broke the news to him that he was helping Sterling's father pedal and manufacture a modified methamphetamine that gave people superpowers. By then, Noah was already in too deep, and when he was told that the latest experiment needed someone who was strong and able, he was ushered into the chair before he could decide.

Reiji told him it would be simple: just take the drug and then develop powers.

If only it had been that easy.

"So, you can get even stronger." *His father patted his cheek on the opposite side from where Carter injected him.* "Come on. You heard him. Chin up."

Noah shook his head. "You just want me dead. Why do you want me dead?"

Reiji frowned. "I don't want you dead. You are my greatest accomplishment, you know that?"

Noah laughed, jerking his head back. "Hai, hai."

Through his teeth, Reiji said, "Noah."

"Maji?"

"Watch your manners. It won't get you anywhere."

In Japanese, Noah continued, "<This is your greatest accomplishment, is it? Your son, the freak of nature? You must be so proud!>"

Before Reiji could reply, he turned toward the sound of footsteps bounding down the stairs. Tom Stevens was shrugging off his blazer as he walked and turned in.

"More experiments, huh?" Tom tossed his jacket over his shoulder.

Carter reached into a messenger bag on the table behind him and pulled out a stack of cash. "Here, we owed you this."

"Many thanks." As he pulled out his wallet to slip the bills in, he said, "How are you doing, Noah?"

Noah spat; it barely missed Reiji's face. Still speaking in Japanese, even though Tom wouldn't understand him, he replied, "<How am I doing?>" He stifled more laughter and added, "<How do you think? Go fuck yourself,>" and then shook his head.

"What's that mean?"

Reiji answered before Noah could. "The gist of it is that he's high, but he's fine."

Noah repeated the word "iya" five times as he rolled his head in a circle, once to the left and then once to the right, so he could crack his neck. Then, he looked at Tom. "Oi. Aho."

With a smile and a small wave, Tom said, "Hello to you too, Noah."

As Noah laughed more, Reiji ran his thumbs along his eyebrows as he sighed and rolled Noah's attitude off. "He's not saying hello, Tom. Just ignore him. Carter, the lighter, please."

Reiji held his hand out so Carter could place it in his hand. Once he had the lighter, Reiji flicked the spark wheel. In English, he said to Noah, "Come on, now. You know what to do."

Noah frowned. "Not this again."

"You can do it. Come on."

"What if I don't want to?" Noah pouted.

Reiji's expression didn't budge; he was as emotionless as ever. "Too bad."

"This shit makes me feel like death, you know that."

"If you can do this, you can do anything," Reiji said. "For five years, you've been fine with matches, but unable to produce the same results with a lighter. There's no reason for that, especially at this stage in the game. You're blocking yourself. Stop it."

"Maybe if you just let me practice without nearly OD'ing, we wouldn't have a problem." Noah looked at the lighter and blew the flame up, so it was

high enough to reach the ceiling, then squashed it with a blink. "That was to spite you."

Carter and Reiji looked at each other and grinned. Then, Reiji turned his attention to Tom.

"Does this mean what I think it means, Ray?"

"It does. Tell Stone Breaker that we're one step closer. This is a cause for celebration."

———

Noah forgot to turn the car radio on when he got in his father's old van. Even if he hadn't, his thoughts occupied him enough on the long stretch of road from Potter Laboratories to downtown Riverpeak. Noah kept the windows down so he could feel the spring breeze on his face as he transported the latest supply of drugs to Amy. Winter was almost over, and he dreaded the days without snow to help him regulate his temperature. Summers were the worst, no matter how many of them came and went.

The more he worked with Amy, the more he questioned everything. He thought his father's death would bring him clarity, and, for the most part, it had thanks to the freedom it provided. But now, he just felt tethered to Sterling instead. While Noah received a pretty penny after his dad died, it wasn't enough to get by on his own, and he wouldn't be off the hook until Sterling achieved his goal: immortality, just like Hematite.

What a waste of a life.

At least his latest mission would make a difference. That was all Noah wanted, after all—to help people, there was no better way to do so than to empower everyone with superpowers of their own. There was no fairness to the current structure, and if Riverpeak could fend for themselves instead of relying on a vigilante, then maybe Hematite would stand down once and for all.

But then there was the issue of the third mystery person. Dr. Potter was hiding something—someone—from him, and it had taken everything in Noah to not burn the lab down just to prove a point. The longer he went, the more difficult it became to exercise his restraint.

He'd been right about everything leading up to this moment, so he was certain he was right once more.

Noah bit his thoughts back when he reached downtown Riverpeak; he wanted a clear head when he saw Amy. After spending his whole life in Riverpeak, trailing after his business owner of a father, he knew the small shops better than he knew the back of his own hand. Despite how much he'd changed, the rows of alternating brick walls and wooden false fronts were the same as ever.

He pulled into the small, dirt parking lot behind the theater; the only other car there was Amy's, which came as a relief. He texted her to let her know he'd arrived and then got out of the vehicle to lift the hatchback. Noah leaned against the trunk as he waited for her to arrive.

Amy opened the back door dressed in her work uniform, a black button-up tucked into matching slacks. She'd removed her name tag, and her red hair was tied back in a small bun on the back of her neck. Amy greeted him with a kiss, making Noah feel even more confused— *how could she feel like this? How could I?*

Do I even have anything to offer her?

What happens after this?

"So, this is it, huh?"

Noah slapped the clear barrel sitting in the back of the van. A dark, amber-colored liquid swirled inside, some bubbles hanging in suspension. "Yup. Here it is, completely liquified. Not too different from the original process. Carter gets the science behind the cooking better than I do, so I'll defer to him for any questions."

"My only question is if it'll work."

"Oh yeah. I had him do a test run with it for me before tweaking it to this dosage, and it worked just as well as the crystallized version at lower levels. Not sure how they pulled that one off since I don't make the shit myself, but I only care so long as it works."

The name Carter sounded familiar, but Amy couldn't remember where she'd heard it. She didn't bother to ask; it wasn't important now.

"How much do they need?"

"Not a ton. We've tweaked it so it's quite a bit easier than the bullshit I had to put up with. I'll help you get it in there so it's just right. You got the label?"

"I do! Here." She reached into her back pocket and pulled out a sleeve with kanji on it. "This will wrap around the handle. The translation is right, yeah?"

Noah read over the Japanese. "Yeah, looks right. Luckily, I don't think anyone in this town could even tell you what *konnichiwa* meant except for my mom and sister."

"Do I get to try it, too?" She leaned against the car with her hip. "I believe that was part of your end of the deal."

Noah opened his mouth to speak, closed it, and then finally said, "Not yet. Let's see how this goes first. I need a very big sample size before I can be sure that this will work, remember?"

"Okay, right. And if it all doesn't go to hell?"

"Then we'll discuss the next steps for you." Noah poked her nose. "Honestly, a lot of this is riding on how everybody handles it. If people get powers, then we'll go from there."

"Do you think anybody will?"

"Shit, I sure hope so. Haven't tested this exact dosage yet. I've been seeing this guy right on the outskirts of town. Dr. Potter, the one who runs a lab. We've been testing, so to speak, but right now, this dosage is all just theory."

"Are there any side effects?"

Noah swallowed. "While I had my fair share of issues, I was also the first lab rat, so I don't think it'll be an issue. Everything stronger than this has been too strong, but everything weaker hasn't been strong enough. There's no way this isn't the sweet spot. Plus, it lines up with some of my old man's notes that Dr. Potter found, and the color looks right. I think we have a winner."

Amy just nodded as she stared at the batch, her hands still on her hips. "If you insist. I trust you."

"I'll do my best to make sure you won't regret it." Noah lifted her chin with two of his fingers and then leaned in to kiss her. "You can still back out if you're having second thoughts."

"Aren't I a little too far deep for that?"

"Not until this is done. Do you want to do this, or is the risk too big for you?"

"I'm sorry, but wasn't there a whole conversation about how once I'm in, I'm in?" Amy rose a brow. "Which is it, huh?"

For a split second, he faltered. Had Amy blinked, she would have missed it. Simultaneously, his jaw popped, and his knuckles cracked. "Situation's changed."

"How so?"

"What, you're gonna make me spell it out?"

"You know, I'd actually love it if you did."

She couldn't help her smirk as his gaze softened. "You already know. No need to get all smug about it."

Amy blushed and forced herself to not stare at her shoes, feeling like she was under a microscope. That was confirmation enough for her to know that he cared about her just as much as she did for him. But she knew better than anyone how difficult putting words to emotions could be.

"In all seriousness, I appreciate the offer for the out, but no way. I've been thinking about what you said about empowering people with this and giving them superpowers. If people like Shawn are going to be born with powers like this, then we need others to help keep him in check. Unfortunately, I don't know that Hematite is able to do that on his own. So, yeah. Let's do this."

Noah smiled. "Happy to hear it."

After all, he didn't know what he would have done if she'd said no. If someone had asked him a few short months ago, he would have said he'd just take care of the problem discretely and be done with it.

But now?

Now, he wasn't so sure.

CHAPTER 12

"We're live in thirty!"

Naomi didn't look up from the tablet on her desk. "Thanks!"

The production assistant raised their hand as they walked off to acknowledge her thanks, not bothering to say any more over the never-ending sounds that echoed through the newsroom. The evening news anchor, Frank, was at the printer behind her cubicle, printing off his news scripts. She'd tried to get him used to the iPad app so they could save paper, but he was old school and set in his ways.

The local scanners were abuzz, everything happening all at once amidst the slight static: the east side was busy tonight. Naomi was just glad it wasn't her job to sit there and listen to them and decipher all the different words and codes, even though she'd memorized most of them by now thanks to years of prolonged exposure. On one of the televisions surrounding the room, a station in Denver played; they were a much bigger market than Riverpeak's small channel but were always helpful to watch to compare story stacks.

"Hey, Sato!"

Naomi looked up from her scripts on her tablet to address her coworker. "Evans now, remember? How's it going, Frank?"

"I'll get the hang of it one of these days." Frank draped his arms on the top of her cubicle wall, his own scripts printed in hand. He'd been at the station for as long as Naomi had been alive and was all too comfortable there, but he meant well. "Cat just showed me something in the editing booth. You might want to take a look before she sends it out on Slack and adds it to ENPS."

"What did she show you?"

Frank ran his free hand through his brown hair, slicking it back as the gel dried the spikes flat. "You'll want to see for yourself."

Naomi stood and kept her eyes on Frank as she moved across the newsroom to the editing booths. "You're not usually this serious, Frank."

Frank walked behind her and set his scripts on his own cubicle desk on their way to the booths lining the back wall. "Well, it's a serious matter. And I figured you'd rather hear it from me and Cat now. Sure beats finding out while we're on the air."

Naomi gave him a look of concern, brows furrowed and lips slightly parted. "Well, thanks in advance, I guess."

"Thank me after you see it."

Naomi knocked on the door before entering the room. Cat slid the headphones off her head, lifting them over the messy bun of dark hair on the top of her head and hanging them around her neck. Cat sat cross-legged in the office chair, her chunky cardigan hanging off the back of it. The only light in the booth came from the computer screens, the black-and-gray acoustic foam panels lining the walls, making the room look even darker and smaller.

Cat said, "You need to see this."

As Frank leaned against the doorframe, arms crossed against his chest, Naomi stepped into the editing booth. She looked at him and then at Cat. "Okay, you guys are never this stiff. Just show me already."

"Your friend Rory was kidnapped by Stone Breaker, right?" Cat asked.

"Yeah, she had some history with Hematite."

"Well, I never turned my Google Alert for Stone Breaker off after last year, and this video got uploaded to his YouTube channel a few minutes ago. Don't worry, I've already ripped it in case it goes offline for whatever reason."

Cat opened the video, showing a black-and-red neon mask. The voice had been altered in post-production, but it sounded distinctly different from Stone Breaker.

"Stone Breaker is back…"

Naomi placed her hands on the desk as she leaned forward, watching the video with intent and wide eyes. Cat rolled her chair aside to make more room for Naomi.

"Didn't Rory find out who Stone Breaker was? Like, isn't that the whole reason why he kidnapped her beyond her business with Hematite?" Cat asked. "Think she can find out who this is?"

Naomi gently shushed her.

"Let me turn your attention to Brick Beast."

Naomi stepped away from the desk. Her hand reflexively reached up to cover her mouth. "Holy fucking shit."

Frank stepped forward to join them in the booth. "I've only heard you swear like that after a few glasses of wine at the annual Christmas party."

"We don't need Rory to figure out who this is. I already know."

Cat rolled her chair back toward Naomi. "Wait, you do?"

Naomi nodded. "Can you send me the link to this? I'd like to send it to Rory. She can pass this along to Hematite, assuming he hasn't already seen it."

Frank rose a brow. "If she's still working with him, do you know who he is?"

The lie came easy. "No. She won't say. To be totally honest, I'm not even sure if she knows who he is."

Frank chuckled. "All right then, keep your secrets."

Naomi grinned. "Very funny, Frank."

"I just sent it. You should have it on Slack."

"Thanks, Cat."

Frank shoved his hands in his pockets. "So, who's the asshole behind the new mask, huh?"

Naomi sighed. "That is most likely Brick Beast's ex-girlfriend. Off the record, please, at least for now, and I don't want to say too much since she's a victim at the end of the day." She also didn't want to blab about Amy's identity without at least running it by Rory and Kane. "My understanding is that he treated her like total shit, so it's only natural she wants revenge."

"How many people do you know that are connected to vigilantes?" Frank asked. "This some sort of trend I should know about? Should I tell my son to put a mask on next time he gives Tinder a shot?"

Cat chortled. "I would pay to see how that goes down."

"Are we reporting on this?"

"Already back to business, I see."

"Well as you said, Frank, this is serious. Do we even want to report this? I mean, they're making vague threats based on view count. I don't think we should give them the attention they so desperately want."

"If we don't report on it, then we're gonna get a thousand emails asking why," Frank said. "I know you already know that."

"So let them email us," Naomi said, snapping her head to look at Frank. "You know what else I get a thousand times a day? I get women telling me to fire my nonexistent makeup artist as their husbands send me emails so creepy, it'd make your skin crawl."

"Touché."

Cat then asked, "Do you think she's acting alone?"

Naomi frowned as she remembered the screenshot of the text message Shawn received a few weeks ago: a shirtless selfie of her brother in Amy's living room. "Probably not. But I'm not sure."

When Naomi stepped out of the booth, she opened Slack on her phone so she could grab the link and text it to Rory. Naomi made her way through the building, ducking down the short hall between the newsroom and where they filmed as she double-checked that the mic clipped on the back of her skirt was turned off. She called Rory as she opened the door to the dressing room, a private, one-person room that was presently unoccupied. She was grateful that Frank's usual co-anchor was out on maternity leave, leaving her to cover for now; that meant she'd have the room to herself.

"Naomi? Aren't you at work?" Rory asked when she picked up.

"Listen, we go on soon so I only have a minute, but you need to see what I just texted you." Even though she was alone, she dropped her voice to a whisper. "Are you with Kane right now?"

"Yeah, he's getting a head start on moving some of his stuff in."

"That's right, that's this weekend. Ugh, sorry, my head's been so frazzled that I forgot."

"Hey, it's fine. I get it. What is this? Is this Stone Breaker's channel?"

"Yes. It's Amy. My guess is that Noah got his login information. Half the video is just her saying Brick Beast is a piece of shit and trying to rack up views so they can dox him or something."

"Kane has the video up now. Where are they?"

"Hard to say. My guess is that house Hannah followed them to last summer."

"We're on it. Are you guys going to be talking about this tonight?"

"I'm pushing for us not to, but I think I'm in the minority with that opinion."

"Well, whatever happens, just keep your guard up."

———

Amy swept the room one last time before she went to work spiking the bar tap system. She wanted to make sure she was alone and felt she could never be too sure, especially with how vigilant her parents were. She was startled by the knocking on the back door, even though she fully anticipated it, knowing it wasn't anyone there to bust her but just Noah arriving to help. When she opened the door, he was standing there with the bartender from the night they met, Carter.

"You brought help."

"Figured you could use a hand," Carter said. "The less time we spend here, the less likely you are in getting caught."

"I already killed the cameras tonight," Amy said, "so there's no need to worry about that."

"Good," Noah said. "You two have met, right?"

Amy nodded. "I remember you from the bar."

Carter nodded in acknowledgment.

"Carter was my father's right-hand man. Now, he helps me out. Don't worry, he doesn't ever really report to Sterling."

"Very few do," Carter said. "I'd say he's pretty uninvolved, but that's not exactly true. It makes more sense to say he's not in the weeds with the rest of us. Noah let me know about your circumstances, at least whatever he was comfortable telling me. I suspect not much. For what it's worth, I'm getting paid, so I'm happy to keep my mouth shut."

If Noah trusts him, Amy thought, *then that is good enough for me.* "Great."

"So where do we need to stand guard?"

"I can hear the back from here, but the front is a whole other story. My parents like to check in after closing sometimes, especially before a big show, so that's going to be the biggest deal."

"I'll head that way," Carter said. "Noah, ping me if you need anything."

"Got it." As Carter made his way to the lobby, Noah wrapped an arm around Amy. "How can I help?"

"Let's get a system going. Come on, I'll show you how this works."

They made quick work of spiking the drinks, working rhythmically in comfortable silence. As much as Noah hated to admit it, they made a great team.

"Hey, before we go, I'd like to see something," Noah said.

"What's that?"

"We need to do something about Hematite. I don't want him ruining our plans."

Amy rose a brow. "Does he even know about them?"

"Not that I'm aware of, but I also don't know what I don't know. Wouldn't you feel better if we played it safe?"

"Of course. So, what were you thinking?"

"We should hold him here. Shit, maybe it'll send Brick Beast to us so we can take him out."

"Hold him here? How are we going to get him here to begin with?"

"I know where he lives," Noah said. "He's moving in with Rory this weekend. We grab him and bring him here."

"You mean kidnapping?"

"Eh, that sounds a bit dramatic, no?"

"I mean, just technically speaking."

"Is that beneath you?"

Amy laughed. "Do you think it is? I just helped you lace a bunch of kegs with supercharged methamphetamines."

"You just seemed less than enthused, that's all."

"Come on. I know where we can hold him."

Noah grinned. "I knew I could count on you."

Amy wiped her hands on her black jeans as she brought Noah behind the stage. As they dodged around the props and costumes waiting in the wings, Amy revealed a door behind the stage.

"Come on. There's a basement backstage."

"Is there an easier way to get there?"

"I'll show you how to get there from the outside once we're downstairs. It's just another stairwell that leads to a hatch. You'll see."

Moving through the backstage area with no one else there gave Amy the creeps. The costumes hanging on the portable racks swayed like ghosts haunting the theater. No matter how many times she came backstage, she'd never get past the chill that it sent down her spine.

When they passed the green room, Amy opened a door next to it in the hallway. She leaned forward through the now open doorframe to flip on a light switch, illuminating the stairwell and what waited at the end of it.

"Like I was saying, we've got our own basement," Amy said. "Not unlike yours, except ours is actually just storage. Old costumes and set pieces that we might reuse, things like that."

When they reached the bottom of the stairs, Noah examined the space. Some plastic storage totes lined one of the walls. More costumes were suspended on racks, mostly in black garment bags, with the exception of a handful that were too large to fit. Those had sheer white garbage bags hanging over them, retrofitted to act as a makeshift protector. Signed Playbills and posters in frames lined the walls, highlighting the shows and stars of past performances. Some chairs were stacked in a corner. Noah grinned as he crossed the room to grab two and set them in the center, so they were facing each other.

"It's perfect."

"Yeah?"

"Oh yeah."

As they made their way out and walked back to their cars, Amy said, "Say, I was thinking. Should we film another follow-up video? Like, in case we do hit our view count? It's getting really close."

"You mean beyond the one with all his shit?"

"Mhm. Maybe a warning?"

"Yeah. Want to come over, stay the night?"

"Sure, I'd like that."

They drove separately to Amy's apartment complex first, leaving her car there so she could hitch a ride with Noah to the suburbs. All the houses looked more or less the same down the rows, alternating only in color, how many stories, or what side the front door was on. When they reached Noah's green house, they went their usual way: bypassing the rest of the house to head straight upstairs. The living room still looked like a photograph, untouched and unused. Amy supposed it was to help keep up the illusion that nothing was out of the ordinary.

"So," she said, as they made their trek upstairs, "how have you managed to not get caught living here if everyone thinks you're dead?"

"One of our customers is Carla Ferrara. Old classmate of yours, I believe?"

"Wait, Carla? Carla, as in your sister's bridesmaid Carla? The real estate agent?"

"The very same."

"She's using?"

"You'd be shocked how many people here are. Can't smoke weed like normal people. No, everyone in Riverpeak wants an extra pep in their step before they go to work."

"Holy shit. How have I not realized?"

"We got it down to a science. The perfect dosage to get people just high enough so that they can go through their day-to-day without it being noticeable. Anyway, she and my old man made a deal. He's got a few properties he owns that he rents out, and he asked her to help him fake a rental sale on the MLS or whatever. So, it looks like the house has a tenant, but it's just my old man's. When he died, Sterling worked with her directly to buy it."

"Holy crap." They entered his room and Amy went straight for the closet, grabbing the clothes she borrowed and the same neon red mask she used last time. As she did, Noah opened his laptop to get YouTube ready.

"Have you seen some of these comments?" Noah whistled. "People are out for blood."

She held the mask in both hands as she rested her chin on his shoulder to read along.

> boris42069: wow fuck this guy ... let's get 'em boys
>
> xXxflamebladexXx: if i see this mothafucka i cant wait to see if he is as strong as he thinks
>
> l33tkiller: I saw him fight with hematite once at UC Denver and even hematite seemed annoyed lmao
>
> kingwalterwhite: nothing worse than a wannabe, can't wait to fuck this guys shit up
>
> waifufucker: who's the new guy tf

Amy pointed at the last comment. "Wait, they think I'm a guy?"

Noah shrugged. "They're incels. It's probably for the best that they do, both for your sanity and your privacy."

"Touché."

"Do you want to introduce yourself? Come up with a name or something? I'll be honest, they're not my strong suit, but your call."

"No, that's not my thing either." Just thinking of Stone Breaker, Shatterstone, and Brick Beast's monikers made her shudder from how cringey they sounded.

"I'm not gonna lie, I'm a bit relieved to hear you say that."

"I'm not even going to address it. Let them keep asking. It'll boost engagement."

"Speaking of which, we should be eligible for monetization soon. This is blowing up."

"Sweet." Amy continued to scan a few more, not wanting to spend too much time reading over the shared sentiment in the vacuum chamber that was the video's comments section, but one in particular caught her eye.

> dansanders93: shit like this is exactly why i left colorado but maybe its time i come back, fuck these wannabe superheroes

Amy pointed at the comment. "Wait, does that say Dan Sanders?"

Noah followed Amy's finger to it. "Yeah, why? You know him?"

"No, but I know of him. Click on his profile. I want to see if this is the same guy."

Once the profile loaded up, his photo made it clear. Amy recognized the pale skin and mousy brown hair, which he'd shaved into a buzz cut in the photo. She remembered it longer, but his face was the same: this was the very Daniel Sanders that went to college with Amy, Rory, and Naomi.

"Holy fucking shit. Small world. Though I can't say I'm surprised he follows Stone Breaker."

"Who is this guy?"

"This is the guy that stalked Rory Miller a few years ago. The same guy that Hematite saved her and your sister from back in college."

"No fuckin' way."

"Yeah! If I remember correctly, he ended up getting kicked out of school and moving out of Colorado entirely. Not sure if Rory ever got a restraining order or if it wasn't even needed since he got arrested for bringing a gun on campus. I think he wound up in Utah or something since he had family out there."

"I'd wager Utah. The only videos he's uploaded are sermons from some church. Looks Mormon."

"Go figure. We should keep an eye on him."

"Pushing my personal feelings about what this piece of shit almost did to my sister aside, should we reach out to him privately?"

"To recruit his help?"

"Someone like that with a grudge against Hematite could be useful."

"Hm. Maybe let's just keep an eye on him for now and see if he continues to comment. I don't want to fall too far down that rabbit hole just yet. Ready to film?"

"Sure." He looked up, and their lips met. "Just say the word."

When Amy slipped the mask on, she instantly felt more at ease. Something about covering her face with a layer of anonymity gave her the extra boost of courage she needed, especially after years of being chastised for wearing her heart on her sleeve. Between the mask and editing her voice, no one knew what she truly felt or how she looked. Her feelings couldn't be used against her like backfiring weapons in an argument. Instead, it provided a bulletproof defense against people like Shawn or her mother.

"Looking good as always." Noah gave her a thumbs up. "Ready when you are."

Amy nodded, unsure of exactly what might come out of her mouth. "If you're seeing this, then Brick Beast, better known as Shawn Jameson of Riverpeak, Colorado, has been defeated. No longer will the false hero of Riverpeak plague our streets with his self-righteousness."

Amy paused, hoping this would come to fruition. If she'd jinxed this, she'd hate herself for it. When she continued, she felt she found her groove now that the initial nerves of being on camera subsided.

"For any other so-called heroes out there who think they are above the law, think again. It is about time we all had equal footing here in Riverpeak. Stand down. Brick Beast had superhuman strength, but it did not stop him from facing his inevitable defeat. You've been warned."

CHAPTER 13

As Elijah opened the last security camera feed, Kane stopped pacing around the home office. Even with Hannah trying to help Kane calm down, he still had too much energy he was trying to burn.

"Well?" Kane asked.

Rory reached for him. Her fingers slid down Kane's forearm until their fingers interlaced. "Relax."

With his free hand, Kane pushed his hair out of his face. It had long since fallen out of his bun. "I don't like this."

"Well, I've got my sights on them," Elijah said. "Here's the confirmation we needed. Interestingly enough, the cameras at the Riverpeak Theater happened to be down, but I can see them from a distance on a camera from Jefferson's Coffee across the way."

"So, Jameson was right," Brad said, as he pinched his nose. "This is bad."

"Well, it doesn't have to be," Naomi said. "I mean, it definitely is now, but we can still turn this around. Besides, the video hasn't hit 100k yet."

"Yeah, but it's not far from it," Rory said. "What are you thinking, Naomi?"

"We could just try talking to her."

Kane laughed. "Talking to her? Her boyfriend, your brother might I add, killed three women, almost killed one of our students, and then—."

Rory squeezed his hand. "Kay, we know. We're angry too."

Kane groaned as he rested his back against the wall next to Rory.

"It's worth a shot to invite Amy over. Just Amy," Naomi said. "Especially with Hannah here. They don't know about her power. Having her will help us keep everything under control if Noah shows up, too. Like a secret weapon." She looked at Hannah and added, "That is, if you don't mind."

"Not at all." Hannah's expression dropped. "But if we just invite her, do you think he'll come too?"

"I do," Naomi said with a nod. "He already knows one of us is Hematite. There's no way he won't go with her."

Rory gulped. "And if he doesn't?"

"Then at least we have Amy. We can ease her into it and explain everything, and hopefully even get her on our side again. Sort of like an intervention. I'm sure she knows at least about the drug and super-powers after being with Jameson, assuming Noah hasn't already filled her in."

"I'm surprised he hasn't killed her," Kane said. "I thought this would just be another one of the cases of missing girls. But he's been seeing her for a few weeks? Months, hasn't he? The fuck is he doing?"

"What if he was successful with her?" Brad asked.

"I've been monitoring her on security cameras since Jameson sent us that photo," Elijah said. "I think he's hesitant, but I don't know why, and it's been driving me crazy. It doesn't seem like she has powers unless they're invisible like Hannah's."

"Speaking of which," Naomi said, "Hannah, I have a question for you. Do you think you can use your power to get Noah to tell me what happened?"

"Probably? I mean, talkative is a feeling," Hannah said. "I can certainly try."

"Get him talking before he leaves if you can, please."

Hannah nodded. "You got it. I'll try to give you a boost, too. Something tells me you'll need it."

Naomi smiled as she typed out the message to Amy and hit send. "Much appreciated."

"Should we loop in Jameson?" Brad asked.

All at once, everyone said, "No!"

———

The woman on the television flashed a seductive smile. "I'm not a program. I'm real."

Amy snorted, hoping the soda wouldn't come back up through her nose. Noah laughed at her reaction. They were both in their pajamas, hair still wet from their post-workout shower together at Amy's apartment. As they cuddled, Amy could feel Noah's transformation; now that he wasn't being force-fed drugs and was working out with her, he'd regained most of the muscle he lost.

"Is she seducing him with corn? *Corn*?!"

Noah shrugged. "I mean, shit, it's doing it for me."

Amy placed her head in her hands. "Oh my God."

"Come on, that doesn't turn you on?"

"You like this crap?"

"The crappier, the better, baby!" Noah grabbed a fistful of popcorn from the bowl balancing between his right and her left leg, eating it with a dramatic flair just to make Amy keep laughing. As the sound of popping corn kernels took over her television, the rain continued to patter against the window of her apartment.

Amy's phone chimed. She lifted it so the screen would stay illuminated as she checked who the message was from.

"Hey, check this out. Your sister invited me to hang out at her house tomorrow."

Noah grabbed the remote and paused the movie. "My sister? What does she want?"

"To hang out, or so she says. I don't buy it."

"Is that not normal?"

"Not really, no. Maintaining friendships was always hard for me after college, especially once Shawn was in the picture."

"Do you think they're onto us?"

"Probably. I can't think of any other reason why she'd ask me to come over. It's not like she and I were ever exactly close past grade school."

"Want me to go with you?"

Amy frowned. "What if they're hoping you will? I don't want you to walk into a trap."

"Hey, hey, don't worry about me." Noah placed his hands on her shoulders. "We've got the upper hand here, alright? Don't forget that."

"Okay, and if it is a trap?"

"You're a lot stronger than you think, sweetheart. You've impressed me a lot since we first met. You're so, so strong, Amy."

"Strong enough for powers?"

Noah gulped. "I think you're close."

She smiled. "Alright then. Let's see what the hell they want."

———

When Noah and Amy pulled up to Naomi's house the next day, Amy felt uneasy. She licked her lips as she set the motorcycle helmet down and looked up at the two-story home in the suburbs, situated on a street where the houses became visibly more expensive. Noah's bike was behind a tree in front of the long driveway, keeping it out of Naomi's view. He leaned against the bumper of Naomi's car in the driveway as Amy collected herself.

"You sure you don't want me to go in with you?"

"Positive. I'll text you when things start to go south."

"If you insist." He pulled his lighter and a carton of cigarettes out from his jacket pocket and lit one for himself. He held the box out to her as an offering, but she shook her head.

"No, thanks. I don't know how fast this will go to shit, probably sooner than I'm hoping, but we'll see."

"At the risk of sounding like my ego is the size of the sun, my guess is they're using you to get to me." He took a long drag and exhaled to the side so the smoke wouldn't blow in her face. "Remember the code we came up with?"

"Yeah. Alright, I'm going in."

Noah lowered his cigarette and, with his free hand, grabbed her chin to kiss her. His kiss gave her a confidence boost, grounding her in the moment and clearing her head. She could faintly taste the ash of his cigarette, the smell enveloping them both as the smoke swirled around them from his hand. "You got this."

"Thanks for the good luck charm."

He laughed as she made her way up the driveway. With a shaky breath, Amy rang the doorbell. Naomi answered right away, as if she'd been waiting by the door the entire time.

Naomi beamed. Her hair was in the usual twin braids that she wore when she wasn't at work. It kept it out of her face, and Amy could already see the family resemblance with Noah, the only differences being their eye color and that Naomi's jaw was slightly rounder.

"It's so good to see you." Naomi's smile grew, closed-lipped but seemingly genuine. She looked like she wanted to give Amy a hug but wasn't sure if she should. "How are you?"

Amy looked around the room just inside the door, trying to get a glance over Naomi's shoulder. Given how much taller Amy was than Naomi, it wasn't hard. "Is he here?"

Naomi shook her head. "No. Of course not. We didn't invite him, nor would we."

"Good." Amy looked behind her, pretending to stretch her neck so that way, Naomi wouldn't notice that she was looking at Noah. He was still at the end of the road, his bike out of view from where she stood. Then, Amy stepped inside, curious as to how long she would last before she felt the need to send him their secret code: a text message with a single thumbs-up emoji.

"I didn't realize that this would be a party," Amy said, as she made her way through Naomi's living room. Everyone—Rory, Kane, Hannah, Elijah, and Brad—looked at her like they felt bad for her, with eyes best resembling that of a forlorn puppy. Hannah's expression was the least obnoxious, and when Amy looked at her, she felt a bit more at ease. Amy hadn't forgotten their conversation at Naomi and Brad's wedding and thus held Hannah to a higher standard than the rest. None of them before had ever asked if she was okay, except for Hannah.

Naomi replied, "Well, we heard that you just went through a breakup. No matter the circumstances, those are really hard, so we just wanted to check in."

"Okay, well, I am fine. I'd been wanting to break up with him for a while. And before you can even say anything, I could not give a shit how he's doing."

"Yeah, that's only natural, I guess." Naomi reached for her glass of wine on the table. "Can I get you anything?"

Amy held her hand up and shook her head. "No, thanks though."

She looked around at everyone in the living room and tried to gauge their reactions. Brad was the most obvious, bad at hiding how he was feeling and fiddling with his thumbs. An empty glass sat on the coffee table in front of him, some suds residue along the rim indicating that it had been filled with beer. She wondered what he needed liquid courage for if this was simply a check-in.

"Oh, okay." Naomi looked like she didn't know what to do with herself or what to say, which struck Amy as odd, given that Naomi essentially talked for a living as a news reporter.

"Listen, if there's something you guys wanna say to me, then just say it." Amy sighed. She took out her phone and quickly sent the emoji to Noah. "I would much rather you be straightforward with me than go through this weird, little awkward dance."

Naomi wanted to say something but stopped herself and looked at Rory for assistance. As Naomi took a sip of her wine, Rory said, "No, no, it's not that. We just haven't seen you in a while, that's all."

"Is this a check-in, or is this an ambush?"

Kane finally spoke. "I think the word Naomi and Rory used when they described it to me was an intervention, which I guess it's not that different from an ambush when you think about it."

Rory sighed. "Kane—."

Amy cut her off. "Finally, some fucking honesty for once."

"I know you're seeing my brother," Naomi said. "So, you want honesty? Okay, I'll give it to you. I know that you're going out with my brother, and boy, do I have a lot of questions for you. All of us do."

The door opened behind them, which brought a wave of relief over Amy. She'd been starting to wonder when he would show up.

"So why not just ask me directly?" Noah didn't bother to close the door behind him, letting the chill breeze and the scent of his cigarette smoke follow him in. The heater was on Naomi's house, and he thought that even he would melt just standing there without the fresh air.

"You were right," Amy said to Noah. "They don't actually care. They were just hoping for you."

"I'm sorry, sweetheart," Noah said. He made a bit of a show of kissing the top of Amy's head. "Can I give the lot of you some advice?" He smirked, and then said, "If one of you is Hematite, then this is the last thing I would do if I was trying to hide a secret identity. And oh boy, am I going to have fun with you." He looked at Kane, locking eyes with him for a second before he turned his attention to Brad. "And you! I had a feeling that you were double-crossing us. Is this any way to treat your new family?"

Brad wasn't sure what to say, so he muttered an apology.

"If you show your face at my house ever again, it'll be the last time you have a face. Understood?"

"Don't threaten him," Naomi said.

"Oh, that wasn't a threat. That was just a warning."

Naomi stood her ground. "Let's talk through this."

"What exactly did you want to talk about? Were you hoping to get Amy here alone so that way you could try to twist her onto your side? Like any of you should be trusted."

Elijah sighed. "It's not like that."

Hannah nodded and added, "Amy, we just don't wanna see you get hurt."

Noah placed a hand over his chest. "And just what are you implying? That I'd hurt her? I bet you wish I would so you could prove a point. Sick fucks."

Naomi was straight-lipped and ready to burst. "So, you admit it?"

Amy rolled her eyes. "No one is denying it, Naomi. Yes, I'm

sleeping with your brother. Give me a fucking break. Can't any of you just be happy for me for two whole seconds? Actually, you know what? I do not have time for this. I don't need to put up with it, either."

Noah nodded. "Come on, Ames, let's go."

As they turned to leave, Rory called, "Amy, please! It doesn't have to be this way. We're here to help you!"

Amy laughed. "You're here to help me? Since when have you ever been there to help me?" She turned back around and took a few steps forward. Noah stayed where he was and kept a close eye on her.

"Amy—."

"No, Rory, shut the fuck up and listen! Where the hell were you guys when I needed help, huh? When Shawn belittled me? When he gaslit me? When he…?"

She gasped violently; the air felt like it pierced her lungs. She couldn't bring herself to actually say the one word that hurt the most.

"When he forced me to do things his way? To do *everything* his way?" Amy said it all with a venom she did not know she had. "Where the hell were you when I needed help? Nowhere, that's where! You always have had each other to rely on. And you know who I've had until now? No one! Not a fucking soul! The only person who had the balls to even attempt to give a shit was Hannah, probably because she's not from here and wasn't afraid of disrupting your little clique."

Naomi went to protest, but Rory stopped her. "You're right." Rory opened her mouth, closed it, and then opened it again. "You're absolutely right. We totally fucked up. We could have been better friends to you. We should have been. I am so, so sorry."

"If you're so sorry, then make sure that piece of shit never gets the platform he wants ever again." Amy wiped some stray tears with the back of her hand. She hated that she was crying; they weren't tears of sorrow, but it was hard for her to convey that they were tears of rage, especially with how fuzzy her head was feeling.

"Come on, Amy," Noah urged. "Let's leave these assholes behind, yeah? They're not worth your time."

She sniffled as she turned to face him. "You're right." As Amy walked with him, she heard Naomi call from behind her.

"Noah, please. Come home."

Noah gave Amy a gentle pat between her shoulder blades and nodded. "Go ahead. I'll be right there, okay?" As she did, he looked over his shoulder at Naomi. "Sorry, sis. But Daddy Dearest made sure I don't have a home to go back to."

He went to rejoin Amy, who was already outside and standing by the motorcycle, but Naomi followed after him. "No! No, you're not fucking going anywhere yet!" Her pace quickened and she grabbed his shoulder, forcing him to face her as she spun him around.

Amy glanced back and looked at Noah through the door, which was still open from when she left. He shook his head, silently letting her know to stay put as he closed the door. Something told him this conversation would be best had private.

"When you went to Hannah's house, I was too shocked to say anything. But I've got a whole lot to say now. What the hell do you think you're doing?"

Noah held his arms out before letting them fall to his sides with a light slapping sound. "What was I supposed to do, Naomi? Huh?"

Naomi balked at him. "See a goddamn therapist! Come to me! Literally anything other than killing people!" She shook her head. "You killed people!"

"You say it as if I did it for fun. They simply weren't strong enough."

Naomi gaped at him. "They didn't sign up for that!"

"Yeah, well neither did I! Don't you get it?" He spoke through his teeth. "I'm trying to liberate people here!"

"So, you kill them, that's it? Were you trying to liberate Dad, too?"

He glowered at her and frowned. "Naomi, don't."

"I know you killed him!"

"I did what had to be done!"

"Why, then? Why?"

"He put me through hell trying to get these powers and then had the audacity to hold me back. Don't even get started, alright? You got to have it all. You got to live a normal life and be happy, with the perfect career and the perfect house with the perfect wedding."

"My life is not as glamorous as it looks."

"Oh, spare me, would you? Boo hoo, you had a few bad days and got a few mean emails. Do you know what I got? I got to be burned to a crisp and live in a fucking meth house as a test subject."

Out of nowhere, Noah's head felt like static fuzz. He tried to close his mouth so he could shut up and walk away, heading back to Amy and leaving Hematite's rag-tag group of friends, but instead, he felt compelled to speak.

"Shit had been going on for years before I died. And let me tell you, a part of me did die that day. All this wasn't even for me! I wasn't just made to stop Hematite. No! I was made to make sure that his boss wouldn't die when he went through what I went through."

"What?"

Noah laughed. "You got that right! Dad guessed on a hunch that I would be able to handle it instead of dying under the pressure. He was willing to risk my life, and I didn't even know that was the case until a few months ago. Imagine that! So, forgive me for not giving half a shit." Noah hissed and then rubbed his temples. "Which one of you has powers that I don't know about, huh? What's with this fucking migraine?"

Naomi was quick to cover for Hannah. "Maybe it's your own guilt for blaming everyone but yourself for what you've done."

"I wasn't born yesterday. Whatever you do, just stay the hell out of my way."

"Or else what? Huh, Noah?" Naomi stood tall. Her brain, too, felt abuzz, but with confidence.

"Didn't anyone ever tell you, Naomi? If you play with fire, you're gonna get burned. Or did you forget already what happened to Dad?"

Noah didn't stick around after that, slipping out the door and closing it behind him. Naomi rushed out behind him, but he and Amy were already back on the bike. Before Naomi could stop them, Noah revved the engine as a final goodbye and took off.

CHAPTER 14

The neon sign outside of the Chinese restaurant down the road flickered and buzzed, on the brink of death. Noah checked his watch as he leaned against the abandoned South Main Burgers restaurant, annoyed by the sound and eager to get his night over with. He watched as the seconds ticked closer and closer to twelve—closer to no longer having to hear the light zapping of an old sign on its last leg. His eye involuntarily twitched as he became aware of his subconscious foot-tapping, soft enough to not make any sound.

That left just him, the restaurant he was reborn in, and the neon sign.

His nostrils flared. "Come on."

Noah still didn't understand why his father bothered to rebuild the restaurant after the fire if he was just going to abandon it anyway. The story he spun to the media when asked was that he had good intentions, but business just wasn't quite the same since the fire, with the usual clientele already used to a new location or restaurant. The truth was that Reiji didn't trust anyone in that building after what happened, and Noah didn't see the point in sinking all that money into the property if he didn't plan on using it again in the first place. The only thing he could justify was to keep it up for appearances, but even that felt like a weak excuse.

The second his watch hit midnight, he pushed himself off the building and pulled out his lighter. He lit it by one of the wooden planks covering a broken window, focusing on it to make the flame grow in hopes of the wood catching fire faster. Once the planks were engulfed, he blew the fire up to wrap around the whole building. Had he blinked, he would have missed it happen—but he wouldn't dare.

"This one's for you, *oyaji*."

Some glass shattered; from the sound of it, it was somewhere in the back of the building. With any luck, this would bring Hematite straight to him, but either way, it certainly felt cathartic. He allowed himself a moment to stare into the flames and watch the building burn. While the back offices had already been destroyed last year, he was relieved to finish the job now.

Noah slunk into the shadows, eyes darting around his surroundings to see if he could spot the blur of black and navy. Everything was aligned: this was Hematite's usual patrol time and place, based on past reports and sightings recorded online, and he knew Kane was looking for him just as much as he was looking for Kane.

"Come out, come out, wherever you are," Noah said to the dark in almost a whisper. "I know you're here somewhere."

Shuffling footsteps caught Noah's attention. Noah strolled over to the building, standing just outside of the light cast by the flames, and pulled his phone out of his pocket. He opened the YouTube app, where the video he wanted was loaded and ready. Noah watched as a hooded, masked figure in all black ran in front of the restaurant, and once he stood still, Noah hit play on the video.

The sound of a baby crying and a woman screaming emerged from the burning building. Hematite pried the door open and ran in, but the moment he did, he was right where Noah wanted him.

"Let's turn the heat up, shall we?"

Noah waltzed in as soon as Hematite was inside, using the sound of the crackling flames to cover his footsteps. As he walked through, he pushed the flames outward from his body, preventing them from engulfing him and ruining his clothing. He snuck behind Hematite in the restaurant, walking with increased trepidation to avoid being caught or heard. Part of him enjoyed the hunt, finding it exhilarating in the same way that killing his father had been, even though he knew his prey wouldn't remain dead for long.

But he didn't need Hematite dead forever. All Noah needed was a few minutes of a guaranteed knockout.

Once Noah was close enough, the chaos of smoke and fire and crying babies still masking his presence, he turned off and pocketed his phone. Hematite stopped, which allowed Noah to reach out to him.

Hematite gasped as Noah wrapped his hand around his throat. He used his arm to pull him close as his fingers pressed into Kane's windpipes. The flames around them felt warm on his face, and now with the body heat, Noah wished his sweat glands would burn away.

"Careful, Kane. I can't imagine your teacher's salary making it easy to buy new clothes as nice as this."

Hematite sputtered, trying to speak but failing. *The trap couldn't have been laid any more perfectly*, Noah thought.

"Come on, use your words." Noah chuckled as he squeezed harder.

Hematite wheezed as his body stiffened in Noah's grasp. He reached up, trying to grab Noah's wrist, but Noah's grip tightened further.

"Yeah, I know, I know. Stone Breaker and my father didn't adequately prepare you for me. A shame, really. I was hoping for more of a fair fight. Now I wonder what will get you first: me or the smoke."

The struggle continued, but Hematite grew increasingly weaker. After only another minute, Noah felt Hematite's body go limp in his arms.

"Oh! Already?" Noah moved his fingers around Hematite's throat to check for a pulse. "Aw, man. That was faster than I thought." He kneeled and then hoisted Hematite up to carry him across his back. It took him a moment to position him since Hematite was taller, but once he had his balance, he released a deep sigh. "Oh well." He turned his head to look at Hematite's face, where the hood continued to cover him due to gravity in the fireman's carry. "We can get this over with."

Before he left, Noah moved through the building, taming the flames as he pushed through to the back. He retrieved the Bluetooth speaker he left on the cashier counter, which had been reduced to a rubble pile on the floor. To anyone else, it would have burned them before they even grabbed it, but Noah was able to lift it with ease. He exited the building with Hematite still draped over his shoulders, then dumped the body in the back of his car before hopping in the driver's seat to drive to the theater.

This one didn't feel like a murder, not like a real one, anyway.

When the Hooters waitressed died, seizing and screaming, it knocked the life out of Noah. All he could think to do was dispose of her as discreetly as he could in his panic, even if it meant there was a risk she'd be found. He'd hoped a mountain lion might smell the parts and nibble at anything that washed ashore, but unfortunately, Hannah and Elijah found her instead. At least the Riverpeak Police hadn't connected her to him anyway.

When his second test subject died—some woman at the bar he'd never met before—it wasn't as off-putting. The fact that she passed out before she died helped, her eyes blowing wide before closing for the last time. Jordan Jefferson's survival shocked him more and irked him that he likely wouldn't get closure or know if she developed powers, but the girl kept her mouth shut, which was good enough for him.

And when he killed his father—his first intentional murder—it came as easy to him as breathing or eating. Perhaps those women died so he'd feel no hesitation when it came time for the only kill that really mattered.

———

From where he stood outside by the windows, Noah could faintly hear the chatter of wedding guests coming and going from the restrooms. He couldn't pick out any lyrics, but he could still follow the melody of whatever the DJ was playing. His cigarette smoke left a bitter taste lingering in the air, which otherwise smelled of freshly fallen snow and pine trees.

The front door of the venue closed so softly, Noah almost didn't hear it. It was quite the contrast from the way Reiji placed a hand on his shoulder and pushed him into the wall, back pressing against the space between the windows. While Noah had made a point of staying hidden, he'd wanted his father to know he was there.

He wanted him to come outside.

"What are you doing out here?"

Noah shrugged his father's hand off him and took a drag of his cigarette. "It's not every day your sister gets married. You honestly think I wouldn't show up?"

Reiji looked around; Noah presumed he was making sure no one followed him out of the bathroom so he could stay his father's best-kept secret. "Who told you?"

"Brad. He's a nervous little fucker, you know that?"

"That is neither here nor there. You need to leave."

"I never said I was going in. Just hanging out. You were a shit father, but you raised me better than to go into a fancy venue dressed like this."

"So, then what are you doing here? Really?"

Noah puffed his cigarette again and when he exhaled, he didn't care where the smoke blew. The cigarette was at the end now, so he dropped the butt and squished it with his shoe like a bug. He retreated his hands to the pockets of his black hoodie. "I told you. Just trying to support my sister in whatever fucked-up way I can."

"Do you really want to ruin what is supposed to be the happiest day of her life?"

"No, I don't. Really, truly, I don't. But unfortunately, Hematite is in that building. The man behind the mask, anyway. And if I'm here now, then that will put him in quite a predicament. Not anything I don't think he can't weasel his way out of, but enough for me to buy myself some time to get some cover."

Reiji stepped closer to his son, speaking lowly. "What predicament?"

Noah pulled his hands out of his pockets, taking the switchblade he'd snuck in there with him. He flipped it open and, in one swift motion, drove it into Reiji's chest with his right hand.

Reiji's eyes blew wide at the shock as he released a short gasp. "I suppose you think I deserved this."

Noah shrugged his left shoulder. "I didn't have some big speech planned, but yeah."

He tried to laugh but spat up blood instead. Reiji's knees gave out. "Perhaps you're right."

Reiji collapsed, lifeless. Noah pulled the switchblade from his father's heart, wiped the blood on his father's white dress shirt, and then walked away. He inhaled the mountain air and, from the heights of Aspen's mountains, felt free.

———

Noah glanced at Kane in the rearview mirror once he hit a red light. "What are we gonna do with you, huh, buddy?" His left leg bounced as he waited for the light to turn. Even though part of him was tempted to just plow through the red light, he made it this far, and he wasn't about to lose everything to a traffic camera.

As he pulled into the back lot of the theater, he checked the clock on his car: it had only been about seven minutes since he left, which meant he had at least three until Hematite woke up, eight at best. Carter was waiting for him outside. Noah swung the bulkhead doors open before returning to his car to fetch Kane's body, lifting him back over his shoulders like a human scarf. Carter grabbed the keys from Noah's hand to lock up as Noah moved downstairs, bringing the faint smell of smoke with him. It hung over him like a cloud, but it was the least of his concerns; he was practically nose-blind to it at this point.

Noah dropped Kane's body in one of the chairs he set up when Amy showed him the storage basement a few days prior. Based on where everything was, no one had been down here since.

Carter returned with a new chair in hand; Noah would recognize it anywhere. The leather straps on the arms and legs of the chair had seen better days, but so had Noah.

"You brought it."

"Of course. You asked. How much time do we have?"

"Assume a minute."

"Fuck."

Noah transported Hematite to the new chair. His body slumped against it, head rolling back and arms flopping out to the side. Carter dropped his messenger bag and rushed to the opposite side to help strap Hematite into the restraints. As Noah tightened them, he tried to swallow back the memories of when his father and Dr. Potter would do this exact thing to him.

"Is he awake yet?"

Noah looked at Hematite's face. His blue eyes were still glazed over. "Any minute now. Get it ready."

Carter moved back to his messenger bag, fishing out the inhaler and the mask that was attached to it. "How'd you do it?"

"Asphyxiation. Sped the process up with some smoke inhalation."

"Brutal."

"Well, I didn't exactly feel like cleaning up any blood." Noah stood and pulled the hood back. He reached into the top of Hematite's hoodie and found the bottom of the balaclava tucked into the undershirt and pulled that off with enough force to nearly undo the blond bun of hair beneath. Kane Kelly's lips were dry, and his neck was bruised where Noah choked him.

"So that smoke I saw was you?"

"Yup, over at the old restaurant. The one my old man ditched after the first fire. Given Hematite and his rag-tag group of friends kept raiding it to look for clues, it was about time that place was dusted anyway."

Suddenly, Kane inhaled, taking in any clear air he could. Before he could do or say anything, Carter shoved the mask in his face, covering Kane's nose as he triggered the inhaler. Kane's eyes rolled to the back of his head as he breathed in the knockdown gas and then closed as he slumped back in the chair.

"That should keep him out for a few hours so you can get some shut-eye."

"Good work," Noah said. "I knew I could rely on you to whip something up."

Carter reached into his bag and grabbed a second mask with another inhaler attached. "If he's up prematurely, just make sure this covers his nose. Totally sealed. I doubt you'll need it, but figured it would be good to have in case his regeneration kicks in. I'm not sure how it would work given all that."

"Got it."

"You sleeping here?"

"Yeah, I don't want to miss a thing. Besides, our pal Hematite here shouldn't have to sleep alone."

"Well, I'm not far from here if you need anything," Carter said. "What are you gonna do with him?"

"Get some closure. I want to see the person responsible for all this mess. If he'd never come on the scene, none of this would have happened. Plus, I need to get a blood sample of his for Potter."

"Fair. How's Amy?"

"Still on board, last I heard. Not gonna lie, part of me expected her to get cold feet once shit got real. But I think Shawn really fucked her up. Personally? I'd like to bash the bastard's skull in myself, but when it comes to it, I'll give her the honors."

"That speaks volumes coming from you."

Noah rolled his eyes as he smiled. "You know I did what I had to do."

"Yeah, I know, I know. All in the name of science." Carter slung his messenger bag back over his shoulders. "You think she's got it in her?"

"For what, this?"

"No, she's already committed to this. No turning back now. I meant to bash Brick Beast's skull in, as you so delicately put it."

"If you asked me that a few months ago? I'd say no way in hell. She's changed since you called me to her at the bar, though. Her sadness turned to rage somewhere along the way. Probably my fault, but if anyone gets that, I do. You'll be with her in the morning, yeah?"

Carter nodded. "My earpiece is ready to go, but I'll double-check it in the morning. If anything goes wrong, let me know."

"What, you wanna come up with a code or something?"

"Might not be a bad idea."

"Alright. If you suspect anything, ask when *Cats* is coming to town. I'll make a reference of that, too."

"*Cats*?"

"Trust me. I'll get it, and Amy will think it's theater talk."

"Roger that. Hey, did you get what you needed for the smoke detectors?"

"Amy had the tool here. They're off as a precaution."

"Sweet. See you in the morning."

Noah saluted Carter as he departed, leaving him alone with Hematite. Once Carter was gone, Noah grabbed a few more chairs from the stack in the corner and placed them all in a row. Once he had enough to lay across comfortably, he grabbed some extra to place on the other side so the backs of the chairs could act as a barrier in case he rolled over in his sleep.

"Good night, Hematite. Sweet dreams."

Once Noah laid back down on his makeshift chair-bed, he turned onto his side so he wouldn't have to look at the old costumes. In the dark, they looked like apparitions, spirits of the people he'd wronged who were haunting him.

At least if he was on his side, he could pretend they weren't there.

CHAPTER 15

s Amy adjusted her name badge in her car the next morning, she tapped her black acrylics across the surface, letting the sound soothe her racing mind until she had to go inside the theater. She focused on converting her nerves into excitement, finding the euphoria of getting vengeance on Shawn.

If other people—myself included—could stand up to people like him, then the world would be a better place.

Right?

She glanced at the digital clock in her car: it was already 10:00. The first show would kick off at one o'clock, meaning she had to get everything ready for early arrivals. The back lot was filling up around her with the cast running in, hoping to get one last read-through of their lines before starting their hair and makeup.

Despite how much she wanted this—wanted to help Noah achieve his dream so she could finally feel powerful enough to stand up for herself and not have anyone question her ever again—she struggled to get out of the car. Her hand lingered on the door handle for too long, but she forced herself to push off and out of the vehicle. The earpiece she wore felt uncomfortable, so she chalked the strange feeling she couldn't place up to that. Carter delivered one to her doorstep late last night, telling her to wear it today.

Her heart raced as she moved through the theater. Whenever one of the actors or set crew said hello, she almost panicked and worried that they knew what was in the basement. After slipping past the door, she slowly went down the stairs to find Noah stretching his neck and shoulders.

"Good morning, sweetheart," Noah said. "How'd you sleep?"

"Better than you, I'd wager." Once she reached him, he pulled her in for a kiss. The warmth of his lips almost made the unusual ping in her gut go away. "He awake?"

"He came to just as we were strapping him in last night." Noah rested a hand on the back of Hematite's chair. "Then Carter hit him with some knockout gas. He wasn't even fully awake yet. But can confirm that this is Hematite in the flesh."

Her heart felt like it dropped into her stomach. "Holy shit. You seriously killed him?"

"Only temporarily, and he handled it well, for what it's worth. Didn't put up much of a fight, either. To be honest, it was way easier than I thought. Not sure why Mark and Doug had such a hard time with him."

Amy ignored the nonchalance Noah spoke with. "Well, at least he's out of the way in case something happens."

"How are you feeling?" Noah moved his hand to her shoulder and let it drape down her arm. It made the tug-of-war in her body worse: on one side, she empathized with him but on the other, something in her mind insisted that this was wrong. The voice reminding her of the danger came back, loud and clear now.

She couldn't believe that Noah was so casual about murder, temporary or not, but now wasn't the time to unpack that. So, she simply said, "Not gonna lie, I'm a bit nervous, but I think it'll pass."

"Hey, don't be." He spoke with that tenderness he reserved for her. "I'm here, okay? Nothing can go wrong so long as I'm here."

Amy nodded, but for as much as she wanted to believe him, she still had a horrible feeling. "I know." She checked her watch. "I should head back up. I've got some cleaning to do before I find Carter."

"Good luck up there. I believe in you."

She forced a smile. "Will do."

As the crowd arrived with their tickets a few hours later, Amy was finally in position by the bar tap. Repeated welcome greetings as security checked people's bags rang through her ears. She wiped her hands on her black dress pants to dry her palms and subconsciously chewed on the inside of her lip.

She stood behind the bar and glanced at Carter, who wore the same all-black uniform as she did. He wore a fake name tag that identified him as Bruce, a former employee from a few years back. Each of their sections had a bar tap covered in a fabric sleeve with Japanese writing on it, indicating the beer they'd mixed the drugs with. Due to its amber color, no one would be able to tell the difference.

It was showtime.

Amy reached up to her earpiece. Carter said Noah spotted Hematite using these and was able to find something similar on Amazon so the three of them could easily stay connected. "Testing."

"I hear you," Noah said. "Carter?"

"Confirming."

"Good."

Amy scanned the theater, looking for familiar faces. The theater lobby was small, so trying to find a specific person in the crowd proved more challenging than she hoped. She thought she spotted Elijah's curls towering over the crowd, but she sighed in relief when she got a better look at his face and saw it wasn't him.

"They aren't here yet, in case you were wondering. No sign of them, anyway."

"That's assuming they come."

"I'm telling you, Noah, I don't think we should underestimate their ability to figure shit out. Your sister's a reporter, Rory's crazy smart, and Elijah is like a fucking wizard behind a computer."

"Noted."

"How's Kane?"

"Fine. He hasn't woken up yet, but I imagine he will soon. Also, we hit our target on YouTube, so I published the second video. Just another way we can keep them distracted. I like our odds better when they don't know which way to look."

"Music to my ears," Amy said. "I'll watch for them."

She put on a fake smile as the first couple of the night approached. She scanned them up and down as they took their time. They were both dressed to the nines, typical for Broadway but fancy for a small, local theater's standards. Both must have been in their early seventies and reminded Amy of her grandparents before they'd passed.

Carter leaned over and whispered, "Not sure if Noah told you, but people who are in really good shape tend to handle it better."

Noah hadn't told her. Amy's eyes widened, and she felt nauseous when she spotted the cane the woman was using to walk. Her husband's hand rested on her upper back, guiding her to the bar.

"What?"

"Yeah. Not, like, bodybuilders or anything. But in good shape, you know? Mentally and physically. I'm surprised he didn't say."

Amy tried to control her breathing before it grew more rapid. If she wanted to avoid being accused of betrayal, she needed to keep her cool in front of Carter.

"Alright. Good shape. Got it."

She mentally wished the couple would order wine.

Her brain fired off what felt like a thousand questions a minute—questions she could never verbalize, forcing her to finally look away from the whirlwind of the last few weeks and accept the truth.

If Noah's goal is to empower people and help them live more fairly, then how is gambling with someone's life fair?

Would it be fair if they died without so much as a willing choice?

The couple reached the bar, forcing Amy to snap out of it. She kept her smile on, grateful for the blush she wore that made it look more natural. "How can I help you?"

"Your second-best red."

"Second-best, huh?" Amy asked, keeping the conversation playful to hide the way relief consumed her.

"It's always better than the more expensive ones," she said. Her husband laughed, and Amy did with him as she poured the wine from the tap into the glass.

"Just the one, or for both of you?"

"No, nothing for me. I gotta drive her home," her husband said in jest, "but thank you."

Amy chuckled along. "Alright then, you wild ones. Here you go. Can I get anything else for you?"

"That's it. Here, keep the change." As the woman paid, Amy ignored the doubt shooting through her. She hoped the woman didn't notice her hand shaking as she passed her the drink.

"Enjoy the show!"

When the couple was out of earshot, Amy leaned back toward Carter. "So, what happens if someone like them tries to order what we mixed up?"

"Don't worry," Carter said. "Stable, I promise. What happened to Noah won't happen to them."

"Do you mean that, or are you just saying that?"

"As far as I know, I mean it."

She hoped he was right.

———

Noah wondered why Carter's audio feed was on when Carter asked, "So, what's your favorite show?"

"Me?" Amy replied. There was a pause, probably Carter nodding. "Oh, probably *Hadestown*. Why?"

"Just curious. My cousin loves *Cats*. They're obsessed with it. That ever come around here?"

Noah perked up.

"Sometimes, yeah. It's too bad it's not playing now, or I'd hook you up with tickets. Personally, I think it's better enjoyed high."

Carter laughed. "Appreciate the offer."

The audio feed was then turned off. Must have been a false alarm. Noah looked back to his phone and saw that the video Amy recorded a few weeks ago finished uploading, and once it did, he pocketed his phone.

Just as he stood to stretch his legs, Kane stirred. The timing couldn't have been more perfect. Noah approached Kane with slow, heavy footsteps. He made a point of emphasizing his movements as he approached an awakening Kane. Noah chuckled as he circled him, examining Kane up and down.

"Hello, Kane. Glad you're finally awake. Can I call you Hematite?"

Kane was silent, maintaining a neutral expression. Noah laughed as Kane took in his surroundings, acknowledging the old theater costumes and props.

"Don't worry, Hematite. It's just you and me here right now. No one else. I haven't told anyone your little secret, except for maybe Cinderella over there." Noah pointed with his thumb to a gown on a rack behind him. "We've known each other for so long, you think I wouldn't have figured it out?"

"Listen, Noah, I'm not sure what you're talking about, but it is great to see you again. We all thought you died, dude."

Noah raised a brow. "Spare me the theatrics. The people upstairs are getting paid for that, not you."

"No, man, I'm serious! You're looking good, all things considered."

"So are you for a man who's died ... how many times has it been now? Let's see ... there was last night, that time that broke the news, then when Mark's friends got you in that dumpster." Noah held a hand up, counting with his fingers. "And a handful of times before that, my associates could have sworn they killed you. Talk about coming back from the dead, am I right? Maybe you can teach me a thing or two about it so I can be prepared for whenever I do kick the bucket."

Kane almost snorted. "Oh, come on now. Do you really think I've got it in me to be a superhero? I barely remember last night. Shit, I don't even know how I ended up here."

"You know, I am so glad you mentioned that. It's surprising how many people fail to see through your facade. It doesn't make any sense. You mean to tell me the man who grew up with deadbeat parents, trying to protect his sister from becoming like them, ended up an alcoholic?"

"We've all got our vices."

Noah pressed his hands on the chair's arms and brought his face only inches from Kane's. They both still reeked of the smoke from the night before. "See, I'm not buying it. Especially in these clothes of yours."

"This is really unnecessary, Noah. Why don't you release me, and we can go grab a drink somewhere—?"

"You may have charmed your way into Rory's pants, but you won't charm your way into mine."

Kane grinned at him. "You sure?"

Noah grabbed Kane's chin with enough force to feel the curve of his jawbone beneath the flesh, which wiped the smirk clean off Kane's face. "Nice try. You're not my type." Noah released him and stepped away. "How is my sister's best friend, by the way? Are you taking good care of her? I heard Stone Breaker gave her the run-around."

Kane swallowed. "Rory's great."

"Is she? I imagine after everything she's been through, she'd be awfully traumatized. Maybe I should pay her a visit." Noah smirked as he saw Kane shift uncomfortably in his chair. "You know, she's quite the beauty now that she's all grown up. Smart as hell, too. Makes me wonder how she ended up with you."

"I always tell her that she's too good for me. There's no need to go visit her, though. I've got plenty of pictures on my phone if you want to see her."

"Oh, is that so? Or are you just trying to get untied?"

"No, I do. Seriously, I take candids of her all the time. I can't help it. She doesn't even know about half of 'em in there."

"Aw, how cute." Noah placed his hands over his heart. "Warming my cold, dead heart with that won't get you anywhere, though."

"Just leave Rory out of it." Kane sighed. "I can't help you and you said so yourself, she's been through enough. She's doing really well in therapy, and I'd hate for her to have a setback."

Noah grabbed the second chair and placed it in front of Kane's. When he sat in it, Noah swung his legs over one of the arms and leaned back against the other. "You think I give a shit about your girl-friend's therapy? Please."

Kane scoffed. "Rude."

"I've got plenty of time."

"Just how long do you plan on keeping me here? This is ridiculous."

"Just twenty-four hours. That's all I need."

"If you're so convinced that I'm Hematite, why haven't you killed me yet? Are you hesitant? Or are you just using me as bait for Hematite?"

"Bait for Hematite? Don't make me laugh, Kane." Noah stood from the chair and crossed the room. "I already know you're him. Caught red-handed … or would it be black-hooded in this case?"

Kane followed him with his eyes and used the opportunity to see if he could fight the restraints, but it was no use; Noah's leather straps were too thick or tight for him to do anything. They showed signs of wear in the places where they once wrapped around Noah's limbs but weren't worn enough to break. Noah didn't like to look at them for too long.

"Where are you going?" Kane said as Noah was walked away.

"Grabbing something. Just to show you how much I mean it when I say I'm not hesitant." When Noah returned, he was holding a fresh needle. Noah tossed the plastic wrapping behind him as he attached the needle to the syringe. "Now if you'll excuse me."

"Is there even anything in there?"

"Not yet. Now be a good boy and hold still. If you don't, I've got another round of gas that'll make you really sleepy. Who knows how long you'd be knocked out for then?"

"Not like I have a choice!" Kane's brows furrowed, making his forehead wrinkle where they met. "What the fuck is this?"

"Relax, you'll be fine. If I could do it countless times over, then I'm sure you'll have no problem this once. You've been through worse. To hell and back!"

Kane had no choice but to comply. He tried to turn his arm, but the straps on his wrists and chest were taut. Noah grabbed Kane's bicep to further hold him in place.

"Awfully muscular for a binge-drinking English teacher, aren't you?"

"It's not unusual to work out, you know."

"Still playing stupid? Hm. Maybe not." Noah injected the needle into Kane's arm. "Just a pinch."

Kane frowned as he watched his blood fill the syringe. "What are you going to do with that?"

Noah smiled at him. "Nothing you need to concern yourself with." Noah moved back to where he retrieved the equipment so he could safely store the sample and dispose of the used needle.

"Do I at least get a Band-aid?"

"You're a grown man. I think you can handle it."

"It was worth a shot."

"What's next, you're gonna ask me to kiss your boo-boo better?"

"I mean, shit, if you're offering."

Noah sucked his teeth. "You're testing my patience." He sat back in his chair, swinging his legs over one of the arms again. "You behave? I'll even consider letting you go after this. This can either be a nice, peaceful meeting of two guys just hanging out, or I can see if your skin regenerates too or if that only applies in life-or-death situations."

"There is no need to set fire to me, I promise you."

Noah raised an eyebrow. "Why, do you know the answer already? Care to share with the class?"

"No, it's not that. Listen, Noah, I'm just a guy. A totally ordinary and normal guy. Some fucking loser English teacher, that's all. Clearly, you have some preconceived notions of me, but I think you need to reconsider them."

"Hmm, no, I actually don't think I need to reconsider a goddamn thing. There's no use pretending, considering I brought you here myself. You know, I started working out with Amy a few days a week. I've gotten a lot stronger. Made it real easy to carry you."

"May I ask why you're holding me here, of all places? You're not gonna set the theater on fire, are you?"

"Who do you take me for, the Phantom of the fucking Opera?" Noah scoffed. "Don't make me laugh. Just have patience and you'll see. Everyone will."

CHAPTER 16

Even though she knew that Kane was okay, Rory still felt sick to her stomach as Elijah drove her, Naomi, Brad, and Hannah to the Riverpeak Theater. Never in her life did she think she'd be donning the Hematite uniform herself. If someone told her nine years ago that would be the case, she'd have laughed. "You're positive he's going to be here?"

"Absolutely," Elijah said, conviction clear in his tone. "There's no way he's not. Brad's intel may be too dumb to realize that he hasn't shown up in months, but he's there all the time. He'd know. And the security cameras being down is just the icing on the cake."

"Besides," Brad said from the back left seat, "it's not like he can die."

"Which is nice, but that's not what I'm worried about." Rory went to chew at her thumbnail but remembered she couldn't when her lips met the rough fabric of her gloves. They fit tightly over the boxing wraps that wound around her knuckles and wrists. "Noah already knows Kane's identity, but if he's got him like this and now all of a sudden, he and Amy are uploading to Stone Breaker's YouTube channel?" Her knee bounced, and Naomi, who sat in the center between

Rory and Brad, placed her hand on Rory's knee. Rory stopped, apologized, and sighed. "Fuck."

Hannah turned around from her spot in the front. "If you're thinking Noah wouldn't upload anything without evidence, I wouldn't be so sure. After all, they blasted Shawn without any care."

"That's different. Hardly anyone knew who Brick Beast is, nor do I think anyone really gave a shit until now. But Kane's Hematite. I think everyone from here to Denver has heard of him. The fact that he hasn't had any copycats or people trying to claim they're him is a fucking miracle."

"Valid point," Brad said. "I can't think of any other reason why he'd kidnap him. He knows that Kane can't die."

"If you can't kill him, kill his reputation," Rory said. "As much as the public loves Hematite, vigilantism isn't exactly legal. The second that's out, his weird coexistence with McMahon is compromised, so his arrest wouldn't be a matter of if, but when."

"Then he could kiss his job goodbye," Brad said.

"Yeah. And so could I, probably. Guilt by association."

"You think the school would do that?" Naomi asked.

Rory nodded. "Absolutely. Aiding and abetting vigilantism would be enough for them to, especially since it's not exactly a secret that Hematite saved my ass. You know the only reason HR didn't care that we started dating was because they thought we already were when we were both hired?"

"The principal wouldn't vouch for you?"

"She likes me, but not that much." Rory sighed. She pulled out her phone, opened YouTube, and refreshed. With no Wi-Fi in the car, it took longer than usual to load. Rory waited with bated breath as she stared at the white screen. Once the feed populated, though, she swore. "Bad news, you guys. They just uploaded another video."

Hannah's brows furrowed. "What?"

"Yeah. They hit their target view count." Rory frowned.

"Probably scheduled it," Elijah said, as he pulled into the theater parking lot, "unless they have a laptop or phone with them here. Either way, it's likely." Once he was out, he moved to the trunk to grab his laptop and pulled up security camera feeds. "Good news! One of these is back online."

"I'm really hoping Kane isn't next." Rory grabbed the balaclava off her lap and kept her head low as she got out of the car. Shawn was already there, leaning against his car. "You know, he was so hesitant to move in with me in case something like this happened."

"Hey, you couldn't have predicted this," Naomi said. "Besides, their beef isn't with Kane. It's with Shawn."

"Well, you know, except the whole fucking drug ring," Shawn said.

Hannah raised an eyebrow. "You are in no position to talk right now, Jameson."

Shawn didn't look Hannah in the eye when he spoke. "They definitely have beef with Kane, that's all I'm saying."

"Not to share more bad news," Elijah said, as he looked up from his laptop, "but I've spotted Amy. I saw her run out back."

"I should go after her."

"Wait, wait, wait. Amy, like my ex-girlfriend Amy?" Shawn laughed. "No way. She doesn't have it in her."

Naomi frowned. "Well, now she does. She didn't look happy to see me when I invited her over the other day."

"She's never happy to see anyone," Shawn countered.

"Well, she wouldn't have doxxed you if she didn't, now would she?" If looks could kill, Shawn would be dead three times over from Elijah's glare alone. "You know, I haven't wanted to ask this, but I think it's on everyone's mind, so fuck it. What the hell did you do to her when we weren't looking?"

"What do you mean, dude?"

"Don't play dumb! You know exactly what I mean!"

Everyone was taken aback; none of them had ever heard Elijah so angry, but they shared his fury.

"Listen, whether you think your powers were a gift from God or," Elijah dropped his voice to a whisper, but the rage maintained its course, "a curse like Hematite does, you're supposed to be fucking helping people with them! What did you do to her?"

"Nothing out of the ordinary. She was my girlfriend, Baron. What do you think?"

Brad pinched his nose, cast his gaze at his shoes, and closed his eyes. "Dude, no. Oh my God."

"That doesn't fucking make it okay!" Elijah exhaled, hoping the tension would leave his body with his breath, and focused on adjusting the beanie on his head. "Listen, I always knew you were a grade-A asshole, but I didn't know you were a full-blown psychopath!"

"Relax, there's no need to freak out." Shawn laughed, but no one laughed with him. He felt all their eyes on him, like his friends were staring into his soul—if they would even call themselves his friends anymore. "Since when did everyone get so sensitive, huh?"

Hannah rolled her eyes. "Full disrespect, but your head is wedged really far up your ass, and I hope you choke on your own shit."

For once, Shawn didn't have a comeback.

Naomi frowned, shook her head at Shawn, and said, "Maybe you should sit this one out."

Rory tied her hair back, slipped the balaclava on, and then tossed the hood up over her hair. "We can't waste any more time. I'm going after her."

"Is your earpiece working?" Elijah asked.

"I hear you loud and clear."

"Anything happens that you don't like, you come right back," Hannah said. "Got it?"

Rory nodded as she grabbed the riot shield Detective McMahon loaned her. "Give me a hit of adrenaline."

Hannah smiled. "Anything for Hematite. Go get Kane."

Rory turned the voice modification switch on as Hannah turned her brain into fuzz, transforming her nerves into more actionable energy. Her voice was distorted, sounding similar enough to Hematite's that the average person wouldn't be able to tell the difference. "Where did she go?"

"When you get to the back of the building, you should see a stage door. Looks like she went in that way."

"Thanks, Elijah."

———

Kane kept a close eye on Noah in the chair across from him. The restraints were made of thick leather and far too tight for Kane to bust out of on his own, so he felt relaxed enough.

"So, what do you want from me exactly, huh?" Kane suspected he knew—to reveal his identity—but didn't want to say anything that might sound like a confession. He knew his clothing was a dead give-away, especially after Noah ripped the balaclava off him with his own hands, but he also didn't want to be too sure. If he was being secretly recorded, a confession could end him.

This could end him even without his admitting anything, but at least since he'd been awake, Noah hadn't pulled a camera out.

"What I want isn't any of your business." Noah shrugged. "I already got it, anyhow."

"So why hold me here?"

"To keep you out of the way." Noah picked at his nails. "I've worked my ass off for far too long. After seven years of literal blood, sweat, and tears, I refuse to let you try to play hero and get in my way."

"What are you going to do?"

"Going to do? No, no, no. You're mistaken. It's already happening." Noah smirked. "I've already won, as far as I'm concerned. Anything that happens after this?" He shrugged. "*Shouganai.*"

Kane huffed. "Okay then, let me rephrase my question. What are you doing? Is it at this theater?"

Noah tutted his tongue. "I get that you're trying to pass the time and probably bored sitting in that chair, but the only one asking any questions around here is me. How'd you get so good at this, huh?"

Kane frowned and shook his head. "No idea what you're talking about."

Noah opened his mouth to speak but stopped when the hatchway opened. Light streamed in, casting a faint orange glow from the sun starting to set overhead, and brought a cool breeze with it that both Kane and Noah were grateful for in their own ways. The silhouette was indeterminable, but as they closed the doors behind them and made their way down the steps, it became clear who they were: Hematite.

Kane's brows furrowed. *Hematite?*

It had to be Rory. There was no other contender. Kane could tell right away; she was the only one with access to his clothes, and the pieces were all just a tad too big on her. But it would be hard to discern the difference to an untrained eye.

Unfortunately for them, Noah wasn't an untrained eye.

The navy scarf wrapped around her neck and mouth where the black hood didn't cover, the sweatshirt being large enough to hide her feminine frame. Kane's black pants fit a bit more snuggly on her thighs than they did on him, but left plenty of space around her calves, which was only saved by the cinch at the ankles. Kane wasn't sure where she got it, but she wore a clear riot shield on her arm.

Noah swung his legs to the ground and then stood from his chair. "Do my eyes deceive me?" He lazily pointed at Kane. "You know, I could have sworn I had Hematite right here."

Kane felt like the wind was knocked out of him. "Holy shit."

"Let him go, Noah. Cops are on the way. There's no point."

Kane couldn't believe what he was hearing. Her voice sounded exactly like his own, but he didn't have much time to marvel at Rory's accomplishment that she must have worked on with Elijah.

"You know, Kane, sending someone in your stead is pretty smart. I wonder if they're immortal, too."

Noah grabbed a match from the table and lit it. He blew on the flame for dramatic effect, causing the fire to burst at Rory in a thick stream. She covered herself with the riot shield, which did its job of deflecting the flames. Kane sighed in relief as she charged forward and stepped her foot out to stomp on Noah's, which caused him to drop the match. As Rory let the riot shield fall so it could take the blunt from the heat, she pulled a taser from her pocket and hit Noah in the neck with it. Suddenly, Kane could feel the flames warm his face from where he sat. His eyes darted from Rory, to Noah, and then to the flames, which began to slowly wrap around the room, licking up the walls.

As Noah collapsed, Rory pocketed the taser and dashed for Kane. As the flame rose up from the shield, creating a wall between them and Noah, she kneeled and made quick work of unbuckling the leather straps.

"Where the hell did you get a riot shield?"

She reached into the mask to turn the voice modifier off as she moved from the strap on his wrists to the ones on his chest. The lack of a microphone also made it so only Kane could hear her. "I called McMahon last night. He let me borrow it from the station. Same with the taser."

"God, I love you."

"I love you too, but we gotta get out of here before we can chat." She flipped the voice changer back on as she lowered herself further down to work on removing the ankle straps. One unbuckled with ease, but the other wouldn't budge. "Fuck. Is he still down?"

Kane craned his neck. "Hard to tell through the flames. They've steadied, but they're still thick."

With a huff, Rory reached into her pants pocket. She fished out the same pocketknife Kane once used to free her from Stone Breaker's restraints to release him from the final leather strap. The thick leather was resistant to cut, so Rory put in as much elbow grease as she could. Kane kept an eye out in front of them and watched as the flames parted for Noah.

He limped over to them, clutching at his stomach as he keeled over, and the fire slowed. Kane blocked Rory's head with his left arm, pushing her head down as he swung at Noah. His right fist landed on Noah's jaw, causing him to stumble backward and further lose control just as Rory freed Kane from the last strap. She'd managed to avoid nicking Kane, sacrificing only a thread or two in his pant leg.

"Do you know which way they took you in?" she asked.

"No. The bastard killed me before kidnapping me, so I was out the whole time."

Rory frowned beneath the mask and then quickly led Kane behind the hanging costumes, using them for cover as the smoke from the fire filled the room. "Stay low. Can't have you passing out on us now."

"There's a stairway around the corner here, I think," Kane said. Rory followed him there, both crouching down until they reached the stairs. The smoke rose further still, filling the room to the point where they could no longer see Noah.

"Smoke detectors gonna go off at this rate."

Kane reached the top first and opened the door for Rory. Smoke followed them out into the backstage hallway. A performer, half-dressed in their costume and reviewing some sheet music, covered their mouth as they gasped.

"Hematite?"

Rory nodded and asked, "Which way out?"

The performer ushered them along, bringing them out to the back door Rory came from. The theater was small, so the narrow, short halls made for a quick getaway. Next to the door, Rory saw the same type of red pull station that Riverpeak High School used. She grabbed it, yanked down on the handle, and then left the building with Kane as the alarm blared overhead.

"Are you okay?" Rory asked him, as they stepped outside. Once they were in the clear, she pulled Kane into a hug, grateful to feel him and have physical confirmation that he was well.

"I've been better, that's for sure. Who would have thought you'd be saving my ass again, huh?" He stepped back to hold Rory at an arm's length. "And look at you! I should get you this in your size."

As sweet as Kane was, Rory was still too high-strung. "What happened?"

"I'm not totally sure. No clue if he had any hidden cameras, but he took a blood sample of mine and then just said he was keeping me down there to stay out of the way. Something is going to happen at this show. I think you just saved a ton of people's lives by pulling that fire alarm."

"He'll come looking for us," Rory said. "We should wait out here for him. He probably thinks we're leaving."

"Good thinking. Remember everything I taught you?"

Rory nodded. "How could I forget?"

He chuckled. "That's my girl." He kissed her forehead through the balaclava. "Just don't overdo it, okay? Know your limits."

"I know. We can do this. Together."

Kane nodded. After what he'd just been through, he wasn't so sure, but he didn't want to place any doubts in Rory's head. So instead, he simply said, "Together."

CHAPTER 17

Before Noah pursued Kane and Rory, he took the blood sample he'd stolen from Kane and hid it in one of the garment bags. It would be safer here, hiding in plain sight, than it would be on his person or with Carter. As he did, a new light source caught his eye, barely visible in the thin cracks of the hatch: red and blue, confirming what Rory said.

He jogged up the steps to the theater with gusto. When he opened the door, he did so as minimally as possible to check for a possible crowd. The actors looked more like a blur of tea-length dresses and sharp sports coats, dress shoes, and kitten heels tapping along the linoleum floor as they scattered about to the back entrance in a flustered whirl. Someone yelped as they knocked over a hot box with warm rollers, which spilled out onto the floor with a clash. Once he determined the coast was clear, actors too busy trying to reach the back door, Noah slipped through the crack and slowly closed the door behind him.

Noah too wore the uniform that Amy instructed: a black button-up and black dress pants. According to his name tag, he was Johnny for the night, which allowed him to blend in as he walked with purpose through the crowd. He'd rolled his sleeves up to his elbows, grateful that the silk of his shirt was lightweight so he wouldn't sweat right through it. With everyone backstage, the air was stale, and the smoke rolling up from downstairs was about to make things much worse.

He'd disabled the smoke detectors with Amy, as a precaution to buy himself some time, but mentally chastised himself for not doing the same with the fire alarm. While he'd prepared to have to use his fire, he hadn't expected Rory to steal her boyfriend's clothing and to get a riot shield from the police. When Reiji received reports from Councilman Stevens, the department didn't even have fireproof equipment.

That detective must have prepared her for him. He made a mental note to pass the information along to Sterling so they could nip this rebel in the bud.

Noah cut through the wings to reach the front of the building so he could get to Amy and Carter as fast as possible. The stage lights were hot, even from the dark shadows of the curtains. Pushing past the crowds rushing in either direction and fighting the current of actors running backstage, he dipped back into the side hallway. When he closed the door behind him reading "Employee Access Only," he pocketed his hands and moved to the concessions bar where Amy and Carter were waiting. The lobby flooded with patrons rushing out the front door, but Amy and Carter stayed behind the bar.

Thankfully, Carter was prepared. He'd left the canister Noah brought the liquid in behind the bar for easy access, and he was already filling it back up so as to not lose any product. Noah mentally thanked his quick thinking. When he jumped up onto the counter and slid over it, Amy stared at Noah with wide eyes.

"What are you doing up here?"

"We gotta go." He grabbed her hand. "Come on."

"What's happening?"

Carter chimed in, "You look like hell."

"Yeah, what else is new? Hematite escaped, pulled the fire alarm, and now his little police buddies are here. There's not actually a fire right now. Well, there was, but that's a story for another time. Point is," he looked at Amy, "I gotta get you out of here." He turned to Carter. "Can I count on you to blend in?"

Carter nodded. "I'm on your six."

"Don't follow me. Stay here until you're done with this." He gestured to the canister. "Get this shit out of here so the cops don't find it and so it doesn't go down the drain."

"On it."

Amy barely comprehended what they were saying. All it took was the word "police" for her heart to race. "Where are we going to go?"

Noah pursed his lips and tilted his head to the side. "Still working on that."

"Did you not come up with a plan?"

"Not for this!" They moved out of the bar and moved back the way he came. "Just promise me you'll remember one thing."

"What's that?"

"These heroes? They're full of shit. Do you understand me? Hematite has enabled Brick Beast so he can try to fulfill his version of the greater good. Well, I say fuck that and fuck both of them. Should anything happen, don't go to them. Know that I will come for you."

Once they reached the Employees Only door, they both broke into a light jog, staying on their toes to be as quiet as they could. The commotion helped cover the sound, and thanks to their uniforms, the performers didn't even give them a second glance. As they ran out of the wings toward the back of the theater, she felt like the breath had been knocked out of her lungs. "Will you?"

"I swear on my life, Amy. I always will. It might take me some time, but I will."

It was hard to hear him above the fire alarm blaring overhead, but she was able to read his lips well enough to fill in the blanks. The sound made her head throb, and as they pushed back through the halls, it crescendoed as they approached another alarm, only offering the slightest reprieve between its speakers.

When they swung the back doors open, the dirt covering the back lot of the theater swirled around them. After being kicked up by so many heels, it lingered in the air, seemingly frozen in time. The sun was already dipping below the mountains, painting the sky a brilliant orange against the tips still covered in the last bits of snow of the season. The bite in the air already returned as the sun retreated. Amy reflexively reached for Noah, desiring his warmth to help her beat the chill.

As the dust and last members of the crowd dispersed, scrambling to the front of the building, Rory and Kane stood before them. Rory was still wearing Hematite's clothing, masquerading as the hero.

"I know that's you, Rory," Noah said when he saw the two. In the spring weather, he was already feeling overheated, a disadvantage he tried to play off. "I'm here to fight your boyfriend."

"Stand down," Rory said. The voice modifier was still on, altering her voice to sound mangled and mechanical. She must have tweaked it to better suit her voice.

Noah grabbed his lighter. "You really wanna do this right now?"

"Hiding behind your lighter again?"

Noah chuckled and pocketed it. "Oh, I see what this is. You want a fair fight, is that it?" Noah stepped forward, standing in front of both Rory and Kane. "Those clothes are far too big on you, but they look like they'd be a great fit for the man beside you."

"Hand over the lighter."

Noah looked at Rory and then at Kane. "What do you think about this, Kane? Huh?"

Kane sighed. "Just hand over the lighter. Backup is on the way. It's already over, dude."

Noah turned his gaze to Rory, looking her in the eyes through her balaclava. He patted his left pocket and then said, "You want it? You're going to have to take it from me."

They stared at each other for a moment that felt longer than it was. Ultimately, it was Rory who made the first move. She reached for his pocket, but Noah stepped aside to dodge the reach. Rory followed by ducking and sweeping the leg, causing Noah to lose his footing. Kane took the opportunity to lunge at him, reaching for his arms to hold him back, but Noah elbowed him in the stomach as he stumbled backward.

As Kane regained his footing, Rory shuffled to stand by his side.

"You've been practicing together. I'd be lying if I said I wasn't a little impressed." Noah looked at Amy and held out his hand. "Stay put."

"We aren't here for her," Rory said. "We're here for you."

Kane moved first, lighter on his feet than Rory was from years of experience. Noah cracked his knuckles and ran to meet him, hoping to get Kane out of the way first. Noah dodged the first punch but fell right into the second. His jaw crunched beneath Kane's knuckles. Noah recoiled and shook it off, ignoring the throbbing in his cheek. He countered, blocking the next hit and throwing a punch, but Kane dodged. As the momentum pulled Noah forward, Kane reached up to flip Noah over his back. He slammed into the dirt and concrete below, groaning in pain as he rolled over and spat out warm blood. The pavement felt gravely and rough beneath his palms, and his burned arm stung from the recent impact.

As Noah went to stand, pushing his bangs out of his face, Rory kneed him in the stomach. It knocked him back down, so he tried to think of his next move as he let his tattooed arm support him to minimize the damage to his burned skin.

Before he could, Kane hoisted him up from behind, underneath the armpits. As he did, Rory unclipped the billy club from the belt holding her pants up. Noah thrust his head back, butting Kane in the nose, and swept his leg up in an arch kick. His foot hit the club, sending it flying across the lot until it clanged against the pavement and rolled away. Noah then stomped on Kane's foot, but Kane still didn't budge.

"My point still stands. You're awful tough for a teacher."

Kane raised his brows, as if the answer were obvious. "You kinda have to be in Riverpeak, thanks to guys like you."

As they spoke, Rory reached for Noah's pocket. He kicked her with his other leg, hitting her in the head. She stumbled to the side with a grunt and, to Noah's delight, Kane released him to run to her side.

"I'm fine," she said.

Rory held her hands up by her face, ignoring the pain and ready for more, and threw a jab. Noah tried to bob and weave but didn't make it in time. Before Rory's fist could reach his temple, he grabbed her wrist with both hands. He moved a hand to her shoulder so he could pull her into an arm lock. As he did, Noah looked behind him and made eye contact with Amy. He nodded at her, and he'd never been more grateful to see someone understand him so well, especially without words.

Amy shuffled toward him, kicking up some dust along the way. When Amy reached him, she shot her hand into his pocket and grabbed his lighter. Amy held it a few inches beneath Rory's chin. To even Amy's surprise, her hand didn't shake, and there was no hesitation.

"Turn it on for me, will you, sweetheart?" Noah turned his gaze to Kane. "Let's see if this version of Hematite can come back from the dead."

"No!" Kane lunged forward, but Noah twisted, jerking Rory with him. Kane held his arms out as he caught his footing. "Don't!"

Noah snapped his head back toward Kane in response to the interjection. "Oh? And why shouldn't I? After all, can't Hematite regenerate himself back to life?" He chuckled. "Don't worry. If this is Hematite, then they'll return to us in the next … how long is it again? Fifteen minutes, give or take?"

"Leave her alone."

Noah laughed. "Why, huh? You got a confession on the tip of your tongue?"

Rory shook her head. "Kane, don't."

"Yeah, Noah, you were right. So let her go. I should have never let her drag herself into this, and she doesn't need to get hurt for my fuck-up."

As if pleading for him to stop, Rory only said, "Kay."

"He already knows, Rory. There's no point." He held his hands out only for them to fall to his sides. "Your life isn't worth my secret."

"Just say the words, Kane, and I will be over the moon."

Before Kane could speak, Rory took a step forward and leaned, bringing Noah with her. Amy shuffled back, trying to avoid getting hit during the sudden change in positions. Noah was caught off guard by the movement and tried to adjust how he held her arm, and she used the opportunity to donkey-kick him with her back leg. He groaned as her foot made contact with his inner thigh and his grip on her arm loosened just enough for her to wiggle herself free. Rory tucked and rolled forward to make a quick getaway.

As Rory stood again, Noah steeled himself and pressed his heels into the dirt. "Amy, now!"

But just as Amy's thumb hit the spark wheel, the sound of sirens drowned out her eardrums. The flame flickered for a split second before immediately vanishing, too quick for Noah to even notice with the new distraction. She turned to see the source of the sudden arrival, and in rapid succession, they heard the sound of tires squelching and doors swinging open, only to immediately slam shut. It was then followed by shuffling footsteps, heavy boots kicking more dirt up along the way in the back lot. The cars read RIVERPEAK PD in large, bold font on the side, superimposed over a blue stripe on the white vehicle. Amy's eyes widened as the officers reached for their guns and pointed them directly at her and Noah.

"Freeze! Hands above your head!"

Amy jumped, dropping the lighter in the process. She cursed at herself for it, saying it out loud on instinct. Before she or Noah could reach for his lighter, Rory kicked it so it slid across the pavement toward the increasing police presence. As the lighter reached the police force, the realization of what Amy had almost done dawned on her.

What the hell was I thinking?

One of the cops grabbed the lighter as another leaned into the radio on his shoulder. "We got his lighter!"

"You're surrounded, Sato." It was Detective McMahon's voice, but they couldn't see him. Amy's eyes darted around, searching for a sign of the detective before determining it must have been on a radio or speaker in a squad car. "Give it up!"

Noah placed a hand on Amy's shoulder and glanced at her. As he did, he heard more police cars speeding in their direction. He gave Amy that smile, the same one he gave her when he first showed her his powers. It was almost as if he was asking if she was still his moth attracted to his flame, and she hoped the look in her eyes told him "yes" a million times over.

"Hang on tight, sweetheart."

CHAPTER 18

As the sound of more sirens grew closer, Noah focused his attention on the police car. He hadn't done this before but figured now was as good a time as any to try. He'd be testing his limits, seeing just how much he'd grown over the last seven years.

As Noah took a deep breath, he ignored the shouts of the officers as they cocked their guns and homed in on the sound of the engines, listening to hear just how many of their cars were still running. He counted at least four, though he wasn't completely positive given everything that was going on around them, but four was more than enough.

After all, he only needed one.

As another final police car pulled up, tires squealing, Noah smirked. It was just within his range now and still running. He wasn't about to deny the additional ammunition, especially at his most desperate hour.

"Thanks, officers." Noah saluted them. "It's been a pleasure."

As flames burst through the hood of the last police car, he took Amy's hand and ran. Noah's smirk grew as he realized the full potential of his power unfolding behind them. Amy ran ahead of him, using his body as a shield from the growing heat. As they bolted, Noah listened to the humming of other cars beneath the sirens, utilizing whatever internal engine combustions he could, starting with the four he identified before then. A few more boomed with their explosions, the heat rising around him and Amy. The tires followed, the smell of rubber melting before the pressure popped and overwhelmed their senses.

The cops were distracted enough by four rapidly engulfed vehicles in a row so Noah and Amy could get away, dodging police detection. Noah kept the flames growing so they were tall enough that all Riverpeak would see what happened.

———

Detective McMahon lifted his smartwatch. He was waiting on the other side of the theater with some computers and a few other officers in the back of an armored van, where he was awaiting further instructions. "You still there, Miller?"

"I'm here. We're a little beat up and my ears are still ringing, but we managed to get out of the way just in time."

"What the hell happened?"

"Nothing an ice bath won't help with later," Rory said. She grimaced on the other line. "Are you okay? I think he concentrated the fire on the cop cars, so it didn't spread to us, but that explosion still looked pretty bad."

"I'm fine. Can't say the same for our vehicles, though, and I think we've got a few men down. Sato's on the move, and I'm sending another crew after him. Any idea where he might be heading?"

"They've got a house."

"Where?"

Rory rattled off the Prescott Road address and then said, "I don't think he'll head straight there, though. Noah's smarter than that. He'll try to find somewhere he can dodge you first."

"You know, I didn't get my raise this year because the department had to get all sorts of flame-retardant gear in response to all these fires over the last year, so we should be able to handle him."

"Well, I'm sure you'll get it once you catch him. He's behind those missing women, too."

"Speaking of which, he's got some girl with him. She's got red hair and a whole lotta freckles. Ring a bell?"

"Yeah, I know her. Her name is Amy. We think he's manipulating her after she broke up with Brick Beast."

"Who?"

"Brick Beast. That guy who helps Hematite sometimes."

"Never heard of him. Should I have?"

"It doesn't really matter."

"Right. Well, we're on our way." He looked to his men. "Make the call. Let's pursue this asshole."

"Thanks, Detective. Get to safety."

"Like I said, we can handle him with the gear we got."

"And like I said, get to safety." Rory sighed. "Your whole department's corrupt and you know it. We thought Eliza Daniels getting pulled out would stop that, but we were wrong."

"How do you mean?"

"Hematite caught a few cops engaging with some known dealers the other day," Rory said. "They're customers. A free hit in exchange for immunity, then they get hooked and come back for more."

"Are you fucking kidding me?"

"I wish I was."

"And nobody told me?"

"Are you shocked?"

McMahon sighed. "I suppose I shouldn't be."

"Anyway, this whole thing goes deeper than Noah, as I'm sure you already know. He's just a very dangerous piece of the puzzle. For Hematite to take them all down, we need you, McMahon."

"Yeah, I know. We'll keep in touch. Oh, and Miller?"

"Yes, sir?"

"That little boyfriend of yours isn't Hematite, right? Sato's just fucking crazy?"

McMahon wasn't stupid, and he knew that the blond Rory came to rescue was, in fact, the masked vigilante he'd been working with over the last few years. But if what Rory said was true, it was just as much his job to protect Kane Kelly as it was Rory's.

Rory didn't hesitate. "Nope. Kane's just a teacher. He grew up on the east side of town, and everyone there knows how to fight."

"Yeah, it's either that or get your ass kicked," McMahon said.

"I don't know what got into Noah; maybe all the drugs are rotting his brain. If we narrowed the list of Hematite suspects down to black hoodies and sweatpants, that would be the entire state of Colorado."

McMahon hid his relief. "You're telling me. Where is Hematite, anyway?"

"Getting people out of the theater," she lied. "I'll have to see where he ran off to and try to rendezvous."

"You do that. We'll take over from here."

———

As Amy and Noah ran, she mentally cursed Riverpeak for being as small as it was. There were only so many places to run and evade the police, which made her nervous about their chances of successfully escaping.

"Where are we going?" She'd hardly call herself religious, but she prayed Noah had an answer as they passed the precinct and city hall. She couldn't help but think that if the police station was right there, then they were going the wrong way.

"Out of here," Noah said. "Come on, I know where we can lose them."

Noah led Amy through the back alleys of the east side of Riverpeak. Sirens blared around them and made her wince, but Noah remained collected and alert. As they paused in one of the alleys, waiting for it to be clear before they crossed the road, Noah's eyes landed on the warehouse on the edge of town. Like most of the businesses in Riverpeak, it was abandoned, and he knew there were still some shelves and boxes collecting dust inside after his father considered buying the space.

"I know where we can go."

"Really?"

"It's abandoned. They won't know to look for us there. This way."

Noah darted across the road, still holding Amy's hand to drag her along with him. They ran around the side of the building, where a side door had a wooden plank covering where the handle once was. There was a small window on the top of the door, but no logo. Noah let go of Amy's hand, and his biceps flexed as he ripped the wood off, allowing him to shove the door open with his elbow. It swung open, slamming against the wall inside.

For once, Amy didn't flinch.

Noah nodded his head toward the inside, gesturing for Amy to move forward. She stepped in and Noah closed the door behind them. As he took her hand again and directed her toward the back of the building, weaving through hallways of tall shelves filled with boxes, her thoughts flashed back to that elderly couple and all of the what-ifs.

Would it be so bad if they did get caught?

"Where do we go from here?"

"Let's wait it out. If we do, then maybe we can lose them."

Amy nodded, lacking the mental clarity to think of another idea. "Yeah, you're probably right. Let's just lay low."

The two of them sat in one of the rows, keeping their heads down and behind boxes. Their shoulders touched as Amy pulled her knees into her chest and wrapped her arms around them. Noah moved a hand to her back and rubbed small circles at the nape of her neck.

"Sorry for this mess. This didn't go how I hoped at all." Noah hung his head. "You were right; kidnapping probably wasn't the best approach."

"Luckily for you, I'm not in an 'I told you so' sort of mood. Does Rory have powers?"

"No. Just nerves of steel."

"If she didn't fuck us over just now, I'd say I'm glad to see her therapy's working."

Noah bit back a laugh. "Yeah. But hey, remember what I told you? No matter what happens, I will always be there for you and have your back. You don't have to worry about a fucking thing with me, alright?"

Noah leaned over and kissed her temple. She looked at him and let him kiss her, which he did with an urgency she'd yet to see. *My mouth will be sore later from this*, she already knew. Amy wasn't sure exactly when, but somewhere along the way to here, their relationship evolved beyond just a fun hookup, and now she questioned if it was for the better or for the worse.

They pulled away as the front door suddenly slammed open. Amy jumped at the sound as the door fell. It landed flat as a group of men yelled at them to freeze and stormed in. Noah and Amy both peered through the cracks of the boxes on the shelves to see who had joined them.

"Is that the fucking SWAT team?" Amy asked in a panicked whisper.

"Looks like it." Noah scanned the officers he could see, evaluating the likelihood of escape. Fighting wasn't an option—had he been alone, he'd set the whole building on fire and not have a care in the world, but getting Amy safely out of there was his biggest priority. He told himself it was because she was his key to Brick Beast, but in truth, that was only part of it. The idea of her being hurt or arrested made him sick.

"Full body armor," he said to her, still speaking in whispers. "I know their riot shields are fireproof, so what do you wager the rest of their gear is?"

"I'd wager everything on that."

Their armor included goggles, something Noah hadn't expected, but it didn't surprise him that they weren't taking any chances with his pyrotechnics. As Noah looked longer, he noticed their goggles were embedded into the black helmets, which wrapped their entire heads and faces in Kevlar. They all carried semi-automatic rifles.

"How many do you see?" Amy asked. "I think there's six."

"They're fanning out to surround us. I spot a seventh." His eyes moved from the officers to around the room, wondering what he could use to evade detection and get Amy out. Using his fire wasn't an option, much to his chagrin, but with everything in the warehouse, he'd be damned if there wasn't some other way.

Then, his eyes spotted their way out. A water pipe wrapped around the perimeter of the building with a few valves along the way. It was only three aisles over, and the officers were looking forward.

"Stay quiet, stay low, and don't let go of me. We have to get to the wall."

"What?"

"Do you trust me?"

Amy hesitated, but ultimately, said, "Yes."

"Just do as I say."

Amy grabbed his hand and ducked with him as they moved through their aisle. Some boxes were missing from a lower shelving unit, so they used that to move back one.

Two to go.

They didn't have the same luck in the new row, so they tip-toed to the spot in the center of the aisle where the shelving gapped. They hugged the shelves, backs to it so they wouldn't be ambushed from behind. Before they turned the corner, Noah felt around in his pockets, only to silently sigh in relief as he checked to make sure none of the officers snuck into the aisle. Once he confirmed it was clear, he pulled her with him to enter the new row.

One to go.

"Where are we going?"

"That valve." Noah pointed to it so Amy could see their destination. "I have an idea."

They didn't have to travel far since they were still near the break in the aisles. They checked one last time for officers to ensure they could move freely. Footsteps approached, letting them know that one was getting closer, but the warehouse was big enough that they still had time to escape.

"Where are we heading after this?"

"Out the way we came. If we can lose them in here, then we can get to my bike and make a run for it."

"Got it."

Now by the edge of the wall, Noah crouched by the valve to spin it open. Water sprayed out, louder than he'd have liked. Amy was still by his side, waiting to see what he would do.

He couldn't let her down. Not now. Too much was riding on this working.

Noah grabbed his spare lighter from his pocket and, upon lighting it, ran the flame along the pipe. He used a hand to gently block Amy from the flames, urging her to take a step back. The flames grew, licking up the sides of the pipe in both directions and enveloping it. The fire grew so quickly that it was hard to tell where it started.

"Where is he?!"

"Who has eyes on him?"

And then, some fog spat out of the valve—just what Noah had hoped for.

He maintained the flames, needing the water to grow hotter still. The humidity stuck to his skin, starting as a thin layer but growing thicker by the second. Amy wiped her glasses as they fogged up, and the action made him smile.

"Bingo."

The fog rolled out of the valve, which was hot to the touch, but the temperature didn't bother Noah. It spread across the room, and as long as Noah held his flame to the pipes, it wouldn't stop. It grew thicker, rising from floor to ceiling, engulfing everything around it.

"I can't see!"

"Take off your helmets!"

"I thought these were fog-proof!"

"There's too much!"

The fog was so thick that Noah could barely see. The only reason he saw Amy beside him as he stood was from the flame wrapping around the pipes.

"Now's our chance. Let's go."

They stayed in their aisle, following the source of light streaming in from the small window in the side door where they came in. The footsteps around them grew louder, but Noah made the flames grow larger.

Once they reached the door, Noah swung it open. Some fog swirled out, coming out in a rush, but he closed the door as soon as Amy was out with him. She grabbed his hand with an iron grip as they stepped forward and her eyes adjusted to the red-and-blue lights.

"Freeze!"

"We've got you surrounded!"

"Drop the lighter, Sato!"

The voices swirled around them like a disjointed symphony. Before Amy or Noah could consider their next move, the door behind them opened and a gun was placed against Noah's back. He stiffened at the feeling and looked to make sure Amy wasn't receiving the same treatment. To his relief, she wasn't.

"Hands behind your head! Now!"

Noah and Amy glanced at each other as they both lifted their hands. Noah dropped his lighter and as it hit the ground with a soft thud, some dirt kicking up by their shoes, and Amy's pupils expanded in fear. As Noah mouthed an apology to her, he saw her bottom lip tremble and tears well in her eyes. Another siren blared, coming to a halt when the police car parked in the grass in front of them.

"I'm so sorry, Amy."

"You tried."

The officer with the gun to his back pushed the rifle, making Noah stumble forward. "Shut up!"

It was over. He failed.

"Leave the girl. I'm taking her in." A red-headed officer stepped out of the car that had just arrived, dressed in the same gear as the others but with his goggles and helmet off. "Amy Brewer, you're coming with me. My name is Detective McMahon. You're safe now, okay?"

As the rest of the officers handcuffed Noah and shoved him into their vehicle, leaving Amy alone again, she didn't feel safe—not at all.

"Please, don't hurt him!" Amy couldn't stop the tears that fell down her face. She hated that she was crying at a time like this; it felt like admitting defeat. The officers sped off without so much as acknowledging her. She looked toward McMahon, who offered her an awkward smile.

"Your friends told me about you. Did Sato hurt you?"

She shook her head. "No. He'd never."

McMahon's brows furrowed and his eyes narrowed in his confusion. "Hm. Well, once we get to the station, I'll have some questions for you. But first, let me read you your rights."

CHAPTER 19

Detective McMahon slumped into the chair across from Amy. He sighed as he looked at her with a look that she couldn't quite read. It was a cross between disbelief, annoyance, and exhaustion, and she wasn't sure what parts were directed at her, at Noah, or at something else entirely.

"Amy Brewer. You are not who I expected to see here, literally ever."

And just like that, Amy felt small. She once again felt the desire to curl up into herself and shrink so she could hide from McMahon's view, not dissimilar to how she felt before Noah saved her from that sketchy man at the bar a few months back. "Yeah, I know. I'm sorry, Detective. The feeling is mutual."

"Now that we've got you booked, I have a few questions that I need to ask you."

"Sure."

"Quick recap: you're under arrest for aiding and abetting Noah Sato on May 15. We have a phone service that runs 24/7 to connect you with legal counsel, which you have a right to. You want a lawyer first?"

Amy shook her head. "No. Probably stupid, I know. But I just want to get this over with."

"Suit yourself. Just a friendly reminder that while you are not obliged to say anything, anything you do say may be given in evidence. So, how would you describe your relationship with Noah Sato?"

"That is a really good question." Amy chuckled, breathy and nervous. "I desperately needed a rebound after breaking up with Shawn. Noah provided that distraction."

"How would you define said distraction?"

Amy knew what he was looking for: a confession. But she wouldn't give it to him, even if it meant sharing only parts of the truth. "Sex, pretty exclusively."

"Your place or his?"

"Does that matter?"

Detective McMahon shrugged. "Maybe it does."

"Mine. I live alone."

It was a lie, but the detective didn't need to know that. Amy knew the second that she confessed to being at his house, it would all be over. The more she could play dumb about what Noah kept in his basement, the better for both of them.

"Even if we have the two of you on security camera together?"

It was a possibility, but Amy didn't sway. She wasn't sure when her nerves developed steel armor—perhaps she was less of a deer in the headlights than she always thought she was—but she stayed the course.

"He was just some guy I was hooking up with." It pained her to reduce him to that, even though at its core, it was at least partially true. Then, she lied, "I don't know where he lives."

He raised a bushy red brow. "Not even 31 Prescott Road?"

"30 Prescott?"

"Thirty-one."

"Prescott..." She leaned back in her chair. "That's in the suburbs, right?"

McMahon sighed, slouching in his own seat. "There's no need to play dumb, Ms. Brewer."

"Listen, Detective, I'm simple. I wake up, go to the gym, head to work at the theater, and then go home. Noah knew my schedule, and we worked around that when we'd meet up."

"For rebound sex."

"Correct. Just rebound sex."

"What was involved in this rebound sex?"

"There some weird law about getting kinky that I don't know about?"

"I meant drugs, Ms. Brewer. Did Noah Sato offer you drugs?"

This was her out. All she had to do was to say yes and this would all be over. It would be as simple as, "Yes, he offered me drugs that would give me superpowers and that's why I slept with him." But something inside of her told her to lie and protect not only Noah but herself.

"No. There were no drugs in our situation-ship."

"So, then what the hell happened at the theater? Your stories better be straight or so help me God."

Amy felt tears welling up behind her eyes, unsure of what Noah might have said. She froze with fear, capable only of keeping her breath steady. Before she answered, she took in McMahon's posture. He was rubbing his eyebrow, not looking at her directly. Shawn's sarcastic words came back to her: "Because Riverpeak PD is known for being the pinnacle of law enforcement."

The realization hit her like a truck. "Have you even spoken to Noah?"

"Excuse me?" McMahon moved his hand from his brow and started cracking his knuckles one by one. The sound echoed in the room.

"Come on. We all know cops lie during these kinds of things." Amy frowned and shrugged. "But that I won't talk to you about without a lawyer, actually."

McMahon sighed. "Fine. We'll resume this conversation at a later date."

As he stood, another officer swung the door open. "Amy Brewer?"

"Yes?"

"Your mother's here."

———

Everything felt like a blur. Amy figured that feeling was probably for the best.

"Absolutely unbelievable."

She looked up from her phone at her mother. Sarah Brewer's hair was neatly trimmed, so cleanly that Amy wagered she'd gotten it cut on her way to pick her up. She'd gotten her dark blue eyes from her, along with the rest of her features. The main difference between them was that her mother's freckles faded over the years, thanks to dozens of different spot-reducing and bleaching skin creams. Amy's, however, dotted her skin, vibrant now that summer was returning.

Sarah looked over at her daughter from the driver's side. "Don't you have anything to say for yourself?"

Amy frowned and shrugged from her spot in the passenger seat. She'd sent a few texts to Noah and tried to call him, but he wasn't answering. After promising he'd be there for her, she felt like a fool, but saying so would steer the conversation with her mother into dangerous territory. Instead, she said, "I'm just glad it's over."

Sarah scoffed. "That's it?"

"I don't have anything to say that you'd want to hear, so I'm not even going to bother."

"I mean, Amy, come on. How could you do this to yourself?"

The question made her feel like she was seven years old again. Amy hated that she knew the answer: after Shawn, she'd been so desperate to believe that someone could be good to her, and Noah was —or, at least, so she thought. Now, she wasn't so sure.

"Do we really have to have this conversation right now? Really?"

"Yes, really. What on earth were you thinking? We raised you better than this. And you love the theater!"

She loved the shows, but she realized she didn't hold that same regard for the theater itself. While the steady income and job security had been nice, it kept her tethered to her parents, giving them the sense of entitlement her mother exhibited now.

"It's complicated, Mom. And not worth explaining. It's neither here nor there at this point."

"I'd certainly say it is."

"No, it's really not, because it's over and done with now."

"And I'm not sure what you were doing with that boy," she spat, ignoring Amy's insistence, "but you should take a pregnancy test if you expect me to ever come to your rescue again. That would be..." She shivered as her voice trailed off.

"Oh, come on. We really don't need to talk about this." It also wasn't possible thanks to her birth control, but she didn't need to get into that much detail with her mother; it would be fruitless since once Sarah started, there was no derailing her. Amy looked out the window as they passed her apartment complex, then the storage facility next to it, and then the church across the way from Constance's Pond.

"Well, I think we do!" Sarah wanted to shout—Amy could tell from her tone—but kept her voice hushed as they proceeded into the church parking lot. "You are in no position to raise a child, and to think what people might say."

"There's no baby on the way, Mom, so you can cool your jets. What the hell are we doing here?" Amy asked. "We haven't gone to church in ages. Me especially, but I know you really haven't either."

"And clearly, we need to start going more often again." Sarah snatched her purse from the backseat and stepped out. "Come on. I need to pray for my daughter, and you should too so you can repent."

Amy rolled her eyes. "I think I'll pass."

"No, you're coming." Sarah slammed her door, walked to the other side of the car, opened Amy's, and grabbed her arm. The seatbelt held her in place, tightening as Sarah did.

Amy smacked her mother's hand away and scoffed. "But *I'm* the one who needs to repent."

Her mother huffed and said, "Amy, just unbuckle your seatbelt and come with me, for Christ's sake."

Not in the mood for a fight, Amy sighed as she unbuckled her seatbelt. Sarah stepped back to give Amy space to step out of the car.

In a whisper, Sarah chastised, "What has gotten into you?"

Amy didn't reply; she knew her mother wouldn't like the answer. Instead, she just stared at the church and didn't feel anything stirring

in her. If Sarah was hoping that Amy would receive some divine revelation, then she would be disappointed.

The church, like many of the buildings in Riverpeak, hadn't
changed much since it was first built in the late 1880s. The small
Carpenter Gothic building recently had a plaque added to the side of
the building's board and batten siding to acknowledge it as a historic
monument. A few small lancet windows gave the white-and-gray exterior walls a pop of color, especially as the sun shone through their
stained glass. On the top of the pointed roof were a bell and a cross,
with a second cross right above the archway over the dark front door.
Behind the church, Amy could see the edges of Constance Pond and
the mountain ranges, still topped with snow but mostly varying
shades of brown and green now that spring was in full force.

Amy followed her mother in. Once inside, Sarah rushed to the front
row, where she fumbled in her purse for her wallet to donate a dollar
in the small box next to the rows of candles. Amy watched as she lit
one and then prayed in the first pew. Amy lingered in the back, sitting
on the edge of the one furthest away. The light-colored oak felt uncomfortable on her posterior and her back. Wood panels shaped into an
arch filled the middle of the wall behind the altar, with a massive cross
filling the space. Otherwise, the church was mostly plain, with beige
walls that looked stained and a few stained-glass lancet windows
along the walls, alternating about every other pew or so. The red
carpet in the center of the aisles dulled from years of use. To Amy's
relief, they were alone. She wasn't sure she could face anyone right
now, not after everything that happened; she was too mortified.

As Amy waited on her mother, she felt restless and uneasy. She
hated church—always had, not for any particular reason other than it
not being her thing—and her mother was a zealot only when it was
convenient, or she felt guilty but didn't want to admit it. Amy knew
her mother's habits enough to not let them bother her as much as they
would have a few years ago, and admitting guilt would be like admitting defeat. So instead of ever apologizing or owning her faults, Sarah
would rush to donate a dollar, light a candle, and pray, much like she
was doing now.

Before Amy could take out her phone so she could do something with her hands other than stare blankly at them, her mother stood up and powered down the aisle. Amy thought about trying to call or text Noah again, but he hadn't answered. Sarah stopped when she reached Amy.

With her nose turned up, Sarah said, "I hope this was productive for you."

Amy shrugged. "Sure."

They made their way back to Sarah's car in silence; the rest of the drive was quiet too. Instead of going back toward Amy's apartment complex, they made their way into the suburbs. As Sarah pulled into her driveway, Amy unbuckled her seatbelt before the car was even parked. The moment it was, Amy opened the door, grabbed her bag, and stepped onto the pavement. While her apartment complex was a short walk from her parents' house, she still found it interesting that her mother brought her here instead of her own complex.

"Don't run from me, Amy," Sarah said. "We need to talk about all of the possibilities here and what happens next for you."

As Amy entered the foyer of the house, she said, "I'm not comfortable with this conversation." She wasn't comfortable at their home, either, wishing she had the energy or strength to just walk away. The photos on the wall acted as a harsh reminder of days long since passed, depicting the perfect family through the generations in front of the theater. She realized now that her freckles were edited out of most of them: the same freckles that Shawn had often teased, and Noah often kissed and doted on, trying to find each and every one of them with his lips.

She stopped herself in her tracks. *No. Can't think like that now.*

"Good! You shouldn't be comfortable! Did you think I was comfortable paying your bail for you? Do you think I'm comfortable having an absolute delinquent for a daughter? Absolutely not!"

Amy sighed through her teeth. "Not what I meant." She turned to move back up to her childhood bedroom, retreating to save her sanity. If she walked out of the house now, the fight would only get worse, so it was the next best thing.

"And where do you think you're going? I brought you here because we need to talk, and your father is about to get home!"

"Yes, because this conversation is so productive right now. I think we both need a few to cool down."

To her relief, Sarah didn't respond; instead, her mother exhaled loudly from her nose, like a bull ready to storm through a fine china shop. The last thread holding Amy together was growing increasingly thin, ready to snap at any second.

She wished she was still in jail. At least then her mother couldn't hold the bail over her head.

When she reached her old bedroom, she closed the door behind her. It hardly looked how she remembered it. The bed was still in the corner, but the sheets had been replaced from the black ones she once had with a boring beige. Any sign of her living here was long gone except for some old tape residue on the wall in one spot that her parents missed, barely visible through the paint job they'd given it after she moved out. They'd once been blue, but now they matched the comforter.

She grabbed her phone, desperate to talk to somebody. Noah wasn't answering her, and she wasn't sure if talking to him was even a good idea right now. So instead, she stared at Hannah's contact information, feeling transported back to the night she dumped Shawn, except this time, she actually called. The phone rang only twice before someone answered.

"Hello?"

"Hannah? Does your offer from the wedding still stand?"

"Amy!" She sounded genuinely happy to hear from her. "Oh my God, yes. Of course, it does. Are you okay?"

"I'm not sure." Amy hated the way in which her voice shook. "Listen, I'm going to cut straight to the point. What do you know about Noah?"

"I reckon you'd know more than I do."

"No, no, I think he manipulated me. Maybe manipulated isn't the right word, but I'm not sure how much of what he told me is a half-truth or a lie entirely or what. Please, Hannah. What do you know? Tell me everything."

Hannah blew a raspberry. "Well, I know he has fire powers but that he wasn't born with them. I also know he's the one that killed those women who went missing, almost killed Jordan Jefferson, and then stabbed his father in the chest."

"Wait, what?"

"Yeah. Mr. Sato's death at Naomi's wedding? That was all him. And as far as those women are concerned, we think he lured them in somehow so he could experiment on them. He's trying to give everyone superpowers, except it's not exactly stable."

"He killed them?"

"That's mainly a theory, but we're pretty sure, yeah. Amy, are you safe right now?"

Amy looked around her childhood bedroom. She wanted to say no, but said, "Safe enough, sure."

"Listen, if I were you, I'd bail. I'm here for you, okay? Do you wanna come over?"

"As much as I'd love to, I don't want to put you in harm's way. I don't know what he'll do next, and now there's potentially a whole bunch of super-powered people waking up to find out what gift Noah gave them."

"What exactly happened at the theater, anyway? Hematite said that Noah didn't get too specific."

"As much as I wasn't super cool with kidnapping, we needed Hematite out of the way. Looks like that backfired. But, uh, we spiked some of the beer at the theater and used that as a mass distribution method. It was my idea, too. Fuck, I'm such an idiot."

"You're not an idiot, Amy, I promise. From what Elijah's told me, Noah was always a bit of a sweet-talker. It's easy to get swindled into that, but it doesn't make you an idiot."

"I certainly feel like one. God, what have I done? Are these people who drank that beer going to die?"

"They might. I wish I had a concrete answer for you. Did he say why he wanted to get it out to everyone? We've got our theories but I'm not sure how on the money we are."

Amy stuttered. "Something about fairness. Trying to even out the playing field. But now that I think about it, I think he just wanted them under his control. Probably wanted to create an army of sorts to help tackle Hematite and peddle the drug. I bet he's less than thrilled about the cops breaking up the whole operation beyond just getting caught."

"How do you reckon?"

"Noah never seemed to give a shit about getting caught. I think he's been hiding for so long that he can't be bothered anymore. But he *did* care about *me* getting caught. Or at least he seemed to."

"Do you think he'll hurt you?"

Amy thought about it and, recalling Noah's concern for her safety, said, "No. Not me, at least." As much as she wanted to feel more empowered, it was why he was hesitant to give her the drug. If he wanted to hurt her, he would have already.

"Are you sure?"

"Completely. I'll be in touch, okay?" Amy wasn't sure how true of a statement that was, but it felt like a good promise to make.

"Okay. Don't hesitate. No judgment on my end, alright?"

"Thanks, Hannah. You know, I really appreciate you. Have a good night."

Amy hung up before Hannah could reply. She tossed her phone on the mattress next to her, watched it bounce against the comforter, and then fell on her stomach so she could face-plant a pillow.

The way she saw it, she had two options. The first was to ignore Noah and go to Hannah, hoping to rekindle a friendship with Naomi, Rory, and their clique, at risk of running into Shawn. But the idea of it made her too nauseous to even think straight, which brought her to her second option: to confront Noah about everything.

I made it this far, she thought. *No sense in giving up now.*

CHAPTER 20

As musty as the prison cell and as thin as the mattress was, Noah slept in worse places than this before. The cell was a few down from Mark's, making him only the second inhabitant of the long and lonely row of wet stone and metal bars. The worst part about it all was how humid it was, the warm dampness of spring sticking to his skin. He'd take the feeling of the mattress springs poking into his spine over the way everything clung to him. The first thing he decided he'd do when he got out of there was to fill a tub up with ice and dunk himself in.

Once the guard delivered breakfast and left, Noah heard Mark cackling down the hall as the echoing footsteps grew softer until they were gone. "Karma's a bitch, ain't it?"

Noah ignored him. Instead of giving Mark the satisfaction of a response, he pinched his nose and shoveled the food—if he'd even call it that—into his mouth, ready to get it over with.

"So much for getting me out of here. Fucking asshole."

Noah rolled his eyes.

"Oh, what, too embarrassed to face me, Noah?"

"You're beneath me, Mark," Noah said, mouth half full of slop. "Shut up before I burn your dick off."

Mark was silent for a moment and then asked, "Can you do that now?"

"Take a wild guess. Your imagination can't hurt you."

Mark said nothing after that. Once Noah was finally met with silence, save for some water dripping outside, he leaned back against the wall and stared at his feet. His mind wandered to Amy; he couldn't help but wonder if she was in a cell as dingy as his or somewhere slightly more comfortable. She'd mentioned she struggled with friendships, and the idea of more hardened inmates ganging up on her made his fists involuntarily clench.

The door to the hall swung open with an echoing clang. Instead of collecting the food trays, though, the corrections offer began to unlock his cell door.

"What's going on?"

He smiled. "You're free to go. Your bail's been paid."

Noah blinked at the officer standing before him. "What?"

"Get out of here." Once the cell door was open, the officer gave him a nudge. "Talk about a silver lining for you."

He raised a brow. "Silver?"

"Silver."

As the officer nodded, Noah understood. He had a few questions, but now wasn't the time to ask them.

"What were you saying about karma, Marky Mark?"

Noah chuckled at his own joke and Mark's lack of an answer.

As the officer led him down the hallway, he swung his hand against Noah's, letting it linger once making contact. Noah opened his palm and felt the cool, smooth texture of his lighter slide into it. He wrapped his finger around it, grateful that he wouldn't need to buy a new one. At the end of the hall, the guard grabbed a plastic grocery bag by the door and handed it to Noah. He slipped the lighter inside.

"There's your effects. Oh, and hold on. Forgot something."

Noah said nothing, not wanting to test his luck. The guard reached into his pocket and pulled out both of his cell phones.

The guard dumped them into the bag and then leaned in close to Noah. When he spoke, Noah could smell the cinnamon gum he was chewing. "McMahon couldn't find these to search through for evidence. Weird how they went missing, huh?"

He chuckled and winked. "Strange indeed."

Noah hadn't expected it to be this easy. The only disruption in his exit was a dirty stare from McMahon, whose arms were crossed by his chest. Noah made a point of flashing him a smile and two-fingered salute on his way out the door, just for good measure.

Now back in his own clothing and free, Noah stepped into the nearest alley and pulled his cell phone out of his pocket. The only missed call was from Amy, and as tempted as he was to reach out to her immediately, he had business to take care of first. That was the priority—it had to be—but he wouldn't pretend that seeing her name didn't bring him some relief.

Instead of calling her back, he called Carter. The phone only rang once before Carter answered.

"Well, I'll be damned."

"You're telling me. Sterling let me out."

"He filled me in. Don't worry, I managed to grab all of our supply at the theater, and then I got the stuff out of the basement at the house. We've moved it for now."

"Wait, what? How did you even get in?"

"Sterling lent me his spare key."

"I mean, I figured that. Was the place not swarming with cops?"

"Well, yeah. Luckily, that Irish-lookin' motherfucker wasn't there."

"The detective?"

"Yeah, him. Sterling went with me. He paid the rest of the force off."

"Fuck." He rubbed his eyes with his free hand. "I owe him big time."

"You got that right, buddy." Carter laughed. "Anyway, they didn't find anything, because of course they didn't. Right? So the house is free and clear. But we're keeping operations split between Potter Laboratories and the backup rental for now. You'll find some beer bottles in the basement. I put any excess we had in those for storage. Would hate for it to go to waste. Thanks to the chaos of the fire alarm going off, no one caught me."

"Wait, hold on. They're cooking at Potter's? You shitting me?"

"Just for now. Sterling thinks it would be best to let the dust settle, plus having everything split will help us stay at least partially protected."

"Sounds like he's officially calling the shots now."

"I think your arrest forced his hand."

"Well, good. Better him than me running the show. But I dunno that cooking out of Potter's lab is a good idea."

"Why's that?"

"Because that squirrelly, little shit is hiding something from me. From all of us. I think he's protecting someone on Hematite's side. One of them has powers and he won't say who or what exactly their ability is."

"Noted. Listen, Noah, I'd head to the backup rental if I were you. Sterling may have paid off most of the cops, but that detective is a determined son of a bitch and, I think, will be waiting for you to just breathe wrong if you go back home."

"Thanks for looking out." Noah's phone beeped, letting him know he was receiving another call; it was an unknown number. "I should take this and see who it is."

"Sure, man. Take it easy."

Noah ended his call with Carter and accepted the other. He didn't say anything at first, wanting to scope out who was on the other line.

"Noah?"

He recognized the voice, as he'd recognize his sister anywhere. "Depends on who's asking."

"Noah, for fuck's sake, I know you know it's me. Please, just," Naomi took a shaky breath and then continued, "just don't hang up. I just want to talk."

He sighed, nostrils flaring, and began to walk toward Constance's Pond so he could cut through to the suburbs with the privacy he needed. "How did you get this number?"

"Elijah found it for me. He's in tech. I've tried dozens of numbers that he found that could be potential matches."

"Yeah, well remind me to chuck this one into Constance's Pond after this."

"Jesus, Noah, with the dramatics. Listen, no one is with me right now. I'm in the yard, Brad's inside, and it's just me. This isn't some set-up or anything, I swear to you."

Noah didn't believe it. *"Maji?"*

Naomi sighed and replied in Japanese, "<Yes. I just want my brother back. This never sat right with me: how you died but Dad walked out without a scratch, how he never talked about it. It's been plaguing me for years, Noah, so yes.>"

Their conversation carried on like this—if she was lying about no one else listening, then they wouldn't understand, at least not without her having to later translate. Noah also liked the idea of no one around him being able to listen in.

"<It's not so simple.>"

"<And why not? Do you know how happy Mom would be to know that you're still alive? Grandma? We don't have to tell them anything, Noah. We can just start fresh. Blank slate. We can lie and tell them that whoever killed Dad kidnapped you or something, or—.>"

Noah frowned and cut her off. "<No, we can't. I wish we could, but we can't.>"

"<Why not?>"

"<You really think your little friend Hematite wouldn't swoop in to save the day?>"

"<We have enough money from Dad's death. We could bail you out.>"

Noah laughed. "<Prison? You think they'd just send me to prison? >" He couldn't stop the laughter. It stemmed from his core, free and feral. "<Oh, Naomi, that's good. You don't think Kane wouldn't bash my fucking brains in at the first opportunity?>"

"<Hematite doesn't kill people. He would never.>"

"<Even if he wouldn't, there's blood on my hands, Naomi. Too much for me to wash off and I don't care to. You don't want anything to do with that, do you?>"

"<Let me help you wash it off!>"

"<You can't!>"

"<I am giving you an out, Noah. What don't you understand about that?>"

"<You are the one who doesn't understand. I know you think that there's a part of me in here crying for help, and maybe it helps you sleep at night to think that, but there's not. Your brother is dead, and your father created me to replace him.>"

"<And Dad is dead now, so what is stopping you from coming home? Is there no love in your heart anymore?>"

There was, but that didn't matter.

"<You know, Naomi, I'm really glad you called.>"

Naomi paused. "<You are?>"

There was hope in her voice. Hope, of all things.

Noah couldn't help but to keep laughing.

"<I am. You've reminded me of why I'm here in the first place. Everything is so black and white for you, but the way I see it, this world is unfair. If I can help even the playing field, then why shouldn't I?>"

Naomi went to say his name, but he didn't give her a chance.

"<Now if you'll excuse me, I have a phone to chuck into a pond.>"

Noah hung up, pried open the SIM card tray so he could remove it, and then tossed the phone into Constance's Pond, as if he were skipping rocks. Everything he needed was on the burner phone he got to contact Amy with anyway.

It reminded him of the missed call from her. *It is promising,* he thought, and he couldn't help but wonder what she would have said should he have been able to answer. At least he knew she wasn't behind bars anymore. The only question that remained was how much she blamed him for what happened. Noah was aware enough to know that she had every right to blame him for everything, but depending on how well he did his job, she might find it in her heart to forgive him.

He pondered it as he walked to the backup rental. The unit was, just like the home he'd lived in for the last seven years, courtesy of his father. When he reached the house, Noah punched a four-digit number into the keypad on the front door by the handle. It beeped in affirmation as it unlocked, prompting him to turn the handle and push the door open with his shoulder. Once he stepped inside, he froze, letting the door swing shut behind him until it slammed.

The living room light was already on, and the ceiling fan ran on its lowest setting, preventing the air from going stale. Sterling sat on the couch with one long leg crossed over the other. His fingers on his left hand rolled across the arm of the sofa, but the tapping sound was almost muted thanks to the leather gloves on his hands. Sterling was, as always, sharp-dressed, more comfortable in a suit than he was in jeans and a T-shirt. For once, his hair—which had turned even grayer since Reiji's funeral a few months ago—wasn't slicked back, but tied back in a short, low ponytail. Some of his bangs fell in front of his face, but even with that, Noah would recognize him anywhere.

Sterling waved and said, "Nice of you to come back."

"Jesus Christ, Sterling. How long have you been here?"

"Not long. Just since you were set for release."

"Down to the minute?"

Sterling raised a brow and smirked. "Come on, Noah. You know me better than that by now. I know everything." Sterling shifted and crossed his ankles as he patted the spot next to him on the couch. Noah wasn't sure if Sterling's causal demeanor made him feel reassured or nervous. "Smart of you not to go back to the house."

"Yeah, well, even an idiot would know better than that."

"Don't worry. Carter called me as soon as you pulled your little stunt and already cleared out the basement."

"Yeah, he filled me in."

"I also heard your little girlfriend got bailed out."

"Yeah, she called me, but I haven't had a chance to call her back yet. Speaking of which, my main cell is currently at the bottom of Constance's Pond. Burner only for now. Do you know if Amy's okay?"

Sterling laughed. "Well, well, well, you perked up like Pavlov's dog."

Noah groaned. "Shut up. What are we, twelve?"

"Since when are you sentimental?"

"She gets it, alright? That's rare for me."

"For the record, I was going to bail both of you out, but her parents beat me to it. Don't worry, I'll make sure any charges against her are wiped so she can have a clean slate."

"Appreciated."

"Of course. She's got a spotless record, so it shouldn't be a problem. I should have figured you liked them innocent."

Noah rolled his eyes and dryly said, "Ha ha."

"You should have seen the look on their faces at the station when they saw someone actually pay your bail, though. I don't think they thought anyone actually would, especially with how high they set it."

"Sorry. I'm expensive."

"Nonsense. It was hardly anything for an asset as valuable as yourself."

Noah wasn't too fond of being described as an "asset," but he brushed it off as he removed his jacket and hung it up on the empty coat rack. "What was the hold-up?"

"I was in Denver on business. Unfortunately, I couldn't get away in time, but I did manage to get you, at least. Forgive me for being caught off guard; I suppose your irrational behavior shouldn't come as a surprise to me. It's why I like you, after all."

"Tch. You can cut the crap."

"I mean it!" Sterling held his leather glove-clad hands up in defense. "Trust me. If I was full of shit, you'd be taken care of already. Did you get what I need?"

"Yeah, but I had to hide it so the fucking cops wouldn't grab it." Noah took slow, long strides to the couch and plopped down next to Sterling, finally accepting the nonverbal invitation. He rested his elbows on his knees and ran his hands through his hair.

"Please tell me you don't mean—."

"Fuck, no! Jesus, what do you take me for? Contrary to popular belief, I have at least an ounce of dignity left."

Sterling laughed. "I'm joking, Noah. Calm down. You can relax."

Noah sighed through his teeth as he glared at Sterling. "I'm not in the mood."

"Well, I am, so you're gonna have to deal. Where is it?"

"The theater."

"You left it with your girlfriend?"

"Not technically. It's down in some storage room, which is in the basement. There's a shit ton of old costumes in garment bags, which is where I dumped the extra sample you and Potter needed. No one will find it; only Amy ever goes down there. If you find her before I do, she can grab it for you."

"Assuming she's allowed to set foot back in that place."

"She will."

Sterling raised a brow. "You trust her, huh?"

"She hasn't given me a reason not to." Noah paused. "Did you know Shawn Jameson's her ex-boyfriend?"

"Brick Beast, right? I know. Dumbest name of the bunch, in my personal opinion."

"You're telling me."

Sterling laughed again. "And here I thought Stone Breaker and Shatterstone were lame. So, what's next for you, Human Furnace?"

"Oh, for fuck's sake." Noah glared at him, and Sterling just winked in response. "I don't know yet. But I owe Amy an apology. She got wrapped up in this mess because of me."

"You do that and keep your head down, got it? I'll have to get my hands dirty."

"How do you mean?"

"I've bought the police department before. Surely I can do it again. You're lucky I still had your cell guards wrapped around my finger." Sterling reached inside his suit jacket for a carton of cigarettes in the pocket. He placed one between his lips and before he could even say anything else, Noah tossed him a lighter. Sterling caught it, lit the cigarette, and then tossed it back. "Thanks. Remember, I'm doing this because I like you."

Noah frowned as Sterling took a long drag, stood, and walked away to leave the house. Once the door was closed behind Sterling, Noah sighed, feeling mentally exhausted to the point where it was starting to affect his physical energy levels. He wasn't sure when the last time he drank any water was, but he couldn't be bothered to stand to grab himself a glass. Noah sat there for what felt like hours, but when he looked back at the clock, it had only been about thirty minutes. He succumbed to his dehydration and decided it was time for that ice bath he promised himself.

Once he emerged, feeling refreshed now that he no longer smelled like prison mildew and regulated his body temperature the only way he truly could, it was time to get back to work. The basement here was a bit smaller and lacked the stench of cat urine, but otherwise bore an identical layout. It made it easy for Noah to get around, but he couldn't bring himself to do anything other than check the inventory. Instead, he found a chair near the front of the stairs and let gravity carry his body to it.

He zoned out again, unsure why. Emotional exhaustion took over, urging him to just go sleep on a real, functioning bed, but too much swirled inside his brain—mostly thoughts about Amy—in order for him to properly command his legs to stand. He lifted his phone and hovered his thumb over her contact, but he was distracted by the sound of the door to the basement stairwell opening. When he looked up, all he saw was the silhouette of a hooded and masked figure in all black.

Without a doubt, Hematite.

"You want to take me out? Go right ahead."

Hematite said nothing, but Noah heard his slow steps down the stairs.

"Or take your sweet ass time. That works too."

"I'm not going to kill you."

"Then what's the fucking point?" Noah brought his fist down onto the table, but it didn't slam; it barely made a thud. His jaw tensed and his shoulders tightened.

The sound of footsteps stopped once Hematite reached the last step, opting to stand there. "This has to end. All of it. That is the point."

"So, how's it gonna end if you're not gonna kill me, huh?" Noah finally looked away from his closed fist to stare at Hematite. "And for fuck's sake, Kane, you didn't have to get all dressed up for me. The voice changer feels like a bit much given where we're at."

"You need to be behind bars, Noah."

"I was. Remember? But look at me now." Noah held an arm out in a grand gesture. "We're sitting here together having a lovely conversation. But you see, we have one tiny, little problem." He held his pointer finger up for emphasis.

"What's that?"

He dropped his hand, letting it join his fist on the table. "I'm really not in the mood right now."

"That's fine. We can just talk. I won't call the authorities unless you give me a reason to."

Noah scoffed. "You say that like we're not in a literal meth lab."

"Yeah, a meth lab that predates both of us. Listen, I get that you want to give people a little power in a town where it's easy to feel powerless. It's all shit, and you benefit from it, but even you know it's shit. But this isn't the way. Quit while you're ahead."

"Naomi already tried to give me the spiel this morning. Just get out of here, Kane. As I said, I'm not in the mood."

"This doesn't have to be a fight. Not unless you make it one."

Noah reached into his pocket. "Then allow me to end it before it even begins." He opened his lighter and turned it on. The flame blew toward Hematite in the blink of an eye, causing him to jump up a few steps to avoid the wall of flames. The fire danced up the wooden railway, leaving Hematite to start his retreat.

"Noah, don't do this."

"Have you ever burned to death, Kane?" Noah was met with silence. "Didn't think so."

"We need to talk."

"No, we don't. The police are about to be under our control again, so your little plan of apprehending me? Consider it squashed. So now, you have two options. You can either stick around and find out if your body can still regenerate if it's been burnt to a crisp, or you can get the fuck out of here. Go home to Rory and tell her that you love her."

"Noah!"

"It's your decision." With his jaw clenched, Noah glared at Hematite through the orange flames that licked dangerously close to the ceiling. "Time to make your choice."

Hematite stared at the fire before him, paused, and then ran away.

CHAPTER 21

When Amy finally emerged from her childhood bedroom, she saw her parents watching the news in the living room. At the sound of her footsteps, Sarah muted the newscast but left it playing. The headline at the bottom of the screen read, "RIVERPEAK THEATER FIRE SUSPECT OUT ON BAIL."

So, he did make it out.

"You finally decided to join us," her mother said. She hadn't even bothered to turn to look at her daughter; her eyes were glued to the television set, even though it was muted. It was a guilt tactic Amy was familiar with.

Amy's father gave her a sympathetic smile. "I made tea. Help yourself. You know where the kettle is."

Amy nodded. "Thanks." She picked at her pointer finger as she moved to the kitchen while Sarah unmuted the television. One of her acrylics was lost in the midst of her arrest, and the glue residue felt rough against her nails. As she poured some hot water into a mug, she could faintly hear the reporter in the other room from the television, but not well enough to make out every word.

"Can you believe this?" Sarah said. "What the hell is our taxpayer money good for, huh?"

"We might as well write checks to Hematite at this point."

Amy gripped the mug so hard she thought the porcelain would shatter, but she stopped herself. Instead, she moved back into the living room, leaning against the door frame.

Her mother shook her head. "This new police chief is no better than the last."

"What happened?" Amy asked.

Her father set his mug down. "That boy you were with, they let him go. Dropped all charges. Won't say why."

"What?"

"They won't say why," he repeated.

"I can only assume someone paid a very pretty penny for that," Sarah said. "A disgrace."

Amy felt like the wind was knocked out of her. "No way."

"Just when we thought things would change." Her father sighed. "It's too bad."

"Your record better get wiped clean, too." Sarah sighed, the long kind that indicated she had more to say. "But that doesn't mean you're off the hook even if it is."

Amy grabbed her phone and texted Noah, eager to get some answers from him and to get out of her house. Since he hadn't answered her calls at his normal number, she tried his burner.

AMY: Where are you?

To her relief, Noah replied instantly. It was an address only a few blocks down from her apartment. Another text immediately followed, reading only four numbers: 0901.

Amy grabbed her bag of belongings from where they hung on the back of a chair in the dining room, but before she left the kitchen, she opened the spare drawer where her father hid a handgun. She stuck it in her jeans and then made her way to the door.

Sarah craned her neck. "Where do you think you're going?"

"I want to bring my stuff home," Amy said. "Then I'm going to talk to my friend Hannah."

Amy didn't wait for them to respond. Once upon a time she would have, but she was twenty-eight years old, not a child. They didn't have the control over her that they thought they still did.

It was a surprise, but a welcome one that Riverpeak's residents weren't enjoying the warmer weather. If they were, they certainly weren't downtown, as she cut through to reach her apartment complex.

Amy swung by her apartment first but didn't bother to stay long. It was like stepping into a time capsule of her life before Noah, except for the genmaicha tea on the island that separated the kitchen from her living and dining spaces. She ditched the bag of her belongings on the couch and then slammed the door behind her.

The address Noah sent her was a house not much different from the one he'd been living in. When she reached the front door, she understood what the four-digit code had been for; there was a keypad right above the handle. She entered the numbers and then a checkmark button. The keypad made a whizzing sound before chiming in approval as it unlocked the front door. When Amy stepped inside, she locked it behind her and took in her surroundings.

This house looked less like a model home than Noah's did. Its emptiness overwhelmed the room, making it feel larger than it was, with only a couch and an overhead light in the space. The only light streamed in through the cracks in the blinds, which highlighted some dust particles lingering in the air. There wasn't so much as a small hole in the wall where a picture might have once hung. As she moved through the house, she saw a broken window in the back.

The only sign of life was the smell of smoke. Amy followed the smell and noticed how it grew stronger by an ajar door. She elbowed the door and felt relief when it wasn't too hot, though smoke rolled out from the sudden movement of the door opening. She stepped aside to let it pass, and once it settled in a slow roll by her feet, she peeked her head in. There was a wall on either side of the stairway, so Amy couldn't make out what awaited her below.

"Noah? You down here?"

"Amy?"

Amy began her descent down the stairs, speaking as she crept. She didn't want him to know how close she was. "I hear the new chief of police is dropping the charges against you."

"Oh, good." She thought he'd be thrilled, but he just sounded annoyed. "Another reason I owe Sterling. Just great."

Amy hovered her fingertips along the burned wood of the railing, not touching it to avoid the risk of splinters. "What the hell happened down here?"

"Nothing you need to worry about now." Noah dropped his lighter on the table; it landed with a clang. "It's been taken care of."

"That's one way of putting it."

"Are you okay?"

Her nose scrunched as she frowned. "What the fuck do you think?"

Noah groaned as he rubbed his eyes. "You're alive and look unharmed, at least. That's what matters. So, what brings you here?"

When Amy reached the bottom of the stairs, she walked through the rows of tables until she found the vials. This basement was almost identical to the last, making them easy to find. She noticed that beneath the table, beer bottles without labels filled some crates. "Give it to me."

"Give what to you?" Noah didn't need to ask, but he couldn't believe it. He could barely recognize the woman standing in front of him. Amy's hair had grown out considerably since they first met, no longer trim and clean but wild with dead ends and some tangles forming. The prim and proper Amy who used to be too afraid to even order her own drink was gone.

Amy answered by swiping a vial off the counter. Noah stood and reached for his lighter, but Amy beat him to the draw. He wasn't sure where she got the gun.

"It's about time we even the playing field." She shrugged a shoulder as she popped off the lid to the vial with her thumb. "Don't you think?"

"Amy. Sweetheart, *don't*. You can put the gun down."

"No, I think I'm going to keep it for now. You get to have powers. For now, this is the best I got."

Noah put his hands out in front of him and still held onto his lighter with his thumb but didn't ignite it. He took a slow step forward. "I understand you're frustrated. Let's talk through this."

"You're not my therapist and you're not Hematite," Amy said. She didn't lower the gun. "One of these bullets and I could really fuck you up."

"Ames, please. Don't." There was desperation in the way his voice quivered and the way his eyes were wide and soft. Amy had never seen Noah like this, but now that she knew the truth, she enjoyed it.

"You roped me into this whole mess and for what? For a big, fat nothing." Amy scoffed. "You tell me at the theater that I'm stronger than you thought, yet I don't get what I was promised? That's bullshit and you know it."

"It'll hurt," Noah said. "You might not survive that, Amy. I don't want you to go through what I did."

Amy gawked at him. "Since when have you cared for human life, huh? I heard about the girls, Noah. So, what about them and their lives? Did you seduce them, too? Was I just another line on your laundry list?"

"God, no! No, Amy, I didn't! Things never went that far. They didn't have to. But with you, it just happened!"

Her jaw clenched. "It just happened?"

He sputtered, "Yes! Fuck, I don't mean it like that, and I know you know that."

"Bullshit!"

"I swear. I don't know how to get you to believe me, but I'm serious!" His breathing was labored. Not once did he shout, but his speech sped up and he started talking with his hands. "You were the first one that Carter brought to me clean. The circumstances were different. And then you tell me Brick Beast is your ex-boyfriend, and then somewhere along the way, I actually started to give a shit about you."

"Because of my ex?"

"No, not because of your ex. Because I saw someone who was just as emotionally distraught as I was, and it made me happy to see you start to feel better and come into your own. And I thought you got it. Got me, that is."

"I also heard about what you did to your father. How you're the one who killed him. If you think I could understand that … as much as I hate my mom, I don't even know what to think about that."

"And if you'd let me, I can explain that, too."

"You can explain killing your own father?"

"I mean, you might not like it, but yes!"

"God fucking damn it, do you have an explanation for everything?"

"Yes, Amy, I do, because I have had nothing but this to meticulously plan for the last seven years! Seven years, in case you forgot, that I had to live in solitude! You think I like being here? Having powers? You think I like this?" He pointed at himself. "I wanted to die in that restaurant that day, as you already know, because I was so fucking sick of this. And then, I'll be damned, it worked! My life has been hell because of this." He gestured to the basement they stood in, his burned arm sweeping in front of him. "I am an abomination of science and greed and a hunger for power, and I never wanted to be. So, if I could give people a small piece of that power, then maybe I'd be able to live with it. If one person could benefit, someone like my sister the day some guy tracked her and her best friend down, then I'd know that this wasn't for nothing."

Amy scoffed. What he was saying at face value wasn't anything she hadn't heard before from him, but now it just felt like lies. Maybe he wasn't meaning to lie to her, but she suspected he was lying to himself. "I'm sorry, wasn't that the whole point of recruiting me in the first place? To give me powers?"

"It went to hell. Listen, let me talk you through this. I owe you the full story."

Her frown deepened. She still maintained her hold on the gun, not lowering it just yet. "I'm listening."

"My father? Yeah, that was very intentional. I won't deny that. And you know what? I'd do it again in a fucking heartbeat. But those women? I didn't mean for them to die. That was entirely an accident, and everything they walked into was on their own accord. The only exception was that Jefferson brat, who saw more than I'd have liked her to. But the others? They knew exactly what they were signing up for."

"Did they, Noah? Or did you manipulate them like you manipulated me?"

"I have not manipulated you, Amy, I swear to God. My intentions may have started off shoddy, but I have always kept your best interest at heart."

"So then why don't I get to make this choice for myself?"

"Because I don't want to lose you! You are all that I have anymore, Amy. Fuck."

"See, there you go again! I don't need a guilt trip!"

"You asked, so I answered honestly! What more do you want?"

Amy yelled, unsure of where the confidence to release her pent-up aggression came from. "To make a decision on my own for once!"

To Noah's horror, Amy moved the vial to her lips. The orange liquid inside swirled slowly inside like warm honey as she tipped it toward her mouth. She tossed the vial aside once she emptied it, licking her lips as the glass shattered on the floor. Amy didn't say anything; she just laughed. Even though the smoke and heat from Noah's flames still swirled around them, she felt a sharp chill shoot down her spine before it extended its reach through her veins. When it reached the tips of her fingers, she dropped the gun, limbs feeling stiff as if she'd just taken a polar plunge.

That made her stop laughing.

The cold within her grew sharper now that it spread through her body. Her hands shook, then ceased altogether, as if they were completely frozen. She stared at her skin with wide eyes as her pale complexion shifted to a ghostly white and then an icy blue. The color was the most saturated in her fingers.

"Amy?"

She looked from her hands to Noah. When she tried to speak, a piercing sensation shot through her lungs until she could see her own breath in front of her face. "What's happening?"

She took a step forward, yearning for his body heat as her entire figure went numb, but her knees wobbled and gave out beneath her. The last thing she remembered seeing before she hit the floor was Noah staring at her, his reaction unreadable. Everything went black after that.

———

"Fuck!"

Noah rushed to Amy, reaching to pull her into his lap, but before he could, a wall of ice formed around her skin. He stepped back, watching to see what would happen. The ice stopped after it was a few inches thick, having encased Amy's entire body.

It worked; she got what she wanted. But he wasn't sure if this ice would kill her or not. He was resistant to heat, but fire still burned if he didn't control it well enough—and Amy wasn't in control of the ice that held her unconscious form.

"Fuck, fuck, Amy, no."

There was only one thing he could think to do. He grabbed his lighter and shot a blast of fire out of it, a slow and steady stream to start melting the ice. If he moved too fast, he ran the risk of shooting straight through it and either burning her or causing too severe of a shock to her system from the constant jumps in temperature.

"Come on, come on, come on." It took everything in him to not shake and hold the lighter as still as possible as he ran it over the melting ice. He watched for the dripping water on the edges like a hawk, desperate to see it work.

Once the ice was mostly thinned out, Noah turned off the lighter, pocketed it, and then grabbed her. Her whole body was stiff from the remaining layer—he feared penetrating it too deeply and burning her skin—but he still managed to cradle her body in his lap.

"Please, Amy. Don't die on me, here. You've come too far. No way you can die after all this."

He hoped his body heat would be enough to continue the thaw, but the process was moving too slowly. He wrapped his arms around her, the chill cold enough to even make him shiver. While her body was heavier like this, it wasn't anything he couldn't handle. He struggled a bit up the stairs with her, but once he made it to the living room, he beelined it for the back of the house.

Noah kicked the handle of the back door, breaking it so he could push his way through. He rested Amy down in the grass and then ran for the tree to snap off some thin, weak branches. Thanks to his powers, it would be enough.

He piled the twigs and sticks up in a pile next to her and grabbed his lighter again, using it to start a fire. It crackled to life until it was large enough to melt the ice again. He sighed in relief the moment he saw the first drop roll onto the grass, leaning back on his heels and looking up at the sky.

Noah sat with Amy's frozen body in the backyard for an hour until the ice fully melted. Once she was thawed, he snuffed the fire out with his power, reducing it to small embers in the blink of an eye. He grabbed her again, carrying her back into the house and bringing her upstairs; while he'd yet to use this house, his father had it set up years ago as a precaution, and now he was glad he did.

Before he put her beneath the bed covers, he took her into the bathroom to remove her clothing. They'd soaked right through from the ice melting, and if he was trying to warm her up, wet clothes wouldn't do any favors. Noah let the wet clothes sit in a sopping pile in the corner, then brought her to the bedroom. He swung open the closet, relieved to find a few spare clothes that Reiji must have left behind. All that would fit her properly was an oversized T-shirt, but it would do while he washed and dried her own clothes. A fleece blanket, folded neatly, was also there. Once the T-shirt was on her, he wrapped her in the fleece blanket, tucked her into bed, and rejoined her once her clothes were on a wash cycle.

"Alright, Ames." He'd brought a chair from the dining room downstairs to sit in and pulled it up to the edge of the bed. "Are you happy now?"

Noah reached up to wipe his eyes, feeling like something was in them. All he found were tears.

"Was it worth it to go through all of this?"

Amy didn't answer. Noah wasn't sure if he was talking to her passed-out body or to himself anymore.

"Was all of this worth it? Are you happy?"

CHAPTER 22

Amy was only sure of one thing when she woke up: she was freezing. Her entire body felt numb, even with the feeling of soft fleece against her skin from a blanket. She couldn't say what day or time it was, nor would she be able to tell anyone how long she'd been out. Based on her surroundings as she blinked her eyes open, she registered she was at Noah's secondary house.

She pulled the blanket up over her body, but it still didn't help. Her clothing wasn't her own, either. She felt frigid, as if icicles replaced her bones. Given what she'd taken, it was plausible, but Noah would have answers.

"What happened?" Her voice felt sharp and dry. "Is there water?"

Noah shot his gaze in her direction. "Oh, thank fuck. You're awake."

He rushed to the bedside and was the only relief from the chill refusing to leave her body; the warmth radiating off of him was a welcome relief. Part of Amy wanted nothing more than to lean into him and wrap her arms around him, but then she remembered everything that happened before she collapsed. She remembered being mad at him for his omission of truths, but the warmth he gave made it hard to resist leaning into him.

"Here." He shoved a straw between her lips. She moaned in relief at the first sips of water, and when she reached for the glass, it froze in her hand.

"What the fuck?"

"It … it worked," Noah said. "When you passed out, you encased yourself in a cocoon of ice. I had to thaw you out of there."

"Ice?" Amy scoffed; leave it to her to be cursed as Noah's opposite.

"That makes us one hell of a team, huh?"

Amy shot him a glare that told Noah she'd rather do anything but team up with him.

Noah gulped. "We'd be a stronger pair together, Amy. I don't want to fight you. I know you probably don't believe this, but I do care about you. You're actually the only person I care about anymore."

She laughed in response. Amy laughed at a few things: namely, at the irony of her powers in relation to his and at Noah suddenly seeming to care. Amy couldn't control her laughter, and Noah just stared at her as she released it all. It bubbled up from her gut and passed through her chest, a steady stream she couldn't stop even if she tried to freeze it.

Her laughter went on for a minute or two, but to Noah, it felt like hours. She only stopped when she grabbed the pillow beneath her, screamed into it, and then chucked it at the wall.

"How could you even say that? You used me!"

"Minor correction: I started off using you. And for that, I'm sorry. Truly. I've used a lot of people, but you…" Noah sighed. "You were different. When you froze up like that, I freaked the hell out. I thought you were going to die. It's why I never went through with it; that wasn't a risk I was willing to take."

Noah swallowed. When Amy looked at him, his brows were furrowed, scrunching the skin between them, and his eyes looked glazed over. It took her a moment to realize it was because they were brimming with tears.

His shoulders hunched forward, making him curl in on himself. "I've lost too much, Ames. I'd scorch the ends of the earth for you, climate change be damned."

"I don't want someone to scorch the earth for me. I just want a nice, normal relationship."

"Well, given our situation, we may have to redefine what normal means, but maybe we can try. Only if you're willing, of course."

"And what if I'm not willing?"

Noah didn't hesitate. "Then you know where the door is. I can't stop you." His shoulders straightened from their slump as he ran his hand through his hair, brushing some of the bangs back out of his face. It was almost long enough to tie back now, and she spotted a five o'clock shadow along his chin and cheeks.

She'd never seen him anything but clean-shaven. It made her wonder how long she'd been out.

Deep down, Amy *was* willing, but she didn't want him to know that yet. Before she made any decisions, she had wanted to see how he would respond, and there he was, giving her the choice. Despite everything, she had hope for him; it stemmed from behavioral patterns and the way he treated her over the last few months. If he didn't care, he wouldn't let her make any choices, and regardless of what happened and his original intentions, he had still been better to her than anyone else in her life.

All the same, she was frustrated at herself, struggling with the idea of needing his help as she navigated new waters. While she felt weak for not wanting to handle this on her own, lacking the confidence necessary for such, she knew it would be better with Noah's help. She also couldn't go to Hematite after everything she'd done. At least now, she was strong enough to get back at Shawn.

Maybe, she thought, *I can find the strength to admit that needing help is okay.*

"You mean it."

He looked up at her, and their eyes met as he nodded. "Yeah, of course, I do."

This was the most genuine she'd seen him—or anyone, for that matter. "Then I'm willing. But you're on thin fucking ice, Sato."

He chuckled at the unintentional pun, one corner of his lips curling up. "Really?"

She rolled her eyes. "Don't even."

"Come on, you walked right into that one." He lost his fight against the smile forming on his lips. "But in all seriousness, you have every right to be so fucking pissed off at me."

"I can tell you mean it, though. Sure, we've only known each other for a few short months, but I haven't seen you worried about anything ever. Not until now, at least. When's the last time you slept or ate something?"

With a crooked smile, he said, "Couldn't tell you."

"You'll have to earn my trust back."

"I know."

"That won't be easy."

"Fully aware. I'm still up for the task." He reached for one of her hands. Amy watched him closely but let him take her hand. "What we had going between us, it was fun, wasn't it?"

No matter how much she tried, she couldn't help her smile when he looked at her like she was his entire world. "It was."

"Despite my horrible intentions at first, it wasn't fake. I swear to you, that was all real. I'm going to prove to you that it was." With the back of his free hand, he wiped his eyes to stop himself from crying.

"Hey." She squeezed the hand she was holding. "I'm okay. I didn't die. We won, didn't we?"

"Not sure I'd go so far as to say we won. We were arrested. Now we have no idea what these people are going to do, or if they even realize they're super-powered..."

"It's in Riverpeak's hands now. This town ... Riverpeak has a weird way with people. No one ever leaves. It's like it draws us to stay and take care of it. We did right by it. Even if we can't control what happens next, at least those who shouldn't have powers won't be able to abuse it as easily."

"That's true." He wiped his eyes again. "Not sure if I'm even capable of feeling love anymore, but this has got to be pretty damn close."

"You don't have to say anything you're not ready to just for my sake. To be honest, it's probably going to take me a while to ever say those words, too. Not because of you. Just, you know. Everything."

"I get that. We can take our time figuring this weird thing out together then."

Amy smiled. "I like the sound of that."

Noah leaned over her to kiss her. His hands gingerly hovered over her face, and the sensation of his fingertips grazing her skin tugged at her heart. Amy grabbed his wrists, craving more of his touch. It was like a reflex she couldn't stop, no different than when her doctor whacked the top of her knee at a check-up. The warmth of his skin brought her back to a normal body temperature. She wondered if she did the same for him.

When Noah pulled away, he stepped back, retreating to the corner of the room. He started pacing, another action she'd never seen from him.

"Noah?"

"This isn't right. It's not fair to you. I ruined your life, Amy. You should want nothing to do with me. Guys like me? We don't deserve to get the girl."

"Does said girl get a say in that?"

"I suppose it really *wouldn't* be fair if you didn't."

"You poured your heart out a few minutes ago. I think I understand why you're freaking out, but I promise you: this is it. We hit some bumps in the road, but we made it out. You succeeded, Noah, and so did I. We both got what we wanted."

"You're right. Just," he clutched at his chest, "something doesn't feel right."

"Did you think you'd make it this far?"

He stopped pacing. "What do you mean?"

"Time for me to play psychiatrist for you. Did you think you'd ever make it this far?"

Noah paused, deep in thought. He dragged his feet until he was at the edge of the bed, where he sat and faced Amy. "No. Never really planned this far or for what happens next, come to think of it."

"And why is that?"

The realization crossed his face with a softened gaze. "Guess I've been impulsive because I never thought I'd make it." He exhaled. "When I was waiting for you to wake up, I had a lot of time to realize that I have a lot to unpack. Don't worry, I'm not going to be one of those guys that expect you to unpack it for him."

"You don't have to go it alone anymore, Noah."

Her phone rang. As she grabbed it, Noah said, "We can finish this conversation later. I bet a lot of people are wondering where you've been."

"It'll give me more time to think, anyway," Amy said. "It's my mother." She stared at the ringing phone.

"Are you going to answer her?"

"No, I don't think I will." Amy rejected the call and then opened her Messages app.

There were twenty texts from her mother, mostly consisting of just question marks, asking where she was and demanding that she call her. The missed calls gave her an idea of how long she'd been out: Noah had been at her bedside for three days.

Another text came through.

MOM: Consider yourself unemployed.

Amy looked up at Noah. "Did you leave anything in the theater?"

"Just one thing. Why?"

"I'm fired."

"Think I can break in?"

"Probably. Between the two of us, I think we can make it work. Honestly, we can probably just walk right in if we go through the back. I think I was the only one who gave the basement any TLC."

"Hold on, 'we'? No, no, Ames. I don't want to make you break any more laws than you already have."

"I'm committed now. And besides, I don't have a job. What else am I gonna do today?" As he smirked, she said, "There's that smile."

"Don't worry about a job, by the way. I have enough money for both of us. It should last us more than long enough to find a new source of income."

She nodded, then looked down at her hands, the coldest part on her body, and for once, she wasn't worried about anything at all.

———

When they arrived at the theater, they stared at the hatch to the basement; it had been padlocked. Amy's set of keys was nonfunctional, jamming in the lock instead of working it open.

"That was fast." She yanked the key out and pocketed them. "Not one of those messages from her was asking if I was okay, either. Just where I was, why I was ignoring her, yada yada yada."

"Forgive me if this is overstepping, but your mom sounds like a real bitch."

"Yeah, I hope you never meet her." Amy cracked her knuckles, then placed them on the padlock. "So, when you set fire to something, you just focus on it, right?"

"Right as rain."

Amy took a deep breath and tried to hone her energy on the padlock. She grinned as she watched her fingers turn blue, spreading ice to the padlock until it was completely frozen over. She looked around and pointed to the other side of the parking lot. "There's some old construction equipment over there. Can you grab me a brick?"

Noah nodded and did as she asked. When he returned, she grabbed the brick and smashed the lock. The icy lock shattered, breaking into chunks and scattering around.

"Alright, now we can head in."

"Bravo. That's one way to use your new powers."

"Thanks. I'll be here all week."

Noah laughed and made his way into the basement with Amy. He beelined it for the racks of old costumes, fishing around inside the garment bags until he found it.

"Alright, this is it," Noah said.

"Amy?"

Amy held back her groan as she turned around. She'd recognize her mother's voice anywhere, and seeing her mother reminded her how much she hated that they looked alike. Everyone used to tell her that she was her mother's little clone or twin. In the past, she'd brush it off. But now, something was different within her—not from her newfound powers, but from the confidence that came with it—that made her understand Noah a little bit better.

Now, she understood why he'd snapped. She wondered just how good it must have felt for him to plunge the knife into his father's chest but shook it off before she could go too far.

"Thought I heard something, and I guess I was right. What are you doing down here? And who is this with you?"

"I left a few things down here. I didn't think it would be an issue." She shrugged and elected to ignore the second question. There wasn't an answer that her mother would like, and she wasn't in the mood to dive into it.

Her mother's hands landed on her hips. "And where have you been the last few days?"

"Doesn't matter. All that does is that I'm alive."

"Since when are you so short with me, young lady?" Her mother gawked at her. "Who did this to you?"

Amy sighed. "No one, Mom. I did it to myself. Are you happy?"

"No, I'm not happy!"

"Yeah, well good thing that doesn't matter, does it?"

"Excuse me?"

"I'm twenty-eight years old and I don't need your money, so don't get all worked up. You know, you're lucky I didn't walk away from this place sooner, but I've finally woken up."

Her mother scoffed and shook her head. "Oh, you've gone cold."

Amy snorted. "You have no idea."

"I mean it, Amy. We all make mistakes and not one of us is perfect. But you are making a choice every single day to be cruel and manipulative by giving us the silent treatment. You are hurting people who have done nothing but love you unconditionally."

Amy rolled her eyes at that. She knew that there was no love between her and her parents, but even if there was, it was absolutely conditional. Her mother's voice was not that of a saddened woman, but that of someone feigning their feelings to hide their bite. Amy knew when her mother's tears were real or crocodilian well enough by now to easily spot the difference.

Her mother continued, "You have become an angry, rude, and cold person. Friends, jobs..." She huffed. "All casualties of your defensive attitude, and your attitude is not what I'm looking for. It's a choice you're making, and your method is abusive."

Noah stepped forward and placed a hand on Amy's shoulder. Amy leaned in and whispered, "This happens sometimes. She'll burn herself out. Just let her run her course."

"I can't trust you, Amy. I can't trust someone that was my daughter to not backstab me or throw me away, to not put a knife in my heart and send a message through your silence that I am meaningless, worthless, and non-existent. That my life has no value in your eyes and the woman who gave you life is nothing. If I hurt you in some way, some way that I'm not even aware of, then I would try and make that right."

The words rolled off Amy's back with ease. She wasn't even sure where her mother pulled most of this from beyond broken expectations, but it'd gotten to the point where Amy knew better than to question it or to fight back.

But Noah's patience was a lot thinner.

"Not to interrupt this monologue of yours, but she was literally comatose. Did you even stop to ask if she was okay?"

"Noah—."

"No, I'm sorry, Ames, I can't listen to this garbage. You might be used to it, but fuck, even my old man wasn't this delusional."

With a sheepish smile, Amy asked, "Do you have what you need?"

He patted his pocket. "Already grabbed it. Let's go."

"No, you're not leaving until I'm done speaking to you," her mother interjected.

But Noah ignored her mother and, to Amy's surprise, scooped her up to carry her over her shoulder. "Actually, we were just heading out. And trust me, lady. My pops tried the whole family business thing but learned the hard way that you really shouldn't mix the two. Sounds like this falling out was inevitable and probably for the best, given you think so lowly of your daughter that you assumed she was ignoring you rather than something being wrong."

"Who the hell do you think you are?"

As Noah walked away with Kane's blood sample in his pocket and

Amy bent over his shoulder at her waist, he gripped her rear and called back, "I could ask you the same thing."

Amy gave her mother a wave goodbye as they went up the back stairs and swung the hatch open. Once they were outside, she said, "Sorry about her."

"The joys of being a millennial, right? Who'd have thought that boomers would make such shit for parents?" He set her down. "Don't worry about it. You alright? Those were some pretty harsh words."

"Nothing I haven't heard before. I'm fine. My mother stopped being nice to me when she realized I had my own sense of self as a teenager."

"Yeesh. Back to the house?"

Amy nodded. "Yeah. Time to leave this behind me for good. Oh, and Noah?"

"Yeah?"

"I think I get it. Why you killed your dad, that is. I do. I'm sorry for judging you for that."

He kissed her temple. "Don't even sweat it, sweetheart."

"I don't think I'm capable. Like, of sweating."

To her delight, Noah laughed. *Maybe things would be okay after all.*

They were quiet the whole way home, which gave her a moment to soak in everything that happened to her. With her arms wrapped around Noah's waist and her ice powers coursing through her veins, she felt, for once in her life, secure.

She wasn't weak anymore. The thought—combined with Noah's brazen display of gripping her ass in front of her mother—was what prompted her to kiss him with every ounce of energy she had. As they stumbled back to the couch, bumping against the arm of it, Noah smirked against her mouth. "Feeling feisty, sweetheart?"

"Just shut up and take your clothes off."

Noah laughed and did as she said. "Who am I to turn you down? I love it when you get all riled up like this."

"You taking forever to unbutton your shirt or do I have to rip it off myself?"

"Careful, careful. I try to avoid scratching either of my arms."

They both laughed as he shrugged his shirt off. In the months they'd been together, he'd gained a significant amount of muscle from their workout sessions, but still remained slender. The muscles of his arms were hard to see past the burned skin on one side and the tattoos on the other, but it was still clear as day that he'd put on weight.

Noah's voice snapped her out of the realization. "Admiring Jolene's work again?"

"And what's beneath her work."

"Aw, you're gonna make me blush."

With a grin and more confidence than she'd ever felt, she said, "I'm gonna do more than make you blush."

CHAPTER 23

The change of pace over the next few days was refreshing for them both. Amy felt like she'd been given a fresh start, while Noah seemed renewed, too, and softer than he was before. While he'd always been gentle with her, careful to never raise his voice or do anything that might startle her, there was a tenderness to his words and to his touch. His fingers always lingered a little longer on her skin, and kisses seemed to last longer, as he was hesitant to pull his lips away.

Her near-death experience fucked him up; she saw that now. But in the spirit of controlling what they could control, she'd encouraged him to train her. They found that their powers worked similarly, except she could produce ice herself whereas Noah needed a preexisting flame.

When she froze a row of old soda cans, turning them into solid ice that Noah was able to chip at, he asked. "So how are you feeling?"

For the first time, she felt strong enough. There wasn't a concise way to word that, so for the sake of brevity, she said, "Like myself for once."

He smiled. "I'm glad that it worked out. And that this wasn't all for nothing." He placed his hands on her shoulders. "Thank you for letting me help you." He pulled her in and kissed her forehead, her nose, and then her lips. "You know, Dr. Potter thinks that there's a reason we get the abilities we get. He reckons Kane got immortality because he needed it to survive the fights he was getting in, and that I got fire to survive the restaurant. Have any inkling as to why you ended up with ice?"

Amy thought about it, mulling over a few ideas. When she opened her mouth to speak, a banging from the front door cut her off. "Are you expecting anyone?"

Noah shook his head. "Anyone who works for me or Sterling already has the code to the keypad."

They went back inside and moved through the house to the front. When Amy opened the door, Shawn was standing before her. Hematite was right behind him.

"What the fuck are you doing here?" Amy asked. The sight of him alone was enough to spike her heart rate.

Hematite spoke, mechanical and warped. "I only brought Shawn here so he can fix his mistakes. Since I understand how deeply he's hurt you, he has no right to call himself a hero, so I won't be working with him ever again. But he needs to right his wrongs."

Hematite left, blending into the patch of woods across the street. Amy's skin crawled as she looked at Shawn, the rage filling her from head to toe. The chill from her anger made goosebumps rise on her arms.

Shawn smiled awkwardly. "Can I come in?"

Amy silently stepped aside. Shawn took that as an affirmation and made his way in. He whistled, too nonchalantly for Amy's liking.

"So, you're living in a drug house now, huh?"

She rolled her eyes. "Shut the fuck up."

"Whoa, since when do you have a mouth like that?"

"I said to shut the fuck up."

"Well then!"

Noah took one of the frozen cans and tossed it at Shawn's head. "You heard the lady."

Shawn caught it before he could get hit. "The fuck is this?"

"Left it in the freezer too long." Noah winked. "The hell are you doing here?"

"Did you not just hear Hematite?"

"So, what, he's turning you in just like that?" Noah raised a brow. "Since when is it that simple?"

"Maybe he's got an ulterior motive," Shawn suggested. "Did you think of that?"

"Or maybe you do," Amy said. "You want your glory? To finally make a name for yourself like Hematite? If you're thinking you can earn that by apologizing to me, think again."

"There is one way, though." Noah pointed toward the first door down the hall. "Everything's in the basement."

Shawn blinked. "What?"

"You heard me. Go on. See for yourself."

As Shawn moved forward, Amy approached Noah and whispered, "What are you thinking?"

"Go get your revenge on that oaf." Noah kissed her cheek. "You're ready."

"Are you saying…?"

"You have your powers. Use them."

She nodded. They both followed Shawn to the basement, meeting him at the bottom of the steps. He was taking photos with his phone.

"Listen, Amy, I'm sorry that I was a dick and pushed you to drugs."

Amy tutted her tongue. "Wow, that is one hell of an apology if I've ever heard one."

"It's not your fault," Shawn said. Then he turned to Noah. "I just gotta get this asshole out of the way and everything can go back to normal."

Noah placed a hand over his chest. "You're talking to me?" He laughed as he spoke. "I am the least of your fuckin' problems, buddy."

"Then who are we dealing with? Who is the head of this, if not you? Isn't that why you killed your dad?"

"I killed my dad because he had it coming, not for some power trip," Noah said. "Get it right. I know you wanna play superhero, but last I checked, heroes don't hurt people, dumbass." Noah nodded his head toward Amy. "You gotta answer to her, not me. Only reason I'm here is to make sure you don't lay a hand on her."

"So, you're not the leader?" Shawn's brows furrowed. "What is going on, then?"

Amy leaned against the rail post as Shawn turned to look at her. "You know, there's a theory that we get the power we really need. That's what Dr. Potter thinks, anyway."

"Wait, Dr. Potter is working for you?"

"Working for us? He co-founded the product. Catch up. Anyway, do you know what it was that I really needed, Jameson?"

Shawn shook his head. "Nope. No clue."

Amy slunk forward, feeling calmer than she thought she would. She placed a hand on his abdomen, just beneath where his rib cage ended. She smirked at him and said, "I've been thinking long and hard about it."

White and blue coated her fingertips as she pressed into his flesh. Even through Shawn's clothes, the frozen feeling penetrated deeper, reaching right into his organs. He stumbled back as he keeled over, gasping for breath.

"What the fuck was that?"

"And then I realized, I've had the answer all along. What I needed was to chill out. Didn't you say so yourself?"

Shawn groaned. "Amy, what did you do?"

She tilted her head as she looked at him. "I froze your liver. I heard it hurts like a bitch to get hit there. Why? Want me to do it again?"

Amy stepped forward, making Shawn stumble back. The back of his legs hit one of the tables, making some of the vials and Bunsen burners fall with a clanking sound. Amy placed both hands on Shawn's chest. Shawn looked up at her with wide, worried eyes; Amy loved that look on him.

"I said I was sorry, okay?"

She grinned. "Oh, that half-baked apology? You're sorry for what, huh?"

Before Shawn could answer, Amy's fingertips turned white and blue again. Shawn went to say something, but he was only capable of cold, short gasps until eventually, his breathing stopped. His face turned as blue as Amy's fingertips, and she only pulled away once she was confident he'd stopped for good. She looked to Noah, to her hands, and then back up at him.

"You're not going to judge me for that, are you?"

Noah shook his head. "Nah. And either way, I'm hardly in a position to. How are you feeling?"

"I…"

There wasn't one answer. Her gut reaction was to say she felt properly avenged, as if she was vindicated but by her own conscience instead of any external source. But as the realization crept up on her, there was panic. Should she be found out, then she'd be behind bars again, and she wasn't sure just how many strings Noah could ask Sterling to pull—especially since she wasn't even sure if Sterling knew who she was.

"We can't be caught."

"Let me see what I can find to help with," Noah gestured to Shawn, "this. I think my dad kept some bags in a closet upstairs."

While Amy wanted to question why there was an emergency stock of body bags, she thought better of it. She could guess the answer well enough, nor was she in a position to critique. "Sure, yeah, thanks."

Once Noah was at the top of the stairs, Amy slumped in a chair. She looked at Shawn's body, unable to look away. The old adage about staring at a train wreck came to her mind, but she was the conductor, not some random passenger in a car speeding by. As she did, the ice around Shawn thickened.

Amy didn't get to stare for too long. The footsteps on the staircase lacked the confidence of Noah's. From the cautious trepidation, her guess was Rory. Amy stood and cracked her knuckles, readying her fingers for another burst of ice. From what Noah told her and from what she gathered from Rory's Facebook profile, she knew better than to underestimate her. Letting her guard down would be a foolish mistake to make, and she wasn't about to make one this late in the game.

"Amy or anyone, if you're down there, I just want to talk."

It was Rory's voice, confirming Amy's suspicions. Rory held her hands up as she finished her descent down the stairs. Her curls were tied back into a ponytail, keeping it out of her face.

"Here on Hematite business?"

Rory grimaced. "Sort of. We lost Shawn's tracker, so we wanted to see what's up. Personally, I didn't want him to go in at all, but you know how Shawn gets."

"You mean how Shawn got."

Rory made the turn around one of the tables and found the body. She stopped, keeping her distance from Amy. "Oh. Yeah. I suppose so."

"I did this. Not Noah. Just me. If anything, Noah tried to delay this for as long as possible."

"Did you ... well, you know?"

"Try drugs? Yeah, I used the dosage we gave out at the theater. You don't need to ask me like it's some dirty word. Anyway, it worked."

Rory looked back at Shawn's body. "Given his skin is actively turning white and then blue, may I ask how?"

"Well, I froze his liver. And then, I froze his lungs. I imagine the cold is making its way through his bloodstream now."

Rory exhaled. "Fuck."

"Does Noah know you're here?"

"No, I snuck in when he went up. Let me guess, he's on his way back down?"

"Probably sooner than later."

"Alrighty then. I'll make this quick. Listen, I obviously don't support murder, but let's face it: Shawn was a piece of shit and he had it coming. I think that people who do things like him deserve it. I am not going to tell anybody, and I'm going to encourage the rest of them to do the same if they do somehow find out."

Amy blinked a few times. She was positive she was hallucinating but Rory was still there. "What?"

"It's the least I can do after everything; it's actually, like, the bare minimum. But I want you to do one thing for me in return."

Amy's eyes narrowed. "Depends. What's that?"

"Don't tell anyone about Kane. So long as no one blabs that he's Hematite, I won't tell anyone you killed Shawn. In fact, when I get back to the car, I'll tell them that he must have snuck out. Deal?"

Amy sighed. She suspected Rory's response had been too good to be true, but it still stung. "Fine. You know that I still can't go back, right?"

"Yeah, I figured you'd say that."

"And that I can't control what does or doesn't come out of Noah's mouth?"

"I'm well aware. But we have our ways of knowing. Small town, you know? Word gets around pretty quick, including who said what. And besides, it seems like he'll listen to you. A casual suggestion might go a long way."

"Okay. I can't make any promises, but I'll try."

"Thank you. I'm just sorry that it came to this. Of all people, I should have known better and should've opened my eyes a lot sooner to what was going on." Rory frowned. "I did really wrong by you and for what it's worth, I'm sorry, Amy."

"I appreciate that." The two women shared a brief moment of silence before Amy said, "Truce?"

"As close to one as we can, given the circumstances, sure."

Amy forced a smile. While she meant what she'd said to Rory, she still wasn't sure how she felt. "Go on. Get out of here and stay out of our way. I didn't see which way you went."

Rory fought the urge to hug Amy and bounded up the stairs.

"Oh, and Rory?"

Rory stopped halfway up to look at Amy. "Hm?"

"I thought you did a pretty good job as Hematite."

She smiled and pushed some curls out of her face. "I'm getting there. Now I'll have to keep up with you."

With a wink, Rory was gone. Amy sat in silence until Noah returned a few minutes later.

"Alright, there's a few ways we can do this. If you'd like, I can cut him up and we can dump his body somewhere. I've got a chainsaw out back that'll do the trick. Or I can burn him. Complimentary cremation, if you will."

Amy shuddered at the thought of having to cut his body up to bits. "Can we just burn him? That feels a lot less messy and like it won't leave a trace."

"Can do. Let me thaw him out. I need to grab something for Potter and get it over to him anyway."

"What's that?"

"One last blood sample. We're trying something for Sterling."

"What's that?"

"We want to see if we can influence the type of power people get. Sterling wants Hematite's, but we obviously have to see if it'll work before we just take Kane's blood and mix it in with the drug to give to him, you know?"

"I'm following." Amy bit the inside of her lip. She guessed what he might say next and didn't like where this was going.

"Potter found a candidate willing to try, and we think he'd be a good match for Shawn's strength." Noah met her eyes and, to address the growing panic, said, "He's a good guy. Sterling's bodyguard. He teaches boxing lessons somewhere between here and Denver. Don't worry, it won't end up in the wrong hands."

"That makes me feel better about it."

"Good. If you weren't okay with it, I'd have just given Potter my own blood sample, but the last thing we need is two pyromaniacs running around this town."

"Valid point. It's fine. Hard for me to believe I'm saying this, but I trust your judgment." He'd been right so far, even about the drug nearly killing her; if he hadn't been there, it most likely would have.

"That means a lot to hear you say that. Thanks. I promise I won't do wrong by you with this. I don't want another Shawn running around either."

"I know."

Noah grabbed his lighter and started thawing out Shawn. Once there was a patch of skin that returned to its normal shade of milky white near the crease of his elbow, Noah stood, grabbed a needle and syringe, and extracted a blood sample. Once it was safely stored, he returned to work. As soon as the last remnants of ice were gone, he pocketed the lighter.

"We gotta bring him outside. It's gonna smell like fucking shit, and I don't want it reeking like a literal rotting corpse in here. Do you want to grab the arms or legs?"

"I'll take the arms."

It took the two of them to lift Shawn's muscular frame, still stiff from death and Amy's freeze, but they managed to drag him up the stairs and out into the backyard. They both dropped his body with a grunt and took a moment to catch their breath.

"Do you want to watch or head in?" Noah asked. "He's a big dude, so this is probably going to take a while."

Amy allowed herself a moment to think it over before she said, "I think I want to watch. I can handle the heat."

Noah nodded. "Alright. Here goes nothing."

Amy zoned out as she watched Noah's fire. The fence in the backyard gave them just enough privacy, and he hadn't been kidding about the smell: it was pungent, a sickly sort of sweet that made her want to lurch, but she endured. She hadn't expected to feel so apathetic after her first kill, but then again, she never thought she'd be saying she took another life.

With her new powers, she was finally everything she wanted to be —even if that meant she was also a murderer. But after everything Shawn put her through, she felt no remorse in her heart. Instead, she focused on how the fire warmed her face, providing some relief from the chill she hadn't been able to shake since she developed her powers.

Whether she liked it or not, she and Noah seemed to be made for each other. Despite their rocky start, there he was, burning the body of her ex that she killed with her own bare hands. She doubted anyone else would do that for her without so much as batting an eye.

"Hey, Noah?"

He looked up at her but didn't stop the flames. Shawn's body was well into disintegration now, parts of him having already turned to dust and others looking like melted wax. "Yeah?"

"Thank you. For everything."

As he smiled, the glow of the flames illuminated his face. "Anything for you, sweetheart."

CHAPTER 24

The rest of the day felt like a blur. Amy stared at what used to be Shawn's body, now reduced to a pile of black ash, as Noah swept it up and poured it into a paper cup he'd grabbed from the kitchen. The sun started its descent over the mountaintops, painting the sky pink and orange.

"Don't want any bad energy lingering around here. Where should we dump him?"

"You have to go to that lab to deliver the blood sample, right?"

"That I do."

"Let's just ditch him along the way."

"Works for me. Coming along for the ride?"

"I'd love to."

"Ready whenever you are. Do you need a minute, or..?"

Amy shook her head. "No, I'm okay. I wasn't sure how I'd feel, but I kind of don't feel anything. Just like everything's finally over, you know?"

Noah nodded. "I get what you're going through." They made their way back inside so Noah could fetch the blood sample from the basement. When he returned, pocketing the sample, he grabbed his keys and said, "Come on, we'll take the van so we can shove him in a cupholder until we get there."

"Good thinking."

"When I killed my old man, I felt the same way. Just kind of numb and detached, you know? I thought I'd feel this rush but instead, everything was just kind of over, like you said. Sure, it felt a bit cathartic, but overall, it was just a thing that happened. Feels fucked up to put it like that, but hey."

"That sounds on the money," Amy said as they reached the van. She slid into the passenger's seat and reached over to grab the cup from Noah so he could buckle his seatbelt. Amy's gaze lingered on the ashes as she put them in the cupholder; they were mixed with some dirt and stray grass clippings from the last time he mowed the lawn. After everything—the way Shawn had isolated her from her friends, only to abuse and then harass her—it was strange to see him as nothing more than dust and dirt. The way they'd been dumped in the cup was so unceremonious, but Amy thought it was a fitting ending for Shawn.

"Do you have any regrets?"

Amy thought about it for a second. "Hm. Only that I didn't do this sooner, to be completely honest."

Noah placed a hand on her shoulder as he backed out of the driveway. "It all worked out though, didn't it?"

"I suppose it did."

As they drove past downtown, she saw Riverpeak in a different light. She felt as if she'd been sleepwalking through her own life, letting events happen as they did up until now. Now, she saw the truth behind her town: recognizing people from not just the theater, but from Noah's line of work and seeing Riverpeak for what it really was. Behind the charm of their small mountain town, hidden in the grasslands and historic buildings, was a sort of corruption that was rotting the town away from the inside out.

As the buildings thinned out and the grasslands expanded into view, glowing golden as the sun set, she watched for the sign reading Potter Laboratories. While she'd never been out this way, Noah seemed to know the roads well.

"So, this is the guy who started it all?"

"Yeah. I have mixed feelings about him. On the one hand, he's a fucking weirdo. On the other hand, he showed me some shreds of sympathy when my father had him running all those tests on me. Part of me blames him, but part of me wants to thank him for not being a completely heartless piece of shit."

"That's valid."

"To be frank, I think you should wait in the car. He'll probably want to do some sort of test or bloodwork on you. I don't think you need to go through that. I'll drop the blood sample off and let you do the honors of dumping Shawn's ashes, and then we can be on our way. Maybe get a drink or something after this if that's alright with you."

"Sure, yeah. I could go for a nice date night after this. End the night on a high note."

"Anywhere you want to go?"

"Maybe just the bar on the edge of town, right before you get to East Riverpeak?"

"If that's what the lady wants, that's what she'll get." He winked at her as he pulled into the lot, and once the car was in park, he pulled her in for a peck on the lips. "Be right back."

They both got out of the car. Once Noah was inside the building—which resembled a tall, silver box—Amy roamed the patch of grass and dirt just on the edge of the pavement. A few flowers were starting to bud in the weeds, yellow petals taking shape.

Amy held the paper cup with both hands. The ashes almost filled it to the brim, the dirt bulking up the cup and giving it some weight. Before she poured it out, she stared at it for a moment, debating on if she had any last words to say.

"If there is an afterlife, which I think there is, I hope you never reach it."

At that, she tipped the cup. She watched every last grain of dirt, sand, and ash fall from it, the grass clippings floating down gently after them. Once it was empty, she heard Noah's footsteps against the pavement behind her.

"All set?"

She turned away from the grass and took a moment to look at him—*really* look at him. Just like Riverpeak, she saw Noah differently now, too. Despite his confident smile, there was a sadness behind his eyes that was almost out of reach but just close enough for her to grasp. What their town thought was a power-hungry drug kingpin was really just a man seeking his own way, not given much else of a choice for the path he walked.

Now, she understood that.

"Yeah, all set."

He grabbed her waist and captured her lips with his. When they were together like this, their own internal temperatures balanced each other out, his radiating heat matching her cold. Whenever he kissed her, she felt the cold subside, making her want to melt into him. Amy reached for his bicep and let her grip linger as he pulled away and said, "Drinks are on me."

As they drove back the way they came, Amy continued to admire the view. The sun completed its dip behind the mountains, leaving the sky a rich shade of purple as the moon took its place. The stars sparkled overhead, showing the promise of a beautiful night. They made a stop at the house along the way to ditch the van and swap to his motorcycle.

The bar hadn't changed at all in the last few months. Amy couldn't believe the passage of time, mentally transported back to the day she and Noah met here. The floors still had odd stains and the patrons all still kept to themselves, the same faces at the same booths. It didn't look as seedy now—not after everything.

"I'm surprised you picked this place."

"Well, we can chat pretty freely since Carter works the bar," Amy said, "and maybe I was feeling nostalgic."

"Really? You, nostalgic?"

"Yeah. When you were burning Shawn, I realized that we met here six months ago today." She licked her lips out of nervous habit, meaning to say more but stopped herself when Carter approached.

"Vodka cranberry?"

She nodded. "Yes, please! Thanks, Carter."

"Me too," Noah said.

Amy couldn't help her smile. "You don't mind that it gets pegged as girly?"

Noah shook his head. "Nah. Since when have I ever given a shit about that?"

They both laughed as their drinks slid across the counter to them.

Noah lifted his glass and tipped it toward her. "Here's to us."

They toasted, glasses clanking softly against the live guitar in the front of the building. As they took a sip, Carter stepped out back, leaving them alone at the bar. As Amy stared at the remaining liquid in her glass, she said, "Still can't believe I ended up your opposite."

Noah flashed his teeth as he smiled at her. "It's like I was meant to be yours."

She giggled and ruffled his hair. "Since when are you corny, huh?"

"Oh, give me a break."

She took a sip of her drink and then asked, "So what's next?"

"I'm not sure. But I'm done."

Amy set her drink down. "Wait. What?"

Noah's smile faltered. "With the drug ring, I mean. Not with you. No, you're not getting rid of me so easily. I'm taking my second chance and running with it."

With a blush creeping on her cheeks, she asked, "What changed?"

"I wanted to help people, but I dunno. Maybe I can't save everyone after all. Not everyone was built for this." He set his drink down and then pinched her cheek. "But I helped you, so at least my experiment wasn't a total failure."

"What about Sterling?"

"I'm keeping him at arm's length for now. It'll take a little time, but I think we should get the hell out of Riverpeak in the near future. What do you think?"

Amy shrugged a shoulder. "I mean, I'd love nothing more than to change my name and go off the grid."

"See? Sterling can help with that. I'll keep you close but my enemies closer."

"Speaking of which," Amy said, "let's keep Hematite's identity close to our chest for now. I'm not sure what you were planning now that we've confirmed his secret."

"I wasn't planning anything, actually. To be completely honest, I just wanted to know." Noah swirled his glass with his hand, making the drink swish. "Naomi and Brad have been together since forever. I played babysitter a lot for them and their friends, including Kane, when we were younger. Kane and I, we always understood each other."

"How so?"

"It's kind of sad, really. He was like a second little sibling to me, and he'd come to me if he needed help with his sister. He'd call or instant message me from Elijah's house when his sister finally went to bed, after they had to get out of their house for the night. So, when the puzzle pieces started lining up, I just had to know." He took a sip of his drink and then set the glass down. "What did you have in mind?"

"I was just thinking that if we're trying to get out, it might be best to not stir the pot. We can keep that in our back pocket for a rainy day in case we need it, but I don't think it would be in our best interest to at this point."

"What happened?" Noah shifted in his seat, so his torso was now completely facing her. "Did somebody say something?"

"Rory knows what I did. She came in the house looking for Shawn. They got worried because he hadn't come out in a while. They hooked him up with a tracker or something and when he froze, so did the tech. She found me in the basement with him and I let her get away. Please don't be mad."

"Hey, hey, hey." Noah reached for her hand and gave her a reassuring squeeze. "Why would I be mad?" He held her hand up and kissed her knuckles. "I trust you had your reasons."

Amy dropped her voice to a whisper. "She promised not to tell anyone I killed Shawn so long as I didn't tell anyone who Hematite was."

"That's a good deal. I'd have taken it, too."

"I'm sorry." Amy pulled her hand away to down the rest of her drink. "One of these days I'll remember you're not some raging lunatic."

"Well, depending on who you ask..."

Amy laughed. "Sure, but you're good to me. Despite everything, you really are."

The corner of his lip twitched up in the hint of a smile. "As much as Sterling wants to stop Hematite, I did what I wanted to do. So, if you think we should keep it our little secret and protect ourselves, then so be it."

"Thanks."

"What about your video?"

"We can still upload it. Hematite's not even mentioned, so I think we should. After all, if we're looking to leave with solid footing and not burn any bridges along the way with Sterling, then we'll need some extra help in the form of weird incels trying to stop anyone in our way. And it'll sell that we're still committed."

"Good point. Okay, one last question. You believe Rory?"

"We know where to find her and we know how to ruin Hematite's life. If she's smart, she'll stick to her word, and Rory is one of the smartest people I know."

"Alright then. You've convinced me. Just remember that there is nothing you can do that will make me mad. Not like how you're used to."

"I mean, I'm sure there's something."

He shook his head. "I've been through some shit, Ames. Trust me. It takes a lot to get me truly mad these days, and you? There's something about you. I dunno, it's like we're cut from the same cloth. We get each other."

Despite her permanent freeze, she felt a warmth spread through her. From the soft look in his eyes and the way he'd treated her over the last few months, she knew he meant it. "Yeah, we do."

"So where do you want to go once we're able to get out of here?"

"I mean, the charges against us were dropped, and our secret is safe as far as Shawn goes. We could go anywhere."

"I haven't given travel much thought, so I'm open to wherever you want."

"We could get an RV and live out of it for a while and then see where we land. Take our time exploring, see where we like."

He smiled, so genuinely that Amy felt it radiate into her chest. "An RV?"

"Yeah! There are a bunch of couples on Instagram that do it. They live out of it so they can travel the country, see all the national parks, and camp out."

"Alrighty then," Noah said. "Once we tie up our loose ends here, we'll get ourselves some new IDs and use them to get an RV and go."

Her eyes lit up. "You mean it?"

"Cross my heart, Ames." He leaned over to kiss her cheek. "If that's what you want, we'll make it happen. Besides, I personally think it could be fun. Could even give us a chance to try this as a normal couple if you'd like."

Amy nodded. "Are you kidding? Of course. I'm sorry I snapped at you and have been harsh after the warehouse. I just—."

"You don't have to apologize. I deserved it."

There was so much more he wanted to say, but his phone rang. On a normal night out, he'd ignore it, but the name on the caller ID was cause for concern: Dr. Potter.

"Sorry, let me grab this. He doesn't usually call me."

Amy nodded and pulled her own phone out. She opened the YouTube Studio app so she could upload the warning video she'd filmed a few weeks prior. *That video wasn't the last time I'd be putting on the mask,* she thought. While the video was uploading and Noah took the call from Dr. Potter, she checked the stats. Their follower and view count skyrocketed, leaving them close to monetization. Even though Noah had both an inheritance and drug money, having something as a backup made her feel more secure.

A notification popped up right after the video completed its upload.

> dansanders93: i want to talk to you, how can we meet?

When Noah answered his phone, Dr. Potter wasted no time. "My apologies for the late-night call, Noah; however, this is an emergency."

"Emergency?"

"Requesting backup at the laboratories as soon as you're able. I'm afraid we have a situation on our hands."

"What do you mean by an emergency situation?"

"You'll see."

Noah swallowed as he hung up. Amy set her phone down, not yet having replied to Daniel's comment.

"Well?"

"We gotta go."

———

For all the theorizing Noah did on the motorcycle ride there, he hadn't anticipated this.

On a normal day, Noah would say Potter Laboratories was orderly, tidy, and so sterile he thought he'd go insane. But tonight, it was none of those things. The window in the front lobby was shattered. Dr. Potter was standing by it and visibly sighed in relief at Noah and Amy's arrival. Glass shards lay around Noah and Amy's feet. Through the window, they could see pens and clipboards scattered on the floor by the desk.

Dr. Potter wiped his hands on his lab coat. "Thank goodness you've arrived."

Noah watched his step as he approached, careful to avoid the glass. "Luckily for you, I'm too nosy to turn away from your cry for help. You alright?"

"I'm just glad it's nearly summer so we won't freeze until the window is repaired," Dr. Potter said. His hair, usually gelled, stuck up in a few odd places. "However, I need your help subduing a subject."

"Subduing? Who's the subject?" Noah asked.

"What happened?"

"It's Sterling's bodyguard, Anthony. Remember how you suggested that we test the fusion first? Well, we did, with Mr. Jameson's samples. It worked. In fact, it worked rather well. Too well." He looked at Amy. "Who's this?"

"She might subdue better than me," Noah said. "Can you control the intensity?"

Amy nodded. "Yeah, I did before."

"Good. Time to put your ice powers up to another test. Where'd Anthony go?"

"Toward the woods. Here." He bent down and grabbed a flashlight. "I know you have your fire, but this may also help."

Amy grabbed the flashlight. "Should we take the bike?"

Noah nodded. "Good thinking. It'll be faster, plus extra light."

They both jogged to the motorcycle and hopped on. The stream from the headlight covered most of the area ahead of them. Noah was careful about dodging around the trees; the area wasn't thick enough for him to evade any, but he still had to go slower than he'd like. Amy used the flashlight to look on either side of them, even occasionally checking behind when they went slow enough for her to turn her torso around.

"To the left."

Noah made the turn and in the center of the headlight's high beam, a silhouette blocked the way. It heaved and looked larger than life, shoulders round and high as it flowed with its breath.

"Anthony, that you?"

Anthony sprinted forward, silhouette barely shrinking as he approached. His wavy black hair looked as if he'd been trying to pull it out but to no avail. His clothes were tattered and ripped in some places.

Noah grabbed his lighter, but before he could do anything, the flashlight whacked Anthony right in the head. As Anthony caught it, Noah saw that it was coated in ice. Anthony's breathing returned to normal as he rubbed his head with his free hand.

"Sato? That you?"

"In the flesh, buddy."

Anthony looked down at himself, examining his clothes and his body. "Where the hell am I?"

"Potter gave you a hit, and then you bolted. At least that's my understanding of it, anyway." Noah pocketed his lighter again. "Do you remember much?"

"Yeah, the fusion test. It's coming back now. I don't remember much after the syringe was empty, though." He held his forearms up.

"My veins felt like they were gonna burst and then? Blacked out, worse than I ever have in the ring."

"I hate to say it, but that's actually a promising sign that all went to plan. Extreme pain seems to be a common symptom."

"If you insist. Who froze the flashlight?"

Amy waved her hand. "That would be me. Sorry about that. You okay?"

"Don't you worry about it, Elsa. Between boxing and watching Sterling, I've gotten enough concussions. I've had worse."

Noah laughed. "So, is this a meth high or your new powers that we just watched? Maybe a bit of both?"

Anthony replied by punching the nearest tree. The wood cracked and splintered around his fist.

"Holy shit," Noah said. "So it did work."

Their road trip would have to wait.

———

Sterling rises to power as tattoo artist Jolene discovers her abilities in ETCHED IN INK.

ETCHED IN INK

RIVERPEAK HEROES
BOOK 4

JESSICA SALINA

*To everyone who has been here since
January 19, 2023. Thank you.*

CONTENT WARNINGS

Etched In Ink is a supervillain romance that includes murder, drug abuse, gun violence, physical violence, blood, depictions of grief, consensual sexual content, and mentions of the death of a parent.

There is also a superpower that involves animals and objects spouting form the body, but no true body horror - but still worth mentioning here in case you get squicked out by that kind of thing so you're not thrown off guard.

CHAPTER 1

S terling Harrison held a vial in his hands, turning it over to watch the amber-colored liquid swirl inside. He watched it closely with narrowed eyes, unsure of what he was examining for exactly. Sterling lifted it to the light, seeing how the liquid almost seemed to sparkle when hit with the laboratory's fluorescent strips overhead. He could hear the rain pattering against the windows. The rain brought a reprieve from the June heat, a dreary day for a Colorado summer, though in the temperature-controlled laboratory, it didn't matter.

All that mattered to Sterling was what was in the vial.

"So, this has Hematite's powers? All I have to do is drink it?"

Dr. Potter went to speak but was interrupted by a scoff from Noah Sato, who leaned against the wall with crossed arms. "You're lucky you don't have to get poked with a million needles. Thank Amy for that discovery."

Sterling looked at the couple and smiled. "I am most grateful for that. Thank you, Ms. Brewer."

"Oh, uh, you can just call me Amy." She scratched her temple with one finger from her spot next to Noah. Sounding exasperated, she added, "Ms. Brewer makes me sound like my mom or something."

"Very well." Sterling returned his gaze to Dr. Potter, who refused to look him in the eye. "What's wrong, Doctor?"

"Nothing, I assure you." Dr. Potter laughed as he fidgeted with his gloved hands. The plastic rustled as he did. "This is just my life's work, that is all. I hope for its success as much as you do, Mr. Harrison."

With a raised brow, Sterling said, "And?"

Dr. Potter noticeably gulped. "And?"

"You look like you have so much more to say." He sighed, bored already. "Well, go on. Get on with it. What are the disclaimers?"

"Well, you see, I have good and bad news. Which would you prefer?"

"Start with the bad. I'd prefer to end on a high note before I take a sip."

"Understood. While I know you were hoping for full immortality from Hematite's sample—"

"Kane Kelly, correct?"

Dr. Potter froze. His silence spoke volumes, causing Sterling to look away from the vial and to the doctor. Sterling lowered the vial, keeping a firm grip on it, and took a step forward. The doctor was taller than most people in Riverpeak, but Sterling still stood about an inch above him, keeping him at eye level. For as much as Dr. Potter tried to look away from him to look instead at his twiddling thumbs, Sterling maintained eye contact.

"You don't have to be frightened, Dr. Potter." He maintained an even tone, sounding as blasé as he felt. "I understand you must feel a certain fondness for him. But don't fret, I have no intentions of killing Kane Kelly. He may be a pest, but as I can't kill him, I have other ways I plan to deal with the situation at hand without involving him." Sterling smiled. "But Hematite *is* Kane Kelly, correct?"

Dr. Potter nodded, the movement staccato. "Yes, Mr. Harrison."

"Splendid. Now, we can speak freely. I tire of secret identities. Anyway, you were saying?"

"The bad news is that Mr. Kelly is not fully immortal. His cells regenerate when he is murdered, but he is still aging, just as we are."

Sterling bit back his disappointment and tried not to frown. He'd been hoping for true immortality, but figured this was a step in the right direction. "Hm. A pity. Though I suppose this will have to suffice for now. You said you had good news as well?"

"Yes. When we gave Anthony the Brick Beast ability from Shawn Jameson—"

Sterling noticed in his peripheral how Amy tensed at the mention of her now-dead ex-boyfriend, Shawn. Noah squeezed her hand.

"—We noticed he developed a second ability as well. Not only does Anthony contain super strength, but he is now bulletproof. A fitting ability for a bodyguard."

"Interesting!" Sterling grinned. "Is his skin impenetrable?"

"Only to bullets. I'm conducting further tests to see if there's a reason for his limitation. But my point is you may develop your own natural power besides Kane Kelly's."

Sterling nodded. "Very interesting, indeed. Well then, I look forward to seeing what opportunities await me. Shall I?"

"Here? Now?"

"There's no time like the present, and I'm surrounded by all of you, who know what to expect and how to help should I need assistance. I don't think there could be a better time or place." Sterling took the cap off the vial and set it down on a metal table beside him. He looked at Amy and asked, "How's it taste?"

Amy shrugged. "Pretty flavorless, but it's thick. Nothing that should make you puke."

"Then I'll dive right in."

Sterling brought the vial to his lips and sipped it as casually as one would drink a glass of water. He was pleased to find Amy was right: there was no taste, but the liquid felt like watered-down honey dripping down his throat. As he set the vial down, he cracked his knuckles and then flexed his fingers. A pins and needles sensation surged through his whole body like an electric current. Sterling kept his gaze on his fingers, which he continued to flex and relax.

He went to speak, but his tongue felt too heavy in his mouth. Upon realizing it was because of the numbness coursing through every muscle and tendon, he looked around for something to write with. When Sterling found a notepad and pen next to the vial cap, he picked up the pen, though he still couldn't feel his fingers.

He wrote his question: "When will it hurt?"

Noah's brows furrowed. "Can you not speak?"

Sterling scribbled the word "numb" on the paper, and when Noah continued to stare blankly at it, Sterling added a question mark.

Dr. Potter placed a hand on Noah's shoulder. Noah brushed it off as Dr. Potter said, "Go warm him up. It should stimulate his nerves."

Noah stood next to Sterling and wrapped an arm around his shoulders. "Not to flirt with you or anything. Let me know if this helps."

Sterling sighed as he regained feeling in his fingers first, spreading from the left side of his body where Noah stood until it washed over him. "Much better. Thank you, my friend."

Noah side-stepped to give Sterling his personal space back. "Yeah, don't mention it."

"Now," Sterling said as he clapped his hands together, "I'd love to test the effectiveness."

There wasn't much color to Dr. Potter's skin, but any semblance of it effectively drained from his face. "Pardon?"

"There's a water chamber a few rooms down," Amy said. "I got to practice in there a few weeks ago."

"Can you show me there, please?"

Sterling smiled at Dr. Potter so earnestly that he was certain it was a threat, so he nodded. "Come along." He pushed his glasses back up his nose. "This way."

The four of them funneled out of the room and down the hall. When they reached the water chamber, Sterling examined the room. There was a clear tank against the wall with a few pipes keeping water cycling in and out of it. It was at least 10 feet deep, enough even for a man as tall as he was to drown. A few metal steps led up to the tank.

Sterling approached it and then moved back to the table where the other three waited for him. The silence bothered him, but he understood why they were quiet. He knew that while Amy still wasn't sure what to make of the doctor, Noah wasn't fond of the experiments that happened within these walls. The doctor was more anxious than he led on, barely hiding it. Sterling could all but smell the fear radiating off of the man with his slouched posture and incessant fidgeting.

"It's perfect," Sterling said.

Dr. Potter cleared his throat. "Surely you don't mean—"

"Oh, but I do. I can't know if it worked without proper testing, now, can I? Not that I doubt your test runs, but it can never hurt to be sure before a potential future gunfight." Before Potter could protest, Sterling kicked off his black dress shoes. As he removed his matching black socks, he said, "Besides, I've got you all here to monitor me. If shit hits the fan, you can just revive me manually. Right?"

Dr. Potter nodded but sounded anything but confident as he spoke. "I have a defibrillator, yes. I also have adrenaline shots. Let me retrieve them as you undress."

"Thank you, Doctor." Sterling waited for him to leave. "Noah. Amy. Keep him in check, will you?"

"You got it," Noah said. "Squirrelly little shit, isn't he?"

Sterling chuckled. "You've always had a way with words." He removed his suit jacket, folding it in his arms and placing it carefully on an empty table. "Forgive my lack of modesty, Amy. I didn't prepare a change of clothes."

Amy waved a hand. "Oh, you're fine. I've seen enough people naked working backstage at the theater that it doesn't even phase me. We did a production of *Hair* one year, so I'm sure you can imagine how that went."

As Sterling's shirt joined his jacket on the desk, he said, "Excellent."

"Can't believe we're getting this for free." Noah winked. "You should start an OnlyFans, Sterling."

"An OnlyFans, huh?" Sterling laughed as he unzipped his pants to step out of each leg. "You'd be the first to subscribe, right, Noah?"

Amy stifled a laugh. "Oh, my God."

Sterling left his briefs on, leaving little to Noah or Amy's imaginations. He climbed the steps in front of the tank, trailing a hand along the small railing. The steps felt cold beneath his feet, and the railing was a lifeless steel that sent a similar chill through him.

"I wonder how long it will take me," Sterling said. "It takes Kane ten to fifteen minutes, correct?"

"About that, yeah," Noah said. "Prepare for pain. None of us have had what I'd call a pleasant experience."

"No?" Sterling looked back and eyed Amy. "You too?"

"When I got my ice powers, I nearly died. If Noah wasn't there, I don't know what would have become of me. And Anthony went all sorts of feral when he got his."

"Hm. Noted. I'm not worried, though. All of you have worked so hard to help me bring this dream to life." He smiled. "Thank you."

"After everything?" Noah reached into his pocket and grabbed a stick of gum. "You don't get to die on us."

"I owe the most thanks to you, Noah. Don't worry. I plan to express my gratitude to you far more than Ray ever did. Just say the word."

Noah nodded. "I'll keep that offer in my back pocket for now."

"Suits me just fine. Say, you had the chance to expose Kane's identity to the world, didn't you?"

Noah smacked his lips as he popped the gum into his mouth. "At the theater, yeah, I did."

"You're not in trouble. I'm simply curious why you didn't."

"He saved my sister when I couldn't." Noah pursed his lips. "All I wanted was closure. To know who the guy was who couldn't die that my father so desperately arrived to turn me into. But after he helped Naomi … I didn't need to ruin his life in the process."

"How unexpectedly noble of you. Well, at least some of us have a heart. Perhaps you'll use that sense of goodwill to subscribe to your poor boss's OnlyFans?"

Noah laughed. "Shut the fuck up."

As Dr. Potter returned, they silenced. Sterling stuck his toes in the water and, upon realizing how cold it was, dunked in to get the feeling over with. As he sunk in, dipping his head beneath the surface, his body's urge to float won over. Bubbles passed through his lips as he fought the desire to gasp for breath as he resurfaced. Once he did, Sterling slicked back his long, silver hair, feeling like a wet cat. Shivering, he collected his breath after holding it against his own will in the water.

"Force me under."

Dr. Potter frowned. "Are you sure?"

"I'm sure." He reached for the doctor's hand and placed it on the top of his head. Water dripped from his own fingers onto his face and the doctor's wrist. "My sense of self-preservation is too strong. You have to force me under."

Dr. Potter ran his hand along the side of Sterling's head until he cradled Sterling's neck. With his free hand, he used his palm to press down on Sterling's forehead. Dr. Potter gulped as he extended his arms and lowered Sterling into the water. They only broke eye contact when Sterling was beneath the surface again. Sterling thrashed, stopped, then thrashed again, going against his own will to survive as Dr. Potter pushed further down on his head.

Dr. Potter swallowed, heavy with nerves. "Noah. Amy."

From their spot along the wall, the two of them straightened their posture at the sound of their names.

"Help me."

Noah and Amy glanced at each other as they pushed off the wall and approached the tank.

"What do you need?" Amy asked.

"I cannot do this alone, I'm afraid." Potter released a mangled sound, a cross between a cry and a grunt. "But he needs to be reborn. I am going to withdraw my hands. Amy, could you be a dear and freeze the surface?"

Amy nodded. "I take it Noah's here to get him out of there when the job is done?"

"That is correct. We need the layer to be thick enough that he cannot break through."

Noah rose a brow. "Is he even strong enough to?"

"He recently convinced Anthony to teach him how to box. Something about learning from his underling's mistakes."

Noah remembered how Rory Miller beat Shatterstone bad enough that, had it not been for Hematite interjecting, she could have killed him. "At least he had the sense to do that."

Amy stood beside Potter and hovered her hands over the water. "Let me know when you're ready. I'll work my way from the other side to give you more time."

Dr. Potter nodded. "Just do it."

Amy lowered her palms and, once they touched the surface, ice spread from the corners of the tank. The water along the back edge froze first, and the ice crackled as it crept closer and closer to Sterling. Amy heard Dr. Potter's breathing quicken beside her, so she sped up the speed of the ice to get this over with. Her face tightened and squeezed as she focused. She sensed if she took too long, he might have second thoughts, and his short, rapid breaths only confirmed that.

"Noah?" Amy looked back at him. "Grab Potter. He's hyperventilating. I got it from here."

Noah slid his arms beneath Potter's armpits and pulled back. Potter released Sterling's head, which remained beneath the surface, as Noah forced him out of the now-frigid space. Amy thanked Noah as she pushed more ice out of her fingers and into the water, making the temperature of the room drop so it felt as cold as the laboratory looked.

With a deep exhale, she stepped back once the entire surface had turned into a thick block with a layer of frost. She studied her handiwork as she swayed, and when she reached for the railing, it froze in her grip. Noah dropped the doctor to rush to her side. He could thaw the handrail, but opted to ignore it in favor of wrapping an arm around her.

He asked, "How are you feeling?"

She sighed in relief as she leaned into Noah. "Better now that you're warming me up. Never froze that much at once."

Noah kissed Amy's temple. "I overheat sometimes, too. You'll find a balance, eventually."

When they looked at Sterling beneath the surface, Sterling smiled. They could see gooseflesh forming along his skin as the water matched the ice's temperature, the cold permeating into the rest of the tank and piercing Sterling to the bone. More bubbles passed his lips, and he'd occasionally twitch as he went against every nerve in his body telling him to fight to survive. When Sterling opened his mouth, he began to choke on the cold water until his dark gray eyes rolled back into his head before closing, and just like that, he floated in limbo.

Dr. Potter bit his thumbnail. "Already?"

"Yeah," Noah said. He patted Amy's shoulder before ascending the steps. As Noah pulled his lighter out of his pocket to manipulate its flame and thaw the ice, he said, "I'm always surprised by how fast it happens, too."

"Please, Mr. Sa— Noah, that does nothing to ease my concerns."

"He'll be fine," Amy said. "God forbid it didn't work, you've got what we need."

Noah asked, "How long should we let him stay out for?"

Dr. Potter replied, "Given this is Hematite's power, I'll worry once it's been fifteen minutes."

Noah stepped back once the ice melted. The three of them watched with bated breath as Sterling remain suspended in the center of the tank, listening to every second of the ticking clock in the room. Sterling's body lowered to the bottom of the tank for a few minutes before, eventually, he floated once more. When he was halfway back up, his body convulsed, seizing beyond control as his skin turned blue.

"It's been ten minutes," Dr. Potter announced. "We should grab him."

But then, as if on cue, Sterling surfaced and his eyes blew open. He outstretched his long arms as he pushed himself to the edge of the chamber and emerged with a sharp gasp. He crossed his arms to lean against it, but as he caught his breath, he smiled.

Sterling Harrison was officially reborn.

CHAPTER 2

The kawaii metal blaring on the stereo was a welcome sound to Jolene Gautier's ears, audible as soon as she opened the door of her tattoo studio. Mornings were never her favorite, but as of late, they were insufferable. More often than not, the high-energy music helped wake her up when paired with her morning latte, and she hoped today was no different. She took one last sip of the matcha as she closed the door behind her.

As the door chimed open, Stella looked up from her tablet. "Good morning, Jolene!" As Stella twirled her stylus between her fingers, the neon sign—shaped like the Japanese kanji for "beautiful"—on the right wall emitted a pink glow that framed her like a saint.

Jolene opened her mouth to speak but quickly covered it with her free hand as a yawn came out instead of a greeting. "Fuck, sorry. G'morning, Stella." She slid the drink tray down on the glass counter at the front of the shop. Tattoo repair gels and CBD-infused scentless creams lined the rows inside the case. "I come bearing coffee."

"Looks like someone still isn't sleeping well." Stella got up to grab her drink and then resumed drawing once she reached her station. She tossed her wavy hair over her shoulder as she took a sip of iced coffee.

Stella and Jolene looked like polar opposites: Jolene's hair, once blonde, was currently bubblegum pink in contrast to Stella's natural brown that matched her cocoa-colored eyes. Black and white tattoos lined Stella's arms, whereas Jolene's were all in color. It didn't stop them from feeling as if they were cut from the same cloth, and soulmates if friends could be considered such.

"Unfortunately, you're not wrong." With her iced matcha latte in hand, Jolene moved to the back wall with its magical girl mural and opened the curtain to the right of the sailor scouts, revealing the hallway where her private workstation was. "I haven't gotten a good night's sleep since I took my mom to see the spring musical at the Riverpeak Theater for her birthday. I'm not sure what the hell is going on with me."

"Have you called your doctor?"

"Yeah, and they were no help." She dropped her messenger bag in the corner of her room and then moved back to the main floor, where she started restocking the snacks on a shelf in the left back corner, where the magical girl mural was connected to a wall completely covered by black and white manga pages. "Clean bill of health, even after getting some extra tests done. Waste of a co-pay."

"Shit. Melatonin?"

"Helps me fall asleep faster, sure, but every morning, I just feel like I've gotten no sleep. At first, I thought there might be something in something I drank at the theater."

"Yeah?"

"I don't drink a lot, but I treated myself to some new beer they had for the event, and it was *great*, but I don't know. It's been a few weeks since then, so I feel like it would already have moved out of my system."

"Hm. Yeah, that's tricky. There's this therapist that I used to see; she might help. Want me to give you her info?"

"A therapist?"

"Yeah. Maybe it's a mental block or something."

"Honestly," she said through her yawn, "I'm so desperate that I might as well give it a try. Text it to me?"

"Yeah, I'll do that now before I forget."

Jolene looked over Stella's shoulder as she made her way to the front of the studio. "That looks fucking sick."

The tattoo in question was of a dead manga character, but red spider lilies replaced the blood from their wounds. Thin, wiry petals swept down the character's forehead and poured out of their sternum. Except for the flowers, the sketch was completely black and white.

"Thanks! I'm so excited about this one."

They both looked up as the door chimed and opened. Annie waved with her elbow tucked into her side as she entered, a wide grin covering her face as per usual. Her dark curls rested in two puffs atop her head and bright pink lipstick popped against her skin.

"I knew that lip color would look gorgeous on you!" Stella clapped her hands together, thrilled about the result of donating makeup she'd only used once to Annie and Jolene last week.

"This is why I encourage your impulses." Annie winked.

Jolene jerked her head toward the front of the building as she said, "Coffee on the counter's yours. I have another present for you, too."

"Aw, Jo! Thank you!"

She normally hated being called Jo—that was what her former mentor called her, and Jolene preferred to not think about him after the way things ended at the old shop—but it sounded so cute from Annie that she didn't mind. Jolene retreated to her station to rummage through her messenger bag until she found the fake skin sheets. As she returned, she handed them to Annie and said, "In addition to those oranges you've been using. This is my favorite brand."

"Slay! Stop, this is so nice of you!" Annie pulled her mentor in for a hug, which Jolene happily accepted. "You are the best."

"Do good enough on those and you'll be tattooing me next."

"Oh, no," Stella said. "We are fighting for that honor of her first."

Annie faked a grimace as she giggled. "Oh, boy."

"Yeah?" Jolene flashed a lopsided smirk at Stella. "I got time right now if you wanna duke it out."

"Should we go to the parking lot out back?"

"Don't make me call HR, Stella."

"You *are* HR, doofus."

"And HR says that all conflicts must be resolved by fighting to the death in Smash Bros."

Stella snorted. "I forfeit. You know I'm ass at that game." Her eyes trailed over to the window and she leaned forward. "Whoa, check it out. Not all at once, obviously. Hot guy alert."

That got both Jolene's and Annie's attention; hot guy alerts happened once in a blue moon, but with the dating pool being fairly small in Riverpeak, it always felt like a treat when they spotted new eye candy. Jolene took her spot up by the front desk as Annie glanced over her shoulder.

Annie whistled as she went to her workstation, getting ready to practice on the fake skin. "Damn, he *is* hot."

Annie and Stella were both right. The man outside their studio was tall, with long, lean legs in well-fitted black slacks. He carried a black blazer over his shoulder, revealing his white dress shirt paired with a thin black tie. He'd rolled his sleeves up to the elbow, showing off taut forearms. With his pale skin and gray hair, he almost looked monochromatic, and Jolene wanted nothing more than to shove him in a chair and get to work—preferably, on those deliciously plain forearms. She'd never seen more of a blank canvas.

"Think he's a virgin?" Jolene's stylus found its way to her bottom lip. "A tattoo one, I mean."

Stella stifled a laugh. "I was gonna say, no way that man doesn't fuck."

Annie nodded in agreement. "Fucks, fucked, will fuck."

Jolene couldn't help her grin. "I know he's just stopped to talk on the phone, but I'd love to drag him in here and get to work."

"We've been through this, babe," Stella said, returning her focus to her sketch. "You can't just tattoo people off the street because you feel like it."

As Jolene continued to observe him, she could have sworn she knew that face, but with his large black sunglasses, it was hard to say for sure. She couldn't hear his end of the phone call, but she did hear him laugh at something said on the other line. His chuckle was low and dark, enough to send a chill down her spine.

"Have you seen this guy before?" Jolene asked.

"No, first I've seen him," Annie said. Stella dittoed her statement.

"Something about him seems so familiar, but I dunno. Maybe I just saw him at the grocery store or something."

As much as she wanted to chase him down and drag him into the shop, she focused on her next client's tattoo and sweep the man from her mind. After all, the last thing she needed was a distraction—and with clients booking her solid, she didn't have time for one, either.

———

While she didn't love driving and she wasn't fond of the destination itself, Jolene never minded the route from Riverpeak to Denver. The golden grasslands spanning out until they reached the Rocky Mountains were a beautiful sight and, with minimal cars on the road, provided for some much-needed quiet time. She drove with the windows down, enjoying the way the sun streamed in on her sunscreen and tattooed-covered arm that rested on the exposed weather stripping. The wind whipped, a headband the only thing keeping her pink hair from blowing in her eyes, and brought a pleasant breeze and the scent of pine and lemongrass in from outside.

To her delight, her destination was on the opposite side of the city from where she used to work.

The therapist's office pleasantly surprised Jolene with its warm and inviting atmosphere, despite her having no prior expectations. Rich mahogany bookshelves and tables surrounded the space, accompanied by green plants that seemed to dance in the sunlight streaming in from the windows. With summer in full swing, the plants must have been thriving.

"Jolene Gautier?"

Jolene smiled at the straight-haired brunette standing before her. "That's me!"

"I'm Dr. Thornton. A pleasure to meet you."

"Pleasure's all mine." Jolene couldn't help but sigh as she sat in the chair. "Holy shit, this is so comfortable."

Dr. Thornton laughed. "So I've been told."

"I gotta get one of these for when I'm not tattooing."

"Is that what you do for work?"

"Yeah, I run my own shop down in Riverpeak. I love it and wouldn't have it any other way, but I'm pretty sure I'll look like the Hunchback of Notre Dame by the time I'm 40."

"I'll have to pay you a visit if I want more work done," Dr. Thornton said with a smile. She grabbed a notebook from a table next to her seat. "So, what brings you in today?"

"My best friend recommended you to me a few weeks ago, actually. She said you might be able to help me find out why I can't sleep."

Dr. Thornton crossed her legs as she clicked her pen once. "Sure. Tell me more about what your typical bedtime routine looks like, so we can use that as a baseline."

"Watching an episode or two of whatever anime I'm trying to catch up on with a cup of chamomile tea, then taking some melatonin supplements I got at Target and tossing and turning for the next hour."

"How many hours asleep do you get?"

"That's the thing. Lately, with the tea and the melatonin, I'm getting at least seven hours. But even then, I'm not well-rested at all. When I wake up, I feel like I've only got seven minutes of sleep, not hours, and I don't look much better either."

"Hm. Well, Jolene, there are two things I'm going to recommend you do to start. Start logging a sleep diary and taking some notes both before you go to bed and immediately after waking up. Second, you're going to set up a camera and film yourself sleeping."

"Wait, why?"

Dr. Thornton shrugged. "Maybe you're sleepwalking. Maybe not. Can't hurt to check."

Remembering what Stella said, Jolene asked, "Do you think there could be anything blocking me? Like, mentally?"

"A mental block? Could be. Has anything been troubling you?"

"Not really. Well, there's money, but who isn't stressed about that? My bills are paid and everything's all good. I just have some ambitious savings goals."

"Okay. How are the relationships in your life? Family? A partner?"

"No partner; I've been single for a few years now, and my ex-girlfriend and I broke up on pretty good terms. No hard feelings either way."

"Why'd you break up?"

"I was moving from Denver back to Riverpeak and my business was growing, which meant no time for a proper shot at a long-distance relationship. On top of it, my books and social media accounts were blowing up, and she wasn't super into the attention I was getting."

"What kind of attention?"

"From fans. It's weird. People act like I'm some sort of celebrity or something, when in reality, I'm just a tattoo artist. There were some issues with my old mentor, too, but I haven't really worried about that in a while. But my split from her was amicable."

"No family issues either, you said?"

"Yeah, my family's really chill. We're super different, but my parents are really nice, and I'm not super close with the rest of 'em. Not for any reason other than that they're mostly older. My brother and I get along, too."

"Film yourself, then. So far, it doesn't sound like a mental block. I'm curious what you'll find."

Jolene was, too.

CHAPTER 3

I f it wasn't for the tint on the windows of the boxing gym, the sun would stream directly in where Sterling and Anthony were sparring—and were it not for that, their session would be utterly unbearable. Sterling exhaled, directing the air towards his bangs to push them out of his eyes. A few gray strands still stuck to his face with sweat. He raised his hands towards his face as he got back into the proper boxer's stance and said, "Again."

Anthony matched Sterling's stance: his right hand by his cheek, the left just by his jaw, and his back foot at a forty-five-degree angle as he squared his hips. Despite the solid stance, he huffed. "You sure? We've been at it for two hours."

"I said again." His own shallow breaths betrayed his words, but there was no question about it—he had to keep training. The rubber boxing mats felt light beneath his feet, simultaneously providing a decent grip for his flat high-tops and a light spring in his step. The row of red boxing bags swung along the wall, their shadows lining the gym as the sun streamed in through the windows.

"Famous last words. If you insist."

Sterling was at Anthony's boxing gym for one reason and one reason only: if he wanted to be the most powerful man in Colorado, he needed the muscle to back it up. For as long as Anthony had been by his side protecting him from the shadows, Sterling trusted no one—not even his bodyguard. With the abilities he had now, he couldn't afford to.

"And don't be afraid to hit me this time," Sterling said. "Even with these powers, I can't afford to be comfortable."

"I punched through a tree trunk, Sterling."

Sterling grinned. "Good thing my cells can regenerate me back to life then, isn't it?"

Anthony shrugged with one shoulder. "Suppose so." He held his hands up by his face, his upper back curving inward as he guarded himself. Anthony wasn't much shorter than Sterling, but by doing so, he made himself a slightly smaller target. His elbows were against his sides, protecting his ribs as he shuffled on his feet, and then he threw the first punch. Anthony stepped into the first jab, but Sterling shuffled to the side just in time, leading with his left foot.

When Sterling would position his toes to turn into his cross, it reminded him of the dance lessons his mother enrolled him in as a child. Boxing was no different from the ballroom in some regards, so the movements felt natural, despite the soreness building in his shoulders and upper back. But rather than his feet gliding across the floor, his steps were elaborate and sharp, meant to strike rather than to embrace.

"Keep your hands up. I know you're getting tired, but keep 'em up." Anthony paused for a breath, a thin sheen of sweat dripping down from his hairline.

As Sterling bobbed, weaved, and swung, his whole body ached. His muscles fought against every moment, desperate for rest, but Sterling swallowed back his discomfort. His enemies wouldn't wait for him to rest, so he had no choice but to push through. While the men responsible for his father's death had long since been taken care of, Sterling knew they weren't the only ones in Colorado with a grudge against him or his operation.

Anthony punched again, still fast to swing as he released short, puffy breaths. His years of instructing and decades of practice meant he had far more stamina than Sterling, who'd only recently begun physically training himself so he could withstand the drug's effects. Sterling panted as he dodged, trying to sidestep away from the punch, but he lost his footing thanks to his exhaustion.

Anthony's fist hit Sterling's shoulder with a reverberating boom. Sterling flung back so quickly that he didn't even register the hit until his back reached a bag. He slammed against it with a loud thud, feeling like a rag doll. While the bag swung behind him, the metal hook rattling above it, Sterling fell to the floor. A sharp pain ran through his shoulder, and when he tried to stand, his arm went numb and collapsed beneath him. As Sterling winced and looked at his shoulder, he could tell that it dislocated.

When he looked back up, Anthony was already running over. "Sterling?"

Sterling hissed, hoping it would release some of the pain. To his surprise, it did. He looked back at his shoulder and watched it readjust, lifting back into place with a click. As the pain subsided, he supported himself on his elbow.

"Are you okay?"

"I'm fine, I promise." He rolled his shoulder, letting it crack and solidify its spot back in the socket. "Can we do that again?"

Anthony's eyes widened and eyebrows down-turned in shock. "I beg your pardon?"

"Hit me again. Break another bone."

Anthony's thick brown brows furrowed as his mouth fell open. "You broke your shoulder?"

"Past tense."

Anthony blinked at him in surprise. "What does that even mean?"

"It means it's not broken anymore." Sterling raised a brow at Anthony, waiting for him to understand. "Break another bone, will you?"

"Is this your second power?"

"Maybe. Can't know unless I try again. I'd like to make sure that wasn't a fluke."

Anthony frowned. "Promise you won't fire me if it *was* a fluke?"

Sterling couldn't help his lopsided smirk. "Don't be ridiculous. I actually like you."

Anthony sighed as he returned to his stance. The moment Sterling stood, Anthony tossed a few punches. Sterling recognized the combination and, testing his bodyguard's resolve, dodged and counterstrike. But Anthony never lost focus and, once Sterling was certain he could predict his next move, he sidestepped and grabbed Sterling's arm.

The air flew out of Sterling's lungs as Anthony kneed him in the stomach and pulled him into an arm bar. Remembering the police report from Noah's arrest a few weeks ago, Sterling realized Anthony must have taught Noah this maneuver. Before Sterling could figure out how Rory Miller slipped out of it, Anthony hammer chopped down on Sterling's arm with all of his might.

As easily as glass, the bone shattered. When Anthony released him, Sterling gasped, though the air felt sharp in his lungs. He breathed through the pain as his father once taught him to do, then focused on his broken arm. As he willed the searing throb in his forearm away, he heard a clicking sound, almost as if someone popped their jaw, and then—sweet relief. Sterling stretched it and smiled wide, feeling a sense of calm wash over him.

"Bone manipulation is a funny thing, isn't it?" The excitement was evident on Sterling's face; he saw his own reflection in the gym's mirrors and could not deny the childlike wonder he felt.

"Think you could do it to other people's bones, or just your own?"

"Are you volunteering?"

Anthony glanced at the clock on the wall. "Don't think I'll have to."

Before Sterling could inquire further, he heard the front door open. While he didn't recognize two of the three people walking in, the brown curls were unmistakably Rory Miller's. She tied it back in a ponytail as she laughed with her fellow boxing classmates over something they'd said, their conversation from outside carrying over into the lobby.

"Looks like our lesson is up," Sterling said. "Thank you, Anthony, as always."

Anthony nodded. "Any time. Need anything before you go?"

"No, I'm ready for a break, anyway."

Sterling retreated to the men's locker room, where he took the fastest shower he could. Once he'd dried off, he put on his button-up and slacks, then tossed his workout clothes into his duffel bag. He tossed it over his shoulder as he walked out, locking eyes with Rory as he did. Rory's posture straightened and her jaw tensed as she took a slow breath, aware of his presence just as much as he was aware of hers.

Neither of them said anything. It was a silent standoff, but Sterling had the upper hand. Sterling didn't look back as he left the building; instead, he took his time putting his duffel bag in the trunk of his black Porsche. As much as he preferred the white vintage Rolls Royce he'd inherited from his father, he was too nervous to drive it outside of Riverpeak.

When he sat on the driver's side, he waited, watching through the window to see when Anthony's boxing class would begin as more and more students trickled through the doors. Even through the window tints on both the building and his windshield, Rory's voluminous curly ponytail was visible from a mile away.

Once they began bag work, Sterling narrowed his focus further on Rory: specifically, on her wrist. As she hit the bag with a hook, she recoiled, clutching onto her wrist. Sterling drove away before Rory could leave, not wanting her to put the pieces together. Unlike Mark, Dougie, and Noah before him, he knew better than to underestimate her wit or her physical strength. *At least now she'd be out of my hair for the next few weeks.*

Using the Bluetooth speaker in his car, he called Dr. Potter, who answered on the first ring.

"Hello, Mr. Harrison! For what do I owe the pleasure?"

"Are you free this afternoon? I've had quite the productive morning."

"Yes, sir. Is everything alright?"

Sterling couldn't help his smile. His amusement shone in his voice. "Oh, more than alright. I have some tests I'd love to run. Trials, even. Anthony and I discovered my second power today, and I'm curious to see if it has any limitations. Its range particularly interests me."

"Understood. I shall look forward to your arrival."

———

Sterling took it upon himself to walk and talk with Dr. Potter, searching for what he needed of his own volition. He poked into some of the different rooms, but they all more or less looked the same with their white walls, linoleum flooring, and silver cabinets and tables.

"So, Mr. Harrison, what can I get for your tests today?"

Sterling also, however, looked for something else: any sign that Dr. Potter couldn't be trusted. Noah's words still rang through his ears, like a soft warning every time the doctor was within his line of sight. If Noah didn't trust him, even after Dr. Potter kept Noah alive when he was so close to the brink of death, then Sterling certainly didn't, either.

Dr. Potter straightened his glasses on his nose and then said, "It may be faster, Mr. Harrison, if I help you."

"Ah, but of course. Forgive my curiosity." Sterling smiled. "I'm just so energized after my discovery, I couldn't help myself. I need bones."

"Bones? As in a model skeleton?"

"No. Actual bones. Preferably not those of a living human."

"Well, I'm afraid I don't keep those handy."

"I wish you'd speak more over the phone. I know you're paranoid about people listening in that shouldn't be, Dr. Potter, but honestly. If you'd let me say so before hanging up, I'd be able to tell you these things before driving out this way."

Dr. Potter bowed his head. "My apologies."

"I suppose we'll just have to use a living subject."

Dr. Potter's pale face turned even whiter. "That's not something I can provide, either."

"Come on, Dr. Potter. You're a man of science, aren't you?" Sterling pat the doctor's shoulder. "You and Ray had no problem testing on Noah. This should be half as painful."

Dr. Potter exhaled through his nose. "Well, I can't argue with that."

"Right. So, without further ado." Sterling already knew he could break a wrist, so he decided for more of a challenge. Focusing on Dr. Potter's left femur, he willed it to snap—clean and far enough from any major arteries to eliminate the risk of death, but still something that would certainly hurt. Noah would, without a doubt, take some pleasure in hearing about this. Sterling was tempted to call him but wanted to prioritize the work that needed to be done.

Dr. Potter let out a pathetic cry as he clutched his leg, crumpling into the nearest chair. The color returned to his face now as bright pink splotches on his cheeks and neck as tears threatened to spill. Sterling watched as the man's breaths shortened, resulting in quick bursts of exhales through his mouth.

"Do you like my new trick?" Sterling watched Dr. Potter wiggle a bit more before he snapped his bone back into place for him. Once he did, Dr. Potter sighed in relief, slumping his head back. "Now, I recommend you stay right where you are."

Exasperated, Dr. Potter said, "You said you wanted to test the range, didn't you?"

"I did. Now, what I'm going to do is call you," Sterling said, speaking pointedly through his teeth, "and you're going to get comfortable using the phone so that way, the next time I need to test something, you've got what we need before I waste my time. Understood?"

Dr. Potter whimpered as he nodded. "Yes, sir."

"Excellent." Sterling smiled at the doctor enough for his eyes to squint. "Now, I could successfully try this from a few feet away, but let me see if I need to even be within the building." As Sterling turned on his heel to leave, he grabbed his phone to call Dr. Potter. He answered right away, and once Sterling was outside, he envisioned the doctor's femur once more. Based on the sharp gasp of pain on the other line, he assumed it worked.

"May I ask," Dr. Potter said between short, staggered breaths, "why, of all bones, you selected my femur?"

"Would you rather your skull? Spine? Neck, perhaps?"

"No. Heavens, no."

"I wanted a challenge, and the femur is thick," Sterling said matter-of-factly. "Don't worry, I'm controlling the break. It's too clean to kill you. After all, you're still of use to me."

When Sterling repaired the bone, he heard the affirming exhale as Dr. Potter said, "Excellent. You don't need to be in the same building."

"I'm sure this has limits, though. I'm going to get in my car and see just how far we can go."

Even over the phone, he could hear Dr. Potter gulp. "How far to start?"

"Let's try a quarter mile at a time." His initial thought was half a mile, but perhaps this would get Dr. Potter to open up about anything he may be hiding. It was one of the many lessons Sterling learned from his father: when all else fails, pain makes people talk.

Sterling switched his phone to the Bluetooth speaker in his car and began driving, pulling over on the long stretch of road that lead in and out of the laboratory. As he did, Dr. Potter said, "Ready when you are."

Sterling picked at some lint on his lapel for a moment, letting Dr. Potter sit in suspension before finally willing his leg to break. Sure enough, Dr. Potter's yelp of pain came through.

"So, Dr. Potter, tell me," Sterling said, "what powers have we seen so far? I'm losing track of everyone."

In truth, Sterling hadn't lost track at all. He was well aware of Anthony's super strength and bulletproof skin, Noah's fire, and Amy's ice. Hematite's immortality was now his twin, and Brick Beast was out of the picture. But Noah suspected that Hematite's crew had a secret that Dr. Potter was closely guarding, and Sterling wanted to know it.

After all, he knew everything else happening in Riverpeak. It was only right that he know this, too. Dr. Potter rattled off the ones Sterling knew and then faltered. His voice trailed off, and while he caught himself, it wasn't quick enough for Sterling to not notice.

"You hesitated, Potter."

"Did I? Perhaps I, too, am losing track."

"Sounds like you got all the ones we know of."

Sterling repaired the break, giving Dr. Potter a rest. He drove another quarter mile down the road and snapped the femur again without warning, not hesitating.

"Mr. Harrison, what are you getting at?"

"Has anyone else in Riverpeak come to you with powers? Perhaps since the show?"

"No, they haven't."

Instead of repairing the bone, Sterling focused on Dr. Potter's right femur, curious if he could break multiple bones at once. The scream that came through the car's speaker confirmed his suspicion.

"Are you sure about that, Potter?"

Dr. Potter did not hesitate, even through his heavy breathing. "I swear to you, Sterling. If you ever find me to be wrong, then you can kill me on the spot. I swear on my own grave."

"Hm. Interesting." Sterling repaired the left femur first, then the right. He drove another quarter mile, repeated the process, and then did so once more. Once he was more than a mile away, there was no more screaming on the other line. "Well?"

"I believe we've found your limit, Mr. Harrison."

"A mile radius. Good to know. Thank you for your time today, Dr. Potter. This was very insightful, indeed."

Sterling hung up and, as he drove home, called Noah.

"'Ello?"

"I just wanted to let you know that I've made Dr. Potter suffer. After he and your father did those live, inhumane tests on you without my knowledge or approval, I thought you would like to know that justice has been served."

Noah chuckled once. "Good. Is the bastard still alive?"

"For now."

"Now you're speaking my language."

"If you ever find out more about that secret you suspect he's keeping, let me know."

"Goes without saying. What did you do to him?"

"Broke his legs. Repeatedly. He's fine now, but he may have trouble walking after this. I've repaired the bone, but I'm sure he'll be sore."

"Well, if you ever *do* kill him, I hope I get to burn the bastard's body."

"I'll give you the cremation honors."

"Appreciated. How'd you break his legs?"

Sterling recapped his discovery to Noah as he pulled into his long driveway. As he pressed the button on his garage door opener, he said, "I'm home now. I'll catch up with you more later."

Upon hanging up, Sterling pulled into his garage and entered his home. As he went through the motions of his routine, he decided to change things up for the evening by grabbing himself a short glass of Scotch and heading to his back patio. He stared out over the mountains, feeling the breeze on his face and the fruity spiced malt on his tongue, and realized exactly what it was that felt wrong. At first, he'd chalked it up to Dr. Potter's secret keeping.

But now, as he sipped his drink and stood still, watching the world from his massive house alone, he knew that was the problem.

He was alone.

CHAPTER 4

J olene tapped her painted nails in rapid succession, from pinky to pointer finger, across her small desk as she waited for the video to load. The sound echoed through the room from her spot in her lavender gaming chair. Next to her laptop was a gray hand towel from her bathroom, stained with a dark substance. She couldn't identify what it was, nor did she remember bringing the towel into her bedroom, but she figured the video would fill in the gaps in her memory.

Still in her pajamas, a fancy silk set she bought along with the first bottle of melatonin to get a better night's rest, she grew antsy. While she wasn't sure if the pajamas helped or not, at least the soft fabric felt soothing on her pale skin. As she waited for the video to load, her phone rang. Her brother's name flashed across the screen, along with a selfie the two of them took a few years back.

"Hey, Chad!"

"Jolene! What is going on?"

"You're only this chipper when you want something."

"Okay, maybe I had a question for you, but I figured I'd check in on you and see how you're doing first."

Jolene swallowed. She knew why he was asking and was grateful that her brother cared enough to do so. But the last thing she wanted to do was talk about the people she'd left behind, especially when now she'd made a name for herself without an ego-inflated prick's influence.

So, she ignored it. "What's your question? Does someone want a tattoo?"

"No, I know to send them to your website to get on your books whenever they open. I don't need that lecture twice."

"Alright, good."

"I've got a fundraiser to go to tonight. My date totally bailed, and I can't recoup the ticket. Shit wasn't cheap. My question was if you wanted to mooch off of rich people and get some free food and drinks tonight with me so I don't look like a total loser."

With a laugh, Jolene asked, "Why the fuck didn't you lead with that?"

"Well, if someone hadn't accused me of just trying to get something…"

"Okay, okay, I'm sorry for jumping the gun. Sure, I'll go. I should wrap up with my client by five today, so you're in luck. When and where is this thing at?"

"It's at 7:30 at the High School. I'll drive."

"Solid. Sounds good." She checked the screen on her computer and saw it had blacked out. She waved the mouse around until it turned back on; the light, even though she expected it, made her squint. "What's the fundraiser for?"

"Some scholarship for students with disabilities. A bunch of us from the dealership are going to support one of the guys. His son gets it every year."

She cooed. "That's so sweet."

"Don't sound so surprised, you ass."

"Yeah, yeah. How fancy do I gotta dress for this thing?"

"I mean, if you have a nice dress, that should do the trick. I'm just wearing a sports coat."

"Got it. I'll cover up the ink."

"I don't think you have to."

"Eh, can't hurt." She shrugged a shoulder. "I'll see you later, then. I gotta get ready for work."

"See ya!"

She turned back to the computer and groaned at the still-loading video. "C'mon, you cheap piece of shit." Her bottom lip found its way between her teeth until the video was ready. As soon as she hit play, Jolene moved her knuckles to her chin and rested her elbows on the desk, leaning forward to get as close of a look as possible without destroying her eyesight.

In the clip, Jolene emerged from bed and walked out around 2:30 in the morning, only to return an hour and a half later with her hair messier than it'd been when she left. She'd wiped her hands on the gray hand towel, drying them before plopping back into bed.

Jolene leaned back in her chair. "What the fuck?" She reached for her mouse and dragged the progress bar back to the beginning. She rewatched the feed in disbelief as she watched the tape back, again, again, and then again, repeating it until she had no choice but to finish getting ready for her workday.

There is no way this could be real, she thought, but there it was. *The recording didn't lie. It can't—right?* She clipped the video out of the larger feed to cut the file size down and then sent it via email to Dr. Thornton. Hopefully, the therapist wouldn't drop her entirely for what she saw.

"Fuck this," Jolene said to herself with a huff. "Oh, man, I need some caffeine."

———

When she stepped inside Jefferson's Coffee, she was relieved to see no one else inside except for Aaron behind the counter, his dark skin warm beneath the Edison lights overhead. He waved at her as he grabbed three cups, setting two aside and getting her matcha started. Aaron wore his usual flannel beneath the navy apron with the shop's logo, matching the cups. At least here, she found some sense of normalcy.

"The usual for the three of you?"

"Yes, please!" As she fished her wallet from her bag, she said, "Hey, can I ask you something kind of random?"

"Sure. What's up?"

She looked around as he frothed the matcha, double-checking that they were, in fact, alone. "You were there for that shit show at the theater a little while back, weren't you?"

"Yeah, I took Jordan to cheer her up."

"Have you noticed anything weird since then?"

Aaron raised a brow, listening as he poured the drink into the plastic cup already filled with ice, vanilla syrup, and oat milk. "Weird like how?"

Jolene trilled her bottom lip as she handed him the cash for their drinks. "Oh, I dunno. Are you sleeping okay? Notice anything disrupting your usual routine?"

"No, I've been sleeping just fine." Aaron returned her change, but Jolene shoved it in the tip jar. Aaron moved to pour the iced coffees into their cups as he asked, "Why? What's going on?"

"So, ever since then, my sleep has been fucked up." She put her wallet back in her bag. "I started filming myself, and get this! I'm sleep-walking! Like, going for walks out and about on the town in the middle of the night with no recollection of anything that happened."

"Jesus. That is weird. Can't say I've had that happen, though. What makes you think it's connected?"

Jolene shrugged a shoulder. "Just a hunch."

With a kind smile, he said, "Maybe that hunch is induced by sleep deprivation."

"Shit, you're probably right."

"Listen, Jolene." Aaron placed all three drinks in a carry tray. "If I were you? Take a day off. Or two. Even three. Get some sleep."

"Easier said than done."

"Believe me, I know. You think growing up here didn't give me a severe caffeine addiction?" He laughed. "I'm sure it's a coincidence. Tell Stella and Annie I said hi."

"Yeah, will do."

On her short walk to the studio, Jolene racked her brain over the footage from overnight. She still couldn't determine what she'd wiped off her hands and onto that towel, and part of her didn't want to know —she wasn't prepared for the potential answers to that question, but not knowing felt worse.

As the bell chimed overhead, she heard Annie's voice greeting her. She was with Stella, practicing her stipple work.

"Hey, guys!" She delivered their coffees before dumping the tray on her way to her space, going through her usual routine and feeling more confused than she had been before filming herself. *Maybe*, she thought, *the night out would help me take my mind off of everything.*

————

At the sound of her brother's car honking, Jolene left her house, taking her time in her heels. She seldom wore them, but she enjoyed how they made her feel just a bit taller, and the dress she wore called for them.

When she opened the car door, her brother said, "Damn, I didn't know I was bringing Morticia Addams."

Jolene rolled her green eyes as she got into her brother's car. Her black gown shimmered in the light and hugged her curves, form-fitting to make up for the lack of visible skin. Only her collarbone and neck were visible, as the long sleeves hid her arms with a subtle batwing. The dress cinched at her waist before slightly flaring out down her legs. Simple, yet elegant.

"When you tell me sports coat, I know better."

Chad scoffed in faux-offense. "What's that supposed to mean?"

"You're always slightly underdressed, but never enough for anyone to say anything." She pinched her fingers together for emphasis. "Without fail."

With a stroke of his blond beard, he said, "But my Gautier charm makes up for it."

Jolene groaned. "You're gonna make me vomit. How old are you again?"

Chad simply laughed as he drove off, leaving the apartment complex to head toward the school.

Jolene hadn't even thought about Riverpeak High School since she'd graduated. It felt like so much longer ago than it actually had been, a testament to how much she'd grown and changed since then. The fundraiser was in the gymnasium, decked out with black, white, and gold banners and balloons for the evening. Matching tablecloths donned the circular tables where a few already sat, waiting for dinner to be served.

"For a function this nice," Chad said, scratching his nose with the same prominent bridge she'd inherited from their dad, "I'm surprised they hosted here."

"Me too," Jolene said with a wince. "They couldn't have found a Hilton or something?"

He snort-laughed, the same that she'd also inherited from their father. "And I see the bar. It's open. Want anything?"

"Whatever's strong."

"Sure thing, Mrs. Addams."

Jolene rolled her eyes as she smirked. "Shut the fuck up."

But Chad just laughed as he pranced off, leaving Jolene to search for their seats. Upon their arrival, they'd received place cards with their table numbers. As she finally found the table and set the place cards down, a feminine voice called her name.

"Jolene Gautier, is that you?"

She turned and saw an old classmate, who wrapped her up in a conversation she wasn't particularly interested in, but paid attention just enough to nod and smile when polite. Jolene didn't even remember the girl's name, but over her shoulder, she saw Chad talking and laughing with a tall, lean man in a sharp suit. From the look of his outfit and his slicked-back gray hair, Jolene realized he must have been the man she saw outside the tattoo studio before.

As he nursed his drink, bringing it to his lips, he glanced over in her direction and caught her staring. Their eyes locked from across the room, and for as much as Jolene wanted to introduce herself, she also knew now wasn't the most appropriate time or place to be checking someone out.

Seeing him for a second time just confirmed it: this was the most attractive person she'd ever seen, man or woman, and she was convinced that she was doomed to fumble. *Besides*, she thought, *someone like him had to be married.*

So, she returned her focus to her conversation for a brief moment before excusing herself to the restroom, feeling the need to dunk her head into a bucket of ice. She contemplated splashing her face with cold water in the bathroom, but as she stared at herself in the sink, she didn't want to ruin her makeup, so she decided against it.

Alone in the bathroom, Jolene posed in front of the full-length mirror by the door. She placed her free hand on her hip, accentuating her figure, and snapped a photo, uploading it with a simple caption: "fit check #ootd"

Before she hit send, she added a single emoji to the end of the caption—the fox—and hoped Hematite would notice.

She pocketed her phone in her clutch as she left the bathroom, returning to their seats. Her notifications were bound to blow up any second now—her Instagram following consisted mostly of feminist women who were past or future clients, but it didn't stop horny men from openly thirsting in her comments section—but at the event, she didn't have time to get check them. Lately, she hardly had time to do anything other than post and close out of the app. When she sat, she saw Chad still chatting with the silver-haired man, the two now walking towards their seats. As Jolene sat down and smoothed her dress, she wondered if he would be at the same table.

When the silver-haired man stopped two tables over, she wasn't sure if she was relieved or disappointed. Her brother slid into the seat next to her and set two rum and Cokes down.

"Do the trick?"

Jolene swiped for the drink and took too big of a sip, leaving a lipstick print on the rim. She didn't care how it made her look. "Most certainly."

"What's got you all flustered?"

"One: being back in high school is weird. Two: whoever you spoke with just now? The girls and I were checking him out the other day. He's so hot. Like, if we weren't here..." She whistled.

Chad nearly spat out his drink. "I wish I hadn't asked."

"Then let that be your lesson not to. I'm just here for the food."

"Not to save my ass?"

"Saving your ass means free food, so, by extension, sure."

With a teasing grin, Chad said, "I can bring him over here if you want."

"No, I'd need far more liquid courage for that, but then I'd say something stupid and fuck up my chances."

"Come on, Morticia. How will you ever get Mom to shut up during the holidays if you don't start shooting your shot?"

"If I remember correctly, it was *you* she was pestering on Christmas about finding a girlfriend and having babies, not me." A couple in their sixties walked by their table, so she dropped her voice to a whisper. "It's fine. I prefer to admire from a distance, especially when they're outside of my tax bracket."

Chad whispered back, "You probably make more money than two-thirds of the people here."

She shrugged her shoulder. "That may be true, but I'm trying to head out to Colorado Springs, anyway. No sense in starting something just yet."

"That's your prerogative, but hey, you never know," Chad said. The couple that walked by sat down, so Chad and Jolene ceased their conversation to introduce themselves. But as they spoke with the couple, her eyes kept wandering over to the silver-haired man's table, noticing the way he spoke—or, rather, seemingly didn't. Whenever she looked over at him, he was listening intently to the people at his table, smiling and nodding. She wondered if he was paying as little attention as she was, getting wrapped up in the fantasy that they were living separate yet parallel lives.

When his eyes darted to her between conversations, she cracked her neck and took a sip of her drink, hopeful not to get caught, but his gaze lingered. There was no way he hadn't noticed her staring, but dinner being served saved her from a potentially embarrassing moment.

At least her fantasy was taking her out of her own head—and the Instagram message she'd sent to Hematite, a silent cry for help that she wasn't even sure would be answered.

CHAPTER 5

At precisely 7:30 that morning, Sterling knocked on Chief Alex Parker's door. He'd completed his usual morning routine, both his workout for the day and some paperwork for a few restaurants completed. But now, he had to attend to the dirtier side of his business.

After Noah and Amy's stunt at the theater went awry, he had some cleaning up to do. After all, Detective Jon McMahon was proving to be a larger thorn in his side than expected. The detective was the one man who evaded his bribery, but if he could sway Chief Parker, then all would be restored—at least well enough until he determined a more permanent solution.

Alex opened the door. Sterling had to look down on him, though he found that to be the case with just about everyone except for Anthony and Dr. Potter. Alex had slicked back his dark locks with pomade, styled almost the same way as Sterling's hair. His face was clean-shaven, and his uniform was already on save for his jacket.

"Sterling Harrison!" He smiled, none the wiser. It almost made Sterling laugh, but he kept his cool composure.

"Chief Parker. Are you well?"

"I am. How have you been? Do you want to come in before work?"

"I'd love nothing more. I was just about to ask if now was a good time."

"Yeah, yeah, come on in. I'll grab you a cup of coffee."

Sterling sat in a deep mauve lounge chair. A coffee table rested between him and Alex, where two coasters and a vase of flowers called home. Sterling glanced up at the fireplace in front of them, built from gray stone. Above it hung a painting in an elegant wooden frame: a massive ship, caught in a tempest. Storm clouds painted the sky as the waves crashed up against the ship, and in the corner, the name Laurel stood out in thin white paint.

"You've settled in nicely," Sterling said.

"Thank you." Alex placed their mugs down. He wiped his hands down his pants as he sat in the chair next to Sterling. "I'm glad you could join me today. For what do I owe the pleasure?"

"You went to university with my father, didn't you?"

Alex smiled as the memories flooded back behind his eyes. "I did. We were roommates during our freshman and sophomore years. He was a great man. Went to his wedding and watched you grow up, until I got transferred out to Wyoming, but it's good to be back in Riverpeak."

"I remember. I used to call you Uncle Alex." He took a slow sip of coffee. "How're Laurel and the kids?"

"Laurel is loving it here. The kids are still in Wyoming, but they visit now and then."

Sterling nodded, taking a mental note of that as he took another sip. "Good. Is she home?"

"No, she's on her way to work."

"Then we can speak freely."

Alex stiffened in his seat. "About what?"

"Do you know why you're back here, Chief?"

Alex frowned, no doubt noting the sharpness with which Sterling now spoke. "Because they needed a new chief after the scandal with Eliza Daniels. Said the entire department was too corrupt for an internal promotion. Still can't believe she was sleeping with a councilman. I met her husband once. A shame, he was a really nice guy. Didn't deserve that."

"No. That's only part of the story." Sterling brushed a speck of dust off of his lapel, bored. "You're here because I willed it so." Not giving him a chance to ask questions, Sterling continued, "You're here because I needed a man I could trust. Someone who I knew could help me set things right again."

Alex shifted as his face went taut. "What does that mean?"

"That means I own you, Alex." Sterling gave him a small smile. "Don't look so horrified. I owned Chief Daniels, too, but she didn't even know it. You should be grateful that I'm giving you the courtesy of a heads-up."

"You're out of your goddamn mind."

Sterling chuckled. "Please, Alex. Let's not pretend that you didn't know exactly what my father was up to. About why he died."

"Oh, what, the meth? I thought he gave that up when he had you."

"Quite the contrary. He bred me for this." Sterling propped his ankle up on his thigh, relaxing in his seat. "Let me tell you something about Riverpeak. It runs on my father's legacy, and I ensure that doesn't stop. Now, don't be mistaken. Working with me will have its benefits, too."

"Like what? Why shouldn't I book you for peddling drugs right now?"

Sterling jerked his head toward the painting. "Your wife. Laurel still likes to paint, does she?"

"Is this a threat?"

"No, no, of course not. It's an offer." Sterling flashed a million-dollar smile. "Your wife gets to spend the rest of her days painting away whatever the hell she pleases. There's some boutique on Main Street that's moving out, right across from the vet clinic. Her art's beautiful. The space would make for a lovely gallery."

"You remember her saying she'd like one someday, huh?"

"I get my observant nature from my mother. Anyway, if you let me and my people do what we need to, then let's just say you may see a nice bonus in your paycheck. I would imagine it could be enough to pay for a gallery."

Alex swallowed with his jaw clenched. Sterling could see some sweat forming on his brow. "And what if I don't?"

"Well, then my offer would have to turn into a threat." Sterling rested his cheekbone against his knuckles. "And I really would hate to imagine what that would do to your children. Losing a parent at a young age fundamentally changes you."

"Get out of my house."

Sterling didn't budge an inch. "And you've settled in so nicely here. I'd hate to see you have to pack up and leave so soon. Seeing as you have a mortgage on this place, I also imagine it would be pretty hard to afford if you were to lose your new position."

Through gritted teeth, Alex asked, "Is this really what your father would want, Sterling?"

"It doesn't matter what he'd want now. He's dead."

"This is sick."

"This is business." Sterling held a hand out. "Do we have an understanding, Chief Parker?"

With a frown, Alex shook Sterling's hand. "Understood, Mr. Harrison."

"Excellent. I'm glad we're on the same page and am looking forward to a fruitful partnership." He stood. "Now, if you'll excuse me, I have a few errands to attend to."

"Come on. I'll walk you out. But if you ever show up here making thinly veiled threats like that again..."

"Oh, please, Chief Parker. I do hate to be the bad guy. Don't give me a reason." With a wave, he said, "Thanks for the coffee."

Sterling didn't bother to look over his shoulder as he left; there was no reason to. He was certain that Alex was fuming behind him, but unable to do or say anything about it. Alex simply let the door swing closed behind Sterling, causing it to slam in his own face.

Instead of heading home or to the safe house, Sterling walked to the woods just outside of Potter Laboratories. The thick trees expanded from Dr. Potter's vast property on the west side of town all the way out to Constance's Pond. Sterling's first errand of the day wasn't so much of an errand as it was practice. The closest gun range was too far of a drive to be worth it when there were plenty of trees and no one around in those woods.

While his aim wasn't perfect yet, it had gotten pretty damn close.

He saw some scars on the trees from past practice sessions. Even though Sterling's father taught him how to use a gun when he was young, he hadn't needed to until about a year ago.

A year ago, he'd missed.

While he hadn't shot to kill Brad Evans and Shawn Jameson, he'd wanted to at least scare and slow down the two young men as they ran from his old car. With Anthony behind the wheel, they'd taken Reiji out for a spin that afternoon, and when they'd passed the old South Main Burgers that Reiji swore had been taken care of, they found the two—alongside Elijah Baron and Hematite—emerging from the front door like they owned the place.

But he'd missed. Message not received.

He wouldn't make that mistake again.

————

As Sterling turned the corner down Noah's street, he took the last drag of his cigarette and pulled the black disposable mask out of his jacket pocket. It barely blocked the smell of cat urine and meth cooking, but he preferred to keep himself hidden as he made his way down the street. Should anyone see him here and things went to hell, he'd have plausible deniability with his face covered.

Though, he thought, *with my hair these days, it's making it harder to blend in.*

But he was confident enough to push the thought back as he entered the numbers on the keypad lock and opened the front door, not yet bothering to dye his hair back to his natural black. He hurried through the house, wasting no time in heading to the basement. Carter, Anthony, Noah, and Amy were all waiting for him there, alongside a few of the cooks that Sterling hadn't bothered to learn by name.

"Look who decided to join us today," Noah said. "What brings you in?"

Sterling pushed his sunglasses to the top of his head. "Just letting you know that I finally finished cleaning up after the theater incident. The police are officially back on our side. I had a riveting conversation over a cup of coffee with Chief Parker this morning."

"Thank you," Amy said. Despite everything she'd been through, she was still so polite. It was no wonder Noah liked her so much.

"Of course. Just doing what needs to be done." Sterling leaned against the back wall. "What's next here?"

"While we know the liquid version works, we're still prioritizing crystal," Carter said. "Though Amy was thinking of taking some left-overs from the theater to the bar. We've been preserving it so it should still be good, but we wanted to run it by you first, actually."

"I think that sounds like an excellent idea. There may be some who are curious, but hesitant to crystals."

Amy smiled and nodded as Noah wrapped an arm around her, pulling her closer to him.

"You don't need to be shy, Amy," Sterling said. "Just a few weeks ago, you killed a man. Rightfully so, if you ask me. Why the sudden change in attitude?"

"This is still just new to me, that's all. Being this involved and all."

"You've more than earned your spot here. Keep your chin up. I'm sure Noah would prefer it if you did, too. Isn't that right?"

Noah glared at Sterling. "Now you're just teasing me."

"Of course I am. It's my favorite pastime. Anyway, go ahead with the bar. It's not like there's anyone who can stop us."

Carter smiled. "Perks of you owning the place."

One of the many gifts from my father's inheritance, Sterling thought. "Do a trial for a few weeks. If it sells and does well, then we may want to make it a regular option. How do we plan on letting people know?"

"We can get the dealers and middlemen to work their magic," Noah said. "Come up with a code word and boom, the rest is history."

Sterling nodded. "Acceptable. Any plans for under-covers?"

"I thought you said you had the police department handled?" Carter asked.

"I do. All but one."

"That McMahon guy?" Carter said, "I'll know him if I see him, don't you worry."

"If you insist. Any leads on potential supers?"

"I'm on that," Amy said, her confidence returning. "My parents were out of town, so I snuck back into the theater to pull some credit card data from that night. I've got the list of everyone's information so we can start there and see if anything's been happening with them."

"Clever. If you find anyone, it would be in our best interest to monitor them and ensure that Hematite doesn't get to them before we can. I don't want to loop anyone in unless it's mission-critical, but we will also need to build trust. Work accordingly."

"Understood."

"Anthony, care to accompany me to a few of the restaurants? I owe them a few visits."

Anthony nodded. "Sure. Ready to go?"

"Whenever you are."

————

Finally ready to unwind after making his rounds at all the restaurants in Riverpeak, Sterling allowed himself to sink into his couch. Before he could claim business was done for the day, he retrieved his phone from his pocket and scrolled through Instagram, monitoring a few people of interest.

Rory Miller's Instagram was still private, and he didn't dare send her a follow request. While Noah's sister Naomi used to be easier to keep track of, she now exclusively shared wedding photos on her Instagram, so it was another one he barely bothered to tamper with.

If Sterling hadn't known any better, he'd have fallen for the story Kane Kelly spun on his Instagram account. But equipped with the knowledge from Dr. Potter, Sterling saw right through every post and caption. His feed looked normal enough: the first three squares on his grid were a carousel photo post of him and Rory bowling at the alley a few towns over; a shot of him and Rory enjoying a warm drink, seemingly tea or coffee, on a triple-date with Elijah, Hannah, Brad, and Naomi; and an old photo of him and his sister Kayla when they were children to wish her a happy birthday. But Sterling knew that there was much more to Kane Kelly than he led on.

After all, Hematite had an image to uphold, and it was no coincidence that Kane and Rory were not only dating but now living together in the aftermath of Stone Breaker's slip-up. Sterling had always hated the little prick, but his father, Tom Stevens, was a valuable asset. Unfortunately, trying to appeal to him—and his son Mark, who wore the Stone Breaker mask before they got arrested—meant the entire house of cards collapsed.

It was a good thing Sterling was an expert at assembling the cards back together.

He returned to his feed, and the first post was a photo of Jolene Gautier. When Noah had his full sleeve done, Sterling followed her to see if she'd say anything out of the ordinary, and so far, she hadn't—but his appreciation for her art was enough to keep him following. The photo of her black gown seemed innocent enough—if not a little sexy, even he'd admit, with the way it hugged her body and her pink hair had been swept up off her neck into a low bun—but the fox emoji caught his eye.

A fox, just like Noah's tattoo, when she seldom used emojis in her captions.

He called Noah.

Noah answered with, "Miss me already?"

"Ask Amy if Jolene Gautier is on that list of hers."

"My tattoo artist?"

"Yes. Look at her latest Instagram post."

"Hold on. Let me switch you to speaker so I can multitask here." After only a minute, Noah cursed on the other line. "You thinking what I'm thinking?"

"I am. Let me know if she is. If Amy finds her name, I may just pay her a visit."

CHAPTER 6

E ven though Jolene had her private space, she preferred to draw out in the shop lobby. It was abuzz with life—quite literally, thanks to the vibrations of Stella's tattoo machine as she and a client laughed over their love of the anime she was tattooing from. It was the piece with the flower petals bleeding out of the character, now etched permanently into her client's thigh. The woman drove over an hour from Eagle County just to get the tattoo. Even with the music playing n the radio—Japanese city pop today—Jolene could hear them from her spot, perched at the stool behind the front counter.

The sun streamed in through the windows, providing a natural light that felt nice on her skin. With summer in full swing, her tattoos finally emerged from hibernation, no longer hidden behind puffer jackets and sweaters. She thanked herself for getting some anti-glare screen protectors online for her tablet. She doubly appreciated the lack of glare today; thanks to her cutting coffee from her morning routine, the withdrawals were kicking in, feeling like her head split in two. The sun bouncing off of her screen and into her eyes would have just made it worse. While the matcha she'd switched to help her ween off, the withdrawal migraine was still nauseating.

But Jolene was distracted from both her drawing and her headache when the door opened before her. A tall man—taller than she'd ever seen—walked in, his dress shoes lightly clicking against the floor. Despite his gray hair, slicked back and out of his face, he looked only a few years older than her, likely the same age as her brother. A closed-lipped smile formed on his long face, making his hollow cheeks look even more pronounced.

With his pale skin, white button-up, black slacks, and suit jacket, she realized this was the monochrome man she'd checked out the other day, and the same from the fundraiser two nights ago.

As he lifted his sunglasses off his eyes, tucking a temple into his dress shirt, she saw that even his eyes were gray, the color of storm clouds ready to unleash their fury. It made her yearn to know what every color would look like painted on his skin.

So, with the most pep she could muster, she said, "Hey, welcome!"

The man nodded curtly. "Good afternoon." His voice was rich and smooth, like honey dripping onto velvet.

"What can I do for you?"

"A colleague of mine had some work done by you. Had nothing but good things to say."

"Glad to hear it. I'm booked out for the next three months, but my books did just open up for the next quarter of the year."

"How much for your time now?"

The question confused her. At her shop, they charged on a case-by-case basis for each piece, and state that on their website. "Excuse me?"

"How much for your time? Say, twenty minutes?"

"For a tattoo? We don't charge by the hour."

"No, not that."

Her brows furrowed as annoyance poked at her, wondering what this man was up to. Maybe she'd been right to keep this a fantasy in her head, but fate seemed to have a different idea for her. "Are you trying to pay your way into a date right now?"

"Oh! No, no, forgive me." He held his hands up to his chest, palms facing her in an act of surrender. "I could have worded that better. Not that you aren't short on beauty. That's just not why I'm here. I understand you're a very busy woman, and time is the most valuable thing we have."

"All right, well, why don't you spit it out, buddy? Your fancy suit doesn't make this any less unsettling."

"To cut to the chase: I have some security camera footage that I believe features you. I'd love to not only show it to you, but offer some help. I understand you've been having trouble sleeping at night?"

Her breath caught in her throat; Jolene wasn't sure how he knew that, but she was so desperate for help that she didn't care. "My price is an iced matcha latte from Jefferson's Coffee. Now."

"Deal." The silver-haired man smiled like he knew the secrets to the universe. "Shall we?"

"Let's go." Jolene turned off her tablet and hid it behind the counter in a locked cabinet. "What's your name?"

"Sterling, like the silver. And you're Jolene, like the Dolly Parton song."

"Sterling … Wait a second. Sterling Harrison?"

"The very same."

"Holy shit. I didn't even recognize you with your hair!" Then she called out, "Stella, Annie, I'll be back soon!"

As they walked out the door together, Sterling raised a brow at her. "Have we met before?"

"It's been years! You and my brother Chad took piano lessons together. I remember you from all of his recitals."

"Well then, Jolene, it's a pleasure to be reunited. I must confess, I didn't recognize you with your hair either, though yours is much more fun than mine."

She laughed, feeling relief wash over her now that she knew this wasn't some creep off the street. "No, no, I quite like the silver fox look on you. It suits you."

He simpered. "Is that a compliment or an insult?"

"Definitely a compliment. You always struck me as so refined, even though you and my brother are the same age."

"Well then, thank you."

"Weren't you at that charity fundraiser at Riverpeak High, too? My brother went with his coworkers and made me tag along when his date bailed."

"I was. Did I see you?"

"I'd covered my sleeves up, so was probably harder to spot me than usual."

"Ah, now that you mention it, I do think I saw you. My apologies for not speaking up. My attention was dragged in a million directions that night."

"Oh, please. Don't sweat it. Do you still play piano?"

"Occasionally. It's something I wish I had more time for."

As they reached Jefferson's Coffee, Sterling held the door open for her. She thanked him as she went inside, the smell of freshly ground coffee beans instantly smacking her like a brick wall. There was no line at the cashier, where Aaron Jefferson prepared a drink for a customer waiting at the bar.

"Hey, Jolene!" Aaron waved as he set the other patron's drink down. He bid them a good day and moved back to the register. "Oh, give me a second." Aaron grabbed one of the clear plastic cups printed with the cafe's brown and blue logo on it and said, "Iced matcha with vanilla and oat milk, right?"

"You are so good at this."

"I know. My dad's wondering when you'll make the switch back to coffee."

"As much as I miss testing his new flavors, I'm having a hard time sleeping as it is, and the caffeine wasn't doing me any favors."

"Totally understand. My mom just quit, too. Also switched to matcha."

"No shit?"

"Doctor's orders. Her cortisol was way too high."

"Oh, with everything going on, I'm not surprised. Is she in today?"

"She's on a supply run now with my sister."

"Give both of them my love, okay? How's Jordan hangin' in there?"

"She's been better, but it seems like she's on the mend." Aaron shrugged as he held back a frown, his lips forming into a thin line and making his dimples more prominent. "Still won't say what happened to her. I've caught her talking in her sleep and it's as good as riddles. She'd make more sense speaking another language."

"Poor thing. If I find any miracle sleep solutions, I'll pass 'em along."

"That'd be great. God knows she could use something like that." He looked at Sterling and said, "Forgive me! Got carried away there. Is there anything else I can get you both?"

"Aaron, oh my God, don't apologize," Jolene said. "This is Sterling. He's a childhood friend of my brother and works with one of my clients. Sterling, this is Aaron. His dad runs the café, of which I am an embarrassingly frequent regular."

"A pleasure to meet you." Sterling gave him a nod as he handed Aaron a hundred-dollar bill. Jefferson's Coffee was the one place his father never acquired, and Aaron's father remained adamant to this day that it stayed in their family. "Whatever she's having, make it two, please."

"Of course. Your total will be $8.49."

"Keep the change. For that sister of yours."

Aaron's eyes widened as he tried to hide the surprise on his face. "Are you sure?"

"Positive." After all, he only felt a modicum of guilt about how Noah's experiments left Jordan Jefferson—but Aaron didn't need to know that.

"Thanks." Aaron stuffed the extra cash in the tip jar on the counter. "I really appreciate it, and I'm sure she will, too."

"Of course."

They moved to the end of the bar, waiting to pick up their drinks. Once Aaron was out of earshot, Jolene said, "That was really nice of you."

Sterling waved a hand. "Oh, please. It's nothing. I heard about what happened to her on the news. That can't be easy on their family."

Once they received their matcha lattes, Jolene said, "I saw a table outside. Want to grab it?"

Sterling glanced out the front window and spotted it. "Looks private enough. That should do."

They sat across from each other at the iron table. Sterling's long legs felt crunched beneath it, but he paid no mind to his comfort. He had Jolene right where he wanted her, and from what he could tell, Hematite hadn't gotten to her yet.

Sterling pulled out his cell phone as Jolene took a sip of her latte.

He opened up the video he'd downloaded of the security camera footage with her, turned his phone so it faced her, and then hit play. In the video, Jolene stumbled in front of Le Petit Chateau and slumped against the window. Lightning zapped around her body like a coil before disappearing as quickly as it'd appeared. Her palm ran down the window, smearing blood along the glass, but when she checked her hand, there were no scars or scratches. Under her breath, she cursed.

Her stomach churned as she processed the footage. Part of her wanted to deny it was her, a kneejerk reaction caused by a lack of memory from that night and a need to protect her reputation. Another part of her knew it was true based on the blood she'd wiped onto her towels, but she was still too stunned by the video to put all the pieces together. The lightning made no sense. She had so many questions, but she felt intelligible when the first one that tumbled out of her mouth was, "You own Le Petit Chateau?"

Because God forbid anyone else, like someone she didn't know or trust, had this footage. At least it was just Sterling.

"As of recently, yes. I bought it after the fire to help them rebuild and renovate." He also bought it to help conceal funds, much like Reiji had at South Main Burgers, but that detail was unimportant to Jolene and, thus, omitted.

"That's not my blood." She showed him her scarless palm. "And unfortunately, I have no memory of this. I'm sorry."

"You've no need to apologize. And if it makes you feel better, we're positive it's from an animal, not a human."

"I'm a vegetarian, so only a little better, I guess."

"Then we can only assume you did it in self-defense. But the blood isn't what piqued my interest. It was the lightning around you. Do you know how you did that?"

She shook her head. "No clue."

"Remembering your parents from the few times I met them as a child when they'd pick your brother up from his piano lessons, they were fairly strait-laced, correct?"

"Yeah, why? What are you getting at?"

"Did you happen to attend a performance at the Riverpeak Theater this spring?"

She leaned forward on her elbows, her torso hovering above her drink. "That's when this started. I was at the viewing that got busted by the cops after someone pulled a fire alarm. Do you know what happened?"

"The Chief of Police is an old friend of my father's. He's like an uncle to me, so he told me everything." Sterling frowned. "I'm afraid to say you were drugged, Ms. Gautier."

Normally, she'd correct him with a, "Just Jolene is fine," but the words felt stuck in her throat as she processed. Instead, she stuttered. "W-What?"

"The beer was spiked with a stronger version of the methamphetamines responsible for Hematite's immortality and Brick Beast's super strength. They falsely accused a colleague of mine, but thankfully they dropped his charges after quickly seeing he wasn't behind it." Sterling spoke with such confidence that no one could tell he'd told a necessary lie. "Unfortunately, the ones responsible are still on the run, but I believe your spiked drink granted you abilities in the same vein as our local vigilantes."

Jolene scoffed and leaned back in her chair, processing the information. "Wait, wait, hold on a second. You're saying," she paused, looking for the right word, and then said, "that I have superpowers?"

"You could call them that, sure. Perhaps you're exhibiting your power in your sleep."

"You think that's how I killed that animal?"

"That is exactly what I think."

Jolene reached for her matcha and took a sip, savoring the earthy tea leaves against the sweet and creamy flavors of the vanilla syrup and oat milk. It slowly provided a reprieve from the lingering headache she'd had for the last few days. While matcha still had caffeine, it didn't have nearly as much as coffee did.

"You're not shitting me with the superpower thing?"

"Do I look like the type of person who would?"

Jolene leaned in again, holding on to her matcha on the table with both hands. The cold plastic brought relief to her hands, always at work and now enjoying a rest against the gradually melting ice. She studied his smirking face, trying to get a better read on him. Despite how sharply dressed he was in his suit and tie, and how his hair was perfectly slicked back with pomade, there was a wickedness behind his gray eyes that hinted he wasn't as serious as he seemed.

It captivated Jolene, curious to see what this gray and silver man's true colors were once she peeled back his layers. When she first saw Sterling, she thought he was a blank canvas. Now, she saw him as the completed painting that he was, covered by a white cloth to not yet unveil the masterpiece beneath.

"No, you don't look like the type to," Jolene said, "but there's something behind that suit that I'm not so sure about."

"Oh, come on, Ms. Gautier. You knew my family, so this should come as no surprise."

"Just Jolene," she said. "Just Jolene is fine."

"If it pleases you, just Jolene it is, then. But, to your point, we're all multifaceted."

Jolene nodded, sensing a secret. "Right. That we are."

"As far as your powers are concerned, I can recommend my doctor. Potter Laboratories have been increasingly helpful in understanding our abilities, and can help you discover yours and how to control it as well."

There the secret was. "*Our* abilities?"

"Ah, I've said too much," Sterling said with a smile beautiful enough to grace a magazine cover. "What is it my associate always says?" His finger tapped against the table as he contemplated it. "*Shouganai*. It can't be helped."

"Noah Sato?"

"Yes, him. Those of us who have gained abilities have come together, so to speak, since the musical. We'd like answers just as much as Hematite does, but it appears he's uninterested in forming a team."

Jolene frowned. "That's too bad. I'm sure everyone just wants to know what's going on with them."

"I'm glad you understand. Dr. Potter tells me he's been helping Hematite for years now, so we should all be in good hands."

"Yeah, give him my info. I'd love to sort this out."

"More than happy to help an old friend. How have you been, anyway? It's been years."

"Great, besides all this. Living the literal dream. I work, like, all the time, but I love it so much."

"That's good. You left Riverpeak for a few years, didn't you? I saw you were working out of Denver when I was browsing your portfolio."

Jolene swallowed her initial thought with another sip of matcha. She didn't care to talk about the shop in Denver. "Yeah, but I'm glad I have my own place now."

"That's the best way to do it if you ask me. Then you only have to answer to yourself. I'm happy for you."

"Thanks. Let me guess: you took over the family business? Your dad owned a bunch of restaurants, right?"

"He did, and you would be correct. I'd been trained for it since I was a child. That's why my mother homeschooled me."

"Oh, shit. Well, at least you got to do some extracurriculars. My brother used to love getting to talk to you after his lessons and at concerts. I did, too."

"Oh?"

She blushed. "Can I admit something kind of embarrassing?"

Sterling leaned back in his chair. He propped his ankle up on his thigh and, without missing a beat, said, "I would love it if you did."

"You may have been my first crush. So yeah, I enjoyed getting to see you play at my brother's piano recitals and concerts."

A faint blush dusted his cheeks as his heart all but skipped a beat, but his eyes never left hers. "That is not what I was expecting."

"I mean, you played a killer sonata, and you just looked so handsome in your suits and your hair slicked back." She took another sip of her drink, halfway through it now. "You still do, not gonna lie."

Through his laugh, that deep one that she recognized from when she first spotted him, he said, "Well, I suppose we're even now for earlier."

Jolene was convinced she was the same color as her hair. "I guess so. Though, now that I know it's just you and not some random creep, you're welcome to comment on my beauty again."

With a raised brow, he said, "Is that so?"

"You *did* say I wasn't short on it."

"And I meant it. Though I'm not sure you'd want an old geezer hitting on you."

She stifled a laugh. "Oh, please. If you're my brother's age, that would make you ... what, thirty-three?"

"That's correct."

"I told you, you're rockin' the silver fox thing." She cracked her neck.

"That sounded productive."

"Oh, yeah. I often find myself sitting like a shrimp thanks to work."

He chuckled. "That's one way to put it. Shall I walk you back?"

She nodded in affirmation, but as they stood from their chairs, a part of her didn't want their conversation to ever end.

CHAPTER 7

When Jolene returned home that night, she nestled on the couch, ready to draw as she watched anime and enjoyed a cup of tea. Before she opened up Adobe Illustrator, she tapped on the Instagram icon with her stylus and, ignoring the countless notifications, went to her profile. As she selected her latest post, Jolene stared at its caption. The orange fox emoji popped against the white screen, reminding her of Noah Sato and her secret Hematite hotline code.

While the vigilante's insights might be beneficial, she wasn't sure if working with Hematite would be in her best interest given how chaotic Riverpeak was; the whole town was on edge since the Riverpeak Theater incident. Sterling seemed to have all the answers she needed, so she tapped Edit, backspaced on the fox, and then hit Save.

If he'd already seen it, she thought, *I could always just say it was a false alarm.*

It wouldn't entirely be a lie, and Hematite had also said to use it if she saw Noah—not if she had any other problems.

She returned to sketching, letting a reality show on Netflix keep her company. Once she was satisfied with her work, Jolene took a final swig of chamomile tea, letting the floral wash over her tongue. It complemented the blackberry-flavored melatonin supplements she took right after, and she hoped it would lull her to sleep quickly.

For once, it actually did.

She wasn't sure when she fell asleep, but she dreamed she was in the bathroom at her tattoo studio. She stood by the porcelain white sink and could smell the lavender from the air freshener they kept in there. When she looked down at herself, she was wearing a white dress she'd never seen before, and her hands—coated in red ink from fingertip to mid-forearm—trembled before her. Some of the ink slowly dripped into the sink from her middle fingers.

But then, Sterling materialized behind her. Instead of his usual white dress shirt, he wore all black, as if he'd just come from a funeral. He'd slicked back his hair in its usual style, and his steely eyes held a sadness she'd yet to see from him.

"Here." His voice was low. "Let me help you, darling."

When she looked back at her hands, the red ink looked richer, felt thicker, and then she realized it wasn't actually tattoo ink.

It was blood.

Sterling reached in front of her to turn on the sink. The running water drowned out the sound of blood dripping off her fingers. As Sterling pumped soap from the dispenser to wash her arms, wrapping his fingers around her forearms, he hummed. She recognized the melody as a sonata he played at a piano recital years ago, and let her head fall back into his shoulder. Sterling massaged the blood off of her hands and forearms, soothing her aching muscles in the process. He asked no questions about the blood: whose it was, how it got there, why she trembled. Instead, he simply washed it clean for her, hummed a calming melody, and then planted a soft kiss on her temple.

That prompted her to wake. She jolted up, checked her hands, and was relieved to find them clean. As she caught her breath, her fingers reached up to her temple, where Sterling kissed her in her dream. She struggled to make sense of what everything meant, but as she got out of bed and undressed, she saw her tattoo of The Star tarot card on her thigh.

"Was this your doing?" Jolene felt ridiculous once the words left her mouth. "Now I'm talking to myself and using my tattoos as a proxy. Fucking great."

As she washed her face, she let her mind run. *Stella,* she thought. *I need to talk to Stella. She always knows what to do in situations like this.*

Her morning routine felt like a blur: she put on some plaid capris and an anime T-shirt, pack her tablet in her bag, and then head out to Jefferson's Coffee for her matcha and two coffees for Stella and Annie. The sun on her skin snapped her out of her trance, assisted by the first sip of caffeine that she snuck while balancing the tray. Summer was officially underway, and Colorado lived up to its colorful nickname in the way the wildflowers blossomed wherever they could and the mountains decorated the clear blue sky with splotches of green and brown.

When Jolene walked into her studio, to her delight and relief, Stella was already there. Jolene left the drink tray on the counter, then tossed her bag in its usual spot in her room before lengthening her stride to head back to the main floor.

Stella, tying her long, brown waves into a ponytail, noticed. "Looks like someone's walking with purpose today."

"Can I talk to you? Like, about something personal I've got going on?"

"You know I'm always here for girl talk. My next client isn't due for another hour. What's up?"

They both grabbed their drinks from the tray. "So you know how I told you I haven't been getting any sleep?"

"Yeah. Have a breakthrough?"

"Yes and no. I'm not sure how this correlates, but it somehow does. Sterling Harrison, that guy that came in here the other day?" She recounted the security camera footage he showed her as she traced her finger around the edge of the plastic cup, feeling the condensation trail behind on her skin. "It was seriously so weird."

"Girl, if you have rabies, I swear to fuckin' God."

"I don't have rabies. Holy shit, do I have rabies?"

"Did Sterling tell you what he thought it was?"

Jolene wasn't sure how much to tell Stella. She trusted her friend, but Sterling and Noah's stories weren't hers to tell. Besides, if Hematite worked alone, the last thing she wanted was for Stella to get the wrong idea—either that Jolene herself was a vigilante or an enemy of one—when they were nothing more than a group of people trying to make sense of who or what they were.

So, all she said was, "He thinks it could have been something at the theater. We're looking into it together."

"Together, huh?" Stella wagged her eyebrows.

"Yeah. I got his number."

"He's that rich guy we saw walking down the street, right? The hot one?"

Jolene fought it, but still smirked. "Yeah, the hot one."

"If you don't report back, then I swear!"

"Only if I don't have rabies. Speaking of him—"

Stella clutched her chest. "Oh my God, for a second there, I thought you were about to be like, 'Speaking of rabies.'"

Jolene snorted. "Fuck, no!"

"Okay, circling back to rich, hot guy."

"Yes. Him. I had a funky ass dream with him last night. You're into interpretation and all that, yeah?"

"Ooh, yeah. Spill."

As Jolene recounted her dream, Stella listened intently. Jolene stared at her friend when she finished, looking for clues on Stella's pensive face. "Well?"

"You know what I think it means?"

"What?"

"It's one of three things." Stella held up a finger for each point she made as she spoke. "One: you feel guilty about whatever wildlife you killed. Two: you've been single too long, and this guy is hot as fuck, so, bonk, go to horny jail. Or, three: both."

Jolene suspected Stella may have been right, but before she could reply, the door chimed as Jolene's first client for the day came in.

———

When Sterling entered the studio that afternoon, the door chiming above him, Jolene was cross-legged in the chair behind the counter. She looked up from her tablet, the light hitting her face and making her pink hair look a shade softer, and smiled at him just as brightly as the sun streaming in from outside. The green-colored kanji on her shirt made her eyes pop.

"Sterling like the silver! What brings you back?"

He half-smiled at her, hoping to push the feelings that confused him down. "I wanted to apologize again for getting off on the wrong foot the other day." Sterling slid an iced matcha latte across the counter. "With vanilla and oat milk, if I remembered correctly?"

"You did." Her smile never left her face as she accepted the latte. He held his own in his hands, a duplicate of her order, as he noticed she had dimples when she smiled. "Thanks, that was really thoughtful of you."

"A pleasure." He wasn't sure what to say. His mind raced: *why am I really here? What am I doing, standing here in her tattoo shop without a plan other than to buy her forgiveness?*

Luckily for him, he didn't need to overthink for much longer.

"Say, my client that just left was getting a *Boku no Hero* tattoo, and it made me think of everything going on. Is there any way to stop these abilities or whatever?"

Sterling shook his head. "Not that I know of. What's *Boku no Hero*?"

"An anime. I'll rewatch it with you if you ever want to get caught up, though you don't strike me as the kinda guy to watch much TV. Anyway, I was hoping we could chat again. I was going to text you when I got home later today."

"Great minds think alike, then."

She checked her watch. "My next client won't be here for another hour. Can we talk outside?"

"Of course."

"Come on, we'll go out back." Making small talk along the way, she asked, "You said you don't really play piano much anymore, but what else have you been up to?"

"An associate of mine is also a boxing coach on the side, so I've been taking lessons with him."

"Ooh, fun! I need to get out more."

"That makes two of us." The breeze cooled their faces as they stepped out back, summer rolling in from the hills. They both rested against the brick back wall, standing shoulder-to-shoulder as Jolene took a deep breath in. Sterling reached into his pocket and grabbed a carton of cigarettes. "Do you smoke?"

"Eh, I picked it up when I was living in Denver, but I'm trying to quit. Stella made it a New Year's Resolution a few months ago and I've been following along in solidarity."

Sterling pocketed them. "Then I'll refrain out of respect."

"No biggie either way, but thanks. So, I've been thinking about what my powers might be. I'm really struggling to connect all the dots, though. Did that doctor ever get back to you?"

"I followed up with him this morning. He can be elusive."

"You mentioned. So, are you in the same predicament as me, or do you know what your powers are?"

Sterling nodded. "I can heal myself."

"Huh. That's useful. How'd you figure that out?"

"Boxing with Anthony. I broke my shoulder and then I unbroke it. I'm not sure that's a word, but you get my drift."

She chuckled. "Yeah, I got you. Nifty."

He thought about telling her about the rest, about his immortality and that he could break bones, too, but decided against it. *Too much at once may scare her,* he thought, and he needed to bring her closer so he wouldn't lose her to Hematite's whims. From what he'd seen on security cameras and heard from his crews on the street, Hematite was also keeping an eye out for additional super-powered people while on patrol. While Hematite wasn't actively looking, it was on his radar, and Sterling fully intended to keep both himself and Jolene off it.

Before he could reply, she said, "I wonder if mine has something to do with sleep, since I've been struggling with that."

"There's a theory that my doctor has been floating around. I'm not sure what I think of it, but if he's on to something, it could give you a springboard to jump off of until he's ready for you. I'm not sure what the hell his holdup is, but that's beside the point."

Jolene looked up at him and focused on his expression. He was looking at her with a gentleness in his eyes that, at first glance, didn't suit his sharp, monotone features. "What's the theory?"

"That the power we get is something we need. Other than a decent night's rest, is there anything you've been needing? Or perhaps something you'd even find useful in your day-to-day life?"

"Hmm." Her bottom lip found its way between her teeth as she thought it over. "Less back pain, maybe." They laughed together. "That's just it, though," she continued. "I sort of have everything I need, beyond some materialistic stuff and an occasional loneliness that creeps up when my mom pesters me for not having dated anyone in a while."

"Are you lonely? Forgive me, that may be too personal."

She shrugged. "You're fine. I brought it up, after all. I am, but I'm also not if that makes sense. God, that sounds so fucking stupid now that I say it out loud." She kicked a pebble aside. "To clarify: I feel such a deep camaraderie with my friends, so I'm not *lonely* lonely. And if I really want to feel connected, my Instagram notifications are blowing up at any given moment. But I'm still sleeping alone at the end of the night, you know?"

"I do know, yes." Sterling licked his lips. "We have that in common, it would seem."

"Oh, come on. A guy like you doesn't have a beautiful woman or a handsome man warming your bed?"

He shook his head. "No. Work beckons too much. I'm sure you understand."

"We're cut from the same cloth, I guess."

"Perhaps we should share a bed some night. Before you look at me like that, I mean so I could follow you. See where you go and what leads to the blood."

"If this was all some elaborate ruse to ask me out, you could have just stuck to the matcha."

He laughed, the most genuinely she'd heard. It was a rich sound that echoed through her ears and rumbled through her chest. "If working together helps us feel less lonely, then I suppose that is an added benefit." The smile he gave her was so soft, a flash of vulnerability. "We're so different and yet, the same. However, I also don't want to make you uncomfortable, either. I'm sure there are other ways we can help each other."

"Don't get me wrong! I actually think it's a good idea. It's just fun to flirt with you."

"And just when I thought I'd heard it all, I'd say that's a first."

She couldn't help her smile, just like she couldn't deny the excitement that bloomed through her chest. "Come over tonight?"

"Sure. Strictly professional, I promise."

———

As Sterling lay in Jolene's bed, he found it more complicated than he initially thought to keep his promise. From their proximity, he could smell the mint toothpaste on her breath and her body wash that she'd used in the shower before he arrived. The notes of lavender and vanilla tickled his nose with every breath he took, the soft fragrance suiting her flowery and sweet personality.

Getting here had been simple enough. They'd brushed their teeth together, standing side by side in relative silence, and they'd changed into their pajamas separately. But with Jolene's pink hair splayed around her like a halo, bringing her scent closer to him, he thought he was going to implode.

That was until Jolene roused from the bed. She stumbled out, her steps sluggish but quick. Sterling kept up with her easily thanks to his long stride, and he filmed her once she made her way out of her front door. Jolene hobbled towards the woods that surrounded Constance's Pond, tucked a little ways away behind her apartment.

When they approached a wild boar—a rare sight in Colorado—it charged for Jolene, spooked by her arrival. As it did, blue and white lightning emerged from Jolene's skin, crackling with warmth and then searing the boar. The animal fell with a high-pitched squeal, collapsing on its side. Its fur was charred, and the smell of its roasted skin permeated the air.

That must have been where the blood came from that night.

Sterling debated waking her. He reached out, but just as his fingers hovered over her shoulder, he withdrew. Should she be in the midst of using her power, he wasn't sure what the repercussions of interrupting her sleepwalking may be.

He wondered what would happen to any of them if they were intercepted in the middle of using their ability, if anything at all. Every time he thought he had all the answers, more questions came to him, and everything moved too slowly for his liking, no matter how much he pushed Dr. Potter to work faster.

He wanted more—*needed* more. But halfway down Main Street, Jolene woke with a sharp gasp and an exclamation of a curse, interrupting his train of thought.

Sterling rushed to her side, having been only a few paces back. Jolene jumped but soon settled at his touch on her back, and she leaned into Sterling once she realized it was just him. The action of her resting her head against his chest made his body physically ache, a sensation he could not name, and he realized her shampoo must have matched the scent of her body wash as the lavender smell came over him once more.

"Where am I?"

"It's okay," Sterling said. "I got you, Jolene. You're on Main Street in Riverpeak."

Jolene looked at her hands, where a few splatters of blood dotted her palms. "Again?"

"You began sleepwalking and went into the woods. When you spooked a boar, it charged, and you summoned some sort of electricity."

"Fuck."

"Let's get you back to bed. No wonder you're so tired."

Jolene nodded. When she didn't pull away from him, Sterling moved his hand on her back so he could wrap his arm around her shoulders. It was then, as they walked home in their pajamas, that he realized she was cold, so he squeezed her shoulders to pull her tighter into his side.

"Say, Sterling?"

"Yes?"

"Can you promise me something?"

Sterling looked at her, their eyes meeting, and he wanted nothing more than to freeze this moment. "If it pleases you."

"It would please me to not hurt anyone or anything else. So, if I get up again tonight, wake me up."

"What if it hurts you?"

"Then it does. But I can't stomach this."

They finished the walk back to her apartment in comfortable silence. Upon their return, Sterling only pulled away from her to grab a washcloth from her bathroom, which he dampened.

"For your hands. Come."

Jolene stood before him and extended her arms to him, too tired to bite back with a flirtatious remark. He missed her banter but understood her exhaustion to his core, which is why he found himself cleaning the blood off her hands for her. When he was done and she thanked him, he held her hands for a moment too long before he finally let them fall.

When they returned to her bed, Sterling did not sleep—but Jolene did not wake again.

CHAPTER 8

As Sterling scoped out Dr. Potter's stark white and silver office, ensuring everything was still in its proper place, he sat in the spare chair and set his briefcase on the desk. He'd been checking in more frequently now—only partially because of his new abilities. Dr. Potter was none the wiser, but Sterling knew Noah didn't trust him and suspected he had his secrets. These days, with how long it was taking to prepare for Jolene's appointment and his lies about knowing of an additional super-powered person, Sterling didn't trust the doctor either.

And after all, his father did always tell him to keep his friends close, but enemies closer.

"Let me ask you, Dr. Potter," Sterling said as he reclined in the chair. "Is it possible, in your opinion, for one to gain multiple powers?"

"Of course. Haven't you and Anthony?"

"Perhaps I need to be more clear. If Anthony or I were to take another dose blended with a super-powered's DNA, what would happen then?"

"Admittedly, I'm not sure."

Sterling leaned forward, propping an elbow on the desk beside them. The steel felt cool, even through his shirt and sport coat sleeves. "I'd love to find out, wouldn't you?"

Dr. Potter removed his glasses to clean the lenses. "The possibility had yet to cross my mind."

Sterling unlatched the buckles on his briefcase. "Well, we're in luck. I've asked Noah and Amy to identify any potential super-powered residents using the credit card information they got at the bar."

"I thought Ms. Brewer was fired from her family business?"

"Oh, please. You underestimate those two. I'm just surprised she hasn't killed her mother yet." Sterling pulled out a vial wrapped in bubble wrap. He peeled the tape holding the ends together off with his thumb and then handed it to Dr. Potter. "Let me know what you find. After a bit of surveillance, we suspect this should grant enhanced reflexes."

"I won't ask how you got their blood sample." Dr. Potter frowned as he prepared a drop for the examination.

Sterling chuckled in his throat. "That's probably for the best."

As Dr. Potter went to work, Sterling closed his briefcase and checked his phone. There was a text from Anthony.

> ANTHONY: Miller will be out of commission for two months, but I doubt she'll step foot in my gym again. But you won't have to worry about her for a while.

> STERLING Broken wrist?

> ANTHONY: She has no idea it was you. She thinks she tweaked it when she punched the bag.

> STERLING: Excellent.

He pocketed his phone as Dr. Potter announced the new dosage was ready. They said nothing as Sterling took the sample and drank it down, much the same as the first time he'd done this. He waited for the feeling of pins and needles to wash over him, but it never came.

Sterling said, "Well, the good news is that I can still speak this time."

"You're not feeling numb?"

"No, not numb." On the contrary, he felt the opposite of numbness. His whole body felt like it was actively being electrocuted by a million small sparks, shooting off at different times. His eye twitched, then his lip, followed by his nose, then all ten fingers in random order.

"Are you alright?"

"Spasming."

"Ah, here." Dr. Potter reached up into a cabinet overhead and grabbed something out of it. He stood, crossing the room to grab an unused water bottle. The doctor handed the bottle and two pills to Sterling, who managed it down with shaky hands. By some miracle, he managed to not spill water all over himself, though some did splash over his shoulder. The twitching slowed almost instantly until his body returned to normal.

"Much better. Thank you."

"Of course. Now here."

Before Sterling could register anything, he saw another bottle hurling at his face. He snapped his hand up so quickly that his arm looked like a blur to catch the empty water bottle, which crushed in Sterling's hand. He stared at the bottle in his hands and set it down on the table, annoyed by the sound of crunching plastic, but too thrilled by the results to let it bother him. "Brilliant."

———

Over the weeks, Sterling added some extra steps to his usual routine. Typically, he'd head straight to either Potter Laboratories or Noah's secret house after checking on one of his properties—a restaurant inherited from his father, the police force he'd earned himself, or rental properties passed on from Reiji Sato—in order to balance both sides of his business. But now, he allowed himself to indulge in a small pleasure: ordering two matcha lattes and bringing them by the tattoo studio for Jolene.

Even though his intention was to lure her to his side and find out what her power was, he found himself drawn in to her. Something about the way she smiled at him like he was just a normal man warmed him at his core. If he was the moon, she was the sun, leaving him to forever chase her in her orbit.

As he delivered her drink, she smiled and set her tablet down. "You are always just in time for a mid-afternoon pick-me-up."

"You know, I'm not sure if you're more excited to see me or the matcha."

As she leaned over, bringing herself closer to him, a mischievous smirk graced her face. "It's a really close call."

Matching her energy, he propped his elbows on the counter, leaning forward so their faces were only mere inches apart. Her lavender scent wrapped around him like a warm hug. "Close call suggests that one of us has a leg up. Dare I ask if I do?"

From this proximity, he could see the glimmer in her green eyes, bordering on hazel. "I would have less tea if it wasn't for you, so I'd say you're in the lead. But only by a hair."

He cocked a thick, dark eyebrow. Unlike the hair on his scalp, those were still black. "Only a hair?"

"One singular, silver strand, yes."

Sterling's smile revealed his perfect teeth. He ran his tongue over one of his canines. "Because it's from you, I'll take it as a compliment."

"As you should."

As Jolene grabbed her tablet again, the door chimed behind Sterling, who looked over his shoulder to see the new arrival. A slender brunette with spiked hair walked in, wearing a worn theme park sweatshirt that mismatched his cargo shorts and made Sterling wrinkle his nose in disapproval. As the brunette approached the counter, Sterling didn't budge, but let him stand next to him. This man was beneath him, after all, and not worth moving for.

Jolene spoke with her best customer service tone. "Hi! How can I help you?"

"I have an appointment with Stella. Name's Josh."

Jolene grabbed her tablet and switched the application open on the screen. With a few taps, she said, "Alright, I've got you checked in. She should be out shortly. We'll just need you to sign the waiver on the iPad by the couch. Feel free to take a seat."

Josh smiled; something about it seemed disingenuous. "Thanks." Sterling anticipated that Josh would go sit on the couch behind them after he tapped away on the iPad, but he returned to the counter and asked, "What's with all the pink?"

Jolene didn't look up from her tablet as she answered. "It's my favorite color."

"Who'd have guessed?"

Sterling rolled his eyes at the awkward attempt at small talk and took a sip of his own matcha, the condensation building up on his black leather gloves. While he'd always just ordered two of the same drink, it was a bit too sweet for his liking. But it reminded him of the woman before him, and the idea of the flavor on her lips made it even more appealing.

He stopped himself. *There was no time for thoughts like that.*

Josh's pestering Jolene snapped Sterling out of it.

"So, what are you drawing?"

"Oh, just a piece for a client coming in later this week while I wait for today's to show up. I like to stay ahead."

"So cool. And what's this?" Josh reached for her drink, but Sterling smacked Josh's hand away. "Whoa. Sorry."

Sterling said nothing. He didn't even look at Josh; the man wasn't worth his effort. To his surprise, when he looked at Jolene, she was biting back a laugh.

"Josh?" Stella peeked around the partition wall next to Jolene. "Hi, I'm Stella! Come on back this way."

Once Josh retreated with Stella, who held some stencils in her hands, Jolene sighed. Her shoulders slumped forward, but then she straightened her posture. Sterling heard her neck crack.

Sterling asked, "Shall I stay?"

"Oh, you don't have to. I'm sure you have better shit to do."

"Nothing urgent today, actually."

She smiled. "There's a second stool back here if you'd like to play shopkeeper for the day."

He stepped behind the counter, dress shoes clicking against the floor. When he slid onto the stool next to her, he perched his feet up on the lower ring supporting the legs, feeling too tall for the seat but grateful for the proximity to her. Sterling couldn't put a finger on why, but a part of him felt a visceral need to keep Jolene safe.

She leaned over to him. He felt her cool breath on his ear, smelling sweet and earthy from her drink. He wanted to lean in closer but fought against the urge as she whispered, "We have a code. If Stella says she's stepping out for a smoke break, that means he's gotta go."

"Understood." He looked at the tablet. "Beautiful, as always. You'll have to let me know which shows I need to watch to fully appreciate your work."

"Thanks. But this one's an original, actually! I love getting to make my own magical girls."

"An associate of mine has a young niece. The same one that's a boxing coach. Perhaps I'll commission something on his behalf one of these days."

"Hell yeah! We can work something out." She looked up at him and smiled. There was a warmth behind her eyes that Sterling wanted to wrap himself in. Her voice dropped to a whisper again. "Thank you for staying, by the way. Fair warning: this could be a few hours. I think he's getting a big piece."

"Well then, I suppose I'll be here for the next few hours." He nudged her shoulder with his. "Please don't let my career fool you. While it certainly keeps me on my toes, I will always have time for you, Jolene."

With a trace amount of sarcasm, she asked, "You say that to everyone?"

"No. Just you."

Some of Jolene's hair fell in front of her face. Sterling tucked the pink strands back behind her ear before she could even lift a finger, acting on instinct.

Jolene smiled. "What makes me so special?"

Sterling thought about it for a moment, seeking the answers in her eyes. After a minute or two, he said, "There are parts of myself that I wish I had more time for, and I see those parts of myself in you."

That, at least, was true. Jolene almost perfectly balanced her creativity with an entrepreneurial spirit. At times, Sterling missed the days when his biggest worry was how much time he'd have to play piano—but his life hadn't been that simple in decades.

She glanced down, trying yet failing to hide her brush. "You know, it takes a lot to get me flustered."

"If it's unwelcome, say the word."

"No, no, it's fine. We may have had a shaky start, but you've grown on me, Ster. Can I call you Ster? Like a nickname?"

"If it pleases you."

They spent the next hour and a half in relative silence: her drawing, him watching, both of them eavesdropping on Stella's conversation with Josh. Jolene had lowered the Japanese city pop playing overhead to better hear. There was a comfort in having Sterling there, Jolene realized, especially knowing he had fast reflexes. She'd seen as much from the way he'd smacked Josh's hand away before she even realized he was reaching for her drink.

As she put the finishing touches on her drawing, she said, "You know, not a lot of people would stick around like this."

"Does this happen often?"

Jolene shook her head. "Thankfully, no. Once every blue moon. Say, what are you doing over the next few days? Are you free at all?"

"I can be for you."

Jolene felt the heat rush to her cheeks again, her face now matching her hair. "Suave, aren't we?"

"My answer remains unchanged."

She licked her lips as she looked him up and down, now unafraid of him noticing that she was checking him out. "I was hoping we could talk more about my predicament. We still aren't sure what I can do, and I wish I knew right about now."

"Naturally. When are you available?"

"I don't have any clients on Tuesday."

"Tuesday it is. I'll text you my address. We'll be able to speak freely there. My doctor said he'll let me know when he's ready for you, by the way. Should be soon. I've put the pressure on him."

"Perfect."

Stella's voice interrupted them, announcing a quick cigarette break.

"Oh, shit. Just give me a sec. I gotta deal with this."

Jolene stepped into Stella's workspace from around the corner. Sterling watched from the partition wall behind the desk, leaning against it with his arms crossed. He watched as Jolene applied some latex gloves and then wiped the excess ink from Josh's thigh, where Stella had tattooed the outline of a horse next to a pre-existing lion. It wasn't until she wrapped it in plastic that Josh sensed something was off.

"Why are you wrapping it? Stella said she was just grabbing a cigarette."

"You need to leave."

Josh's face squished together in his confusion. "What? Why?"

"Because we don't let people talk to us like that here." Jolene stood and looked down at him, a bundle of well-controlled pink rage with her arms crossed just beneath her chest. "You've made both of us uncomfortable. Now go."

"But I'm in the middle of my tattoo."

"You think I care?"

Sterling debated stepping in, but Jolene had a handle on it. Her voice never wavered, nor did her conviction. Given the spiked beer at the theater had worked on her, he wasn't surprised: after all, one needed extreme physical and mental fortitude for it to succeed.

"Can we at least finish my piece?"

"No. Grab your shit and get out of my studio. I've got security cameras outside and in the lobby, so don't even think about pulling any shit, either."

Josh sighed as he stood. "Fine." He patted his pockets to ensure he still had his wallet and began to walk out. He slowed once he reached Sterling and turned back to Jolene. "Do I at least get my deposit back?"

Her eyes narrowed. "What do you think?"

Before Josh could say much else, Sterling said, "I'd suggest you quit while you're ahead, but that would imply you've been ahead at all."

Josh scowled as he departed. He swung the front door open, hoping it would slam behind him, but the automatic closer slowed the door's return to the frame.

"Thanks for the backup," Jolene said, already moving her way to the back door to let Stella back in. "I swear, some guys don't listen to women until another man repeats what we've said."

"An unfortunate truth. My mother struggled with the same when my father passed. It's why I inherited the business as young as I did."

"They raised you well." She winked at him as she opened the door, letting Stella back inside.

Sterling asked, "Do either of you need anything?"

Before Jolene answered, she looked at Stella, who said, "I'll be okay. Thanks, both of you."

Jolene nodded and approached Sterling. Despite being more than half a foot taller than her, she took him off guard when she stood on her tiptoes, grabbed him by the collar, and planted her lips on his cheek. "Tuesday?"

Sterling nodded, hoping his cheeks didn't look as warm as they felt. "Tuesday. Door code's 1-1-0-7." Listening to his instincts once more, his hands cradled her face as he pulled her in closer once more, leaving a kiss on her forehead. "Should anything happen in the meantime—"

"Call you, I know."

Sterling smiled as he left, departing with a final wave above his head. He was pulled off of cloud nine when he spotted Josh ambling down the sidewalk. Sterling had planned to follow the man home and luckily, the fool had walked, making it easier for Sterling to blend in. After he missed his shot at Brad Evans and Shawn Jameson last year, he'd been working on his aim but still preferred to not be in a moving vehicle.

As they neared an alley, Sterling picked up his pace—easy to do with a stride as long as his—so he could catch up. Before Josh could register what happened, Sterling placed a gloved hand on his shoulder to force Josh down the alleyway. Before he even looked him in the eyes, Sterling shoved Joshua against the brick wall.

"You're the guy from the tattoo shop."

Sterling cut straight to the point. "Do you always speak to women like that?"

"Oh, come on. You followed me all the way here just to talk about this?"

"No, of course not," Sterling said. "I came to kill you for it. Men like you shouldn't exist, let alone procreate. I fear what may become of our society so long as people like you roam the earth."

Sterling focused on Josh's neck, and with a snap, Josh crumpled to the ground. Taking a last sip of his matcha, Sterling left the alleyway and went home.

CHAPTER 9

As Jolene returned to the front desk, Stella's heels clacked with each step. Stella smirked as she placed her hands on her hips, standing next to Jolene in front of the partition wall. "Okay, so we're kissing each other now? What did I miss?"

"Not gonna lie. I wasn't sure how he was going to react to that." It was a gamble, but it had paid off as far as she was concerned. The way Sterling's long fingers curled around her face as he'd placed a gentle kiss on her forehead was forever etched into her memory.

"Really, now?"

With a lopsided grin, Jolene said, "Come on, Stella. Can you blame me for shooting my shot?"

"Not at all." Stella giggled. "Isn't the Harrison family loaded, too?"

"Yeah, he comes from old money. But I could give a shit about that. He's a total gentleman and super hot. Plus, he's been helping me with my sleeping problem."

Stella cocked an eyebrow, her tone teasing. "Oh?"

"Not like that, for fuck's sake."

"Girl, you had me fooled."

"I mean, like I said, he *is* super hot, so I wouldn't mind if it takes that turn."

She cackled. "Listen, whatever you do on Tuesday, just take it slow. Some people are great about hiding their crazy."

Jolene shrugged a shoulder. "For sure, but I knew Sterling when we were kids. He's got good roots. What's the worst that could happen?"

———

As Jolene stared at Sterling's front door on Tuesday, part of her admittedly felt nervous. While her family had always done well, this neighborhood in Riverpeak was known for affluence. She saw the former police chief, Eliza Daniels, pulling into her driveway on her way home from the grocery store on the way up to the front steps from Sterling's long driveway. Down the street, she knew, was the Stevens' family home—tackier than the others in the row—as well as Naomi and Brad's home, which she'd visited once for a birthday party a few years back.

But Sterling's home was the nicest of the bunch. There was a subtlety to it thanks to his class, an attribute of his that leaked out into every facet of his life. His two-story home had a gray and brown-colored stone front with a dark roof, flawlessly fitting a more modern Colorado aesthetic. The front door had a keypad beneath the lock, and she remembered the code he'd told her before he left the tattoo studio the other day. She punched in the numbers 1-1-0-7 and then smiled as the door chimed. She tried the handle and found it unlocked.

As soon as she opened the door, she heard a piano playing. The grand piano was in the back corner of the room, where the stone from outside encroached on the front entryway as an accent wall. A window covered the entire back wall of the house, revealing a small, rectangular in-ground pool with a sweeping view of the Rocky Mountains.

It was the most beautiful view Jolene had seen. She couldn't help but to transfix her eyes on that as she listened to the music. Jolene felt so wrapped up in it that she hardly paid attention to the simple yet high-quality, luxurious furniture around her. She only wished that one day, she'd have a view like this to call her own, whenever she opened up her new shop. Jolene leaned against a support beam, wrapped in stone like the outside of the house and the accent wall, and zoned out with her eyes focused somewhere between Sterling and the Rockies.

As the music stopped, Sterling spoke. He wore round reading glasses, but took them off and set them down next to the sheet music. "I know you're standing there."

She smiled as she stepped forward, arms swinging by her side as she met him by the piano bench. "That was beautiful, but sounded rather melancholy."

Sterling shifted to make room for Jolene on the bench. As she sat beside him, their thighs touching through her skirt and his pants, he said, "Melancholy is a good way to put it, yes."

"I know you invited me here to talk more about my ... recent developments, but I'd like to talk about you, too."

Sterling lifted his gaze from the piano to look at her. His long, bony fingers fell from the keys and into his lap. "About me?"

"Mhm." She nudged his arm with her shoulder. "Are you feeling melancholy?"

Sterling's eyes never left her own. "More often than I'd like to admit."

"Oh. I wasn't expecting that from you."

"Yes, I suppose I do a great job hiding it. May I confide in you, Jolene?"

"Of course."

"I struggle with feeling adequate more often than not. Between you and me?" He'd posed it as a question. "I'm one of the most powerful men in Colorado. And yet, I often wonder if it's enough and if my father would be proud."

"Having big shoes to fill is never easy, but I think he would be." Unsure how he'd respond but deciding it was worth the risk, Jolene reached for his thigh. She squeezed it right above his knee as she said, "And for what it's worth, I think you're more than enough."

Sterling's cheeks flushed red. "That's very kind of you to say."

"Yeah, well, I mean it. I think you're pretty great."

"Would you believe me if I told you that was the nicest thing anyone's ever said to me?"

Her heart broke for him. It made sense—his parents groomed him to be the heir to a tycoon who died far too young, forcing Sterling to become a man far too early. "I would. But it doesn't have to stay that way, you know." The words fell from her lips, heart effectively on her sleeve now. "You've been doing so much to help me, Ster, and you've been so selfless about it. Of course, I think you're great."

"Jolene." He said her name with the weight of the world.

"Hm?"

His gaze finally broke from her eyes, darting to her lips and lingering a moment too long for her to not notice. "You are a bright spot in my life, you know that?"

The words left her speechless. Instead of responding, she examined him. His lips were slightly parted, pink like his cheeks from how she'd flustered him. The crease he usually wore between his brows faded with his softened expression, though those dark gray eyes of his—flitting between her lips and her eyes—maintained their focus. For as much as Sterling was an enigma, she was grateful he'd opened up to her and shared his inner turmoil.

Jolene realized she'd never released her grip from his thigh, so she instead reached for his forearm, where his rolled-up sleeves exposed his skin. His forearms were cold, but goosebumps didn't form on them until her fingers trailed along the inside of his arm.

Sterling said her name again, this time through gritted teeth. It almost sounded like a threat, but in a way that blew her eyes wide with excitement. "I must admit that when you touch me like that, it makes it exceedingly difficult to refrain."

She rose a dark blonde brow. "Refrain?"

"That's correct." Sterling swallowed.

"Well, whatever it is," she said with a sly smile that let him know she knew *exactly* what it was, "I wish you wouldn't refrain around me."

Her statement was a loaded gun, even more so than she realized. "Be careful what you wish for."

Sterling's hands moved from his lap to grip her face and kiss her. Jolene smiled as he did, reciprocating with fervor. Sterling's lips were soft and cautious, despite the way he clung to her. As one of his hands fell to her side, desperate to feel her beneath his palm now that he knew what her touch felt like, part of her wondered if he'd kissed anyone before in his thirty-three years of living. There was something about the way he held her with trepidation that gave her the sneaking suspicion he was inexperienced, but if he was, he was a natural.

Jolene deepened the kiss, darting her tongue out to swipe at his bottom lip, and Sterling went rigid. When she pulled away, Jolene could have sworn she heard a suppressed whine in the back of his throat, surprising her after he'd frozen. She reached up, brushing his hair out of his face; he hadn't gelled it back today. When she trailed it down his cheek, he leaned into her touch with closed eyes.

"Ster?"

"Yes?"

"Are you okay?"

When his eyes opened, they were soft. She'd never seen him look so relaxed. "Better than ever."

————

When Sterling pulled her in for another kiss, he felt as if time somehow moved even slower than before. His head swirled with confusion, at war with himself. One thing he'd always been told was he'd have plenty of time for romance once he achieved all his goals. He'd never so much as had a partner before, instead prioritizing his studies to become a successful heir. But instead of listening to the doubts swirling in his mind, he focused on what felt good: the softness of Jolene's lips, the way her touch sent a spark through his skin, her fingertips brushing against his scalp.

Sterling knew why he existed: he was the successor to his father's local empire. As such, it was no surprise that his parents ever got together in the first place. He got the sense that his mother did eventually come to feel love for his father, and his father taught him to treat women with the utmost respect, but their marriage was for one purpose and one purpose only: to produce an heir.

To produce him.

At least I was wanted, he thought. But in the process, love was the only unfamiliar territory to him. Sterling knew how to play Chopin as well as the composer himself, to manipulate a ledger, and to flay a man like a fish without killing him for the sake of extracting information.

While he was so close to Jolene that he could practically taste her, she'd said he was 'more than enough,' and it had him wondering if he really could have it all at once.

But he couldn't. He needed more power if he wanted to get Hematite out of his way and maintain his control over Riverpeak. *He needed—*

But as one of Jolene's hands rested on his thigh and her mouth warmed his own, Sterling felt completely lost, his thoughts drifting away like the wind. A chill shot up his spine, wrapping around each individual vertebrae on the way to his tight shoulders. Sterling wasn't sure how to relax his stiff muscles and kiss Jolene at the same time. As he rolled his shoulders back, his lips slowed.

Jolene pulled away again. Sterling leaned into her, letting his body act on his impulses as he captured her lips again. The new sensations almost overwhelmed him, leaving him drunk on her kiss and her touch, but he couldn't stop now that he'd begun. Sterling felt breathless as he kissed her, feeling as if he was stuck in a dream. She smiled into it, but placed a hand on his chest to stop him.

"Ster."

His eyes fluttered open. "Yes?"

"You are *so* tense. Are you sure you're okay?"

He smiled shyly. "These are uncharted waters, that's all."

"Don't take this the wrong way. When's the last time you kissed someone?"

"Approximately thirty seconds ago."

Jolene rolled her eyes. "I mean before me."

Sterling felt heat rise to his face. He didn't even know he could blush until he'd met her. "As I told you, these are uncharted waters."

"Hold on, you didn't actually answer the question." She simpered. "You just repeated yourself."

"You know, I usually don't let people make me do that."

"But I'm not *making* you repeat yourself. Is that embarrassment I smell on you?"

"*Smell?*"

"Mm, it's mixing in with your cologne somewhere between the sandalwood and citrus."

As he played along, the corner of his lips turned up into a smile. "That doesn't sound right. I'll have to inquire about a refund."

But Jolene never broke his gaze. If they were in a staring contest, she'd have won. "You're avoiding my question."

"I think I answered it already."

"Was I your first kiss?"

"That is correct. Entrepreneurship is all I've known, and I haven't had any partners before now. Probably not what you expected at our age, but I simply haven't had the time for it."

He spoke so formally that it took Jolene a moment to process his words. She blinked once, then twice, and then said, "Hey, no biggie if you're a virgin, Ster. Everyone's timeline in life is different. No judgment on my end."

"I appreciate your understanding. Hopefully, my inexperience doesn't show."

"You seemed hesitant, but otherwise, no. Something tells me you'll be a quick study."

"Oh, am I your student now?"

"Given how much you've been helping me learn about my power, I think it'd only be fair for me to return the favor."

Sterling rose a brow. "You don't owe me anything. You do know that, right?"

With a grin and a dollop of sarcasm, she said, "It's called flirting, Ster. I'm flirting with you."

Sterling nudged her long nose with his own. "It's working, but also a terrible distraction."

"You can help me after we make out a little more."

Sterling chuckled. "If it pleases you."

He wrapped his arms around her waist and pulled her closer yet, lifting her from beneath her rear to lift her into his lap. Jolene hiked her skirt up so she could comfortably wrap her legs around his hips, feet perched behind him on the piano bench he now straddled. As he leaned up to kiss her once more, one of her arms dangled lazily across his back as her other hand ran through his long hair, mussing up the silver locks.

The sensation of her nails on his scalp combined with their bodies this close made him feel dizzy. His hands ran up her back, long fingers splayed across her spine until he gripped at her shoulders. The physical need for her made his whole body ache in a way that was unfamiliar. It was what ultimately caused him to pull away from her after only a few moments—for as much as he wanted to kiss her for the rest of the day, there was work to be done.

"Shall we get to work?"

She smiled and nodded.

"Come, then." Sterling helped her off the bench and then held a hand out to her. She took it. "To my study."

CHAPTER 10

From the looks of Sterling's study upstairs, Jolene got the impression that he didn't spend a tremendous amount of time there. Dark shelves lined the white walls; one shelf acted as a desk, spanning the entire length of the room. A few plaques from his concert piano days stood proud on the shelves, alongside some books —some for business, some for pleasure, others for sheet music. She also spotted a photograph of him with his parents after a piano recital.

Now that Sterling was older, he was the spitting image of his father, though his father hadn't gone prematurely gray. They shared the same dark eyes, charming smiles, and almost gaunt cheekbones. When Sterling was a preteen like he was in the photo, he'd shared his father's black hair too, the polar opposite of his mother's sandy blonde locks. In the photo, Jolene noticed, with the way he stood between his parents—already taller than his mother at that age—and they each had an arm around him. They looked happy.

Jolene turned her gaze from the photo to the rest of the room. In the back, she noticed a balcony overlooking the pool and mountains. She said, "Your home is dreamy, by the way."

"Thank you. I grew up here, though we recently remodeled it. My mother left it to me when she moved out of town."

Jolene's gaze darted back to the picture. "Where'd she go?"

"Steamboat Springs. Mother loved nothing more than dipping in the hot springs after a day of skiing. She offered me the house since I was living in an apartment up in Denver. I'd grown tired of the commute, so I wasn't about to turn her down." As his fingers traced the desk, he said, "It's lonely since it's just me with all this space, but I'm hardly here anyhow."

"Well," she said, drawing out the vowel, "now that I know your key code, I can keep you company, so you're not so alone."

Sterling's gaze softened. "I'd hate to trouble you."

"Trouble me? Don't be ridiculous." She approached him as he turned around, the two of them only a few steps apart. "So, how can we test what my powers are?"

"I've been pondering that over the last few weeks. Other than your strange sleep patterns, have you noticed anything else? Any other symptoms, perhaps?"

"None."

"Hmm." His thumb ran across his chin as he pondered. "Then may I suggest something that may sound a bit strange?"

"Define strange."

Before he made the suggestion, Sterling leaned forward at the hips to examine the tattoos scattering her arms. His lips pursed as he did, judging by a criterion she wasn't aware of. Sterling's gaze made her feel nervous, the uncertainty of what he was looking for eating at her.

After what felt like a never-ending minute, Sterling tilted his head and looked up at Jolene like a confused puppy. "You have tattoos on your legs, too, correct?"

"Yeah, a bunch."

"May I see them up close?"

Jolene's face grew hot as she nodded and attempted to play it cool. "Yeah, sure."

And at that, he dropped to his knees so he could be eye-level with her thighs.

The sight of Sterling on his knees in front of her made her mind race to what else he could do from this position. As Sterling bunched the fabric at the hem of her maxi skirt in his lanky fingers, Jolene felt a lump form in her throat. His touch was feather light as he hiked her skirt up, and once it reached her knees, she grabbed it for him. His face was so close that she had to stop herself from thinking too perversely. But with Sterling's prominent nose barely grazing against the skin of her thighs, she almost forgot that he was doing this with a specific purpose.

Jolene struggled to swallow back her assortment of feelings: confusion, nerves, arousal. She wasn't sure what his expectations were, but based on the twinkle of wonder in his eyes, he seemed pleased enough.

"I don't know who this is supposed to be," Sterling said, pointing to the tattoo of the red Japanese thunder god, Raijin, surrounded by blue orbs of lightning. "But would you kindly focus on this for me?"

"Focus on it? How do you mean?"

"Really envision in it your mind's eye." With a grin, he said, "I have a feeling that you have quite the gift."

"Alright. Here goes nothing."

As Jolene stared at Raijin on her thigh, she cleared her throat and, unsure of what else to fixate on, she thought of the electric orb in his hand. Looking at the tattoo, she saw the orb pulse on her leg.

No, that can't be right, she thought. *That's not possible.*

A single bolt of lightning extended out of the ball of light, rippling up her thigh until neither of them could see it past her clothing. It faded after only a minute. Jolene stared at her leg, unsure of what she just witnessed and wishing she'd had a camera filming the whole thing.

Sterling broke the silence as he straightened his stance. "Well, I'll be." From the way his brows and the corners of his lips both raised, Jolene would wager he was proud, but for what exact reason, she couldn't say. The glow from the lightning reflected in his dark eyes, making them appear almost white, like shooting stars.

She looked back at her hands, watching the lightning run in a figure-eight motion between her palms. There was no shock or heat from it, but just a tingle at the center of her hands. "Is this really happening?"

"Right as rain, darling." He pulled his phone out of his pocket. "Let me see if Noah is available. You tattooed his arm, so perhaps you have some control over his ink as well."

"You think so?"

As he texted Noah, he said, "Unsure. Only one way to find out. In the meantime, I'm curious if it works on any of your other tattoos." He put his phone away and then pointed at the tattoo next to Raijin of the geisha in a floral kimono holding a katana with butterflies instead of a steel blade. "What about this one?"

Jolene spread her hands, watching the lightning stretch like a string, mesmerized by the way the blue and white glowed before ultimately bursting. The light scattered around them like tiny fragments, fluttering like butterflies.

Not like butterflies—they *were* butterflies, Jolene realized. One perched on her nose, tickling her skin, as another landed on Sterling's shoulder. Jolene looked down at her leg, watching as more of them sprung from her skin and swirled around her and Sterling in a carousel of pink, blue, and purple. Her eyes followed the butterflies as they danced around them, unsure how something so beautiful came to life with a single thought. Curious as to the full reach of the power, she willed one of them to land on Sterling's head. Ten did as she instructed, lining his head in a crown of butterflies that made her giggle.

With the softest smile she'd ever seen, he asked, "What's so funny?"

"Nothing. Just a sight I'd never thought I'd see."

Sterling reached up to his head, offering a finger for the butterflies there. Two of them fluttered over to their new perch, and as he held his hand forward, he didn't look at them. Instead, he looked straight at Jolene.

"You are magic. Don't you ever forget that."

The butterflies on his finger and head flew off, joining their brethren in circling them. The one on her nose followed as she stepped closer to him, closing the gap. There were so many butterflies now that she could no longer see the room behind him, only a swirling wall of wings and the man before her.

She had so much she wanted to say: how she'd been called many things, but never magic; how she saw him, the real him, beneath the business attire and sharp features; and how she wished this moment between them and the butterflies could last forever. Instead, all she could muster up was, "Am I dreaming?"

Sterling gently pinched her arm, not enough to hurt but enough to feel her skin against his nail. "Have you awoken?"

She laughed. "If I haven't and this is just a dream, I hope I never do." Jolene stood on her tiptoes to kiss him, not wanting to wait a moment longer to feel his lips on hers. The butterflies tightened their circle around them as they did, and only when they pulled away for a breath did they slowly dissipate into a thin wisp of smoke.

Sterling's phone ringing broke their moment. He apologized as he grabbed it from his pocket, answering the call on speaker. "Noah."

"Hey, boss man, I've been standing outside for the last five minutes. Does your doorbell not work?"

"My apologies. The keypad combination is 1-1-0-7. Help yourself in."

"My fuckin' birthday?"

"Something I could easily remember that others may not guess. Try not to let it get to your head."

"Too late," Noah said. From the other line, they could hear the keypad ding in the affirmation that he'd input the right code. "If you were in love with me, you should have said so sooner. Pretty sure Amy'll claw your eyes out and then freeze 'em if she's gotta fight you for me."

Sterling stifled a laugh. "We're in my study." And then he hung up.

Noah joined them only a minute or two later. "Good to see you again, Jolene."

"Yeah, you too. Sterling filled me in on your group, I guess. It's too bad Hematite works alone."

Noah shot Sterling a quick glance that Jolene couldn't quite iden-tify. It almost looked like apprehension. "Well," he said, switching to a smile, "at least I don't have to catch you up to speed. What's up?"

"Jolene has powers of her own," Sterling said. "She was at the theater that night." The two men exchanged another look, and Jolene wished she could get inside at least one of their heads to know what the raised brows and subtle nods meant. "We'd like to test something and require your help."

"Yeah, what's up?"

"Jolene, you know what to do."

As she looked at Noah's arm, she didn't dare close her eyes, not after the way the butterflies had blossomed from her skin earlier. If the snake and fox would do the same, she wanted to see every moment of the process. Noah's rolled-up sleeves revealed his forearms: one burned, the other tattooed. Where the snake tattoo coiled around Noah's arm, his skin raised. Scales formed, glimmering like emeralds when the overhead light caught them just right.

Noah's eyes widened as the scales on his arm lifted further, detaching from his body to form a living, breathing snake. "What the hell?"

The snake wrapped around his arm, growing in size, before it unwound and plopped onto the ground. Its body continued to sprout from Noah's arm until it was around ten feet long, its body winding as it approached Jolene. The snake's teeth stuck out and protruded from its face, looking more like the stylized version on his arm than any real, living creature.

She mentally willed the snake to stay put, and once she did, it wrapped around itself, awaiting further command. Then she focused on the next part of Noah's tattoo: the kitsune, hidden beneath the sleeve of his dress shirt.

Noah stretched his arm and, once he lowered it, pink cherry blossom petals fell from his shirt sleeve. They floated in a nonexistent wind, billowing in front of their faces. With the petals, she saw some short strands of orange. At first, she thought it might be a strand of Amy's hair, but the strand joined the others in the breeze she couldn't feel to form a fox.

"Okay, what in fresh hell is this?" Noah looked at his arm, seeing the tattoo exactly as it was, and then at the snake and fox before them. The snake hissed at the fox, baring its fangs, but before the fox could pounce, Jolene willed them away. The sakura petals picked up once more, carrying the snake and fox away in their private breeze.

Sterling just clapped his hands together. "Bravo, Jolene."

"Tattoo manipulation?" Noah whistled. "And I thought my fire was impressive."

"This is great," Jolene said, "but still doesn't explain why I'm struggling to sleep."

"Correlation doesn't always equal causation, but we can see what Dr. Potter has to say. There may be a caveat to your power that we don't know about yet."

"When can I see him?"

"As helpful as he is, he operates on his own time. Thankfully, he prioritizes my appointments, so I'll get you in under my name. Should only be a few weeks at most."

It took all her willpower to not balk. "Weeks?!"

"He must be working on something I don't yet know about, but I'm working on getting to the bottom of it. At least now you know what you're working with."

Noah pointed at them, wagging his finger from Jolene to Sterling, and then back to her. "Are you two..?"

Sterling sneered. "Is there a problem, Noah?"

"No, no, not at all. Just a little ironic based on some past conversations we've had, that's all." As Sterling continued to scowl, Noah said, "You see, Jolene, this one gave me so much shit when Amy and I got together. Glad to see you loosen him up a bit."

"Thank you, Noah, for your assistance today." Sterling forced his face to contort into a smile, though it was as clear as day that it pained him to do so. "Jolene and I will take it from here."

Noah wiggled his eyebrows. "I sure hope you do. Later."

Sterling sighed as Noah left. "I apologize on his behalf."

"Don't. My friends roast me way worse than that."

"I'm afraid in this case, Noah could quite literally roast me."

"Then consider it an excuse to invite me over more often. We could cool you off in that pool."

"I've never used it."

"Never?"

"Not since I was a child."

Jolene took his hand and wordlessly led him back downstairs. As they moved down the steps, passing family portraits, he asked, "What are you doing?"

"It's criminal that you haven't used that in God knows how many years, and we're having a beautiful summer."

"Are you even wearing a swimsuit?"

She didn't answer, but simply rounded the corner once they reached the bottom of the stairs. Jolene said nothing, just dropping his hand so she could reach for her shoes. She didn't bother to stop as she beelined it for the backdoor, leaving a trail of her shoes and socks. She then reached for the hem of her T-shirt, which she dumped on the floor with her skirt.

"Jolene?"

She glanced over her shoulder as she removed her undergarments, which she let fall to the floor by the door. Sterling's skin turned a pale shade of ghostly white, lips parted and eyes blown wide. Instead of replying, she just laughed as she slid open the glass door and then ran for the pool, jumping in with a splash.

Sterling stepped outside, watching as she floated on her back for a moment. She noticed his eyes trained first on, and then just below her chest. She realized he must have never seen the ornamental tattoo on her sternum before—and that her nipple piercings likely caught his eye, too. From how frozen he was, she wondered if he was focusing on the tattoo to avoid looking anywhere else. He looked as if he'd short-circuited.

"Water's great, you know," she said.

"What are you doing?"

"Helping you loosen up."

He scoffed and shook his head, but couldn't stop the grin on his face. "Alright, fine." He unbuttoned his shirt first, draping it across the back of one of the pool chairs on the deck. Jolene shifted from floating to wading as she watched him undress. She noted the taut muscles in his abdomen and arms and the strength showing in his long, lean legs. Once his clothes were all neatly on the chair, he sat on the edge and then slid into the pool.

She studied his face and saw nervousness behind his smile, hidden in the furrow of his brow and the wrinkle between them. So, she said, "We don't have to do everything at once, okay?"

Sterling nodded as he swam to her. He reached for her but faltered.

"You can touch me. It's okay, Ster."

His body relaxed as she washed away his nerves. His hand reached for her waist, pulling her closer as his thumb latched onto the space just beneath her breast. Jolene lazily draped her arms around his shoulders, making eye contact as the world went still around them. Thanks to the high wood fence in the yard, it was easy to forget about anything and everything other than each other.

Sterling said, "Thank you."

"For what?"

"For helping me loosen up."

She giggled as she kissed him, feeling that draw to him she had since she first laid eyes on him. Sterling's free hand went for her face and brushed back until his fingers interwove with her wet hair. Their kiss turned open-mouthed as his grip on her hair and ribs tightened, shooting warmth through Jolene's body despite the cool water surrounding them.

Between kisses, Sterling said, "Come by every Tuesday."

Without hesitation, she obliged.

CHAPTER 11

I f it were up to Sterling, he'd have never stopped kissing Jolene. The warmth of her mouth against his own brought him a surprising comfort that he craved as he made his way to the safe house the following day. As he did, he yearned to both toy with her newly discovered tattoo manipulation and to bask in her affection. It left an ache in his chest he'd never felt before. He wasn't sure what to do about it.

Noah and Amy still occupied the secondary safe house. The first was still too unsafe to continue working in again—at least as long as Detective McMahon watched his every move, regardless of the new chief's orders to stand down. Detective McMahon would be the death of him—metaphorically, of course.

When Sterling descended into the basement, he frowned beneath the black, disposable face mask covering his nose and mouth. He always wore one when he came to his *real* work; the stench of drugs was too much like cat urine for his liking, and the filter provided some relief.

Beyond the usual cooks, Sterling only recognized Carter, the bartender who worked directly under Noah. Anthony slunk down the stairs behind Sterling, having followed closely yet out of sight as he'd been instructed. Sterling moved past the rows of long, metal tables, where the dim lighting overhead reflected on the surface until he reached Carter. One good thing that came out of the theater incident was Amy and Noah's mass distribution method. Liquid proved popular with most of their customers, who preferred to be more discreet.

Reiji should have listened to his son a long time ago, Sterling thought, *but at least it's one less person to split the bill with.*

"Where are the others?" Sterling asked, only partially muffled by his face mask. "I thought all hands were on deck today."

"Noah and Amy are on their way, sir. They said they had someone to meet and didn't say much else, so your guess is as good as mine."

Sterling moved to another station with the cooks. "Hm." He grabbed a chair and sat at the end of the table, giving him a view of the entire production. "I suppose we'll wait for them here, then." With a wave of his hand, he encouraged Carter and Anthony to do the same at the other tables.

At the sound of footsteps leading down to the basement about half an hour later, Sterling stared at the new arrival: a man with mousy brown hair and a stocky build. Sterling didn't recognize him, but he accompanied Noah and Amy, so he just waited. Patience was a virtue that his parents drilled into him. He found it almost always paid off.

"Hey, boss man," Noah said, "we brought someone who wanted to meet you."

"Oh?" Sterling turned in his seat to face the group. Noah and Amy retreated as the newcomer approached Sterling with a bold show of confidence. Neither of them looked thrilled to be with him; Amy kept her gaze on her shoes, and Noah—while he kept an upbeat tone—bore a scowl.

"I've been following the Stone Breaker channel since day one," he said with a wide grin. His demeanor reminded Sterling of Josh. "Huge fan. Consider me your newest recruit."

"A recruit, you say?" Sterling stood and held a hand up when the man continued to approach, stopping him in his tracks. "Personal space, please. What's your name, son?"

The newcomer straightened, but still didn't match Sterling's height.

He had a few inches on Noah, but so did most men. Sterling looked down at him as he introduced himself as Daniel Sanders.

"Sanders, hm? You're not from here."

"No."

Sterling's eye twitched. "No, *sir*."

Daniel frowned. "Excuse me?"

"Show some manners. Not all have earned the right to use the casual tone with which Noah speaks to me." He brushed some dust off his jacket. "Anyway, what brings you to Riverpeak?"

Behind Daniel, Amy and Noah shared a glance. Amy whispered something in Noah's ear, and while Sterling couldn't hear her, he didn't need to in order to know she didn't feel sure about Daniel.

"I want to help you take down Hematite," Daniel said.

"And why is that? As we've established, you're not from here. What's it matter to you?"

"I went to school in Denver. When I had a crush on this girl in one of my classes, Hematite stood in our way."

Sterling rose a brow. "Ah, so you're the one who gave Rory Miller post-traumatic stress disorder."

As expected, Daniel's expression lit up at the mention of Rory's name, ignoring the rest of the sentence. "Wait, you know Rory?"

"Mm, I do." Sterling's hands clasped behind his back. "She nearly killed one of my men. Did you know that?"

"Who, Rory? Nah, she'd never."

"It's true. Hematite took the fall for her, but Douglas Doerr's nose has never been the same. It curves now, with a nice little scar where some plastic from his mask dug into his face." Sterling ran his thumb along his own nose, feeling the straight bone beneath his glove and mask. "The only reason Douglas walked away with his life is that Hematite showed up just in time. After all, his one rule is he won't kill."

Daniel laughed. "No shit?"

Sterling sneered at him. "But do you know something?"

"What's that?"

"I have no such moral code."

Before Daniel could fully understand what that meant, Sterling reached inside his suit jacket. In one swift motion, Sterling pulled his gun from his shoulder holster, pointed the barrel between Daniel's eyes, and pulled the trigger.

As the echo of the gun firing dissipated, it left the room silent. When Daniels's lifeless form fell, Amy jumped back with wide eyes. Noah placed a hand on her shoulder as he looked at Sterling, who frowned as he looked down at his suit. The blood splattered on his white shirt, freckling it with red.

"A shame." Sterling slid his gun back into its holster. "I just had this dry cleaned."

"Are we good?" Noah asked.

"Oh, the both of you are fine. You couldn't have predicted his disrespect."

Amy tried to hide her exhale, but Sterling still caught her show of relief.

"Unless this is the result you were hoping for. In that case, I applaud you." Sterling met Noah's eyes as he grinned. "Your sister was with Rory that night, was she not?"

Noah nodded. "Yeah. She was."

"Ah, I see. What a clever little trap you set."

"Though I must admit, I wasn't expecting this so quickly. Not complaining, though. One less asshole in the world."

"Well," Sterling said as he straightened his jacket, "now that he's dealt with, I'd like to set our sights on our next target."

Carter asked, "Not Hematite?"

"No. Carter, Noah, Amy. I need you three to get me every piece of information you can on that detective, Jon McMahon. I've already got the new police chief wrapped around my finger, so it shouldn't be an issue." He turned to Amy. "You've been putting out those Stone Breaker videos, correct? Put a target on his back like you did to Brick Beast. I'm sure one of your followers knows something."

"Will do, yeah," she said. "Between that and whatever intel Carter can get from the bar, we should be able to track him down."

"Good. I don't just want to stop him. I want him to hurt."

Carter said, "If you know who Hematite is, why not go after him?"

"He can't die. What's the fun in that? Besides, this will hurt him where it counts. Without McMahon in the picture, Hematite loses his connection to the Riverpeak Police Department. No detective friend means no more free rein to play vigilante. At the risk of sounding like a hypocrite, what he's doing isn't exactly legal."

Amy asked, "What about Jolene? Can we use her yet?"

Use her. Sterling tensed at the verbiage, even though that was exactly what he'd planned on doing. He cleared his throat and said, "It would appear I owe you an apology, Noah, for my harsh judgment of your timing before. Ms. Gautier isn't viable yet. We have yet to perfectly unlock her tattoo manipulation, though we're close."

"Was that a softer tone I heard?" Noah bore a shit-eating grin. "Don't lie to me because you know I'll call you on it. You finally got a girlfriend, Harrison?"

Forcing a neutral expression on his face, Sterling replied, "While I am unsure of how Ms. Gautier would feel about that title, yes, something like that. Regardless, she trusts me after the last few weeks of us working together while I wait for Potter to act." He looked at Amy. "Let me know if you need help with the video about Jon McMahon. I can access his work schedule and files from the police department, but I want to know every minute detail. When he takes a smoke break, where he picks up dinner for his wife, when his wife gets home from work down to the second, when he takes a shit. Understood?"

"I'll see what the followers can come up with. They're all fucking weirdos like Daniel was, so I'm sure they'll find something."

"Excellent."

————

When Sterling returned home that evening, sinking into his couch with a glass of red wine and a fresh shirt on, he opened YouTube to see the video already posted. Amy wore the usual red neon mask and baggy black clothing to conceal her identity. The voice modifiers she and Noah used changed with every video, likely to keep Elijah Baron on his toes.

Sterling had to admit he much preferred Amy as Stone Breaker over the Stevens brat.

"Our vigilantes aren't the only corrupt ones drunk on power here in Riverpeak," Amy said in the video. "Did you know that Detective Jon McMahon has been helping Hematite this entire time? Men like him abuse their power to help men like Shawn Jameson get away with their power trips. If Jon McMahon is helping Hematite, then we can't trust him. And if we bring him down, then the whole vigilante operation might as well be over. Self-appointing himself to Hematite cases feels like cheating, doesn't it? So let's give him a taste of his own medicine and appoint ourselves to his case. If you know anything about McMahon, share it in the comments below. Let's make sure he knows that corruption isn't welcome here in Riverpeak, regardless of who is behind it."

Sterling leisurely sipped his wine as he watched, making a mental note to compliment Amy later on yet another excellent video. He was willing to admit he'd been wrong about her at first and that he shouldn't have doubted Noah.

Now, with Jolene in the picture, he understood.

I should call her, he thought. *I should call her and tell her everything that's happening here so she can know exactly what it is she's getting herself into.*

But when he stared at her contact information on his phone, he froze. Never had Sterling felt such a lack of confidence, at least not since he watched his father die, helpless to stop it. Something—he wasn't sure what, but it stemmed from that same pang in his chest—told him Jolene may not be so receptive to what lurked in the basements of his storehouses. So instead, he set the phone down and waited for next Tuesday to come.

On Tuesday, he could experience bliss. While he wasn't sure he believed it, he even told himself he deserved it.

———

When Tuesday rolled around, Jolene let herself in with the number to the keypad. Sterling didn't mind that she did. To his own surprise, he enjoyed having someone he could share the more personal parts of his life with.

They sat on the back patio, feet dipped in the pool. Jolene ditched her pants entirely, sitting on the edge in just her underwear from the waist down, but still fully dressed from the waist up. When he'd gotten a glimpse at her bare hips and rear in the high-cut garment, Sterling hid his blush with his hair. His bangs fell in his face as he rolled up his pant legs to his knee.

She said, "I can't believe I forgot to bring a swimsuit after last time."

"It's just the two of us. If you really want to go in again, I'll be the only one to see you."

"Sitting like this with you is nice too, though. Stella and Annie have been forcing me to keep up with the news since I guess all sorts of crazy shit is happening in Riverpeak. It's got me nervous. But when it's just the two of us? My brain doesn't go into overdrive."

Sterling leaned down to kiss the top of her head. He ran his fingers through her pink hair, which faded in the weeks since they reunited. "No one will so much as lay a finger on the three of you. Do you understand?"

"You know, I have no idea how you have such a wide scope, but I believe you when you say that."

"When you're in my line of work, you get to know just about everybody."

It wasn't a lie—just an omission of the truth. *It's good enough for now*, he thought, *and more than I should say, but this will satiate her.*

"Yeah, that makes sense."

"Regardless, with your tattoo abilities, I don't think you really need my protection. But I'm watching over you, anyway."

"So much of this just doesn't make sense to me. I know we wanted to just hang out, but do you mind?"

"Not at all. What's troubling you?"

She shifted to face him. "Hematite doesn't want to work with us. But he had no problem coming to me for something before I had powers. This was a while ago, like, before Naomi and Brad got married. He comes walking into my shop, asks if I've tattooed Noah, and starts asking me the meaning of the sleeve he got. It felt pretty random, but he said he was hoping to uncover some motives or something. I don't remember exactly, but he told me if I ever saw him again to put a fox emoji in my Instagram caption."

Sterling feigned surprise. "He did?" *So it was just as I expected.*

"Yeah, but then get this: he never helped me when I actually did. I put the emoji up in a caption, and then you talked to me and told me Hematite works more or less alone, and then he still didn't reach out to me, so I just took the emoji down."

He laid his hand on her shoulder. "Well, I'm glad I found you when I did. You needed help."

She smiled. "I'm glad you did, too."

"Perhaps he forgot. Unfair to you, but you're right. It is strange, though I suspect it may have to do with Brick Beast. He went missing."

"That guy sucked. Good riddance. But blows for us."

"It would, but we don't need Hematite's help. We can get through this."

"And did you see this Stone Breaker guy?" She spoke with her hands, flailing them in each direction. It made the pine tree tattoos on her forearm look like a blur. "He got some replacement for his YouTube channel and he's asking for information on some local detective. I mean, ACAB and all that, but what the fuck is going on?"

For as much as Sterling wanted to admire how impassioned she was, the conversation steered in a direction he'd rather avoid. More often than not, he could talk around her questions, but this was more direct.

"It appears he found an important link in Hematite's chain. Objectively speaking, if Hematite can't die, then I suppose that would be the best way to go after him. Personally, I try to just stay out of it."

"We should lie low. God forbid that weirdo found out other people had powers, too."

Sterling nodded and said, "We'll keep our experiments confined to my home and Dr. Potter's office. No one will suspect a thing."

He admired Noah for being upfront with Amy from the beginning and wished he'd done the same: just told Jolene what and who he really was in full from day one. Perhaps he wouldn't feel guilty as she curled up to him if he'd been able to tell her everything and that every-thing was happening just as he willed it. Then he wouldn't need to fret whenever she questioned things.

The idea of losing her felt like too big of a burden to bear. Losing his father devastated him, even all these years later. He couldn't lose her, too.

CHAPTER 12

As Rory and Kane graded papers, Kane soaked in and savored the moment. Rory's apartment—*their* apartment, now, something he still hadn't gotten used to saying—hadn't changed much since he moved in except for the Hematite gear in their shared bedroom closet. The entire room smelled like a mix of the vase of fresh flowers and twin mugs of coffee on the table in front of them. Rory poured herself a second cup a few minutes ago, and the steam still swirled from the top.

He wished he could freeze the moment. But with Sterling getting his hands dirty and a replacement Stone Breaker going after the one and only authority figure on his side, he didn't let himself wish for too long.

Once Sterling was out of the picture, Kane would retire. He'd decided that after moving in with Rory, wanting to spend as much time with her as he could to make up for the eight years of pining. His body ached so deeply from years of fighting that he felt it in his bones, sometimes literally. As he looked at her, sitting on the floor next to him in between the couch and the coffee table, he felt peace. Sunbeams streamed through the nearby window, highlighting her brown curls. When her bottom lip slipped between her teeth as she read a student's essay more closely, he couldn't help but reach out and tuck a stray strand of hair behind her ear.

Rory looked up at him, eyes wide. "What's got you looking all dreamy?"

"You're sexy when you're hyper-focused."

She rolled her eyes as he snaked his arms around her waist, but made no move to resist him. Instead, she leaned into his touch with a smile as she set the essay down. "Please." Rory wiggled one of her arms free from his grasp. With her hand that wasn't partially encased by her wrist cast, she brushed some of Kane's straight blonde locks out of his face. With his forehead now bare, she kissed it.

Kane asked, "Your cast gets to come off soon, right?"

"Just another week."

Both of their cell phones vibrated on the table, interrupting their small moment of peace. They leaned forward to examine the names on the screens.

Kane picked up his phone. "I just got a text from Potter."

"Funny you mention. I just got one from Amy about him."

"Amy? Amy Brewer?"

Rory swallowed as she grabbed her phone and skimmed the text. "Yeah." Her tone darkened. "Looks like Potter blabbed."

Kane's brows furrowed. "What do you mean, he blabbed?"

"Apparently," Rory said, enunciating each syllable in aggravation, "Dr. Potter told Sterling who you are. Remember him from the funeral? So much for doctor-patient confidentiality. What the hell does Potter want?"

"He didn't say, just that he has something to tell me in person, but I'm definitely going to see him now. What the fuck was he thinking?" He sighed and tied his hair back into a small bun. "Is Amy okay? I'm surprised she texted you."

"I'm surprised, too, but maybe she feels a little guilty after everything got so out of hand." Rory knew that with Shawn, there was no guilt there—but she'd made a promise, and so far, Amy held up her end of the bargain.

RORY: How is everything? You okay?

AMY: More than okay, I promise. Thanks for asking though.]

Rory told Kane that Amy was fine. "I'm not about to look a gift horse in the mouth."

"Fair. Probably best to not push it. We'll get the answers we need from Potter, anyway."

Rory stood and grabbed her mug. "I'll switch to a to-go cup. Want one for the road?"

"No thanks. I'm jittery as is."

———

When Kane and Rory entered Potter Laboratories, the front desk looked long abandoned. For such a large facility, Kane wondered why there was so much space for just one doctor. After they moved through the hall, Rory swung open the door to Dr. Potter's office; it hit the wall with a jarring thud. She turned to Kane and nodded, so he stepped through the doorway, unsure if he was emotionally prepared for their conversation.

Dr. Potter jumped with a startle at the sound of the door slamming open. He looked up from his desktop computer as he adjusted his glasses on his nose. "Ms. Miller and Mr. Kelly! What a pleasant surprise!"

"Don't greet me like nothing is wrong." Kane bit back his anger, but it was clear just from looking at his clenched fists and tight jaw that, if he were alone instead of with Rory, he'd hold back far less. "You told Sterling Harrison about me?"

Potter stood. He walked back with every step forward Kane took.

Kane continued, "The leader of the drug ring? The very same drug ring that has made my life a living hell?"

"That is why I called you here, Mr. Kelly. I ... I'm afraid I have done so wrong by you and all of Colorado."

Kane's brows furrowed, intensifying his scowl. "What the fuck did you do?"

"Mr. Harrison—"

"Oh, we're calling him Mr. Harrison now?"

"He's my employer! His father and I..." Potter's voice trailed off as he struggled to find the words, now backed into the corner of the room.

With a gruff edge to his voice, Kane said, "I'm waiting."

"We created that drug together, Mr. Kelly. Sterling's father and I, that is. He came to me in need of something to make his competition obsolete. We were roommates at university for two years, and who would I be to turn an old friend down?"

Dr. Potter held his hands up to his chest as he looked to the ground. Kane said nothing, too disgusted to quip back, so Potter continued.

"And then ... we created this. We didn't even know it was giving people abilities until you came into my office and told me that whenever someone killed you, you simply awoke a few minutes later. You, Mr. Kelly, were the catalyst." Dr. Potter finally looked back up, his eyes meeting Kane's. Despite the fury he saw, he said, "You were my finest masterpiece, Mr. Kelly, and I saw your plight and felt ashamed of what I'd done. But that brings me to why I've called you here today."

"Have you been feeding my information to Harrison this whole time?"

"No. He already suspected it was you and simply asked me for confirmation. Why do you think I always preferred to talk here, in person, and not over the phone?"

Rory ran a hand through her curls, pushing some out of her face. "Fuck."

"But you must understand, Mr. Kelly. Whenever peddlers would beg you for mercy, they weren't talking about Stone Breaker. They weren't even talking about Noah or Reiji Sato. They were begging for mercy from Sterling Harrison."

Kane scoffed. "What more could you possibly want from me?"

"I never realized just how far this would go. It has been decades since I first helped Sterling's late father, and..." Dr. Potter clutched his chest. "I am so, so sorry."

"How did Sterling know?" Rory asked. "Who else knows?"

"He didn't say. I did some investigating of my own and it would appear Sterling's connections run even deeper than just the restaurant industry and our local police. I suspect he got the coroner's report from the night you died a few years ago."

Kane rubbed his eyes. "Shit." His flannel, open to reveal his graphic tee beneath, billowed around him as he moved his hands to his hips, widening his silhouette.

"Noah Sato and Amy Brewer were with him when he asked me to confirm."

"So what now?" Kane asked. "We just hope my identity doesn't get blasted all over the news? We can ask Naomi to protect me and Rory at Channel 10, but that doesn't account for the rest of the stations."

"I am hoping you'll allow me to redeem myself. You see, I have a proposition. If you could bring Jordan Jefferson here, we could give her the answers she needs to heal."

Rory spoke up, protective and fierce over her former student. "Why the hell should we trust you with Jordan? That poor girl has been through enough and after you tell us all this, you expect us to believe you to actually help?"

Dr. Potter simpered in Kane's direction. "Have I not been of use to you over the years, Mr. Kelly?"

"You have, but Rory's got a point. How do we know you won't just take that information and give it to Noah so he can finish the job? He meant to kill her, remember?"

"I will take down no identifying information about the patient. We will simply observe her condition to understand where she stands and what happened to her after Mr. Sato's failed attempt. You can even monitor the sessions."

Kane looked at Rory. "Can I talk to you?"

Rory nodded and grabbed a hold of Kane's hand. "Yeah, come on. We'll talk through this in the other room."

Hand in hand, they left Potter alone as they moved out into the hallway. Once they were outside the door, Kane never dropped Rory's hand. Each of them leaned a shoulder against the wall as they faced each other.

Kane said, "If we're present, then I'm comfortable with it. Potter *has* helped me a lot over the years, and Jordan is fucked up. He's her only chance at closure."

"I hate it, but you're right." Rory frowned. "Hematite should be the one to bring her here. She loves you, Kane. Poor girl wants nothing more than to hook Hematite up with a free coffee."

Kane's expression softened. "And she loves you, too. You think I didn't notice that she went to you instead of the school counselor?"

"She knows I get it, to a degree. So even though she doesn't want to talk about it, I think she feels better knowing that someone at least partially understands. Now that she's graduated, I'm worried about her. She said she's taking a gap year to just work at the cafe with her parents and Aaron, but I think she's too scared to do much of anything." Rory sighed. "Did I tell you what she said to me one day when I was grabbing a coffee from her?"

"No."

"I can't believe I forgot to tell you. It was just the two of us there and she just broke down out of nowhere. She reminded me of myself when I was going through it, you know? And she asked me if it ever gets better. I told her that yes, with lots of therapy, things do get better, but it broke my heart to see her like that."

"Then here's what we'll do. Thanks to all of that Stone Breaker bullshit hitting the news a year and a half ago, she and just about this whole town knows that you've worked with Hematite. Offer to bring her to me, and then Hematite can explain the situation to her, and if she accepts, then we bring her here."

Rory nodded. "Sounds like a solid plan."

"I just worry that we're about to get in way over our heads."

"When haven't we, huh?" Rory squeezed his hand. "Just know that no matter what you have to do, I'll be right by your side, okay?"

Kane frowned. "No matter what?"

"No matter what."

"Even if I have to kill him?" He winced, the words alone enough to pain him. "If Sterling is as ruthless as Potter says, and it comes down to it…"

Kane's glance averted to his feet, but Rory used her free hand to cup his chin and force eye contact. Her cast lightly scratched Kane's jaw.

"Then I trust you'll do whatever it is you have to."

Kane swallowed with enough force that she could see his Adam's apple bob in his throat. "Even that?"

"Yes, even that."

In a whisper, he asked, "Hon, do you hear yourself?"

"Let's be real, Kane. If you hadn't pulled me off Shatterstone when you did, I don't know that I would have stopped. I could have killed him."

"Rory—"

"It's true. From the look on his face in the mugshot photos, I think I almost *did* kill him. We've all gotten our hands dirty, so know that I will never judge you if you need help cleaning blood off of yours."

Kane rested his forehead against her own, nudging her nose with the bridge of his. "Thank you."

With a reassuring smile, she said, "Now let's get this son of a bitch."

CHAPTER 13

After tattooing for eight hours straight on Tuesday with minimal breaks, Jolene looked forward to heading to Sterling's home after work. Her client that morning came in for an intricate sleeve, a fusion of anime meets traditional Japanese, and her upper back was screaming at her for the way she sat. The idea of sitting with Sterling, catching up with one another after their years apart, appealed to her tired spine.

They always had enough to talk about to fill the silence, but when they weren't talking, they'd found other ways to keep occupied.

Ever since their first kiss, Sterling seemed to cling to her. Jolene found it endearing to see the lanky man—now more muscular, making his suits fit tighter—blush as he kissed her. Sterling left his lips wherever he could, and now that they'd kissed, it seemed Sterling didn't want to stop.

Before she left the studio, Stella ran up front, calling her name. Jolene turned at the sound of it, smiling until she saw the way Stella simpered like she had bad news and wasn't sure how to soften the blow.

"Stell?"

"Remember the guys from Denver?"

"What about them?"

"Well … look at our old teacher's Instagram Story. I figured you'd want to hear about it from me instead of someone else."

Jolene grabbed her phone from her back pocket and opened the Instagram app. She had to search for his username, but once she got there, she nearly dropped her phone in horror. In his Instagram Story was a photo of Jolene and Sterling at the shop, enjoying some matcha. Sterling was behind the counter with her; it must have been taken when Josh was there.

The text written over the photo made her stomach lurch.

"When someone who fucked you over and claims they weren't in it for the money shags the richest guy this side of the Mississippi, makes you wonder!"

Jolene scowled and said, "What the hell is this? How did he even get a photo like this?"

"I don't know," Stella said. "Seems like he's keeping tabs on you."

Her lip curled. "How the fuck did I fuck him over?"

"You didn't. He's just a jealous prick! Half of his clients left for us. That's the only thing I could think of."

Jolene sighed. "I don't need this right now. But thanks for telling me. Hopefully, this doesn't blow back too bad."

She was sure it would, but she waved goodbye to Stella with a smile, anyway. On her walk to Sterling's house, she tried to push the Instagram post out of her head, but the image was as good as burned into her mind's eye. Even though she was tempted to ask him what the hell that was all about or to respond online, she also didn't want to give him the satisfaction. Her relationship with Sterling was hers and Sterling's alone.

When she arrived, she found Sterling wrapping up a pasta dish for two; the savory vegetables and cream-based sauce smelled as good as it tasted. After eating, they moved to the back patio to stargaze. Sterling and Jolene kept their feet in the pool until their toes long since shriveled and they could practically feel the dampness from within. Now, instead of the mountains and clouds reflecting in the waters, they only saw the night sky when they glanced at the pool. Some constellations sparkled brighter than others.

"You walked here, right?" Sterling asked.

"Yeah, straight from the studio."

"If you don't want to walk back at this hour, I can drive you home or you can stay the night with me. Your decision."

Jolene smirked, a twinkle in her eye. "And what happens if I stay the night?" This was exactly what she needed after that Instagram Story. She hadn't told him about the social media drama. But from the way his irises blew wide, she was tempting Sterling's restraint—reason enough to accept his offer.

"If you were to stay the night, darling, I would invite you to join me in the shower for us to rinse off this chlorine. There, I'd take great pleasure in massaging your scalp while washing your hair for you." Sterling ran his fingers through her pink locks, giving her an idea of what was to come. Jolene closed her eyes and hummed at the sensation as he continued, "And then, I would take you to bed, where I'd touch every square inch of your body so I could learn what makes you tick."

Jolene licked her lips. "And if I said yes?"

"Then I would do everything in my power to make sure you feel at ease."

After everything he'd done to help her, she trusted Sterling. Navigating her new powers could have been a mental toll and had been prior to meeting him when she didn't know what was going on. But with Sterling, everything felt secure, like she didn't need to have a care in the world. So Jolene leaned into him and said, "Then I'd very much like to stay the night, if that's okay with you."

Jolene stretched her arms above her head and then emerged from her seat by the pool, shaking her feet over the water to not drip it everywhere. She doubted he'd give a shit if she did, especially after she managed skinny dipping with no repercussions a few weeks back, but she still didn't want to be rude.

As Sterling stood and stretched his legs, Jolene took a moment to admire him. He was made for the night, with his dark eyes and silver hair that shined in the moonlight. The lighting in the pool illuminated his features, long fingers rolling down the pant cuffs on his rolled-up long legs, and the silhouette of his side profile.

He asked, "Something on your mind?"

"Can I draw you?"

His head cocked to the side like a cute, confused puppy. "Beg your pardon?"

"Just stay here, okay? I brought my tablet."

Jolene scurried back into the house and all but leaped for her bag, where she kept it in a dedicated sleeve. She clutched it to her chest as she scurried back outside. She took up residence in a chair as she opened the case, retrieved the stylus from its holder, and then opened her drawing apps.

"Pretty please?"

Sterling chuckled as he flexed his fingers. "Alright. I have a hard time saying no to you. What should I do with my hands?"

"Keep 'em out. At least the one facing me, anyway. Do whatever with the other. You just have such gorgeous hands, so I'd hate to not capture at least one of them."

He pocketed the left. "Erm, thank you?"

"Oh, that one in your pocket creates a nice shape. Hold that pose. Or sit. I dunno how long I'll be."

Why he entertained her, she had no idea. Not just this whim, but all of them. Jolene tried not to think about it too much as she sketched away, starting with a rough outline that she polished after a few minutes. Sterling remained standing, occasionally shifting his weight as he looked off in the distance. Occasionally, he'd cast his gaze to her, not daring to turn his head—but she could still see his eyes dart over.

"What about this moment made you so quick to grab your tablet?" Other than his voice, the only sounds were some crickets and the grass rustling in the gentle evening breeze.

Jolene played with the color selector until she was happy with the shade of blue for the lower half of the background. As she did, she said, "The moonlight is mixing with the light from the pool. Like a watercolor in real life, and it suits you."

"I'll be stylized, I take it."

"In that same kinda style that I draw my custom magical girls in, yeah."

"Does that make me a magical boy?"

She giggled as she added some extra details to his hair, emphasizing the fallen wisps of bangs. "Do you have a transformation sequence with a catchphrase?"

"I transform into a total sap when I'm around you, if that counts."

Jolene cooed. "That was so fucking cheesy. But so cute."

Blush dusted his cheeks, and she rushed to add a faint tint of it to the drawing. It gave a subtle, warm touch to an otherwise cool, monochromatic color palette.

She littered the night sky behind him with stars on her tablet. Jolene replicated a few of the constellations she recognized: Perseus and the Big and Little Dipper. She left a break in the stars where the shadows of the mountains blocked them, making Sterling stand out against the starry night, illuminated by the blue glow as he was in real life.

"You know," he said with a hint of amusement in his voice, "most people would just snap a photo. I think I prefer this. It's much more sentimental."

As she felt her cheeks heat up, she felt a similar warmth in her heart. "All done."

Sterling approached her with long strides and then looked over her shoulder at the work. Her 1990s anime-inspired style complimented him, especially his long and narrow features.

"So," she said, drawing out the vowel, "do you like it?"

Jolene didn't care much if people approved of her work; as an artist, she understood that not everything was for everyone. Her clients chose her because they liked her style and knew she could pull some of the cleanest lines in Colorado. It made it easy for her to ignore the trolls calling anime cringe in her Instagram comment. But she really hoped for Sterling's approval, fully aware that her little crush had developed into something much more serious.

When he nodded and kissed her cheek in response, she felt a weight lift from her chest. She could finally breathe again when he said, "Are you kidding? Darling, this is beautiful. Is that really me?"

"Yeah, you dork. Of course, it's you."

"You made me far too pretty."

"I don't think I could ever draw you too pretty."

She looked away from the tablet to finally meet his eyes. Their noses were close enough to touch, but instead of kissing her lips as she expected, Sterling's lips moved up to her forehead as he extended a hand to her.

"Shall we?"

Jolene turned her tablet off, tucked it under her arm, and took his hand with no hesitation.

————

When they sat on the couch in his den, Jolene nuzzled right into Sterling's side, like a comfortable cat offering its affection. Moments like this felt so simple that he wished he could freeze the moment. In another universe, maybe their life could be like this all the time. At least, that's what Sterling wished.

In this universe, it was much more complicated. His legacy made sure of that.

Jolene's voice snapped him out of his thoughts. "I haven't had a sleepover since high school."

"Does it still count as a sleepover when you're in your thirties?"

"Sure it does," Jolene said. "They're actually even better now because we have adult money, which means we can use that money to buy the shit we always wanted at sleepovers when we were kids. Like better snacks and the fluffiest pillows."

Their Target run after their poolside time had been productive. The closest one was forty-five minutes away but open late enough for it to not matter, and Jolene and Sterling didn't mind the drive. Jolene introduced Sterling to some of her favorite Japanese bands and sand along, knowing the lyrics but having no clue what any of them meant.

She'd stocked up on everything necessary for a charcuterie board. Sterling offering his wallet willingly and without limit. Now, they were curled up in his den, the couch fully reclined and a blanket over their laps. Each of them had a glass of red wine, one that Sterling paired perfectly with the cranberries, raisins, nuts, and various flavors of vegan cheese.

He asked, "Did you have sleepovers often growing up?"

"Every now and then. My friend and I used to just gather around in our sleeping bags when we should be sleeping, playing video games and talking about who we had a crush on or what teachers we hated."

"Did you tell them about that crush you had on me?"

Jolene blushed as she hid her face with her hands. "Oh, God. You're never gonna let me live that down, are you?"

Sterling chuckled lowly as he pulled her closer to his side. He kissed the top of her head as he steadied the charcuterie board. "Never."

"But to answer your question, yes. Yes, I did."

As they watched an anime, they picked at the charcuterie board until it was empty. Once it was, Sterling set the tray aside. With it out of the way, Jolene's legs—mostly bare in her shorts that she'd changed into for comfort—draped across his lap.

Sterling dared to run his hand up and down her leg, starting at her thigh and then ghosting down past her knee to her calf, ankle, and then back up again. She hummed as he did and after his hand made the round trip a few times, she leaned in to kiss his cheek. Their noses grazed against each other as he turned his head to look at her. When their lips pressed together, Sterling could no longer hear the Japanese dialogue coming from the television in front of them. Instead, he could only hear his own heart pounding in his ears.

Jolene shifted her legs so she could straddle him and deepen their kiss. Sterling once again relied on his instincts as he wrapped his around her and pulled her closer, their bodies now flush together. The only thing preventing their chests from pressing together was Jolene's hands, which already trailed down the front of his dress shirt. When they lowered to his thighs, he felt his entire body tense. Her fingers pressed in, and the sensation shot through him even with his slacks acting as a barrier.

Sterling could feel heat rushing towards his lower body to pool in his groin as his heart rate quickened. The feeling was familiar from nights of loneliness triggering his natural urges, but it had never been quite this all-consuming. Jolene only heightened it pulling away from his lips so she could trail her own down his jaw. When she nipped at the spot between there and his throat, he was certain she could feel the stiffness beneath her.

"Before we proceed," he said as she kissed his neck. Her hands trailed to the collar of his shirt so she could unlatch the first button, making it hard for him to focus on his breathing. "I have a confession I must make."

Between kisses, she replied, "Oh?"

His hands gripped her waist as he thought of what to say, hoping to convey that he didn't want her to stop. "While I'm no stranger to self-pleasure, I am not as confident as I'd like to be when it comes to making you feel good."

"Why don't I take over and show you the ropes?" An innocent question; she didn't seem bothered by his inexperience.

Sterling swallowed. No one ever took over, at least not really. When Reiji and Noah were in control, at the end of the day, they still reported to him. But as Jolene's soft, nimble fingers unbuttoned his shirt, he nodded. "I'll let you lead the way."

As his now-open shirt exposed his torso to her, she trailed her kisses down to his chest. He wondered if she could sense how quickly he breathed and how his heart thrummed against his ribs as she pressed her lips against his bare skin.

As Jolene slipped out of her black tee and stood to remove her plaid pants, her movements were slow enough to make Sterling feel as if his skin were on fire. He couldn't help but scan her body, eyes landing on her sheer black underthings, including a bra with no liner, so he could see her pierced nipples right through it.

Reaching for her, he cupped her face with his hands as he kissed her again, then let his hands on her cheeks trail down to her breasts, which he cupped over the thin mesh. When his thumbs grazed over her nipples, shaking from trepidation and nerves, he felt a boost of confidence when they hardened beneath his touch. As she whimpered into his kiss, Sterling felt a chill on the back of his neck. Jolene dragged her fingertips down his chest and abdomen, not stopping until she reached for his belt buckle.

"May I?"

The way she looked at him through her lashes as she said it made him certain his heart would stop. *At least,* he thought as he nodded his affirmation, *if this kills me, I'll come right back.*

As he sprung free from his pants, he only felt minor relief. While the lack of fabric restricting him felt wonderful, he could still feel his heart beating in his throat. Jolene stepped out of her panties and lowered herself onto one of his thighs. As she moved her hips, Sterling groaned, the sound so guttural and deep that he didn't even recognize it as his own.

"Are you sensitive?" Jolene asked as she splayed a hand on his chest, pushing him further back into the couch. With the other, she reached for him, tending to his arousal. "It's okay. I'm sensitive, too."

He'd pleasured himself before, but it felt so much different with her hand than his own. Jolene's skin was softer, her touch gentler, her fingers more delicate. Sterling felt entirely out of control, but to his own surprise, he didn't even mind. For once, his mind wandered away from his duties and ambitions. His only ambition now was to taste every inch of Jolene's skin. His curiosity piqued over the difference in the sensation between her breast and her piercings.

Once she was finally in his lap, he had easy access to her chest. He ran his tongue over her nipple, gentle with the piercing there, and continued when she dug her fingers into his shoulders in response. His hips met hers, finding a slow, steady rhythm that he tried to mimic with his tongue.

If he wasn't careful, he'd get lost like this.

When he found his release, Jolene didn't relent. Instead, she grasped for his chin and kissed him.

At that moment, Sterling Harrison had never felt more alive.

CHAPTER 14

When Sterling entered the back of the bar, he brushed some dust and lint off his jacket's lapel. Anthony lingered behind him as Noah and Carter led them into one of two storage rooms. One was legitimate, but they reserved the other for moments like this: moments when to remain discreet, they couldn't bring someone to the safe houses.

The room was empty save for the chair in the center and the sound-proofing around the walls. Amy stood behind the black-haired man duct-taped to the chair. Ice encased his wrists over the handcuffs, and a similar cocoon coated his body from the thighs down, leaving him frozen in place.

"Aw, look," Amy said as they entered. "You said you were too cold, right? Looks like help is on the way."

Noah grabbed two cigarettes as he said, "Good work, Ames." He kept one cigarette for himself and handed the other to Sterling.

"Who do we have here?" Sterling asked, holding the cigarette out for Noah to light it.

"We got some leads on Detective McMahon and we found this little traitor warning him," Amy said. "We thought you might like to talk to him yourself."

"You'd be correct," Sterling said. He stuck his free hand in his pocket and leaned back on his heels. "So, what's your name?"

"Martin."

"Martin," Sterling repeated, drawing the man's name out. "Now, Martin, tell me. What would compel you to let Detective McMahon in on our little plan?"

"My brother and I have worked for you for years. And then, when he got his ass beat by Hematite outside that abandoned office building a few blocks down, you finished the job. Was that really worth killin' him over?"

It felt so long ago, despite only having been a year and a half ago, that Sterling barely remembered it. But after two drags, he recalled the man who'd returned from a standard delivery beaten and bruised. "So you've been plotting your revenge ever since?" Sterling clapped thrice. "How admirable. You've really played the long game here."

Martin jerked his head toward Amy, who was still behind him. "You gonna shoot me like that guy she recruited off YouTube?"

"No," Sterling said. "No, I killed him swiftly because he was a waste of my time and a disrespectful little prick. I save the slow, painful deaths for traitors." He looked at Noah. "Unfreeze him. Do your worst, but leave at least a little behind for me."

Noah smirked. "It would be my pleasure." He stalked toward Martin, circling the chair as he set his cigarette between his teeth and took his lighter out. "You said my girl made you a little too cold? Let me take care of that for you."

Fire shot out of the lighter in a rapid burst. The stream of it hit Martin's legs, melting the ice with ease, but also catching on his pants and burning through to his skin. Martin opened his mouth to scream, but Amy slapped her hand over his face. When she pulled it away, a thick layer of ice coated Martin's lips, preventing him from making noise.

"You don't have to stick around for this, you know," Sterling said.

Amy shook her head. "I'll be fine." From her flat tone, Sterling could tell she meant it.

"Suit yourself." He and Noah both approached the flames that slowly died down on Martin's lap and used them to light a new cigarette. Sterling took a long drag, keeping his gaze at the ceiling, and then looked down at Martin. "Was your revenge fantasy worth it?"

Martin shook his head.

"Good."

Sterling willed Martin's left and right femurs to break. Martin yelled in agony, muffled against the ice blocking his lips, and once he stopped, Sterling did the same to both of his arms and then, finally, his neck.

Once it was done, Sterling sighed and ran a hand through his hair, pushing back the stray strands that had always defied his pomade. "Burn his body so we don't leave a trace," he instructed. "And delete any security camera footage that might show us coming in. McMahon will come looking, I'm sure."

"Understood," Noah said.

"Now, if you'll excuse me, I owe someone a visit before they wrap up for the day."

———

As Jolene sprayed the countertop, she tried to think about anything other than her old mentor's comments on social media. Her thoughts wandered to Sterling—particularly, the night they spent together a week and a half ago. While she saw him nearly every day since, he was unavailable to swing by at his usual time because of a work meeting. She tried to dismiss the way she'd missed him, not wanting to over-think or overcomplicate their relationship. But when the door chimed, she snapped out of her thoughts.

Sterling waved as it swung behind him. "Just me."

"What brings you in tonight? Did your work meeting go okay?"

"Beyond just wanting to see your beautiful face?" Sterling grinned as he took two long strides to the counter. He thought better of leaning against it with his elbow since she'd just cleaned. "It did, thank you. I was actually wondering when you were opening your books. I'd like to throw an idea at you."

Jolene thought her jaw might drop. "Wait, *you* want a tattoo?"

"A shock, I know. But you're a phenomenal artist and you've

inspired me to take some steps out of my comfort zone recently, so I figured, what the hell?" He smiled. "How far out are you booking?"

"Sterling, it's you. I'll tattoo you right fuckin' now."

"No, you don't have to do that."

"Listen, I'm booked for the next three months, and then when I *do* open my books again? They fill up like that." She snapped for emphasis. "If you wanna wait, I'll respect that, but you're here now and I was just about to close up, so no one's coming in."

"As tempting as your offer is, I'd hate to make you stay later than necessary."

Stella laughed as she moved through the studio, keys jingling in hand. "She practically lives here. Take the offer, buddy."

With a lopsided smirk, Jolene pointed to her fellow artist with her thumb. "She's not wrong. My only other plan for the night was to watch reality shows on Netflix. See ya later, Stella!" She turned back to Sterling. "What were you thinking?"

Sterling pulled his phone out from his inner jacket pocket and quickly opened up a photo. "Black and white nemophila."

"Nemophilia? That a kink I don't know about?"

As she grabbed the phone, Sterling blushed and smiled, casting his gaze at his feet before looking back at her. "Nemophila, not -ia. It's a flower. They were my father's favorite."

She smacked her palm over half of her face. "Oh, fuck. I'm an asshole. I'm so sorry."

To her relief, he laughed. "It's fine. You're not an asshole. You didn't know."

"These are beautiful flowers. Where do you want 'em?"

"How's the forearm? Does that hurt?"

"Nah, that's a good spot to start unless we get too close to the wrist. Everywhere hurts at least a little, but it could be worse than there. Mind texting me this photo?"

"Not at all." He took his phone back and did just that.

"Okay, and hold your forearm out for me real quick?"

Sterling removed his jacket and hung it on the coat rack in the corner by the door. He returned to the counter with his sleeve rolled up.

"You sure you want them in black and white?" Jolene grabbed her tablet and stylus, saved the image, and then switched to Procreate. "Your skin is like porcelain, Ster. The blue tones of the petals would really pop."

"Maybe we can start with the outline and then I'll see if you can convince me on the blues."

She smirked, confident in her element. "I can work with that. Come on, let's head on back. Keep your sleeve up for me, too, if you don't mind."

"Anything for you."

His words held more weight than just keeping his sleeves up, and Jolene sensed that but didn't dive too deep into it. She grabbed her tablet and led him to her room in the back, past the manga wall and neon signs. She pushed a door open with her hip, revealing a pink and purple room that looked like something out of a magical girl anime.

"This one's yours, huh? It suits you."

Jolene snorted as she sat in a small desk chair and got to drawing on the tablet. "What gave it away?"

"The walls match your hair, for starters."

A knock on the doorframe interrupted them. Annie stood there, leaning in. "Hey, Jol. Mind if I stay here and work on some fake skin tonight?"

"Only if you order some delivery for the three of us." Jolene winked. "My wallet's in the top drawer. Grab the blue card. You pick the restaurant."

"Sweet." Annie reached in for the drawer and grabbed the pink wallet. "Thanks!"

"Yeah, of course!" As Annie stepped away to order something, Jolene resumed drawing. "So, you said these were your dad's favorite?"

Sterling nodded. "They were. Despite their marriage being what most would call arranged, he and my mother were good for each other. Every week, he'd bring her a bouquet. I'm not sure how he got just this specific flower every time, but he did."

"That's so sweet. He passed, what, about 20 years ago now?"

"About that, yes. It's hard to believe it's already been that long." He swallowed. "I was there when he died."

His words hit like a battering ram to the chest. "Oh, Ster, I'm so sorry to hear that."

"Thank you." He frowned, unsure of what to say or how much to divulge.

"Do you want to talk about it?" Jolene looked up from her tablet to meet his eyes. Sterling couldn't say why exactly, but he found comfort in the swirl of blue and green in her irises. "You don't have to," she added, "but if you want to, I'm here to listen. A lot of people treat tattoo appointments like therapy sessions, so I've gotten really good at this."

The corner of his lips twitched up. "I was just shy of my thirteenth birthday. We were at a restaurant he owned and a competitor shot him in the heart. He pointed the gun at me next, but the restaurant manager beat him to the second draw."

"Holy fuck." Jolene paused her drawing to examine his forearm again. When her hand wrapped around his wrist, Sterling felt as if a jolt of electricity shot through him. "That's awful."

"You're the first person I've told that to, by the way."

"Well, I'm glad you felt comfortable enough with me to do so." She withdrew her hand, and he wanted to do nothing more than grab it again, but he let her continue working. "And I'm glad you're here. These are gonna be the best flowers I've ever tattooed in my life, just for your dad."

He smiled wistfully. "I'm sure they will be. If there's anyone I'd want to permanently alter my skin, it's you."

She laughed. "I'm honored. Seriously. Do you have a favorite story with him?"

As Jolene drew, Sterling shared multiple stories from his childhood until she printed out the stencil. She held up three sizes to his forearm, asking for his input on each.

"The middle one. Not too big, but still a decent size."

"Alright." She reached for a cardboard box to grab some disposable gloves and then slipped them on her hands. "You ready?"

When he nodded, she began the process, which felt more like a ritual. First, she washed the area with a soap bottle, then shaved some of his forearm hair to ensure the area was smooth. After wiping that area down with some alcohol, she hovered the stencil over where she wanted it to rest on his forearm. With a red marker, she made a few marks, then grabbed a plastic green bottle.

"It's a gel, so it may be a little cold."

"Got it."

The gel didn't quite send a shiver through him, but the slight chill was still a relief; he didn't realize how warm he felt until it smeared across his skin in a thin layer. Then she applied the stencil, straightening it on his arm and then applying light pressure with her palm.

"Last chance," she offered.

"I'm already in your chair. That means I'm committed."

She couldn't stop smiling as she slowly peeled the paper off, revealing the stencil beneath. "Look good? I've got a mirror if you want a better look."

"It's perfect."

"Alright. Stay still so that doesn't get wiped off on your clothes. While that dries, I'll get your ink set up."

She felt his eyes on her as she grabbed her ink cups and bottles, holding them in place on a sheet of plastic wrap with some clear gel. He watched as the black, gray, white, and blue inks filled the cups.

"Blue?"

"In case I convince you. I'm pretty confident."

"Yeah?"

"Mhm. Color is my specialty, after all. But worry not, I can still do a bitchin' black-and-gray." She prepared the tattoo machine, which Sterling watched with fascination, and then she turned it on. The buzzing sound filled his ears, and he noted the way the sound made a light smile cross her face. She wheeled her chair over to him and then hovered over his arm. She glanced up at him through her eyelashes and said, "We'll start with a small line. Let me know how it feels, okay?"

Jolene was so close to him that he could faintly feel her breath on his body as the needle met his skin. The sensation felt akin to a cat scratch, but he ultimately didn't flinch. After freezing to death and breaking his own bones, he'd experienced far worse pain.

She asked, "You good?"

"Fine, yes. You're light-handed."

"So I've been told. The last thing I ever wanna do is tear someone's skin up, so I try to be gentle. A woman's touch, I like to call it."

He chuckled as she proceeded. As she tattooed him, she was close enough to press her lips to him. As she tattooed him with her right hand, she used the left to hold his arm in the exact position she needed.

"What made you want to become a tattoo artist?"

"I always loved art, but I was always drawing weird shit. Well, all of my childhood interests are mainstream now, but it was weird shit when I was a kid. My parents were supportive and always made sure I had whatever tools I needed so I could consistently improve. And then, when my high school teacher asked what we wanted our major to be in college, I totally panicked. The idea of being stuck in a cubicle just seemed so soul-sucking to me. I watched my parents just work that office life and, I dunno, it just sucked any creativity out of them."

"That makes sense. So what brought you to tattooing from there?"

"One of my brother's friends was working at a shop up in Denver. The guy running the place was open to working with apprentices, so I went for it. My parents weren't sure what to think about it until they asked me how much the guy charged for a piece. Alright, sit real still. We got a few long lines coming up."

"Yes, ma'am."

"Ooh, say that again sometime."

He bit his laugh back for the sake of sitting still. The door rang out front, and they could hear Annie call out, "That's our food! I got it!"

"Thanks, Annie!" Jolene replied. "This shouldn't take too long, but let me know if you need a break to eat. I'm guessing an hour and a half or so."

"Is that with or without color?"

"With. I told you, I'm confident."

"I can wait to eat. Don't worry."

"Sweet. I'll keep chugging along then."

Within the hour, the outline was done. Despite it looking just like the stencil, it exceeded his expectations already. The leaves on the stems almost looked fuzzy from how realistic the detailing was.

"So," she said as she turned the tattoo machine off, just when he'd gotten used to the buzzing sound. She grabbed a spray bottle and pointed it at the tattoo, then wiped the excess ink and soapy water with a paper towel. "There's more detail I want to add to the flower petals, but it'll depend on if we stay with the black-and-gray or if we add some color."

Jolene stared at him expectantly as she awaited his answer. After the longest minute of her life, Sterling finally said, "Work your magic. I trust you."

She squealed and leaned up to kiss his cheek. "You won't regret this."

"The look on your face alone makes it worth it."

She'd been right: the blues *did* pop beautifully against his skin. When she turned off the tattoo machine, she set it down and then sprayed the tattoo with some more green soap. Sterling took his time gazing at the tattoo, all of his father's good deeds and sins alike etched in ink on his arm with a few simple, elegant flowers. The details on the petals were exquisite, but not so detailed that they'd become a mess of lines in a decade.

"The redness and swelling should go down within a day or two. Typically, I'd say only a day for something that size, but since it's your first and I don't know how sensitive your skin is, it may take an extra day."

Jolene's voice snapped him out of his thoughts, his memories lingering on his father.

"Wonderful. It's beautiful."

"Happy to hear it. Mind if I grab a photo?"

"Go right ahead."

Jolene wheeled her chair to the back of the room, where she grabbed a light bar from the corner. She scooted back, holding it over his arm with one hand so she could snap a quick photo and video on her phone. "Yeah," she said as she filmed, "this came out clean."

Once she took pictures, she set the light bar back down and then reached for something in a drawer. She cut a piece off of the roll and explained, "Think of this as a second skin. I'm going to put one on now and then give you another sheet. When you wake up tomorrow, the first one is gonna be nasty. Plasma and blood and excess ink are gonna show, but don't panic, it'll all wash off. Are you a night or morning shower kinda guy?"

"Night, typically."

"If it's too gross or leaks, take this off when you shower tomorrow night. Let the water run on it and peel towards you, not away, so you don't hurt yourself." Jolene carefully applied it, being gentle with his arm as she did. She prattled off the aftercare instructions and then said, "I've got a healing lotion that I swear by. I'll grab from my bathroom and give you next time I see you."

"Thank you," Sterling said. "Truly."

"Any time. You want another one, you know where to find me."

"Here," he said, reaching into his pocket for his wallet. He grabbed ten hundred-dollar bills. "Is this enough to cover it?"

"Oh, that's way too much for this. Normally I'd quote—"

"Whatever you charge, keep the change." He reached forward to shove the money in her pants pocket for her. "Because I know you won't accept it otherwise. This means a lot to me and you're worth every penny."

Not wanting to insult him by fighting it, she said, "Thanks, Ster. Come on, let's grab our food and check on Annie. I just gotta clean up real quick."

As they both stood, he brought his hands to her face to capture her lips in a kiss. "I can't thank you enough. Not just for this, but for everything."

CHAPTER 15

A few days later, as soon as Jolene finished cleaning up her personal room in the studio, she made her way to Annie. Annie was drawing up some additional flash pieces for Jolene to approve. Jolene reviewed the first few sketches last week, but was eager to see more; Annie was proving to be an incredible artist.

"Hey, Annie! Remind me. What day is it?"

"Saturday." Annie looked up from her tablet. "Why?"

"You up to anything tonight?"

"No, my evening's free."

"Okay. Ready to tattoo actual skin?"

Annie's entire expression lit up, with her brown eyes blown wide and her smile as bright as the pink neon sign behind her. "For real?"

"Yeah, for real. Lemme see that flash you worked on."

Annie reached for her phone in a frenzy, opening her Instagram Story highlights as fast as she could. She swiped past the informational posts until she reached the first page of flash art and handed her phone to Jolene.

"This one." Jolene took a screenshot of a design of a self-defense keychain that looked like a cat with some flowers. "I should have just enough room on my ankle for this one."

Besides, she thought. *This could come in handy.*

Jolene guided Annie through the prep process until the needle was ready to go. While she did, Stella came running over with her film videos for social media.

"Okay," Annie said, "ready?"

Jolene nodded. "Whenever you are. Take your time. You know what to do."

The familiar hum and buzz of the tattoo machine made Jolene feel right at home. She relaxed in the chair as Annie pulled her very first line on real skin. All the while, Stella filmed the milestone. If Annie was nervous, she didn't show it. Her hand was steady and her gaze determined, laser-focused on the stencil.

Annie asked, "I'm not going too hard, am I?"

"No, you're very gentle. I barely feel it."

"Okay, good."

"I'm proud of you. You're doing great."

"Learned from the best. Seriously, Jolene, thank you for everything."

"Please don't get all emotional on me because if you do, then I might start crying, and I really wanna sit still for you."

Annie paused her work to laugh, then resumed. Jolene confirmed some technical questions for her along the way until she added some color. Once completed, she wiped it clean and then grabbed the ring light to get plenty of photos. Jolene and Stella did the same.

"You like it?"

"Fucking love it!" Once out of the chair and with her ankle wrapped, Jolene pulled Annie in for a hug. "You're a damn natural."

"I'm just grateful that I got to train with you and get to work out of here now."

"I cannot wait to see what you do." Jolene pulled away from the hug. "Now I'm going to pay you and buy you dinner. Stella, you come too."

Stella perked up. "Hell yeah! I don't have anything else going on."

"We haven't had a girls' night in forever. Let's go."

The three women made their way to the Japanese izakaya-inspired restaurant on Main Street, only a few buildings down the road from the tattoo studio.

"You are officially open for business, Annie," Stella said. "How's it feel?"

Annie blushed as she took a sip of her beer. Some of her bright pink lipstick rubbed off on the glass. "Amazing. I can't even believe it."

"You're gonna kill it," Jolene said. "Just like I am about to kill this crab rangoon coming out."

They laughed, toasted to Annie, and dug in.

————

When they left the izakaya, Jolene tilted her head up toward the sky to feel the warm breeze on her face. With not a cloud in the sky, all the stars sparkled overhead, dotting the deep navy with flecks of white. As Stella shrugged her red coat off and draped it over her arm, she asked, "Are you still planning on moving to Colorado Springs?"

Jolene turned to look at her and Annie, who walked on the other side of Stella. "Eventually, yeah. I've been squirreling away."

"What'll happen to the studio here?" Annie asked.

"Do you want to stay here or go to Colorado Springs? Both of you." Jolene quickly added, "No right or wrong answer."

"A lot of my regulars are local," Stella said. "I'll probably stay for them."

"Then it'll be yours," Jolene said. "No reason we can't treat it like a franchise, right? We'll figure something out when the time comes, and I bet Sterling can provide some good insights. But no sense crossing that bridge right now when I still have a way to go."

Annie said, "I'm open to going wherever. Maybe I'll follow you to Colorado Springs."

"You'd be more than welcome to."

Before they could say anything else, they heard a low whistle behind them. At first, all three of them ignored it, but then, an unfamiliar male voice called, "What are you ladies up to, by yourselves this late?"

It was only around ten according to Jolene's smartwatch, but that was beside the point. "Ignore it," Stella said under her breath.

"This town is falling to shit," Annie whispered. Jolene nodded in agreement.

"Hey," another man said. "I think I've seen pinky pie with the boss."

"Oh shit, you're right. That is Harrison's girl. I saw her in that guy's Instagram Stories."

As the men laughed, Jolene's heart felt like it was stuck in her throat. As much as she wanted to call Sterling for help, there was no time—and if she pulled her phone out now, the risk that they would smack it away was high. She swallowed her fear and some rising bile that threatened to pass up her throat to steel herself.

She took a rapid-fire mental stock of all her tattoos, running through which would be the best to use in this scenario. The first that came to mind was The Star card on her leg: likely a nonviolent choice, but she wasn't sure what exactly would happen. Curious about its effects and seeing now as the perfect time to test, she summoned it in her mind, not daring to close her eyes. To her delight, the two men froze, yawned, and then swayed until they collapsed.

Jolene huffed out a sigh, feeling out of breath from the adrenaline coursing through her veins. As she looked at her friends, her eye fell on the chain tattoo that wrapped around Stella's wrist—one that she'd tattooed years ago.

"Stella, I'm sorry if this hurts or tickles," Jolene said. Before Stella could ask her to clarify, Jolene summoned it. The chain lifted from Stella's skin, the tattoo coming to life. Jolene jerked the chain from Stella—who nearly stumbled but caught her footing just in time—and used it to handcuff their would-be attackers together. As she did, Stella just stared at her wrist, where the tattoo remained despite having very much emerged from her body.

"What the fuck just happened? Did I get drunk?"

"No," Jolene said. "That was me. I can explain. Just … here." Jolene reached into her back pocket and held her phone out behind her. "Can one of you call Sterling?"

Annie snatched her phone and, with a few quick taps, found Sterling's number. Before Sterling could pick up, Annie put him on speaker.

"Jolene, darling. What a surprise. Home from your dinner?"

"Hey, Sterling, it's Annie from the studio. Can you, uh, come down and hook us up with a ride? We're near Le Petit Chateau."

The women heard shuffling and then the jingle of car keys. Sterling's tone dropped from jovial to serious. "Is everything alright?"

"Uh, Jolene has some freaky fucking magic or shit going on, but it was definitely a slay."

"I don't know what that means, but I'm on my way. Are any of you hurt?"

"No, we're okay."

"Where's Jolene?"

Stella spoke up. "She brought one of my tattoos to fucking life! Some guys followed us after dinner and one of them said they thought they saw Jolene with 'the boss' or something? I dunno. They followed us back to the shop, and next thing we know, they're on the ground asleep and Jolene's wrapping a chain around them."

Sterling asked, "They're still there?"

Jolene finally stood and wiped her hands on her plaid pants, satisfied with her chain work. She held her hand out and Annie passed her the phone. "They are. It's me, Ster. I just wanna make sure these two get home safe."

"Have you called the police yet?"

"No. Do you trust them in this town? They don't do anything."

"I'm close to the chief. I think I told you, he's an old friend of my father's. Let me call the station on your behalf. They'll make sure those two assholes get taken care of properly if I make the call."

"Thank you."

"Hang tight. I'll be right there, okay?"

"Will do. I'll see you soon." Once Jolene hung up, she saw both Annie and Stella staring at her expectantly. She chuckled nervously and said, "I guess I owe you both an explanation."

While they waited for Sterling, Jolene filled Stella in on the details she'd previously left out and told Annie the entire story. The only parts

Jolene omitted were Sterling's powers and his connection to Noah and Amy, not wanting to share a story that wasn't hers to tell.

Stella shook her head and asked, "So you mean to tell me that you got drugged at a theater and walked away with superpowers?"

Jolene nodded. "It's why I was struggling to sleep. It's been keeping me up at night. Sterling's been helping me a lot since he has so many connections, and through that, we've really bonded."

As if on cue, his car pulled up right in front of them. He emerged from the driver's side and beelined it for the three women. Sterling placed a gentle hand on Annie and Stella's shoulders as he asked them once more if they were okay, but when he reached Jolene, he carefully looked her over.

"You're sure you're not hurt?"

Jolene nodded. "I'm positive, Ster. I thought fast. You taught me well."

He sighed in relief as his long arms encased her torso, pulling her close to him. "I was so worried." When Sterling pulled away, he kissed her forehead. "Come on. I'll drive you all home."

Since they all lived in the same apartment complex, it was easy enough to drop them all off. Sterling drove by Jolene's unit last. Before she left the car, she looked at him and asked, "Do you want to come in? At the risk of sounding silly, I think I'd feel better with you here, not gonna lie."

"Anything for you." He reached across the center console and brushed some of her hair back. "You don't sound silly in the slightest."

As they made their way out of the car and into her apartment, she asked, "Did you know them?"

"I recognized them. They're cooks. Well, were. They won't be anymore." His jaw tensed as he clenched a fist, then released it. "I'm sorry if I put a target on your back."

"It's not your fault." She turned the key and opened the door, letting him in. "Riverpeak just fucking sucks. What the hell is going on with this town?" Jolene huffed. "And I thought Hematite was patrolling at night. What, because more people have powers now, we're all left to just fend for ourselves?"

"That's what Riverpeak gets for putting him on a pedestal, I suppose."

"Yeah, I guess. I can't believe I ever thought that guy was cool."

"He recently had some massive failures," Sterling said. "Perhaps Hematite is too embarrassed to show his face after the theater incident."

"I can't wait to get out of here," Jolene said as she collapsed on her couch. She kicked off her boots, letting them fall to the floor with a plop by her coffee table. "Colorado Springs is looking nicer by the minute."

Sterling removed his shoes by the door, then grabbed hers and placed them next to his own. She thanked him as he joined her on the couch, wrapping his arm behind her. "You know," he said, "I am out that way for work pretty often."

"Good. Then I don't have to give you up whenever I go." She smiled at him. "I enjoy having you around."

"I can't fathom why." He winked at her, and she playfully shoved his shoulder in response.

"Thanks again for the ride tonight, by the way."

"I'd hate to see you all alone after that. It was nothing."

"You're reliable. That's why I like having you around." Jolene curled up into his side, the soft fabric of his dress shirt providing comfort. She reached an arm around him to grab the remote but didn't pull away from his waist after she put the television on to return to the anime she'd convinced him to watch. "Everything here has just gotten so out of control. Is it so much for me to just want this?"

Sterling stroked her hair. "No. It's not much to wish for at all."

"What do you wish for? At the end of the day, I mean. I know you inherited your father's businesses, but what gets you out of bed in the morning?"

"Hm." Sterling kissed the top of her head as he thought about his answer. "I understand my position comes with great privilege. I'm just trying to leave this town a better place than my father left it." He sighed. "Though these days, I'm not sure I've done any good at all."

"Why would you think that?"

"It's complicated and not very fun to talk about."

"Well, I've got all night."

Sterling chuckled. "Not tonight. In due time. Let's turn our brains off for a few, shall we?"

Jolene couldn't help but feel that Sterling was hiding something, that there was so much more to his work than managing restaurants, but she didn't press. She'd find out in due time. "Yeah," she said, "I could really use that."

"Did something else happen? You haven't seemed yourself lately."

"How so?"

His lips twisted as he thought of how to word it. "It's like you've got a weight holding you down."

"Well, yeah, there is something I haven't wanted to talk about because I don't think it's worth the energy. That guy I used to work with in Denver, remember how I mentioned him? He's kind of starting a feud, I guess. Not sure why. Stella thinks it's just because he's jealous and can't keep a client, so he's got to blame someone instead of reflecting internally."

"What's he doing?"

"Someone took a photo of us at my shop and he insinuated that I'm with you for the money. Which, for the record, I'm not."

"I know you're not," Sterling said without hesitation. His jaw visibly tightened. "What's his name?"

"It's not worth it," she reiterated. "Responding will just give him the attention he wants. Unfortunately, my social media is a fucking shit show as a result. I can't log in without people calling me a gold digger or an attention-seeking greedy whore." Jolene sighed after she said it; speaking the words out loud enough released some of the pressure off her shoulders, but not quite enough to completely free her of it.

Sterling cupped her face, biting his anger back for her sake. Jolene recognized that from how strained he sounded when he spoke, and appreciated it since she needed comfort above all else.

"You are none of those things, darling," Sterling said. "And you've done nothing to deserve this. Just promise me you won't let it get to you, okay? They don't matter. Your clients will know better."

Jolene drummed her fingers against her palm; they felt empty without a stylus or pen to fidget with. "Thank you. I just ... I just like keeping my head down and doing good work, you know? I'd like to think that I'm a good person. What the hell is this all about? I think this is all making me extra antsy."

That very thought was why she doubted herself sometimes with Sterling. She went back and forth, like a game of tennis in her mind. It was hard to tell if Sterling was too good to be true and was hiding something, or if everything was fine and she was just overthinking.

"That's understandable," Sterling said. "But for what it's worth, you *are* a good person, and know that I'll keep an eye on it. I've got friends everywhere. Don't you worry."

"I don't need you to clean up my mess."

"I know you don't, but allow me to lift some of your burden, anyway." He kissed the top of her head. "It's the least I can do."

Jolene didn't know what Sterling had up his sleeve, but hearing that made her feel better, regardless. She thought, *Maybe I am over-thinking after all.*

CHAPTER 16

When Jolene closed up at her tattoo studio, grateful to wrap up early on a Tuesday for once thanks to lucky client scheduling, her phone rang. Her brother spoke the moment she answered. "Hey, Jo! What is up?"

"Just about to head home." She held her phone up to her ear as she cut through the small strip Riverpeak called its downtown. The rows of shops and restaurants were mostly closed by now save for one or two places to get dinner. "What's going on?"

"I have some potentially scary news," he said, his pitch dropping. "So, uh, some detective showed up at my work today."

Jolene scoffed, not in the mood for her brother's antics; all she wanted was to relax and unwind. "What did you do?"

"I was just about to ask you the same question! Did you know that one of your clients was found dead close to your studio?"

Jolene's stomach flipped. "Wait. What?"

"Yeah. And oddly enough, there weren't any functioning security cameras. No footage or anything. He's trying to figure out who did it."

"Fuck." Jolene ran a hand over her face. "I had no idea. Who died?"

"Some guy named Jason? Or was it Josh?"

"Wait, Josh?" Despite the summer air warming her skin, a chill shot down Jolene's spine. "He's dead?"

"You don't sound too devastated. Did you kill him?"

"No, of course not, but that guy was a dick! He came in here all creepy and shit. He was one of Stella's clients. Fuck, I should call her. How'd he die?"

"Someone snapped his neck in some back alley."

Jolene exhaled. "*Fuck.*"

"Oh, it gets worse! According to the detective, he had a half-finished tattoo sleeve still covered in plastic wrap."

As Chad told her everything about his conversation with an officer named Detective Jon McMahon, Jolene frowned and rubbed her eyes. When Chad finished, she said, "Well, fuck me, I guess."

"I'm just saying, if you see a detective knocking on your door, don't be surprised."

"Great. Thanks, I hate it. I think I'm gonna puke."

"Well, please don't do that on the phone. Listening to that would make me do the same."

Jolene groaned. "So helpful."

"Yeah, you're welcome for warning you."

They hung up when Jolene reached Sterling's neighborhood. She took her time walking down the street, unable to focus on the mansions around her as she texted Stella to warn her.

STELLA: Wtf do you mean he's dead?!

JOLENE: Someone took it upon themselves to break his neck. Chad was just questioned by Riverpeak PD. Keep an eye out.

STELLA: This is so fucked

JOLENE: Tell me about it. As if I don't have enough going on right now…

STELLA: Let me see if the news has said anything about it.

> JOLENE: LMK what you find. I'm on my way to Sterling's.

Less than two minutes later, Stella's texts came through in short bursts.

> STELLA: Holy shit

> STELLA: This is a nightmare

> STELLA: fml fml fml

> STELLA: The cops think the local crime ring is involved

> JOLENE: Then why was Chad interviewed?

> STELLA: Maybe they think we're connected?

> JOLENE: No way. There's nothing incriminating us because we didn't do shit. I don't feel bad about kicking that motherfucker out and you shouldn't either.

> JOLENE: If he was wrapped up in some shit he shouldn't have been in, then that's on him.

> STELLA: Yeah you're right you're right

> STELLA: I just

> STELLA: FUCK

> JOLENE: I know. It's a lot.

> STELLA: LMK if a cop reaches out to you. I'll do the same. Thank you for letting me know.

> JOLENE: Of course. You know I've got your back.

When she opened the door to Sterling's home, the sound of his piano filled her ears and made her heart swell with a joy she desperately needed. With the chaos from just a few moments ago, it grounded her, washing a feeling of peace over her. She knew he didn't play as much as he should, so to hear him back at it felt like a small victory. While it made her feel like a hypocrite to think it, there was more to life than work, so to see him come out of his shell was a step in the right direction.

Jolene leaned against the doorframe as she watched Sterling play. She was grateful for the temporary distraction from the detective-sized bomb her brother just dropped. Sterling wore just a white button-up shirt and black slacks, accentuating his long legs, and round glasses that gave him a youthful air. Despite the light, jocund notes of the scherzo Sterling played, there was a sadness to the melody and the melancholy way his fingers glided across the keys.

Without removing his gaze from the piano, Sterling said, "Come. There's room on the bench for us both."

She approached as he played the finishing notes and scooted over on the piano bench for her to join him. As she sat, he pulled his eyes from the keys to her face. Sterling's instincts took over as some of his fingers curled beneath her chin to pull her in for a kiss.

"That was beautiful," she said.

"You're too kind. I'm rusty. I don't have much time to play these days."

"You just took the second skin off, right? How's your tattoo healing?"

"Very well, thank you. Here, I'll let you see for yourself." He took his glasses off, then rolled his left sleeve up to reveal the ink. The tattoo shined in the light thanks to the gel he'd applied earlier that day; she'd given it to him when he swung by the studio with matcha for her. "Is it supposed to itch this much, though?"

"Yeah, that's normal."

"I wasn't expecting that, nor the skin flakes to just shed off every time I shower."

"You're not alone." She leaned over his arm, fingers resting on his wrists so she wouldn't touch the still-healing lines. "I've had many a panicked client call about that. You're not picking at it, though, right?"

"No, I'm not. Don't worry, I can follow instructions."

"Consider yourself in the minority on that one."

He chuckled. "Well? Artist's assessment?"

"Yeah, it's looking good. That recovery gel is my favorite. Your skin took to the color well, too. I'm so glad you went with it."

"I wasn't expecting to like it this much. With the color, I mean. I never would have thought it would suit me so well."

Jolene looked up at him with wide eyes, an undeniable glimmer in them as she spoke. "Thank you for trusting me."

Sterling mulled over the phrase in his mind as she continued to examine her work. *Trusting.* Sterling wasn't sure if there was anyone he trusted anymore, save for Jolene. There was an innocence about her that he found endearing, and an honesty he could rely on that shone through in her art, including the nemophila flowers on his forearm.

The realization dawned on him as quickly as the thought came: *he trusted her.* The last two people he trusted, his father and Reiji Sato, both died. His jaw clenched as unfamiliar feelings pulsed through him.

"Damn, I think that's the straightest line I've ever pulled. Anyway, you'll probably be good to go in, like, a week tops."

"Good to hear. Are you still looking for a tattoo shop in Colorado Springs?"

"I am, yeah. When I was an apprentice, I was working out of a shop up in Denver, and as nice as it is to be back in Riverpeak, there's just so much more business in the cities. But I'd rather head out that way instead of Denver again."

"May I ask why you left?"

Jolene leaned back and brushed her hair back with her hand. Sterling already missed the contact. She said, "I mean, it's not a happy story. Let's just say this business isn't the greatest for women."

"No?"

"Not at all. You know Stella from my shop, right? Well, she and I both apprenticed with the same artist. He's a local legend, so we were both stoked, but he turned out to be the biggest asshole. Total misogynist, but he was Instagram famous, so he got away with it. When we went to the other guys or some friends at a neighboring shop ... none of them were of any help. It was just us against the world."

"Jolene, I'm so sorry."

"It is what it is. That's why I run the shop I do. I wanted a safe place for women like us. Stella followed me here so we could at least stick together."

"Well, I'm glad you're safe now. Should anything else arise that goes beyond what happened last night? You call me right away, you understand?"

Jolene rose a brow. "What, you gonna box 'em?"

"If I can't, my bodyguard will."

Jolene's eyes widened. "Wait, you have a bodyguard? How have I not realized this?"

"Because he's good at his job. It's on my order that he's discreet. The less attention I can draw, the better."

"What the hell goes on in the restaurant industry that I don't know about? And here I thought tattoo shops had drama."

He smirked as he rolled his sleeve back down. "You'd be surprised. But I mean it. Offer stands."

"You continue to surprise me, Sterling. I like that about you." She licked her lips, which suddenly felt dry. "I like a lot of things about you."

"If you'd like, I'll buy your shop for you."

She leaned forward again, thinking she'd misheard him. "What?"

"How much?"

"Very funny."

"I'm not joking. How much is it?"

"Between the cost of the building and moving all my shit, I'm trying to save up at least $35,000. Part of me wants to buy a place, but my dream spot is only available for rent, and that's just the tip of the iceberg."

"That's nothing."

"Sterling, *no*. Seriously, you don't have to do that. I'm getting close to my savings goal. I've been taking on extra clients and everything."

He shrugged with a nonchalance that Jolene couldn't understand. "It's just $35,000. That's a drop in the bucket for me. Say the word and it's yours. And forget the rent. I'll just buy the building out from the landlord if it's the space you really want."

Jolene blinked at him; he said it as simply as he would have if he was going grocery shopping or picking up dinner. "Sterling, I appreciate it. Really, I do, but I like you for reasons other than you being rich."

"Forgive me. I didn't mean to insinuate that you did."

"It's fine. You see the world so differently than I do, so spending time with you is really fun. It lets me see the world differently, too."

"I could say the same about you. Opposites attract, so they say. Though I suppose we both have our creative streaks."

Jolene ran her fingers across a few keys. The notes softly ascended. "What made you start lessons? My brother got shoved in them because my mom was hoping it would calm him down. He was such a bundle of energy. It didn't really work, at least not in the long-term."

"My mother played, but she was a terrible teacher. Self-proclaimed." They both laughed. "I wanted to play with her. Since I spent so much time with my father, I thought it would be nice to have something to share with her." His fingers grazed the tops of the white keys, never actually pressing them until he reached Jolene's lingering hand. "It's funny how different pieces of them break off and come together to create us, isn't it?"

"I'd love to know which pieces of my parents I got. I don't think we could be any more different."

"Were either of them creative?"

"Not particularly. My grandmother was, though. My parents are fine, just very... normal, I guess?"

"Well, there's enough extraordinary about you to make up for it."

Jolene blushed, feeling the heat rise to her cheeks. "You think so?"

"I know so. Your art comforts some and excites others. And you have a good heart. Meanwhile, all I've got to show for myself is an old car I'm too scared to use often and some gray hair."

"When did you go gray, anyway?"

"Almost ten years ago. Noticed the first few silver streaks when I was 24. The last few black strands made the switch last year. My physician says it's from stress."

"Speaking of stress," Jolene said as she shifted in her seat. "I have something to ask you. You left not long after Josh did that day. Remember that pervy client?"

"I do, and yes, I did. Why do you ask?"

"Did you see where he went after he left the studio, or was he long gone by the time you left? Some detective, I think his name was McMahon, just questioned my brother and is probably going to be talking to me or Stella next. Apparently, they found him with his neck snapped in an alleyway right after his appointment, only a few blocks away."

Sterling rose his brows. Jolene couldn't decipher his expression. "That's unfortunate. I'm afraid I didn't see him. I'm sorry, darling."

His phone rang. Sterling checked the caller ID on his smart watch and groaned.

"My apologies. I have to take this." He planted a kiss on her forehead and stood from the bench. "If you'll excuse me."

Jolene nodded as she watched Sterling answer the phone. He said nothing as he walked into the other room, leaving her to look at the piano they'd bonded over so many times. Bored after a few minutes, she stood to pace the room, observing some of the art on the hallway walls. From here, she could faintly overhear Sterling on the phone.

"That detective continues to infuriate me." He sighed, agitated. "How hard is it to track one man down?"

Jolene couldn't help but wonder what he was talking about.

"Keep tracking. I'm preoccupied at the moment, so I'd much prefer you not make me do this myself. You know how I hate having to do things myself."

Sterling hung up at that. As Jolene heard his footsteps lightly pad against the hardwood floors, she made her way further down the hall, not wanting him to think she was intentionally eavesdropping.

But when he returned, he wrapped his arms around her waist from behind. Sterling dipped his head to kiss her temple, then said, "I should replace these old things with your art."

"We can work something out." Jolene winked. "Everything okay?"

He sighed once more. "Things are getting dangerous in Riverpeak. The crime ring on the east side is gaining power, and Hematite has been more active than ever. It wouldn't surprise me if Josh was wrapped up in all of that and the timing of his death was mere coincidence." Sterling paused, weighing his next words. "You should stay with me for a while."

Jolene hadn't expected to hear that. "Define 'a while.'"

"Until all of this blows over. A few weeks, perhaps. You'd be safe here."

"Is something wrong with my apartment? Who was that on the phone?"

"A colleague. Rumor has it Hematite lives there. While you have your tattoo abilities, I'd hate to see you caught in the crossfire if the situation continues to escalate. But you don't have to. Just an offer."

If she was honest with herself, she was torn. The idea of leaving her apartment made everything happening to her and around her all the more real. Being able to conjure butterflies and lightning was all fun and games until a vigilante war broke out on the streets of her own town, which was why her heart urged her to accept Sterling's offer.

But it felt wrong all the same, like he gave her an incomplete puzzle set. The only certainty was that she would, in fact, be safe here, so she said, "I would hate to impose."

"Oh, nonsense. You could never. Besides, the two of us are worka-holics. I reckon both of us will hardly be here."

"Hey, if you really just want me to stay the night more often, you've got me convinced." She smirked, hoping to brush off the strange feeling settling in her stomach. Part of her once more sensed that there was so much more beneath the surface. After all, there was no logical reason she could think of for why Sterling would have a bodyguard, or for how Sterling seemed to be so connected to every seat of power in Riverpeak beyond his money. *There is something he isn't telling me*, she thought, *but he's doing a damn good job of hiding it.* But it didn't stop her from saying, "I'll pack a day bag."

"Good. You'll be safer with me. There are dangerous people roaming our streets, right beneath our noses."

It is *safer with him,* she thought, *but maybe this way, I can get a better grip on what's going on.*

———

As Jolene sat in bed, waiting for Sterling to finish his shower, she scrolled through her phone. Money bag emojis overwhelmed her Instagram notifications. There were too many to delete manually, but she was too proud of her work to take the posts down, so she just changed her settings to turn comments off. Jolene was sure she'd get called a coward for that, too. Just as she saved the setting, Sterling grabbed her phone and pulled it from her hand, only to set it face-down on his bedside table. She hadn't even heard the shower turn off in her spiral.

"Stop checking that. It's not going to get any better, you know."

She sighed as she looked up at him, hovering over her with a few wet strands of silver hair falling in his eyes. The shadows of the dimly lit room made his cheekbones look almost gaunt.

"I know. Guess I can't help myself. It's hard when I'm used to being glued to that thing for work, you know?"

"Then allow me to distract you."

As Sterling kissed her neck, Jolene sighed in pleasure, and said, "I would be more than happy to take you up on that." His touches were delicate, designed to tease her and build anticipation so she could let the thoughts of her phone drift away. As she felt a familiar pressure building between her thighs, she asked, "Do you want me to lead, or would you rather take charge?"

"Hm." He pondered it for a moment. "As tempting as it is to let you guide me again, I'd love to explore your body for myself and see what makes you feel good, if that's alright."

"Fine by me."

"I will definitely take you up on the role reversal at a later date, though."

She grinned, eager for the distraction. "Rain check granted."

When Sterling kissed her once more, he ghosted his hands up and down her body. Eventually, he reached her hips, and when he gripped them, Jolene's hands flopped up above her head. Sterling enjoyed the way she writhed and moaned against his kiss as he inched his way between her legs, the anticipation making her squirm. Sterling moved one hand back up, but kept the other by her thigh to knead at her soft flesh.

His hand gripped her wrists, long fingers encasing the joints, and her breath hitched in their kiss. Sterling pulled away to examine her face, seeing how her pupils blew wide when he gave her wrists a squeeze. He withdrew his other hand from her leg and now that it was free, he reached for his tie, loosening it.

"Do me a favor and keep your hands like that, would you?"

Heat rose to her cheeks. "Sure."

With a short tug, his tie snaked off his neck. He wrapped it around Jolene's wrists before tying it. The satin felt smooth on her wrists, despite being bound a bit too tightly.

"Maybe a hair looser, please?"

"Only because you asked so nicely." Sterling kissed her forehead as he slipped a finger into the knot. "Better?"

"Much, thank you."

"Now, where were we?"

Sterling took his time undressing her, exploring her exposed skin with his fingertips and lips. With her hands tied overhead, Jolene felt every sensation heightened. She wanted nothing more than to run her fingers through his hair and grip at his shoulders, but like this, she was at his mercy.

She loved it.

She loved it even more when his mouth moved between her legs. Sterling didn't withdraw until her legs shook with pleasure, until all of her worries were a distant afterthought. As Sterling straightened, sitting on his knees between her legs, he unbuttoned his shirt. He tilted his chin up as he looked down at Jolene, one corner of his lips curled up into a smile. "Atta girl."

Jolene swallowed as her heart thrummed in her chest. "Oh, this is unlocking something in me."

"Is that so?" Sterling shrugged his shirt off and tossed it behind him, letting it fall to the floor. "I'm surprised. Despite your personal style, you strike me as the type to be on your best behavior."

At his words, she felt a zap straight into her abdomen. "Keep talking like this and I will be, that's for sure."

He chuckled, low and dark. "You're marvelous. Seeing all the things that make you tick fascinates me. *You* fascinate me."

She tugged her wrists fruitlessly against his tie and said, "Why don't you show me how much?"

Sterling smiled, flashing her his perfect teeth, and said, "Oh, I assure you, darling. You'll see just how much you fascinate me tonight."

CHAPTER 17

The sunset over the graveyard cast an orange glow over the rolling hills. The cemetery was just outside of Riverpeak, stuck between various small mountain towns and municipalities, much like their own. On her way to find Sterling's father's resting place, she weaved through the rows, looking first at some of the more elaborate tombstones; some of them dated back to the 1800s.

Eventually, she found Sterling. He sat before a beautiful tombstone with an angel statue, intricately carved with her arms outstretched and gown blowing in the breeze. As she beelined it for Sterling, she noticed Reiji Sato's grave, finally settled after a few months.

All these rich, powerful men, and yet they all met the same fate as everybody else.

Jolene tip-toed around some headstones, not wanting to startle him when he looked so fragile. He must have been there a long time because even from a distance, she could see the dirt coating his typically spotless black slacks. While he'd extended one leg in front of him, he'd propped his other knee up so he could rest his arm on it. A cigarette dangled between his pointer and index fingers.

When Jolene came closer, he looked up at the sound of the paper bag in her hand, rustling as she adjusted her grip. With her free hand, she waved. In response, he beckoned her over with the same hand holding a cigarette. When she reached him, Jolene pulled the small bouquet—including nemophila, matching his tattoo—out of the bag. She rested them across the dirt in front of the spotless tombstone. All the graves in this row were impeccable. Upon a closer look at Sterling, she saw a small wooden brush sticking out of his jacket pocket. He must have been the one to clean them.

"Hello, darling." His voice was almost hoarse. A red puffiness had snuffed out the usual sparkle in his eyes behind his round frames. Tear stains ran down his long cheeks, drawing attention to his chapped lips.

Jolene leaned down, cupped his face, and kissed his forehead before she sat down next to him on the grass. She suspected she knew the answer, but asked anyway, "Do you want me here or would you rather be alone?"

He responded instantly by moving his cigarette to his right hand and reaching for her with his left. He clutched her bicep, desperate for her touch. "Stay. Please. Though I'm sorry you have to see me like this."

"Don't worry about it. Today's the anniversary, right? That's gotta be hard."

Sterling nodded and, with a shaky breath, extended his left leg to join the right. As he snuffed out his cigarette in the dirt, he leaned his head on her shoulder. "It's been decades, but it still doesn't get any easier." Still holding her arm, he squeezed it. "Probably doesn't help that I often hold this in. After all, I've got a reputation to uphold. But I suppose that's something I should unload on a therapist, not you."

"Well, I'm here if you want to talk about it. And I also can recommend a therapist up in Denver, if you want."

He chuckled once. "I may take you up on that. But for now, thank you for being here. I make it a point to come out and see him every once in a while, even if it's just to have a quick cup of coffee, but I'm always alone and today is usually more difficult."

"Least I could do was pay my respects. I wasn't sure if you'd be here when I came. But I'm glad I caught you."

She brought her focus to his arm, where she'd tattooed the nemophila and willed them to life. Their blue petals blossomed on his skin, softening it before rising up. As Sterling plucked the flowers from his arm, his lips twitched into a smile. "He would have loved you as much as I do."

The confession slipped past his lips so fast that, based on his unwavering expression, Jolene didn't think Sterling even realized he'd said it. So, she said nothing about it, not wanting to make him feel uncomfortable in his vulnerability.

"Even with all my tattoos and unprofessional hair?"

Sterling chuckled. "Especially with your tattoos and unprofessional hair. You've made quite the name for yourself through your hard work. With the way he thought, he'd chalk it up to branding and applaud you for it."

They both laughed. Jolene then said, "I never did get to meet him at piano recitals or anything like that. Just your mom."

"No. He was at every single one, but my mother was always better at playing the socialite. He was always all business, all the time." A wan smile came to his lips as the memories came to him. "But he involved me in everything, no matter what. For better or for worse."

As more tears fell from his eyes, Jolene wiped them with her thumb. Sterling leaned into her touch.

After a moment of silence, he said, "It appears I've just told you I love you, haven't I?"

"You sort of did, yeah."

"While this wasn't how I ever thought I'd tell someone that for the first time, I mean it. Truly. You are so open-minded and thoughtful, with so much compassion, that I can't help but love you."

Jolene looked at him, crumpled against her side with his heart and soul bare for her, and smiled. She sensed she was the first person to see Sterling like this, and understanding him beyond the glamor of his suits and ties, she said, "I love you too, Ster."

They sat in silence for a few more minutes. The setting sun warmed their skin until it dipped beneath the horizon, leaving only remnants of the pink and purple sky behind. When Sterling checked his watch, he allowed himself a final deep breath.

"I've been here for hours. Shall we head home?"

Home, she thought. Despite all of her doubts and uncertainties, Sterling was home, and from the way he looked at her as she nodded, she knew he felt the same way.

———

The following morning after breakfast, Sterling declared there was something he wanted to show Jolene. It was her day off, so she obliged.

This is exactly why I agreed to stay, she reminded herself. For as much as she cared about him, especially now that he'd opened up to her more than he had anyone else, all she wanted was to find out who he really was.

Sterling led Jolene to a room tucked away in the hallway next to his bedroom; she had thought nothing of it before. Since the door always remained shut and he never called it out before, she'd assumed it was where he kept his central air conditioning unit. But as he unlocked the door from the outside with a key, she asked, "May I ask what's in here?"

"My family's safe," he said as he unlocked the door. "This isn't the main attraction. I just need to grab something from it first."

The only thing in the room was the safe embedded into the wall and a pad next to it. Sterling lowered his face to it and she watched as it scanned his eye and then clicked open.

"So what's in there?" Jolene asked. "An eye scanner seems pretty high-tech."

"Family heirlooms, mostly."

"And..?"

"And a few things for work. Nothing exciting."

"So then, why is it behind an eye scanner?"

"If you sold the heirlooms in here, you'd be able to buy the whole town. But you wouldn't need to, seeing as the deeds and paperwork all live here."

She whistled. "I guess that does require a little more security than a locked file cabinet."

He chuckled and grabbed a key from the safe. "There's also this. This is what I'd like to show you." Sterling locked the safe and held a hand out for Jolene. She took it, letting him lead her to the room across the hall from his. Once he'd unlocked the door, Sterling swung it open and let Jolene in first.

She could hardly believe her eyes as he flipped the light on. The room illuminated to reveal dozens of screens, more than she could count. They covered an entire wall, with a wire running along the floor to a large computer.

As Sterling crossed the room, Jolene's eyes followed him. Across from the screens, a massive bookshelf dominated half of the wall. The desk next to it, where the computer was, matched the dark wood of the shelves. While none of the spines were cracked, the edges were just worn enough to show they'd been read and loved.

Sterling made it to the desk with only two long strides, turning the computer on to show what was waiting for them on the screens. As they flickered to life, Jolene's eyes widened. Some of them were in black and white, others in full color, but they were all undoubtedly security feeds. It went beyond just the restaurants she knew he owned, but random street corners and the outsides of multiple houses.

She asked, "What is this and why are you showing me?"

Sterling walked towards her with his hands in his pockets. He only stopped when they stood shoulder to shoulder, and as much as she wanted to look up at him, she found her eyes glued to the screens.

"This is my office, which includes an overview of Riverpeak, as I like to call it, plus a few locations in Denver and Colorado Springs. I'm showing you because I trust you and want you to understand the scope of ... well, my life. I'd say my business, but this has been my entire life until you."

"Beyond basic security, what do you need an overview of Riverpeak for?"

"I know a lot more about everyone than they realize. Don't worry, I've never kept tabs on you in that regard. But this was how I spotted you on that security camera that day. So should you need anything, just say the word. I'll know where to find you."

If it were anyone else, Jolene would be horrified. But with Sterling, she found it endearing in that sometimes strange way he showed he cared.

But she still didn't understand why all of this was necessary. Maybe someday soon, he'd tell her.

———

As Sterling drove Jolene to Potter Laboratories, they sat in comfortable silence. Jolene brought her tablet with her, drawing up some tattoo sketches even on her day off in the passenger seat. It gave Sterling a moment to think.

More than anything, Jolene seemed curious about his family safe and the security room. Sterling sensed that Jolene—who wanted nothing more than a quiet life in the tattoo studio of her dreams—wouldn't approve of his lifestyle. Introducing one facet at a time to her would be the way to success. If he overwhelmed her, she'd leave.

Never before had he wanted someone to stay so desperately.

The thoughts clouded his mind as they entered the lab and as he watched Dr. Potter perform some tests on her. As he stared at her in the harsh fluorescent lighting of the lab, he couldn't help but wonder if there was a way to make her even stronger or if there were limits to her powers.

If she could use anything she tattooed and bring it to life, then where did it end?

Sterling was snapped out of his thoughts when Dr. Potter said, "Well, no wonder you're exhausted, Ms. Gautier." Dr. Potter stepped away from the compound microscope and cleaned his glasses with his lab coat. "Your body is rejecting your powers. The added stress on your body is making you restless."

"What do you mean, rejecting?" Jolene asked.

"It looks like the old tattoo ink in your skin is reacting to it. This is likely why you can manipulate your tattoos—the cells in your dermis layer are fighting back. You must have one strong immune system."

"What about Noah?"

"You tattooed him after he gained his fire powers, not before."

"Okay, so what do I do to stop it so I can finally get some sleep?"

"Marijuana, Ms. Gautier."

She blinked. "Wait, seriously? That's it?"

"If you get a prescription, the employees will make sure you won't get high if that's what you're worried about. But living in Colorado, you don't need one."

"Well then," she said with a huff. "Maybe I'll just tattoo a pot leaf on myself or something."

"Is there another power we could give her?" Sterling asked. "Perhaps something to help her body not reject it?"

"That may help, or it might make it worse," Dr. Potter said. "If her body is rejecting it as it stands, there's no way to predict how it might react to introducing a secondary ability."

"I'm willing to try," Jolene said.

"Find the ability you wish to test with and I'd be happy to monitor."

Sterling frowned. "Have Noah and Amy not been sending you blood samples to test?"

"They have. However, there is more testing I wish to do with them yet."

"Like what?"

Dr. Potter blinked once, then twice, and then said, "I am studying the properties of the various powers to see what determines an ability, much like we discussed in regard to Anthony's powers. Perhaps there's a correlation between heritage and type."

"What are you really testing, Potter?" Sterling sneered. "You think I can't tell when you're lying?"

Dr. Potter held his hands up in defense and waved. "Oh, no, Mr. Harrison. My deepest apologies. I simply haven't wanted to say anything until I have concrete answers. You understand, don't you?"

Sterling's teeth clenched as his dark brows furrowed. "I expect results from you by the end of the month. If I don't hear from you by then, I'm afraid we must evaluate our working relationship and where it stands. You understand, don't you?"

Dr. Potter swallowed and then bowed his head. "Yes, Mr. Harrison."

"Good." Sterling cracked his jaw as he smiled at Jolene. "Come along, darling. I believe we're all set here."

Jolene nodded, smiling back, but it didn't reach her eyes. "Yeah, I think so. Thanks, Dr. Potter."

"A pleasure, Ms. Gautier."

Sterling kept a hand over her upper back as they left the building, and once they returned to the car, Jolene exhaled. She hadn't said a word since leaving until now. "What the hell was that all about?"

"He's hiding something. Noah suspected it for months. It infuriates me that I have yet to find out." He ran a hand through his hair. "I'm sorry that you had to see a glimpse of that side of me."

"What do you think he's hiding? Help me understand."

"There's someone else with powers that he won't tell us about. Someone or something he's protecting. Noah and Amy surveyed everyone in town that was at the same show you were. So far, there's still no sign of who or what it may be."

Jolene frowned. "You'll get more flies with honey than you will with vinegar, you know."

Sterling leaned over to kiss her cheek before pulling out of the parking lot. "Perhaps."

They spent the car ride in stiff, uncomfortable silence.

CHAPTER 18

When they returned home from Potter Laboratories, Sterling had finally mustered up the courage to properly apologize. He and Jolene sat on his back patio, lounging together as she wrapped up her drawing.

"I should have been more transparent with you," he said. "I can see how that would have taken you off guard."

Jolene brushed back a loose bang and smiled at him, her eyes crinkling at the corners when she did. "I appreciate you saying that. Sorry that I was quick to judge. He just helped me figure out what's been plaguing me for months, so I guess I was feeling a little defensive."

"I understand. But thank you for trusting me."

She kissed the corner of his lips. "Likewise."

He made it up to her by taking her to bed and exploring her with his mouth. Sterling learned when to use the tip of his tongue versus laying it flat on her body to incite the best reaction out of her. From the way she gripped at his hair and arched her back, he wagered she'd forgiven him.

They fell asleep in each other's arms, neither setting an alarm for the first time in months. When they awoke, Sterling fully intended to pick up where they'd left off the previous night, but the doorbell ringing interrupted them.

"Are you expecting anyone?"

Sterling shook his head. "No."

Jolene made to stand, but he held a hand up to indicate he had it covered. Jolene waited as he did, first pulling up the security camera application on his phone. Outside was a face he knew all too well, the very detective he'd been trying to track down to eliminate. He'd combed his red hair to the side and heavy bags lined his eyes.

"Who is it?" Jolene asked.

"A detective."

"Probably here for me," she said. Before Sterling could stop her, she stood to dress, then walked to the door and opened it. Sterling winced as she did, then took a deep breath. As he stood, he focused on his breathing so he could maintain his composure while he quickly dressed in some slacks and a button-up shirt.

"Jolene Gautier, is it?" McMahon flashed her his badge. "Detective Jon McMahon with Riverpeak PD. Is it okay if I ask you a few questions?"

"My brother told me you interviewed him," she said. "I take it you're here about Josh?"

"That's correct."

Sterling stepped in behind Jolene and propped his hand up on the doorframe. "Everything okay, Detective?"

"Mr. Harrison," McMahon said with a nod. "Just asking some questions, that's all. Standard part of an investigation. As of right now, Ms. Gautier isn't in trouble."

"Come on in," Sterling said, despite how much it pained him to say it.

Sterling cracked his jaw as he forced himself to release the tension he held there. Whatever game McMahon was playing, Sterling was already aware. There was no reason the detective couldn't have flagged Jolene down at her tattoo studio, where she spent most her time.

No, Sterling thought, *there's a reason McMahon conducted this interview while she's at my house.*

As the three of them took a seat in the dining room, Sterling clenched his fists beneath the table, where he sat next to Jolene and across from McMahon. The detective arriving like this in Sterling's own home was an insult. After all the help he'd provided Hematite and somehow gotten away with it, Sterling resolved one thing: the detective would pay twice over.

The interview started simple enough: McMahon had Jolene confirm when Josh's appointment was, for starters. Then he asked, "Did Josh seem like he was under the influence?"

"No, that wasn't an issue. If he was, I would have kicked him out a lot sooner. We refuse to tattoo anyone who's even had a little bit to drink or smoke. I'm pretty good at spotting that right off the bat."

"So what happened for him to leave with a half-finished tattoo?"

"He made one of my artists uncomfortable," Jolene said. Her fingers fidgeted on the table, twirling an invisible stylus around. "He made both of us uncomfortable, actually. It's not out of the ordinary for guys to come in and treat their tattoo appointment like a speed dating session. So I kicked him out after he repeatedly hit on both myself and the other artist."

"And where did he go after that?"

"No clue. We stayed inside the shop after he left, so I couldn't tell you anything after that."

"Security camera footage is down from that entire day," McMahon said. "How can I know you stayed behind?"

"I was with her," Sterling said. "As was the other artist. After making sure they were okay, I looked outside to see if he was still around. He wasn't. I went right back in." He shot Jolene a glance when he said it. He hadn't, and she knew he hadn't, but she squeezed his hand beneath the table. His cover was safe with her. Internally, he felt relief, but did not let it show.

"And how do I know you were really there and aren't just trying to protect your girlfriend?"

"I thought she wasn't in trouble," Sterling replied. "And, if I may." He pulled out his cell phone and opened up his credit card statements. After scrolling for a moment, he said, "I bring her a latte every day at work. See? I'm sure Aaron Jefferson could confirm that for you if needed."

McMahon sighed. "No, that's unnecessary."

"There's also a photo of us that someone took," Jolene said. She grabbed her phone and opened her Photos app, where she'd saved a screenshot of the initial Instagram Story in case she needed it for anything. "See? This was from that day. We were in the shop."

The detective just nodded as he stood. "Very well. Thank you both. I'm going to check in with Stella, but thank you again for your time. I'll see myself out."

Sterling leaned back in his chair and watched McMahon's every step until the man left. Once they heard the door close behind him, Jolene slumped back in her chair with an exhale. "I didn't do anything wrong, but that's still nerve-wracking."

"Of course it is." Sterling kissed the top of her head. "You've been working yourself to the bone, and this is what you get. Despicable."

She shrugged. "It is what it is. God, I need a break."

"Do you want to go out of town for a few days? A vacation could do us both good, even if just for the weekend."

She ran her hand over her face. "That would be nice. Where could we go?"

"My family has a vacation home in Telluride." His parents bought the Telluride house when he was five. Situations like this were why: so they could make a quick getaway when things got dicey, but still stay close enough to maintain control.

"It's pretty down there. I haven't been since I was a kid. We tried skiing once, but Chad hated it."

"It's beautiful in the summer, too. We could fly if you'd like."

"To Telluride? That would be the biggest waste of jet fuel, especially since you have an electric car. Absolutely not."

He chuckled. "Alright, fair. Pack a bag for the weekend. Don't worry about anything other than the clothes you want to wear. I've got the rest handled. Let me know when you're ready to go and I can make it happen."

"I had some clients cancel next weekend, so I could take a few days. Friday?"

"Friday it is."

———

When they pulled up to the vacation home, Jolene stared up at the three-story townhouse as they waited for the garage door to open. The modern exterior, which blended wood and stone with a glass balcony in the front, reminded her of his home in Riverpeak. The mountains stood tall behind them, their pines green and alive as the summer sunset painted the sky lavender and pink.

Since the first story was just the garage, they made their way up to the second floor, where the interior also didn't stray too far from his Riverpeak home. *Clearly,* Jolene thought, *the Harrisons have a style preference.* The main difference, Jolene noticed, was the use of lighter-colored woods and stone throughout the interior, though the fireplace remained the focal point. Cream couches and rugs blended in with the white and tawny colored walls and hardwood flooring, warm and bright in a way that felt infinitely inviting.

"This is so cozy," Jolene said. "Do you come down here often?"

"Not as often as I should," Sterling said as he set their luggage down. "I'll wheel these into the bedroom."

"Thanks."

She soaked it all in as he did, half-tempted to follow him to see the rest of the townhouse but drawn into the view of the mountains from the balcony on the second floor. If she craned her neck to the right, she could see the tops of the shops and cafes on Main Street from there.

After a few minutes, she heard Sterling's dress shoes clicking against the hardwood floor, then the tile of the balcony. His arms wrapped around her from behind, hands clasping in front of her stomach as he dipped his head to kiss her jaw.

"Is it to your liking?" Sterling asked.

"What do you think?" She looked up at him and smiled. "It's lovely. I'm looking forward to unwinding here for a few and taking my mind off of everything. It's been so overwhelming, between saving for the shop and figuring out my power and now this bullshit with Stella's client."

He kissed her jaw again. "It must be. But you deserve this. As I said, I'll take care of everything, okay?"

Sterling gave her a quick tour of the townhouse: two bedrooms, two bathrooms, a kitchen, dining space, and a sitting room. No hidden closets. When Sterling excused himself and stepped into the primary bathroom, Jolene explored the walk-in closet. She ran her fingers along the row of dress shirts, none of which had a single wrinkle. Behind them, she found at least half a dozen bulletproof vests on hangers. Her heart raced in her chest and she could feel some sweat building on her palms. She couldn't remember the last time she'd felt this way—maybe not since she'd left Denver. As she yanked a bulletproof vest off of a hanger, she tried to identify the exact feeling, stuck at the crossroads of anxiety and unadulterated fear.

When she heard the toilet flush, Jolene scurried back into the bedroom and shoved the vest in the bottom of her bag that she'd ditched at the end of the bed. Her gut told her she'd rather have it than not need it, and that she'd rather be proactive.

After all, she thought, *if Sterling needed them, then wouldn't I?*

Sterling opened the door as she grabbed her toiletries case out and then zipped her day bag. "Mind if I set this up in there?"

"I don't mind at all. My home is your home."

Jolene smiled as she made her way into the bathroom, setting her bag down with a gentle sigh, too soft for Sterling to hear. It wasn't him that she was afraid of—she had the feeling that Sterling would rather die than so much as accidentally bump into her shoulder when walking side-by-side, never mind letting harm befall her. Despite all her unanswered questions, Sterling still felt akin to wrapping herself in a warm blanket inside a pillow fort: safe, secure, and cozy.

It was what was outside of their pillow fort that frightened her, but she knew they couldn't stay in their cocoon forever.

"Can we go for a walk?" Jolene asked, feeling suddenly claustrophobic despite the size of the townhouse. "Just a little stroll."

"All the shops are closed by now, I think," Sterling said, "but we can if that's what you'd like."

"I'd love to stretch my legs after that ride, that's all."

With a nod, Sterling offered his arm and led the way outside. The breeze held a crispness to it, hinting that autumn would arrive sooner than later. Jolene could smell garlic wafting through the air from a restaurant on the street.

"Say, Ster?"

"Hm?"

"The last few months have been really fun. Don't get me wrong. I just can't help but feel like I'm missing something, you know? Like I missed a memo or I don't know what."

She studied his expression, hoping to be clued into what was really going on. She was dying to know why he had bulletproof vests, and why his father's competitors really tried to kill him nearly 20 years ago. But Sterling's expression remained neutral—flat, even—with no sign of emotion behind his eyes. His lips and brows didn't even so much as twitch.

"My business can feel rather intense," Sterling said. "Admittedly, I shield you from much of that, mainly for my work-life balance. Besides, you'd probably find it rather boring. There's always a mountain of paperwork in my inbox."

Jolene sensed it was a lie: he was too cool and casual for it to be the truth. Even if he were being honest, there'd be some hint of feeling behind his words, some weight to what he said. But she couldn't make any sense of how paperwork meant his job was intense.

"That feels contradictory, but I think I get it," she teased, hoping he'd say more, wishing for anything but to have to rummage through more closets. She wasn't sure what skeletons she'd find in them.

She wasn't sure if it was out of nerves or in genuine response to her teasing, but Sterling laughed. The airy sound filled the surrounding silence. "I suppose that's true. I'm sure most of it is in my head, given what happened to my father."

Finally, he frowned, the first sign of identifiable emotion since they started their walk down Main Street. The mountains at the end of the road were bathed in dusk's red light as thin, short strips of violet clouds floated by, matching Jolene's mood.

"I'm sorry," she said, feeling like an insensitive idiot. *Of course*, she thought, *this was because of his childhood trauma*. Everything about him was. "I should have guessed."

"No, no, I don't expect you to read minds," Sterling said. "And I'm sure with everything, you've been overwhelmed. But that's why we're here." He squeezed her hand. "Relax, Jolene. Allow yourself to relax."

"You're right, I should." She hoped she wasn't wrong for continuing to trust him and decided to at least enjoy the walk for now. She deserved that much, at least.

———

All it took to clear Jolene's head was an evening stretch and an hour to sketch the view of the meteor shower streaking above the mountains. Disconnecting from the pressures of her phone refreshed her, especially with her Instagram comments still feeling like a war zone. Allowing herself space from that helped her nerves about Sterling subside.

Once she'd finished sketching, she took a moment to study the stars without her tablet balanced precariously on her lap. Sterling was already stargazing in the chair beside her on the balcony. He hadn't bothered to bring his phone, unplugged for once, so they could watch the lights flash before their eyes in long, thin strips. A small, black mosquito landed on her arm, but it punctured her skin and flew off before she could swat at it.

"Mosquitoes are coming out," she said. "Wanna head on in?"

"You can't knock them out with one of your tattoos?" He winked. "Come on."

But once they were back inside, her mind felt plagued again. There was a darkness looming, something engrained in the walls and buried beneath the floors, but it was there, weighing heavy on her soul. Jolene stared at her phone in the corner, hoping it wasn't just the inevitable comments that awaited her taunting her, but she shook it off. While her imagination was worse than whatever awaited her on TikTok or Instagram, this, she knew, was coming from the Harrison family townhome.

I'll get to the bottom of it, she thought. *There's bound to be something in this house.*

CHAPTER 19

With the car window down, Jolene and Sterling could both smell the snow as the crisp mountain air tickled their ears. They sped down the highway, making their way back to Riverpeak from Telluride. From the window, Jolene saw a sea of pines 50 feet tall atop a white blanket of snow, hiding the red rocks beneath.

She said, "Thank you again for this weekend. I couldn't tell you the last time I took some time off."

He chuckled as he interlaced their fingers, sending a warmth down Jolene's spine. "My pleasure. You work too much, even by my standards." But Sterling's expression dropped as he peered in the rearview mirror. "Do you see this?"

Jolene looked in the side view, wanting to be subtle. "This cop is on your ass. Wait, hold up. Does that say Riverpeak? All the way out here?"

Sterling scowled. "I think he followed us here."

Before she could ask why a police officer from Riverpeak would follow them all the way out to Telluride, the sirens assaulted their ears. Even with the breeze whipping in through the windows, the noise was far too loud, making Jolene wince. She thought for certain she'd settled things with Detective McMahon. The police lights flashed, alternating between red and blue.

"Are you going to pull over?"

Without hesitating, Sterling replied, "No."

"No?"

"This isn't a traffic violation."

"Then what the hell is it?"

Before Sterling could answer, Jolene saw for herself. She ducked on instinct at the sound of a gunshot and cradled her head with her arms, bending at the waist so her head wasn't in view of the window. After she yelped, she asked, "Did they just fucking shoot at us?"

"I'm sorry, darling. Luckily for me, Anthony isn't the 'I told you so' type. Don't worry, I'll handle it. Hang tight, now."

Sterling accelerated the car, pressing his right foot down on the gas pedal. As Jolene's body lurched, her arms and strengthened center of gravity prevented her from whacking her head as he swerved. She wasn't sure where to look. For as much as she wanted to peek out the window to see what was happening, she also couldn't take her eyes off Sterling from her semi-fetal position. He'd steeled himself with perfect posture, a focused gaze, and knuckles taut on the steering wheel, looking as white as bone. For as collected as he sounded, he was tense.

She asked, "What the fuck is going on?"

"Do you trust me?"

"What?"

"Do you trust me, Jolene?" She'd never heard him sound so serious. He moved his left hand to the armrest on the inside of the driver's side door, activating the switch that would roll her window up.

She wished she had a straightforward answer. Her mind moved as fast as the car was, but as he slowed their pace, her pounding heart finally return to a normal resting rate.

"Yeah, I trust you."

Sterling glanced at her as he smiled, but immediately returned his focus to the road. "I'll tell you more once we're home."

"Once we're home?"

"Yes."

"And why not now? We have a few hours to go until we're back in Riverpeak."

"Because I'm not sure if he's working alone. I'd wager he is, but with you in the car with me, I can't be too sure."

"What do you mean, with me in the car? Can't be too sure of what?"

"Your personal safety is a bigger concern than my own." It was why Sterling didn't just snap McMahon's neck from here. While the detective was in range, he didn't want to risk the car crashing into his own and hurting Jolene.

"No offense, but given your sense of self-preservation, I'm surprised to hear that coming from you."

"Just trust me, will you?"

The roads wound, and even though Jolene couldn't see them through the windshield, she could feel it thanks to their increased speed. She jumped at the sound of a second gunshot.

"The windows are bulletproof, as are the doors. You can sit up."

Why he had a bulletproof vehicle was another question that floated in her mind, but she was hardly sure she could articulate that. *This*, she thought, *goes deeper than his trauma from his dad's death.* "I think I like it better down here, actually."

Sterling said nothing, opting instead to drive. After a minute that felt like hours, a smirk teased at his lips. For what reason, Jolene was unsure.

He only said one word: "Perfect."

"What is?"

"There's a runaway truck ramp."

Her mind went straight to the worst thought. "Please tell me you're not thinking of jumping it."

"No, of course not. I'd never put you in harm's way like that. Our little friend behind us is going to need it, though."

Sterling tapped on the car's touchscreen dashboard a few times. From what she could see, he'd turned on autonomous driving. As the car drove for them, not reducing speed, Sterling hit another button.

The sunroof slid open, moving back silently and excruciatingly slow. Once it was open, Sterling unbuckled his seatbelt, making the car beep in a warning. As the alert continued, Sterling reached into his jacket, retrieved a pistol, and then pushed himself up so he was almost standing. All Jolene could see were his black slacks now, so she uncurled her body from the fetal position to watch out the window.

As they took the curve, Sterling shot twice in rapid succession. The first bullet crashed through the front windshield. The second struck the front tire, causing the patrol car to spin out and slide up the runaway truck ramp. Jolene nearly leaped in her seat as the cop car crashed into the impact attenuator. A massive plume of smoke billowed from the hood upon striking the rail.

When she looked over, Sterling had already returned to his spot in the driver's seat. He tapped away at the dashboard, turning off automatic driving as he said, "There. Now there isn't anything to worry about."

"Nothing to worry about? You ... I'm pretty sure you just killed a guy! A cop!" She wanted to scream, but it felt stuck in her throat, buried by her surprise.

"Correct; that detective should be dead. He wasn't the first and most certainly won't be the last, I'm sure."

"What?!" Jolene couldn't believe what she'd just heard, especially with how easily the words had fallen from Sterling's lips. He was as casual as he would be if she'd commented on the sun feeling nice on her skin. From the precision with which he'd aimed, she wondered just how many times he'd done this before and thought, *How have I been so blind?*

Sterling shrugged a shoulder as he sheathed the gun. "What?"

"Do you see nothing wrong with that statement?"

"I see only necessity."

Jolene gawked at him. *"Necessity?"*

"Yes. Necessity."

"What exactly about that was a necessity?"

"Simple. That detective was the only thing standing between me and my goals. His department recently blew all of its budget on fire-proof equipment, so I happened to know his car wasn't bulletproof. No different from calling pest control when you have a rodent problem."

"Something tells me you're not talking about the restaurant industry anymore."

"No, my dear, and I'm so sorry for keeping this from you for so long." Sterling tried to smile, but his lips barely curled up and it didn't quite reach his eyes. "While I have not lied about my father being a restaurant tycoon, I have failed to share the full truth with you. Surely you're familiar with methamphetamines circulating through Colorado, stemming from the eastern side of Riverpeak?"

"Don't tell me."

"They're not truly methamphetamines, at least not anymore. My father partnered with a colleague of his from university to create something stronger and, thus, profitable. I don't know why my father started it. I never got the chance to ask him. All I know is that he passed it down to me, and I watched him suffer during his last breaths. And then, one day, a vigilante pops up on the streets. Hematite. My father's men tell me that no matter how many times they squash him like a roach, he wiggles out from beneath their shoe."

Sterling glanced at her in his peripheral. He'd never seen someone alive go so pale.

After a few beats of silence, Jolene said, "Ster, I know you said you'd explain at home. But I swear to god, if you don't fess up right now and tell me how this is all connected, I'm going to jump out of this car."

"You wouldn't do such a thing."

"How do you know that?"

"You'd scuff up your tattoos. You wouldn't dare ruin years' worth of artistry, at least not with a childish act of defiance."

Her jaw cracked as it tensed. "Okay, touché, but my point still stands. If you want me to trust you, you can't keep secrets from me, not of this magnitude. How is Hematite connected to you killing a cop and telling me not to worry about you?"

"A few years ago, I went to my father's business partner. We ran some tests and unlocked the possibility of infinite power. Hematite's cells regenerate every time we try to kill him, bringing him back to life. After seeing what happened to my father from being in this line of work, I knew I needed to get my hands on it for myself." Sterling looked at Jolene with a soft smile. His eyes grew brighter and twinkled like a dying star. "And I did it. You don't need to worry about me, Jolene, because I am untouchable."

"Wait, what?" Jolene ran both of her hands through her pink hair, suddenly tempted to shave it all off. She dismissed the impulsive thought as soon as it came, tucking it in the back of her mind to revisit when she wasn't on the verge of a mental breakdown while speeding on the highway with her murderer of a boyfriend.

"My reflexes are faster than most people's, as you just saw, and I never lied about the ability to heal my broken bones. But I bear other gifts as well, including Hematite's immortality. I can also break and repair bones within a mile radius."

"This is … Holy fuck, Ster, this is a lot to process right now."

"I know, and for that, I am deeply sorry. Everything I do, I must do in an act of self-preservation, as you so perfectly said it. But please know that my self-preservation extends to you. Should anyone know about your newfound powers, I fear what they may try to do to you. A power like yours has the potential to be limitless, don't you think?"

"So that beer at the theater that gave me my tattoo magic … that's why? It was laced with fucking methamphetamines that your people put in there?"

"Yes. Noah was testing a mass distribution method."

"Without telling anyone? What the hell for?"

"In order to liberate Riverpeak from the need for vigilantes in masks playing superhero."

"Are you even fucking hearing yourself?" Jolene's hands moved from their spot in her hair, sliding down her face until they covered her mouth. "This whole time? You were behind this the whole time?"

Her words were muffled against her palms, but Sterling understood every word. "The whole time."

"You were a God damn drug kingpin the whole fucking time?"

"Yes."

"When we get home, I think I need a moment alone." She shook her head. "You warned me about what lurked here in town, about dangerous people on the streets … that was you, though, wasn't it?"

"I suppose that's true. Many would call me a dangerous man. But no harm shall come to you, Jolene." As much as he wanted to pull over and reach out to her, to hold her tight, he knew that now was not the time. Doing so would only push her away further. "It's only natural for you to be frightened. Do whatever you need."

Her hands fell from her mouth, landing at her sides. "Are you just saying that?"

"No. I never say anything I don't mean. It's a waste of time to play games like that, don't you think?"

"That is very ironic coming from you."

"Ah, I suppose you're right."

"When was your first kill? Do I even want to know?"

"I was eleven, I think. It was about a year before my father died. He left me at one of Reiji Sato's restaurants, and we were the only ones there besides the employees. Someone tried to rob the place. I'd been studying for one of my mom's tests, so I took the textbook, snuck up behind the robber, and whacked him in the back of the head. As Reiji grabbed his gun, I hit him again, and again, until he stopped moving. Let's just say Reiji never needed to pull the trigger and my mother was furious that the pages got ruined."

"Is that why you haven't introduced me to your mom? Because she's a fucking psychopath?"

"She's also not in Riverpeak anymore, but that is certainly part of it."

"Oh, my God."

Sterling glanced over and studied her, letting his car drive itself. Her face contorted into something between shock and horror, with parted lips and furrowed brows wrinkling her forehead. But it was the look in her eyes that all but broke his heart, something he never wished to see again. She wouldn't even look at him, her gaze lingering on his hand—the same hand that, just moments ago, held the gun.

Sterling frowned and returned his attention to the road. "I don't like the way you're looking at me."

She snapped. "Well, I'm sorry. Can you blame me?"

"That's the thing. I can't. Just," he sighed, "please know that no matter what, no harm shall ever come to you. Ever."

"I'm just having a really hard time wrapping my brain around this."

"That is entirely understandable. If you need time to process, I will respect that."

Jolene scoffed. "Yeah, okay." The sarcasm dripped from her voice, practically thick enough to cut with a knife. "Don't people who walk away from the mob usually end up dead?"

"You weren't involved with the mob. You were involved with me. Just me. And regardless, as I've said, no harm shall ever come to you. Ever."

"Even if I walked away forever?"

Sterling gripped the steering wheel tighter, but nodded. "Even if you did, yes. You mean a great deal to me, Jolene."

Jolene wasn't sure what made her feel more nauseous: what he'd just done; the fact that she knew he meant it; or the fact that, despite the dead man on the runaway ramp, a part of her still loved the man sitting beside her.

CHAPTER 20

Sterling shoved his hands in his pockets as he looked out to the mountaintops. He envisioned his father among their heavenly peaks, almost within reach but too far to touch. As he shifted his weight, his long legs cast a wiry shadow behind him, making him look even taller than he was and larger than life. Constance's Pond sat below, some ripples in the water showing a promising night for any anglers—except there were none. It was just him, alone with his thoughts, wondering if Jolene would show up.

It'd been a week since he'd killed Detective McMahon. Sterling gave her two weeks to process without bothering her, not so much as even delivering lattes when she was working. He figured any reminders of him would be too much for her, so he gave her the space she needed.

But after two weeks and a glass of wine too many, he couldn't stop himself from sending the text, asking her to let him explain in more detail and where to meet him.

At the sound of footsteps rustling the grass, he turned to see Jolene making her way up the small incline. Her pink hair matched the sunset behind them—a romantic pastel sky—but her eyes held none of the same softness. He'd never seen her gaze so steely or her lips in such a hard frown.

"You came."

"Well, you asked nicely," Jolene said. "And I figured I'd at least hear you out." Her face contorted in discomfort as she cracked her neck, though he suspected the stretch wasn't what caused her visible pain. "Well, on with it, then."

"Everything I've done has been to obtain eternal life," Sterling said. "Watching my father die left an unimaginable impression on me, especially so young. If I could prevent that from happening to me, then, well ... that would be magnificent."

"So you killed how many people to make sure you got to live the rest of your days carefree and in comfort, huh?" Jolene shook her head. "How many people?"

Sterling sucked his teeth as he thought about it. "I wish I could give you a number."

Jolene hiccuped. "Were you ever planning on telling me?"

"In small doses."

Jolene wasn't crying, but she was on the verge. She wiped her eyes with her knuckle. "This isn't a drug you can micro-dose. There are consequences to your actions, Sterling. You understand that, right?"

"Of course I do. I'd say my father was living proof of that, but he's dead for it."

"Stop playing the dead dad card for five minutes, will you?" Jolene groaned. "Fuck. I'm sorry. That was harsh."

He closed his eyes for a moment, took a deep breath, and then opened them again. "You were right to be harsh."

"So, what was the initial plan, huh? Was any of this real between us, or was I just another step in your immortality plan?"

"Jolene, no. What I've felt for you has been unlike anything I've ever felt before. My love for you is more true than anything else, do you understand?"

"I wish I did. But this whole situation is so fucked." Jolene's voice cracked as tears welled behind her hazel eyes. "It's beyond fucked, and I don't even know what to say to you, because you mean a lot to me, you know? You helped me get my head out of my work and look at the bigger picture. Which has been extremely helpful in reaching my goals because I work better when I'm rested, might I add. But this? It's too much."

As she rubbed the pine tree tattoos standing tall on her forearm, Sterling felt his heart race. His chest rose and fell rapidly, enough for him to notice, and he was certain Jolene had, too. In full earnest, he said, "My sincerest apologies if I've disappointed you."

"That's one way to put it," she said with a nervous laugh. It turned into a sob. "Did you kill Josh?"

"Jolene—"

"Answer the question."

He nodded, so slowly and subtly that his head almost looked still. "That's correct. I used my power and snapped Josh's neck in that alley. He died quickly and did not suffer for long."

Jolene rubbed her eyes again and bent at the waist, curling into herself. "'For long?' You've got to be fucking kidding me. Is that why you killed that detective, then?"

"Jon McMahon was on my radar long before he showed up at my door to question you." She hiccuped another sob, but Sterling knew it was better to give her the truth. There was no sense in hiding anything from her anymore. "But protecting you did factor into my decision to kill him when I did, yes."

When Jolene stood again, she wiped her hands over her face. Black smeared beneath her eyes. "Jesus fuck."

"If you want out, I'd understand." He hoped she wouldn't, but the words he feared she'd say followed.

"It's just hard to put my feelings into words right now. I'm so conflicted, but if you're going to be some kingpin? Then no, that's not for me. This isn't goodbye. I just … I need some time."

"You're special to me, Jolene. I'll hold you to that." He cleared his throat. "Non-threateningly, I assure you."

Despite everything, Jolene couldn't help but laugh. "Sure. Sorry, I didn't mean for that to sound sarcastic."

"You've nothing to apologize for. Nor do you have anything to be afraid of."

She nodded. "I'll, uh, call you or something, I guess."

Even though it pained him to, even though he wanted to reach out his hand and grab her by the wrist and beg her for whatever it took, Sterling watched her walk away. The grass muffled the sound of her shoes until she faded from view, dipped beneath his viewpoint on the hill overlooking Constance's Pond.

Just like that, she was gone.

Before Sterling could mourn the loss of her by his side and debate if he should run after her, his phone rang. Noah's name flashed across the screen. He sighed, considered letting it go to voicemail, and then thought better of it. For as much as he wanted to, he couldn't let everything he'd done be for nothing.

"Yes?"

He felt his teeth clench and grind as Noah spoke. Sterling huffed out his nose and closed his eyes, feeling the tension build in his neck.

"Come to me again when you have proof, Noah, and I'll consider your claims. Until then."

———

As Jolene walked home, her day bag in hand, her mind raced. She felt the urge to change her hair color, find a spot to squeeze in another tattoo on her skin, and go for a long drive, but none of those things would satisfy her. While they'd provide pleasant distractions, she'd still have to face her thoughts at the end of the day.

It didn't stop her from swinging by the local pharmacy to grab a box of pink box dye: it would freshen up her roots and scratch the itch, she told herself. Anything to distract her from her conversation with Sterling.

When she arrived at work the next morning, Stella handed her something as she accepted her iced coffee and said, "You. Me. Let's go in two weeks."

Jolene looked down at the slip of paper Stella handed her: it was a concert ticket for a show at Red Rock Amphitheater. Jolene didn't recognize the band, but Stella continued, "They're one of my favorite metal groups. I got a targeted ad on Insta that they still had seats available. You've been spending too much time with Sterling."

"Not anymore. We got in a fight." Jolene swallowed. "I need this. Thank you."

Stella's eyes widened as she wrapped an arm around Jolene's shoulder. "Oh, shit, Jolene. What happened?"

"We just don't see eye-to-eye on some things. So I'm taking a breather before deciding on what to do next. There's a chance things might change, and I don't want to walk away without seeing if he'll follow."

"Eye-to-eye on what?"

"Just work-life balance stuff. Nothing too major, but enough for me to take a step back and take a breather, so things don't escalate."

It isn't a total lie, Jolene thought, *but Stella doesn't need to know the details.*

"Well, good thing I grabbed these tickets this morning."

"Yeah, I'm glad you did."

———

When they finally reached their seats, Jolene sat on the bench embedded into the cliff with a long sigh of relief. "God, I forgot how many stairs this place has."

Stella giggled. With all the red rocks jutting out around them, encasing them in the amphitheater and bathing them in the sunset, her dark complexion took on an amber hue. "Good thing you wore comfy shoes. My dumb ass wore heels."

"I'm imposing a two-drink limit for you, missy. Can't have you breaking an ankle."

"Thank you for driving," Stella replied with a sing-song voice. "And for being the best friend I could ever ask for."

"You've had two sips and you're already getting sappy on me?"

Stella rested her head on Jolene's shoulder. "These are sober thoughts, thank you. I'm just really glad we found each other. I dunno, being back in Denver always gets me in my feelings. So much happened here, but it's still such a cool city, you know? Like, how can I hate it when we have this," Stella swept an arm out in front of them, nearly whacking the couple sitting in front of them in the head, "as a concert venue? We could be in some boring stadium right now!"

As Jolene appreciated the sight before them, she nodded in agreement. The sunset over the stadium gave the entire amphitheater an orange glow as its rays bounced off the bright red sandstones. The rolling hills behind them, dotted with bright green pine trees, became harder to see as the sun dipped below the horizon. Red rocks jutted up toward the cotton candy-colored sky in sharp points and ridges. Despite the name suggesting Red Rocks was only varying shades of red, there was so much color that she wished she could draw the scene to capture it in eternity. She didn't work on landscape tattoos anymore, but it could make for a nice skateboard design.

Somewhere along that horizon, those who hurt her and Stella were just mere specs in the distance. They seemed so close, yet so small and insignificant as Jolene beheld nature around them. As a Colorado native, she made an effort to not take it for granted.

She felt like she had lately.

"I need to get out of Riverpeak more," Jolene said. "Let's try to do more when the shop is closed."

"I'd love that. Fuck Sterling."

Jolene chuckled. "I'm not *that* mad at him. Like you said, it's hard to be mad when you've got something so beautiful right in front of you."

"If you don't mind me asking, what's he like? Other than handsome and rich."

"Tortured, I think. He hides it well, though." Jolene frowned. "But being out here, taking it all in, I wonder if he liked me for me or because of some status thing."

"Oh, because you're a popular artist?"

"Something like that."

After all, her tattoos would make her the ultimate weapon, should he need it. Jolene realized that now. It was no wonder why he wanted to keep her safe and sound in his house. Part of her wanted to say that she knew him better than that and he did, in fact, care. After all, he'd let her walk away, and they hadn't spoken since she said she needed to think two weeks ago.

But she also knew he had eyes and ears everywhere, and was almost positive he kept tabs on her with that wall of security cameras of his. He hadn't been trying to scare her, but to reassure her, and while it worked at the time, she wasn't sure how she felt anymore.

"Well, it seemed like he really cared about you," Stella said. "Oh, I think the band's coming out!"

The crowd cheered as the guitarist strummed their first note.

After a few hours of heavy metal and rock lyrics being screamed-sung, Jolene felt clear-headed. Stella had been listening to them for years, and now she knew why. They were silent on the way to the parking lot to give their ears a break until they got in the car. The stars shone over the back roads on the way back to Riverpeak, reminding Jolene of the view from Sterling's pool and backyard. She'd rather not think about him, but continue to keep her mind as clear as she had during the concert. But as she reflected, she couldn't help but now see all the signs that she'd turned a blind eye to when she was naïve, in love, and too busy obsessing over crap on Instagram.

A silhouette blacked out the stream of light from the car's head-lights, pulling her from her train of thought. It stood on four legs, but from this distance, it was hard to tell exactly what it was.

"What the hell? Is that a moose?"

"It's huge," Stella said, leaning forward in the passenger seat. "Looks like it's hogging both lanes." The animal stood in the middle of the road, not budging, even as they approached.

Jolene eased her foot onto the brake pedal until they came to a stop a few feet away, where the animal just continued to stare. No one was behind her, but she put her hazards on. From this close, she could now see the moose's dark gray fur and curved antlers.

"Think I can go around if we hit the shoulder?" Jolene asked.

"Probably," Stella wagered. "Just be careful."

Jolene backed up to give themselves some extra room, but as soon as she did, the moose laid its ears back and took a step for every foot Jolene moved the car.

"Oh, you've got to be fucking kidding me," Jolene said. "Alright, I'm gonna have to beeline it."

"Why not use your powers?"

"I don't want to hurt it!"

"Do you have any for self-defense?"

Jolene tapped her lip with her finger and then had an idea. "Alright, hold on." She rolled her window down and summoned some butterflies from her leg, hoping they could provide a distraction or some cover. The butterflies fluttered out of the window, starting as a thin stream but eventually pouring out in a thick column. Once the last left the car, Jolene rolled the window back up and willed the butterflies to head toward the moose.

To her delight, it worked. The moose followed the butterflies out into the grasslands on the other side of the road, giving Jolene just enough time to speed her and Stella down the road.

Jolene sighed. "God, I'm a fucking freak of nature."

"Hey, hey, you aren't a freak of nature."

"Those were magic butterflies, Stella. They came out of my skin!"

"And? Listen, you're not a freak. That was so cool!"

When they stopped at a red light closer to town, Jolene hit her forehead against the top of the steering wheel. Her forearm pressed against the horn, and the accidental honk made her jump and straighten her posture.

She didn't need Sterling—not to protect her or to use her power. But she certainly wished he was there, consoling her and telling her that everything would be okay.

What she needed from him was to tell her how to live with her powers, how to adjust, and how to cope. Part of her envied his ruthlessness.

At the red light, Stella glanced out the passenger side window and looked down an alley. Jolene felt Stella smack her arm to get her attention.

"Look," Stella said. "Hematite!"

Jolene looked out Stella's window and saw the same vigilante who'd entered her shop last year, asking questions about Noah Sato. Feeling as if they had unfinished business, Jolene pulled the car over to a parking spot and got out.

"What are you doing?" Stella asked, now following close behind.

"Settling something I should have settled a long time ago." Jolene kicked a pebble down the alley, hoping to make some noise. As it scattered down the brick, she shouted, "Hey! Asshole! We need to talk!"

Even with his hoods and scarves, she could tell he looked right at her. Hematite reached for his billy club clipped to his belt, but Jolene summoned some lightning first.

Stella yelped. "Jolene, Jesus!"

"Let's chat, Hematite. No need to fight."

Through his voice changer, he sounded inhuman. "Prove it."

"Move your hand away from the billy club. You know me. I cooperated when you had questions about Noah. Well, now it's my turn."

Hematite placed his hands beside his head, letting her know he'd complied. She withdrew the lightning in response.

"I posted the fox emoji just like you told me to, and then you never came," Jolene said. "You never came, and then I got swindled into helping Sterling Harrison without even realizing it. Deep down, there's good in him, I know it. But I'm gonna need you to tell me everything you know about him and what your relationship is."

Hematite slowly dropped his hands. "Sterling is the kingpin. His father and Dr. Potter over at the lab on the west side of town created a weird version of methamphetamines. Now, Sterling makes his millions off of it."

Jolene gawked. "Millions?"

"An associate of mine got remote access to his safe when you were in Telluride. We didn't take anything, but we found millions."

"There's an eye scanner on that thing. How'd you get in?"

"Unimportant. He's good at his job."

Jolene swore under her breath. Then, Hematite told her everything he could while remaining anonymous: about his mother's drug addiction being the reason he couldn't die and why Brick Beast had the gift of super strength, about Reiji Sato's experiments on his son Noah, and then Noah's experiments on the theater with Amy Brewer.

Jolene's jaw clenched and felt tears well behind her eyes. Some of it, she'd already known, but Sterling had left the bulk of the story out. "Fuck, I think I'm going to throw up."

"What happened to you, Jolene?" Even with the voice modifier, Jolene could sense Hematite's concern. "Were you drugged?"

Jolene nodded and choked back tears. "That conniving little piece of shit." Her heart felt as if it had ripped in two. It had been so easy to fall in love with the charming, sad man who played the piano and grieved his father—and perhaps that had been his plan all along to rope her in. She wished it would be just as easy to hate him, but she couldn't bring herself to, not even as she cried in the alleyway. Despite it all, there was a tenderness to him she suspected was real among the lies and omissions.

"Do you think he killed Stella's client?"

"I know he did. He told me himself that he snapped the guy's neck." She wiped her eyes, letting the mascara and eyeliner smear on the back of her hand. "I feel like my entire summer has been a lie."

"Will he hurt you?"

"No. Maybe? I don't know. Probably not."

"Stay safe then, will you? And if you need anything, Rory Miller has my direct line. You know her?"

"Yeah, we're Facebook friends."

"Contact her. Tell her I sent you."

Even though she didn't think she ever would, Jolene nodded. "Sure."

"And Jolene?"

"Hm?"

"Don't let your guard down."

Hematite leaped up to a fire escape, and when she blinked, he'd already disappeared into the night.

CHAPTER 21

As the weeks went on, instead of turning social media comments off on each individual post, Jolene had to turn them off altogether. They just wouldn't stop: money bag emojis, people outright calling her a gold digger or a whore. Most of the trolls went back to her older posts to call her a coward for turning the comments off on her newer posts, so she turned them all off in their entirety. She tried to tell herself it didn't bother her. But when she woke up in her bed—finally, back in her own bed, where she should feel safe but felt so alone—and scrolled through her notifications, she just cried.

She couldn't help it. It *did* bother her.

What bothered her more than anything was the sheer irony in everything. No one criticized Sterling for dating her. There were no claims that he was just using her for her social media fame or to get free tattoos. No one said that the men leading the charge against her were conniving snakes, or jealous or too emotional, even though it was true.

And even though she knew it was true, the dogpiling with no end in sight still hurt.

She forced herself to get out of bed and dressed, struggling through the motions. The drive to Denver felt like a struggle, too, making her look over her shoulder more than she'd like to. The last thing she needed was for anyone to see her walking into a therapy appointment; it would give them an indication that they'd bothered her and thus won.

Dr. Marissa Thornton's dark hair was tied back into a bun this morning. Her expression faltered at the sight of her as they sat in their usual spots: Marissa in her chair, and Jolene in the one across from her.

"Your eyes are a little red. What's going on?"

Jolene picked up a pen to twirl it in her fingers, needing something to do so she could release her energy. She choked out a sob and then bit it back for the sake of just saying it instead of wasting the appointment crying in contextless silence. Once Jolene filled her in, Marissa nodded.

"I'm sorry to hear that, Jolene. That's fucking awful."

"I don't even know what to do. I thought being quiet would be the right thing to do, you know? Don't want to give him what he wants."

"Seems like you're damned if you do, damned if you don't. What's the risk of speaking up?" Marissa was calm as she spoke, a voice of reason that Jolene desperately needed. Stella and Annie had told her the same thing, but it felt different hearing it from an unbiased professional. "Are you worried it'll further damage your reputation?"

Jolene nodded. "I just always wanted to be a good person. And I thought that if I was a good person and I could do good things for the women in this industry, then good things would follow. Just keep my head down and do good work and offer a safe space kinda deal, you know?"

"How's your relationship with praise?"

Jolene blinked a few times as she processed the words. Faced with Marissa's hard-hitting question, she realized just how deep-rooted this all was. She remembered Sterling calling her a good girl. She remembered how she felt when she first reached a million followers, when she received awards at tattoo shows, and when she made her first $10,000 on her own at the shop. "I guess I rely on it for validation, come to think of it."

"So what happens if everything falls apart?" Marissa asked. "If the praise stops coming, then what?"

Jolene swallowed. "My reputation is tied directly to my success. If it's tarnished, I'll stop getting clients, and then I'll stop making money."

"But what else is there for you besides money?"

Jolene felt her chest heave as she thought about it. "Without the money, how am I supposed to create the safe environment that we so desperately need?" Another sob broke through. "I'm not even doing a good job at that, apparently. Creepy clients. Someone found one of them fucking dead outside of my shop and now the cops are questioning us, even though we had nothing to do with it. I just … I'd have nothing." She wiped her tears with the back of her hand, grateful that she thought better of putting her usual heavy eye makeup on before the appointment. "My community. My dreams. It'd all be gone."

"What about your family? Your boyfriend?"

Jolene shook her head. "I'm not talking to him right now, and my family … I wouldn't drag them into this."

"Oh, my apologies. What happened?"

Jolene was half-tempted to confess to her witnessing Detective McMahon's murder. But she didn't want to sink herself into any deeper of a mess than she was already in. "He keeps a lot of secrets," she decided on saying. "That's the best part about this, though, isn't it?" Jolene scoffed. "I'm not even talking to him right now and I still get the gold digger accusations."

"That is hard. I'd suggest leaning on your family. They may not understand, but I'm sure they'd be happy to be there for you."

Except, Jolene thought, unable to voice the concern, *what happens if that puts them in harm's way?*

———

Jolene picked at her bottom lip with her teeth as she stared at the tattoo parlor in the strip mall she sat outside of in her car. She wasn't sure what compelled her to come here, but she found herself there anyway, at the place where it all began. The red sign, simply reading TATTOO above the front door, was coated in dust, and the building needed power-washing. Just sitting there made Jolene feel dirty, especially as she remembered everything that happened to her and Stella here.

All the ridicule, harassment, and rampant sexism came flooding into her memory, making her wish she could peel her own skin off. She'd been so sure of herself when she walked through those doors for the very first time, only to leave with her tail between her legs.

But it all worked out.

Jolene knew that whatever she was going through with Sterling would, too. She always made it work.

But for now, she could at least enact some karma.

Jolene rolled her window down and let the butterflies sprout from her leg. They tickled her skin as they fluttered out of the car in a heavy stream—not unlike how she'd done with the moose in the road. As a tattoo client left the parlor, the butterflies swarmed together to enter, moving past the client and entering the shop. Once inside, they continued to multiply until all Jolene could see through the window was a wall of pink, blue, and purple. In a tight space like this, there was no doubt they'd become territorial, making them more prone to attack one another.

Even from her spot in her car, with her window rolled down, she could hear the commotion from inside the shop. A few people yelled profanities. One person screamed at a pitch that likely bothered a few dogs. Something—a tattoo machine, from the sound of it—dropped to the floor with a clang.

With shaky hands, Jolene grabbed her phone and texted her old mentor a single emoji: the butterfly.

Then, she tossed her phone in the passenger seat after she hit send, backed out of the parking lot, and drove away. In her rearview mirror, she could see him exit the shop, but the light was green. He'd never see her.

Once she was back on the long stretch of road in the middle of the grasslands, almost back to Riverpeak, she laughed. It started as one chuckle but grew into unadulterated manic laughter. Her hands still trembled, even with her tight grip on the steering wheel, and they hadn't stopped since she'd sent the text. Her phone buzzed incessantly in the passenger seat for the entire ride. The text message notifications popped up on her car's display since it was connected via Bluetooth®. Jolene ignored them all.

Her laughter eventually turned into tears. She couldn't help but think that Sterling rubbed off on her. Maybe witnessing someone she loved murder someone in near-cold blood fundamentally changed her, much like her experiences at that shitty old tattoo parlor did.

———

When her client arrived that afternoon, Jolene allowed herself to get lost in her work. The buzzing of the tattoo machine and the Japanese metal playing overhead took residence in her head, not leaving room for any other thoughts.

"So," she said to her client, a young woman with blonde hair swept back into a messy braid, "this is your first tattoo?"

"It is! I'm super stoked. This means so much to me."

"I'm happy to hear that. You can talk about it if you want, but no pressure to if you're uncomfortable."

"Oh, it's nothing that out of the ordinary. I've got religious trauma out the ass, that's all. I moved out to Fort Collins a few years ago, but finally feel like I'm mentally free of it, not just physically. A lot of therapy helped."

"You drove all this way from Fort Collins? Holy shit."

"Yeah! You're worth it."

Jolene swallowed back tears; at least her reputation hadn't been completely tanked. People were still coming in and she hadn't lost any clients yet. The fact that they were still coming in from Fort Collins spoke volumes. "That means a lot. Thank you. Seriously."

"Like I said, worth it. I trust you with this. Long story short, my parents were part of this extreme church in Utah. Getting out meant having to walk away from everyone and being denounced and disgraced. I just thought there was so much more to life than getting married and popping out seven kids, you know?"

"Fuck yeah. Good for you."

"Thanks. It was just so tough. It's like, my parents and the church groomed me for it, so having to deprogram has been one hell of a ride. I turned to magical girl anime to feel empowered, and when I saw you did original ones, I got so excited."

"Girl, you're gonna make me cry. Shit." They both laughed. "You should write a book or something. That's so inspiring."

"Oh, you're too kind."

While Jolene added the color to the magical girl, she thought about Sterling. *He and this woman weren't too different in a fucked up sort of way,* she thought. The thought wouldn't leave her head for the rest of the appointment, even as the girl paid, gave her a hug, and then was out the door.

As Jolene cleaned down her station, she heard the front door chime out front. She recognized the sound of the footsteps, the familiar gentle clack of Sterling's dress shoes on the floor audible even over the music. When she looked up, he was already in the doorway, leaning against it with his arm propped up on the top of the frame. Dark bags lined the bottom of his eyes and his cheekbones were more pronounced than she remembered. She spotted a wrinkle in his dress shirt, something so uncharacteristic for him that she knew he wasn't well.

"Hi," she said, wanting to break the silence. A part of her wanted to run for him, to wrap her arms around his waist and cry into his shirt with its single wrinkle as she told him everything that happened today. But she held back, not wanting to crumble so easily.

"Hi," he said, the word hardly a breath. "I heard about what happened at that tattoo spot in Denver." His voice was hoarse. "News spreads fast."

"I heard about that too," Jolene said. "Come in."

"You sure?" He stayed where he stood. "I don't want to impose. When I heard about that, I just thought, maybe … I don't know what I thought, actually."

"I'm sure. Close the door behind you." She set down the cleaning products and crossed her arms, unsure of what else to do with her limbs. Sterling crossed the threshold and did as she asked, and once he shut the door, she said, "I scared the shit out of myself. It's like I blacked out and just went there and did that."

"He apologized on his Instagram Stories," Sterling said. "Anthony has been monitoring the situation for me."

"Your bodyguard, right?"

"Right."

"What were you going to do if I didn't? Kill him?"

"No," Sterling said. "Especially after Josh, I wouldn't want to put that kind of spotlight on you. It would look suspicious."

"And if they hadn't questioned me about Josh?"

"Then we'd be having a different conversation," Sterling said, pocketing his hands. "But that's not what I'm here to talk about. I just wanted to see if you were okay." His voice nearly cracked.

"Have you been eating?" Jolene asked.

"Don't concern yourself with my well-being."

"Have you been eating? Sleeping? Anything?"

"Hematite has kept me too busy for such things," Sterling said, running a hand down his face. "And when I do finally get to rest, I worry about you. But that is my own cross to bear. As I said, don't concern yourself with it."

Jolene frowned. "I've been a mess, too, for what it's worth. I'm paranoid as fuck."

"I'm sorry to hear that."

"Listen, Ster. I'm just going to address the elephant in the room, okay? I know you were raised for this lifestyle and your parents isolated you from the rest of the world, so I can sympathize with you. Really, I can. Deprogramming is probably gonna be one hell of a ride for you. So if you promise me you'll tie up some loose ends, then we can make something work."

As his gaze softened, his lips parted in the slightest; Jolene almost didn't notice. Sounding defeated yet hopeful, he asked, "You mean that?"

"I do. Just ... I didn't sign up to sell drugs or be a part of a crime ring. I just want to give good tattoos and be a good person. Live a quiet life and all that. So if that's something you're willing to do with me, then I'll be waiting."

"Loose ends. Right." Sterling nodded. "I'll tie them up, I swear it.

Just … I have one last thing I need to do. Let me finish that and then maybe we can get you that shop in Colorado Springs."

"For real?"

"I promise."

Jolene smiled. "Good. Call me when you do."

He leaned down to kiss her cheek. "I will." The ghost of his kiss lingered as he left, leaving Jolene to wonder if he really would choose her over his power.

CHAPTER 22

n the harsh light of Dr. Potter's office, Naomi tapped on her smartwatch and nodded. "Alright. The timer is on."

When Hannah slid off the examination table and landed on her feet, she cracked her neck and sighed in relief. "Well, I think the inhibitor worked."

Elijah removed his thumbnail from his teeth. "You can already tell?" Kane and Rory were on his left, with Naomi and Brad on his right. Even Brad's hand on his shoulder hadn't been enough to ease his nerves as he watched Doctor Potter testing on Hannah. She'd been the obvious choice since her powers weren't as high stakes as Kane's, but it didn't make him feel any better about it, regardless.

"I'm as clear-headed as ever," Hannah said, "so I think it did."

"Try changing one of our moods or something." Rory smiled. "Make Elijah chill out."

Hannah nodded and focused on him. "Okay," she said to herself, "just like you practiced with Elijah and Kane." After focusing for a minute, she exhaled. "Okay, I give up. How do you feel, hon?"

"Still like shit."

"Yeah," Kane said, "it worked, all right. That was quick."

"Now we see how long it lasts," Naomi said. "What's our projection?"

"It should work for at least two minutes," Doctor Potter, who was standing in the corner fidgeting with a clipboard, said. "Though that's just my hypothesis based on the strength."

"How are you feeling, Hannah?" Kane asked. "Any side effects?"

Hannah shook her head. "Nope. I'm fine."

Elijah asked her the same question, but in Hebrew. When she replied with an affirmation, she grabbed his hand and squeezed it. Only then did Elijah relax.

"Do we know this will work on him? Sterling, I mean?" Hannah asked. "I've got one power. He has multiple."

"It should, since it's based on the cell response. I'll spare you the gory details, but while there's a chance it'll only neutralize one, it should work."

Hannah sighed. "Great." She didn't sound too convinced.

Rory turned to Doctor Potter, examining his body language only to find him hard to read. "Did you ever get Jordan's results, by the way?"

"I did," Dr. Potter said. "Her DNA suggests she may have a super-power of her own after all. However, her brain chemistry is compa-rable to someone with severe post-traumatic stress disorder. Her trauma is blocking her from unleashing her power, whatever that may be." Dr. Potter looked at Rory and said, "Based on your own experi-ence, Ms. Miller, I suggest you speak with her."

"I'll continue to," Rory said.

Hannah looked at Naomi and said, "Time, by the way. I can feel it fading."

"Two minutes," Naomi confirmed. "So that's our window."

"Potter, who has powers and works for Sterling?" Hannah asked. "What exactly are we up against?"

Dr. Potter offered Hannah a sympathetic smile. "As I told you when you arrived, Sterling has multiple gifts, as does his bodyguard, Anthony. Anthony has super strength and bulletproof skin. Then, of course, you already know about Noah and Amy. Those four are the only ones, as far as I know."

"What can Sterling do?" Hannah asked. "You haven't said."

"He may have been responsible for Ms. Miller's wrist."

Rory's brows furrowed as she rubbed the spot where the brace had recently come off. "What?"

Dr. Potter continued, "Sterling has both impeccable reflexes and an ability to break and heal bones. Have you run into him at all?"

"I did, right before a boxing class. I broke my wrist when I hit the bag ... oh, shit."

"So," Hannah said as she paced the room, examining different vials and bottles on the counter, "even if we do get the inhibitor to work on Sterling, we're seriously outmatched. What the hell do we do? I can sway people to leave us alone and to lay down their arms, but not on more than one person at a time."

Rory said, "Hannah's right. We're outnumbered and will get our asses kicked. Kay, if they kill you first, that gives them ten to fifteen minutes to do whatever the hell they want with the rest of our mortal souls."

"Let me set some cameras up in here," Elijah said. "I can watch. Hannah, would being in the car put you within range if necessary?"

She picked up a vial of neutralizer and pocketed it. No one questioned her. "It should."

"That's great, but it's not enough," Rory said.

Before they could decide what to do, the alarm blared, then silenced. They heard a boot kicking down a door, followed by Noah's voice.

"Come out, come out, wherever you are!"

Dr. Potter looked at Rory, Kane, and their friends and said, "Run. If you go to the hallway, you'll find a back door. The keypad is 1977."

"Thank you," Rory said. "Come on, let's go."

They left before Noah could find them, but when the door closed behind them, they looked around and saw Dr. Potter wasn't with them.

Kane sighed. "Fuck."

———

Noah whistled as he made his way through Potter Laboratories. Amy's hands were still blue with the chill of her ice, which she'd used to freeze the alarm system. As they walked side-by-side, he played with the lighter in his right hand. Sterling and Anthony flanked them.

"I saw their car, Doc," Noah called. "We know they were here. No sense in hiding."

"You heard him, Potter," Sterling called. "We just want to talk."

Noah lifted his combat boot-covered foot and kicked down the door to Dr. Potter's office. There, he saw the Doctor standing alone.

"Gentlemen. Ms. Brewer. How may I assist you today?"

"Don't play stupid, Potter," Noah said as a wicked smirk graced his face. "You want to be frozen or burned? We'll let you pick."

"Oh, there's no need," Dr. Potter said. Sterling just chuckled and focused on Dr. Potter's leg, snapping it at the shin. The doctor howled in pain as he collapsed, clutching at his calf, but Sterling pushed past Amy and Noah to approach him.

"If you don't want them to do my dirty work for me," Sterling said, "then I'll just have to do it myself." He placed his foot on Dr. Potter's head. The black dress shoe shined in the fluorescent light above.

"Please," Dr. Potter said. "Please, I can still help."

Sterling sucked his teeth. "Do you really think your begging will help you now?"

The doctor stuttered, then shouted, "I've been using them! I have a way to stop them!"

Sterling lowered his foot, bringing Dr. Potter's head closer to the linoleum with it. "Speak fast, Potter."

"It's in my pocket! You can take it! It's a neutralizer that inhibits powers! Use it against Hematite if you must."

Sterling looked up and nodded at Anthony. "Grab it." His bodyguard did as commanded. "How long is it good for?"

"Two minutes."

"So I'll have two minutes to kill him if I hit him with this?" Sterling extended a hand to Anthony, palm open and facing upward. Anthony placed the vial in Sterling's hand. With his other hand, he pinched it with his fingers to lift it to the light. "What a beautiful shade of blue. Reminds me of the ocean on a clear day."

With a grin, Noah teased, "Since when are you waxing poetic?"

Sterling chuckled. "Jolene's artistic nature must have rubbed off on me."

"Is two minutes enough, sir?" Dr. Potter asked with a stutter. "I-I can strengthen it, if you'd wish."

"No, no. Two minutes is plenty. I'll only need two seconds to kill him. Now, the question is how?"

Sterling looked down at Dr. Potter, seeing his wicked smirk in the reflection of the doctor's glasses. Beneath Sterling's foot, Dr. Potter trembled.

"Perhaps I could snap his neck just like I did to that vermin who dared enter Jolene's studio. But that wouldn't be very original, now would it? Should I just shoot him in the head? Maybe I'll get him there and in the heart for good measure. Then there's Noah and Amy. We could burn him alive or freeze his organs. Or we could make that little girlfriend of his do it. Now that would be interesting, wouldn't it?"

Dr. Potter opened his mouth to speak, but he only whimpered.

"What's the matter? Is it all too much? Do you view the boy as your little Frankenstein freak of a creation?" Sterling put more of his weight on the foot that was on Dr. Potter's head. "Why else would you protect them?"

"I ... I ... I..." Dr. Potter dry-heaved. "I don't have a reason."

"Then tell us where they went."

"Out the back. I suspect Naomi and Brad will leave."

"We'll let those two go. I wouldn't dare hurt family, after all, and I know how much Noah cares for his baby sister."

Noah sighed in relief, so quiet it was barely audible.

Sterling lifted his foot from the doctor's head and then kicked him in the mouth, rendering Dr. Potter unconscious. "Let's move. They can't have gone too far."

Sterling asked, "The one he's hiding from me, is it Rory Miller? Has she truly become a little Hematite 2.0?"

Noah shook his head. "No, I don't think so. I've been keeping an eye on them. Kane would stop her before she could go that far."

Amy spoke up, feeling less timid than usual. "Great, but we should get them before they leave. We should split up. We're stronger than they are. So even if there's less of us, we'd still stand a chance."

"Clever girl," Noah said. "We can take the lobby in case they circle back around."

"Go," Sterling said. "Carter, Anthony, and I will go toward the back."

With a nod, Noah and Amy departed, leaving the other three men to head down the hall. Sterling sent Carter off to branch into the other hallway, leaving just him and Anthony to find the other way out.

The halls held more rooms than Sterling had been in; most of these, he wasn't even sure if the doctor used them. He lingered outside of one with his father's name on the door, the plaque dull and rusted: the only unclean thing in the entire building. Sterling scowled and kept moving forward, aware that he couldn't afford to become sentimental now that he had his chance to put an end to this.

"What's the plan?" Anthony asked.

"I need to get Hematite alone, preferably. We won't show our hand right away. The neutralizer from Potter is already in a syringe, so once I can, I'll stab him with it and be done with him."

With Hematite gone, there'd be no more obstacles. Whereas before, he'd been content to unmask the fellow and ruin his career, but now there was the opportunity to finally kill him. What was once impossible was now within his grasp.

CHAPTER 23

Nothing helped Jolene's paranoia.

She tried visiting a dispensary like Dr. Potter mentioned, and while it helped lull her to sleep, she still struggled during the day. Even though no one bothered her anymore on social media—she'd turned comments back on with no backlash—it still weighed heavy on her mind, especially since those thoughts were tangled up with Sterling's business dealing and Josh's murder.

Though she supposed with Detective McMahon dead, Josh's murder shouldn't be a concern anymore.

But it didn't stop her from looking over her shoulder every time she crossed a street. She was positive Sterling wouldn't hurt her. Despite it all, it felt as if there was a constant battle between her logical mind and the irrational fears and beliefs that took over.

As Jolene left Jefferson Coffee with an iced matcha latte in hand, she tensed at the sight of the stranger approaching her. The man was around her height and, thanks to his baseball cap and disposable face mask, she couldn't recognize him. Despite the summer heat, he wore a plain long-sleeved T-shirt and jeans.

"Jolene Gautier?"

Jolene hesitated. She wasn't sure who he was with; if he was the asshole who took that photo, if he was with Sterling, or worse: one of Sterling's enemies. "Who's asking?"

"I have the information you'll want. About him."

Jolene swallowed. "Do you..?"

"Work for him? I'm on his payroll, but no, I don't. I can explain momentarily."

She sighed. "Follow me, but from a distance, so we don't look suspicious. I can get us somewhere private."

"Where? There are cameras all over this town."

"Not all over. I've seen 'em. Just be quiet and follow me."

Jolene took the long way to the studio before making her way around to the back. The man in the hat came around the corner two minutes later.

"Who the fuck are you?" Jolene asked. She'd already summoned the self-defense tool that Annie tattooed on her, now gripping it in her knuckles with her free hand. In the other, she could feel the condensation from her iced matcha latte already building up on her palm.

"Not sure we've officially met." He removed his hat, revealing dark curls, and lowered his mask to show his face. "Alex Parker."

"You're the new chief of police," Jolene realized. She didn't loosen her grip on the self-defense tool, the cat's ears sticking out from her fingers. "Why come to me like this?"

He looked over his shoulder. "We're truly hidden back here?"

Jolene nodded. "I swear, and the cameras out front are mine, so we're clear."

"Good. I've seen you around town with Sterling Harrison. Am I right in my assumptions?"

"What are your assumptions?" It sounded more like a demand than a question with her flat tone.

"That you're special to him. Is he special to you?"

She frowned and took a sip of matcha. "You could say that, though I'd say my definition of special might vary."

"I did some digging on you. Despite what that self-important asshole leading the smear campaign has said about you, you don't strike me as the type to be okay with Sterling's line of work. Detective

McMahon had his suspicions and I feel like a fucking asshole for not warning him more."

"You're right. I'm not okay with it. But it should be over soon. He told me he's tying up some loose ends and then it should be done."

"You gave him an ultimatum?"

"I did."

"Well, I'm sorry to say it, but I think he crossed you, Ms. Gautier."

As she took another sip of her drink, she gnawed at her straw. "How do you mean?"

"I trailed him going to Potter Laboratories this morning. Listen, I can't go after him. He threatened me, and the last thing I want is to put my wife in harm's way. We've both seen what he's capable of."

"Unfortunately." Jolene crossed her arms over her chest, unsure of what to do with her hands in her anxiety. "How long have you known about him?"

"I knew his father was into it, but I've only known he took over for a few months now. I—"

But Jolene cut him off, her brows furrowed and a scowl forming on her face. "Wait a minute. You've known about Sterling for months? He threatened you months ago and you've done nothing about it since?"

"He threatened my family!"

"You mentioned you're on his payroll. Is he paying you off like he is the rest of the department?" When Alex didn't reply, Jolene scoffed. "Oh, my God. Why not take the money to get your family out of town for a week? Treat them to a little vacation out on some island or something where they won't have cell phone service, and then do your damn job?" She shook her head. "See, this is why everyone fucking hates you guys. When you're not harassing people for simply existing, you're letting people like Sterling give you hush money. Well, now your detective is dead. Maybe if you did something sooner, none of us would be in this mess and McMahon's wife wouldn't be a widow."

Alex pointed a finger at her, but dropped it. "I ... you're right."

"Yeah, I know I am. What the hell was McMahon doing in Telluride, anyway?"

"He thought Sterling might have another base of operations there. That's why he followed you. He also was convinced the only way to get the job done was to leave Riverpeak, given the entire department has been in on this since well before I got here. What were you doing there, anyway?"

"As you're already aware, I had a jealous piece of shit start beef with me on social media. Sterling was trying to help me relax and unplug, because it was stressing me the hell out. No drug deals involved. You know, maybe he wasn't half as bad as you all thought."

"Are you forgetting the part where I said he threatened my family?"

"And are you forgetting the part where I said you're all to blame for letting him?"

"Maybe, but that doesn't change the fact that he owns this town, and we might as well call him Don Harrison."

Jolene rolled her eyes. "You're missing the point. Well, thanks for the tip. Now if you'll excuse me, I'm gonna go do your job for you. I expect a check in the mail from your department if I succeed."

As she turned away, Alex called her name.

"What?"

"I know you're not a gold digger."

"Yeah, well, maybe I should start leaning into the rumors. I'll get some ridiculous jewelry or something."

"If you were going to do that, you would have already."

"You don't know me well enough to make that judgment call." She'd never admit it, but the chief of police was right. "But I've got more pressing matters to attend to, anyway."

"Good luck, Gautier. You're going to need it."

He was right about that, too.

———

When Jolene pulled her car into Potter Laboratories' parking lot, she felt hot and heavy as she stepped outside. The bulletproof vest she'd swiped from Sterling didn't fit her perfectly, but well enough to protect her. The bulky material was enough to make her sweat as she made the walk from her car to the lab, and she couldn't help but squirm within it as she tried to adjust it. She gave up once she reached the front door, accepting that her chest would feel constricted and that she'd just need to take a cold shower to cool off when she got home.

Unsure of what exactly she'd find inside, the fluorescent lights blinded her from overhead. Inside the lobby, Jolene saw Noah and Amy standing side-by-side, guarding the entrances of the two main hallways in the building. They turned at the sound of the front door opening.

"Jolene?" Noah sounded as surprised as he looked, golden eyes wide and dark brows raised.

Amy brushed her red hair back and frowned as she looked Jolene up and down. "What are you doing here?"

Jolene kept her tone even, not wanting to hint at her internal panic. "Looking for Sterling."

"How'd you know we were here?" Amy asked.

"I had some unexpected help. Don't worry about it."

"Is anyone else coming?" Noah asked. "Are you alone?"

"I'm alone. It's just me, I promise. Where the hell is he?"

"He just made his way to the testing room," Noah said. "Where the water tank is."

"What's he doing there?"

"Luring Hematite over. Anthony went with him."

"And where's … what's his name? Carter?"

"Going after Hannah and Elijah," Amy said. "They've been working remotely to back up Hematite."

"No one needs to die today," Jolene said. "No one. I don't care what side anybody is on."

"Listen, Jolene, you're preaching to the choir," Noah said. "Those are my sister's friends. Shit, for all I know, she and my brother-in-law aren't far from here, just waiting for some signal. You really think I wanna see them get hurt?"

"So what do we do?" Jolene asked.

"Just protect yourself and see if you can reach him," Amy said. "Sterling loves you. If you get a hold of him, he'll listen to reason."

Jolene nodded, but turned at the sound of footsteps approaching them in the lobby. From one of the two hallways, a silhouette resembling Hematite formed. When they grabbed their billy club, Noah grimaced and said, "Jolene! A little help here before you go?"

Jolene frowned as she watched Amy create a protective barrier of ice. On the one hand, she didn't want to fight, but she also didn't want to see her friends get hurt. As her mind raced, her heart pounded loud so loud that it became the only thing she could hear. She wondered what she was even doing here.

Were those assholes on Instagram right? Jolene couldn't help but think to herself that they were. *Why else would I be here, fighting for Sterling if not for the fact that he could help me get to Colorado Springs? I witnessed him kill somebody just for driving behind us. What the fuck is wrong with me?*

Overhead, the fluorescent strips flickered off. Noah flipped open a lighter and grew the flame just enough to offer some light, but kept it away from Amy's ice. Now, Jolene didn't have time to chastise herself for finding her way into this predicament and would have to resume her internal lament later. She didn't have time for her panic, either.

"If I had to guess, I'd say Elijah probably got the lights," Noah said. "Are you gonna help or what?"

"Fuck, sorry." Jolene focused on Noah as she summoned his snake and fox. "This shit trips me up. Are you guys used to this?" The scales lifted from his arm first, forming new skin as the snake plopped to the floor with a thud. The fox followed, orange fur floating in the firelight.

"Eh," Noah said, voice cracking, "you start to expect it, but it still keeps me on my toes."

The snake slithered down the hallway as the fox pranced after it. It turned a few corners before, in the distance, they heard a feminine shriek as the silhouette fell out of view, blending in with the shadows.

"That wasn't Hematite," Amy said. "That was Rory. She's probably heading for him."

CHAPTER 24

n the dark, Jolene heard Noah shout, "We need to get the lights back on."

"I'll find them," Jolene said. "Stay safe, okay?"

"Need a light?" Noah asked. "I carry a backup lighter."

Jolene summoned a ball of lightning from her Raijin tattoo. The blue and white glow illuminated the surrounding space. "I'll manage. Thanks, though."

She darted into the hallway, where she saw the snake and fox traverse. Her stomach was in knots, her nerves worse than ever as she wondered how she ended up in this situation. The life she knew as a normal woman was long gone, but if she played her cards right, she could get things back on track. Ideally, she'd steer Sterling in the right direction, too, but she was prepared for the worst.

I never asked for powers, Jolene thought. *But I guess Hematite didn't, either.*

It took a few rooms, but Jolene eventually found the breaker. The lights flickered back to life, and Jolene slumped against the wall with a sigh of relief.

As she turned down the hall, Jolene spotted a hooded and masked figure. They dressed identically to Hematite, but their frame was shorter and curvier; the hoodie almost hid their shape, but the way the pants fit around the thighs gave it away.

"Rory?" Jolene asked. "Is that you?"

There's no one else it could be, Jolene thought. Rory didn't answer, but stalked forward.

Jolene held her hands up and took a step back. "Wait!"

"For what? For you to hit first? I don't think so."

As Rory grabbed the billy club clipped to her belt, she extended it with a snap, making it questionably lethal. Upon a quick evaluation, Jolene determined that one hit wouldn't kill her, but would hurt well enough to wonder how many strikes would do the job.

She didn't want to find out the answer to that question.

"Listen ... Rory, that *is* you, right?"

Rory stepped forward. "Whatever you say better be good."

Jolene kept her hands by her face as she walked backward, hoping to guard herself against Rory. She juggled that with thinking of what tattoos she could use that would be best for defense. Raijin on her thigh was out of the question, but she summoned the butterflies surrounding the geisha on her leg to buy herself some time.

As Rory lifted the billy club, purple, white, and pink butterflies swarmed around Jolene, emerging from her calf to encircle her and block her from view. She couldn't see Rory past the thick wall of them, small wings fluttering in a massive blur. As the last butterfly to spring from her skin tickled her calf, she remembered the tattoos on her other leg.

"What's with the butterflies, Jolene, huh?" There was a bite to Rory's voice that Jolene didn't find promising.

The fantasy sword and shield were some of the first tattoos she'd ever gotten nearly a decade ago. Jolene summoned the shield and watched it materialize on her arm from a bundle of light. The fluorescent strips overhead reflected in the silver border of the shield, nearly blinding Jolene when angled just right.

It gave her the perfect idea.

"Do you not like butterflies, Rory?"

"I mean, I do, but not like this." With a swipe of the billy club, a diagonal strip dissipated into thin air. It left behind a narrow trail of smoke that whirled in their place before that, too, faded. Through the line of missing butterflies, Jolene could see Rory over the top of the shield.

"A shield?" If Jolene didn't know any better, she'd say Rory seemed amused.

"I don't want to fight you."

"Yet you're here."

"I came here to ask everyone to knock this shit off. Sterling seems to listen to me."

"Yeah, sure."

"Rory, I'm serious. Come on, we went to school together. You know me better than this. I told Sterling it's either me or this shit show. He told me he was wrapping things up. I had no idea that *this* is what he meant by that. Please, hear me out."

"I'm not sure I should."

"Why not?"

"Sterling has killed people, Jolene! Including the only decent cop in this town! Why should I believe he'd listen to anyone?"

Jolene tilted the shield, letting the light bounce off into Rory's eyes, the only part of her face that wasn't covered. As Rory lifted her arm to block the light, Jolene ran, knowing it was too late to reason with her.

She needed to find Sterling before he could hurt anyone else.

———

As the door behind him closed and Sterling lit a cigarette, Kane frowned. The aqua chamber was full of water, but a tarp covered the top of it.

Kane said, "You shouldn't smoke those things. It'll fuck up your lungs."

Sterling grinned from ear to ear, the cigarette still between his teeth. "And so what if they do?" He grabbed it with his middle and index finger and pointed at Kane with it. "My lungs will just regenerate, anyway. Just like yours, isn't that right?"

Kane's brows furrowed. "What?"

Sterling laughed as he sat in one of the folding chairs and leaned back in his seat, crossing his legs with his ankle on the top of his thigh. He took a long drag of his cigarette and puffed out a long string of smoke. "We have a mutual friend, you know. You were so eager for answers that your tunnel vision blinded you to the bigger picture."

Kane's fists clenched. "What are you talking about?"

"Dr. Potter had all of your blood samples, cell swabs, and you name it. You were so trusting." Sterling held the cigarette over the ashtray on the table next to him as he continued to laugh. "Allow me to let you in on a little secret. Noah wasn't just built to handle you in a fair fight. He was my life insurance policy. Between his sacrifice and your little oversight, I have finally accomplished my dream. This whole operation is so much bigger than you."

In the corner of his eye, Sterling caught sight of Carter. The laboratory door swung shut behind him as he moved straight for him.

Sterling asked, "Did you deal with the tech?"

Carter frowned. "I'm afraid the tables have turned, sir."

Sterling sighed as he assessed Carter's body language. Carter continued to cross the room with tense shoulders and balled fists.

Sterling demanded, "What happened?"

"I... I'm being controlled."

Sterling sighed. *So Noah had been right to think Potter was hiding someone from us*, he thought. Reaching into his shoulder holster, Sterling removed his gun and shot Carter once. The bullet lodged in Carter's shoulder, making him stumble back. Sterling tutted his tongue, disappointed at himself for missing, and then shot again, this time hitting the once-loyal brunette in the heart.

Carter's body hit the floor with a thud. Sterling stood and strolled over to Carter, gun still in hand and hanging at his side.

"Which one of them sent you after me, hm?"

"The writer. The blonde girl." As Carter choked the words out, blood spat up and dribbled down his chin, painting his lower lip bright red.

"The blonde girl?"

Carter nodded as he took his final breaths. "Thank you."

Kane stepped forward. "I'm sorry. Did he just thank you for killing him?"

Sterling shrugged a shoulder as he looked around the room. "Some of us like to go out like real men, I suppose. While I'd rather not die at all, I'd prefer to do so with honor if I had to, not with someone else adjusting the dials in my head."

As Sterling checked his bullet chamber, ensuring there was still at least one more in there, he walked to the hall. Kane followed him and said, "Hold on. We weren't done speaking."

"Well, can you walk and talk? I find myself suddenly preoccupied."

"I won't let you kill Elijah."

"Oh, I'm not going after Elijah, nor am I going after his girlfriend." He proved it by walking past the main lobby, instead taking another turn down the hall toward Dr. Potter's office. "They're in the car monitoring you with cameras, correct? Anyway, Hannah Cohen is far too high-profile. However, I don't take well to liars."

Before Kane could interfere or say anything, Sterling pushed open the door to Dr. Potter's office, pointed his gun, and shot for the third time. Dr. Potter slumped over his desk, crimson spilling out onto the metal and dripping onto the floor, rapidly forming a large pool.

Kane felt his own blood run cold. "What the hell have you done?"

"Oh, come on, Kane. Don't sound too disappointed. This snake in the grass couldn't decide which one of us should be his prey, so I've eliminated the predator altogether." Sterling looked at Kane and smiled, a wicked grin that seemed inhuman. "I should be thanking you, you know."

"Thanking me? What the fuck for?"

Sterling made his way back to the aqua chamber, sheathing his gun. Kane followed. "If it wasn't for your little schtick as Hematite, we'd have never discovered the full possibilities of my father's creation with Dr. Potter. It was your emergence that alerted us to the possibility of superpowers."

Kane swallowed, remembering how Dr. Potter once told him the same thing, and couldn't help but wonder if he could have avoided all of this.

"Thanks to you," Sterling said, "I've reached my full potential. You coming back to life in that shed all those years ago changed our town forever."

"You're full of shit," Kane said, fists clenched despite knowing it was the truth. "You're just trying to get under my skin."

"Why would I lie to you, Kane? Especially now? Especially when you're too late to do anything to stop me?"

"We're not too late."

"Then why haven't you attacked me yet?" Sterling asked. "Are you waiting for me to show my hand?"

Instead of answering, Kane groaned in frustration. "Where the hell is Jameson when you need him?"

"Jameson? As in Shawn Jameson?" Sterling cackled. "Surely you've assumed the worst by now. You'd have been right."

"Wait, what?"

"That's right, Hematite. Your friend's muscle lives on only in my bodyguard now. How do you think he got so strong?"

"What?" The blues of Kane's eyes darkened. "Are you telling me Jameson's dead?"

"Oh, so you didn't bother to look for him over the last few months?" Sterling took a drag of his cigarette. "Some friend you are."

"I had no intentions of maintaining a friendship after I found out what he did to Amy."

"But didn't you wonder? You're a cat that curiosity can't kill. It didn't get to you?"

"So you killed him for your bodyguard to steal his powers, is that it?"

"Oh, no. Amy did the honors. Her quest for vengeance just so happened to work in my favor. I still owe Noah my thanks for his quick thinking of taking Shawn's samples before they gave him a complimentary cremation."

Kane scoffed as he shook his head. "You know, I thought I'd heard it all, but you are a heartless motherfucker."

"I get that a lot. Your lack of creativity disappoints me. If you were hoping to insult me, I'm afraid you'll have to do much better than that."

Kane went to speak, but Rory swung open a door, beating him to the punch. "Maybe she can talk some sense into you, then." Walking side by side with her was a frowning Jolene.

Sterling froze. He wasn't sure how Jolene would greet him after some brief time apart, but this wasn't what he'd expected.

With her arms extended out by her sides, Jolene yelled, "What the actual fuck, Sterling?"

As he stepped toward her, he dropped his cigarette, stepping on it as he extended his hands to her. "Darling, it's not safe in here."

"Because of you!" Jolene swatted his hands away. "I know what you've done. I know the whole story. You can't talk your way out of this one."

Sterling looked to his right, where Anthony stood near the water tank. "Get her out of here."

Sending her away pained him, but it was too late to recruit her now. Perhaps in another life, she'd have fought by his side as the greatest weapon in Riverpeak. But Jolene didn't understand what he needed to do. She defined wrapping up loose ends too differently from him. When he walked in the door, he thought he could get away with it and have it all.

He knew better now, but would always cherish the taste of love she'd given him. If she'd have him again, he decided, he wouldn't deny her. He wasn't sure he ever could deny her—except for when it came to this.

"No!" Jolene stepped forward, summoning the self-defense tool tattooed on her ankle as she did. Anthony scooped Jolene up with powerful arms, and she reached over to his neck to hit him with the cat-shaped weapon.

The pointed ends of the cat's ears dug into Anthony's skin, causing him to drop Jolene. As she fell from his grip, she dropped the self-defense tool, which hit the ground with a clang before it vanished into dust. Jolene scrambled to her feet, using her hands to help find her balance as she did. But before Anthony could grab Jolene again, she summoned the sword from the back of her leg. It felt heavy in her grip, and the fluorescents bouncing off the steel gave the sword an illusion that it glowed, but she stood firm as she said, "Don't get any closer to me."

But Anthony obeyed Sterling's command, attempting to grab her once more. "Come on, Jolene. You know me," Anthony said. "We don't have to hurt each other."

She swung the sword, but Anthony caught the blade with his hand. His powers prevented him from getting hit by bullets, but he wasn't immune to blades. After only a few seconds, Jolene could see red drip from his closed palm and dribble down his wrist.

Jolene immediately felt guilty and unsure of how Sterling stomached it. Maybe the first kill made him numb to it, made the next ones easier and easier, but it was a feeling she couldn't fathom. At the sight of his blood, she choked back a sob, her breath feeling heavy in her chest.

In her hesitance to do much else, Anthony grabbed the blade with his other hand and then snapped the steel in half. The sword dissolved from Jolene's hand once he did, and he used her shock to his advantage by wrapping an arm around her waist and lifting her over his shoulder.

She didn't fight him this time.

There was no point.

"I'll tell you whatever you want," Anthony whispered. "You deserve to know. Just wait until we're outside. Understood?"

Jolene sighed, feeling deflated. She understood why Anthony had to play this smart, but she still criticized herself for failing. "Fine."

———

Once they were gone, Sterling turned to find himself face-to-face with Rory Miller; even in her own version of the Hematite gear, her curvier stature and brown eyes gave away her identity, especially when next to Kane. Whether or not Jolene had known it, she'd served as the perfect distraction for Rory to sneak up on Sterling. Rory's eyes, filled with hate, leered at him as she sunk a needle into his neck. Sterling pushed her back, causing her to stumble until Kane caught her, so he could reach for whatever it was she'd just administered.

"A gift from Dr. Potter," Kane said. "You yourself said he was a traitor. Consider this his last act of defiance."

"The neutralizer." Sterling grinned. "You must think you're so clever."

"Well, now you don't have any powers." Kane and Rory both stepped forward, matching black techwear standing out against the bright whites of the laboratory. They both procured their billy clubs, and before Sterling could act, they struck in a coordinated attack. Sterling fell to his knees as his rib cracked from where Rory hit him particularly hard. He tried to will it to repair, but it was no use. Kane frisked his torso and pulled his gun out of its holster.

The neutralizer worked.

Rory said, "Don't even think about moving."

As Kane pointed the gun at Sterling's forehead to hold him in place, his finger away from the trigger, Hannah and Elijah ran in. They stopped in the doorway as they saw what unfolded, then side-stepped against the wall to keep their distance. Meanwhile, Rory took a few steps behind Kane, covering him from behind.

Kane said, "You're going to enjoy a long time in prison, asshole."

Sterling barked a laugh. "Prison? Of course, you would think that. Don't you know? Prison isn't for people with money! I all but own this town, you hear? There's only one way you can put a stop to me." Sterling laughed, cold and manic. "So can you do it, Hematite? Can you take your first kill and claim your first life?"

Kane pulled down his mask and frowned. The truth was that he couldn't, and he was almost positive that Sterling knew that as Sterling pressed his own forehead to the gun barrel.

"Sterling."

He smirked, eyes so dark they looked black. "Can you?"

Kane glanced behind him at Rory, seeking her approval. But before she could say where her moral compass pointed, Sterling's dark laughter rang through the halls.

"You can't, can you? Not without the guilt weighing you down!" He spat his words with a venom that could rival a snake's. "It's why you looked at her, isn't it? Worried you won't be a hero anymore after this?"

Sterling threw his head back as he laughed, crazed and unfiltered. It echoed off the walls, reverberating in his own ears. But now that he'd lost, he'd also lost all of his sense. When he leaned forward, he grabbed Hematite's wrist, pulling the gun closer to his forehead once more.

"Go on! Send me to my father! Or do you not have the guts?"

Kane continued to stare down at him. Sterling's pupils blew so wide that the black almost overwhelmed his blue irises. Kane held the gun with a steady ease that did not match his short, rapid breaths that matched the rise and fall of his chest.

Seconds felt like hours before the gunshot rang, sending Sterling to the floor as everything went black.

CHAPTER 25

Kane's hand shook as Sterling slumped forward in a pool of his own blood. It spilled from the back of his head and stained his silver hair a deep maroon, spreading out until it hit Kane's feet. As the blood wrapped around his shoe, Kane looked for the source of the gunshot, finding it directly in front of him: Noah Sato. Amy Brewer stood behind him, fingertips frosted white and ready to go on the defensive for him if need be.

"What have you done?" Kane hand's trembled. He looked back at the gun in his hands and then at Noah, whose expression was blank and impossible to read.

"Spared you from having to kill the bastard." Noah lifted his wrist to his face to check his watch. "Perfect timing." He slid the gun into a holster hidden within his jacket.

"Noah, I…"

"Please, Kane. No need to thank me. I didn't do it for you." Noah slung an arm over Amy's shoulder and ushered her along, heading back the way they came. "Come on, sweetheart. Let's get the hell out of here."

As they left, Amy's voice echoed down the hall. "Does Jolene know?"

With a dejected sigh, Noah said, "I'll break the news to her."

Their voices fell out of earshot after that. Kane still held Sterling's gun, now staring at it and the body at his feet. At the sound of a footstep behind him, he held his arm out and back, shielding whoever it was from the sight.

"I'll meet you outside."

But Rory's footsteps grew louder as she approached him. Her hand felt heavy on his shoulder. "It's going to be alright, Kay," she said. "There's nothing you could have done. Let's get out of here before things somehow get worse. I'm sure they're bound to."

When Kane turned to Rory, he was aware of the tears in his eyes—tears he'd wanted to spill for years, but never felt he could. For so long, he'd had to be strong for everyone: first for Kayla, then for Rory, and inevitably their entire town. He was exhausted, but it was over. He should be happy.

It was over—but at what cost?

———

Anthony set Jolene down once they reached her car in the parking lot. The dirt picked up in the warm, late summer breeze, dirtying their shoes and pants as they stood there.

"Don't run," Anthony said. "Listen, I know I don't usually say much, but let me answer any questions you have, okay?"

"I just want to know on what fucking planet this is considered tying up loose ends."

Anthony trilled his lips. "Sterling has wanted it all ever since I first met him. He's never *not* had his cake and eaten it too."

With sarcasm dripping from her voice, she bit back, "Yeah, tell me something I don't know."

"He adores you, Jolene," Anthony said. "I know that doesn't make any of this right. But I truly do think that, at the end of the day, he genuinely just wanted to help you."

"And what for? To be some pawn in his game? To be a lackey like you? No offense."

"None taken. He wanted to get to you before Hematite could.

Something tells me if you hadn't changed your Instagram caption, things could have gone very differently."

She bit back a sob as she leaned against her car and crossed her arms. "Un-fucking-believable."

"Everybody lies, Jolene," Anthony said. "Hematite lies. Sterling lies. We've all done it. The way I see it? I'm in no position to throw stones from a glass house."

"Are you the associate with the niece who wanted a magical girl mural?"

Anthony blinked at her a few times. "Huh?"

Jolene closed her eyes and took a deep breath. "Sterling told me he had an associate with a niece. He mentioned commissioning me to do a mural. Is that you?"

"He never mentioned it, but yeah, I've got a niece who is into all of that."

She dragged her palm down her face, not caring that some of her makeup trailed behind on her fingertips. "So at least he didn't lie about everything."

Anthony opened his mouth to speak, but paused at the sound of a gunshot. After confirming another wouldn't follow, he said, "He wanted you out of there so you wouldn't get hurt. And to be honest, I've never seen him act the way he does around you. I don't think he's ever loved anyone or anything, at least not like this."

"Yeah, well, he's a grown man. It's not my job to hold his hand as he figures out that murder might turn a girl off."

"That's not what I mean, and you know it."

She sighed. "I know. I'm sorry. Fuck."

"Do I agree with every decision he's made? God, no. But he doesn't pay me to agree with him. He pays me to make sure he doesn't get himself fucking killed. Something he's probably doing as we speak."

"Why even tell me that? To try to guilt me or something?"

"No. But you deserve to know the full scope of the situation. He's in way too deep to let this go, at least so long as Hematite is around. I don't see both of them walking out of that building today. It'll be a fucking miracle if they both make it out alive."

"Neither of them can die."

Anthony rose a brow. "You think that'll stop 'em?"

Before Jolene could answer, the question lingering in her mind like the dust on her shoes, the front doors swung open. They both turned as Noah and Amy emerged. Once they saw Anthony and Jolene, the two broke out into a light jog.

"Jolene!" Noah called. "Good, you're still here."

"Is it over? We heard a shot."

Amy nodded. "Yeah, it's over."

Before Jolene could release a deep breath, Noah cut her exhale off. "Just don't go in there. Not yet, anyway."

"Why not?"

"So, no easy way to tell you this, but Hematite thinks I killed Sterling. And from the looks of it? It's a convincing story. He and Potter worked on some sort of inhibitor and they hit Sterling with it so he couldn't use any of his powers. That also left him without his immortality."

Jolene felt the color drain from her face. "Is he okay?"

"He's okay. Just don't go in there," Noah reiterated, stressing the command. "Shit got real ugly. And there are a few people in there who *aren't* okay. Potter is dead. Carter's dead. Fuck."

The news felt like a punch straight to Jolene's gut. "I'm so sorry for your losses. It shouldn't have been this way."

"You're right," Amy said, "it shouldn't have. Things got way out of control. That's why Noah and I are getting the hell out of here."

"If you need us, we'll be renting an RV. Sterling will know how to contact us if times are tough, but I recommend the two of you do like we are. Get a new identity and start over. He's got a contact for that. You probably don't have to worry about that, but he will, just so you're aware."

Jolene went to ask where Hematite and the rest of them were, but a car pulled out from around the back of the building.

"Good," Amy said. "They left."

"Just give it another ten, fifteen minutes," Noah said. "The inhibitor that they used, or whatever the hell you wanna call it, it had a time limit before it wore off. Hematite and Sterling were going at it, and things weren't looking too good for us. Sterling ... He snapped a bit, and Hematite had a gun to his head, and it was impossible for me to tell if Hematite would pull the trigger or not. So I waited for the exact minute that I knew that damn neutralizer would have worn off to make it look like I killed the bastard. Spared Hematite the kill and bought us the opportunity to get the hell out of there."

"How'd you know they used it?" Anthony asked. He'd been so quiet that Jolene almost forgot he was there.

"We made our way down the hall and then overheard them talking about it. Our window was two minutes. I timed three to be safe."

Despite everything, Jolene didn't think Sterling deserved to die. There was still so much left unspoken between them that the thought of it being too late left her weak in the knees. When she spoke, her voice cracked. "Noah, please tell me he's not dead. Please tell me you're sure."

"I'm sure, Jolene. Don't worry. Just give it another ten, fifteen minutes, tops. I promise you, he'll come stumbling out of there. If you still want him, that is."

"I still have a lot I have to talk to him about. And I think he's willing to get on the straight and narrow."

Amy smiled. "If anyone understands, it's us."

"Thank you," Jolene said. "Thank you for saving him."

Once Noah and Amy left with Anthony not far behind them, Jolene did as Noah suggested. She checked her watch every few minutes, counting down the seconds until the fifteen-minute mark appeared. If he didn't come crawling out at that point, she'd assume he was either dead or had descended back into his need for power.

But after twelve minutes, she saw his silhouette before his body, but he *did* shuffle out of the building. His body slouched with exhaustion and his suit jacket was scuffed up, but despite his dishevelment, he was fine. He was alive.

Sterling stopped in his tracks when he saw Jolene leaning against her car. Jolene pushed herself off of it, taking slow steps in approaching him. After everything that happened, she wasn't sure how he'd receive her. There was no knowing how he'd changed, even though part of her hoped the boy from the piano recitals was still there.

When they were finally within arm's reach of each other, Sterling collapsed to his knees and buried his face in her hip. His hands reached for her sides, clinging to her clothing as his sobs cracked through the air. Blood caked his silver hair, staining some of the silver strands maroon and pink where Noah must have shot him.

"I don't deserve you, Jolene."

For as much as she wanted to push him away, she couldn't bring herself to. Listening only to her instincts, she stroked his hair. "You're right. You don't. But beneath it all, Sterling, I do think you have the capacity to be a good person. You were given a second chance. Don't waste it."

He opened his mouth but found himself incapable of speech. Jolene quickly pieced together that he hadn't expected to see her here; with the way he held on to her, there was no questioning it. She lowered into a crouch, bringing herself to eye level with him. She didn't care if the dirt coated her clothes, not when Sterling broke before her. After she wiped his tears with her thumbs, she cupped his face with her palms.

"Hey," she said, trying her best to toe the line between gentle and commanding. "Look at me."

"Why?" To call it speaking would be disingenuous; Jolene thought it sounded more like a frog's croak. "Why did you stay?"

"Because it felt like the right thing to do." Jolene simpered. "Listen, I'm not here to fix you. That's not my job. But I didn't want you to crawl out of there alone, with no one here for you. I think the consensus is that the operation is over. And for what it's worth, you helped me. And now, you're gonna need all the help you can get. The least I can do is return the favor."

"What do I need to do in order to not lose you?"

He'd asked it so earnestly that Jolene's heart wrenched. She brushed some of his hair back and said, "Change your name. Get a fake ID. Move to Colorado Springs with me and start seeing a therapist. I almost have enough money to pay cash for a place, so we should be able to get out of here in another month or two. You'll have to lie low at my apartment until then."

"I'll give you the cash," Sterling said. "I'll give you anything."

A part of Jolene thought she should have taken that offer, but she couldn't shake the gold digger comments out of her mind. "I don't need your cash. By the time you have your new ID, we'll be ready to go."

"I don't care if you don't need it. Take it. Please." He spoke with such desperation that Jolene sensed he was hinting at more. He continued, "Even if you don't want it, it's yours anyway."

"What do you mean?"

Sterling hiccuped. "I wrote you into my will and added you to my life insurance weeks ago. While I never anticipated that this would happen, I always preferred to be prepared."

Jolene sat back on her heels as she processed the information. "Fuck."

"It's yours. My mother will get enough to keep her satiated, and the rest goes to you."

"What do you mean, keep her satiated? She's not gonna take me to court, will she?"

"No. I would never do that to you. We have an agreed-upon amount," Sterling explained as he collected his breath. "A number that she knows means I'm fine and just needed to disappear."

"What about the rest of the logistics? Everyone's going to look at me."

"They won't." His confidence was returning. "I have my contacts. Leave it to me. Sterling Harrison is dead as far as the rest of the world is concerned. He failed." His voice trailed off. "I failed."

"Sounds like the perfect thing to talk to a therapist about. The lady I see in Denver offers virtual appointments, you know."

"You're right. And I will."

"It's for your own good. But it's not too late to start over, you know."

"I know. And I also know I'm on thin ice with you. After losing everything, I can't lose you, too. Just give me time." He reached for her and grasped her shirt, clinging on to the collar. "If you can give me time, then I swear to you. I'll be a whole new man in a year."

"I believe you." *And even if I didn't*, she thought, *I have little choice.*

People are going to ask me questions I don't want to answer if I don't get the hell out of here with him.

But she did believe him, deep in her heart. When she sifted past the hurt and the rage, she believed every word.

"Anything you want, darling, and it's yours." As he spoke with swollen, bloodshot eyes, Jolene saw the scared little boy sitting at a piano bench, mourning his recently deceased father. "Just say the word."

He needed help. He'd needed it for the last twenty years.

She knew she didn't need to—that she owed him nothing. But for no reason other than wanting to, for the sake of being a good person, she extended her hand to him. "Let's start with getting out of here."

He hiccuped another sob as he took her hand, and she noticed just how dry his skin was and how cracked his cuticles had become. As they stood, she could see just how much of the dirt from the parking lot covered their clothes. A thin sheen of yellow dust covered both of them, but Sterling paid it no mind.

"There are a few things I'll need from my house," Sterling said, "but we can go straight from there to your apartment."

"I want to grab a few things, too," she said as they helped each other stand, "but it's probably better if I shop online. I don't want to risk you being seen anywhere."

"Such as?"

As Jolene opened the driver's side door to her car, she grinned. "I think it's time we add a little more color to your look, don't you?"

CHAPTER 26

As Sterling held the keys out to Jolene, he didn't focus on the view of the mountains reflected in the windows. He paid no attention to how warm the sun felt on his skin or the smell of coffee and freshly baked bread wafting over from the cafe across the street. The sound of locals and tourists chatting behind them as they walked to work or left their hotel filled his ears, but he drowned it out.

He'd been to Colorado Springs enough times to know how the city felt. Soon, he'd be a part of its beating pulse. So now, instead of taking in his surroundings, he was only concerned with one thing: the expression on Jolene's face.

When she took the keys from him, she looked at them like she couldn't believe they were real. She looked up at the shop, then behind them at the mountains. Pikes Peak stood tall and snow-coated amongst the lower green ranges and red rocks in the distance. And then she looked at him, smiling wider than he'd ever seen anybody smile. That expression alone made everything worth it.

There was more to life than just his ambitions. He knew that now. Sterling had both Jolene and Dr. Thornton to thank for that.

"I can't believe we're here."

Sterling kissed the top of her head. "Welcome home, darling."

"The view is phenomenal. I don't even want to know how you got it."

He chuckled. "Legally and with no threats, I promise."

With mischief in her tone, she asked, "Do you mean that, or are you just trying to make me feel better?"

"Everything's in your name and your name alone. I wouldn't dare risk your reputation like that."

Jolene laughed, carefree. "You've done too much for me as it is."

"Nonsense."

She playfully smacked his chest. "I'm serious!"

"You have shown me the world, darling, so it is only natural that I want to give it to you in return."

Jolene softened. "Come on. Let's get in already, shall we?"

He'd purchased both floors so the downstairs unit could act as her new tattoo studio; Stella and Annie took over the shop in Riverpeak. The first floor had enough room for at least four chairs in the lobby, with three rooms in the back that could function as private tattoo or piercing spaces. There was a lot of work to do if she wanted the space to look as whimsical and feminine as her old shop, but Sterling already offered to put in some elbow grease with her.

"So, as my new Shop Manager, there are a few things we need to do to you," Jolene said as they walked around. Jolene had her phone in hand as she jotted down some notes about how she wanted to paint each wall or structure the space. "Nothing major."

"Define 'nothing major.'"

"We're dying your hair and getting you some more ink. And before you argue, don't say I didn't warn you about this back in Riverpeak."

His lip twitched into a smile. "I suppose you did. Alright. I'll let you pick my hair color while I decide on some more tattoos."

"Wait, for real?" She looked at him, beaming like she didn't have a care in the world. "That was way easier of a sell than I thought it would be."

"It'll help me not get recognized. Besides, I just got this position. I'd very much like to keep it and my makeover sounds like a job requirement."

"It is a standard part of onboarding, yes." She giggled. "And I may have already gotten the hair dye."

"Knowing you? I'd figured as much. Do I get to know what color you got for me?"

"Is it okay if I surprise you?"

"Sure. I put my full trust in you, darling."

"You know, I'm excited that we're here and doing this. Together, specifically."

"Hm?"

"This is everything I've wanted. It's nice to share it with someone I love, I guess."

Sterling's gaze softened as his heart soared. Neither of them had spoken those words since his graveyard confession. He hadn't dared since everything exploded in his face two months ago, not wanting to say anything that may make her feel uncomfortable. She'd given him a chance, and he wasn't about to look that gift horse in the mouth.

"I agree," he said, letting the warmth flutter through his chest. "It is nice."

———

The upstairs apartment was small enough to be cozy, but spacious enough that they never felt cramped. They spent the night getting their furniture together since Jolene was eager to get started with the work downstairs. Sterling was just grateful that he had something to do. By helping her, he felt useful.

It was something Dr. Thornton told him: help others and maybe he'd find purpose again. He'd started seeing her once he had his fake ID and a new name, only setting appointments up virtually and conveniently never having a working camera on his laptop. Sterling wondered if Marissa knew he was lying about the camera and just didn't care. He kept things vague and nondescript with Marissa as much as he could; he'd told her about how witnessed his father's murder, but never the details or who his father was. Marissa didn't ask more than necessary, which he appreciated.

He planned on donating to a few charities anonymously once he and Jolene settled in. But for now, helping her and feeling himself sweat beneath his activewear as they assembled furniture in the living room together was a good start.

The following morning, after waking up as a mess of tangled limbs, Jolene ushered Sterling to the bathroom. She'd wasted no time in dragging a barstool from their kitchen so she could get to work on dying his hair. Her fingers felt heavenly against his scalp, providing a satisfying scratch as she covered his hair with dye. Sterling hummed and leaned into her touch, closing his eyes to keep himself from stealing a look at the box.

Sitting on the edge of the tub wasn't the most comfortable, but it allowed her to rinse everything out of his hair. She'd dyed her own hair, too, using a mix of the leftovers from his box and a blue box she'd set beside the one she got him.

"I can get this myself if it's easier, you know."

"Nope," Jolene said. "I want to."

"If it pleases you, love. I certainly won't deny the free scalp massage."

Once she set her mind to something, there was no stopping her. They were alike in that way, Sterling realized. He'd followed her lead in channeling that into something beautiful and life-changing instead of the bleak future he'd created for himself back in Riverpeak.

"Okay, you're all set. I'm gonna rinse mine out while you dry your hair, okay?"

He turned to kiss her cheek. "Thank you. For this and for everything."

She beamed, proud of her work and touched by his words. "Thank you for letting me."

When Sterling emerged from the shower, he wrapped a towel around his waist and grabbed the hair dryer, only looking in the mirror once it was mostly dry. As he ran his fingers through the dark lavender strands that now reached his shoulders, two months' worth of change hit him like a violet-colored freight train. He didn't even notice the shower turning off or Jolene standing beside him until she wrapped her arms around him from the side, resting her head on his shoulder.

The blue popped brightly in her hair, and her ends transitioned into the same purple that covered his entire head.

"Do you like it?"

He nodded. "It's far from subtle, but no one will guess it's me, that's for sure."

She kissed his shoulder. "Contrary to how it may seem, you'll blend right in with this downstairs."

"It's perfect." He kissed the top of her head. "It'll take some adjusting, but I do like it."

"Okay, good." She sighed in relief. "Ready for your tattoo?"

"Might as well get all the change over with at once, right?"

It was far from ceremonious, but Jolene prepared their living room like she would her studio downstairs once they'd gotten dressed. They were still waiting on a shipment of tattoo chairs, so when Jolene brought the chair back to the kitchen, she ushered Sterling along to the living room. There, she'd wrapped the couch like she would have done to the chair in her studio.

"I'm impressed," he said. "Here I thought we'd just wait until downstairs is ready."

"Oh, you'll be getting another one then, too," Jolene said. "We'll need to break the place in, after all. But this? This is identity management, baby." She reached for her tablet on the coffee table. "Did you think about what you wanted?"

"I did," he said, "and I want you to do whatever you want. Artist's choice."

Her eyes widened, the hazel looking extra green in the natural light that streamed in through the window. "No way."

"Seriously. Whatever you think would best fit, go for it."

"Hm." She tapped her finger on her bottom lip. "Oh! I have an idea. Sit down and get comfortable. Let me sketch something up really quick." After thirty minutes, she'd finished sketching on her tablet. "Okay, take a look."

Sterling gasped. "Wow. It's beautiful." Seldom did anything take his breath away, but this was one of her finer pieces to date—and she hadn't even tattooed it yet. "It's also massive."

"It's a full sleeve. This will take a lot longer than the little nemophila I did for you a few months back. We can break it up if needed, but I've got all day if you can sit."

It couldn't be worse than being shot in the head, he thought. He also thought better of saying that out loud. "Well, it won't kill me, so let's go for it."

———

After six hours, they took a break for a late lunch. She finished the full sleeve after another seven. Once she wiped down his arm one last time, Sterling looked down and smiled at the piece. On his arm, Japanese fans with golden frames and orange leaves filled in the space between red-crowned cranes in flight.

"Why the cranes?" He asked.

"Legend says they live for a thousand years and can bring good fortune." She grabbed her recovery wrap from the table as she continued explaining. "Maple leaves are all about fresh starts, and fans can show all the different paths our lives might take. I've seen all the progress you've made in such a short time, and we've still got a long way to go, but I'm really proud of you."

"Thank you. That means the world coming from you."

She kissed his temple. "Of course. Now, I don't know about you, but I'm starving. Come on, let's eat."

Once his arm—as sore and stiff as it was—was wrapped, he helped her clean up the space. Even though she insisted he relax, it felt good to stretch his legs after sitting for so long. Once they settled on the couch together with their lunch, Jolene tucked her legs beneath her body as she balanced her food on her thigh. She grabbed the remote, turning on the news.

"Breaking at ten: a crime ring bust."

"Riverpeak Police tell Channel 5 the vigilante Hematite captured and delivered over two dozen gang members…"

Sterling nearly choked on his pizza in disbelief. "Gang?"

"I mean, you kind of were, Ster."

The male anchor continued, "who sold a modified form of metham-phetamines. Police did not recover any materials when searching their safe houses."

"In an encrypted statement sent to Channel 5, Hematite claims to have safely disposed of the drugs so no one can get their hands on them. We have a crew on their way to Riverpeak as we get more details. Count on Channel 5 for the latest."

Jolene looked at Sterling, transfixed on the television. He took one slow, deep breath and then looked at her. "Well, I suppose it's done."

She set her plate down on the table. Seeing that his own was long abandoned to his train of thought, she did the same for him. "Are you okay?"

"I will be." He flashed a wan smile.

"Do you want to talk about it?"

"It's strange. On the one hand, that was all I ever knew and my father's pride and joy. But on the other?" He grabbed one of her hands. "Now I suppose I get to find out who I really am beneath the superpowers and with no ambitions to answer to."

"Well, I think I've gotten a glimpse at you." Jolene shifted and swung a leg over his body to straddle his lap on the couch. It forced his attention away from the news, which had already moved on to another story. "You mean well beneath it all, Ster."

"Thank you. Truly."

"Do you think there's anyone out there who will still recognize you?"

"Anyone Hematite hasn't gotten arrested has been dealt with. Anthony texted me last week to assure we wouldn't have any problems before he left for Italy."

She tried not to think too much about what that meant, but she understood it had to be done. "Good. That's good."

"I have one more gift for you. However, should you reject it, I would completely understand."

"What is it?"

"Reach into my left jacket pocket. Your right. Don't worry, I'm not carrying right now."

Jolene slid her hand across his chest beneath his jacket lapel. She felt a small bottle inside, no larger than an alcohol nip. "What's this?" She stared at the amber liquid swirling inside.

"The last of it."

Jolene looked away from the bottle to meet Sterling's eyes. "Wait, what?"

"You heard me. It's the last of my life's work. My father's, too." Sterling took a deep breath and his jaw tensed, but he forced himself to look at Jolene. "And not just that. It's combined with my DNA. If you drink this, you'll have more than just your tattoos to protect you. For as much as I'd love to be glued by your side at every waking moment, that's not realistic. You'd grow sick of me."

He chuckled at his own joke. Jolene ran her free hand up his torso and could feel his heart pounding beneath her touch. His chest rapidly rose and fell with his breath, which he was trying to keep under control.

"But if you drink this, you'll have the same powers as me. In fact, with your tattoo manipulation, you'd be ever stronger than I am. While I hope my past doesn't follow me here, the ability to predict the future has eluded me." He grabbed her hand and kissed each knuckle as he regained his composure. "And besides," he said into her skin, "if you drink this, then you know I can't return to my old life. However, if you'd rather dump it down the sink, I'd understand."

"Ster, are you … are you joking right now?"

"If only that I were."

"What will happen if I drink this?"

"You might feel numb. But if you use your abilities, you should be able to get yourself out of it. Noah had to warm me up to stimulate my nerves, but I imagine your butterflies or lightning would have the same effect."

Jolene nodded. "Right. Right. You'll talk me through it?"

"If it pleases you."

In one swift motion, Jolene twisted off the cap and chugged the amber liquid. Sterling watched as it made its way from the nip past her lips. Once it emptied, she leaned over to place the bottle on the end table next to the couch. When their eyes met and she straightened, Jolene smiled.

"You didn't think I'd turn that down, did you?"

Sterling shook his head. "I'd hoped you wouldn't, but I had no idea how you'd react. But know that I am grateful." His fingers wrapped around the back of her neck as he pulled her down for a kiss, feeling closer to her than ever before now that she'd drank the final vial.

Now, Noah could be freed from his past, and Hematite freed from fighting.

Sterling, too, was free—not to evade death, but to live despite it.

NOT READY TO LEAVE RIVERPEAK, CO?

Additional content is available for my newsletter subscribers! Each book in the Riverpeak Heroes series has a bonus chapter. Sign up at jessicasalina.com.

ABOUT THE AUTHOR

Jessica Salina is an award-nominated romance author based out of Washington state. As someone with fibromyalgia and CPTSD, Jessica strives for positive mental health and disability representation in her writing. Her goal is to make sure that no one feels alone and always knows they're worthy of love. When she's not writing, you can find Jessica taking pictures of cool mushrooms on hikes, chasing waterfalls, or  cosplaying from her favorite anime, video games, and Marvel comics with her husband.

ALSO BY JESSICA SALINA

Stuck On The Slopes

Riverpeak Heroes

Not My Time

To Be Normal

Play With Fire

Etched In Ink

Short Stories

Fly Agaric (featured in Unapologetic Love)

Coming 2026

Eyes of Molten Silver

www.ingramcontent.com/pod-product-compliance
Lightning Source LLC
Chambersburg PA
CBHW061936130726
47909CB00013B/1801